MICHAEL KIMBALL

MOUTH *to* MOUTH UNDONE

BCA

LONDON NEW YORK SYDNEY TORONTO

This omnibus edition published 1999
By BCA
By arrangement with Headline Book Publishing
A division of Hodder Headline PLC

CN 5438

Printed and bound in Great Britain by
Mackays of Chatham PLC, Chatham, Kent

CONTENTS

MOUTH *to* MOUTH

For my son Jesse

And in memory of three good men:

Al Pope, my father-in-law
Dr Bob Mackey
Professor Terry Plunkett

They were warm, joyful, hard-working, open and caring people. They made life much better.

THANKS

Rich Connor, Chris Fahy, Nancy Graham, Glenna and Jesse Kimball, Tabby King, Chuck Landry, Paul Mann, Howard Morhaim, Nessa and Pete Reifsnyder, Brenda Reimels, Frances Sullivan and Mildred Schmalz . . . for wading through early drafts and telling me what was right and wrong.

Howie Nielsen, Karen Wachtel Nielsen and Glenna Kimball, for listening to an oral version of this entire novel while imprisoned in my car on a drive back from Montreal.

Aaron Bourassa, the esteemed professor Bob Steneck, and the folks at York Beach Scuba, for diving info.

Nancy Graham, for help with computer-editing in the home-stretch.

Sarah Haskell, for her knowledge of tapestry-making and weaving.

Susan Hayes, Nanny Kennedy and Joe Miller, for answering my questions about sheep.

Arthur Kyricos, for his knowledge of firearms.

Fred Muehl, of York Harbor Marine Service, for answering my boat questions.

Pat and Al Philbrook, for medical and engineering info.

Stan Ross, of York, Maine: good man, hard-worker, straight-shooter, for helping me find a house.

Reverend Betty Stookey, for her help with biblical questions.

Jill Schultz and the Maine Writers and Publishers Alliance.

The Automatics, for their permission to quote from 'Hangin' Out at EJ's,' the quintessential pop-punk song of the twentieth century (from their CD, The Automatics, Mutant Pop Records, 5010 NW Shasta, Corvallis, OR 97330).

Special thanks to Jennifer Hershey, my US editor, and Bill Massey, my UK editor, for their patience and encouragement.

Abner Stein, my UK agent.

As always, to my US literary agent Howard Morhaim . . . and to fisherman Earl MacVane, Jr, for pulling him out of the ocean off of Peak's Island one day and not throwing him back when he found out he'd rescued a New Yorker.

And, as ever, to Stephen King, for his uncommon generosity.

Neglected last time:

Alan Williams, my first editor, for teaching and encouraging me.

Note: In order to sell a few more books, I borrowed some names from my friends; however, personalities, relationships and events in the novel are completely fictional.

Revenge is a kind of wild justice . . .
Francis Bacon

. . . I will repay, saith the Lord.
Romans 12:19

CHAPTER ONE

On the crest of the hayfield, outside her sheep pasture, Ellen Chambers stood under a green canopy tent passively smiling while her son-in-law asphyxiated her daughter with wedding cake. Randy was apparently teaching Moreen the first lesson of their married life, a public punishment for the way she had fed him, mashing purple frosting into his sculpted goatee. The wedding guests laughed. Even Moreen's high school friends thought it was funny, the way her back bent over the table and her belly showed her swollen navel through the silk. But when Randy wiped his hands on Moreen's dress, then stalked away from her, Ellen lost her smile and went to head him off at the beer keg.

'Is it my imagination, or is the groom not the son-in-law of your dreams?'

Ellen heard the caution in her friend's voice. In her heels and close-fitting skirt, Maddy was doing her best to keep pace with Ellen.

'He's twenty-seven years old,' Ellen said. 'She's a junior in high school.'

'Shy girls always marry outlaws,' Maddy said. 'You did.' She took hold of Ellen's arm, a gentle grip meant to dissuade. 'Anyway, you don't want to make a scene today, not with all the cameras.'

Ellen stopped walking. She shut her eyes, took a heavy breath. Madeleine Sterling was a psychotherapist, twice divorced, and Ellen's closest friend since high school.

'So,' Maddy said, turning them around, 'do I see more sheep in your pasture?'

Ellen laughed, finally grateful for her intervention. 'We need the wool,' Ellen told her. 'The phone company's threatening to shut us off, the barn's falling in. It's just a matter of time before Scott loses the store.'

'Interesting. The minute Moreen moves out, you expand your flock.'

'Oh, Maddy, not today.'

Ellen turned away and found herself making eye contact with a young man standing in the shade of the oak tree beside her house. She averted her eyes, as she had done twice already. He'd been there for some time, nursing a Styrofoam cup of coffee. Sizeable and strikingly handsome, he had dark eyes and long black sideburns, a thin black necktie. The cuffs of his white shirt were rolled up.

'No one seems to know anything about him,' Maddy said quietly.

'I'm sure you've asked.'

'Discreetly.'

Ellen mustered a smile. Actually, she'd wondered about the young man herself, the brooding way he'd been watching her.

'*His hair*,' Maddy said in a low voice, covering her mouth. 'Would you call that wavy or curly?'

Ellen's own hair was mahogany-colored and lustrous as a girl's, and it fell down the middle of her back in a single thick braid that reached the base of her spine. She was taller than most women, but with a subtle fullness of hip and breast. Her face was soft, her nose lightly freckled. Her eyes were deep green, quick and vibrant, and her jaw well-defined. At thirty-six, Ellen felt strong and healthy and young – too young to be a grandmother.

'How old do you think?' Maddy asked, eyeing the dark young man. 'Thirty-three? Not a day younger than thirty.'

'Dream on. Twenty.'

'Oh, but look at the body. Imagine the progeny.'

The young man glanced over at Ellen again, and she turned to look for Scott, her husband, spotted him leaning against the paddock fence talking with Randy, their new son-in-law. The two men were smoking cigars and talking intently about something. Scott, with his dark good looks, his easy manner and ready smile, he worked hard to make sure nobody in Destin disliked him. It bothered Ellen to see him working at it with Randy.

She heard a burst of singing, turned to see Moreen standing at the beer keg with her friends, posing for snapshots with their arms around each other and jumbo cups of beer in their hands, Moreen swaying and singing along with the three-piece band: 'Wonderful Tonight.'

Unavoidable, the way she mirrored Ellen's own young life: the rebellion, the recklessness, the careless pregnancy, the misfit, misunderstood husband. But somehow, across all these years, the reflection seemed so warped – almost as though Moreen was knowingly orchestrating her own destruction.

'I feel like she's drowning herself, and there's nothing I can do to save her,' Ellen said.

'Don't you think that's a wee bit overstated?'

'Maddy, I don't even know her anymore,' Ellen said. 'It's like I just opened my eyes, and here we are.'

Maddy gave her a look. 'That's called life,' she said.

'Call it what you want,' Ellen said. 'It's not the life I wanted. For her or me.'

She turned away from Maddy and peered off past the people, beyond her leaning, sway-roofed barn, down the pasture hill toward the pond.

'Must be a friend of Randy's,' Maddy said, once again focused on the dark-haired young man. 'He looks too intelligent to be a relative.'

Ellen looked back. 'Looks too intelligent to be either.'

'You know, I'm very intelligent, myself. And under the right circumstances, I can be extremely sultry.'

Maddy's hair was straight and jet black today, cut to her jaw line, and she wore deep red lipstick. Her upper body was wrapped in designer silk, richly black and revealing. She earned a healthy salary on top of her divorce settlements and spent a good deal of it on her wardrobe.

'Ladies and gentlemen, get out your hankies,' the singer announced, his amplified voice booming out over the valley and echoing back off the wooded hillside. By now Ellen's sheep had flocked to the furthest corner of the fenced-in pasture, over to the right, where the stream came down out of the woods. Ellen imagined the wool shrinking on their bellies, their milk drying up. She imagined the gray coyotes slinking down the hill beyond the fences and stream, stalking them.

'Because right now, ladies and gentlemen, I'd like to get the bride and her father up here on the dance floor—'

Ellen turned, saw Scott stub his cigar out on the gate, set his drink on top of the cedar post and start walking toward the canopy. Of average height and hoarding what was left of his youthful charm – his Tourmaline stud and black ponytail countering the fullness of his face – everyone knew his hardware store was going under, this, after being one of Destin's most prosperous young men only ten years ago, but he carried himself with a staunch, countrified dignity as he searched the crowd for his daughter. When he ducked under the canopy and stepped onto the dance floor – nine sheets of parquet set on the grass – Moreen was there waiting, dark eyes staring off drunkenly as she reached for him, wrapping her arms around his neck and laying her cheek against his chin. Daddy's Little Girl.

'You gonna cry?' Maddy asked.

Ellen folded her arms, not answering.

'I just hope Randy knows how to waltz.'

'Why?' Ellen looked askance at her.

Maddy patted her arm. 'Be sweet,' she said, moving off. 'I'm going off to do my sultry thing.'

Ellen turned, spotted Randy sauntering toward the beer keg with his hands stuffed in the pockets of his leather pants. With his matching leather vest and dark shades, the purple bandana wrapped around his head, and the cropped orange ponytail hanging out the back, he must have imagined himself swashbuckling.

Waltz? They'd never even had a conversation. Not that Ellen had made the effort, even though Randy was closer to her age than to Moreen's. He claimed to have studied art at some community college in Florida. Yet he worked as a tender for a part-time urchin diver, his best man. On the side, Randy made airbrush paintings depicting endangered animals killing humans – building up his portfolio, Moreen had explained the night she told Ellen and Scott she was pregnant.

Really, what was there to say to Randy? I'm so happy that my daughter has chosen you to father her children. And it was so cool how you wore your shades to the wedding. And that little nod you and Scott exchanged when he brought Moreen to the altar (*Sacrifice*, Ellen had thought at the time, with chilling clarity).

Ellen had avoided Scott since then. And now, as she watched him dancing with their daughter, she wondered again how he'd given his consent so easily, while she tried to talk to Mo about adoption and even offered to help raise the child herself, to keep Moreen in high school – and to keep her from marrying Randy. But the conversations had been cut off each time by Moreen's breezy optimism, by Scott's reluctance to argue with her, by Ellen's steadfast willingness.

Ellen gazed at her daughter. Dark-haired and beautiful as only a pregnant Irish-American farm girl could be, Moreen had the black hair and deep brown eyes of her father, a dusting of freckles on her nose like her mother, and a pretty, cherubic mouth that was all her own.

Moreen had told her mother that Randy was an uneducated genius. She said he was sensitive and ambitious and funny, and that he'd be a wonderful father. Moreen told her mother a lot of things. For instance, she told Ellen that the first time in her life she'd ever felt loved was the first time Randy looked at her.

Right now, Randy was at the keg making another girl feel loved, judging by the way she picked the frosting out of his goatee. She was maybe fifteen years old, with spiked bleached hair, a thin white tank top that didn't reach the bottom of her rib cage, and worn denim shorts ripped off so short they seemed to have no crotch.

'Now I'd like to have the groom and the bride's mother join in,' the singer announced, snapping Ellen from her reverie. While she watched Randy wrap his arm around the girl and fill her cup from the keg, Ellen set her glass on the gift table and came forward to the dance floor. She looked for Randy again. He glanced over while he fed the girl her first sip, spilling the beer down her chin.

The singer leaned into the mike: 'Randy, your mother-in-law is waiting for you. Get used to it, man.'

Some of the men laughed heartily, some women booed. Randy kept feeding the girl.

Ellen looked toward Moreen, who rolled her eyes. Randy was just so independent. Ellen eyed Scott, wishing he'd rescue her, but he just gave her a look, a shrug. Don't sweat the small stuff. Then a hand touched her back.

'Dance with me,' the voice said, and before Ellen could decline, her right hand was firmly in the young man's left, her left hand was on his shoulder, and they were dancing.

His arm was solid, as was his back. His fingers were thick and long. His face was symmetrically constructed, his nose straight, his chin square. Though cleanly shaven, she could tell his beard would be heavy in a few hours. She could detect a tinge of fresh perspiration about him, a close, energetic scent. She could feel the champagne she had drunk.

'He may not be the groom,' the singer announced, 'but I don't think you mind, do you, Mom?'

Ellen felt the heat flush her face as she glanced up at her partner. He gave her a slightly bemused smile which she took for sympathy. His brown eyes, she noticed, were as dark as Moreen's.

'I guess your son-in-law has one redeeming quality,' he said to her.

'What's that?'

'He left you unattended.'

His smile was warm and easy. She was careful with the smile she returned.

As the small dance floor filled with other couples, Ellen became aware of the young man's fingers spreading on the small of her back, and she felt her heart pump. However, wanting to show no encouragement, she moved her own hand slightly higher on his shoulder and inched away from him, then felt conspicuous doing so.

'I'm Moreen's mother,' she told him.

'I know,' he said. 'Your name is Ellen. And you've been standing over there wondering if it's possible to get away with murder.'

'Close.'

'Actually, it is,' he said quietly.

She pulled back another inch, to study him, to ascertain that he was joking. He laughed a little, to show that he was.

'Are you a friend or relative?' she asked.

'Relative, you might say.'

'Brother? Cousin?'

'Cousin.' His eyes glinted, as though he were harboring a secret.

'Okay,' she said, tiring of the game.

'Of the bride.'

Ellen stopped dancing. She pulled her hands from him, his features suddenly snapping together like puzzle pieces. His smile broadened.

'It's nice to see you, Aunt Ellen.'

She captured his arm first, his sleeve, then she embraced him. 'Oh, Neal,' she said breathlessly.

'I wasn't about to miss my only cousin's wedding day,' he said, as he took her hand again and they continued dancing, Ellen's heart drumming, her mind whirling, remembering Neal the last time she saw him, at his father's funeral, two days after his twelfth birthday.

Now she held him tightly, suddenly wanting the song to end, wishing Scott was near so she could tell him – *Neal is here* – then wondering whether to tell him at all.

'She'll be so happy you came,' Ellen said.

'I wouldn't have recognized her.'

Ellen sighed, but said nothing in response. They danced some more, while they both absorbed the reunion.

'And Uncle Scott – I heard he's still running the hardware store.'

'Fifteen years now,' Ellen said.

Neal gave her a look. 'Or it's running him—?'

Ellen looked closely at him and saw the knowledge in his eyes. 'Into the ground,' she said quietly.

'I probably should mind my own business. Anyway, there's another reason I came here today. I didn't know if you heard about my mother.'

Ellen looked up at him again, then pulled him closer and rubbed his back as they kept dancing.

'Now that she's gone,' he said, 'you're the only family I have – well, *sort of* family – you and Mo and Uncle Scott, and I was hoping we could, you know, exchange Christmas cards at least.'

'Oh, Neal,' she said again, wishing she could think of something else to say, trying to rectify her feelings in the face of the old wounds, the persistent scars, finding herself caught between this young man whose touch only moments ago had excited her and this boy trying to reclaim the lost fragments of his life.

'Mind if I cut in?' Scott said, one hand on his nephew's shoulder, the other on Ellen's.

'Not at all,' Neal replied, backing away, giving her a furtive glance, Ellen recognizing in that instant their camaraderie in all of this, hers and Neal's, their alliance with the past.

She took Scott in her arms, held him in a familiar way, felt the softness of his back as he began moving his knees in time to the music, scuffing his soles across the wood.

'Holding up?' he asked. Ellen smelled the cigar on his breath, tinged with whiskey.

'I'll be glad when it's over,' she answered. *Tell him. It's his past too, more than mine.*

He drew her closer. 'They'll be okay, El. Don't forget, you were the same age.'

'Have we been okay?'

He gave her a look, deepened by whiskey. 'I think we've been great.'

She nestled her face against his.

'So who were you dancing with?'

'Neal,' she answered, just as the song came to an end and the drummer began a disco beat.

'Neal a friend of Randy's?'

Moreen's arms around Ellen's neck interrupted them. Ellen let go of Scott, turned and took her daughter in a hug. Moreen was not quite as tall as Ellen, and so drunk that she almost pulled Ellen over, but it didn't matter. It was a hug from her daughter.

'You look so beautiful today,' Ellen told her.

'So do you,' Moreen said. 'Are you happy for me?'

Ellen closed her eyes, exasperated with herself, and she pulled her daughter closer. 'I'm trying, Mo. I really am.'

Moreen turned out of her arms, moving to the music and nearly falling in the process. Ellen tried to hold on.

'You're gonna love Randy once you get to know him,' Mo said.

'Come on, Mo. What do you want me to say?'

A short scream answered her, coming from the barn. Ellen looked over, saw her sheep trotting down the hill toward the pond, their bells jangling excitedly.

'Jesus,' Scott said, heading for the barn.

'Who *is* that guy?' Moreen asked.

Neal, in fact. He was standing beside the paddock fence with Maddy, who was bending toward him with one hand covering her eyes and the other out in front of her face, as if to keep Neal from touching her.

As Ellen fell in step with Scott, hurrying to see what had happened, Neal lowered his head and walked away.

'What the hell is she doing now?' Scott grumbled, as if Maddy had single-handedly ruined the entire afternoon. Ellen reached her friend first.

'Mad?'

'I'm fine,' Maddy told her, though she rubbed one of her eyes with her fist, and her cheek was wet.

'What happened?' Scott asked, watching Neal disappear around the barn.

'I'm fine,' Maddy repeated. 'I touched your goddamned fence and got rum in my eye.'

A few other wedding guests gathered around to see what was wrong. 'She got bit, that's all,' Scott told them.

'Bit by what?' Sugar Westerback asked. He was the town's only full-time policeman, here as a guest, holding a twenty-ounce plastic cup of beer in his hand.

'By the fence,' Scott explained.

'If you want, ma'am, I'll arrest that fence,' Sugar said, and he laughed along with some of the other guys. Sugar was two inches shorter than Ellen and built like a hydrant, with massive arms. His hair was shaved within an eighth-inch of his skull, and he wore loose-fitting, clownish pants, the kind favored by weight-lifters, with a pager hooked to his belt and a black, tight-fitting T-shirt that said **D.A.R.E. to keep kids off drugs**.

'So glad I can entertain you all,' Maddy told him, squeezing her eye shut. 'Does anyone have a napkin?'

Scott pulled a clean handkerchief from his pocket and handed it to her. 'Sure you're okay?'

'I'm not going to sue, if that's what you mean,' Maddy replied, dabbing the corner of her eye.

Sugar nudged Scott with his elbow. 'Scotty, I think you need to hire this woman,' he said. ''Cause if this fence don't keep them kii-otes away from them sheep, that scream of hers sure as hell will.' Sugar laughed louder than anyone, then he grabbed the fence with his hand, saying, 'Hey, I don't feel any—'

An arc of beer lifted out of his cup, its frothy head splashing off the ground.

'Whoa,' Sugar breathed, staring in drunken awe at the single strand of wire. The guys laughed some more.

'Entertainment's that way, folks,' Maddy said, returning the handkerchief to Scott. 'God.'

As the small audience dispersed, Ellen found Maddy's plastic drinking glass a few feet away in the deep grass, went over to pick it up.

'I thought it was a very sultry scream,' she said to her friend.

'Here he was, all by himself, and I'm coming over, of course not noticing him at all, doing the walk – remember Kathleen Turner in *Body Heat*? – and just as I start to pass by, I stop dead in my tracks, look over at him like he's a bug and say, "You don't have an older brother, do you?" Then I lean against the fence and throw my drink in my face.'

'In *your* face?'

'Of course.' She blinked her eye, still working the sting out.

'And now you're thinking he wasn't impressed.'

Maddy scowled 'El?' She turned to the fence and stared. 'He was holding onto it.'

'Holding what?'

'No, the fence. The electric fence. He was standing right here, leaning against it, holding it in his hand.'

'Are you sure?'

Maddy looked up at Ellen in disbelief. 'The entire time he was standing here, he was baiting me.'

Ellen turned toward the barn. 'Remember Neal?'

'Neal?' Maddy scowled darkly. 'Neal, your nephew?'

'Well, Scott's brother's son.'

Maddy gave her a look. 'Does Scott know he's here?'

Ellen shook her head.

'Well, I hate to be the one to tell you, kid, but Scott's brother's son could use some serious professional help.'

'And you just happen to know a psychotherapist with free time?'

Maddy shook her head grimly. 'Not on your life,' she said. 'That's way more than I can handle.'

While the crowd was distracted, Neal Chambers walked into the barn. There were two rows of stalls running down the left and right walls, with a small dusty window lighting each, and a double door on either side of the barn that opened onto the ewes' and rams' paddocks. A thick chain and hook hung down from the center beam. As he passed under the hook, a kid stepped out of the last stall on the right.

'You want something?' the kid said, meaning to stop Neal's approach. He was Neal's size and build, possibly a year or two younger. His face was puffy and yellow-tanned, his sandy hair crewcut. He seemed to have a southern dialect. He tipped a bottle of Pabst Blue Ribbon to his mouth in a way that flexed his biceps.

Neal kept coming. 'Before I left, I wanted to say goodbye to Randy.'

The kid cocked his head. 'Wait outside. He's busy now.'

But Neal didn't stop, he walked right up to the kid and looked into the stall where Randy was kneeling in front of an overturned wooden craft. The young girl with spiked, bleached hair sat on the crate, with her knees pressed tight against Randy's sides. She looked up vacantly at Neal while Randy loosened the slender rubber tube that was tied around her left arm.

Randy's glance over his shoulder, however, was far from vacant. 'Good fuckin' job, Gator,' he said. A hypodermic stuck like an arrow in the head of a green hummingbird tattooed on the girl's forearm.

'It's okay, Randy,' Neal told him. 'I'm Mo's cousin.'

Randy peered up suspiciously at Neal.

'I wanted to say goodbye before I left,' Neal said, stepping through the narrow doorway.

Watching Neal closely, Randy left the needle hanging from the girl's arm, reached around behind her and picked a double-edged razor blade off the crate. 'You want to say goodbye?' he said, rising to his feet, shifting his weight to his left side.

Neal came toward him, extending his right hand.

'Randy, finish me,' the girl protested.

Randy stuck out his left. Had to, the razor blade was in his right. He rotated his open hand palm down.

'One other thing,' Neal said, clasping the hand in his own.

'Yeah?'

'Well,' Neal said, 'I guess I'd appreciate it if you'd start showing a little more respect for the family.'

At first Randy didn't react beyond a slight narrowing of his eyes, as if he were trying to read the glint in Neal's eye, wondering what would make a guy who looked so smart act so stupid, especially outnumbered as he was. The hesitation was also a timing thing – speedballs did wonders for timing. Now the corners of Randy's goatee lifted in a kind of grin. He blinked his eyes. Once. Twice. Then he snapped Neal's hand around and laid the razor blade flat against the pale underside of Neal's wrist. Timing.

'Stay very still, cousin,' Randy whispered, and he steeled his grip on Neal's hand to make his point. 'Very, very still. 'Cause now I have something to tell you.'

'Randy, are you gonna finish me?' the girl complained, pushing flaccidly to her feet. Gator snickered, leering over the stall at her.

A bright speck of red winked on Neal's wrist where the point of Randy's blade touched his skin. Neither man saw the blood, however, intent as they were on each other's eyes. Neither did they see Gator sidling into the stall with a three-inch punch blade protruding from his fist. 'See, I don't know what your actual problem is,' Randy continued. 'Fact is, maybe I didn't even hear you right – '

'Ran-dee,' the girl sang, knees bending, holding the syringe in her forearm.

With the hand that held the punch-blade, Gator reached out and caught the girl's nipple between his thumb and finger. She let go of the syringe, clutched at his wrist as he pulled her toward him.

'You're kind of a little brat,' Gator said, giving her nipple a twist until she rose onto her toes. 'Anyone ever teach you not to interrupt?'

Tears welled in the girl's eyes. He plucked the syringe from her arm, then released her. She staggered two steps backward, into the door post. 'Asshole!' she screamed. Gator jumped at her with his punch-blade, and she ran out of the stall.

Turning back to Randy and Neal, the southerner raised his fist and squeezed the punch-blade until the veins on his arm rose fat and blue. Holding the syringe upright in his other hand, he tapped the barrel with his ring finger, then sank the needle into his bloodstream and pushed the plunger. He inhaled through his teeth as the drug went in.

'Well, then,' he said, tossing the syringe on the floor as he studied Neal and Randy. 'Looks like we got ourselves somebody else that needs a lesson in manners.'

He pushed himself off the rough-boarded wall and ambled closer to them both, pale eyes shining intently.

'See, I got no name,' he explained, his voice slowing to a drawl. 'No identity. Where I come from, everyone thinks I'm dead. Which means I can do just 'bout anything I want.' He stopped an arm's length from Neal, staring at his neck the same way he had stared at the girl's breast. Even as his punch blade flashed with the window's reflection, Neal kept his eyes fixed on Randy. 'Like maybe someday I might wanna be a surgeon – '

Suddenly Randy flinched.

'*Fuck!*' he spat, and he looked down at his razor blade, one corner of which was buried between the bones of Neal's wrist, while the opposite corner had risen unnoticed deep into the fatty bend of his own index finger. Momentarily dumbfounded, Randy watched the blood pool eagerly out of both of them. Then he returned his scowl to Neal's steady stare. 'What are you, some kind of mental case?'

'*Hey!*'

Suddenly Gator jerked backwards, snagged in the oversized hand of Rooftop Paradise, who yanked him out of the stall.

'This is a wedding,' Rooftop scolded, ducking back into the stall and leaving Gator behind.

Rooftop stood over seven feet tall. The stall's ceiling was six-six. Rooftop, whose real name was Rupert Paradise, owned the diving business where Randy worked. He'd been Randy's best man. As the giant made his way toward Neal, his back rubbed the old, cobwebbed boards clean. He placed his hand firmly on Neal's shoulder and spoke in an unnaturally low voice.

'Your business done here?'

Neal's eyes left Randy's but didn't meet Rooftop's. Instead, they tracked Gator sidling into the stall again, his punch blade peeking out of his fist.

'I said behave, you,' Rooftop told him, his long right arm swinging back, stopping Gator short.

The kid looked up at him with a lazy sparkle in his eye that suggested he might have been grinning. He wasn't.

'And put that thing away.'

With a smirk, Gator turned out the door and was gone.

'And you,' Rooftop said, returning his attention to Randy. 'It's your wedding day. You're supposed to be out there with your wife.'

'Fuck,' Randy said.

Rooftop turned to Neal again. 'Okay now?'

'I think I made my point,' Neal replied, backing into the cobwebbed corner of the stall, casually taking a handkerchief from his pocket and pressing it against his wrist, though his eyes remained keenly focused, watching Rooftop, watching Randy, watching the stall doorway where Gator had exited.

Randy tried to flick the razor blade off his bloody fingers. 'Dipshit,' he said, finally flinging it toward Neal's legs. 'Stick around, maybe you can give me some more marital advice later on, when we won't be interrupted.'

Rooftop gave him a look, then peered down at something on the floor. He wore small wire-rimmed glasses that looked tiny on his face. He slid his huge wingtip shoe forward and nudged the syringe out of the hay, then bent his head toward Randy. 'What the heck is this?'

'How should I know?' Randy answered. 'It's a sheep barn, probably some vet left it.' He did not make eye contact with the giant, who took a clean handkerchief from his back pocket and stuffed it in Randy's hand.

'I don't know what that little girl was doing in here, but she's young enough to get all you guys locked up. Now go take care of that hand.'

'Since when did Ann Landers die?' Randy grumbled, wrapping his finger with the handkerchief.

'Cop,' Gator said, sticking his head in the door.

'Mind your manners,' Rooftop said quietly, pointing a long finger first at Randy, then Gator. 'Let's go.'

Gator shot Neal a final, menacing glance, then left the doorway. So did Randy. As Rooftop turned toward Neal, he gouged his shoulder on a nail sticking out of the ceiling.

'If you were planning to leave, I'd go ahead with my plans,' he said. Then he ducked out of the stall.

'Jesus Crow, what do they feed you?' Sugar Westerback stood about ten feet inside the barn with his hands on his hips. 'You gotta be, cripes, eight foot tall.'

Rooftop made a noise in his throat, as polite a response as he could muster, as the three men approached.

'Anyways,' Sugar said, 'we got a little girl come runnin' out of here a minute ago all upset about something. You boys know anything about that?'

Randy raised his nose, his etched scowl deepening on his brow. 'What are you, a fuckin cop?'

'Off-duty fuckin cop,' Sugar answered, as the men came together. He looked down at the bloody handkerchief in Randy's hand.

'Old barn,' Randy said, and he grinned at Sugar. 'Nails stickin out every which way.'

'So you boys don't know anything about the girl,' Sugar said.

Randy shrugged, then nodded to his two cohorts. 'My associates were just giving me some pointers for my wedding night.'

'No, but they had to take that cake knife away from her,' Sugar said. 'The girl I'm talkin about. She had it in for somebody.'

'Not me,' Randy said, then he pointed his red finger toward

Sugar's ear. 'Hey, I thought you said you're a cop. What's this?'

Sugar touched the tiny silver post in his ear. 'If it's good enough for Bruce Willis, you know?'

'Fuckin Bruce,' Randy said. 'Fuckin *Die Hard*,' and he started walking toward the door.

'I just got it done last night,' Sugar said, walking with him. 'People in this town already think I'm crazy, what the heck?'

As they proceeded toward the daylight, Gator moved around behind Sugar, his right hand buried in his pocket. Rooftop inserted himself furtively between the two.

' "Dare to keep kids off drugs," ' Randy recited, reading Sugar's T-shirt.

'That's me,' Sugar said, turning back. 'I go into the schools dressed up in a dog suit.'

'You piss on the monkey bars too?' Gator said.

Sugar turned. 'Nah. Kids, you know?'

Gator snickered.

'But you know what I got in my car? Pot. About this much.' He spread his thumb and finger an inch apart. 'I show the kids what it looks like, you know, in case somebody offers 'em any.'

'That's good,' Randy said, as they emerged into the sunlight. 'You keep this fuckin town safe for law abiding citizens like us.'

'That's what I do,' Sugar said, and he gave Randy a wink. 'So I'd watch myself, if I were you assholes.'

CHAPTER TWO

For Ellen, who taught at the local school, the last days before the summer break passed slowly. Home in the afternoons, she worked in her garden, picking rocks, preparing the soil for another planting of green beans and late corn. On Tuesday a customer came by and bought two brown fleeces at $16 a pound, and she was able to make a payment on her phone bill. With shearing behind her and her spring lambs almost ready for weaning, the sheep required little of her time, besides feeding and watering.

At five o'clock every day, she went into her pantry where her weights were set up and put herself through a brutal workout. Where normally she'd lift every other day for forty minutes, this week she worked out every day for an hour. She also raised her bench weight from one hundred twenty pounds to one-twenty-five. The exhaustion did her good.

Evenings she graded final exams and filled out report cards, and if she finished at a reasonable hour, she'd go up to her spinning room and work on her tapestry, a seascape commissioned by a Portsmouth interior decorator. She didn't read this week; she didn't watch television. As much as possible, she avoided the living room.

In fact, she avoided Scott, and she was aware of this. At first she thought it was Moreen's glaring absence, the reason she preferred her solitude. But there was more to it. Even on the weekend she had barely spoken to Scott when they awoke in the morning or passed in the kitchen. Maybe she didn't want to tell him about how it felt to be grading papers of kids who were Moreen's age and planning for college, when Moreen was pregnant, married and gone. Maybe she didn't want to confront her husband about his cavalier attitude in giving their daughter away. Or maybe she was afraid she might tell him what she'd been thinking, that without Moreen home to care for, there wasn't a whole lot keeping her there anymore.

No matter. He never asked her what was wrong, so she kept it to herself.

But on Sunday afternoon, a week after the wedding, when she went into the pasture and found her oldest ewe bloodied and sprawled on the crest of the hill, Ellen's cry rang full of her frustration. It also sparked a movement below them, which she spotted with a heart-thumping start. *Coyotes*. Three of them, gray as sticks, slinking down at the far right corner of the pasture, where they'd gotten through the fence. Timid as coyotes tended to be, these must have been famished beyond reason, the way they stood their ground.

Ellen glanced behind her at the rest of her sheep, tightly flocked in the paddock. She turned back to the coyotes, realized they were edging up the hill toward her. She thought of Scott's revolver in the bedroom but was afraid to leave her sheep to fetch it. For the first time this week she wished Scott was here.

'*Go on!*' she shouted, tearing off her baseball cap and waving it at the predators. The dying ewe raised its head and Ellen put her hand on its bloody shoulder, then saw the blood-saturated grass under its belly. Its gut was torn.

Halfway up the hill, with seeming calculation, the coyotes separated. Bowing their heads, fixing their yellow-brown eyes on Ellen, they spread left and right. Ellen raised herself high on her knees, although she realized that the visage she presented was hardly threatening: a woman in a green tank top and frayed jean shorts, her only weapon a faded green baseball cap.

Hearing the familiar diesel engine slowing up on the road, she was almost afraid to hope it was Scott. To her relief, the old Mercedes pulled into their driveway. She waited until the door closed, then she called for him. When he didn't answer, she yelled louder.

'Wait a minute!' he yelled back, wounded by her week of silence, emboldened by whiskey.

'*Get the gun!*' she cried. As if understanding her words, the coyotes stopped. They sniffed the air.

'Where are you?' Scott shouted.

'Down here! Get the gun!'

Scott came to the paddock fence. 'What's the matter?'

She pointed down the hill. '*Coyotes!*'

'Ellie, get out of there!'

But Ellen wasn't about to leave her sheep. Besides, as close as the coyotes were, and as bold, she had a better chance standing and fighting than turning and running. Scott remained at the fence, holding his briefcase, as if wondering whether or not to just, fuck all, charge down after the predators barehanded and resolve this silence between them with a burst of reckless machismo. Instead, he turned and ran for the house.

Katie let out a mournful bleat and tried to get up again. Ellen held her down. She knew the ewe could smell her killers nearing. Then Scott's voice called out:

'Ellie, where the hell did you hide the bullets?'

Ellen shouted back: 'In the freezer!'

She looked towards the coyotes again and saw them resume their skulking ascent up the hill. She got to her feet, presenting her full height, grateful for the additional half inch her work boots provided. She raised her arms over her head. The coyotes balked.

Ellen looked back, as the side door of the barn opened against the wide flock of sheep pressed together there, and Scott came marching through their midst, holding the revolver at his shoulder.

Seeing him, the lead coyote hunched his bony shoulders and lowered his head.

Scott stopped walking, straightened his arm and aimed. The animal's ears went back. Scott fired, the gun kicked. The coyote wheeled and ran downhill toward the corner of the pasture. Scott ran a few steps, then got off a second shot. A divot sprayed up to the left of one of the remaining two animals, and they too bolted for the gully. When Scott reached the crest of the hill, right in front of Ellen, he fired again, three times, the echo of his shots slapping back off the opposite hill, as the trio pushed under the livestock fence and disappeared into the tangled gray shadows of the stream bank.

'Nice shot,' Scott said, disgusted with himself.

Ellen knelt beside Katie, running her fingers gently over the stiff, cropped wool beside her ear. Scott turned toward her, blowing a sigh that was tinged with frustration. 'Want me to call Merrifield, see if he can fix her?'

For the first time, Ellen noticed that Scott's ponytail was gone. In fact, his hair had been barber-cut and parted neatly down the center. And he was wearing what appeared to be a uniform – light-blue blazer, red necktie. An insignia embroidered on his breast pocket read ***Mainely Hardware***, under which grinned a dancing stick figure holding a hammer in one hand and pipe wrench in the other.

'I'm buying into the franchise,' Scott said, responding to her stare. 'First thing they said, no earring, no ponytail.' He raised his brow in a show of futility.

Ellen looked off beyond him. Scott must have seen a change in her eyes, because he turned and said, 'Who's that?'

They watched the young man duck under the electric fence and come steadily down the hill, black hair, black wool sweater, black corduroy jeans.

'Do we know him?'

In her week of silence, she hadn't mentioned Neal's presence at the wedding. 'It looks like Neal,' she said, fitting her cap back on her head and pulling a loose strand of hair behind her ear.

'The kid from the wedding?'

'Neal,' she said. 'Your brother's son.'

Scott turned fully toward the barn, peering off against the low sun. When he looked back at Ellen again, he was still squinting, as if trying to register too many facts through too much alcohol.

'Wolves?' Neal called.

Scott watched him with a scowl.

'Coyotes,' Ellen replied.

'*Neal?*'

'Hello, Uncle Scott,' Neal said. 'If you want to go after them, we'd have better luck with a shotgun.'

Scott reached the pistol behind him, tucking it in his waistband. 'Jesus Christ,' he said, grabbing Neal's hand, grinning, then looked at Ellen again, his face registering the reasons she hadn't told him.

'Pistol's the only gun we have,' Ellen said. 'We keep it hidden.'

'You want to go after them?' Neal asked again.

'Nah, we'd better get the sheep to the vet,' Scott said. 'I'll bring Ellie's truck down.'

Neal knelt beside the animal, placing his hand gently under its shoulder and raising it a little. He laid his face on the ground and peered underneath the sheep, then said matter-of-factly, 'You can't save her.'

'You don't know Jake Merrifield,' Scott told him. 'For fifty bucks, he'll bring the dead back to life.'

Neal got to his feet again, shaking his head. 'They've opened her gut,' he said, and he looked intently at Ellen, as though for her decision. She became aware that she had no bra on and that, bending over the sheep, her tank top was opened to him. She straightened, kneeling upright. 'Neal's right,' she said to Scott. 'She's dying.'

'Want me to bring her to Justin?' Scott asked, consolation in his voice. 'Justin Briscoe, the butcher,' he explained to Neal.

Ellen shook her head. 'They might've had rabies.'

'Not likely,' Neal replied. 'Rabid animals travel alone.'

He reached behind him and withdrew a knife from a sheath, a four-inch blade with a worn leather handle. 'At least we can save the pelt.'

'Wait—' Ellen rose to her feet.

'Go up to the house if you want,' Neal said, 'but we need to take care of her. She's suffering.'

Ellen noticed his hands, strong and tanned.

'Uncle Scott, can you lift her?'

'Why kill ourselves?' Scott said, pulling the revolver from his waistband.

'Scott—'

'El, go on up to the house,' he told her gently, then turned to Neal. 'This is the only thing she lets me do on the farm, but she hates me when I do it.'

He placed the barrel behind Katie's ear, but Neal reached out and touched his hand. 'The other sheep are spooked enough,' Neal said. 'I've done this before. Lift her by the hind legs, backside to you.'

Scott looked down at his uniform.

'Quickly,' Neal said, taking the revolver from Scott and setting it in the grass. Scott, nonplussed, nevertheless stooped and got his arms around the animal's flanks. He grunted once as he raised the sheep off the ground.

Neal knelt in front of the ewe and held the back of its head. Ellen felt her knees shiver. Neal looked up at her. 'Okay?'

Despite the way Ellen might have thought of Neal at the wedding, all traces of boyhood had vanished.

She nodded. Although she had never watched when Scott put down one of her sick or injured animals, there seemed something less offensive about Neal's doing it.

His questioning look on her lingered. She nodded again. Then he turned back to the sheep, threaded his knife blade carefully through the wool at her throat.

'Hold her still,' he said softly to Scott.

'Got her,' Scott replied.

Neal's arm barely moved. The sheep kicked once, and Ellen saw a dark flow of blood gulp over Neal's wrist before she turned and left them, walking quickly toward the barn. She moved through her flock, hiding the still warm revolver under her arm, then hurried through the paddock, across the dusty dooryard and onto the porch, into her kitchen, where she closed the door behind her, wondering why she had stayed to watch.

She went into the pantry, stepped around her weights and slid the pistol on top of the cupboards, then returned to the kitchen, where she washed the ewe's blood off her hands, then sat at the table and unlaced her boots, pulled off her wool socks. Through the open windows, she could hear Scott's voice out in the barn, the dull clatter of the chain being dragged across the same wooden beam that Neal's father had used to hang himself.

She went into the bathroom, stripped off her top and shorts and stepped into the shower, lathered and rinsed herself thoroughly, wanting to wash away every trace of Katie's death.

When she was through, she wrapped a bath towel around herself and went upstairs to dress, putting on a crisp, white long-sleeved shirt and pair of faded jeans. Wide leather belt. Rolled-up her shirt cuffs. She liked the look.

She returned downstairs to the pantry, where she kicked a ten-pound dumbbell out of her way and took some frozen lamb chops out of the old chest freezer. Part of farming, she told herself. All part of farming. The screen door opened.

'That animal did not feel pain, I guarantee it,' Scott said, tossing his new blue blazer on the kitchen table. His khaki slacks glistened red and brown. He seemed to study her.

'Take off your pants,' she said. 'I'll throw them in the wash.' The old linoleum felt cool under her feet.

'You okay?' he asked her.

'I've had better days,' she answered, even though there was more to his question than her slaughtered sheep. They both knew it.

'Toss me a couple brewskies?' he said.

Ellen opened the refrigerator, found two cans of Pabst and put them in his hands. He smelled of sheep, of fresh blood. It bothered her, the thought of them drinking beer over Katie's carcass, but she didn't say so.

'Neal's got some ideas about the barn,' Scott said, going back out the door, his pants riding low on his hips. Ellen followed him out, went around the side of the house to her salad garden, where she picked some spinach and chives, then returned to the kitchen to rinse them.

'Amazing,' Scott said, coming in again behind her. 'I mean, it was like he was putting her to sleep.'

'Mm.' *You told me*.

Scott unzipped his pants and stepped out of them as he went into the bathroom, turned on the shower and came out with the water still running.

'I invited him for dinner,' Scott told her, naked. 'I didn't think you'd mind.'

She took a knife from the maple holder. 'Scott, you never told me about the franchise.'

'It's business,' he said, stopping to give her a kiss. 'I didn't tell anyone.'

He went back into the bathroom, then called out to her, 'You know, Neal's a carpenter by trade.' This time when he stepped out of the bathroom, Scott had a towel wrapped around him. 'He's built a couple of barns before, post and beam, he's got pictures. Beautiful.'

Ellen started cutting the chives, her back to him. A moment passed.

'El, is this hard for you?' he asked. 'I mean, Neal showing up.'

'It's not hard for me.' She kept the knife moving.

'Maybe it's a little uncomfortable for me.'

'Maybe it is.' *Should be*. Chop, chop.

'He looks so much like my brother.'

'I thought he looked like April.'

Scott paused. Ellen could feel his eyes on her. 'Anyway,' he said, 'he's between jobs, and he was talking about fixing up the barn. Actually, building us a new one.'

Ellen stopped cutting.

'He says it'll take less than two weeks. We buy materials, give him room and board, that's all he wants.'

Ellen turned. 'Scott, where are we going to get money for lumber? We can't pay the bills we've got.'

'Hey,' he said, scratching at his new haircut, 'we're middle-class now. I get a salary.' It was hard to ignore the defeat in his voice.

'Are you going to tell me where you got the money to buy into the franchise?'

'El, how does any business get money? I took out a loan.'

'With *our* credit?'

'It's not important. Look, you've been telling me for years the barn's falling in.'

'But have him stay here?'

'Mo's room is empty. Why not?'

Ellen took a breath and let it out. How hard, really, was this going to be, Neal showing up?

'I didn't say yes,' Scott said. 'I told him I'd talk to you.'

Ellen scooped the cut chives into her hand, sprinkled them over the spinach, then brushed her hands together over the wooden salad bowl. She chose her words with care. 'Scott, if this is your way of making up to him—'

'Free labor, that's all it is.' Scott took his beer off the counter and took a long swig, then tossed the empty can in the waste basket, bouncing it off the wall. 'That's what the silent treatment was about, right? Neal shows up and you get a chance to crucify me a little more.'

'Scott, you brought Katie into the barn and hung her from the beam,' Ellen said. 'With Neal standing there.'

Footsteps on the porch silenced them, Neal outside the screen door, looking in.

'Here he is!' Scott said, finding a welcoming grin. 'Come on in, man.' He threw the door open and Neal caught it, then stood awkwardly in the doorway, wearing a black T-shirt, his black sweater bunched in his hand. His arms, Ellen noticed, were long and sinewy, like a swimmer's. His neck and shoulders were strong.

'Name your poison,' Scott said, opening the refrigerator. 'Another brew?'

Neal lingered at the threshold, looking in at Ellen. 'Maybe I picked a bad time.'

Scott waved his hand. 'Don't be crazy, come in. Hey, show her the picture of the barn you built. I've almost got her talked into it.'

Ellen looked over at Scott, and he pretended not to notice.

'Seriously,' he said, 'Ellie and I need to talk it over. Have dinner with us. Tonight you can sleep in Mo's bed. In the morning we'll have a decision for you.'

Neal looked at Ellen again, checking for consent.

She smiled at him. The smile he returned was tinged with sympathy.

'Hey,' Scott told him. He threw a quick punch at Neal's arm. Ellen heard the slap of it connecting.

She served broiled lamb chops, along with the spinach salad, last year's broccoli and some fresh-baked rolls. She used her good stoneware, and Neal ate heartily. To Ellen, the meal felt like those when they'd first bought the farm from Scott's parents, and Moreen was just learning to walk. The old farm kitchen was meant for meals like this, with its cast-iron cookstove and old oak chairs.

'So, Neal,' Scott said. He was wearing a white T-shirt, working on his second whiskey and ginger. 'Where did you learn so much about sheep and barns and things?'

'When I was fourteen,' Neal answered, 'I spent a summer on a sheep farm in Vermont and helped them build a barn. It's basic stuff.'

'What were you doing in Vermont?' Ellen said. 'I thought your mother moved to Greenfield, Mass.'

'The state sent me off to boarding school when I was thirteen. I don't know if you heard, they checked Mom into the hospital.'

Scott doubled his chin.

'She had a nervous breakdown. Well, more than one.'

Ellen studied him in a glance, thinking of her own mother.

'Look at that stupid thing,' Scott interjected. He was turned in his chair, looking at his blazer folded on top of the washing machine. '*Mainely Hardware*. Isn't that clever? Mainely. Mainely bullshit.'

Ellen caught his eye, furtively.

'So, Uncle Scott, when's the grand opening?' Neal said.

'Hold on,' Scott said, laying his fork on the table. 'If you're gonna live here, you can't be calling me "Uncle".'

This time Ellen wasn't so furtive. She got up from the table and started collecting the serving dishes.

Scott crumpled up his napkin and tossed it at her. 'Come on, hon, you know you want that barn.' He turned to Neal with a grin. 'See, she refuses to look at the picture.'

And there it was, stuck to the refrigerator with a Destin Hardware magnet, a beautiful building, tall and stately and bone-white against the dark green hills, almost churchlike the way its silo rose up above the peak. Hearing the silence in the room, Ellen turned to see both men watching her.

'Don't play hard to get,' Scott told her. 'You know you want it.'

Ellen laughed a little as she shook her head. 'Neal, I'd love you to stay here and rebuild the barn.'

Scott responded by sitting back in his chair, turning and giving Neal a wink. Neal smiled, but he kept an uncertain eye on Ellen.

'So what's for dessert?' Scott said.

'Yesterday's rhubarb pie,' Ellen answered. 'Neal, do you want some?'

'I'll get it,' Scott said, standing. He put his hand on Ellen's back. 'Can I get some for you, dear?' He was teasing, and she shot a playful elbow into his side.

'Maybe later,' Neal told them, sliding his chair back. 'I want to get started on the barn tonight.'

'Hold up, I'll give you a hand,' Scott said.

'Know how to handle a hammer?' Neal asked, straight-faced.

Ellen laughed.

'Hey,' Scott said. ' "*Mainely Hardware*: Serving Maine's hardware needs." '

'Ellen, thanks for dinner,' Neal said. 'It was wonderful.'

'Very wonderful,' Scott added.

'Yeah, yeah,' she said, waving them off. Despite her slight annoyance at the way Scott had discounted her, Ellen felt good about how the two men were getting along. Still, she couldn't help but wonder just how much Neal knew about his uncle – or the day his father died.

CHAPTER THREE

'Next left,' Rooftop Paradise said, and Randy turned the dark panel truck onto the Phipps Road, its headlights sweeping over the thick, green woods. A magnetic sign attached to the side of the vehicle read XYZ DIVERS – DIVING IS OUR BUSINESS. But tonight, fifteen miles inland, the men were not looking for water.

Rooftop moonlighted as a collection agent for Ray LaFlamme, a seventy-two-year-old financier who owned the Belle Atlantic Restaurant in Old Orchard Beach. LaFlamme's philosophy was simple: Property in southern Maine, particularly around the southern coast, was gold. Although he owned thousands of acres of it, he knew there were still farmers and fishermen who owned thousands more. And there wasn't a farmer or fisherman alive who wasn't in some kind of financial dung-heap. LaFlamme would loan them as much money as they wanted – for whatever reason. At twenty percent interest, what did he care? As long as they put up their property as collateral.

'Turn left up at the curve,' Rooftop said. 'Then look for a big potato barn and a mobile home in front of a burned-out foundation.'

Randy worked for Rooftop in both ventures, collections and diving, not that Randy had any particular expertise in either. A year earlier Rooftop had hired him after finishing a three-year stint in Thomaston State Prison for a drunk-driving, resisting-arrest conviction in which the giant had taken two bullets in the thigh and another in the chest, and still managed to send four state troopers to the emergency room.

Their job tonight was not a collection, per se, but what Rooftop liked to call an encouragement session – meaning after it was over, the borrower would seriously consider signing his deed over to LaFlamme. A couple of guys named Humphrey and

Jimmy Burdock who lived in a trailer on sixty acres of land in Eliot – they'd borrowed forty thousand dollars from Ray LaFlamme to start a company – and they still hadn't made the first payment, which was not all that surprising, given the homemade product they were attempting to market was pickled french fries. By the time the message reached Rooftop through one of LaFlamme's bodyguards, it was garbled and vague, but the upshot was they'd get an even four hundred bucks for a routine, ten-second beating.

'Two of 'em. Maybe we shoulda brought Gator-Aid along,' Randy suggested as he turned onto the old farm road.

'I don't know,' Rooftop said. 'That Gator's pretty bad. I think he gets a thrill out of hurting people.'

'What, like you on a drunk?'

Rooftop leaned forward in his seat and watched the mobile home slide past them, sitting in front of a pair of white block chimneys spaced thirty feet apart. A huge satellite dish stood at the edge of a rocky, overgrown field. A wooden, hand-painted sign banged into the front lawn said:

BUrDOCK'S FAMOUS FrICKLe'S
LIVe BAIt WeDDINg CAKe'S

' "*Frickles*," ' Rooftop said. 'That was the place.'

' "Wedding cakes?" ' Randy added with a smirk. 'Prub'ly a couple of faggots. Hey, I'll pound faggots for free.'

'Actually, I think these guys are brothers,' Rooftop said. 'They got the same last name.'

'Whatever. They borrow forty grand from Ray LaFlamme and then blow it all gambling, they deserve a pounding.'

Rooftop shrugged. 'Some people can't control their instincts.'

'Fuck. Then they burn down their own house for the insurance money, and the fire investigators find three points of origin. They deserve a beating just for being so stupid. Besides which, *pickled* french fries?'

Randy drove on to the dead end of the road, where he turned the van around, then stepped on the emergency brake. He looked over at Rooftop and said, 'What do you do it for?'

'Do what?'

'Fuck people up.'

'I don't believe I ever hurt a person for fun,' Rooftop said, 'even when I was drinking.'

Randy snorted. 'So how come you're still working for LaFlamme?'

Rooftop stared straight at him. 'Mister LaFlamme helped my mother put me through Saint Joseph's. I'm paying him back for my education. That's the only reason I do it. Plus sometimes I feel like I'm educating others in return.'

'Gator-Aid'll educate your ass,' Randy said. 'Doctorate in pain.'

They shared the rearview mirror and straightened their hair. Sometimes they'd pretend to be Jehovah's Witnesses, but in neighborhoods like this you never knew, the people answering the doors might be Witnesses themselves. Not to mention if these guys had wives or kids living there, like when one of them goes for the gun while the old man's busy getting beaten. One thing Rooftop had learned, people that lived in places like that, with the junk cars and mud-strewn yards and NO TRESPASSING signs – they always had guns. Some of them were fearsomely dumb, some were downright crazy. And you never knew which wayward relative might be lurking in the shadows.

'I don't give Gator much in terms of life expectancy,' Rooftop said, as they got out of the van. 'Personally speaking, I wouldn't be associated with him if he wasn't related to Mister LaFlamme.'

'Who isn't related to Ray LaFlamme?' Randy said, sliding the side door open. 'Some alcoholic bastard third cousin got a stepson in Baton Rouge, Louisiana, supposably swallowed by alligators escaping from his chain gang. And we get to show him the ropes.'

'Like I said,' Rooftop told him, 'I got a debt to Mister LaFlamme. If he says, "Show the kid the ropes," that's what I do.'

He lifted the carpet and pulled out the pair of magnetic signs that said MAINE STATE LOTTERY COMMISSION and stuck one to the side of the van. Randy took the other sign and stuck it to the other side. Then they got back in.

'You know what I think?' Randy said, as they drove back to the trailer. 'I think LaFlamme's groomin the Gator for bigger things.'

'What bigger things?'

'I don't know exactly, but I get a very dark feeling,' Randy said, shifting into neutral and stepping on the parking brake. 'Call it a premonition.'

They left the motor running while they climbed the two porch steps and knocked on the aluminium door. Randy reached in his jacket pocket and took out a small, green jalapeño pepper and popped it in his mouth. Rooftop knocked again. June bugs and spindly-legged flying spiders bounced off the bare yellow light bulb. Chewing the jalapeño, Randy's eyes watered, his cheeks reddened.

When the door opened he smiled warmly, as if he was about to make this guy rich. But it was a woman who stood there, wearing a blue, threadbare bathrobe, possibly the smallest woman Randy had ever seen. Not that she was a dwarf, but she definitely looked undernourished. Her hair hung straight to her shoulders, her eyes were sunken and ringed with dark, concentric circles. In fact, one eye was bruised, as though she'd been punched. Her cheeks were hollow. She could've been seventy, could've been twenty-five.

'Whadda you guys, goin fishin need worms?' she said, squinting up at them. Cases like this, Rooftop would usually detain the wife while Randy walked inside and did his business with the old man. Rooftop hated doing that, the way some of these wives fought. He was afraid of accidentally breaking their arms.

'Is Humphrey or Jimmy at home?' he asked.

Sweat ran down Randy's forehead. He looked back over his shoulder, working up a fiery saliva as he checked the dark road.

'Right here, I'm Jimmy, whaddya want?' the woman said, her speech a rapid-fire burst of syllables. She peered out at their van. 'What's this, I win some kinda gimmick or what?'

Rooftop looked at Randy, then back at the woman. In all the jobs he did for Ray LaFlamme, he'd never had to collect from a woman. He said, 'I thought Jimmy was a man's name.'

'No friggin man around here.'

'No Humphrey?'

'You lookin for Humphrey, you can find him on the gamblin ferry tomorrow night,' the woman said. 'And you can tell him for me that I don't want him back.'

Randy didn't say anything, just hauled off and spat a greenish spray in the miniature woman's eyes, then followed with a quick hard punch to the face. Rooftop saw one of her bony feet lift out of her slipper as she shot out of sight.

Rooftop gaped at his partner, amazed, then looked into the trailer, where the woman was sprawled out in her kitchen, just starting to move. Her cigarette smoldered on the floor beside her.

'For crying out loud,' Rooftop said to Randy. Then he ducked into the kitchen, picked up the cigarette and dropped it in the sink. Turning back to help the woman up, he saw that she'd already pulled herself onto one elbow. Blood ran thinly from her nose down her cheek and lips, but she seemed more concerned with her burning eyes, squinting and rubbing them with her flimsy bathrobe sleeve, like a raccoon washing itself.

'Dirty bastard,' she slurred.

'Never mind that,' Rooftop told her. 'You need to take responsibility for your financial obligations.'

He stooped and gently lifted her to a sitting position. Indeed, she weighed about as much as a raccoon.

'See, when you borrow money from a man and don't pay him back, you might as well be stealing that money from him,' he said to her. 'Now you people have missed your second payment, which means you owe Ray LaFlamme five thousand dollars, plus six hundred in late fees. I don't think anyone's going to complain if you pay half now and half on the weekend.'

'Uh,' the woman replied, reaching her skinny hand into the pocket of her bathrobe.

'This'd be cash, not check,' Rooftop explained, but then he saw that what she pulled out of her pocket was not a check or cash but a tiny revolver, and he hunched up his back and charged through the door, knocking into Randy just as the shooting started, *bang-bang-bang-bang-bang-bang*. She fired the gun like she talked, all six shots popping off before the men had made it down the steps.

'You hit?' Rooftop said as they jumped in the van.

'No, you?'

'Nope.'

'Christ, who keeps a gun in their bathrobe?' Randy said, ramming the shift into D and screeching the tires on the road. Rooftop looked back at the trailer's lights as the van tore up the country road.

'That's what I call paranoid,' Randy said. 'She in pursuit?'

'Nope.'

Randy checked his rear-view. 'Want to go back?'

'What the heck for?'

'I only hit her the once.'

Rooftop shook his head. 'Once was once too much for a lady. What's the matter with you?'

'Some lady,' Randy said. 'Friggin witch, if you ask me. We best get home anyway. I don't want the wife askin a lot of questions. I told her we had to dive in the dark tonight so we wouldn't upset the sea turtles.'

'What're you gonna tell her about tomorrow? Looks like we'll be spending the night on a gambling ferry.'

'I don't know, some story. Dumb bitch believes anything I tell her.'

Rooftop gave him a look, kept right on looking at him until Randy said, 'You got a problem?'

While Scott and Neal worked on the barn, Ellen folded laundry and finished her report cards, then made her way up to her spinning room. She had two looms and a spinning wheel in the room: the smaller loom for her commissioned pieces, and the larger one, which Scott had bought for her ten years ago, for her art. She'd been creating this piece for almost two years now and figured it would be done by summer's end. It was her homage to parents, hers and Scott's, all of whom had died in recent years.

As soon as she sat down, she lost herself in her work, lulled by the sounds of the night, the water falling over the dam, an occasional sheep crying, its bell ringing, the creaking and banging of her barn coming down. She might have worked for three hours or more, only dimly aware of the time, when she realized that the hammering had stopped and the men were downstairs talking softly. She vaguely heard the ring of dishes and silverware, the footsteps on the stairs, and the door opening behind her.

'You are amazing.'

Startled, Ellen turned to see Neal standing beside her, staring over her shoulder at the tapestry. With Scott snoring across the hall, she hadn't heard him come into the room.

'I plug away,' she said.

'You plug away,' Neal replied with gentle ridicule. 'That's a museum piece.'

Ellen smiled, unsure how else to respond. It was a wide tapestry, four feet at the borders, and nearly five feet high. Centered in the work was a scene from an old photo, of her mother crouched in the Ogunquit dunes on a misty day, beside a sand sculpture she had made of an Indian woman lying on her back, watching the stars. Ellen's woven image was done in undyed wool, the natural browns, blacks, whites and off-whites of her own flock, made to resemble an old, sepia-toned print. In both the photo and the tapestry Ellen's mother appeared uncomfortable posing. She had been thirty-six at the time and quite beautiful. But while her sculpture gazed skyward, her own head remained bowed self-consciously.

'How many hours do you have in this?'

Ellen shrugged. 'I haven't counted.'

'And I thought you were so practical.'

'I am, about most things.'

'Is this your mom?' he asked, pointing.

'Yeah. She was a sculptor. Metals mostly. She died a few years ago, choked to death on a lemon sour ball – candy.'

Neal was silent for a moment.

Ellen laughed. 'I'm sure she always thought she'd be struck by lightning.'

'I hope you don't mind the interrogation,' he said.

Ellen turned, shrugging off his concern. 'I'm flattered that you're interested.'

Along the top quarter of the tapestry, where Ellen had yet to inlay the shed, the bottoms of five sepia-toned wheels showed. In the top right-hand corner, the bottom of a full, yellow moon sat in a black night sky. Ellen had made the yellow dye with the skins of onions she had grown.

The entire bottom border was a frozen lake. A jagged break in the ice revealed swirls of creamy white water. From the left and right corners grew gnarled, bare-limbed trees that crackled upward like flames, the tops of which protruded through the central image as dune grass.

'White water?' Neal ventured.

'The reservoir, where Scott's parents were killed.'

'They drowned?'

Ellen nodded. 'Christmas morning. Your grandmother was helping Rolley deliver his milk – she did every Christmas. It was snowing and his truck slid off the road.'

'So that's going to be the milk truck?' Neal guessed, pointing to the pair of wheels on the upper left, where four butterflies of different-hued yarn hung from the unfinished image.

Ellen nodded.

He touched another butterfly, one that hung from a larger wheel in the center. 'This is a spinning wheel?'

'Scott's mother's. Your Grandma Chambers taught me to spin and weave.'

'And?' Moving his finger to the right.

'My mother's motorcycle, an old black BMW.'

'So tell me,' he said, putting his hand on her shoulder. With his other hand he reached over her and tapped the yellow butterfly with his long finger, set it gently swinging. 'Is this the moon or the sour ball?'

'I haven't figured that out yet,' Ellen said, turning to look up at him.

His hand remained on her shoulder, it felt good there, and his dark eyes met hers intently, with either admiration or sympathy or a combination of both. Then he removed his hand and stuck both hands in his pockets. 'Ellen, I feel like you were coerced into letting me stay here.'

She shook her head with a dismissive scowl. 'I don't handle surprises well,' she told him. 'But you're family, Neal. You're always welcome here.'

'I may be Scott's family,' he said. 'As far as you're concerned, I'm just the son of someone who used to be your brother-in-law.'

'Whoever you are,' she replied, conceding the point with a smile, 'I'm glad you came.'

He returned her smile, easily. 'So am I,' he said, and then he sighed. 'Well, I guess I'll leave you alone and try to get some sleep.'

'Neal, how long do you think it'll take?' Ellen asked, hoping he wouldn't take her abruptness for anxiety. 'I mean, realistically.'

'Realistically? Twelve days.'

'Twelve?' Was he teasing her? She met his eyes again.

'Twelve,' he repeated. 'Why?'

She shook her head. 'You seem very confident, that's all.'

He shrugged. 'What can I say? This is the first of July. I'll be done on the twelfth.' He gave her a last look, a kind of polite smile, then he left the room.

'Night,' Ellen said, hoping she hadn't insulted him.

When Ellen got into bed, Scott stopped snoring. He lay still for a moment, then rolled over to face her. 'He's just like his father was, another Superman. Supposedly he's gonna help me too.'

'Help you what?'

Scott smirked. 'With the business.'

'I thought Mainely Hardware would be making all the decisions now.'

'Hey, between them and Neal, how can I go wrong?'

'*Shh.*'

Their bedroom door was closed. Ellen could see the light under the door – she had left Mo's bedroom light on for Neal. She glanced at the clock. One eleven. She rolled over to face Scott, ran her fingers through the soft warmth of his chest hairs. He covered her wrist with his hand. She could feel his heart beating.

'Scott, he's your family,' she said quietly. 'If you'd rather not have him here, tell him we've changed our minds.'

Scott sighed. 'I've got to admit, the kid's a hell of a worker,' he said. 'Incredible energy.'

Ellen softened her voice to a whisper. 'I didn't tell you what Maddy said.'

Scott grunted again. It was as much interest as he could muster in anything Maddy might have to say.

'At the reception, she told me that Neal was holding the electric fence.'

'How the hell could he hold onto the electric fence? And *why*?'

'I don't know. To make a fool out of her.'

'She doesn't need any help there.'

'But if it's true—'

'Ah.' Scott rolled over, facing away from her. 'I don't know what you see in her.'

Ellen rolled onto her back and listened to the quiet night. Just a sheep's bell jingling down in the pasture and the waterfall whispering beyond.

'Do you think he knows?'

Scott took a breath. 'Doubtful,' he said quietly. 'I know his mother wouldn't have told him.'

Ellen closed her eyes, listened to the waterfall. So many years. Let it go.

Second of October. Thirteen years ago, almost. Why keep the date? But you do. A Tuesday afternoon. Ellen's first year teaching. Neal's twelfth birthday.

Scott's older brother Jonathan, convinced that his son's behavioral problems were the result of his unchallenged genius, had bought the boy a state-of-the-art computer for his birthday and stored it at Scott and Ellen's. April – Neal's mother – had arranged to pick it up the day of Neal's birthday, while the boy was at school.

Over the years, Ellen came to believe that intuition had brought her home that day. At the time, however, she believed it was her sheep. A hurricane had been moving up the coast all week and was due to hit Maine sometime in the evening, but it had reached New England hours ahead of schedule, and Ellen wanted to make sure the sheep were safe in the barn.

The wind was already loud when she pulled into the dooryard. Seeing April's Jetta parked beside Scott's Mercedes – Scott often came home for lunch – Ellen stopped in the house to say hi and to see if April needed anything for the birthday party later.

Despite the rain and wind outside, the farmhouse was very quiet when Ellen went inside. In the living room she found wrapping paper spread on the floor, the carton containing the monitor sitting in the middle of it. Then she heard a noise upstairs.

'Where are you guys?' she called and started up the stairs, not suspecting a thing, until her bedroom door slammed shut.

'Be right out,' Scott yelled, but when Ellen went up the rest of the way and pushed open the door, she found the two of them standing on either side of the queen-sized bed, their backs to her. They were getting dressed. April turned first, with a kind of smile – an anticipatory grimace. Ellen did not remember looking at Scott. What she did remember was the sound of his voice as she left the room and escaped down the stairs, through the house and back onto the porch into the loud wind, where the watering pails had overturned beside her black rubber boots and piles of brownish clouds tumbled angrily over the barn.

Leaning on the porch rail, staring wildly off at her farm, the entire scene flattening before her eyes, Ellen finally heard Scott's words. 'You didn't see anything,' was what he had called to her.

Then it was raining and she was in her car, turning onto Main Street, a calendar-image, double-wide New England boulevard bordered by white colonial homes and wide sidewalks, crimson and yellow leaves ripping from ancient maples, while Ellen's new white pickup truck – her anniversary gift from Scott – came slicing through it all, the rain, the plastered leaves, rippling this perfect place with confusion.

The white-pillared town hall stood on one end of the town

commons. A white-domed bandstand sat in the center of the wet green. At the other end of the commons stood the white Assembly of God Church and parsonage – April and Jonathan's residence – the all-good Reverend no doubt closed in his oakwood study, preparing Sunday's fire-and-brimstone sermon.

Ellen pulled into the driveway without a thought about what she was going to say to Jonathan. She hadn't planned to come here. She had told herself she would return to school and try to finish out the day. But here she was, at Jonathan's house. Pastor Johnny, Scott called his brother, though never to his face.

Jonathan was a charismatic faith healer who had recently earned his master's in theology from Harvard Divinity School. Brad Beecham, Destin's first selectman, claimed that Jonathan had cured his throat cancer with a touch of his hand. Marianne Clancy, a receptionist at the tax office, swore that Jonathan had driven the muscular dystrophy from her body. Similar testimony of his healing powers issued from scores of adults and children from as far away as Virginia, who had been cured of their ailments at Jonathan's hands. His church boasted nearly 500 members, 475 more than the Congregationalists who had attended services in 1985, before he had taken it over.

Maybe it was because Ellen felt like she needed healing that day, the reason she went to Jonathan and not to her best friend, Maddy Sterling – who, after all, was a counselor by trade – or to her mother, who would have only acted like she'd seen it coming. Perhaps Ellen believed that Jonathan could heal her.

When Jonathan let her in, she asked if she could use his phone.

'Is everything okay?' he asked as she dialed.

In fact, she could not think of a single aspect of her life that was okay or would ever again be okay. Everything was poisoned. She called the elementary school to have the bus drop Moreen off at Scott's parents' house up the hill from the farm. Then she called the high school. When Arlene Glanville, the secretary, answered, Ellen told her that something had come up and she wouldn't be back. Arlene told her not to worry, that school was letting out early because of the hurricane. Arlene asked if everything was all right. Fine, Ellen said.

'Because Scott just stopped by, looking for you,' Arlene said.

'Thank you,' Ellen told her, then hung up.

All the while, Jonathan stood across the kitchen table from her, watching with growing concern. 'You seem troubled,' he said. In years to come, Ellen would wonder if this was a brotherly thing – Jonathan, older than Scott by six years, academically superior, athletically superior, morally and spiritually superior, the favored son . . . was this Scott's way of compensating?

At the time, Ellen did not wonder. In fact, standing there in the pastor's kitchen, she felt embarrassed that she had come here. Furthermore, she knew if there was any hope of salvaging any of their lives, that hope would be dashed if she told Jonathan. But here she was.

'Did something happen to April?' he ventured.

A short laugh escaped Ellen. April's betrayal did not surprise her. President of the Destin Historical Society, the Concerned Citizens' Coalition; April, with her gray Jetta, her colonial home and community standing. No, April did not surprise her.

But Scott—

—who had always ridiculed his brother's high and mighty attitude, his sister-in-law's hypocrisy. More honor among thieves than preachers, he'd say. At least a thief only wants your money.

Jonathan leaned his fingers on the table, his face clouding with concern. 'Ellie, what is it?'

'Nothing. I just found them in bed together.'

Disbelief now, Jonathan raising his long body, seeming to float on his feet.

'Scotty?' he answered. Wind rattled the windows. 'Scotty and April?'

Ellen gave him another sort of laugh, as if this were Jonathan's own fault – or maybe she'd just thrown him an affliction that he couldn't heal. He pulled a chair back from the table as if to sit, but he leaned heavily on its back. 'Are you sure?'

'I don't even know why I'm here,' Ellen said, turning to leave. Then the door blew open and April flew in with the wind, carrying a cardboard box that read MONITOR.

'She didn't see anything,' April said to Jonathan. Then she wheeled to Ellen, who flinched, thinking April was about to throw the box at her. Her lipstick was smudged, her cheeks a deathly white.

Jonathan left the room.

April dropped the box on the counter and pursued him, saying, 'Jon, she didn't see anything!'

As her voice trailed away, Ellen saw Neal's head pass the window. The door opened.

'*Aw-right!*' he said, seeing the monitor on the table. Then he must have read the turmoil in Ellen's face, because for the moment they just stared at one another while the trees roared outside the house and the rain beat at the windows. Neal was a bright boy, lean and dark and exceptionally gifted, and Ellen wondered if he had any idea how his life was about to change. 'Maybe you should go outside and play for a while,' she told him.

'Yeah, in a hurricane,' Neal said, and he turned toward the living room just as the footsteps drummed down the stairs, April's voice echoing through the parsonage, '*Jon, would you wait?*', Jonathan bursting into the kitchen with a white shirt and wide black necktie, his trench coat flung over his arm, Neal tracking his father silently as Jonathan threw open the storm door, his shoulder banging off the frame.

'*Jon, are you going to listen to me?*'

Neal studied Ellen, as his mother trailed off in pursuit of his father, the sound of her voice chiming against the glass.

'It'll be okay,' Ellen told him. Then she left. Out in the driveway, in the rain, she walked past April while Jonathan started his car.

'You didn't see a *thing*!' April yelled at her.

Ellen got in her truck and followed Jonathan's car out of the driveway, past the white church and down the road. When Jonathan turned right, Ellen went left, and she drove for the rest of the afternoon with no destination, the trees waving her wildly on, the rain and wind buffeting her pickup, the road signs shivering, windshield wipers dashing madly. Everywhere she went, houses were plastered with yellow leaves, roads littered with branches, limbs torn from trees.

Sometime that night, in the full violence of the storm, she made her way to York and knocked on Maddy's apartment door.

Maddy was a counselor then, with the Department of Social Services, and she had a small, private practice in the basement of a pizza place. She was in the process of divorcing her first husband, an anaesthesiologist, while waiting for her next husband, a surgeon at the same hospital, to divorce his wife.

When Maddy opened the door, she just stared at Ellen, an odd mix of fear and curiosity on her face. 'Everyone's looking for you,' she said, trying to hand Ellen a cordless phone. As if they'd all met and sorted it out and now were going to have a prayer session.

Ellen gave a sneering laugh. 'Do you have something to put me to sleep?'

'You don't know?' Maddy asked her.

'Know what?'

Maddy took a breath, kept her eyes on Ellen. 'Call Scotty.'

Ellen heard the gravity in Maddy's voice and her heart checked.

'Jonathan,' Maddy told her. 'He hanged himself.'

Ellen felt the building shake with a gust of wind, and she thought it was going to collapse around them. Hanged himself . . . She wanted to ask if Jonathan was dead, but she wasn't able to get the words out. Then she didn't need to.

'He did it in your barn,' Maddy said. She paused, staring soberly at Ellen, then added, 'El, school let out early today.'

Ellen expelled a long breath of air, vaguely wondering what school letting out had to do with Jonathan's hanging himself. Then it hit her.

'*Moreen*?'

Maddy was already nodding and she took hold of Ellen's arms. 'Mo found the body. She's okay.'

'Oh, God, no,' Ellen said, and she leaned heavily against the door jamb.

'Moreen's okay,' Maddy said again. 'The bus dropped her off at Scott's folks' house, but they weren't home, so she walked down the hill.'

Ellen turned. 'Have you seen her?'

'I've been waiting here for you. Ellie, what happened?'

'I've got to go,' Ellen said, opening the door.

'Talk to me.'

Maddy captured her, held her in her arms. Ellen could feel herself trembling, spiked to the hilt with adrenalin, way too much to manage. 'I've got to see Moreen,' she said.

'She's at Jonathan's.'

'At Jonathan's,' Ellen said, but the words didn't register. Jonathan was dead. Hanged himself.

Maddy nodded, kept their eyes connected. 'Everyone's at Jonathan's. April and Neal, Scotty and Mo. Scott's parents are there too . . .'

Again Maddy tried to hand her the telephone, but Ellen would not take it.

'Scotty doesn't know where you are. He wants you to call him before you go over.'

Ellen shook her head, not wanting to talk to anyone, least of all Scott.

Maddy's eyes darkened. 'If this is what I think it is,' she said, handing Ellen the telephone, 'you'd better get your stories straight before you go over there.' She seemed confident in what she was advising, so Ellen took the phone and dialed.

Scott picked up after the first ring. 'Ellie?' he said anxiously.

She didn't respond.

'Everyone's here.' His voice was low and serious and slightly slurred, as if he'd been drinking. There was talking in the background. The television, Ellen realized.

'Is Moreen okay?' Ellen said.

'She's fine.' There was a pause, and then the background noise quieted. Ellen pictured Scott closing himself in a closet so no one would hear him. 'El, I know we need to talk,' he said softly, and then he paused. 'Did you say anything to Maddy? Nobody here knows. It'd kill my parents.'

Ellen listened angrily, not about to answer.

'I wish it was me,' he said. 'Babe, I love you so much—'

Ellen hung up the phone.

The steeple bell was pealing and a vigil gathering outside the parsonage when Ellen drove down the street, townspeople wearing rain gear, substituting flashlights for candles in the rain, looking like they were preparing to storm the stockade fence, a structure that had been originally erected in 1711 as a defense against Indians, but now protected only the parsonage swimming pool. Not wanting to talk to anyone, Ellen considered stealing into the church and entering the parsonage through the secret tunnel that connected the cellars of both buildings, but, in deference to her claustrophobia, she drove into the driveway, keeping her eyes straight ahead as she parted the mourners.

Scott was waiting in his brother's kitchen, his face deep with remorse, when Ellen came through the back door. He wore his tweed jacket and tapered slacks – his dressed-for-success look – and he came forward to hug her, whispering, 'I told them one of the sheep got hurt in the storm and you brought it to the vet's. I'm so sorry.' She held out a hand, to keep him back.

'Where's Mo?' she said.

'Up in Neal's room reading,' he answered. 'She's okay.'

Ellen started to walk away from him, but he took hold of her jacket sleeve. 'Ellie,' he whispered, and she smelled the alcohol on him. It took all of her restraint to keep from lashing out at him. She pulled away and walked through the arched doorway, where she saw Scott's father Rolley sitting on the carpeted stairs, leaning forward with his arms on his knees, staring down into the living room; Neal sat over in the corner, on the piano bench, working intently at his new computer. Scott's mother Thelma was sitting on the couch beside April, both of them absently watching a medical drama on TV. There was a box of tissues on the coffee table between vases of flowers and plates of cookies and brownies. A few used tissues lay crumpled on the couch. When Ellen walked into the room, April's eyes shone intensely at her. Ellen could tell that she was keeping the secret too.

Thelma lifted herself off the couch and met Ellen in front of the coffee table, where they embraced.

'How can you believe this?' Thelma said, the bones in her back suddenly seeming very frail. Scott came into the room then and placed a hand on both of them.

'That was Jonathan,' Thelma said. 'Never complain, never burden others with his troubles.'

Except for hanging himself in his brother's barn for a child to find, Ellen thought bitterly. She looked over at Neal, whose eyes remained fixed on his computer monitor. She said to her mother-in-law, 'I need to see Moreen.'

Thelma backed away, nodding. 'You go see her,' she said. 'I left her in Neal's room, away from the adults and all the blubbering. It must have been such a shock for the poor thing, but we're all very proud of her, she got right to the phone and called nine-one-one.'

Thelma released Ellen. Scott didn't.

'How's the sheep?' he said, feigning concern, anxiously massaging Ellen's shoulder.

Ellen paused, to decipher his words, to decide how to answer him, indeed, whether to answer him at all.

'Was the leg broken like you thought?'

Ellen saw the halting glance Thelma gave her son at that

moment. Then the old woman turned her gaze to April, whose own stare remained riveted on Ellen. There was no flash of revelation; in fact, it was the way Thelma's eyes sank, unfocused, to the floor that told Ellen her mother-in-law had just seen through the charade. Ellen backed away from her then, ashamed to have been part of it, and she went up to find Moreen.

Rolley glanced up at her as she passed him on the stairs. 'Some God, huh?' he said. 'Let the good one go.'

Ellen was stunned. Although she'd never heard her father-in-law say a kind or complimentary word about Scott, he had always been the most unquestioning believer Ellen had ever seen, a fearsome Christian, the eldest son of parents who believed that every form of enjoyment was a sin. Now Rolley chuckled bitterly, as if every belief he'd ever held had just vanished along with his favorite son. 'Yup, he's a real beaut.'

In that moment Ellen realized that nothing would ever be the same, not with any of them: Rolley sitting on the stairs so small and devastated, Scott standing in the middle of the floor pretending he hadn't heard the old man's invective, Neal eyeing Ellen from behind his new computer, April watching her too carefully, and Thelma walking off to the kitchen, knowing everything. Thelma would not tell Scott what she knew, Ellen was sure of that. She would not even tell her husband.

And six years later she would die with the secret.

CHAPTER FOUR

Two o'clock. Ellen stared up at the darkness while Scott slept fitfully beside her. Although the waterfall spilled steadily and loudly over the dam, to Ellen the sound was as quiet as breathing. With Moreen gone, the farm seemed quieter than ever.

Aware of a faint illumination in the room, Ellen raised her head and saw a line of light bleeding under the door. She got out of bed, careful not to disturb Scott. Putting on her robe as she opened the door, she walked down the hall and discovered that Neal was not in Mo's bed.

She went downstairs, thinking that he might have fallen asleep on the living room couch, but the room was empty. She went into the kitchen, took the flashlight off the counter, then opened the back door and went onto the porch, where she heard the jingle of a single sheep's bell.

She walked down the steps and across the dooryard to the paddock fence, saw one of the ewes pacing nervously, pursued by two of her lambs. Opening the gate, she went in to quiet them – and her heart jumped.

Peering down past the pasture fence, she saw something – was it Neal? – sitting up on the crest of the hill. She aimed her flashlight, but the beam was weak, so she crept through the bustle of ewes and quietly pushed open the pasture gate. Again she shone her flashlight down.

He appeared stationary on the crest of the hill. But as she crept closer, his body suddenly took shape, wrapped in a blanket, his right elbow moving rapidly up and down.

Ellen stopped abruptly, felt her heart beating in her chest, wondering whether to come ahead and risk embarrassing him, or to turn and leave (and risk embarrassing him even more). She cleared her throat loud enough for Neal to hear, but his arm continued moving.

Then he turned his head.

'I didn't want to wake you,' Ellen said from her distance.

He turned back. She wondered whether she should just turn and go back to the house, but she found herself venturing a few steps closer, until she was no more than ten feet away.

'I got worried,' she said. 'You weren't in the bedroom.' She drew a breath and shone the light on him. Reflexively, she drew a sharper breath, this one in relief.

Wrapped in his blanket, he was spinning yarn with a drop spindle, alternately feeding wool from the bundled dark fleece he held in his lap and working the spindle with his right hand. She stepped closer, shone her flashlight onto the fleece in his lap – Katie's, she guessed. He stopped spinning and took Ellen's hand, directing her flashlight down toward the right, the gully. Four tiny eyes shone back at her like stars. Ellen's muscles clenched. Coyotes. He moved the light thirty feet to the right: another pair of eyes. The rogue, she guessed. She lowered herself to her knees.

'What are you doing out here?' she whispered.

'I'm presenting them with a dilemma,' he explained. 'They're very hungry, and I'm very confident.'

'Oh, Neal,' she said, hearing her own words coming back at her.

'Don't apologize,' he told her. 'A stranger comes to your house, you have a perfect right to ask how long he intends to stay.'

'You're not a stranger,' she said, putting her hand on his shoulder. 'Now will you please come back inside?'

He continued spinning the yarn. 'When the sheep are safe, I'll sleep in the house.'

Ellen sighed. A breath of wind came up, rippling the pond on its way over the dam.

'Besides, it's too beautiful out here,' Neal said, 'the way the moon reflects off the water.'

'Back when Scott's parents moved up on the hill, and we first had the farm to ourselves,' she said, 'we used to have parties down there all the time. We'd build a fire, and Scott and the guys would play music, and we'd all get wasted on homebrew and blueberry wine and go skinnydipping.'

Neal gave her a look.

'There was nothing sexual about it.'

'Of course not.'

She detected the sarcasm in his voice, subtle though it was.

'Sometimes Scott and I would wake up in the middle of the night and be the only ones left. And we'd just lie out under the stars listening to the frogs and the nightingales. Those were the best times. Mo was a baby, I was finishing school, we had lots of money.'

'Want some?' He dropped the blanket off his shoulder so it fell on her knee. She knelt up and pulled it underneath her. He gave her more. She moved closer to him and pulled the corner up over her shoulder. In the paddock behind them, the sheep kept moving. Neal's arm felt good against her, generous and warm.

'Can I ask you something?' he said.

'Yeah?'

'Did you have a chance to make amends with your mother before she died?'

Ellen took a long breath and let it out, while she considered her responsc. 'We probably never talked about what we needed to talk about.'

'What's that?'

'I guess I hoped she'd let me off the hook,' Ellen said.

'For what?'

'I don't know. For not measuring up. But I don't think she ever forgave herself, either.'

Neal kept spinning. 'Forgiveness isn't all it's cracked up to be.'

They sat quietly for a few moments. Then Neal stopped spinning and looked at her.

'Is it true your dad was an astronaut?'

Ellen laughed a little. 'That's the family mythology, isn't it.' She said. 'On my sixth birthday my mother took me to a restaurant and told me that my father was either a space explorer or a convicted murderer. Evidently, she only consorted with men who held titles.'

Neal smiled, resumed his spinning.

'She was an art professor in Baltimore at the time,' Ellen continued. 'NASA had commissioned her to do a piece to commemorate the country's first manned space flight. At the dedication she met candidate number one – the astronaut. Candidate number two was a guy who had two original Cézannes hanging in his bedroom. He had stolen them from a gallery in New York. At the time he was the most wanted art thief in America – I guess it inspired the romantic in her. Four years later he killed two museum guards in a holdup and got two life terms in prison.'

'You must be curious,' Neal said.

'About which one of them was my father? It mattered when I was younger,' she admitted. 'Being an optimistic kid, naturally I was convinced it was the astronaut. Then when I was in junior high, he did a space walk. Colonel Drew McDermott. I told all my friends, and my teacher brought a television into the classroom so we could watch him. I never felt so proud. But then they interviewed his wife at home, and I saw that he had two daughters of his own. When they cut back to him walking in space, I wished his tether would let go. That was the end of my father fascination.'

'Fathers can fuck you up,' Neal said.

'I got over it. But sometimes at night when I'd look up at the sky, I'd feel like I had something in common with the stars that no one else could possibly know.'

Neal looked up. She saw him smiling contentedly. She lay back on her elbows, raised her face to the blackness, the infinite billions of bright, silent worlds. 'Mothers can fuck you up too,' she said.

She remembered the restaurant in Baltimore. Their table was at a window, high enough so they could see the Atlantic stretch out beyond Chesapeake Bay. While they ate strawberry shortcake with birthday candles, her mother told her they were moving to Rome. She showed her a picture of bone-white pillars; she showed her the sculpture of David, naked.

Instead, they moved to Maine.

She remembered her mother kneeling in a shower of sparks outside a ramshackle garage they rented from a fisherman. Ellen was a girl sitting in the window loft, watching her mother surround herself with sparks, backed by the cold ocean, wearing leather work boots and a T-shirt drenched with sweat, making shapes of abandoned iron and steel, decorating the muddy yard with strange machinery that would never work.

Another memory: her mother hanging laundry in an April rainstorm, saying, 'This way we don't have to wash them.'

Then Ellen remembered lying in the cove one September evening, her long, fourteen-year-old body draped perfectly over the smooth rocks, watching the airplanes returning to Maine from Boston, New York, Baltimore, Rome, playing dot-to-dot with the stars.

She remembered the afternoon when she was called to the guidance office and told that her mother had been taken to a hospital and that she would be living with the Nielsen family for a while. Later she learned that her mother had tried to drown herself in the ocean and how the waves kept driving her back.

She remembered walking into this clean, spacious house, the way the family – husband, wife and daughter – stood in front of the kitchen table while Mrs Nielsen introduced them. The table was set in a bay window with a view of perennial gardens and a small duck pond. One of Ellen's mother's sculptures – it looked like an exploded lighthouse – stood on a small rock island in the center of the pond. That's what Mrs Nielsen wanted Ellen to see. What Ellen saw instead was that the way the table fit into the bay window, there was room for only three chairs. So for the nine months that Ellen lived with the family, Ellen straddled the corner leg. Ellen remembered their first dinner, and the way Mr Nielsen didn't say anything until his wife had left the room to get dessert, and then he looked straight at Ellen and said, 'Please do your best to limit your bathroom time to three minutes.' She remembered waking up the first morning in her new house, realizing she had wet the bed, a studio couch they had carried from the basement up to Halley's bedroom.

Ellen took the blanket off her shoulder and rolled up to her knees in the pasture grass. 'Neal, we have a bedroom for you. It's no inconvenience. Come on, I don't want you sleeping out here alone.'

He laughed softly, pulling the blanket around him. 'If you don't want me sleeping out here alone, go get your sleeping bag and join me.'

An image intruded on Ellen unexpectedly, the two of them cradled in each other's arms. It surprised her, and she pushed to her feet.

'We'll wake up with the frogs and nightingales,' he teased.

'Yeah, and them?' She waved her flashlight down toward the gully, moving the beam down the green hill to the thick, gray brush . . . but there was no sign of the glowing eyes.

'I told you,' he said, 'we have an understanding.'

Ellen sighed a kind of laugh. She really did admire his confidence. For a moment, she almost considered sleeping out here beside him, curled up in her musty old bag. But she had to work tomorrow, her last day of school—

'Ellen.'

'Hm?'

'Go to bed.'

She smiled, shone the light once more down along the stream bank, the pond, the dam.

'Please be careful,' she said, touching his shoulder again. He reached for her hand, but she drew away from him and walked to her house.

CHAPTER FIVE

Ellen awoke to the sound of hammering the next morning. Scott's radio was playing, he had gone to work over an hour ago. When she saw it was seven-forty, she jumped out of bed, gathered her clothes, ran downstairs to brush her teeth, grabbed her car keys and cap and was out the door.

She spotted Neal high off the ground, straddling a roofing truss, pulling nails out of the ribs. Amazingly, the barn was stripped to its posts and beams on two sides. Looking straight into the sun, Ellen pulled the visor of her cap down. 'You be careful up there.'

Neal raised his hammer to wave, and she caught her breath.

'Always,' he replied.

She noticed that he had removed the paddock fence from the corner of the barn and constructed a temporary pen for her two rams inside the ewes' pasture.

'Think it's safe having them so close to the ladies?' she called, watching Buckminster, a small but Muscular brown Merino with curled horns and extremely valuable wool, pacing incessantly inside the pen, intermittently springing at the Z-boarded gate with a loud *whack*. Mike, the less passionate of the pair, huddled in the slim shade of the barn, content to blaat his lustiness over the nervous bawling of the ewes around him.

'I thought we could add some excitement to their lives,' he replied, looking down at her with a sort of scowl. 'You're not going to school—?'

She figured it was because of her clothes: khaki shorts and a baggy cotton shirt; red Converse All Stars on her feet. No socks.

'Last day,' she explained.

'In July?'

'Class trip. We lost two weeks in January, with the ice storm.'

'Class trip sounds like fun,' he said.

'I'll trade places with you.'

Hearing a car pull off the road, she looked back to see the dark green panel truck coming in, hauling an open, 17-foot Boston Whaler.

XYZ DIVERS
DIVING IS OUR BUSINESS

Randy pulled the van just short of the porch, and Rooftop Paradise unfolded his seven-five mass from the passenger side, to let Moreen out. She looked curiously at the dismantled barn as she came and gave Ellen a quick kiss on the lips. 'The guys need neckties. Can they borrow a couple of Dad's?'

'Neckties? Come on in,' Ellen said, glaringly aware that she had just invited her daughter into her own house.

Moreen walked up the steps, seeming to labor under the weight of her pregnancy. Despite the hazy warmth of the morning and a forecast for a record-breaking heat wave, she wore a black, long-sleeved jersey under a black wool shift. Her forehead and cheeks shone.

'Oh, Mo, you look so hot,' Ellen said. 'Let me find you something cooler.'

'That's okay, they're in a hurry,' Moreen said, coming into the kitchen, the silver ball in her tongue clicking against her teeth as she spoke.

Ellen led the way into the living room then started up the stairs. 'What color ties?'

Moreen remained below. 'Anything,' she answered. 'They've got a meeting, and they want to look spiffy.'

Outside, the van's horn blared. That didn't take long, Ellen thought, but she kept it to herself. She went up to her bedroom, found a couple of Scott's older neckties, then went into Moreen's room to find something short-sleeved. Downstairs the horn blew again.

'Mom,' Moreen called up to her.

Ellen sighed. She left Moreen's room and brought the neckties down. 'Thanks, thank Daddy too,' Mo said, reaching for the ties, but when her sleeve pulled up, Ellen saw a dark bruise in the crook of her arm.

'Mo, what's that?'

'What's what?'

Ellen caught her sleeve and lifted it, revealing four distinct marks on the inside of her forearm, side by side, like fingerprints. The horn blew again.

Moreen shrugged. 'Must've bumped it, I don't know, Mom, I've gotta go.' She pulled the sleeve back down and headed for the kitchen.

Ellen followed closely, her mind tripping over images of Randy grabbing her arm, wondering if the reason Moreen came in the house was to show her the bruise.

'How do you bump the inside of your arm?' Ellen persisted.

'I'm coming,' Moreen called, pushing the screen door open. 'Gotta go,' she said to her mother.

'Wait, before you leave,' Ellen said, coming onto the porch behind her, suddenly hating to see her daughter go back to that van. 'Is it okay if your cousin uses your room for a week or two?'

'Not my room anymore,' Moreen answered with a shrug, then she looked askance. 'My cousin?' She peered over the rail at Neal, who was standing beside the van, talking with Randy. 'You mean that guy at the wedding was Neal – who used to babysit me?'

Randy blasted the horn, glaring up at her.

'I'm coming,' Moreen called patiently again, then turned and gave Ellen another quick kiss. 'I'm gonna be late for work.'

'Work? We've got school.'

Mo wrinkled her nose. 'You don't think I'm gonna spend the day at Funtown—?'

Ellen sighed. 'Honey, I hate to see you hurt.'

'Love you,' Moreen said to her, then started down the steps, the horn wailing.

Rooftop hadn't seen Neal at first. He'd been staring at the farmhouse and sucking on his asthma inhaler when he heard the noise behind him. And there was Neal, claw hammer in hand. Rooftop was over a foot taller than Neal, and a good deal heavier, and when he recognized Neal he aimed a ready stare through his thick glasses.

But Neal ducked down to see Randy inside the van. 'How's it goin'?' he said, and he walked around the front of the vehicle, with Rooftop following close behind. As he approached the driver's door, Randy sat slightly back in his seat, taking his hands off the wheel, keeping an eye on Neal's hammer.

'Listen, I was way out of line the other day,' Neal told him, offering his hand toward the window.

Randy replied by leaning on the horn.

'I was hoping we could get started on a better foot,' Neal said.

Randy regarded him sullenly. 'You wanna discard that thing?'

Neal looked down at the hammer in his other hand and gave a self-effacing smile. 'Sorry,' he said, and tossed the hammer on the ground. His right hand remained offered. 'Really, no hard feelings?'

Randy smirked. He looked away as he stuck his hand out the window.

'So, where you guys diving these days?' Neal asked, shaking hands.

'Here and there,' Rooftop answered. 'Got a couple of moorings to put in down in Kittery.' His deep voice was drowned out when Randy blew his horn again.

Up at the house Moreen came onto the porch. Ellen caught the screen door behind her.

'I'm coming,' Moreen called, and Randy blasted the horn at her, glaring while she said something else to her mother, then came down the steps showing him the neckties.

Ellen leaned on the railing, watching, as Moreen walked toward the van, studying Neal, then stopped about ten feet from him. 'Hey,' she said. 'Don't you remember me?'

A smile formed slowly on Neal's face, and he replied, 'Of course I do. But if I remember right, you weren't pregnant then.'

'Hah!' she said, giving him a thumbs-up. The horn started up again then, and kept blaring, even when she got in the van, and Rooftop ducked in beside her.

Moreen draped the ties around Randy's neck. When Randy whipped them off, Mo grabbed her eye, lowered her head, and poked him with her elbow.

The horn stopped, the van rocked, and Ellen, without planning to, bounded down the steps and was there at the van reaching through the window, bunching Randy's white shirt in her fists.

'*What are you doing to her?*'

'Hey, fuck.' He started to laugh, raising his arm to deflect her.

But Ellen yanked him toward the window, ripping his shirt open. That's when he stopped laughing.

'Mom, I'm okay,' Moreen told her.

'Don't you touch her,' Ellen said to Randy.

'Mind your own business, bitch.'

'Just go,' Moreen told Randy, who found the shift, gunned the accelerator.

'Love you,' Moreen called, as the van shot back toward the barn. Ellen spun away. Neal caught her, kept her from falling. Then the van jumped ahead again, swerving as it sprayed gravel back at the boat, then chirping onto the black top and roaring up the hill.

'God, I'd like to kill him,' Ellen said, as she watched her daughter going away.

'Proverbs sixteen, thirty-two,' Neal replied, taking a hand off her and waving cordially, as the van dipped out of sight. ' "He that is slow to anger is better than the mighty." '

He reached behind her and retrieved her cap, which had fallen back off her head and hung from her braid. He threaded her hair back through, then squared himself to her and fit the cap on her head, giving her a glint of admiration as he did so.

'Which means let's take our time.'

Agitated as she was, Ellen's heart swelled in her chest. Had Neal just let her know he was planning some kind of revenge against Randy, like maybe picking a fight with her sometime when Rooftop wasn't around to defend him? Ellen couldn't deny that she disliked Randy with an intensity that she'd never felt towards anyone. It bothered her, even frightened her sometimes to feel like that. But her hatred for Randy – and her frustration with Moreen for getting pregnant by him and then marrying him – had been building for months. She loved Moreen with all her heart and would have done just about anything to protect her – as any mother would. Still, something Ellen had heard in Neal's voice had chilled her, even dampening her rage somewhat. Or maybe it was the way he was smiling as he looked up the road where the van had gone. *Let's take our time.* His words echoed round her head. Already late for work – and not knowing Neal well enough to ascertain if he was serious or just posturing – she turned away from him without saying a word and walked to her pickup truck.

Still, it wasn't Neal that distracted Ellen as she stood there in Funtown, watching her kids dressed in bathing suits and shorts and sunglasses and sandals, running from ride to ride. It was

Moreen, shadowing her all through the bright, hot day, like a storm cloud looming.

'Moreen?' Scott had said in disbelief when Ellen called him from the teacher's room. 'She's the biggest tomboy that ever lived. Don't worry, Mo's not gonna take shit from him or anyone else. Are you kidding?'

He was right about Moreen. Having grown up on a farm, even as a little girl Mo had been tough and fearless and physical. Ellen could remember her stacking firewood when she was five; trying to carry a wayward lamb back to the barn, hauling pails of water to the trough, even throwing hay bales onto the flatbed. When she was older, between mosh pits, skateboarding and ice hockey, her body was constantly bruised – not to mention the rings and studs she'd had poked through her flesh lately. Ellen had no doubts Moreen was a tough kid.

But it wasn't toughness or fearlessness Ellen had seen this morning. Behind Mo's cheery smile and easy kisses, Ellen had seen a girl showing her mother that she was out of her care and living with a dangerous and remorseless man. And Ellen had no idea why.

The front doors were propped open on the sidewalk, but the store wasn't open for business. Beside the '50% Close Out Sale' poster was a much larger sign, proclaiming in day-glo orange: '**Another Mainely Hardware COMING SOON!**'

Inside the building, a crew of laborers moved walls of shelves, unpacked crates and carried trash out to the dumpster, while carpenters sawed and hammered. Down in the back, across the alley from the laundromat, Scott unlocked the back door to let the young men in. Randy wore a jacket and tie. Rooftop carried a briefcase. Scott locked the door behind them.

The back room was brightly lit by a bank of fluorescent tubes along the center of the ceiling. Aisles of steel shelving stood stripped of merchandise, except for a few snow shovels and bags of rock salt.

'Feel like old times,' Randy said, 'us giving you money for a change.'

'Feels pretty friggin good to me,' Scott replied, leading them through a door to his office. Rooftop and Randy sat on the leather couch in front of a wide, glass-topped coffee table. Rooftop hunched over his briefcase and pulled out a manilla folder, started thumbing through the papers inside.

'Mister LaFlamme's attorney did a title search and found everything in order,' he said. 'We didn't need a survey. No building inspection, either. Randy's seen the house. We know you're making improvements to the barn. That's good.'

Scott wheeled his desk chair over to the table.

'Oh yeah, we took a couple of your ties,' Randy told him. 'Hope you don't mind.'

'As long as you don't take my house,' Scott said with a laugh.

Randy chuckled with an air of authority. 'No way we're gonna let that happen, Scotty.'

Rooftop gave him a look, then slid a document in front of Scott. 'This is your promissory note,' he said. 'You can read it if you want. Basically, it states that Mister LaFlamme is loaning you the money, eighty thousand dollars, at twenty percent interest, to buy into the Mainely Hardware franchise.'

Rooftop took a red pen from inside his jacket. 'This is the mortgage deed, and you need to sign this binder agreeing to keep a hundred percent damage insurance on your home and name Mister LaFlamme as the mortgagee, same as you did with the store.'

Scott looked the documents over. 'So now I owe him a hundred and a half.'

'Well, plus the interest,' Rooftop told him.

'I know it probably feels like a big risk,' Randy said.

'Yeah, you know that, huh? Like if the franchise goes belly-up, Ray LaFlamme not only gets the store, he gets my house and farm too? Is that what you mean?' He looked at Randy straight-faced for a moment, then winked.

It took Randy a second to realize that Scott was pulling his leg. 'I like that sense of humor,' he said. 'See, we think alike, us two.'

'Just don't tell Moreen about the loan,' Scott told him.

'Hey,' Randy said, raising his hands in mock surrender.

'I don't want my wife to know, either,' Scott added.

'Be discreet. Exactly.'

Rooftop set a certified bank check face up on the coffee table, turned it to face Scott.

'Mainely Hardware, here we come,' Randy said, picking up the check and handing it to Scott. 'Really, I think this is a very wise move.'

Scott took the check as he stood up, folded it and stuffed it in his pocket. 'Guys, thank you very much. Tell your boss thank you. I'd invite you to have a drink with me, but I'm a company man now. No drinking on the job.'

'Just as well,' Randy said. 'You ever give this guy a drink' – he hitched his thumb at Rooftop – 'you best be sure you're either caught up on your payments or you're in a fast fuckin car.'

By noontime, the temperature had swelled to ninety in the shade, and the school bus back from Funtown felt like an oven. As soon as Ellen's classroom emptied out, she loaded her pickup truck with cartons of her personal things and headed for home – and summer. Unfastening the third button of her cotton blouse as she drove, she fanned the fabric away from her chest to let the air circulate around her skin. She pulled her shorts up to the tops of her thighs. She couldn't wait to get her underwear off.

Before her truck was within sight of her farm, she heard the miserable crying of her sheep and she knew that Neal had begun the weaning. She pulled into her dooryard and saw that her ewes were separated from their lambs into their respective pastures, both groups bustling at the wire mesh fence that kept them apart, all of them bawling frantically.

Ordinarily, she would have isolated the ewes in the cellar of the barn and withheld their water until they dried up, but now the barn was almost completely skeletonized, stripped to its posts and beams and a few stalls standing off the old wooden floor. She spotted Neal carrying a wide plank from the barn to an area beside the tool shed, where he had stacked the lumber in four separate piles. Despite the overwhelming heat, he was still wearing the same clothes: black wool sweater and corduroy jeans.

'How can you stand all that crying?' she said to him as she pulled off her sneakers.

'I've heard it all before,' he answered.

She got out of the truck barefoot, the fine gravel of her dooryard burning the still tender bottoms of her feet.

'How was your last day?' he said, heaving the plank onto the pile. His sweater was covered with sawdust and wood chips, his hair and face similarly caked.

'Hot. Want something cold to drink?'

'In a while.'

Ellen watched him walk back to the barn, thinking she should talk to him about Randy. But deciding that he didn't look like a young man contemplating murder, she went out to the pasture to feed the sheep.

She started with the rams, hoping to quiet them while she tended to the others. The gate of their pen was fastened with rope at the top and a hook-and-eye on the bottom. Showing Buckminster the bucket, Ellen unfastened the rope from the top of the posts and pulled the gate back just enough so she could fit the pail through. She kept her bare foot behind the post. But the instant Bucky spotted his food, he sprang with enough force to not only split the diagonal board and rip the eye-screw from the post, but knock Ellen to the ground, pinning her ankle beneath the frame. As both rams escaped, immediately all thirty-seven ewes broke for the pasture with Bucky in feverish pursuit, burrowing into their ranks, mounting one after another. Mike, less aggressive, nevertheless took advantage of the stragglers at the back of the flock.

Ellen's ankle burned and bled. Afraid it was broken, she raised herself onto her elbow and reached to gingerly lift the gate off it, when she heard the bells of her flock and saw them charging back up the hill toward her.

She pushed the gate off her ankle and started to pull herself up, when Neal's arms went around her, lifting her effortlessly to her feet. He wheeled away from her and snapped the gate's broken board off its frame, then went wading into the marauding flock. While Bucky was preoccupied with one of his nieces, he swung the board down hard, driving two nails into Bucky's rump. The ram twisted and let out a sorry blaat, raising his face in protest, at which instant Neal smashed the side of the lumber down on his ear, and the animal's legs crumbled beneath him. Dropping the board, Neal lifted the ram by its horns and heaved mightily, swinging him into his pen. Dust flew. The other ram, Mike, trotted into the pen of his own accord. Neal shouldered the gate closed, looped the rope over the tops of the posts, then propped the broken board against the front of the gate, securing the bottom.

He turned to Ellen, who was leaning on the pen for support.

'He's got a beautiful fleece,' she said, flexing her toe to test her weight on the ground, 'but a nasty disposition.'

'Then you have to be nastier,' Neal said. He glared into the pen, and the ram let out a sorry complaint.

Allowing a little more weight on her foot, Ellen tested her ankle.

'Okay?'

Taking a couple of cautious steps, she said, 'Once summer's over and I see how the ram lambs develop, maybe I'll replace him.' She wanted to show Neal that she could be practical about these things. He took hold of her shoulder and brushed off the back of her blouse, then, more tenderly, the back of her arm.

'Sure you're okay?' he asked, and he kneaded her shoulder a bit with his thumb. She took a deep breath and released it, allowing the tension to spill down through her chest. She flexed her neck. His hand remained on her shoulder. She took a deep breath. *Tell him.*

'Neal, I appreciate your help—'

She turned to face him, caught him looking at her breasts. Then she noticed that two more buttons of her shirt had come undone; she fastened them.

'I'm talking about Randy,' she said. 'And Moreen. I guess I want to figure things out for myself.'

He gave her a look she couldn't quite decipher, almost paternalistic in the affectionate way he frowned.

'What's going on with her?' he said, bending to brush the side of her shorts, the side of her leg. She reached back and dusted off her own seat.

'You know, Neal, we're not exactly the Brady Bunch here, in case you haven't noticed.'

He shrugged. 'At least you're a family.'

'Just let me deal with Moreen and Randy in my own way. Okay?'

He looked up at her, then turned away and pushed on the angled board, securing it against the gate. Behind them, the lambs kept bawling. Ellen straightened her cap, folded the sides of her visor down. 'I'm sorry,' she said. 'It's the heat. And I can't stop thinking about Mo.'

'I know,' he told her. 'Wanna take a swim, cool off?'

'I've got way too much to do.'

He smiled. 'No one's gonna see you, Ellen.'

His dark eyes glinted playfully at her, but she disliked the way he questioned her truthfulness.

'Come on, you've got the whole summer off.'

She sighed. 'Maybe,' she told him, 'if I can find my bathing suit.' She turned for the house. 'Do you want one of Scott's?'

'I thought we'd go skinny-dipping.' He raised his eyebrows at her, still teasing.

'I'll get you one.'

'There's nothing sexual about it,' he called after her.

She climbed the porch steps and went in the house, favoring her sore ankle. She stopped at the telephone and called Moreen's house, let the phone ring several times, but no one answered. Hobbling upstairs, she pulled off her blouse and dropped it in the straw laundry basket, then slid the cardboard box of summer clothes out of her closet. The room was easily ten degrees warmer than outside. A line of perspiration ran down Ellen's arm.

The first suit she found was a faded denim two-piece, one she'd had since high school. These days the top showed more cleavage than she cared to reveal, and the bottom rode too low on her hips. She still liked to wear it when she was alone, down at the pond or in the garden, never in public.

The suit she found at the bottom of the box was one she couldn't remember buying, a black one-piece. She unbuttoned her shorts and stepped out of them, pulled off her bra and panties and stepped into the suit. It was snug in the thighs and the elastic was strong, which she was glad of. When she fit her breasts in the cups and crossed the straps over her shoulders, she went to the mirror with apprehension, but was pleasantly surprised. She turned to the side. A slight rounding of her abdomen, but not bad for a thirty six-year-old who ate three meals a day. Hang it, her body was her own, she was too hot to worry about it. She pulled Scott's bathing suit from the box, checked to see that its netting was intact, then went downstairs and grabbed two clean bath towels from the linen closet.

Making her way barefoot down the dusty farm road and around the cinder-block pump house, the farm pond came into view. She could see Neal doing a lazy breaststroke up the middle of the narrow pond, working against the current, his body long, white, muscular, fully naked. She stopped for a moment to rest her ankle, which had begun to throb, and from the corner of the pump house watched him. The pond water looked brownish against his back, his firm white buttocks reflecting the sun. His shoulders were broader and more muscular than she had imagined, his biceps solidly defined. She imagined a strong, lean buck. Then he looked back at her, as if he'd known all along that she was watching him.

Embarrassed, she lowered her head and followed the dusty tire tracks down to the water, aware that Neal's eyes were on her all the way, conscious of her long white legs, her hips. She hobbled up the grassy bank onto the granite blocks of the dam abutment.

'I brought you Scott's suit, if you think you can keep it up.'

He gave her a pointed look, and she threw the suit to him with a smirk. 'Behave yourself,' she said. 'How's the water?'

He retrieved the bathing suit then lowered his arms and legs underwater. In a moment, he was swimming again, the bright orange suit reflecting the sunlight from below the surface.

'Great,' Neal said, watching her.

'I'll bet.'

Neal dived underwater again, disappearing into the darkness, and the water pulsed over the dam, splashing down on the other side. The pond was little more than forty feet long and only twenty feet wide at its widest, but quite deep at the dam. The body of water had once been a sleek granite cascade along the Agamenticus River. In 1828 the river was reduced to a stream when its headwaters were dammed to create a reservoir for the town of Destin. About the same time, Scott's industrious great-great-grandfather – the first of four generations of dairy farmers to inhabit the property – decided to dam up the gorge to restore his water supply.

He constructed the dam of granite blocks eighteen inches thick and bowed in toward the pond, its arch effectively resisting the tons of water that pressed against it. In 1930, after a midwinter earth tremor had realigned some of the blocks, Scot's grandfather had pumped the pond dry and sealed the upstream face of the dam with four inches of cement. To aid future repairs, he also embedded iron rungs down the left side and installed a drainage pipe at the bottom.

Because the sides of the pond were steep, a natural granite gorge, there were only two ways in: climbing down the rungs or diving. Not given to slow torture, Ellen always chose the latter, so now she sat on the edge of the abutment and lowered herself down to her diving rock as Neal rose out of the water, shaking the hair from his face. 'You're stalling,' he said, his eyes fully on her.

She took a breath, braced herself for the shock and sprang out, arms stretched over her head. She hit the water with hardly a splash, knifing down where it was icy and dark, then turned upward and kicked hard, breaking into the sunshine with a yell.

'*Not cold?*'

She slapped the water at him. Neal laughed and splashed her

back, his hair laying down his forehead in shiny black ringlets. She started a lazy sidestroke, and as the sun warmed her cheek and shoulder she experienced a sudden and unexpected feeling of euphoria. School was over, ten weeks of freedom. '*Ohhh!*' she cried, and plunged again, straight down where the water was cold and dark enough to draw the tension from deep inside her. She opened her eyes and looked up to see Neal's silhouette rippling the bright sky, then scissor-kicked powerfully, shot up toward the light and broke water beside him, taking a deep breath of air.

'Feel better?' he said, smiling affectionately at her.

'Mmm,' she said, a luxurious moan. She took another full breath to buoy herself and rolled over on her back, floating on the surface so she could feel the sunshine soak into her black suit.

Neal let the current carry him to the bowed center of the dam, where a clear sheet of water, maybe four inches thick, flowed over. The top of the dam was a flat surface of concrete that overhung both sides of the dam by six inches, to enable foot passage across the top during the dry months. Five heavy-duty eye bolts reached out of the lip, suspending a steel cable twelve inches above, to keep swimmers or stray animals from being swept over the top.

With his back to the dam, Neal reached up and grabbed hold of the cable, spreading his arms wide and pulling himself up out of the water so she could see the thick cords of biceps and the hard ripples of his stomach.

'Careful up there,' she said. 'It's a long way down the other side.'

Neal glinted down at her.

She looked down at herself and saw the bulge of her nipples showing through the bathing suit. She let herself sink in the water.

'I saw the coyotes again,' he said.

'Today?'

'Just now, up in the woods. Don't you have a shotgun around?'

'I got rid of it a few years ago,' Ellen answered.

'Where does Scott keep his revolver?'

'He hides it in the bedroom.' A wild notion came to her that he might have had Randy in mind, so she swam away from him.

'The bedroom where?' Kicking off the dam, Neal skimmed across the surface on his back, pursuing her.

'I don't know. He hides the gun, I hide the bullets.'

'And the plan is, once the burglars break in, you'll have a meeting.'

She rolled over and treaded water as he swam past. 'Scott had some trouble with depression a few years ago, after he went into bankruptcy.'

They moved around the center of the pond, circling one another, Neal holding his bathing suit up with one hand, Ellen enjoying his playfulness.

'Well,' he said, swimming toward the bank, 'If I'm going to finish that barn on time, I'd better get back to work.'

'Why twelve days?' Ellen said, swimming behind him.

'Twelve,' Neal answered, pulling himself onto the diving rock. 'Twelve is the heart of the universe.'

'Yeah, how's that?'

Sitting on the rock, he looked down at her matter-of-factly. 'Twelve months in the year.'

'That's because the moon revolves around the earth twelve times.' Using the strength of her arms, Ellen hoisted herself onto the rock beside him.

'Twelve hours on a clock, twelve inches in a foot,' he said. 'Twelve in a dozen.'

'Maybe it's because twelve is so versatile,' Ellen suggested, 'divisible by two, three and four. It was probably good for trading.' She reached up to the abutment and grabbed her towel.

'So you're saying twelve is practical,' he replied. 'There are twelve tones in western music. That's not practical, it's sound waves. Pure physics.' He grinned up at her, eyes sparkling.

'Twelve-volt battery,' she offered, pulling her long braid over her shoulder and wrapping it in the towel, loving the sun's heat on her back. 'Twelve-step program for alcoholics.'

'Twelve-bar blues, twelve signs of the Zodiac, twelve Caesars, twelve tribes of Israel.'

'Twelve disciples,' Ellen said.

Neal's eyes snapped at her, suddenly intent. 'Christ knew all about the twelves.' He seemed to enjoy instructing her, and it put her slightly on edge. 'You've heard of the twelve legions.'

She shook her head.

'Christ's fatal mistake,' he explained, standing up on the rock. 'When the Romans came to arrest him at Gethsemane, Peter sliced off a guard's ear, and Jesus told him to put down his sword. Remember that? Jesus said, if he wanted to, he could summon twelve legions of angels to slaughter every last one of his enemies.'

'That's right,' Ellen said. 'He was teaching us to forgive our enemies.'

Neal smiled at her, then dived into the pond again. When he surfaced, he turned to her and said, 'That's the popular misconception. Actually, what Christ was teaching us was that forgiveness can cost you your life. That's the real lesson of the New Testament.'

Ellen shielded her eyes from the sun and peered down at him, to see if he was kidding.

'Come here,' he said, and he jackknifed down.

Ellen dropped the towel at her feet, took a full breath of air and dived into the water after him, deeper and deeper, until her ears plugged up and the sunlight all but disappeared. She could see Neal descending further, the pale kicking of his feet, but when her lungs called for oxygen she turned and pulled for the light, yawning to pop her ears on the way up. She surfaced and held onto the cable at the top of the dam as she caught her breath. She looked down in the water, expecting to see the brightness of Neal rising, but the sun's rippled reflection obscured the view. She waited. She watched.

Suddenly afraid that he might be in trouble, Ellen filled her lungs and dived for the bottom, kicking and shoveling the water with all her strength, and as her world grew steadily darker and colder, she spotted him. He appeared to be working at something at the bottom of the dam. When Ellen's lungs demanded air this time, she ignored the call and pulled herself deeper, until finally she touched his arm. He turned and nodded, then pointed his finger upward. Together they sprang off the rocky bottom for the surface. Ellen broke water first, with a gasp. Neal came up beside her.

'Are you okay?' she cried.

'Yeah, why?'

The current carried their bodies against the dam face, and both of them reached up for the cable. When Neal turned to face her, his thigh came forward in the flow and stopped against hers. She drew her leg away.

'It's almost twenty feet deep there,' she said. 'I thought you were trapped.'

He laughed at her. 'I have exceptional lung capacity.'

'Neal, you're so talented,' she said, unable to resist the sarcasm.

'I've known a couple of women who think so,' he answered, giving her a look.

She flicked water at him. He laughed again.

'Did you see that pipe in the dam?' he asked.

'It's for draining the pond,' she told him.

'So if you wanted to drain it, you'd have to hire a diver, wouldn't you?'

He was talking about Randy, Ellen knew it. The way the pond pounded down the other side of the dam, she felt some comfort in the fact that their words would never be overheard. But she felt his eyes lingering. Aware that her nipples were standing up again, she thought about letting go of the cable, but the current was so strong she was afraid she might be swept over the top of the dam.

'Neal, do me a favor,' she said, looking straight at him. 'I asked you not to get involved in this.'

His dark eyes stared back fully.

A cry sounded in the distance. They turned their heads toward the pasture and heard it again, along with the sudden ringing of bells.

'It's Mo,' Ellen whispered, and she called out, '*Down here!*'

Ellen looked up. At the top of the hill, her flock of sheep came thundering down the hill, Bucky the ram in hot pursuit.

'Mo?' she shouted. She waited only a moment for a response, then dropped off the cable and grabbed one of the rungs on the face of the dam and pulled herself up to the abutment. Hobbling down the bank barefoot, then across the farm road, she tore open the pasture gate and started up the green hill, ignoring the burning in her ankle. Reaching the crest of the hill, she could see Moreen sitting just outside the rams' pen, her head bowed, holding her stomach. Ellen ran to her, fell to her knees.

'Honey, what's the matter?'

Doubled up in pain, Moreen sank to her side in the grass.

'Bucky got out,' she moaned. 'I think I did something.' She looked up at her mother, her eyes swimming in fear, her hands pressing up on the underside of her rounded belly, as if trying to hold her pregnancy in place. She was strikingly pale and soaked with perspiration.

Bells suddenly pealed, and they heard the drumming of hooves. Ellen looked back and saw Bucky herding the flock toward them.

'*Hey!*' Neal shouted, vaulting the fence with one hand on the post, the other hand holding the oversized waist of his bathing suit. Fixing his eyes on the ram, Neal stalked forward. If sheep possessed any degree of reasoning, it was clear that Buckminster was putting his to use, the way he nonchalantly dismounted his partner and trotted back to his pen. Mike, his cohort, followed eagerly. Neal pursued them both and swung the gate shut behind them, pushing the looped rope down over the top of the two posts, then fastening the hook and eye at the bottom.

Ellen looked up at him helplessly. 'We have to get her to the hospital.'

Neal came and knelt beside them, laid his hand on Moreen's knee. 'Where did he get you?'

She moaned, as the ewes moved in closer to watch.

Neal pressed his thumb on Mo's ankle. 'Can you feel this?'

She winced.

'This?'

'*Hnn!*' Hunching up, Mo reached for her mother.

'Oh God,' Ellen whispered.

'I'm going to see if you're bleeding,' Neal told her. 'Okay?'

Moreen peered at him fearfully. He lifted her dress, looked underneath. 'No blood,' he said to Ellen, 'but she's cold. And pale. I think she's going into shock.'

Miscarriage, Ellen was certain of it. 'We've got to call an ambulance,' she said.

Neal shook his head. 'Speed takes precedence,' he answered. 'I'll drive her.'

Ellen stared at him, aware that she was too frightened to think clearly, aware also of how she was relying on him. 'Mo, honey?' she said helplessly, touching her daughter's face.

'Tell Randy I'm sorry,' Moreen gasped.

'You're going to be all right,' Ellen told her.

'Okay,' Neal said, fitting his right arm under Moreen's thighs, his left under the middle of her back. 'Ellen, hold my trunks,' he said.

Distracted, Ellen didn't understand. She was thinking that if she had been in the house or working in the garden, this wouldn't have happened.

'I'm going to lose 'em,' Neal said, rising with Moreen in his arms. The bathing suit fell halfway down his hips. Ellen grabbed it, pulled it back up as he started walking, and she kept pace, holding the back of his trunks with her right hand and brushing Moreen's hair with her left.

'Don't tell Daddy, okay?' Moreen said. She was beginning to sound delirious, and it scared Ellen.

'Honey, try to relax,' Ellen said. She thought about her reason for keeping the ornery ram – to get another few pounds of fleece, another few dollars.

'What were you doing?' Moreen whimpered.

'What, honey?'

'You're wearing my bathing suit.'

Ellen shook her head. 'It was the only one I could find,' she said. 'I thought it was mine.'

'It looks good on you,' Moreen said, wincing as she tried to smile.

'Open the door,' Neal said, reaching his truck. Ellen did, and he ducked inside, gently laying Moreen on her side. 'Try to keep still,' he said.

Ellen started to get in with her.

'Go in and call the hospital,' Neal said. 'Where is it?'

Ellen ducked out of the cab, trembling. 'Sanford,' she told him. 'Take Route 91 from the center of town.'

'Tell them we're on the way,' he said. 'Meet me there.'

Before Ellen could question him, he started the engine.

'Love you,' Mo whispered between breaths. Ellen looked fearfully at her.

'Tell Randy I'm sorry,' Moreen said again.

'Sorry for what?'

'Just tell him.'

Ellen called 911 and told the dispatcher to watch for Neal's pickup truck. Then she drove her own truck to the hospital, made it in fifteen minutes, and left the motor running in front of the EMERGENCY ENTRANCE NO PARKING sign.

Neal was waiting when she came limping through the door. The receptionist looked sympathetic. A nurse appeared behind them and brought them into a small room that had a table, a television, and a small refrigerator and microwave on a counter. 'Moreen's placenta became separated from her uterus,' the nurse said after she had closed the door.

Ellen tried to grasp the meaning. 'She lost the baby?'

The nurse picked up the remote control and clicked off the TV. 'Would you like to sit down?'

Ellen stared dizzily at the table under her hands.

'In order to stop the bleeding,' the nurse explained, 'the doctor had to remove the uterus. It was the only option.'

A great breath escaped from Ellen's lungs. *The* uterus, not *her* uterus, as though it were a thing apart now, discarded. Neal put his arm around her back. 'Sit down,' he said. He pulled a chair up and Ellen dropped heavily in it. She looked down at the floor between her bare feet.

Hysterectomy.

The nurse continued talking, but Ellen barely heard her. She stared numbly, feeling as if there was not enough oxygen in the room.

'We were able to leave her ovaries,' the nurse said.

Ellen nodded.

'Here,' Neal said, handing Ellen a cone-shaped cup of water. She took the cup, touched it to her lips and drank, grateful for its coldness, despite how she shivered from the air conditioning. She had thrown a white T-shirt over her wet bathing suit. She noticed that Neal's bathing suit was held up with a wind of duct tape.

'It would help if we knew what happened to her,' the nurse said. 'Her pelvic area is bruised.'

'My ram attacked her,' Ellen said. She turned to Neal and said, 'Didn't you tell them?'

Neal nodded. 'It was the ram,' he said.

Ellen gave him a look.

The nurse said, 'I know you'd like to be with Moreen in recovery, but we're keeping her pretty heavily sedated. She'll probably sleep through the night.'

'I'll stay,' Ellen said.

The nurse studied her, looking like she had more to say, but Neal placed his hand gently on Ellen's shoulder. 'Want me to call Scott?'

Ellen heard him vaguely. 'No,' she said, remembering Moreen's plea. 'If he gets home before I do, tell him I went to see Maddy.'

An hour later, in the recovery room, Moreen opened her eyes.

'How are you, hon?' Ellen asked, taking her hand.

Moreen stared for a moment, tried to smile, then closed her eyes again. An IV tube was taped to her wrist. Ellen watched the fluid dripping slowly into her arm. She watched the slow rising and falling of her daughter's chest. Inside her own chest she could not relieve the terrible weight of her negligence. She sat at Moreen's bedside for another two hours, then left the hospital.

She didn't cry driving home. It wasn't exactly sadness she felt, more a deep sense of regret. She was thinking about all the ways she had neglected her daughter over the years, the way she had filled her own life with work, with her art and her animals, and now one of them had robbed Moreen of her own motherhood. It felt as if something had been torn out of her own womb.

She pulled off the highway onto Reservoir Road with one thought. She would call Justin Briscoe the minute she got home, she would have him come and haul Buckminster to the slaughterhouse and be done with him. She'd give Justin the meat in return for his services. She did not want the animal even in her freezer. Pulling into her driveway, she got out of her car and walked directly into the house, picked up the telephone and started to dial.

'Ellen, wait—'

Neal's voice startled her. He came in from the living room just as Briscoe answered his phone. 'It's Ellen Chambers,' she said to the butcher. 'Can you come over and take care of my ram?'

Neal put his hand on her arm. 'Tell him you'll call him back.'

She looked at him.

He nodded, with some urgency.

'Justin, I need to call you back,' she said, then pressed the cradle with her index finger while she held the receiver to her ear. 'What?' she said to Neal.

He withstood her frown. 'Ellen, the gate wasn't broken.'

She closed her eyes and took a breath, to calm herself. 'Neal, I don't blame you,' she told him. 'I should have gotten rid of that animal a long time ago.'

'Do you think the ram let himself out?'

Ellen's scowl deepened. 'What are you saying?'

'I'm saying that Moreen let Bucky out.'

He reached out and took the receiver from her hand.

'Ellen, Mo was hurt when she came over here,' he said, lowering his voice. 'Your ram did not do that to her.'

Ellen stepped back, her mind whirling, her head shaking in disbelief.

'It was a boot,' Neal said.

Inside Ellen's chest, a boiling started, slow but volcanic in its intensity. Leaning forward on the kitchen counter, trying to catch her breath, she felt as if her body was gathering energy from the atmosphere. She pictured Randy the way one pictures an enemy, alone and defenseless. In furious glimpses, she beat him to the ground with an iron pipe, she smashed his face, she stabbed him through the heart with a carving knife, she strangled him with the strength of her fingers and thumbs. It was relentless, the destruction she wreaked on her son-in-law, but it gave her no relief. Adrenalin tore at her heart.

'You don't know that,' she said. 'You don't know he kicked her.'

'Do you want a drink?' Neal asked softly.

She noticed he was once again dressed in his black sweater and corduroys. She turned away from him, went to the kitchen table and sat down, feeling all the day's heat pressing in around her. She tore her arms out of the T-shirt, pulled it over her head and flung it across the room, then sat there in her bathing suit trembling. Moreen's bathing suit. She jumped out of the chair.

Neal set a juice glass beside her, filled with whiskey. 'Have a sip,' he said gently.

Ellen picked it up and took a sip, coughing after she swallowed, feeling for a moment like she was going to vomit. She would have welcomed it. Get rid of this bile any way she could. She drank again, forced down the whiskey, then spun away from him and threw open the door, stormed onto the porch, intent on, what – walking? running? getting in her car and going after Randy?

As Neal came out, she turned and pushed past him, went back inside to the phone.

'What are you doing?' he said, coming in behind her.

She started to dial. 'I'm going to have him arrested.'

He thumbed the cradle down.

'Neal, stay out of this.'

She glared at him, her chest heaving.

'Take a walk with me,' he told her.

'*I don't want to walk.*'

'Ellen.' He placed his hands on her shoulders, ran his right hand gently down her left arm and took hold of her hand, tugging her toward the door.

She closed her eyes, not releasing the phone. 'Please let me handle this,' she told him evenly.

'Fine,' he replied. 'But first we walk.'

'Neal—'

'Take the bottle with you,' he said softly, letting go of her. 'Or put it away. I'll wash the glass so Scott doesn't see.'

Scott.

Moreen had begged her not to tell Scott. Ellen knew what he would do. Go over there with his gun. He would, too, and nothing and no one would be able to stop him. Though Ellen had fired the revolver only once, she knew well its incredible power, the way flames shot from the muzzle and the gun jumped in her hand. She imagined the black satisfaction of shooting Randy in the chest, firing all six slugs through his body, then watching him collapse to the ground and melt out of Moreen's life.

'Ellen,' Neal said. He was holding the screen door open.

She sighed. She replaced the phone in the cradle and came out on the porch. The sun had set and the greens of the pasture and woods were already darkening.

'Down back,' he said. 'We don't want to be seen on the road.'

She didn't answer, but went reluctantly down the steps and headed left, around the pump house and down the farm road, not talking. A pair of ewes inside the pasture fence started following them, bleating.

'I forgot to feed them,' Ellen said.

'I took care of it,' he told her.

They were walking fast, Ellen setting the pace, heading down toward the stream below the pond, feeling only a dull throbbing in her ankle, the whiskey already blurring her pain. But it had done nothing to suppress this wild electricity inside her.

'Why are we doing this?' she said.

'Because I don't want you going after him.'

'I told you, I'm going to call the police.'

'Do you think Moreen will press charges against Randy?'

She stopped but did not answer him. Then she started walking again, turning right and heading toward the pond. The waterfall grew louder, a heavy black sheet oozing over the dam and crashing on the rocky bed below, boiling and foaming away down the granite hill.

'I'll press charges myself,' she said.

'On what grounds? You didn't see him hurt her.'

She stopped walking, and finally the surge rose up from her chest and closed her throat. Tears burned at her eyes and she turned away from Neal, gulping a deep breath to keep from crying.

She felt like collapsing. Once again his hands found her shoulders.

'Let me help you,' he whispered. 'Let me help Moreen.'

The roar of the waterfall was like the roar building inside Ellen's head. She looked at the water moving, at the woods pressing darkly in beyond it. Sharply aware of what he was proposing, she felt blood rush to her brain. Without answering him, she started up to the farm road again, returning to the house.

'I'm going back to the hospital,' she said, walking away from him.

'Scott's going to be home soon. What should I tell him?'

'Don't tell him anything. I'll call him from the hospital.'

'Ellen—'

She paused, not turning.

'Tell Scott she had a miscarriage,' he said.

She looked back at him, saw a look of arousal in his eyes that made her heart skip.

'Tell him,' Neal repeated.

She resumed walking.

CHAPTER SIX

Ellen took the winding road to Sanford, her mind spinning in blackness. Although she no longer had any doubt that Neal would murder Randy if she so much as nodded, she forced the notion from her mind, vowing to do everything in her power to convince Moreen to have Randy arrested for what he'd done, and then to divorce him. What to do about Randy was clear enough.

It was the idea of Moreen's infertility that Ellen could not grasp. Her mind refused to accept the information all at once, same as when she'd heard that Jonathan had hanged himself, or that her mother had choked to death on a piece of hard candy. Logically, it was not incomprehensible. Moreen would not be the first woman to live her life childless – nor was she the first woman to marry a man who beat on her.

When Ellen got to Sanford, instead of driving to the hospital as she had intended, she followed the back roads that led to the house where Moreen was living with Randy and Rooftop. She came to a stop at the railroad crossing, then turned left onto Basin Road. The neighborhood was poor and rural, a smattering of old mobile homes interspersed among older farmhouses, a seemingly random assemblage of mismatched additions and roofs surrounded by overgrown fields and undernourished woods. Sheds were collapsed. Cars and pickup trucks sat on blocks.

The evening was warm. Ellen had on a beige T-shirt, a brown cotton skirt and sandals, and she'd tossed her white blouse in the cab in case it cooled off.

A mile down the road stood an abandoned chicken barn, easily a hundred feet long. On the other side of the barn was the old house that the chicken farmer had built in the 1940s, sided with green asbestos shingles.

Ellen stopped her pickup truck in front of the house and looked out at Randy's new black Cherokee parked in the driveway. What was she doing here, anyway? Looking for a confession? An apology? She shut off her lights and engine and opened the door, slipping her blouse over her T-shirt as she stepped out of the cab – not that the evening had grown any cooler, but she wasn't wearing a bra, and she was afraid of what she might do if Randy started gawking at her breasts. She walked up to the back porch.

Emboldened by anger, she didn't knock but pulled open the screen door and walked into the empty kitchen. A half-eaten chicken sat on the counter, surrounded by flies. Dirty dishes lay strewn across the table. The house stank of stale smoke and old beer.

She tiptoed through the doorway into the living room, where three of Randy's paintings hung. Framed in rough pine lathing, and airbrushed on black velveteen, they depicted a bull moose upending a woman canoeist in the river; a brown bear rearing up over a doomed female camper; an elk butting a woman off a cliff. In all three paintings, the victims were homesteading, back-to-the-land type women wearing skimpy shorts and tops that had either ripped open or come unbuttoned.

Ellen walked into a hallway off the living room, where she noticed an open door with dim light coming through. A red fire extinguisher was fastened to the right side of the doorway. He was in the cellar, she realized. She stepped softly to the door and looked down. A plywood hatch cover on barn hinges was raised over a two-foot-square opening in the floor, where a set of open treads, a ladder of sorts, led down to an oily, earthen floor. Ellen listened for another sound but heard nothing. A dank, musty smell rose up over her. She stepped down to the first tread, wishing she had worn something other than the skirt. Her legs felt vulnerable.

She stood there listening for a moment or two. Then, moving quietly, she took three more steps. As soon as her head ducked below the floor joists, a hand shot from between the open treads and grabbed her ankle. Ellen cried out and started to fall but caught the stairwell wall above her head. She kicked with the heel of her other sandal, caught the side of his hand. Then another hand emerged through a higher tread, wrapping around the front of her thigh and pulling back on her.

'Feels like my lucky day,' the voice said. It wasn't Randy, Ellen realized as he slid a rough hand off her thigh and ducked under the riser, rising up at the bottom of the stairs. Then he grabbed her swollen ankle with his free hand and jerked her leg in the air. She hobbled and had to hold the walls with both hands to keep from falling.

Ellen recognized him instantly, one of Randy's friends from the wedding, the one they called Gator. He was solidly built, about Neal's size but younger, maybe nineteen or twenty, with baby fat under his chin and a menacing gleam in his eyes as he looked up her skirt.

'I'm Randy's mother-in-law,' Ellen told him, jerking her leg. He jerked back, and her ankle flared with pain.

'Now I know where Moe-reeen gets such long legs,' he said, a southern twang to his voice.

'Where is he?' she demanded. 'Where's Randy?'

He leered up the length of her leg with a dangerous grin. All her adult life Ellen had wondered how she would feel and what she might do if she were attacked by a man. Now she knew. She wanted to kick him in the face as hard as she could, break his nose if she got the chance.

'You need to let go of me,' she said, hoping her change of voice would deter him. 'The police know I'm here.'

He released her ankle and folded his arms, still grinning. 'There, you're let go of. But, funny, I don't see you leavin.' He grinned, and she saw that one of his bottom teeth was missing. Evidently, he'd been kicked before.

Blood pumped behind her ears. Adrenalin surged. But she restrained herself, afraid that if she made any sudden move, he'd tackle her and haul her down. Backing up a single step, she said, 'Just tell me where Randy is.'

He placed his foot on the bottom step. 'Ever have one of those dreams where you could do anything you want, to anyone you want?' His eyes settled high on her thighs. 'See, that's me.'

Ellen glanced behind her, saw that she was three steps from the top, with four steps separating them. She lifted herself one more tread, and so did he, his eyes rising to her breasts.

'Yup, far's the gov'ment's concerned, I was swallowed by alligators two years ago. Far as they're concerned, I'm just some family's dirty little secret.'

She took another step up, and her head rose through the opening. Shifting her eyes, she saw that the hatch cover beside her was held up by a makeshift latch, a small wooden block that swivelled around a nail.

'We in some kinda hurry?' Gator asked. ''Cause the boys took off a little while ago, and I don't 'spect 'em back till tomorrow sometime. Far as I know, they went out fishing for stripers, lookin to catch the midnight tide.'

Ellen turned to face him, targeting the underside of his nose.

'Which means you and me got the whole place to our—'

She saw the flash in his eyes, but her foot was faster, glancing off his nose with enough force to snap his head to the side. He lunged blindly for her legs, but she was already bolting up the last two steps just ahead of his hands, which slapped at the treads behind her heels. Leaping out of the stairwell, she punched the wooden latch with the heel of her hand, then spun around to slam the hatch cover down.

He caught her swollen ankle in his hand. Fueled by fear, she jerked her leg, yanking his arm out of the hatchway. In the same motion she threw herself back onto the hatch cover, the plywood slamming off his shoulder and landing with a satisfying crack on the wrist that still clutched her ankle.

He called her a cunt. His fingers opened and she scrambled to her feet. Just as the cover flew up again, she grabbed the closest thing – the red fire extinguisher – tore it from its rack and swung it by its valve just as Gator's face rose into its arc. The steel cylinder bounced with a hard ring across his forehead.

'*Hah!*' he said. Still grinning, he groped at the air for a second, then dropped noisily down the stairs, as the hatch cover slammed down.

Ellen stepped back, keeping the fire extinguisher in her hand, ready for the hatch to open again. In a moment or two, once her adrenalin subsided, she picked up her sandal and walked quickly out of the house, trembling.

'Moreen had a miscarriage,' Ellen explained to Scott over the telephone.

At first Scott didn't reply. It was almost nine thirty.

'I'm at the hospital,' she told him.

'What happened?' Scott said gravely. 'I'll be right there.'

'Nothing *happened*,' Ellen told him, sounding more defensive than she wanted. 'She had a miscarriage.'

'Okay. I don't know about these things.'

Ellen sighed. 'I'm sorry, it's been a shitty day.' She had already decided to keep her encounter with Gator secret, since, technically, she had entered his house uninvited and may have fractured his skull, not to mention his nose.

'All things considered,' Scott said, 'a miscarriage probably isn't the worst thing that could've happened to her. What room is she in?'

'Scott, she doesn't want you to know.'

'Is that what she said?'

'She's embarrassed.'

For a second or two, Scott remained silent.

'I'm going to stay with her tonight,' Ellen told him. 'She's going to be asleep all night anyway.'

On the other end of the line, she heard Scott sigh. 'I guess it happens, huh?' His voice was soft, as though he were nervous, or close to tears. Or maybe relieved.

'It happens,' Ellen said. 'I've got to go.'

'America Sings and Dances' was the name of the stage show aboard the ferry. Rooftop and Randy sat at a table toward the back of the lounge, where it was dark. Randy worked on his fifth hurricane, the rum concoction the crew was pushing, while Rooftop drank diet Pepsi. An overnight gambling ferry wasn't the best place in the world for a recovering alcoholic. Small wonder – no casino ever lost money making people drunk. And this casino sure wasn't losing money tonight.

The low-ceilinged room smacked of makeshift luxury, with its royal red carpeting and hundreds of stuffed captain's chairs surrounding little round tables. In the center of the floor, a chandelier hugged the elevated ceiling above a circular stage, where a ring of young, sequined dancers kicked to the beat of a four-piece stage band. Running the length of the interior wall, a polished cherry bar was decorated with fish netting and nautical brass – in case the sliding ashtrays or occasional stumble of the dancers weren't enough to remind passengers that they were fifty miles from land, muscling their way through a dark and frigid and particularly unfriendly Atlantic. Already during the show two members of the audience had staggered between the pitching tables vomiting into their napkins.

At one in the morning when the show ended, a couple of crew members wheeled a Karaoke machine onto the stage. By now, the seaworthy audience had dwindled to maybe thirty, and they were all pretty well tanked, all but Rooftop Paradise.

The cocktail waitress started things off by singing 'Top of the World', by the Carpenters, smiling and nodding confidently through the whole thing. It wasn't hard to see she'd sung the song before, probably every night of the week.

'I'm thinking about getting out of the collection business,' Rooftop said after the first chorus.

'And do what?' Randy asked.

'Dive full-time.'

'No future in divin for an asthmatic.'

'Well,' Rooftop said.

'Well,' Randy said, lighting another cigarette.

'I happen to like diving,' Rooftop told him. 'Anyway, ever since I quit the booze, this other stuff's not settin right with me.'

'Tell you what don't set right,' Randy said. 'Me, tending on your diving jobs for seven bucks an hour. That don't pay a married man's bills, not to mention I got payments on my Cherokee and a baby on the way.' The ashtray slid over to Rooftop; he slid it back.

'Nobody said you had to quit collections.'

'Fuck. Only way Ray LaFlamme even tolerates a non-frog like me is cause I work with you.'

Rooftop took his asthma inhaler from his pocket and sucked on it, as he looked left and right, to make sure they weren't overheard.

'You know what I mean,' Randy said. 'Anyways, how the fuck does Gator, that asshole, get made a bodyguard, while you keep doin' the freelance shit. You got seniority over that punk.'

'Gator's family,' Rooftop said.

'No, there's more to it,' Randy said. 'LaFlamme's got something going with the Gator.'

'Like what?'

'I think he's got Gator-Aid doin hits. Terminations.'

Rooftop scowled, looked over his shoulder. 'Keep your voice down.'

'That's what it is,' Randy said. 'LaFlamme knows you wouldn't go that far. That's the only reason you got passed over.'

Rooftop sipped his Pepsi skeptically.

Randy leaned forward on the table. 'Hey, what do you think LaFlamme pays for a hit?'

'I wouldn't know.'

'Ten, fifteen?'

'Not in Maine.'

'Six or seven thousand, I bet. That's some serious re-muneration, bud. Work five days a year, spend the winter in Hawaii, dive to your heart's content.'

Rooftop shook his head soberly. 'We'll educate this guy tonight. Then I'm giving my notice.'

Randy stared at him, sat there staring and smoking and thinking. 'This guy tonight,' he said, 'Humpty Dumpty?'

'Humphrey Burdock, the potato farmer.'

'Yeah, pickled french fry farmer, real fuckin noble vocation. He takes a huge loan from Ray LaFlamme which he's got no intention of payin back because he's too busy feedin LaFlamme's money to slot machines, not to mention he's probably sleeping in his truck because he beat the shit out of his old lady once too many times because he's a drunk and a low-grade character. And you seriously got a problem inflicting pain on this asshole?'

'You're the one that hit his wife,' Rooftop said, 'which was way overboard as far as I'm concerned.'

'Yeah, overboard, huh? I say we throw Humpty Dumpty overboard, make a little example to LaFlamme's other deadbeat clients. Who knows, maybe if LaFlamme sees you got the gonads to do the deed, you know? Little promotion?'

Rooftop took a wheezing breath, then sat there staring right back at Randy through his thick lenses. 'You're not God. Neither am I. Besides, you don't kill a man that owes you forty thousand dollars.'

'Well, then, I think it's time he had some major whip-ass laid upon him.'

Rooftop sighed.

There was a couch in the recovery room, which the nurse had made into a bed for Ellen, with a light wool blanket and cotton sheet. The room was warm and lit with a small night light. Ellen lay in the semi-dark for hours, listening to the steady rhythm of Mo's breathing, hearing voices in the hallway that would rise and fall with her own consciousness.

Periodically she would get up and check her daughter to make sure the blankets hadn't fallen off or that her IV tube wasn't crimped. When it got to be three o'clock and Ellen was no closer to drifting off than when she'd first lain down, she gave up trying. She concentrated on her breathing, as she'd learned in yoga. Deep breath in . . . Deep breath out . . . Pause . . . Peace . . . Repeat.

For some reason, she pictures Scott's mother Thelma walking down the road to their house. It's twelve years earlier, on a cold autumn day, two weeks after Jonathan's burial. Scott is off working at his store. Moreen's upstairs reading. Ellen stands in the pasture, surrounded by her sheep, watching the old woman hobble down the road.

She has known that Thelma would come eventually, to sit in her kitchen. In fact, she's been waiting. Now, while Ellen builds the season's first fire in the cookstove and they talk about the twenty new sheep Ellen has bought, they hear Moreen close her bedroom door upstairs, and Ellen thinks it curious the way Mo has been avoiding her grandmother since her uncle's suicide, especially considering the special relationship the two of them always shared.

'I'm so scatterbrained lately, I can get lost in my own back yard,' Thelma says over her cup of tea. 'But I think I know what happened with my boys that day.' The women avoid each other's eyes at first. Thelma looks out at the barn and pauses for a number of seconds. 'Oh, I don't doubt April felt neglected, as much time as Jonathan devoted to his ministry. And Scotty, such a troublemaker, always trying to put one over on his older brother.' Thelma turns back to Ellen at that point, indeed seems to study her. 'Now Scotty's done a terrible thing and he's torn right up about it. Any mother could see that. If his father ever suspected—'

Thelma closes her eyes and breathes deeply.

'When it comes to holding a grudge, I've never in my life seen anything like these Chambers men.'

She pulls the kitchen chair close to Ellen's and looks in her eyes.

'Ellie, don't you be like that,' she says. 'Scotty's going to have to live the rest of his life knowing what he did, and I know how it'll eat right at him.'

Ellie looks away from the woman, raises her face defiantly to stop the aching in her throat. Thelma puts her hand on Ellen's arm.

'I don't want to lose both my boys, dear. Scotty loves you more than life itself, and he needs you to forgive him.'

Ellen stares implacably down at the wood-grained table.

'Life's a long road,' the old woman tells her. 'If you don't come to terms with what he did, you may never be able to get past this awful way you feel.'

Clench as she does, Ellen can no longer hold back the tears. She pulls away from Thelma, raises her hands to her face and cries for a moment or two, until she's able to stop. Then she dries her face with her flannel shirt sleeve and stands up.

'I can forgive him,' she says. 'I can try. But I don't think I'll ever get over this.'

The old woman rises from the table, far more hunched than Ellen has ever seen her, and makes her way to the door. As she takes hold of the latch, she turns her head and says one thing more, something that Ellen will not understand.

'Forgiving Scotty is only the beginning, Ellie. If you want to save Moreen, sooner or later you're going to have to face the truth. And then you'll need to forgive yourself.'

With that, the woman walks out the door.

'Forgive *myself?*' Ellen says, to herself, and she throws open the door and strides out to the porch, catching the rail in her hands.

'The truth about what?' she calls, but the woman walks on.

At three in the morning the casino manager shut the power off, and that's when Humphrey Burdock tried to pull the slot machine over, which was about the time the Jamaicans escorted him from the casino. It took all four of the little uniformed bastards, too, and then they locked the door on him, so Humphrey went out on the deck to smoke a cigar.

Three in the morning. The Karaoke music had stopped. The bells from the slot machines had stopped, the loudmouthed drunks from Massachusetts had gone to bed, and now Humphrey stood alone under the lifeboats watching the ocean rush past him, trying his damnedest to light his cigar against the gale that whipped across the deck, while this monster of a ship hummed and vibrated and crashed its way through the waves, its twin smokestacks blackening the low clouds above.

Twenty bucks to his name. So tomorrow when he got off the boat, maybe he'd stop at the liquor store and buy Jimmy a big bottle of coffee brandy. At least he'd have something to give her for their anniversary . . . if she'd let him in when he got back. Wouldn't surprise him one bit if she'd already changed the lock on the door. Couldn't blame her, really, after he went and lost the gas money on Megabucks the week before, then blew two hundred at Grange Casino Night, then belted her one when she complained about it. And now losing the rest of the Frickles money on the gambling boat?

Humphrey hunched over his last match. The wind snaked around his shoulders and snuffed it out, then laughed in his ear. He stuck the cigar back in his pocket.

Yup.

Change of luck, that's all he needed. Like maybe in the morning he takes that last twenty to the Wheel of Fortune. Why not? One shot, forty-to-one. Now there's a story. The day I won your grandma back.

Behind Humphrey, the door slammed open in the wind and someone came out on the deck.

'They rob you too?' Humphrey said.

'Humpty, right?'

Humphrey turned. In the instant of understanding, Randy stuck out his chest and let fly a full spray of pepper juice. Problem was, he spat against a wind that whipped the acid back over his own shoulder.

And Humphrey, seeing Rooftop duck through the door, raised himself to his full height, his head grazing the overturned lifeboats. 'We're in international waters,' he said. 'You got no rights out here.'

'Keep your voice down,' the giant told him. 'Mister LaFlamme needs his twenty-eight hundred tonight.'

'Yeah, well, I had it a minute ago,' Humphrey said. 'Anyway, I'm planning to talk to the old man tomorrow about reconfigurin my loan repayback schedule, so to speak. I didn't figure advertising in my budget.'

'Oh yeah? Well, reconfigure this,' Randy told him, and he launched his steel-toed boot at Humphrey's groin.

It wasn't the first time someone had tried to kick the farmer. He sidestepped and caught Randy's heel in one hand and stomped Randy's crotch with his own boot, dropping him in a pile on the deck. Then he wheeled around to take on Rooftop, whose huge fist caught him square in the shoulder, knocking him spinning off the side of the ship, but he sprang back at Rooftop like a bee-stung

Angus, his wild backhand swing catching Rooftop's ear and knocking the glasses from his face.

'Everyone stop,' Rooftop said, dropping to his knees, his blind hands crawling around the deck in search of his glasses. But Humphrey was too busy trying to step around Rooftop and get to the door – and his big rubber boot came down with a sickening snap. For the moment, everyone did stop. Randy lay on the deck groaning and holding himself, while Rooftop paused on his hands and knees and angled his ear toward the crunching sound he had heard.

Humphrey lifted his boot. 'Okay now?' he said, toeing the broken glasses toward Rooftop. 'You ready to listen to reason now? What I'm tryin to explain is, there's a company in Portland that can get me on television – marketing, promotion, the whole works – they'll give out free samples all over New England. All's I need's another twenty thousand.'

Rooftop squinted blindly at the rubber boots in front of his face. Then he wrapped his arms around Humphrey's legs. At first it seemed that the giant was only trying to raise himself to his feet. But as he stood, he lifted the farmer clear off the deck and lumbered toward the rail with the man slung over his shoulder.

Humphrey reached up and grabbed the seat of the overhead lifeboat. 'What I'm saying – hold on a minute—'

Rooftop never heard a word. He pulled toward the rail with all his might, and the big farmer held onto the seat with all his might, as the lifeboat slammed back and forth on its cables.

'Slow down,' Humphrey said. 'No one said I can't get by on ten thousand.'

Behind them, Randy rose unsteadily to his feet, stuffing another jalapeño in his mouth and starting to chew. Then positioning himself under the lifeboat upwind from Humphrey, he raised his face and blew a thick, hot spray into the gale. The farmer's head snapped back. He let out a howl and lost his grip on the lifeboat, rubbing his eyes with one fist and beating Rooftop's head with the other, while Rooftop hoisted him over his shoulders like a log, then let loose with a mighty grunt and hurled him, flailing, over the wet, upturned hull of the overhanging lifeboat. Somehow Humphrey managed to catch the far gunwale on his way down, and he hung there by one hand, flipping in the wind like a gaffed tuna while the ocean raced past far below him.

'I'll get your money!' Humphrey shouted. 'I'll have it by Friday, every dime!'

'You had your chance, you dumb potato-farmin prick,' Randy said, dragging a deck chair over and setting it down underneath the lifeboat.

Rooftop squinted over as Randy climbed up on the chair. 'I guess we'd best pull him back,' he said. 'He's only made half a payment.'

But Randy, caught up in the moment, jumped into the air and caught the near gunwale in his hands. The lifeboat rocked back and forth, squawking like a parrot.

'You want the farm, take the farm!' Humphrey bellowed.

Randy kicked his knees up to his chest, his body coiled as though in a single, taut C-shaped muscle.

'You call that a farm?' he shouted. 'A barn full of pickled fuckin french fries!'

With that, Randy launched into a vicious, full-bodied convulsion that set the lifeboat slamming back and forth against its moorings.

'Whoa, whoa!' Humphrey objected, then without another word, he dropped off the other side.

Amidst the noise of the engines, he didn't make a sound hitting the water, and if he hollered for help, nobody could've heard him. He swam after the ship at first, his powerful arms pumping frantically in the widening wake of the ship. But after a dozen strokes or so, his arms gave out, and then he bobbed up and over a giant swell in the darkness, watching all those hundreds of stern lights getting smaller and smaller, like so many stars in the sky, while high up on the third deck Randy and Rooftop leaned over the rail and watched him disappear into the night.

'Sucks being him,' Randy said.

'I guess,' Rooftop replied with a heavy wheeze. 'But not half as much as it's gonna suck being us.'

CHAPTER SEVEN

'I lost the baby, didn't I?'

Ellen was on her feet before she was fully awake, startled by the brightness of the sunlight in the room. She put her hand on Moreen's warm face, the events of the previous day clamoring into her consciousness like jagged shards of a nightmare.

'How do you feel, hon?'

Moreen shrugged and tried to smile. Her eyes were glassy.

Ellen looked up at the clock. It was eleven. 'I guess we both slept late,' she said.

Moreen reached a hand up. Ellen took hold, as Moreen stared up at the ceiling.

'You never wanted to be a grandmother anyway,' she said.

'Don't say that,' Ellen said, touching Mo's face, trying to make eye contact. 'Don't even think that.' She took hold of Moreen's hands. The left hand, the one the IV tube was attached to, felt cold.

Tell her.

Ellen hadn't intended to. Not now. But here they were. She took a breath. 'Hon, the doctor,' she began, and Moreen's eyes met hers, questioning.

'Mo, he had to do a hysterectomy.' Right to the point – like a slap. Ellen kept her eyes on her daughter, watching for comprehension. Moreen scowled slightly.

'They did a hysterectomy on me?'

Her dark eyes lost focus for a moment. Ellen nodded, keeping hold of her hands.

'They had to, honey. You would have bled to death.'

Moreen swallowed dryly while she processed the information. 'So I can never have a baby—?'

Ellen tried to sound optimistic. 'They left your ovaries.'

She watched for a tear, some sign of emotion, wondering if Mo's complacency was the effect of the painkillers.

'You can always adopt,' Ellen said. 'When you're ready.'

Moreen's chest jumped with a laugh.

'Does Randy know?'

'Honey—'

Ellen waited for eye contact, but Moreen kept staring off.

'Mo, honey—' She touched her hand lightly to Moreen's brow, and their eyes met again. 'Did Randy do this to you?'

Moreen closed her eyes.

'Hon, you've got to tell somebody.'

'Why are you asking me that?'

Ellen let out a sigh. 'The doctor told me it looked like you'd been kicked.'

'*I told you,*' Moreen said, her eyes opened and piercing, her voice lazy and loud, '*your stupid fucking ram Bucky did it. Just because you hate Randy—*'

'I don't hate Randy—'

'Lie. So now, instead of taking the responsibility for yourself—'

'Mo—'

'Now we can pretend it's Randy's fault!'

The door opened behind them. Ellen stiffened, stared at her daughter. She'd never heard Moreen swear, never heard that kind of anger in her voice.

'You're speaking,' the nurse said, the same red-haired woman who had admitted Moreen the day before. 'That's a good sign.' Mo turned her face to the sunlit wall. 'But I think we need to keep the patient quiet today, okay?'

'I feel like sleeping anyway,' Moreen muttered.

The nurse checked her IV, felt her cheek, then gave Ellen a wink. 'It's the medication,' she mouthed, then she left the room.

Ellen took a deep breath of the antiseptic air. She looked down at her daughter, touched her arm. Moreen kept her face to the wall. Maybe it was the medication, Ellen thought. But it felt like the sun had just burned through a fogbank and illuminated a great chasm that existed between them. She leaned over the bed and kissed Moreen's head.

Mo sighed sleepily, opening her fingers. 'I know Bucky didn't mean it,' she said.

Ellen gave her hand a gentle squeeze. 'I'll come back and check on you later,' she said softly.

'Love you,' Moreen breathed.
'Love you too,' Ellen replied.

Randy opened his eyes and looked at the light on the low white ceiling. The ship was moaning and vibrating beneath him, and it took a few seconds to recall where he was. Then he remembered drowning the farmer they were supposed to beat up and he felt a deep, dull movement in his bowels. Actually, if anyone asked, the dumb bastard jumped overboard when he saw them. They tried to stop him. They would have called for help, but sharks got to the guy the minute he hit water. Yeah, and Ray LaFlamme's dumb enough to believe it.

Randy got out of bed and headed for the toilet with nothing on except his wristwatch, which told him he had slept through docking, the hour when the ship ties up in Yarmouth and the tourists go into town looking for souvenirs. Outside the port hole, the ocean rushed past and the sky shone yellow.

'Hey, Skyscrape,' he said, kneeing Rooftop's mattress on the way to the can, but Rooftop wasn't in bed.

He went to the bathroom, then put on his Hawaiian shirt and Dockers, and he slipped his Ray Bans over his eyes, real sharp, in hopes that some single ladies might be aboard. He went up to the restaurant to look for Rooftop, then searched for him near the duty-free shop and in the casinos, finally found him up on the second deck, leaning out over the rail watching all the crooked, colored houses sailing away from them in the distance. The giant was drinking a hurricane, his broken glasses balanced on his nose by one stem. Randy leaned on the rail next to him, staying a couple feet away.

'Been drinkin all night?'

'Fuck you.'

'Yup.'

In his entire life, Randy had never seen anyone as powerful as Rooftop Paradise, nor as tough, and when Roof started drinking, nobody came anywhere near being as mean. Nowhere near.

'I thought those glasses was shatterproof,' Randy said, noticing that one of Rooftop's lenses was missing.

'Only man I ever killed,' Rooftop replied.

'He was still alive last time I saw him,' Randy told him, 'if you think about it the right way.'

Rooftop turned with that look, the way those wide-set eyes of his could blur over. 'You got a dangerous mind,' he said.

Randy shrugged. 'So what do you got in the bag?'

Rooftop took a deep wheezing breath and let it out, refusing to talk.

'What's the big secret?'

'Something for you to give your wife,' Rooftop said.

'What?'

'Thermometer.'

'What for?'

Rooftop pushed the bag along the rail and Randy took it, looked inside: a tomahawk made of lacquered pine, with a weather thermometer glued to its handle. The blade said COME TO CANADA.

'Not all that sharp though,' Randy said, running his thumb across the wooden blade. 'Why would I want to give this to Moreen, so she can scalp me?'

Rooftop gave him an ugly look, then turned his gaze back to the shoreline. 'I'm not beatin up any more Mainers,' he said.

'Think LaFlamme's gonna let you quit?'

'Ray LaFlamme is an evil man.'

'I'm just sayin. I wouldn't be surprised if LaFlamme has Gator-Aid whack the both of us for expiring ol' Humpty, owing him the kind of scratch he did.'

They stood there in silence for a few moments, then Randy said, 'Matter of fact, I had an inspiration last night.' In truth, the idea was just occurring to him.

Rooftop took another gulp from his drink, then just stood there looking out at the retreating island.

Randy said, 'We rummage up the twenty-eight hundred for LaFlamme, you know, like it come from Humpty Dumpty. Then when Humpty turns up missin – and even his own wife can't locate him – Ray and the boys'll figure he absconded with the rest of the money. We had nothing to do with it.'

'I'm not lying to Ray LaFlamme,' Rooftop said.

Randy gave him a look. 'Last night we fed a man to the sharks, but now you don't want to lie.'

Rooftop turned toward Randy, stared at his chest. When Rooftop was drunk, you seriously never knew what his mind was up to.

'You know Herbie Handcream? He bodyguards for Ray

LaFlamme,' Rooftop said. 'He's got one stub of a hand he's always rubbing lotion on, all scarred up and shiny. Ever see him?'

Randy shrugged. 'I'm not part of the inner circle.'

'He used to do collections, like I do,' Rooftop explained. 'One time Ray LaFlamme caught Herbie lying about gas mileage or some little thing that didn't amount to twenty-five cents. Next thing you know, a couple of guys deep-fry Herbie's arm. Right there in LaFlamme's restaurant, with the french fries and clam fritters. They stuffed two big biscuits in Herbie's mouth to keep from scaring the customers downstairs.' Rooftop peered hard at Randy. 'Mister LaFlamme's been fair to me. I intend to tell him the truth.'

'Yeah, you tell LaFlamme we drowned a man that owed him forty grand, and he *will* have Gator whack us. You oughta contemplate on this sober.'

'You oughta be nicer to your wife.'

'Here we go.'

Rooftop kept staring at him. 'You need to think about being a better man.'

'Yeah, like you, throwin people in the ocean.'

'I'm gonna dive for charity,' Rooftop said.

'Dive for charity.'

Rooftop got that vulture look that made Randy wonder if it was his turn to get thrown overboard.

'So what do you think?' Randy said. 'Get LaFlamme the twenty-eight hundred like it come from Humpty, save our asses from the Fryolator—?'

Rooftop reached his souvenir glass over the rail and let it fall to the lower deck. Even with the sound of the engine and the wind and waves, the breaking glass was loud. Then a couple of people started yelling.

'I wouldn't start anything,' Randy said. 'Nobody knows we're here. They do a head count and find Humpty missing, we probably got his DNA all over us.' He looked over the rail and called down to the passengers, 'Go on about your business.'

Rooftop gave Randy that look again, straight on. 'You don't have any goodness in you,' he said.

'Me?'

'You treat Moreen like a dog.'

'That shit again. Here.' Randy handed the bag back to Rooftop.

'You give it to Moreen, you want her to have it so bad.' He folded his arms and looked off at the bright horizon. 'I'd like to see how nice you'd be with a crazy fuckin' teenage pregnant wife that's trying to restrict your freedom.'

'You're the one that married her,' Rooftop said.

'Oh, like I had a choice. When Ray LaFlamme says marry the bitch, what the fuck am I supposed to do? I married the bitch.'

Rooftop wheeled drunkenly, and Randy reared back, thinking he was about to get his skull split with the tomahawk. But Rooftop fixed him with a scowl.

'You be good to that girl, I'm telling you right now.'

'Fine. I'll be Mister Jiminy Fuckin' Cricket, if it makes you happy. Now are you gonna go along with my plan, or do you want to go to sleep every night wonderin' if you're gonna wake up with the Alligator man in your bed?'

'I don't care one little bit.'

'Fine then. Just lend me the twenty-eight hundred to pay LaFlamme off, so we don't get our asses deep-fried.'

Rooftop shook his head. 'I'm done with this business.'

'Fine then,' Randy said. 'Maybe I'm done with your diving business.'

'Fine with me.'

'Fine with me,' Randy said, 'perfectly fucking a-okay.' He walked away from Rooftop, across the sundeck and on down the steel stairway, his boot heels ringing. Two minutes later he came back.

'Okay, I'm gonna ask you one more favor.'

Rooftop stared off over the ocean.

Randy said, 'Give me three days to procure the money. I've got a plan. Just tell LaFlamme I'm taking over for you – no, I'll tell him, that way you don't have to *lie*. I'll speak to him personally. I'll say you got seasick and slept in the cabin all night, and I collected from Humpty on my own. Understand my thought process here? I'll give LaFlamme the twenty-eight Cs and tell him it's from Humpty. But you gotta give me three days.'

Rooftop didn't answer.

'Okay then,' Randy said.

When Ellen slid open the glass door that said DESTIN POLICE, Wes Westerback, the chief, was sitting at his desk tying a Gray Ghost. His son Sugar, who was spackling about sixteen feet of newly constructed wallboard behind the desk, glanced over his shoulder at Ellen, a thick line of joint compound oozing down his thumb.

'Hot enough for you?' Wes said. Without looking up, he reached around the side of his desk and shook a sleeping cat out of a chair. 'Take a load off,' he said to Ellen.

The two men comprised the entire force, maintaining their office in the basement of Wes's split-level ranch, which backed up to thousands of acres of woods near the reservoir. A small plastic sign on the desk said PLEASE COOPERATE WITH US. A wooden sign above the front door of the house said HEAVEN.

Wes was sixty-eight, old enough to retire. But in a town like Destin, Maine, the chief of police didn't have a whole lot to do, and the position came with decent benefits, so he kept the job. Wes spent most of his time down here anyway, surrounded by oak display cases that housed one of the finest collections of antique fishing lures anywhere in New England. Fact was, Wes made considerably more money buying and selling lures than he did on police work.

'I'd like to know what the process is for having my son-in-law arrested,' Ellen said, still standing.

Wes kept working at the fly, peering through a freestanding magnifying lens that was ringed by a circular fluorescent tube. The top of his pink head, ringed by fine white hair, was perfectly smooth. The intricate wrinkles on his hands glistened pink under the light, and Ellen could see that his fingers shook a little. 'Jeez, for what?' he said.

'He beat up my daughter.'

Wes looked up at Ellen for the first time. 'That's right, you had a wedding there a week or so ago. I guess I'll hold my congratulations.'

'She was pregnant,' Ellen said.

Now Sugar looked at her too.

'Mo's in the hospital now. She lost the baby and had to have a hysterectomy.'

Wes set his pliers on the desk.

'Sounds like a young man with a problem,' Wes said.

'Not that young,' Ellen said. 'He's twenty-seven. Moreen's seventeen.'

'So when did this take place, the fight, I mean?'

'What fight? He kicked her. Yesterday afternoon. His name is Randy Cross.'

'Want me to take it, Dad?' Sugar said. Sugar himself had just gone through a divorce in which he'd lost the house it had taken him ten years to build. Ellen guessed he was making himself a bedroom down here.

Wes picked up a pencil. The tip was newly sharpened and it snapped when he started writing in his notepad. He opened his desk drawer and took out a small plastic pencil-sharpener.

'You were a witness?' he asked, leaning over the waste basket while the peel of wood curled out of the sharpener in his hand. 'You saw it happen?'

'Not the actual beating.'

Wes dropped the pencil-sharpener in the drawer, kicked the basket back under his desk. Sugar turned and resumed spackling.

'Moreen came to my house afterwards, and we drove her to the hospital,' Ellen continued. 'She would have died if we hadn't gotten her there when we did.'

'You and Scotty drove her?' Wes said.

'Our nephew drove her. I called ahead to the hospital, then met them there.'

Wes looked up. 'Your nephew?'

'Neal,' she said. 'Jonathan's son.'

The older man scowled as he concentrated on his pad. 'I remember the boy. His mother and him moved to western Mass, didn't they?'

'Greenfield,' Ellen said. 'Neal's helping us rebuild our barn.'

Wes nodded. 'Now, was he a witness to the beating?'

'To the actual beating,' Ellen explained, 'there were no witnesses. It happened in Moreen's house, in Sanford.'

'So she told you about it – your daughter, I mean – she told you that her husband kicked her?'

'She didn't have to tell me. It's obvious he did.'

Sugar looked back at Ellen again. ' "Obvious" don't always stand up in court,' he said. A former all-state running back at Destin High, he had been given his nickname by his football coach after setting Maine's western division record for running yards. Recruited by the University of Maine, he had broken his leg in three places during a preseason scrimmage and ended up quitting college before the first semester ended.

Ellen appealed to Wes. 'Look, I know he kicked her. I also know they're both going to deny it.'

Wes put his pencil down. He looked over his notepad, considering what she'd told him. 'How did Moreen claim she got the injuries?'

'She said a ram at my farm butted her.'

'At your farm. Were there any witnesses to that?'

'To what?' Ellen felt her stomach knot. 'It didn't happen.'

'Were you home at the time she claims the animal hurt her?'

'I was outside.'

Wes looked puzzled.

'She was in the pasture. I was down at our farm pond.'

'What about your nephew?'

'He was with me. It was hot. We were swimming.'

Wes nodded thoughtfully then picked up his pencil and started writing again. He tilted the pad away from Ellen. 'Huh,' he said. 'Then what?'

'I ran up the hill and found her lying there.'

'Was the animal out, the one she claimed hurt her?'

'Yes, but that was just her excuse.'

'What about her husband? Where was he during all this?'

'I told you, no one saw Randy kick her.'

Wes sat back. He took his glasses off and gave Ellen a smile. 'Ellie, you're doing your level best to lead this information the way you want it to go. Now I'm trying to determine what the heck happened here. When you found your daughter in your pasture, with her injuries, and the animal was there – at that point in time, where was Randy then?'

'I don't know. Out fishing for stripers. He and his friend Rooftop Paradise.'

'Wouldn't be the first fight started over stripers,' Sugar said, giving his father a look.

Wes cleared his throat. 'What does Randy do for a living?'

'He works for Rooftop. Diving.'

'Huh,' Wes said. 'They're not local boys. 'Least I don't recognize the names.'

'They live in Sanford,' Ellen answered.

'Do you know what time they left yesterday?'

'Obviously after Randy beat up Moreen.'

'There's no need to get sarcastic with me,' Wes told her.

Behind him, Sugar spoke up again. 'Moreen and him ever have any trouble before, domestic violence, this sort of thing?'

'They only got married a week ago,' Ellen said. 'She wouldn't have told me anyway.'

Sugar scraped his trowel on the rim of the white bucket, then dropped it on the newspapers under his feet.

Ellen said. 'She had a bruise on her arm the other day, like she'd been grabbed. I asked what happened, she wouldn't tell me.'

'Is that what she said, she refused to tell you?'

'She said she bumped it.'

Wes sighed. 'Did the doctor say anything about the bruises that might substantiate your claims?'

Ellen closed her eyes.

'Ellie, you got no witnesses,' Wes told her. 'If your daughter claims an animal gave her the injuries—'

'Forget it, I'll call the state police,' Ellen said, standing.

Wes shrugged. 'They'll only tell you the same thing. We're all bound by the law, which says we can't make an arrest without sufficient evidence, which in this case would be a statement from your daughter, at least. Even then, where it's her word against his, about the best you can hope for is to get Randy into counseling, which is all a judge would probably do if he was found guilty. But with the circumstances here, unless one of them owns up to it, there's not even enough to make a charge. Fact is, if Moreen sticks to her story, they might even have a case against you, for negligence with your animals.'

Ellen turned for the door.

'But hold on,' Sugar said.

Wes's chair squeaked as he leaned back to look at his son.

Standing behind him, Sugar picked up a rag and wiped his hands. In his T-shirt he displayed a barrel chest and massively muscular arms, but he hadn't grown any taller than he'd been in high school, about five-eight, and he walked with a slight but permanent limp.

'Tell you what,' he said to Ellen, scratching his chest. He leaned over his father and tore the sheet of notepaper off the pad. 'They've probably had their fill of fishing by now. Lemme go have a talk with Randy, see if I can't get him into counseling myself.'

'What if he refuses?' Ellen said.

Sugar gave his father a look. 'I can be pretty darn persuasive,' he said.

It was a confident gesture that made Ellen feel, for the first time, that she was not alone in this. She turned to go.

'Ellie,' Wes said.

Halfway out the door, she turned slightly toward him.

'You're not planning to see Randy yourself, are you?'

'Why?'

'I think it's best you steer clear of him till we get this settled.'

'Yeah, just go home and sit tight,' Sugar added. 'I'll give you a call after I talk to him.'

She looked briefly at both men, giving no assent.

'I'd go easy on your daughter too,' Wes told her. 'If what you say is true, the last thing she needs now is someone else forcing their will on her.'

Ellen wasn't in her truck five seconds before she realized that the day had grown even hotter than the day before. Keep busy, she told herself. Heat or no heat, she made up her mind to start working the minute she got home, and keep working. Weed the garden, mow the grass, do the laundry, lift her weights, clean the house, work on her tapestry. Exhaust herself till bedtime and then go to sleep. There was nothing she could do about Moreen, not today anyway. And Randy? She'd give the Westerbacks a day.

She pulled into her dooryard and stopped beside Neal's truck. The bucket loader was sitting in the spot where she usually parked. Deep, wide pits had been dug alongside the left and right sides of the barn: the foundation holes for the additions, she guessed. And somehow he had moved the silo from the right side of the barn around to the back, where he centered it, making the structure appear pleasingly symmetrical.

She got out of her truck and walked straight to her porch, avoiding the lumber pile and the new cellar holes – avoiding Neal. *Something I'd rather work out myself*, she'd say if he asked.

Her first thought when she got into the kitchen was to pour herself a shot of tequila, to calm her nerves, then she'd take off the skirt she had slept in and get into some shorts. She opened the liquor cabinet and brought down the tequila, picked a shot glass out of the cupboard and poured it almost full, tossed it down. Turning, looking around the kitchen, she was surprised to see how clean everything was. The floor had even been washed. She capped the bottle and was reaching to put it back when a noise came from upstairs. She stopped.

'Hello?'

She walked into the living room and started up the stairs, ignoring the pain in her ankle.

'Neal?'

The rustling continued. Reaching the top of the stairs, she turned the corner. Pushed open her bedroom door. Caught her breath.

Neal's shirt was off, his back to her. He was rummaging through her dresser, her underwear drawer, his back shining with perspiration.

'What are you doing?' she asked.

'Looking for your shells,' he answered, turning.

She stared.

'Bullets,' he said urgently. 'Where do you keep them?'

She noticed her closet door opened and plastic bags of clothes strewn on the floor. In the same moment, she saw the black butt of Scott's revolver stuck in the waistband of Neal's corduroys. Her heart bolted.

'Neal, tell me what you're doing.'

He dropped to his knees and felt around under the dresser, seeming to read her mind. Coming up with the small plastic box, he hurried from the room.

She hesitated, afraid to pursue him, but then she thought of Gator, imagining that he'd come looking for her and found Neal instead. Or maybe it was Randy—

'*Neal, wait!*'

She wheeled out of the room, and her ankle flared. Limping down the stairs as fast as she could, she made her way through the living room and kitchen, banged out the screen door and stopped on the porch, looking out over the pasture for him, her heart pounding.

'Neal?'

She saw her sheep tightly pressed together inside the near fence, trampling their feeding trough, oblivious to her shout. Then a slight movement to her left – black boots in the grass behind the pump house. She hobbled down the steps and hurried over to him, but before she could speak he grabbed her behind the knee and pulled her roughly to the grass. Her ankle shot through with pain.

'*Jesus!*'

His left hand covered her mouth, and he pulled her down beside him. '*Shh*,' he whispered in her ear.

The elbow of her white blouse ground into the dirt. Her skirt was up to her hips. She raised her head and looked past the pump house, down toward the stream, and she froze. The coyotes were there, three of them in a tight cluster, greedily working at—

'*Neal!—*'

She tried to fight him, but he climbed on top of her. His thigh pressed against her pelvis and a spark of arousal intruded on her fear.

'*Ellen*.'

It was one of her sheep that had gotten outside the pasture fence. The coyotes were tearing at it. Neal's right arm extended stiffly against the side of her face. He was aiming the pistol.

'Don't move,' he breathed.

Her blouse had come open, and she could feel the heat of his bare chest radiating through her T-shirt. She could smell his perspiration. Don't move? As he slowly rose off her, his thigh ground between her legs. Then he went crawling through the high grass along the fence.

She pulled her skirt down and turned onto her side to watch, as he moved along the fence line, working his way downhill until he was even with the ridge, meticulously stalking. The feasting coyotes did not see him.

Ellen raised her face high enough to see a pair of curly horns flop up and down, and then she realized: They were feeding on Bucky. She saw the ram's brown leg kick listlessly in the air, and she got to her knees. A coyote turned, his ears perked.

The gun fired. Once, twice.

A coyote screamed. Another collapsed. The third bolted, leaping onto the farm road that ran alongside the stream, racing for the far corner of the pasture. Neal rose out of the grass and fired twice more. The animal screeched and tumbled, then scrambled up again and staggered for the fence,

Ellen pushed to her feet and limped down the farm road after Neal, her chest pounding. In her heart she wanted the animal to escape, wanting to see no more death – despite how these predators had ravaged her sheep. In fact, the animal was gaining fair distance from Neal, who was only walking after it. When it had pulled within twenty paces of the fence, Neal took the pistol in both hands, sighted down the short barrel and fired one more shot. The coyote leaped off the other side of the road, his tail slipping into the bright gray and green thicket.

'Neal, just let him go!'

Ellen hobbled down the farm road toward her ravaged ram, not thinking about the dangers of approaching the wounded coyote, the first one Neal had shot. Seeing Ellen closing in, the animal tried to stand and run, but his crippled hind quarter would not comply. He twisted back to look at himself, then bared his teeth at her.

'Stay away from him,' Neal called as he came. The coyote turned to face him, attempting a growl that was pitched too high to be taken seriously. Neal walked directly to the animal, straightened his arm and fired.

'*Jesus, would you stop!*'

The coyote flattened on the grass, eyes dead, silver-glazed.

Ellen stood there, suffocating in the heat. Two coyotes lay sprawled before her, with her poor ram at her feet, throat torn, his brown wool matted and shining, his chest heaving sporadically. Ellen bent over her animal. His black eyes stared. Neal's shadow fell over her.

'How did he get out?' she asked.

'I put him out.'

She straightened, turned to face him. This was no accident, no chance encounter. He had sacrificed the ram to bait the coyotes.

He pulled his hunting knife from its sheath, placed the handle in her hand. 'You need to do this,' he told her.

She stared at the blade and shook her head, but Neal bent behind the ram, got his arms around its hind legs and lifted the animal into the air.

'Ellen, he's suffering,' he said quietly.

The knife felt so heavy, her hand so weak, she could hardly lift it. It was as if all the heat and all the tension of the past two days were finally crushing down around her.

Hoisting the animal under one arm, Neal placed his other hand firmly over hers and directed the knife to the ram's throat. Blood from its wool smeared the underside of her wrist as the blade slipped into the fleece. She felt the stiff wool scrape her knuckles, felt the steel stop against the ram's flesh. She resisted. Her heart pounded in her ears. It was far too hot.

'Ellen—'

She flashed her eyes up at him, squeezed the knife in her hand and plunged. The ram barely flinched as the knife sank into its neck. Ellen's arm hardened. Neal let go of her, and she sliced swiftly across the throat, hot blood throbbing out over her wrist, splattering her ankle. Then it was done. She stepped back, stood there dizzily.

'Did you think I couldn't do it?' she said in a low voice, then flung the knife on the ground.

Neal smiled gently as he lowered the animal to the grass. 'I knew you could,' he replied. 'You needed to.' He bent to pick up his knife. 'You've protected your flock and made your world a safer place,' he said, wiping the bloody blade on the ram's wool. 'You've achieved justice.' Standing, he gave Ellen a look of intense satisfaction. 'And now,' he said, sheathing the knife, 'now is the time to forgive.'

Revenge is a dish best served cold. The proverb came to Ellen unsolicited, as she looked down at the dead animals. Indeed, this was no accident of nature, but a meticulously planned execution. In the rising, rippling heat she could smell their fresh blood. Her blouse was covered with it. So were her skirt and legs. Another wave of dizziness hit her, and she took a deep, shaking breath to dispel it.

'Do me a favor,' she said to him. 'Don't tell me how to live my life.'

She turned and started walking back up the farm road toward the house, but as she passed the pump house she staggered and had to stop. The heat wrapped around her like a fat snake, cutting off her oxygen. She reeled dizzily and leaned on the pump house, then started to kneel, when Neal grabbed her from behind.

'Hold onto me,' he said, turning her into his arms.

She did so, helpless to refuse, her hands sliding down his slippery back. 'It's okay,' he said, supporting her. 'Everything's all right.'

Ellen hated to cry, but now she seemed utterly helpless to resist. Her body trembled and tears burned from her eyes. She laid her head heavily on his shoulder. 'Nothing's right,' she whispered angrily, even though she knew they had done what any competent shepherd would have done: killed a pack of predators and culled a bad animal from her flock. But it had been done with such treachery.

'You've got company,' he said quietly.

She stepped back and wiped her face with her arm.

Ellen turned to see the polished black Cherokee back sliding hard into the dooryard and skidding to a stop, gravel dust rising all around. Incredibly, she felt a fresh wave of anger shoot through her.

'Let me take care of this,' Neal told her.

'You stay out of it,' she replied, marching up to the dooryard. With the back of her arm she wiped the sweat off her forehead, as she watched Randy get out of the Jeep.

'Do I look like a nigger to you?' he yelled. He was wearing a Hawaiian shirt and a purple bandana around his head.

She started walking toward him, imagining what she might do if she had a rock in her hand, while Randy came straight at her, his arms bulging out from his shoulders.

'Huh? Do I look like a nigger to you?'

'Did you *kick* Moreen?' Ellen snapped, abandoning whatever control she might have had. They came within three feet of one another, and she would have kept coming, but Neal grabbed her arms.

'Because I ain't no lower class you can throw in jail for something I didn't do.'

'*Did you kick my daughter?*' She pulled against Neal, but he held her tight.

'You got just what you wanted!' he shouted in her face. 'You got your abortion, you should be happy now.'

Ellen's mind reeled, stunned as if he had kicked her.

'*Ellen—*'

Neal's arms wrapped around her waist, her chest, and he turned her away, while she threw her elbow at him. 'Slow down,' he said, taking hold of her arms.

Randy, sensing the damage he had inflicted, puffed up his chest, seemed to grow larger in front of her. 'Fuckin call the cops on me,' he said with a sneer, then turned away from her and went back to his Cherokee.

Ellen spun toward him but Neal held her fast.

'I did you a favor, asshole!' she said. 'Because if you ever hurt my daughter again, I won't bother with the police—'

'*That's enough*,' Neal said in her ear.

'You stay out of this!' she snapped, wheeling on him. He took hold of her forearms, pulled her toward him.

'Go cool off,' he said firmly. His dark eyes bored into her, making it seem urgent that she do so.

She saw the reason, as Randy turned from his Jeep holding a shotgun in his hands, a frightening thing, black and thick and heavy. However, she stood her ground, bristling beyond fear, knowing enough about Randy to know that he lacked the resolve to shoot either of them. But when he swung around to face the pasture, a chill washed through her.

'Go in the house,' Neal said, turning her away from Randy, all the while watching him carefully, saying, 'Randy, we already put the ram down.'

Randy sighted down the barrel, aiming at a cluster of about twenty lambs in the distance. 'I oughta annihilate the whole fuckin herd,' he said, his finger sliding into the trigger guard.

Before Ellen could speak, Neal released her and stepped directly in front of the muzzle—

'Neal!'

He deflected the barrel with the back of his hand, and made eye contact with Randy, who regarded him haughtily.

'Get yourself killed that way, cousin.'

Neal wrinkled his nose in a friendly way. 'You don't want to start shooting the sheep,' he said.

'Demented fucking moron,' Ellen added, which started Randy's head nodding.

Neal kept his hand on the barrel. 'Ellen, would you please go inside? Thank you.'

She did as he asked, walking close enough past Randy to make him lean back, then across her dooryard in front of the Cherokee, resisting the urge to pick up a rock and smash his polished fender. She climbed the porch steps without looking back, went inside the kitchen and threw open the liquor cupboard.

'I'm no fuckin nigger,' Randy said, his shotgun jutting in punctuation.

'She's upset,' Neal told him, putting his hand on Randy's shoulder and leading him back to his Jeep. 'You can understand that.'

'Nobody said I did nothin, except her. Bitch.'

'I know,' Neal said. 'So you're square with the cops now?'

'Yeah, fuck them too. They think I'm gonna go to a fucking

psycho doctor cause they plant a bag of reefer in my kitchen? Fuck em all!'

Neal nudged Randy with his elbow. 'You know what the problem is?'

'Fuckin call the cops on me.' Randy swung the gun toward the house. '*Bitch!*'

Neal put his hand on the barrel, calmly eased it down. 'I don't think she respects you,' Neal said.

'Like I give a flyin fuck.'

'You know why, don't you?'

Neal stopped walking, and Randy stopped. Neal glanced back at the house, then leaned toward Randy and said quietly, as if confiding, 'It's your diving job.'

Randy screwed up his face, like he'd chewed on something rotten.

'Six dollars an hour?' Neal said.

'Excuse me, eight plus overtime,' Randy told him. 'That's cash money.'

Neal smiled. 'You're still a grunt,' he said. 'You fetch for the guy making the real money.'

Randy went around the passenger side and slid his shotgun behind the seat.

'Think about it,' Neal told him. 'She doesn't think you've got the brains to do the work yourself.'

Randy walked around the front of the vehicle and jerked himself up behind the wheel. Neal closed his door for him, then looked right at him. 'You know the way a woman's mind works.'

'Hey, I *know* the way they work,' Randy said, glaring off toward the house as he started the motor. 'Take your freedom and all your money, then throw you in fuckin jail. Well here's a fuckin news flash: Not this boy. Not this boy.'

Standing at her kitchen sink, Ellen rinsed the blood from her hands, then poured herself a small glass of Cuervo and drank it down. Her hand trembled. Her arms shone with perspiration. She poured another glass, this one fuller than the last, and drank it half down – deep breath in, deep breath out – waiting for her rage to go away.

Noticing the answering machine blinking, she went over and played it back, heard Moreen's voice, distorted with drugs and volume, slurring, 'Why are you doing this?' she practically sang. 'Do you think you're helping me?'

Ellen stood there as the machine beeped off and the tape rewound, her thoughts as scrambled as the sound of the tape rewinding. She turned away, looked out the window and saw Neal talking with Randy, smiling.

She dialed 911. The phone rang six times before Wes Westerback answered. 'What's your emergency?' he said.

'No emergency,' Ellen answered, and she identified herself.

'Why don't you hang up,' he said, 'I'll have Sugar call you right back.'

She did as he asked, and in a few seconds the telephone rang.

'Yeah, I caught up with your son-in-law at his house,' Sugar said. 'Turns out Randy's got a police record. Thought you'd oughta know. A couple of arrests for assault, and one for drug trafficking, which he did nine months for, back a year or so ago.'

'What did he say?'

'Oh, pretty much fussed and fumed, they all do. But I sat right on him there in his kitchen and gave him his choice: either start seeing a counselor or I'd arrest him and haul him into court on other charges.'

'What charges?'

'Oh, guys like him, they're usually up to no good, whether you catch 'em red-handed or not. I used a little professional prerogative, which is to say, I got him to see things my way. I figure a little counselin never hurt anyone. Just some people are afraid of what they might find out about themselves.'

In the moment of silence that followed, Ellen wondered if Sugar had just referred to himself, his ex-wife, or her – and she felt a trace of resentment. She looked over at her glass of tequila.

'Anyways,' Sugar continued, 'I gave him twenty-four hours to get himself a counselor, so I'll check back with him tomorrow.'

'He's here now,' Ellen said, turning to the window as the black Cherokee pulled out with a screech and a flurry of dust. Neal was standing there waving at him with that same smile. 'Actually, he's leaving.'

'You want, I'll come lock him up right now. 'Cause I told him to stay away from you.'

'Oh, he swore at me, threatened to kill my sheep, that's all.'

'He threaten you personally in any way, touch you or anything?'

'No.'

'Okay, but if he comes back, you call me. Tell Moreen to call, too, if she has any trouble with him. Day or night.'

'I don't think Moreen wants me in her life right now,' Ellen said.

'Yeah, I think that's one of the syndromes. But nobody should live in fear.'

'Yeah, thanks,' Ellen said, and she hung up. *Live in fear*.

She finished the glass of tequila, then poured a third.

Sufficiently numbed, she went into the bathroom and peeled off her sweaty T-shirt, used it to wipe under her arms, wipe her chest and breasts. She took off her skirt and underpants, then stepped into the bathtub and took a long, hot shower, lathering every inch of herself, letting the heat of the water burn into her body. For the first time in days, it seemed, she felt her body begin to relax, lulled by the heat. She remained in the flow for fifteen minutes or more. Then she dialed the water cold and rinsed herself.

Wrapping a thick bath towel around herself, she went into the kitchen, where she poured another shot and drank it down. Then she climbed up to her bedroom and dried off. She could hear the backhoe churning outside her window, looked out the window and saw the gray exhaust rising from down by the dam. A slight breeze came in through the screen, and she dropped her towel to the floor, reached behind her head with both hands and pulled her hair back, let the air cleanse her. Then she opened her dresser and found a barrette she'd taken in trade at farmers' market, made of blue sea-glass. She fixed the barrette in her hair, then examined herself in the full-length mirror: Tall and tanned, her skin seemed to shine. Her shoulders and biceps were strong, her hips classically squared, her breasts full, her nipples dark and erect. Maybe it was stress, she thought, or her run-in with Randy – or just the effects of the tequila – but she was feeling stimulated and sexy.

Pulling a pair of silk bikini briefs out of her dresser, she stumbled a bit stepping into them, then went to her closet, where Neal had spilled her boxes of old clothes (she wondered what he thought of her stiletto heels), and found her old denim cutoff shorts. She stuck her foot in, barely noticing the pain in her ankle when she balanced on it. Although she suspected the shorts would be ridiculously tight, she pulled them over her hips and zipped them, surprised she was able to do so. In fact, they hugged her perfectly. Then she sat on her bed and pulled on a pair of red wool socks, then her leather work boots. She picked through the clothes on the floor and found her old brown tank top. She shook the dust out of it and slipped it down over her shoulders, left the top two buttons undone, then walked out of the house and down to the stream, where Neal labored beside the old yellow backhoe, taking apart the old stone wall.

'I took care of the ram and coyotes.' he said. 'Feel like lugging some rock?'

She looked beyond him, saw the freshly turned soil and realized he had used the machine to bury the animals while she showered. She was amazed by his efficiency.

She began working alongside him, hoisting the heavy rocks one by one off the old wall and carrying them to the bucket, neither of them speaking while the pond water spilled over the dam and raced noisily past them. Although the day still weighed heavily with heat, at least the sun had finally angled behind the treetops. She could smell coolness in the mist that rose from the waterfall. Aware of the silence, Ellen came to appreciate Neal's not intruding on it. She liked working with him, and she liked watching him work. He was sure and strong and absolutely steady. When they filled the bucket with rocks, Neal would drive the machine up to the barn and dump the load, then return to the stream again, where they would load the bucket again.

The pasture fell slowly into shadow as they disassembled the stone wall. Despite the lingering heat, the strain on Ellen's biceps and shoulders energized her, and it wasn't long before she had worked up a vigorous sweat. Her long legs glistened, the veins stood out on her arms. Her tank top grew wet on her back and chest.

'Set?' he said when the bucket was full.

'Set,' she replied, and Neal climbed onto the machine and turned the headlights on.

'Want a lift?' he said.

She climbed onto the loader with him, planted her feet on the grated steel step and bounced along, holding onto the back of his seat as he drove. She liked the exhausted glow in her arms, liked the way her breasts jostled as they rode up the hill, liked the way her tank top opened. When Neal turned toward her, she turned her head away, to let him look, and she felt her heart beating freely. As the lights of her house rose into view, she suddenly and inexplicably felt a glow of euphoria. In the face of all her troubles, the feeling made no sense. Yet night was falling, frogs were peeping, the air was perfect. She wondered why Scott was so late getting home.

They pulled into the dooryard and turned left toward the barn. Neal cut the throttle and braked twenty feet from the new foundation. 'Everybody off,' he said, and Ellen climbed down, jumping from the step, feeling no trace of pain in her ankle. In fact she flexed her foot a couple of times, and realized that even her memory of the pain had disappeared. The way Neal watched her, it occurred to her that he may have somehow healed her, and she wondered if he had inherited the gift from his father.

He smiled, then hit a lever and revved the engine, and the hydraulics started. The bucket curled over, dumping the heavy rocks noisily onto the grass. Then he shut off the engine and climbed down, wiping his face with the sleeve of his sweater.

She leaned back against the machine beside him. 'Thanks for getting me away from Randy before,' she said. She watched while he lifted a heavy rock out of the bucket and dropped it on the ground with a resounding thud.

'But when I was in the house,' she said, 'how come you were out here acting like you were his best friend?'

He turned to face her, then wiped his hands vigorously on his corduroys. 'Turn around,' he told her. She did, and he unfastened her barrette, then gathered her falling hair in his hands.

'Romans twelve, twenty,' he said, folding her hair carefully on top of her head. ' "If thine enemy hunger, feed him; if he thirst, give him drink; for in doing so thou shalt heap coals of fire on his head." '

He slipped the barrette back in, then stepped around in front of her, inspecting his work. His gaze lowered from her hair to her eyes, and her heart surged.

In other circumstances, the look he gave her might have been taken as lustful. Indeed, in the first instant, Ellen felt a stirring and told herself, 'He's Scott's nephew, not mine.' However, it was not lust he was conveying, not exactly, though it was every bit as fervent. The look he gave her had to do with Randy. Ellen held his gaze long enough to understand this, but she gave nothing in return, not a shadow of affirmation.

'Ellen, you need to drop the charges,' he said softly.

'You need to take off your sweater,' she answered.

In the brief hesitation that followed, she detected surprise in him. Indeed, she had surprised herself. She had not intended to say that.

Neal looked at her darkly as he crossed his arms in front of himself, took hold of the thick wool and pulled it up over his head. His chest was full, his nipples dark and round. Ellen reached up and pushed the sweater up his thick and slippery arms, breathing in the smell of his perspiration as she pulled it off his hands.

'Give it to me, I'll wipe you off.'

Neither had she intended to say that, but she took the sweater from him, heavy and moist, and bunched it in her hand.

'I don't know why you wear this thing when it's ninety degrees,' she said, raising his arm and running the wool roughly down his underarm and side. 'Turn around.'

He did and she wiped his back, holding her left hand on his shoulder, suppressing the sudden urge to lay her mouth on him, to lick the salt from his skin. She ran the sweater straight down his spine as her free hand slid down his solid arm.

Once again he turned to face her. Or maybe she turned him. She moved the sweater under his neck and he raised his face. Her heart pounded.

Headlights swung in off the road, the diesel engine.

Ellen backed away from Neal, disconcerted by how abruptly she moved. She thrust his sweater into his hands.

'Does he know?' Neal said, practically in a whisper.

'Know what?' she asked casually, turning and walking toward the house.

'About Moreen?'

She turned her head slightly toward him. 'Only that she lost the baby,' she answered. Ellen walked toward the Mercedes as Scott got out, his Mainely Hardware jacket slung over his shoulder. His tie was undone, his shirt untucked.

'Sorry I'm late,' he said. 'I went to see Mo.'

Ellen stopped. 'Scott, I told you—'

'I had to. I brought her some flowers.'

She studied him as they walked up the porch steps together. She could smell whiskey.

'How is she?' she asked, mind spinning.

'Asleep. They wouldn't let me in.' He turned as Neal came

through the door. 'Hot enough for you, guy?'

'I like the heat,' Neal answered.

'Must run in the genes,' Ellen said. 'You can both have it.'

'Better than twenty-below,' Scott said. 'Who wants a beer?'

So unsuspecting, Ellen thought, so single-mindedly absorbed by his business. Maybe it's what endeared him to her, after all. She leaned to kiss him.

'I'm all sweaty,' he said.

'So am I,' she answered, and she kissed him on the mouth, moving her own lips softly, opening them, using her tongue.

'Mmm,' he said, either in enjoyment or protest, breaking the kiss. 'Looks like you started without me.'

She gave him a look, feeling the flush of guilt wash over her face, then realized she'd left the tequila bottle on the counter. 'You don't look that far behind,' she said.

'You're right. Screw the beer. Let's get loaded.'

She gave him a smile, subtle and seductive.

CHAPTER EIGHT

Scott made them each a margarita before dinner, while Neal made pasta and prepared a rich Alfredo sauce from scratch. Scott opened a bottle of Merlot for dinner and poured three glasses. While they ate, Ellen tried repeatedly to catch his eye. When she finally did, she leaned back in her chair and pushed her breasts out against her shirt. 'It's been a long day,' she said. 'After I do the dishes, I think I'll take a shower and go up to bed.'

'Tired?' Scott said.

She didn't answer, waiting for him to catch her eye again.

'I'll do the dishes,' Neal said. She saw him suppressing a grin.

Scott looked up. 'I miss something?'

Ellen shook her head pitifully at him. 'You are getting old.'

'Yeah, well, I guess I'm tired too, now that you mention it.'

Another smile from Ellen. It was met with a look from Neal, something akin to consolation. Ellen lowered her eyes to her plate.

'I sure miss your dad,' she heard Scott say to Neal.

Ellen concentrated on her food. She'd wondered when Scott was going to get around to it.

'He was a pretty incredible man,' Neal said. 'Imagine how many more lives he would have saved if he'd lived.'

'Your mom ever say why he did it? She have any idea?'

Ellen heard a silence then, and when she looked up, Neal was looking straight at her, smiling, gesturing that he needed to swallow his food. She smiled back, not wanting to appear anxious, but her teeth clenched so hard she could hear a humming in her ears.

Scott raised his wine glass to drink again, but it was empty. He grabbed for the bottle and poured himself another glass, then reached to fill Ellen's again. She shook her head.

Finally Neal swallowed.

'My mother never said,' he answered. 'Although she has suggested on several occasions that it must have been my fault.'

'Your fault?' Scott said. 'People get depressed, they need to get help. In this town, everyone put your dad up on a pedestal. He was too proud to tell anyone his problems.' He took another drink of wine, shooting Ellen a glance over the rim.

'You have to admit, I caused my share of trouble,' Neal said.

'It's no wonder. Look who you're related to,' Ellen said, with a nod at Scott.

'Ah' – Scott waved off the suggestion – 'boys are supposed to cause trouble. Hey, do you remember the time you and Mo found that Indian tunnel in your basement and snuck over to the church. We looked and looked all over for you. Christ, I thought you'd been kidnapped. Then the steeple bell started ringing. Jesus Christ, was your father mad. Saturday night – the holy rollers all thought he'd gone Catholic.'

'I think Neal was the best friend Mo ever had,' Ellen said.

'Hey, is it true that my father healed Grandpa Chambers' bursitis?' Neal asked.

'That is true, sir,' Scott said, raising his glass. 'The same day our parents moved into the house I bought for them up on the hill. Dad said it was the best day of his life, gettin rid of that fuckin bursitis.'

Ellen and Neal both looked up at him.

'Hey, not that I'm bitter,' Scott added.

They laughed, grateful for the relief.

'Oh, by the way,' Neal said, 'do your fire insurance rates depend on the farm pond?' It was all very casual.

'Big time,' Scott answered, swallowing more wine.

'Because I think the dam's leaking.'

Ellen's fork stopped momentarily in her plate. Her heart stopped too.

'It better not be leaking,' Scott said.

'Ellen, pass the pepper, please,' Neal said. She reached the pepper mill to him, eyeing him as he took it. 'Have you noticed that the water seems lower?' he asked her.

'Not really.'

He turned back to Scott. 'When do they usually raise the flashboards up at the reservoir?'

'Late August, September, when it starts getting dry,' Scott said. 'They don't release again till the spring thaw, usually March.'

'That's what I was afraid of,' Neal said. 'When that stream dries up, you might lose your pond.'

'Always something,' Scott said.

Scott and Ellen made love that night for the first time since before Moreen's wedding. In fact it was two periods ago, on a Sunday morning, and then they'd been interrupted by a phone call from Sugar Westerback who was looking for a sub for his softball team. Even though Scott had declined the invitation, after he hung up he put on his bathrobe and went downstairs to start the day.

All other mornings – Monday through Saturday – he was up and out by dawn. Nights he was usually too tired, or so their routine had developed. Tonight was no different. As much as Ellen desired the absolute fullness of him, Scott was unable to maintain an erection for more than ten minutes, either lost in thought or dozing. As the backhoe scraped and pounded outside their window, Neal replacing the water line to the barn, Ellen worked on Scott with her hand, then with her mouth, then she sat astride him, doing her best to keep him aroused. She was energized by the tequila and wine, she supposed, and by all the insanity of the past two days. She did her best to imagine Scott when he was younger and daring and tireless, and he always had a defiant glint in his eye.

Expelled from high school for selling pot he had grown here on his parents' farm, he ended up leasing a small storefront in the village, where he rented the movies out for a dollar fifty and put the town's existing video store out of business in less than a year. That spring – Ellen's junior year – she started working for Scott after school and on weekends. One of her jobs was to make copies of the latest movies, which Scott sold under the counter for ten bucks. He told her it was legal. Ellen didn't believe him, but she didn't care. He was self-assured and beautiful, and though he was only seventeen, he seemed to be making his way in the adult world and doing it on his own terms.

Scott had a girlfriend, Ingrid, who was twenty-nine, from Long Island. She ran a crafts and clothing boutique in the same building, called Wool 'n' Things. The two shops shared a back room, which quickly became a hangout for a number of Ingrid's friends.

Ingrid was a sort of retro-beatnik who wore black lipstick and spent her days at her spinning wheel, perched in the storefront window. It didn't matter that Scott was a farm boy at heart, Ingrid soon had his black hair tied back in a ponytail and his left ear gleaming with a bright green tourmaline. She called him her country stud.

Most of Ingrid's friends were musicians and artists who would hang out in the back room listening to jazz and reggae, doing cocaine and drinking tequila. For Ellen, who was tall and aloof and beautiful, it was the first time she had found people who intrigued her, and soon she started working for Ingrid too, stringing necklaces of razor clamshells, painting seagulls on sand dollars, and carding the raw wool for Ingrid to spin.

Even when Ellen wasn't working, she'd tell her mother she was, and she'd do her homework in the back room. She liked the conversation. She liked the music. More than anything, she liked to watch Scott handle these people who considered themselves his intellectual and cultural superiors. While they snorted their coke and drank their shots, he smoked his homegrown weed and drank Moxie. After they'd listen to jazz, he'd put on George Jones and turn it up loud. They considered themselves artists. But Scott was an artist of commerce. He envisioned money and made it materialize with a creativity and intelligence that Ingrid's friends couldn't begin to understand. Unselfconsciously. Unapologetically. Even at seventeen, he seemed to always know exactly what he wanted, and he got it.

One night that winter, just after Scott's eighteenth birthday, he must have realized he wanted Ellen. She had closed Ingrid's shop and gone into the back to get her coat, when she found Scott with a lone candle burning and Frank Sinatra playing on the stereo. *One for My Baby*. Scott told Ellen he had just broken up with Ingrid and asked her if she wanted to go out for a coffee. She was going to say yes. Instead, she dropped her coat and went over and kissed him.

Ellen had made out with boys before, but only ever let one get his hand inside her bra, some college kid from California who was at the beach, an angelic, tanned surfer, and she'd stopped him when he tried to unbutton her shorts. Standing there in the back room with the candlelight and the music, and Scott with his sad green earring, Ellen decided then and there to go as far as the feeling took her. In fact, it was Scott who stopped them, and that's when she fell in love.

As it turned out, Scott hadn't actually broken up with Ingrid, not in a way that Ingrid understood. And, as it turned out, Ingrid had been more than a girlfriend – she was also Scott's legal business partner, who held the lease on both shops. By the time Ingrid realized that their relationship was over, Scott had bought the building from the owners and then helped move Ingrid's store to Destin Plaza and paid her first three months' lease. Then he sold all his videotapes and proceeded to knock down the walls that had divided the two stores. He was tireless then. He did all his own carpentry, his own wiring, plumbing and painting, his own accounting. He worked day and night and hardly ever slept. By month's end, he had opened Destin Hardware. Ellen remembered the pride she felt seeing his picture in the newspaper, accepting awards from the Rotary club, the Chamber of Commerce, The Small Business Association, with his ponytail and earring and the black wool sweater that she had knitted for him, with the green star on the left shoulder.

But tonight, while Scott moved lazily inside her, it was the bucket loader outside her window that spurred Ellen on, churning and growling and shaking the ground, indeed shaking the mattress under her. And it was Neal who occupied her mind: the smell of him, the way his glistening body had felt under her hand, the way the humidity had risen off him. It was his long, muscular stomach. It was the relaxed way he talked and the way he watched her. It was his competence, his steadiness, his conviction, all the things he had done for her, and the thing he was willing to do . . .

Or perhaps her arousal was simply her way of denying what treachery might be in motion – she was aware of this, even as she made love to her husband, aware not of the treachery itself but of the curious way a person could overlook such a thing.

When Scott finally climaxed he'd been soft for several minutes, and the only way she knew he was ejaculating was by the way he moaned and then tapped her thigh to let her know he was done. Then he was snoring.

But Ellen was not ready to stop. In fact, she was feverish, and she rolled off of him and masturbated herself, listening to the backhoe burrowing into the ground outside, churning and churning, and all at once this furious pleasure took hold of her, this dazzling ecstasy that swept up through her body and back, again and again, as though it would never stop. She gasped, she stiffened, she grasped herself, her passion so great that even the small sensation of moving her fingers out of herself sent her into spasms a second time, and she gripped herself with both hands and rolled onto her side, her knee knocking against Scott's back.

'Hey there,' he said.

She reached up to her night table for a tissue and wiped away his earlier offering, then lay on her back again. The backhoe had stopped. Through the open windows, above the steady whisper of water running over the dam, she heard the small sound of bells moving lazily through the night, one or two of her ewes up walking and she suddenly felt more alone and alienated from Scott than she had before they'd begun making love.

Slick with perspiration, Ellen peeled herself off the sheet and took her nightshirt from the clothes tree, pulled it over her head and went downstairs to shower. Leaving the stairway lights off, she made her way through the living room in the dark, went into the bathroom and closed the door.

Pulling off her shirt, she looked in the mirror. Her cheeks were flushed and vibrant, her skin moist. The sun had darkened the freckles on her nose, and her eyes were sharp. She folded her hair on top of her head as Neal had done, thinking she might wear it like that for a while, at least when it was hot. Or maybe she'd cut it all off. The way she was feeling lately, anything was possible.

She let her hair fall down her back and she stepped into the bathtub, twisting the old faucets and pulling the shower valve up, expecting the usual trickle. But the water exploded out of the nozzle full force, and it startled her. Evidently, Neal had climbed down into the pump house and fixed the old water pump, the one Scott had been promising for years to fix. She adjusted the temperature warmer and ducked her head under, luxuriated under the hot pounding on her back, the sensation flowing down her shoulders and thighs. Turning, she let the water beat against her face, curl down under her chin and run over her breasts. She washed and rinsed her neck, her underarms and breasts, her stomach and abdomen and vulva; then, feeling the slipperiness there, she raised her face against the steady hot flow, and started all over again, though she never meant to, her fingers moving slowly at first, deliciously slow, the clean water pounding, running out of her mouth and down her chest, licking off each nipple, those three good fingers pressing in, moving hard and round as she arched her back and let the waves wash over her. When she'd caught her breath again, she lowered her head and let the water massage the back of her neck. Finally sated, she shut the shower off.

She dried herself with a thick towel, then slid her nightshirt back on, the sensation of cotton brushing over her nipples stimulating her all over again. When she opened the door and stepped out of the steam, Neal was there. Standing just inside the back door, wearing only his black trousers.

Although it was too dark to see his face, Ellen could nevertheless make out his expression. Or perhaps it was the attitude of his body, his shoulder slightly cocked, outlined in a faint, glistening light. She felt a bright flutter inside her stomach.

They stood there saying nothing. Despite the noise of the waterfall outside and Scott's loud snoring upstairs, she could hear her own heart beating. She was sure he could hear her too, or that, with the bathroom light behind her, he could see the pounding of her chest through the light fabric, and now she became acutely aware of her breasts, her nipples, as if all the nerve endings in her body were focused there. The smell of his fresh perspiration aroused her, and she knew at that moment she should get away from him, but she stayed, opening her mouth so he wouldn't hear how hard she was breathing, and now she was afraid to think that she was breathing his body heat in, but she breathed deeply, and this rocketed her into a powerful state of arousal. It was astonishing the way she wanted his hands on her, but she knew that if she took a single step toward him right now, what a lifetime of trouble would follow, here in her husband's house (*Scott snoring, snoring*), here with his nephew . . .

She drew a quick breath and held her shirt down while she stepped away from the bathroom door, and now the light fell upon him, the pale ripple of his stomach, the dark bulge of his trousers.

'I thought you were in bed,' he said softly.

'It's too hot up there.'

A second or two passed, while Ellen felt the sensation growing deeper in her abdomen, this dark and lustful ache.

'It's nice outside,' he said.

She looked at him there, imagining how easy it would be to open his jeans and pull them down to the floor. She knew that he was feeling the same thing, she could see the way his chest heaved. She hesitated another moment and then turned away from him and was walking into the living room, back up the stairs, back to the heat of her bedroom, her mind throbbing, wondering how she'd ever let herself get that close. Stripping off her shirt and dropping it on the floor, she slipped into bed beside Scott and felt a sharp pang of fear. She pulled the sheet up over her shoulder, then rolled toward her husband, took his arm in her hands. He kept snoring, and Ellen lay there quietly breathing the oppressive air, waiting for sleep to overcome her while she listened to the restful sound of her pond spilling over the dam . . . and remembered the day Neal was baptized.

At the time it was unclear what had precipitated Jonathan's decision to anoint his son, since it was customary practice in any charismatic church to baptize only adults. Neal was only eleven. Scott and Ellen had laughed about it at the time. Although neither April nor Jonathan ever divulged anything about their problems with Neal, Ellen and Scott were aware that the boy was usually under the confines of one punishment or another – which meant that whatever Neal enjoyed in life, his father found a way to take it away from him. Because Neal loved books, his library card was revoked. Because Neal loved to swim, he was banned from the parsonage swimming pool for his entire tenth summer. So, when the invitation came announcing Neal's baptism, Ellen and Scott saw it as another of Jonathan's attempts – clearly a desperate one – to discipline his son.

The baptistry was a formidable tank embedded in the back wall of the altar, like a giant aquarium, four feet high and eight feet wide. Stairs descended into the tank from dressing rooms on both the left and right sides.

The ritual had an almost otherworldly innocence. As the congregation sang 'Nearer My God to Thee', and the parish lights came down, a pair of heavy burgundy curtains parted to reveal the baptistry tank, which fairly glowed in its own blue light. The water was three feet deep.

Ellen remembered the way Neal stared at his father as he descended the steps into the water, his burgundy robe floating up around his knees. Anyone else might have been moved, mistaking the stare for the fervent look of a boy surrendering to absolution at the hand of his father. Ellen knew the stare for what it was: staunch defiance.

Moreen, who was five at the time, reached for Ellen's ear and whispered, 'Why are they wearing their clothes?' They were sitting in the front pew, along with Scott and his parents and April and her mother, who had driven up from western Massachusetts.

'Uncle Jon is just going to dunk Neal,' Ellen whispered.

'God is forgiving Neal for all his sins,' April said, leaning over with a strange, wide-eyed smile.

'That's their religion,' Ellen explained quietly, and she took Moreen's hand to quiet her.

Jonathan was already speaking. A microphone attached to the top of the tank broadcast his seemingly disembodied voice throughout the chapel: 'Neal Rolley Chambers, have you accepted Jesus Christ as your personal Lord and Savior?'

Standing up to his waist in the water, Neal stared out through the tank. Moreen raised her hand and gave him a timid wave. 'Can't he see me?' she whispered.

'Shh,' Ellen said.

'Neal Rolley Chambers, have you accepted Jesus Christ as your personal Lord and Savior?' Jonathan asked again. 'And you say, "Yes." '

Neal kept staring.

'And you say, "Yes," ' Jonathan repeated.

'Yes,' said Neal.

'And are you trusting in him today for your eternal life?'

Neal kept his eyes on the congregation.

Without waiting for his response, Jonathan took his son's head in one hand, the other holding his nose, and he said, 'Upon your confession of faith I now baptize you in the name of the Father and the Son and the Holy Spirit.'

When he tipped Neal's head back under water, Moreen reached for Ellen's arm.

'He's just dunking him, hon.'

They both jumped as the organist struck a chord and the burgundy-robed choir stood to sing 'Amazing Grace'.

Ellen had seen the ritual only once before, when Jonathan baptized his father in the stream behind the farm. The anointing was over in a second. A quick symbolic dip, then out. But this was different. Now savior was the father, staring sternly into the water, and sinner was son, staring back, unrepentant.

'He's holding him under,' Moreen said, and a few people close enough to hear laughed a little, nervously.

By the end of the hymn's first chorus, and what was obviously meant to be the end of the song, Ellen realized that Jonathan was waiting for Neal to close his eyes.

'Mommy?'

'It's okay.'

A few of the singers ventured ahead with the hymn's second verse. Others in the choir, looking less confident, nevertheless joined in.

Jonathan's demeanour remained steadfast as usual, with the unshakeable faith in his mandate from above that, if necessary, he would allow his son to drown – if that was the path that Neal chose.

Ellen did not know how long Jonathan held him under. Thirty seconds may have seemed like five minutes. A minute may have seemed like ten. It was long enough that Scott glanced over at Ellen with an incredulous scowl. And by the time the second verse had ended, a murmur was building in the church. Now Scott looked over at April, and Thelma looked over at April, and the murmur became explicit.

'Maybe someone oughta go up there,' a man said, as Neal stared out of the tank.

Even the choir members were glancing nervously at one another.

Finally April rose to her feet and called sheepishly, 'Let him up?'

Inside the tank, Jonathan could not hear. Neither would he pay attention when April climbed the altar stairs and approached the tank. His eyes remained locked on Neal's.

She rapped on the glass with her rings. 'Jon, just let him up,' she said. In the congregation, people were standing. But Neal would not submit.

In the end, it was Jonathan who gave in. When a spray of bubbles exploded from Neal's mouth, his father pulled him, choking, out of the water, and Neal's dark eyes swept right to Moreen as he coughed.

'Dry off and go home,' Jonathan told him. The small loudspeakers in the church did not miss the anger in his voice.

Neal turned and climbed the stairs out of the water, quietly victorious, while the organist played the introduction to 'Christ the Lord is Risen Today', and the congregation started singing, and April walked off the altar to her right, the way Neal had gone. She did not return.

★ ★ ★

Mouth To Mouth

In the dark dawn, when the radio came on, Ellen was already awake. She slid her hand down Scott's stomach and took him warmly in her hand. He hardened immediately.

'Mmm,' he said. 'Sorry about last night. I've been taking something to help me sleep.'

'You did fine,' she said.

'So did you.'

'Scott?'

'Hm?'

'Let's go up to Mount Katahdin for our anniversary. Remember the way we used to?' Her thumb inscribed little circles on his glans. 'I'll pack the tent—'

'You're kidding.'

'It's a long weekend. I'll get the sleeping bags, the old camp stove—'

'What about the sheep? The garden?' His erection flagged.

'Neal can take care of it. Do you know how long it's been since we've gone away, just the two of us?'

'But now?'

She squeezed him playfully and said with a seductive warble, 'All by ourselves. Just us, the moose and the deer.'

'Uh.' The way his eyes closed, the way he softened –

'What?'

He reached down for her hand, held it in his own. 'I meant to tell you last night, but I didn't want to spoil the mood.'

She kept her eyes on him.

'I'm not going to manage Mainely Hardware.' He watched her closely, while she waited for him to continue. 'I'm buying Walter Bolduc's place, on the highway.'

'The boarded-up tire place?'

'It's prime location.'

Ellen raised herself on her elbow, propped her head in her hand. 'You're buying it? You couldn't make ends meet where you were. That's why you were going with Mainely Hardware—'

'Hey, I'm trying to explain,' he said, raising his voice. He stopped; sighed. 'I'm getting out of the hardware business altogether.'

'Scott, you're not mortgaging the farm—?'

'I already did that,' he said.

'You mortgaged the farm, the *house*, and you never talked to me?'

'It's just temporary. I used it as collateral to buy into the franchise.'

'Jesus, Scott.'

'I had to get money somewhere. You know the banks wouldn't do business with me. I had to go through a private loan company.' His fingers pressed up toward the ceiling, then fell back. 'I was going to tell you.'

'Why didn't you use the store as collateral?'

'How do you think I've managed to buy inventory for the past two years? My credit's shot. We were about to lose the store. I had to make a move.'

Ellen lay down again, rolled onto her back.

'Look, we've worked out the details.'

'Who's we?'

'Neal helped me.'

Now Ellen sat up in bed. 'So maybe you can tell me now.'

'It's a little complicated.'

She waited.

'Like I said,' he continued, 'I decided against buying into the franchise. Instead, I'm going to use loan number two to pay off loan number one and get the store out of hock. That leaves me ten grand.'

'And a house and farm in hock—'

'Listen. Then I *sell* the store.'

Studying him skeptically, Ellen detected a remnant of his once-confident glint.

'We ran the numbers,' he said. 'Mainely Hardware is gonna buy me out clean – a hundred-twenty-thousand for everything, property and inventory.' His eyes on her lingered with meaning. 'See? Then I turn around and buy the tire store for eighty, and I've got fifty grand in ready cash to work with.'

'Scott, the farm.'

'The farm is safe,' he said. 'This is a sure thing, the chance I've been waiting for.'

Ellen closed her eyes, took a deep breath.

'Look, Mainely Hardware can't last in this town, you know it and I know it, I don't care how cheap they can buy their merchandise. They can't compete.' Ellen could hear him leading up to something, and it worried her. 'These days the only way to stay alive is to specialize, to carry merchandise the big boys don't have.'

'Just tell me, please.'

'You're not going to like it at first.'

She looked at him, a heaviness descending in her chest.

He blinked.

'Guns.'

Ellen stared as if she hadn't heard him. But she had. Outside the window frogs stopped chirring, morning birds stopped singing, the bells of her sheep stopped ringing. The single word was all that remained. *Guns.*

'You're serious.'

He was moving his hands like a conductor. 'Ellie, it's a great opportunity. I'll have something that nobody can compete with – not WalMart, not K-Mart, not the Trading Post or any of the other small shops.'

'Scott, they all sell guns,' Ellen said.

Scott looked straight at her. 'But they don't have firing ranges.'

Ellen got out of bed, walked to her bureau naked.

'Just listen, El. The garage is a perfect size for an indoor range. Plus there's a four-acre gravel pit out back. This is going to be state-of-the-art: skeet and trap range, even sporting clays. We'll take in guns on consignment, used, antiques, small manufacturers. That's another thing you can't get at the big stores. And I don't have to wait for a dealer's license. There's a guy in North Berwick, Tommy Spampinato, who's closing his shop. He's agreed to be my silent partner for a few months, until my license comes through, so I can start buying and selling. I don't even have to pay him. I'll just sell his remaining inventory out of my store and give him half.'

Ellen took a pair of black underpants out of her dresser and stepped into them. 'I don't believe this,' she said.

Scott sighed. 'Ellie, you know this is a great idea. It's the break I've been waiting for. Anyway, I already put down earnest money on the tire store. I'm closing with Mainely Hardware tomorrow.'

Ellen wouldn't look at him. 'You never even talked to me, Scott.'

He got out of bed, went to his underwear drawer. 'Look, we were going to lose the farm eventually, whether you admit it or not. We're paying property taxes on forty acres that aren't paying us back.'

Pulling on a dark blue T-shirt, she opened the closet and snatched her denim shorts off the hook. 'So you rebuild a barn to pacify me, while you gamble everything we own on a gun shop.'

'That's not the way it happened.' He pulled a beige, short-sleeved shirt over his head. 'You know, you could support me once in a while.'

'You want to sell guns, I'm not supporting that. Guns to criminals, guns to fanatics and paranoids, guns to assholes like Randy?'

Selecting a necktie from his closet rack, Scott said, 'I'm selling guns to hunters and farmers.'

'Oh, *farmers*.'

'While we're at it,' he said, 'I might as well tell you something else that you're gonna hate. I'm thinking about taking Randy into the business with me.'

Ellen stopped, so stunned she barely heard what he said next, something about giving the kids a start.

Moreen had to have a hysterectomy! Ellen wanted to scream it, but she didn't, keeping her promise to Mo. She shook her head, all but speechless.

'Moreen told me what caused the miscarriage,' Scott said to her. 'Your fuckin ram attacked her, that's what she said.'

'No!' Ellen snapped. 'Randy kicked her.'

'Come on, don't you think Moreen would know if Randy kicked her?' They were both getting louder.

'He hits her. I've seen him.'

'You saw him kick her in the stomach—?'

'I've seen him get physical with her.'

Scott threw his hands up. '*When? Where?*'

A flash of heat forged Ellen's response. 'Don't you cross-examine me,' she said, and spun to leave the room.

'You don't turn your daughter's husband in to the police! They're broke as it is. El, I want you to tell the cops you overreacted.'

Ellen spun back, stared at him with disbelief. A humming broke from the back of her neck and filled her head as she gazed at her husband. It astounded her to think how far apart they'd grown.

'I don't know you anymore,' she told him, then walked out of the room, suddenly feeling very unsteady in her bare feet.

'If you think you're helping Moreen by having her husband arrested,' he called after her, 'you're crazier than I thought!'

She walked down the stairs and through the house in a mindless blur. Banging out the kitchen door, she marched down the porch steps and directly to the cellar hole at the left of the barn, where Neal had dug a square alcove off the new foundation and was troweling cement on the foundation wall around two water pipes that protruded through the rocks.

'How do you like your new root cellar?' he said, looking up at her.

'Neal, do me a favor,' she answered. 'If you and Scott plan something that affects *my* life, have the courtesy to let *me* know about it, okay?'

She walked away before he could respond, went off to the tool shed and let the lambs out into the pasture. As she followed them out and overturned the water trough to hose it down, she saw Scott walking up the hill from the pond. He came directly to her and said, 'I think the outlet pipe's leaking, but it's hard to see through the waterfall. I'm going to call the water district and see if they'll raise the flashboards up at the rez so we can get it repaired.'

She ignored him, and he walked away. Momentarily she heard his car engine start, and she went into the shed for grain. As she scooped her pail into the grain barrel, the door opened behind her.

'Ellen, I'm sorry,' Neal said to her, 'but I can't tell you something that Scott told me in confidence.'

'Fine,' she said, kicking open the door to the pasture.

'If I did tell you,' he said, 'you'd never be able to trust me with your secrets.'

She stood in the doorway for a moment, knowing they had nothing more to say to one another, then she went outside.

For the rest of the day and all of the next, Ellen and Neal worked together in silence, Neal laying stone on the foundation walls of the root cellar and new additions, Ellen mixing the cement in the wheelbarrow. Emotionally, she was determined to keep her distance from him. If they spoke at all, it was only a word or two about the work they were doing. They did not discuss Ellen's concerns about Moreen, nor did they bring up Scott's gun shop or Randy – or the leaking dam. Certainly they did not talk about what had almost happened between the two of them the night before.

They worked hard and steadily hour after hour, and gradually the frames of two symmetrical shed-roofed additions, twelve feet wide and running the length of both sides of the barn, rose over the expanded foundation. For the longer beams, Ellen stood in the bucket holding the end of the timber on her shoulder, while Neal carefully raised her into place. He would position the bucket just so, the notch would slide into the groove, and Ellen, with her three-pound hammer, would drive the wooden pins through the holes. It was dangerous work, and Scott would never have permitted it had he been there, but with Neal at the controls, Ellen never felt at risk.

Finally, late on Thursday afternoon, Neal lowered Ellen to the ground and shut off the bucket loader.

'Twelve Days of Christmas,' he said.

Ellen tossed her hammer on the ground. 'Twelve-gauge shotgun,' she answered wryly as she arched her back, stretching.

'Twelve Days of Christmas,' Neal repeated.

'You just said that.'

He smiled as he climbed off the machine. 'Did you know I was born on October second, which is exactly twelve weeks before Christmas?' He grabbed the plastic pitcher of water and took a drink.

She looked at him, saw the glint in his eye. 'Is that significant?'

'October second: ten-two,' he explained. 'Twelve.'

'I think maybe that's stretching it, Neal.'

'Maybe.'

They heard a car engine downshifting out on the road, then the mashing of gravel under wheels, as a glossy black BMW Z3 convertible pulled into the dooryard, sending up a low cloud of dust. Ellen looked curiously and recognized Maddy Sterling behind the wheel, wearing a cream-colored power suit, her hair razor-cut and dyed to match the car. She pulled up to the porch and stepped out of the car. 'Looking good,' she said, looking over the barn.

Ellen unbuckled her tool belt and let it fall to the ground, then walked across the dooryard to meet her, while Neal remained behind, shirtless. Maddy eyed him for a moment, then turned abruptly and walked up the porch steps. When she was behind the wooden rail, she turned back again and stared over the tops of her sunglasses, shielding her eyes with her hand, as Neal started hand-sawing a wide, oak plank.

'You and *that* alone every day while Scott's off at work?' she murmured as Ellen mounted the steps.

'He's Scott's nephew, remember?' Ellen said quietly.

'Don't give me that. He's not blood-related to you, and you're just as human as I am.'

'Maddy, we go skinny-dipping together every day.' It was a fabrication, but one that Ellen could not resist.

Maddy stared at her. 'You lie.'

'It's completely innocent.'

Maddy looked at Neal again. 'And what time do you do this?'

Ellen smiled. 'Want a drink?'

'No, I actually came over to tell you that I have a new client.'

'Yeah?'

Maddy took off her sunglasses and gave Ellen a long, almost accusatory look. 'Mo has a hysterectomy, and you never so much as call?'

Ellen scowled. 'You're not counseling Mo—?'

'No, I'm counseling Randy. The police called to set it up. Mo gave them my name.'

'I wish you'd counsel her,' Ellen said. 'Convince her to have him put away.'

'I talked to Mo a little,' Maddy replied. 'Ellie, what made you think that Randy beat her up?'

'I know he beat her up.'

'I'm not defending him. I just want to know how you're so sure it was Randy and not your ram that hurt Mo.'

Ellen looked away.

'El, mother's intuition is one thing. But if Randy didn't do it, this is something they really don't need in their lives right now. If he doesn't show up for his counseling session this afternoon, I'll have to turn him in. He says he's not coming.'

'Good.'

'But what if you're wrong?'

Ellen felt her stomach twist. She pushed herself off the rail and turned for the door. 'I've got to get supper ready.'

'You're telling me to leave?'

'I'm telling you that Moreen is my daughter, and I don't remember asking for your help.'

'You didn't, El. And I'm a little pissed that I had to find out from the cops.'

Their eyes locked for a second or two, then Maddy put her sunglasses on.

'I hope you know what you're doing,' she said, then she left.

Randy pulled his black Cherokee into the woods and drove down the dirt road until he reached the chain barrier and NO TRESPASSING sign, courtesy of the Destin Water District. After looking around, he got out of the vehicle and hid his ignition key under a dusty rock in the grass. He stepped over the chain and started walking, keeping his right hand casually in the pocket of his trousers but tightly on his snubnose .22. When he turned a corner so he could see the gate house and dam up against the reservoir, he stopped. Turned.

Scott was off to his right, thirty feet away, leaning against a white birch, holding a fat, pink Dunkin Donuts bag. The doughnuts weren't what interested Randy, however. It was the way Scott's other hand was stuck in the pocket of his tweed sports coat.

'I didn't touch her,' Randy called, his finger slithering inside the trigger guard. 'Thought we'd oughta establish that right off the bat.'

'What are you talking about?' Scott said, as he left the tree and started walking over. Randy's pants were loose enough and his pistol short enough so he could raise it and fire without pulling it out of his pocket. Scott's sports coat pockets were wide, too, which neutralized Randy's confidence. Scott took seven or eight steps toward him, then stopped at the weedy edge of the road, his Dunkin Donuts bag swinging from its weight. Randy remained on the grassy hump between the tire tracks, about seven feet away.

'If I don't report to this friggin' counselor today for something I didn't do,' Randy said, 'the cops are gonna be out lookin' for me.'

Scott shrugged. Randy thought he detected a smile on his face. 'Mo says you didn't hurt her,' Scott said. 'That's good enough for me.'

Randy gave his father-in-law a long, suspicious gaze. He didn't like the look of those doughnuts. Nor did he like the way Scott kept looking over his shoulder.

'Rooftop with you today?' Scott said.

'The Roof's retired from the collection business,' Randy answered. 'Same as I'm gonna be, just as soon as I can, you know, I'm researching college opportunities – thinkin' about it anyway, the art professor routine. You know, play the game, quote unquote.'

Now Randy started looking over his own shoulder, looking all around. 'So, what's with the doughnuts? And how come you wanted to meet me out here in the willywags instead of at your place of business?'

'I don't own the hardware store anymore.'

'You're the manager. Same thing just about. Got any chocolate-covered in there?'

Scott's hand came out of his jacket pocket, opened the doughnut bag and reached inside. Randy leaned back, aiming his gun, bulging his trousers. But it was a stack of hundred-dollar bills, not a weapon, that Scott pulled out of the bag, a much thicker stack than Randy might have expected.

'I want to pay off my debt,' Scott said.

'That's why I called you,' Randy told him. 'Like I said, Ray LaFlamme personally authorized me to give you a ten percent reduction in interest for an early payment.'

'I mean I want to pay all of it,' Scott explained.

'All what?'

'A hundred-fifty thousand and change, everything I owe – principle, interest and late fees. I'm done. I'm selling thc store to Mainely Hardware.'

Randy stared at the Dunkin Donuts bag a moment longer, his synapses beginning to fire. 'Wait a minute,' he said. 'You brought all of it?'

'Yeah, minus the ten percent discount.' Scott held out the doughnut bag to him. 'Take the money, Randy. I don't need it anymore. I got a bank loan.'

Randy reached out skeptically and took the bag in his hand. 'I don't know how this is gonna go over,' he said.

'Count it up,' Scott told him. 'I want you to sign a receipt that I paid in full. You can tell LaFlamme for me it's been sweet, but I couldn't see a future in the hardware business.'

Randy glanced up at him. There was too much information coming at him, and too fast: bank loan, discount, receipt, a hundred-fifty grand. Not to mention he could actually smell the currency through the waxy bag. He opened the top and peeked inside at the stacks of Franklins, and his heart surged. His racing thoughts ricocheted off the inside of his skull.

'So I sign a receipt, then what? You whack me and take the receipt and the money.'

Scott reached into his jacket pocket.

Randy dropped the doughnut bag on the road and went for his Dockers.

Scott pulled out a ballpoint pen.

Randy pulled out his gun. Then, seeing the pen in Scott's hand, he said, 'Boy Scout motto: "Be prepared." '

'Yeah, you're a Boy Scout, Randy. For Christ's sake, I'm your father-in-law.'

'Don't give me that Mister Innocent routine,' Randy shot back. 'I know how you made your money – back when you had it. Wheelin and dealin, take a man's business right out from under him and never bat an eyelash. You think I don't know things? I'm married to your daughter, don't forget.'

Scott regarded Randy for a long four seconds.

'Put your gun away, Randy. Even if I thought you hurt Moreen – which I don't – I'd never in a million years make my daughter a widow.' Scott handed the receipt and pen to Randy. 'Just sign the receipt and go make your boss happy.'

Randy studied the receipt, studied Scott, then pocketed the revolver. 'Just like that, huh?'

Scott eyed him for a second or two. Then a smile came over his face. 'Just exactly like that.'

At about seven o'clock, when Neal went down to swim, Ellen called the hospital and was told that Moreen had gone home. When she called Mo's house, the phone rang but no one answered, so she went into the garden to pick greens for a salad. The day was ending with a pleasant calm, swallows darting about in the sky, peepers just beginning their evening song.

As she started picking through a thicket of Swiss chard, she thought of Mo as a little girl and remembered how they would lie together in bed every morning after Scott left for work. She could almost hear the sound of the little bare feet bounding down the hall, and the way the old bedsprings would bounce when she landed, the way they'd snuggle under the blankets until their bodies fit perfectly together. Ellen could feel Mo's warm little head nestled in the hollow of her neck. They'd lie together like that for the longest time, making plans for the day. Or just talking about anything that came to mind. Sometimes they'd just lie there without saying a word until they both fell asleep again.

Working in her garden, Ellen became aware of an almost perfect silence in the air. At first she equated it with the tranquility of her thoughts. Then she realized: the waterfall had stopped.

She held her breath to listen, then stepped out of the garden and walked into the pasture with her weeding fork in her hand. Reaching the crest of the hill, she looked down and saw Neal swimming in the pond naked, and she saw the concrete top of the dam, gray and dry.

She heard the diesel engine then and turned to see the old Mercedes pull into the yard. She walked toward the barn as Scott got out of the car. He was dressed in a business suit, and he came toward her with a long, purposeful stride. They met just inside the pasture gate, where he took her in his arms.

'I'm all dirty,' she told him, but he pulled her close and kissed her on the mouth. It was hard to resist. She dropped her fork and kissed him back, loving the warmth of his lips on hers, his hands on her back. When the kiss ended, he reached inside his jacket and withdrew a banded stack of hundred-dollar bills.

'I've been a jerk,' he said. 'I'm sorry.'

'What's this?'

'First Federal likes my gun shop.'

A slow, beautiful smile came to his face, a look of confidence she hadn't seen on him in years.

'Scott, you got a bank loan? You got the farm out of hock?'

'Yes I did. I've put this family through hell for too long,' he said softly. 'I'm going to make it up to you—'

'The cement around the pipe is all eaten away,' Neal said behind them, and Ellen flinched away from Scott as if she'd been caught doing something wrong.

Neal eyed her cautiously. 'We're losing water fast,' he said to Scott, 'and it's only gonna get worse.'

'Got it covered,' Scott said.

Ellen looked at him. So did Neal.

'Randy's coming over tomorrow,' Scott explained. 'He's gonna give us a hand.'

Neal shrugged. 'Might as well keep it in the family.'

Ellen bent for her weeding fork, keeping her objection casual. 'Don't you think you should hire someone more experienced?'

'Probably not a bad idea,' Neal said.

His remark surprised her, and she tossed him a glance.

Scott shook his head. 'It's not like he's gonna be welding down there. All he has to do is take a pipe wrench down and unscrew the cap off the pipe. When the pond drains, we can pack some fresh mortar around it, put the cap back on, and we're back in business.'

Neal shrugged. 'Should be safe enough.'

'Besides, the Water District's only gonna give us two days before they lower the flashboards down again. They're afraid the reservoir'll overflow its banks and flood the roads up there.'

Neal did not respond. Ellen headed for the house.

'Hey,' Scott said, and she turned back, avoiding Neal's eyes. 'There's a bottle of good champagne in the car. We're back in business, Babe.'

Ted's Clam Shed was about to close for the night when the dark green panel truck pulled in. XYZ DIVERS – DIVING IS OUR BUSINESS. Two other vehicles were already parked in the lot, spaced a hundred feet apart, a white Taurus from Quebec and Randy's black Cherokee, which sat off to the right, out of the range of the yellow bug lights.

When Rooftop pulled in beside the Cherokee, Randy looked over, raised a cardboard tray to the window.

'The heck's that?' Rooftop said out his open window.

'Twin lobster,' Randy told him. Motioning with his head for Rooftop to come over, he leaned over and pushed the passenger door open. He was wearing a bib in the shape of a double-wide lobster.

Rooftop deliberated, then opened his door and came over. Randy held the tray on the dashboard for him, beside a cardboard bowl of broth and two plastic cups of melted butter. The clawless bodies of two other lobsters lay on Randy's lap.

Rooftop ducked into the vehicle and Randy handed him the tray, saying, 'I see you're drivin again. I thought you lost your licence for ten years.'

'Special dispensation,' Rooftop explained. 'To and from work. No night driving.'

Randy grinned. 'So you're already breakin the law.'

Rooftop remained somber.

'Anyways, how's life in Destin? Probably never see each other again, now that you're in the same town as my in-laws.'

Rooftop shrugged. Randy raised a slender red leg to his mouth and sucked out the meat. 'Dig in, man.'

'Moreen okay?' Rooftop said. 'I went to the hospital to see her, and they said you brought her home.'

'She's alright,' Randy said. 'But that's a whole nother goddamn story, which I'm not about to comment on at this point in time.'

Rooftop gave him a look. He was wearing his new glasses, which were larger and rounder than his old ones, making his eyes look even bigger, but Randy didn't comment on that either. Instead, he tossed the little hollow leg out his window, then reached in front of Rooftop's knees and popped open the glove compartment. 'S'cuse me, big guy.'

Rooftop spread his legs, and the glove box fell open. Stuffed inside was the bulging Dunkin Donuts bag and Randy's snub-nosed .22.

'Know what that is?' Randy said with a grin.

Rooftop angled his head to see in. 'Dessert?'

Randy shook his head. 'Money.'

'A good deal of it, by the looks,' Rooftop said.

'That's us gettin off the hook,' Randy replied, as he closed the glove box again. 'That's us not worryin about Ray LaFlamme or Gator or anyone else.'

'I wasn't worried in particular.'

Randy sat back in his seat. 'I just got back from Old Orchard,' he said, giving Rooftop a cocky frown. 'I took care of things with Ray LaFlamme. Not LaFlamme personally but one of his bodyguards, some big frog by the name of Marcel something . . . quote, unquote. You know what I mean. Frenchman.'

'Marcel Desjardin. Used to be a prison guard.' Rooftop cracked a claw in his hand, releasing a small flood of broth into the tray. 'You don't want to fool around with Marcel.'

'Who's foolin? I gave Marcel the twenty-eight hundred, like it came from Humpty Dumpty, and another four grand off of Scott Chambers' account. And I slipped him a hundred for himself you know, good will and all that.'

'So what's that in the doughnut bag?' Rooftop asked, gesturing to the glove box.

Randy shrugged. 'A little additional something that I didn't turn over at this point in time.' He gave Rooftop a look. 'What I was wonderin here, you and me with a hundred thousand dollars, huh?'

'What?'

'Well, I thought we might go into business for ourselves, you know, buy a little product? Just the once, bangity-boom, then we get out. I got a couple of assholes I can unload it on, triple the money in a day. Pay LaFlamme the difference maybe next month and hey. Huh?'

Rooftop pushed the pink-speckled meat out of the tail and dipped it in the melted butter, then dropped it into his mouth. 'I'll stick to my diving,' he said.

Randy shrugged. 'Three hundred grand, that's a lot of diving.'

Rooftop kept chewing.

'Who knows? After I pay off LaFlamme, I'm thinkin about diving school myself. Maybe after I get my certification, the two of us can buy a boat and hunt up some pirate treasure.'

'Like I told you,' Rooftop said, 'I'm figuring on living right for a change.'

'No, I'm definitely down for that,' Randy said, tossing an empty claw out his window. 'Matter of fact, I'm doin a little diving job for the family tomorrow – strictly charity work.'

Rooftop gave him a look.

'I thought you'd like that. Wanna give me a hand?'

'Can't,' Rooftop said. 'I joined the town's volunteer firefighters, and we're taking part in the parade.'

'Good ol' Fourth of July on the sixth of July,' Randy said. 'Only in Destin, Maine. Anyway, best we keep this between the two of us – the cash, I mean.'

'Doughnut bag in your glove box isn't the safest place to keep that kind of money, you want my opinion.

'Safer than home, with that friggin wife of mine layin around, kinda mood she's in. Man, I thought fuckin PMS was supposed to be bad.'

Rooftop pulverized another claw with a sharp snap.

'Not to mention Gator-Aid,' Randy added. 'I 'specially don't want Gator to know.'

'He's the last person I'd tell anything,' Rooftop agreed.

'I mean, like, *Hello!*' Randy laughed. 'Anyways' – he wiped his right hand on his pants and stuck it out – 'I just want to make sure there's no hard feelings between us. Any man lucky to call someone his best friend ought not screw it up, know?'

Rooftop looked at the hand, looked at Randy, then wiped his

hand on his napkin. 'Kinda sticky,' he said.

Randy gave a shrug and took his hand. 'Good lobster, though.'

'Real sweet.'

At ten o'clock, when they'd finished eating dinner, Neal went out to work on the barn. Scott poured himself another whiskey and ginger and retired to the living room to watch television. Ellen did the dishes, sober. When she finished in the kitchen, she went into the living room and sat on a corner of the couch. Scott was stretched out in his corduroy recliner, already fast asleep and snoring. An old black and white Elvis movie was on TV. Ellen leafed through the papers and magazines on the coffee table and picked up her journal, *Fiber Processing*. It had come in the mail back in May and she still hadn't found the time to look at it. She opened to an article about vegetable dyes and started reading, but found when she'd reached the bottom of the page that she couldn't recall a thing she had read. She took the TV remote off the coffee table and hit MUTE, silencing the movie.

'*Don't you!*' Scott blurted, lurching awake. Looking around dazedly, he sat forward in the chair and hunched his shoulders, then sniffed deeply as he struggled off the recliner to his feet. 'Goin to bed,' he said, climbing up the stairs.

'I'll be up in a while,' Ellen said. She started reading again.

Presently Scott began to snore upstairs, a five-drink concerto, by no means his loudest. But with the waterfall stilled, it was loud enough to distract her, to remind her how unwittingly he'd been drawn into Neal's plan – indeed if there was a plan. She wished he'd roll over and stop. Then he did.

The back door opened. Ellen listened to Neal's footsteps cross the kitchen floor, then he stuck his head in the doorway. 'Night,' he said. His hair was tousled and he wore a white T-shirt, his sweater draped over his arm.

'Goodnight,' Ellen replied, looking down at her magazine again. She listened to him walk back through the kitchen, listened to the door spring stretch and contract and the door slap shut. If Neal was plotting against Randy somehow, there was no hint of it in his behavior, no telltale glance, nothing unusual in his mannerisms.

Against the silence of the night, now Ellen could hear every detail of sound: the rattle of the clothesline reel jiggling against the side of the house as Neal took his sleeping bag off the line; the short squeak of the pasture gate opening and closing.

There hadn't even been a glint in his eye.

Ellen made up her mind to stop worrying. The leaking dam was only that: a leaking dam and nothing more; a coincidence. She closed her magazine and turned off the lamp and listened closer to the night outside: a sheep's bell tinkling, the peeping of tiny tree frogs off in the distance. Absently, her attention turned to the television. Elvis, young and lean, talking to a girl who was tall, blonde and cone-chested. They were standing very close.

Ellen lay back in the corner of the couch arm and pulled the afghan over her body.

Elvis's eyes shone dark and lazy. The girl gazed up at him, awestruck. Elvis gave her a surly half-smile. Enraptured, the girl parted her lips. The King of Rock 'n' Roll looked deeply in her eyes and suddenly threw his hip to the right, shutting his eyes and grimacing. The girl stood there transfixed. His elbows went out to the sides, like they were suspended on wires, while his left leg shook and his hair, stiffened with grease, flipped up and down.

Ellen's right hand slid down her stomach and unfastened the button of her shorts, then pushed her zipper down.

Elvis moved into the girl, fingers snapping, his dark eyes riveting hers. The girl stepped back in rhythm as if she were afraid of him, and he pursued her to within an inch, but they never touched. His hips went round and round.

Ellen propped her right foot against the edge of the coffee table. She took a full breath of air through her nostrils and closed her eyes. The silver light of the television beat against her eyelids while her fingers moved inside her and the night around her grew deep and dark, and the only thing she could hear was her own breath pouring out her mouth and the glistening sounds from under the afghan. Her orgasm was quick and riveting. As she pressed back in the couch catching her breath, she thought with vague bewilderment, *I don't even like Elvis.*

CHAPTER NINE

Friday morning rose sunny and blue, with barely a breath rustling the trees. It was the third day of a four-day Independence Day celebration that started on July fourth, featuring a softball tournament, road race, bike race, pig scramble, pie-eating contest, wood-cutting contest, parade, firefighting demonstration, arts and crafts fair, baked bean dinner and Casino Night at the fire station, all culminating in the fireworks display at the high school's athletic field on Saturday night.

For the parade, Scott and the other volunteers had polished up the town's two red fire trucks and trained for their annual firemen's muster on the commons. Knowing he'd be home all weekend working on his dam, Scott had agreed to be on-call so the other firefighters could attend the celebration.

At eleven thirty in the morning, Randy arrived, an hour late, having gone to the coast to fill his tanks at Gary Pope's dock. Gary operated the town's marina and owned his own compressor. Randy had told him that the air was for Rooftop. When he got to the farm, he put on his wetsuit in the dooryard, working out of a long black duffel bag in the back of his Cherokee.

Ellen went up to the bedroom so she wouldn't hear the men talking, but when Randy's voice came through the window, she started the vacuum cleaner. She vacuumed the room, then put clothes away and made the bed, which she normally did only when she changed the sheets. This morning she even dusted the bureaus. Then she went downstairs to her pantry, where she lay on her bench and started lifting. She hadn't planned to, so she wasn't dressed properly: barefoot, short-sleeved blouse, khaki shorts. Nevertheless, she did all her reps then repeated them, straining, trying to concentrate on nothing but her breathing, but acutely aware of every minute that passed.

When the footsteps finally came drumming up the porch and the door banged open, Ellen caught her breath, suddenly and chillingly aware of what she had known all along.

'*Ellen!*'

She lowered the bar into its cradle and slid out from under it, walked into the kitchen, sweating. Scott was pacing in his bathing suit, puddling the linoleum with water, the mobile telephone pressed to his ear. He turned away from her.

'It's Scotty,' he gasped into the phone, throwing open the door and heading back outside, waving Ellen to follow him. 'No, my son-in-law – he's caught in our dam!'

Ellen went along numbly, avoiding the water on the porch.

'He's stuck, he's running out of air!' Scott yelled as he ran to Randy's Cherokee, a set of keys in his hand. He jammed the key into the liftgate lock, and when he finally got it open he found another scuba tank and diving mask. He thrust the mask into Ellen's hands. 'Bring this down to Neal,' he told her, 'hurry,' then continued yelling into the phone as she ran barefoot through the pasture, scattering her sheep, 'Well, find somebody! Nothing happens to him!'

Randy was twenty feet down, his left arm sucked into the drainpipe to the top of his shoulder. As deep as he was, the pressure of twenty feet of water trying to rush through the pipe prevented him from pulling his arm out. So now he sat twisted on the rocky bottom, his head crooked against the concrete, facing the bright, rippling sky. His wetsuit was torn at the top of his shoulder, where the threaded end of the pipe had cut into his flesh, and blood darkened the water around the wound, oozing like smoke out of the tear in the suit. But Randy could no longer feel any sensation in the arm, which had gone from cold to practically numb. His right arm curled around his chest, trying to warm himself. His whole body shivered.

As Neal swam down toward him, Randy gazed up listlessly, his chest rising and falling, bubbles of carbon dioxide breaking quietly from his regulator. He watched Neal stop about three feet above him, hovering there. Randy unfolded his left arm from his body and gave him a thumbs-up sign. You got me, bub. You win.

Neal held up five fingers, then tapped his wrist – five minutes, in diving code – which meant help was on its way.

Randy nodded, gave him another thumbs-up. Hope I can wait five minutes, man. Matterafact, I'm ready to go up now.

Neal turned away and kicked for the surface. Randy watched his dark body grow smaller as it rippled up into the light. Then everything got quiet again. No sound but the cold air coming out of the scuba tank into his lungs, then going out again. In and out. In and out. And the ridiculous fucking cold. Randy rubbed his chest briskly with his free hand. Didn't do much good. He was shivering like crazy.

So, five minutes and they'd get him out. Probably Rooftop was on his way. Randy looked down at his gauge. Five minutes, it said. Cuttin it kinda close, boys. In fact, it was already getting harder to breathe, as if someone was standing behind him, pinching his air hose. He looked at the gauge again, trying to see if it was five minutes or four. Looked more like four. He raised his face to the sky, watching for Rooftop. Then a sudden thought came to him, uninvited and entirely unwelcome. More than a thought, it was a feeling, and his entire body jerked with a monstrous jolt of fear.

'He's got five minutes!' Neal shouted when he broke the surface. The water was an inch lower than the top of the dam. The pond was still.

'Maybe we can winch him out,' Scott said. 'Hook up to one of those trees.' He stepped down to the diving rock, beside Ellen, and dropped the scuba tank in the water.

'You'll tear his arm off,' Neal told him, swimming over to retrieve the tank. 'There's probably five hundred pounds of pressure trying to pull him through the pipe.'

'Well, what the hell are we gonna do?' Scott yelled.

'Is it just his arm that's stuck?' Ellen asked.

'Up to his shoulder,' Scott answered. 'Give Neal the mask.'

She dropped the mask into Neal's hands. He spat on the glass and rubbed it around with his fingers, then pulled the strap over his head.

'Pump it out,' Ellen said.

Neal stared up at her. She turned to Scott.

'Get the fire trucks down here. If we can lower the pressure—'

'The trucks are in the parade, they'll never get here in time,' Scott told her. He clawed the top of his head with both hands.

'Can we break through the dam?' Ellen asked him. 'From the

other side – break through to relieve the pressure?'

Scott looked down at Neal, questioning.

'Rock and concrete,' Neal said skeptically.

'It's worth a try,' Scott said. 'Neal, go down and tell him we're gonna get him out. Ellen, stay by the phone. I'll get the pickaxe.' Scott climbed back up the bank, then ran off toward the house.

Ellen looked down at Neal in the water, the telephone tight in her hand, her body shivering intensely despite the full sunlight on her back. While birds sang obliviously all around her, she watched a flurry of bubbles break against the dam. She thought of her wounded sheep sprawled in the pasture waiting to die, the way it had breathed.

'Neal, get him out,' she said evenly.

'We're doing everything we can.'

She stared at him. He gave nothing away. Gulping a quick breath of air, she dived into the water and, when she'd surfaced, said, 'Give me the tank.'

'Ellen, don't go down there.'

'Give me the tank.'

Their eyes met.

'Okay, sit on the rock, I'll help you put it on,' he told her. She swam over and hoisted herself up, and Neal handed the heavy tank up to her. She fit her arms through the straps, then pulled the weight belt around her waist, snapped the latch and pulled it tight. Neal stripped the mask off his forehead and handed it to her. She pulled it down over her face. Then she fit the regulator in her mouth.

'Breathe normally,' Neal told her.

She slipped off the rock and went under, pulling a deep breath of compressed air into her lungs and blowing it forcefully out, as she turned and kicked for the bottom. At first, she saw Randy only as a vague, black shape in the surrounding darkness, but the deeper she swam, the more acclimated to the darkness she grew, so by the time she was five feet from him, she saw something that made her stop just out of his reach.

He was sitting stiffly on the bottom with his right side pressed tight against the dam and his left fist clenched against his shoulder, facing up at her with his eyes shut and a horrible grimace on his face. Ellen might have thought him dead, were it not for the quick, shallow bubbling from his regulator or the rapid rise and fall of his chest. Then she realized what he was doing. His wetsuit was sliced open in three places at the shoulder, like the gill slits of a shark, and slender threads of blood curled off the blade where he held a knife to his flesh.

She let herself descend another inch, until her shadow darkened Randy's face. His eyes opened. Suddenly the knife blade flashed up at her. She pushed herself back. But she knew by the sorrowful look in his eyes that he was not attacking her. He was trying to hand her his knife. He motioned to his shoulder, his eyes desperately pleading. He wanted her to amputate his arm.

She shook her head adamantly.

He waved the knife at her, insistent.

Equally insistent, Ellen refused again.

Behind his mask, his eyes seemed to glaze with sadness. He looked down at his shoulder again, then turned back to Ellen as if to continue the argument. She gestured back at him, that she wanted to give him the tank she was wearing. As she reached down to unbuckle her weight belt, suddenly his eyes flared and he lashed out, knife flashing. She kicked back, just as a hand shot past her and captured Randy's wrist. In the flurry of bubbles, Ellen saw Neal pulling Randy's arm upward, while Randy's knife pecked furiously at him. Then Randy swung his legs up, as if trying to wrap them around Neal's neck, but when his right knee kicked up, his knife pierced his own thigh. Ellen saw a burst of bubbles expel from Randy's regulator as the blood inked thickly from his leg.

Clutching Randy's wrist with both hands, Neal pressed his feet against the convex face of the dam and pushed. From above, it might have looked like he was trying to pull Randy out of the pipe – if the men could have been seen, which they could not, as deep as they were.

Down in the dark, Ellen could see the knife tremble in Randy's hand; she could see the contortion of his face and how his arm actually seemed to stretch as his wetsuit ripped wider, the blood rushing out of his shoulder cut and streaming into the pipe. A sudden pop sounded, then a gurgling scream from Randy, and his wetsuit sleeve snapped free at the shoulder and was sucked into the drain. In the same instant, the knife dropped from his hand and floated to the bottom. Then Neal released his wrist and swam down to retrieve the weapon.

Floating in the fog of stirred-up silt, Ellen could nevertheless see

Randy's eyes through his mask, gazing longingly at her, conveying a desperate understanding of his fate. She started removing her tank again, but Neal took hold of her arm. When she wheeled around and shook her head at him, he knocked on the tank, pointed to his wrist, then pointed up. She understood. Maximize the air in both tanks. She kicked for the top.

She broke into open and pulled the regulator from her mouth as Neal surfaced beside her, looking all around.

'Take this,' he said, poking her hand with the handle of Randy's knife. 'Hide it.'

She scowled at him.

'Ellen, now,' he said urgently.

She tore the mask from her face and slapped it on the water between them. 'You get him out of there,' she whispered.

'Ellie!' Scott shouted, appearing on the ledge above them with a pickaxe in his hand. 'What are you doing?'

She felt the knife handle slide into her palm again, and her heart pounded. She refused to take it.

'What are you doing in the water?' Scott shouted again, his face a bright, burning pink. He slammed the pickaxe onto the abutment under his feet. 'I told you to man the phone!'

'We were trying to pull him out,' she answered.

'Neal and I already tried. We need to conserve the air in that tank, now get up here.'

Treading water, Ellen threw her shoulders back and wriggled out of the diving tank – Neal helped pull it off – then took one powerful stroke to the diving rock and pulled herself onto her stomach. Lifting herself to her feet, she couldn't believe how her legs were shaking.

'How is he?' Scott asked her.

'Cold,' Neal answered. 'The seal's gone in his wetsuit.'

'Don't either of you go down there anymore,' Scott told him. 'Neal, stay on the surface and watch his bubbles so you'll be ready to change tanks when he runs out of air.' He turned back to Ellen as she stepped up onto the bank. 'I know it goes against your goddamned nature,' he told her, 'but right now you've got to do what I say.'

Jerking away from her, he marched around the end of the dam and dropped the pickaxe over the side. it rang angrily when it hit the rocky stream bed below. As he started lowering himself down the granite bank, Randy's knife clattered on the rock at her feet.

She turned back to the pond and glared at Neal, who was floating on the scuba tank.

'Ellen, get rid of it,' he said quietly. She wanted to kick it back into the water.

'*Ellie, where are you?*' Scott shouted.

'Right here!'

She kicked the knife underneath Randy's duffle bag as she stepped onto the abutment, where she could see Scott on the other side of the dam, balancing along the greasy stream bed with his pickaxe.

'Can you see Randy's bubbles?'

'Yes,' Ellen answered, positioning herself so both Scott and Neal were in her sight. In fact, the curve in the dam allowed Ellen to see part of both faces of the structure: the near half of the pond face and the far half of the dry face, where the outlet pipe was located, a dark, eight-inch hole embedded in the granite blocks about three feet off the ground.

Scott chose a spot about five feet beyond the pipe, secured his footing on the slippery rock, then swung the pickaxe. The impact on the rock did nothing to the dam, but Ellen noticed a movement inside the pipe and realized, to her horror, that she could see the tips of Randy's fingers beckoning, like pale earthworms, for the light. She visualized the thickness of the dam and imagined how far his arm must have been stretched.

'Ellen,' Neal called quietly.

She ignored him.

Scott swung the pickaxe again, with a loud grunt. This time its tip stuck between two keystones and held fast. 'Bastard!' he cursed, shaking the handle until the pick came free.

Knowing the way the keystone rocks fit together – the structure was actually strengthened by the force of the water – Ellen wondered how Scott could hope to break through. She looked down to the duffel, saw sunlight flash off the tip of the blade. If Randy died with a wound in his leg, she thought, and the knife were found . . .

Hide it where? She looked back toward the pasture, the house, the barn, the pump house . . .

'Scott?'

He attacked the dam again.

'Scott, I know how we can drain the pond!' she yelled. She bent and grabbed the knife from under the duffel bag, then ran down the bank and on up the farm road.

'*Ellie, where are you going?*' he shouted.

The pump house was eight-by-eight, windowless, constructed of cinder blocks. Two water fixtures protruded through the side. One fed the garden hose, which stretched across the pasture to the sheep's temporary paddock. The other was a two-inch fire hose fitting, which the family had never needed, until now.

Ellen opened the wooden door, then bent and threw open the hatch. A ladder led ten feet down into the darkness, where the two pumps sat: one tapping the farm pond and providing water for the barn; the other connecting the deep well to the house. She descended to the cold concrete floor, feeling her way between the cold, cobwebbed wall and the two water pumps. Finding the narrow space between the two pumps, she dropped the knife down, heard the incriminating click it made against the floor, then made her way back to the ladder. Climbing out of the dank hole, she shut the hatch behind her, then went out in the sunlight, around the side of the pump house, where she opened the ball valve on the fire hose fitting. Instantly a thick jet of water sprayed thirty feet out into the pasture.

Running back down to the pond, she climbed the bank and called to Scott, 'I turned on the fire hose at the pump house.'

'Ellie, we need you here!' he yelled, his pickaxe ringing hard off the granite. He had taken his shirt off, and his shoulders and arms shone with sweat. 'How's Randy?'

Ellen looked over the pond side of the dam, where air bubbles broke alongside the top of the dam. As she turned back to answer, she was distracted by the sight of someone coming around the pump house.

'*How is he?*' Scott shouted.

'The same,' Ellen yelled back, peering up the hill.

It was Maddy, walking sprightly down the farm road, wearing a red summer dress and large dark sunglasses. She had a picnic basket over her arm.

'He's going to need more air in a minute,' Neal called.

'Are the EMTs here?' Scott shouted, striking the dam again and again.

'I brought a little peace offering,' Maddy called, as she

approached the bank, lifting a bottle of red wine out of her basket.

'Mad, we've got an emergency,' Ellen said to her, hoping to turn her back.

'Who are you talking to?' Scott yelled.

Maddy mounted the bank and looked down one side of the dam, at Neal treading water with the scuba tank strapped to his shoulder, then down the other side, at Scott attacking the rock wall with his pickaxe.

'What is he doing?' she asked with distaste.

'Get her out of here!' Scott warned, grunting as he struck the dam again. The impact jolted up through Ellen's legs.

'It's Randy,' Ellen explained to her friend. 'He's caught in the dam.'

Maddy's face changed. 'You're serious—?'

'His arm's caught in the outlet pipe.'

'God,' Maddy breathed. 'Wait a minute. How—'

'*Shh*—'

Ellen listened.

'Scott, stop—'

The dam rang with one more blow of his pickaxe, then everything was perfectly quiet. The bubbles had stopped.

'Neal!' Ellen yelled, spinning toward the pond, but Neal was already underwater, his kicking feet darkening to a deeper green-brown. She turned back to Scott. 'He's out of air!'

'God,' Maddy said again, putting her hands on Ellen's back, as together they watched the unbroken surface.

'*What's going on up there?*' Scott shouted.

'Is his hand still moving?' Ellen called down to him. 'Check his hand!'

'His hand?' Maddy breathed.

Scott dropped the pickaxe and fell to his knees in front of the pipe, staring into the dark hole. He raised his face and cried out: '*I cannot do this to my daughter!*'

In the echo of his shout, the silence was pervasive. Even the birds stopped singing. Ellen felt Maddy's grip tighten on her arm.

Then a burst of bubbles broke the surface, quickly followed by more.

Ellen turned toward the pond as Neal splashed into the air with Randy's spent tank in his hands.

'He's only got a few minutes,' Neal gasped.

'Five minutes!' Ellen yelled down.

Scott grabbed his pickaxe again and swung it mightily, striking the same bruised keystone again, dead on, the impact staggering him. He regained his footing but his shoulders slumped, and he looked like he was about to collapse. But he reared back and swung again.

Maddy stared straight at Ellen, her eyes like lights.

Ellen turned toward the pasture. Now someone else was running down the hillside, a short, stocky man in a baseball uniform, no cap, his muscular arms pumping . . . Sugar Westerback, yelling as he charged down the hill, 'Rescue units on the way!'

'He needs scuba tanks!' Ellen shouted in reply.

'How much air's he got?' Sugar asked, pounding up the bank.

'Five minutes,' Ellen said. 'Less than five minutes.'

'What, *left*?'

He looked down at Neal treading the water, the empty tank discarded on the rocks.

'What's wrong with that one?' he said.

'Empty,' Neal answered.

The pickaxe clanged against the dam. Scott's grunt sounded like a sob. Sugar stared down. 'Scotty, you trying to break him out?'

Ellen looked at the policeman, thinking he might have been drinking. In fact, she could smell beer on him. The words BRISCOE'S MEATS was emblazoned on his softball uniform in deep red lettering.

'He's trying to let water out,' Ellen explained. 'To relieve the pressure.'

'That's not gonna work,' Sugar said matter-of-factly, still looking down at Scott. Then his head jerked, and he gaped down at the black pipe, the white fingertips inside beckoning.

'Whoa,' he whispered, while behind him, Randy's breath bubbled up.

Sugar lowered his head for a moment, scowling in thought. Then he turned toward the house. 'Okay,' he said, 'bring your truck down. We'll hitch up a chain and haul him out.'

'Won't do any good,' Neal said. 'We've got a winch up in the shed. But you'd only pull his arm off.'

'I don't mean *through* the friggin pipe,' Sugar told. 'I mean haul him out by his feet.'

'There's too much pressure,' Ellen explained. 'You pull on him hard enough, you'll rip his arm off.'

Sugar frowned again. 'Huh.' He looked at his watch and said, 'They should be here any minute.' He took a deep, thoughtful breath, his eyes absently roaming Maddy's dress. 'I'm in the middle of a tournament,' he said. 'Luckily, we're between games.' He folded his arms, rubbing his biceps with his hands while his eyebrows went up, went down, and then he scowled deeply. 'Garden hose!' he blurted, clapping his hands. 'He can breathe through a hose.'

'He's down twenty feet,' Neal said, on the other side. 'The pressure'll collapse it.'

'Screw the pressure,' Sugar said. 'I don't hear any better ideas.' He pointed at Neal. 'You, go get twenty-five feet of garden hose. On the double. Bring that winch down too. What the hell, you lose an arm, it's better than losin your life.'

Neal gave Sugar a doubtful look.

'Move it!' Sugar barked. 'Splashin around down there sure ain't gonna help.'

'Just do it, Neal,' Ellen said. Neal swam to the diving rock and climbed up to the bank.

'Hurry up,' Sugar told him, then he stepped to the downstream side of the dam and called, 'Scotty, we got a plan up here!'

But Scott did not hear. He was toiling in a panic, sweat pouring off his face as again and again he swung the heavy tool into the granite, not even noticing Maddy above him stepping out of her dress, revealing a fiery red bikini underneath, then climbing down the rocks toward him. But Ellen noticed.

'Maddy, you'd better not,' she said, wanting to keep her friend away from Scott.

But Maddy was not to be dissuaded. Stepping down into the slippery, puddled rocks, she made her way over to the outlet pipe, where she knelt on the granite bed and reached into the pipe, taking hold of Randy's fingers.

'God, his hand is freezing,' she called.

Scott glanced over to her. *Keep working*, Ellen thought.

To her small relief, he said nothing, but reared back with the pickaxe and slammed it into the wall with a terrible grunt. Chips of granite flew. Maddy ducked. Then she whipped her head up at Ellen.

'He's writing something!' she cried.

Ellen looked down.

'Whoa, his finger,' Sugar breathed, leaning over the edge.

Ellen saw the bent finger moving on Maddy's palm.

'M!' Maddy called up. 'He made the letter M.'

'M,' Sugar echoed.

Behind Ellen, the bubbles breaking on the pond sounded like low, taunting laughter.

'U!' Maddy called.

'M-U,' Sugar said.

Scott stopped pounding at the rocks. He looked over, as Maddy gazed into the pipe. Ellen stared down, paralyzed, as the finger continued moving like a planchette over Maddy's palm. She could feel her heart pounding down through her feet.

'That it?' Sugar said. 'M-U?'

'R,' Maddy said. 'M-U-R—' She watched intently, as the white finger continued inscribing on her palm. Suddenly her eyes rose up to Ellen, horrified.

Ellen felt a wave of lightness come over her. 'M-*O*,' she said, correcting Maddy. 'M-*O*-R . . . *Moreen*. Is that what he's spelling? *Moreen?*' She stared down at Maddy. And Maddy stared back, speechless, her eyes turning glassy. She nodded.

Scott started bashing the dam again with his pickaxe.

'Moreen?' Sugar said.

Ellen could feel his eyes settle on her. She realized she was holding her breath.

'Wait a minute,' Sugar breathed. 'That's *Randy* down there?'

Suddenly Maddy's mouth sprang open. If she had meant to scream, her voice was not cooperating.

Ellen watched her, terrified. 'Mad?'

'My hand,' Maddy gasped.

'I think he's got ahold of her,' Sugar suggested.

Ellen turned toward the pond. The bubbles had stopped.

On the other side of the dam, she heard Maddy gasp. 'He's breaking my—' Then she fell backward, as if repelled from a shock, landing hard on the rocks. Scott dropped his pickaxe and ran to the outlet pipe, sank to his knees and thrust his hand in.

Behind Ellen, a great burst of bubbles broke on the pond.

At that moment, Neal came running onto the bank with the winch in his hand and a long section of garden hose coiled around his neck and shoulder. Immediately reading the situation, he dropped the things on the abutment and dived in the water.

'Oh boy,' Sugar said, folding his arms, looking up at the sky.

Ellen stared down at Scott holding Randy's hand, his forehead laid against the dam.

Beside him, Maddy numbly raised herself off the rocks.

Scott took a deep breath, then withdrew his hand from the pipe and sat heavily on the basin. He turned his head toward Maddy and said, 'You alright?'

Maddy met his eyes.

'You okay?' he asked again.

'Fine,' Maddy replied, and she looked up at Ellen, who turned to the pond to see Neal rise to the surface. Ellen made eye contact with him, seeking the confirmation she didn't really need.

'We lose him?' Sugar said.

Neal nodded, then climbed onto the rocks, saying to Sugar, 'He pulled the regulator out of his mouth.'

'Yeah, what's that?'

'The thing you breathe through.'

'What do you mean he pulled it out?'

'There was no air left in the tank,' Neal explained and he pulled himself up to the bank. 'Probably like trying to breathe through a bent straw. His lungs overruled his brain, told him to breathe. So he breathed. Water.'

Sugar winced.

Neal went over to Ellen, put his cold hand on her arm. 'We did everything we could,' he said softly. As she withstood his touch, she caught Maddy looking up at them both. Then she heard a siren. Two sirens.

'Here they come,' Sugar said. 'Right on time.'

It was an ambulance and one of the two town fire trucks, trailing red, white and blue streamers behind. Sugar looked at the truck, then turned and stared hard at Ellen. A wave of fear charged through her body, though she tried not to show it. Then Sugar threw a furious punch in the air, the force nearly toppling him off the bank.

'*Stupid!*' he cursed himself. '*Pump it out!*'

The state police followed the fire truck in, and a battery of men directed the police down the farm road to the pond, where the fire truck began pumping. As Ellen stood watching, she couldn't stop picturing the knife on the floor of the pump house. Finally she turned away from the pond, picked up the coiled garden hose and headed for the house.

'You okay?' Scott asked her.

'I need the bathroom,' she answered. 'Can I turn off the pump now?'

Scott looked at the trooper, who shrugged and said, 'For all the good it's doing.'

She walked briskly away from them, followed the gravel road up to the pump house as if she were sleepwalking. She shut off the water at the fixture, then went down inside the pump house and retrieved the knife from the cold floor and stuffed it inside the bundled hose. Climbing back out of the pump house, she carried the concealed weapon up the farm road, walking stiffly past the gathering crowd of police and emergency workers and townspeople who were just getting the news.

She climbed the porch steps and went inside with the hose, into the pantry, where she opened the freezer and buried the knife under the plastic bags of last year's vegetables. Then she used the bathroom. When she walked out of the house again she saw Rooftop's panel truck parked in the dooryard – XYZ DIVERS. Rooftop himself was leaning heavily on Randy's black Cherokee, his long chin resting on his arms.

He knew. The way he stared at Ellen, she was sure he knew. When he raised his face off the roof of the Jeep, the sky flashed off his glasses.

'Your daughter's here,' he said to her.

Moreen and Scott were together when Ellen reached them, down below the dam, Moreen kneeling on the rocks with her hand inside the drainage pipe, quietly crying, Scott standing at her side, idly stroking her hair. The fire truck's two hoses snaked down the bank beside them, then stretched thirty feet along the stream bed where, weighted down by blocks of granite, they sprayed pond water down the gorge.

Ellen stood above Moreen and Scott for a moment, looking down. Loath though she was to admit it, along with the sorrow she felt for her daughter, it pained her to see the two of them so close, while she felt so utterly estranged from them both. It was as though they shared some mystical pact that she could not be a part of.

But who had raised Moreen while Scott was away at work, at Rotary or some other meeting? And where was Scott when Moreen needed rides to Girl Scouts, to 4-H, to softball, hockey, soccer, to school concerts? And all those nights when Moreen was sick, who sat up with her while Scott snored obliviously in his own bed? Who cooked Moreen's meals, bought her clothes, read to her, brought her to the beach? Yes, and who murdered her husband?

Ellen tingled with awareness of her crime, as she climbed down the bank and balanced over the slippery basin to her daughter. Before she could think of a thing to say, Moreen reached out for her. It was like the pull of gravity, the way they came together, the way Moreen's crying suddenly made her seem like a little girl again. As much as Ellen's mind stormed with guilt and fear, she relished the privilege of holding Mo while she cried. She sank to her knees and kissed her cheek, while Scott continued stroking her hair.

'I'm so sorry,' Ellen whispered. 'I'm so sorry.'

'It's not your fault,' Moreen cried.

When Duane Ramsey, the deputy medical examiner, climbed down to the bottom of the dam, he took Randy's hand from Moreen, felt for a pulse, then climbed back up and signed the death certificate in the presence of Sugar Westerback. Ramsey asked whether Sugar's father Wes was on his way, and Sugar told him that his parents had gone up to Lake Winnipesaukee to visit his sister, as they did every Fourth of July. Sugar didn't think they needed to be called back.

Interviews were conducted in the house, away from the noise of the fire truck. While Ellen, Scott, Neal and Maddy sat around the kitchen table, Sugar leaned against the counter with a pad of paper and pen he had borrowed from Ellen, and he interviewed them together. Scott, speaking for the group, told Sugar that while Ellen was cleaning the house, he, Randy and Neal had gone down to the dam to drain the pond. While he and Neal stayed on the bank with the equipment, Randy went down to unscrew the cap with a two-foot pipe wrench and three-pound hammer.

'Then he came up and said he got it unscrewed but he needed an axe or a crow bar,' Scott explained, 'something to knock the cap out of the way.'

Sugar said, 'Okay.'

'So I went up and got the crow bar,' Neal said.

'That do the trick?'

'Must've,' Scott answered. 'The water came gushing out for a second. Then it stopped. We figured Randy capped it again for some reason, and we waited awhile, but he wasn't coming up.'

'Did you see what happened?'

Scott shrugged. 'Too deep.'

'How you think he got sucked in?' Sugar said.

'The only way I can figure it,' Neal said, 'he used the crow bar like a lance.'

Sugar scowled. 'What, he threw it?'

'A spear you throw,' Neal said. 'A lance you hold onto.'

'Sir Lancelot,' Sugar said.

'Probably when the cap gave way, the momentum carried him forward,' Neal continued, 'so he held out his arm to stop himself.'

Sugar straightened an arm and leaned forward in his chair, then stopped and did it again. 'I can see that,' he said.

Ellen studied Neal, thinking the theory plausible. In fact, if Neal had actually caused Randy's death, she had no idea how.

'Then what?' Sugar said.

'When he didn't come up,' Scott said, 'I went down to see what happened.'

'You went down in the water and found him stuck?'

'I tried to pull him out.' Scott shook his head soberly. 'We all tried. Even with Neal and me together, we couldn't budge him. So I ran up and called you, got your answering service.'

Sugar turned to Maddy, who was once again wearing her sun dress and sunglasses.

'You have anything to add?' Sugar said to her.

Maddy shook her head. Her tan had given way to a greenish pallor.

'Maddy only got there a minute before you did,' Ellen explained. 'Are you okay, Mad?'

'I'm fine,' Maddy answered.

'You don't look so hot,' Sugar said. 'Unless you got anything you wanna say, you don't have to stick around.'

Maddy stood up and went out the door. Sugar watched her for a moment or two, then turned back to the others, his gaze stopping on Ellen, who was distracted by what she was seeing out the window: Maddy and Moreen huddled beside Randy's Cherokee, quietly conferring.

Sugar leaned forward to see what she was looking at.

'Lucky you got a friend who's a psychologist,' Sugar said looking out the window. 'Moreen can probably use someone to talk to.'

Ellen gave him a sideward glance.

'Almost done,' he said, sliding back in his chair and looking over his notes. 'Hey, anyway, how do you spell Moreen? M-O?'

'It's a type of wool,' Ellen explained.

'Huh,' Sugar said.

Sugar scratched the back of his head. 'Anyone have anything else to say?'

For a moment, the only sound in the kitchen was that of the fire truck pumping out the pond.

'I guess not,' Scott said.

'Good, we're done,' said Sugar, closing the pad.

Maddy was gone when Ellen went outside. Moreen was once again down at the dam, holding Randy's hand. For the remainder of the afternoon and well into the evening, Ellen, Scott and Neal stood vigil on the banks of the pond, silently watching Moreen, while Sugar Westerback and a State Police trooper kept visitors away.

Channel 6 News from Portland had sent a crew to film the recovery of Randy's body – so had a station from Boston, along with local reporters and photographers – but the police would not allow the media or anybody else get close enough to bother the family. However, when a neighbor showed up with three cheese pizzas from Ruby's Pizza, Sugar brought the food down to the dam, along with a tray of red, white and blue Jell-O and a huge bowl of potato salad that other townspeople had dropped off. Chuck Young, who had worked for Scott at the hardware store, sent down a six-pack of Heineken, which Scott started drinking immediately.

Eventually a carload of Moreen's friends came to take her away. Moreen declined at first, wanting to see Randy when he was pulled from the water, but after drinking half the thermos of coffee sombrero they'd sent down, Moreen went off with them.

Rooftop came back, too. This time Gator was with him. When Sugar Westerback caught them going through Randy's Cherokee, he threatened to arrest them. Gator replied that Randy had borrowed some of their diving equipment, which they needed back. Sugar told Gator that unless his name was on the Cherokee's registration, he had no business there. When the state trooper came along, Rooftop interceded and convinced Gator to shut up, and they drove away again.

Randy's corpse was not freed from the dam until well after nine that night, when the water level had sunk to five feet above the drain pipe. By then the crew was working with floodlights. Once the body was removed to the morgue, the fire truck returned to the station and the pond continued draining through its outlet pipe. By ten-thirty, when everyone had finally gone, Ellen and Scott went in the house.

Scott, who had polished off the six-pack, made himself scrambled eggs and toast and downed it with a stiff whiskey-and-ginger, while he watched the reports of Randy's death on the eleven o'clock news. Ellen stayed in the kitchen and poured herself a small bowl of cereal but was unable to eat. She was waiting for Moreen to come home, or at least to call. Eventually she heard Scott begin to snore. Then the screen door closed behind her. She knew it was Neal, but she just sat there, refusing to turn and look at him. He waited a few seconds, then went outside again. Ellen waited until two, but the phone didn't ring. Finally she went up to bed.

CHAPTER TEN

Ellen buried Randy's knife the next morning, the first chance she had. Scott had left the house at five, to work at his gun shop. Ellen stayed upstairs in Moreen's room, getting the room ready for Mo's return, all the while listening to Neal outside, hammering in the barn. When she heard the hammering stop, she went into her bedroom and looked out the window, watching him carry Scott's red bucksaw down the farm road toward the pond. Seeing her opportunity, Ellen hurried down to the pantry and retrieved the knife from the freezer, then scrubbed it thoroughly with a soapy sponge while she kept her eye on the window.

She wiped the knife dry with a paper napkin, then tossed the napkin in the cookstove and dropped a match in. While the fire burned, she went out on the porch and looked for Neal again, spotted him moving up in the woods on the other side of the stream. She had no idea what he was up to. No matter. She stuffed the knife upside-down in her back pocket and walked out to the tool shed to get a shovel, then went around to her vegetable garden and dug down between two cucumber hills, as deep as she was able, about sixteen inches – deeper than her tractor's tines would reach. In a couple of weeks, she knew the cucumber vines would cover the spot. When her shovel hit hard clay, she lay flat on the ground and stabbed the knife into the bottom of the hole.

A sudden crunching of gravel alerted her. She turned to see Randy's black Cherokee skid to a stop beside the porch. Rising to her feet, she casually kicked some of the soil back in, as Moreen stepped out of the Jeep. Ellen waved her dirty hand.

'Hello,' Mo said with a tired, almost apologetic smile.

'Oh, Honey,' Ellen said, heading over to her, refraining from asking where she'd spent the night or why she hadn't called, refraining also from giving Mo a hug because of the dirt on her hands. 'How are you doing, hon?'

Mo groaned. 'We pulled an all-nighter,' she answered, giving Ellen a light kiss on the lips. Then she turned back to the Cherokee and opened the liftback. When Ellen saw the cardboard boxes inside, a small wave of happiness came over her. Moreen was coming home.

She heard footsteps behind her and turned to see Neal walking up the farm road toward them. He was carrying his boots, his pants rolled up below his knees, his legs wet. As he passed the pump house he glanced over toward the garden.

'What were you doing in the woods?' Ellen asked, hoping to distract him.

'Cutting some brush,' he answered.

When she turned back to the Jeep, Moreen was carrying a box up the porch steps.

'Mo, wait,' Ellen said, hurrying up the steps and taking it from her arms. 'Honey, you shouldn't be lifting that.'

'It's not heavy,' Moreen replied, opening the screen door for her.

'Come in and sit down, I'll get the rest,' Ellen told her, as she went into the kitchen and set the box on the table. When she turned around, Moreen was back at the Jeep, pulling a bulging trash bag out of the back.

'Mo, be careful, you'll rip your stitches,' Ellen called, but Mo hoisted the bag over her shoulder and carried it up the steps, turning her body so Ellen couldn't take it from her. Behind her, Neal followed with two more boxes.

'That's everything,' he said.

Ellen held the screen door, and they both walked through.

'How are you?' Neal asked as they set the things on the table. His compassion seemed sincere.

'Hello,' Mo answered brightly, as if nothing in the world were wrong.

Reacting to Ellen's gaze, she said, 'Mom, I'm fine.' Then she turned and gave Ellen another kiss. 'I'll call you later, okay?'

'Wait,' Ellen said. 'You're not going to work—?'

'I quit,' Moreen said, tossing the screen door open. 'Either that, or they fired me, I'm not sure which.'

Ellen took the door from her, held it open. 'Mo, we need to make funeral arrangements.'

'Oh, can you do it?' Moreen said, giving her a pleading look. 'I'll pay you back when I get another job.'

'It's not that,' Ellen told her. 'We'll pay for it. Hon, if you want, I'll take you shopping so you can find something to wear.'

'I've got clothes,' Mo sang, laboring down the steps. 'Thanks, love you.'

'Mo, wait—'

Moreen turned at the bottom of the porch and gave Ellen a look, raised eyebrows, sparkling eyes, carefree and innocent.

'Honey, where are you going?'

Mo shrugged her shoulders, as if the answer were obvious. 'I've got to find a place to live.'

'Here,' Ellen said. 'You live here.'

Moreen steadied herself on the railing post. 'Mom, I'm meeting someone for breakfast, and I'm already late,' she said, then turned for the Cherokee. 'I'll call you later.'

Ellen stepped to the railing. 'You're not even old enough. What are you going to do for money?'

Moreen opened the door without turning back. 'Sell the Jeep, I don't know. Stop worrying.'

'Hey,' Neal said.

Moreen turned, gave him the same look she had given Ellen: blinking eyes, pleasant smile; beautiful indifference. Ellen saw Neal's own eyes search uncomfortably for the right words. Ellen already knew the right words did not exist.

'Your mom wants to know where you're going, that's all,' he said, stuffing his hands in his pants pockets. 'She loves you, and she's concerned about you.'

Mo's smile brightened. 'I'm fine, really,' she repeated, pulling herself into the Cherokee. 'I'm fine, I'm fine, I'm fine.' Then she shut the door and drove away.

Neal stood dumbly, watching the dust settle on the lawn. 'I've just decided never to reproduce,' he said.

Ellen didn't laugh. 'Neal, what are you doing in the woods?'

He glanced back. 'Making a road.'

She studied him. 'A road for what?'

He shrugged. 'If you want to lead someone somewhere, make a road.' Giving her a parting, cryptic glance, he walked off the porch and headed back down toward the pond.

As Ellen watched him, a sudden and profound feeling of regret came over her – or maybe it was fear – that Moreen had told the truth about the ram; and that Neal had made a road for Randy, wide, straight and paved, that led straight to his death.

. . . and that she had lost Moreen forever.

A perfect peace. Draped in cool green placidity, Rooftop Paradise soared slowly over a miniature forest of red, green and brown trees, while banners of kelp twenty feet long waved in the current. This quaint forest, which teemed with minuscule crabs and sea urchins, grew thickly over a wide, expansive ledge that dropped down over several desk-sized steps into darkness.

In his hand, Rooftop held a white plastic quadrat, a square-meter outline, which he would systematically toss onto the ocean floor and then take a census of the lobsters within its borders – size, sex and number. He was working off of the Cape Neddick lighthouse as a research volunteer for the University of Maine. On his left arm he wore a white plastic cylinder, onto which was taped plastic mechanical drawing paper and a plastic pencil, for recording the information. Having depleted his fourth and final scuba tank – two hours of diving – he floated up through forty feet of water feeling a fine tranquility, hearing nothing but his own satisfied breath, while scores of shrimplike amphipods flitted around his mask, and a school of foot-long pollack darted out of his way. As the sun flattened against the ceiling of water, outlining the wide hull of his Boston Whaler, his quadrat broke the surface, and it was immediately snatched from his hand by Jake, a student from the University of Maine's School of Marine Sciences. Rooftop took hold of the dive ladder, then handed up his writing cylinder and weight belt.

'I think somebody's here for you,' Jake said, struggling to pull the weight belt from the water.

Rooftop took the regulator out of his mouth, lifted the mask off his face. The kid handed him his glasses, then pointed toward the shore. 'Over there on the rocks.'

Rooftop pulled himself around the stern and looked. The two men stood above the surf spray: one short, one tall. The shorter man waved his arm over his head, the greasy stump of his right hand glistening in the noonday sun.

An hour later Rooftop was escorted up a set of circular stairs into

Ray LaFlamme's private dining room. Rooftop had changed out of his wetsuit in his van and now wore a plain white short-sleeved shirt and black doubleknit trousers, along with a stiff pair of black wingtips, his entire wardrobe mail-ordered from a supply house for tall men's clothing in the Bronx.

In LaFlamme's rooftop dining room, glass was the prominent feature, covering three walls, floor to ceiling, facing the beach and ocean. The bar, which ran half the length of the fourth wall, was jet black, with a row of mother-of-pearl crucifixes inlaid along its top. The wall behind the bar was red, as was the carpeting. Tablecloths and linens were also white, with silver crucifixes embroidered along their borders.

When the men entered the dining room, Ray LaFlamme was still eating his lunch, seated alone at one of ten square tables, staring up at a wide-screen TV beside the bar. *NYPD Blue* was on, dubbed in French. The old man matched the room's decor: red-framed glasses and a red-plaid flannel shirt, white linen slacks and white suede shoes. His wavy white hair was combed diagonally over the top of his head, his white mustache trimmed square and close to his lip, and his white napkin, spotted and splattered with sauce, was tucked into the collar of his shirt.

'That's okay,' he said when the men opened the door. 'Come on in fellas, sit down with me.'

LaFlamme ate his lunch out of two cast iron frying pans. The smaller of the two contained quartered red potatoes with mushrooms and mussels in a cheese sauce; in the larger was half a blackened duck in a broth, surrounded by mussels. Ray LaFlamme loved mussels with just about anything, and he always ate his meals directly out of frying pans. He considered it his trademark.

Rooftop was led to the table and seated across from the old man, with his back to the bar and kitchen doors. Marcel Desjardin, the larger of LaFlamme's two bodyguards, sat on Rooftop's right. Herbie Handcream sat on his left and leaned his arms on the table. It was hard for Rooftop to understand how Ray LaFlamme could eat with Herbie's shiny stub staring him in the face.

'You hear that?' LaFlamme said. He grinned at the TV with his oversized, overwhite teeth. 'I love that Sipowitz,' he said. 'He's so, you know, sarcastic.'

'Sarcastic,' Herbie Handcream said. All three men had mustaches.

'He says, "Hey, it's great to see you," when what he really means is, "Hey, seeing you really upsets my stomach," you know? Sarcastic. Stop it a minute.'

With his good hand, Herbie grabbed the remote off the table and aimed it at the TV. One click and a boxing match came on.

'Tone it down,' LaFlamme said. The TV went silent. He gave Marcel a nod and the big man stood and frisked Rooftop, up the legs and sides, along the arms. Dressed in a brown suit, the big man had a bulldog's face and disposition. He was fifty years old and looked like he could bench 400 pounds any time he felt like it.

'New policy,' LaFlamme explained to Rooftop after Marcel had sat down. LaFlamme himself was a small man, made smaller with age, and a slight tremor shook his hand whenever he raised his silverware. For a few moments, while he tried to sip broth from his teaspoon, nobody watched him and nobody spoke. Rooftop thought of the kitchen behind him, and the Fryolator, and he realized that the kitchen was silent. He wondered if LaFlamme had someone hiding back there.

LaFlamme set his spoon down and wiped his mustache and chin with a corner of his napkin, then snapped the napkin out of his shirt. He had a silver crucifix pinned to his pocket. 'Anyway, you want a nice glass of Merlot, Rupert?'

'No thank you,' Rooftop answered.

'Beer?'

'I don't drink.'

'Soup or something? You like mussels?'

Rooftop shook his head.

'I bet you can put away the mussels.'

'He's a big one, ain't he, Ray?' Herbie Handcream said. 'Bigger than you, Marcel.'

Marcel looked Rooftop over. The man was built like a refrigerator, with a neck as thick as a normal man's thigh.

LaFlamme lifted his place mat and slid out a greeting card. He smiled gently at it. 'So you're not happy working for me. Gonna get a real job, what's the story?'

'I decided to make a career change,' Rooftop said.

'He sends a thank-you card,' LaFlamme said with a big white grin.

'Thank-you card,' Herbie Handcream said.

'It was a nice card, nice sentiment. Of course, most employers require a two-week notice.'

LaFlamme set the card down, then picked a mussel out of the broth. Taking the shell between his thumbs, he pulled it apart, spattering broth on his shirt. Then he snatched the meat with his fingers, dunked it in the cheese sauce and popped it in his mouth. He lifted his napkin as he chewed, wiping his mustache. Outside the windows, the hot sun shone out of a sky that was bluer than possible and glared through the glass onto Ray LaFlamme's back. The dining room, however, was powerfully air-conditioned. When Rooftop took a breath, it shivered leaving his lungs.

'Hey, didn't you make a collection for me right around this time last week?' LaFlamme said, swallowing his food. He tapped his finger on the thank-you card. 'You know who I mean, the gentleman with the pickled potatoes.' He smiled again.

Rooftop cleared his throat. 'We met Mister Burdock on the gambling ferry.'

LaFlamme nodded. 'Your assistant, the redhead, he came by the other day and turned in the payment. Friday – the day before he drowned. It's in the book.'

Rooftop cleared his throat again. His lungs were tightening up from the cold. He didn't like the way Marcel and Herbie were staring at him.

'You want some water?'

'I'm okay.'

'Here's the funny thing about that. Not ha-ha funny, though. Mister Burdock's wife – what's her name?'

'Jimmy,' Herbie said.

'Jimmy – stupid name for a lady – anyway, she called here looking for her husband yesterday. Marcel, tell him what Humphrey Burdock's wife Jimmy told you.'

Marcel looked straight at Rooftop and said, 'They had a fight and Humphrey left the house and never came home.'

'That's what she said, and the night he disappeared was the night we found out he was going out on the ferry boat,' LaFlamme said. 'So I thought what, maybe he got off the ferry boat in Canada and didn't come back, you know, to avoid paying his debts. What do I know? I'm just a dumb Frenchman.'

'I guess we're all dumb Frenchmen, Ray,' Herbie said, and he laughed like a woodpecker.

Rooftop didn't like Herbie's giddiness. He pulled his inhaler from his pocket, uncapped it and sucked the medication deep into his lungs.

'But the funny thing here,' LaFlamme continued, 'the woman told Marcel that her husband left without, what, shaving kit, clothes, toothbrush—'

'Shaving kit,' Herbie echoed.

'Me, if I was leaving home, I'd take my toothbrush. Unless I was planning on returning home the next day.'

'I'd take the shaving kit,' Herbie said.

'Mister LaFlamme?' Rooftop began.

The old man leaned on his elbows as if to listen, but he kept talking. 'Herbie, clear the table. Marcel, help him. Cold, mussels get tough.'

The two men got up and grabbed Ray LaFlamme's frying pans off the table like they were having a race, then grabbed his wine glass, his silverware, his napkin, his bread basket, the wine bottle, clearing the table completely. All the while LaFlamme leaned on his elbows, eyes glinting intently at Rooftop.

Rooftop's heart pounded. 'Mister LaFlamme,' he said quietly, 'we put him off the boat.'

'What, you put Mister Burdock off the boat in Nova Scotia?'

'No, the ocean.'

'What do you mean?'

'We put him over the rail.'

The old man studied Rooftop hard.

'How far out?'

'Pretty far.'

LaFlamme turned to Marcel like he was going to start laughing. Then he turned back to Rooftop with a frown. 'The man that owed me forty thousand dollars, are you saying he's dead?'

Rooftop nodded, the sun making a blinding halo around the old man's head.

LaFlamme nodded too. 'Then you sent me the letter of resignation. And left your friend in charge.'

'Randy Cross,' Herbie said, 'who's also kaput.'

Rooftop's chest ballooned with a long, constricted wheeze.

The old man started nodding as he stared at Rooftop, a slight gleam appearing in his eye.

'This is the first time for you, isn't it?'

Rooftop's chest pumped like an overworked bellows.

'First time's always the toughest,' Herbie counseled.

'Plus you lost your best friend,' the old man said. 'See, I think you've got a little case of depression, that's all. But they got drugs now, Rupert, wonderful things, wonderful things.'

'Mister LaFlamme, I won't do your work any more,' Rooftop told him.

The old man suddenly pushed back from the table, as the side of Rooftop's head erupted with a deafening ring.

'*Tabernac!*' the old man cursed.

Rooftop got to his feet, at least he meant to, but the pain radiating through his skull dropped him back in his chair. He saw Herbie Handcream standing beside him, the small frying pan in his hand, dripping cheese sauce onto the floor.

'I'm talking to this man!' LaFlamme said to Herbie. 'Since when are you so independent?'

'Sorry, Ray.'

'Don't apologize to me. It's him you hit.'

Herbie looked contritely in Rooftop's direction, his shoulders slumped. 'Sorry, Roof. Guess I jumped the gun.'

Rooftop raised his arm to his head, and he saw Marcel standing on his other side, holding the large skillet.

'Rupert, how's your head?' LaFlamme asked, still frowning at Rooftop. He gave Rooftop his napkin.

'Okay, I guess,' the giant said, but he felt like he was going to throw up. He adjusted his glasses as LaFlamme's wizened smile returned to his face. 'People that know me know that I'm not a very religious man,' he began.

'Yeah, not much, Ray,' Herbie Handcream said.

LaFlamme chuckled. 'All right, maybe a little religious.'

'Maybe a lot,' Herbie said.

'Okay, Herbie,' LaFlamme said. 'The point I'm making here' – he leaned in closer to Rooftop, his gray eyes crinkling – 'I'm not going to heaven when I die. I've done too many wrong things to expect that. But – and this is what I'm saying here – the wrong I've done, I've done for the girls and for Joanne, if you know what I mean, so there'll be a place in heaven for them when they die. I figure, who knows, if I ask God to forgive me when it's my time to go, maybe he'll take that into consideration.'

Rooftop's head throbbed, but he shook it resolutely. 'I'm sorry,

Mister LaFlamme. I've got to live right.'

Ignoring him, the old man reached into his shirt pocket and came out with a folded piece of paper. 'Now as far as Humphrey Burdock is concerned, we're covered. Dead or alive, he defaulted on his loan, now I own a potato farm and a tractor and so forth. Big deal. It's not a great location, but we can make something of it, okay? That's not what's upsetting me.'

He unfolded the paper. The crackling made Rooftop's head hurt more.

'It's your assistant, the man you put in charge, what's his name again?'

'Randy Cross,' said Herbie.

LaFlamme kept his attention on Rooftop. 'When Randy Cross was here Friday he also turned over a monthly payment from another one of your clients, Scott Chambers, the gentleman with the hardware store. Did you know that?'

Rooftop turned and saw that the kitchen door was opened a crack. Dazed as he was, he didn't hear what LaFlamme said next, until the old man slid the piece of paper across the table to him.

'Saturday's mail,' LaFlamme said. 'The very next day.'

'The day your buddy drowned,' Marcel said in Rooftop's ear.

'It's a receipt, signed by your assistant – see, "Randy Cross" – saying that he received Scott Chambers' balloon payment on Friday. Right here: "One hundred fifty-and-so-on thousand dollars, paid in full". But Randy only turned over what?'

'Four thousand,' Marcel said.

The old man examined Rooftop for another second, then pushed back from the table as though he was finally through with his dinner. 'My men do not deceive me, Mister Paradise,' he said, just as a frying pan slammed against the back of Rooftop's head. Reaching back, the giant grabbed at Herbie's arm, but his greasy stub yanked through his palm, and Marcel bounced the large skillet off the side of Rooftop's head, knocking him to his knees, the floor spinning under his hands.

'I did not lie to you,' Rooftop said in a very low voice.

'In this business, you live by the sword, you die by the sword,' Ray LaFlamme said, his own voice distant and shadowy, as another frying pan popped against Rooftop's ear and seemed to crush his face into the carpet. He tried to get up, but more blows fell in quick succession, one on the shoulder blade, one on the hip, another on the back of the head, like a hailstorm, until Rooftop imagined himself lying in a gutter, spinning down the drain.

'Croquet shot,' he heard Herbie Handcream say, then the water swallowed him.

'Breathe now.'

Rooftop felt the mist rush into his throat. He tasted the vapor and inhaled gratefully, as the old man's face rose to a blur in front of him: the red glasses, the bushy white mustache.

Rooftop took the inhaler into his own hand and pushed the top, sucked deeply, filling his lungs. The adrenalin kick-started his heart, and his head began to throb violently. He felt a knifelike pain in his shoulder when he tried to move. His ear burned. He tasted blood in his mouth. His eyes teared. His glasses were gone.

'On the grave of your mother, Rupert, do you have that money?'

Rooftop snored, but it was unintentional. He shook his head.

'Do you know who has it?'

'Uh.' Shaking his head, he thought his jawbone was going to spill out of his mouth.

A raspy southern drawl rose up behind him. 'Hey, how's your buddy's young widow? How's Mo-reeen?'

Rooftop angled his head up to see Gator standing in the sunlight behind Ray LaFlamme. Rooftop's head lolled, swimming in pain.

'Hey, I think the big bastard's got a broad,' Herbie said, and he laughed.

Now Marcel moved in closer. 'Yeah, now that her husband went and drowned himself.'

Ray LaFlamme sat on the edge of his chair and leaned forward, until all four faces seemed like they were connected. 'Pay attention, Rupert,' the old man said.

Rooftop swallowed dryly.

'Number one, you will find the money that Scott Chambers paid to your assistant. It is my money, and you will turn it over to me. Are you listening?'

Rooftop tried to focus his eyes.

'Number two, I'm going to have Gator go with you, to make sure you do the right thing.'

Even without his glasses, Rooftop could see the depraved grin on Gator's face. He wheezed in a short breath, then shook his head.

'I won't do your work for you,' he said, perfectly synchronized with another skillet blow to the ear.

The men behind Rooftop grabbed his arms and pulled him upright. One of them was Gator, with a punch-knife in his fist, angled at Rooftop's neck.

'No blood, fellas,' Ray LaFlamme said, standing up.

Rooftop's shoulders slumped. His head hung down. His big, blurry hands spread before him on the tablecloth like twin skillets. The word *bloodfellas* echoed round his head.

'Rupert, look up here.' The old man hovered beside him until finally Rooftop raised his head. Then LaFlamme gave him a warm, sympathetic smile.

'Rupert, whether you like it or not, you've already chosen your path,' he said. 'God's got no place in heaven for killers. People like you and me, all we can do is make a better life for our loved ones here on earth.' He slipped Rooftop's glasses back on his face and said, 'What's her name again?'

'Mo-reeen,' Gator breathed.

'Nice name,' LaFlamme agreed, and he lined up Rooftop in his vision. 'Now I know you want to make life better for Moreen, and I know you want to keep her from harm. So I'm going to give you three days to get that money.'

Gator looked over the old man's shoulder with a grin. 'Just remember, we'll all be thinking of Mo-reeen.'

CHAPTER ELEVEN

It was a budget funeral. No limousine, no organist, no church. The service was held in the smallest of Chernack's Funeral Home's three chapels. Ellen wore a navy blue suit over a white shirt and sat alone with Scott in the front row of chairs, waiting for Moreen to arrive. Randy's father sat across the aisle from them, looking more uncomfortable than grief-stricken in his short-sleeved shirt and jeans. Gradually the small room filled with many of the same people who had attended the wedding. The only one who seemed particularly distressed was Randy's friend Rooftop Paradise, who sat alone on the right side of the chapel with dark sunglasses on, occasionally blowing his sizable nose.

Moreen arrived five minutes after the service was scheduled to begin. She came in with her friend Keirsted Rawlings, who, last Ellen knew, was sleeping in the woods by Myers Pond with some other kids, most of them homeless, middle-class. Apparently, there was an old shack there, or the remains of one, and a junked van that someone had hauled in. Keirsted, whose family owned a hotel in Wells, had supposedly been kicked out of the house in April after declaring herself a lesbian. She moved in with her girlfriend's family for two weeks, until they broke up. Now she was sleeping wherever she ended up at night. Seeing Moreen with her, Ellen's heart fell.

The two girls came down the aisle together, Keirsted talking loudly, and they sat heavily in the front row, beside Scott.

'Sorry I'm late,' Moreen said, as she turned and faced Ellen. Two blue teardrops were tattooed on her left cheek. Scrawled, they looked less like teardrops than tiny nooses.

'I told her not to do it,' Keirsted explained, wracked.

Moreen smiled helplessly at her mother. Look at the stupid thing I did now. She seemed drunk.

Ellen did not respond. 'Mo, did you find a place to stay?'

'I'll talk to you later,' Moreen whispered, gesturing to the minister, who had just come to the pulpit.

Ellen traded a glance with Scott, who only shrugged.

Then the music stopped, and the minister asked the assemblage to stand and join him in silent prayer. As Ellen stood, she turned and saw Maddy standing alone four rows behind, her eyes riveted on the closed casket, refusing to acknowledge Ellen. As Ellen started to turn back to the pulpit, she spotted Neal standing in the shadows of the doorway. He caught her eye with a fleeting yet loaded glance, and it made Ellen turn away so fast she grabbed onto Scott to keep from falling. He took hold of her hand. She stood there tingling.

When the service was over, Ellen took her place in line, dazedly accepting hugs and handshakes and condolences from the assembled mourners. Moreen stood on the other side of Scott, leaning against the wall and maintaining some degree of decorum through her stupor. A full, hot July sun shone through the open front doors, and the taped music was loud and liberating, more befitting a wedding than a funeral, Ellen thought, but then she never did understand funerals.

The line moved steadily and Ellen was glad to see its end, disconcerted as she was to see Maddy and Neal approaching. Ellen watched as Maddy embraced Moreen and spoke quietly to her, then moved uncomfortably to Scott. When she got to Ellen, they embraced and Maddy whispered furtively, '*We need to talk.*'

Ellen released her while she watched Neal kiss Moreen on the cheek and say something in her ear, to which Moreen blinked her eyes and nodded thoughtfully. Then Neal was shaking Scott's hand. 'I'll see you back at the house,' Ellen heard Neal say, as he moved on to her. Their eyes met briefly. Neal put his hands on her shoulders and leaned in to kiss her cheek. Ellen closed her eyes to convey her detachment. But then his lips met her mouth. She stiffened, wanting to push him away, but she knew she couldn't. Then the kiss was over and he was holding her and she was holding him. 'He'll never hurt her again,' he whispered hotly in her ear. Her heart pumped harder as his sweater sleeve slid through her hand, then someone else was taking his place.

★ ★ ★

The reception was held at the Eagles Club, where Randy's father was a member. The club sprang for a round of drinks and four pepperoni pizzas. Except for Randy's father, nobody stayed once the pizza was gone. Maddy didn't attend the reception at all, nor did Neal. For that matter, Moreen and her friends spent the hour outside in the parking lot.

When most of the funeral guests had left and Ellen was collecting the paper plates and plastic forks, a voice behind her said quietly, 'Mrs Chambers, we need to talk to you.' She turned and gasped. It was like she was staring up at a building with a gargoyle staring down. Below the frames of his sunglasses, Rooftop's cheekbone glowed with an egg-shaped, purple bruise. His forehead appeared swollen and similarly discolored. She looked beyond him and spotted Gator standing in the doorway to the bathrooms, watching her through dark sunglasses.

Abruptly Ellen moved away from them both, wanting to run out of the building.

'Hey, Mister Bear!'

Moreen's voice startled her. She turned to see her daughter come through the door and wrap her arm around Rooftop's waist. Even as tall as Moreen was, she did not reach his armpit. But she stretched up on her tiptoes to kiss him, saying, 'You gonna miss me, Bear?'

Rooftop put his long arm around her shoulder and closed his eyes as he held her there. Moreen flung her other arm around his waist and laid her cheek on his chest. They stood there like that for several seconds. 'I can hear you breathe,' Moreen said, smiling curiously at the sound. Like a baby, Ellen thought, studying her daughter's tattooed, jeweled face. She almost cried.

Rooftop leaned forward and kissed the top of her head. Moreen kissed his chest, then pushed away. 'Watch out for the sharks,' she said, then stepped over to the bar and gave her father a kiss.

'Mo?' Ellen said, coming over beside them while they hugged. 'Where can we reach you?'

'I don't know, I'll call you,' Mo answered, turning to kiss Ellen, then spinning away and heading back out to the parking lot. 'Thanks for the funeral,' she called back over her shoulder. 'Love you.'

'Love you,' Scott told her.

Ellen turned. Gator was standing in the same place, outside the women's room, beckoning her with his index finger. Ellen felt her insides seize. She also felt a sudden urge to pee.

'Hit the road?'

She stiffened. Scott put his hand on her shoulder and gave a gentle squeeze. 'Let's go home and open a bottle,' he said, his warm, beery breath in her face. 'We deserve to get seriously wasted.'

She took his arm.

When they pulled into the driveway, Sugar Westerback was there waiting.

'I just now got here myself,' he said, stepping out of the patrol car. He was wearing his softball uniform again and carrying a Polaroid camera by its strap. 'You prob'ly heard, we made it to the finals,' he said. As he spoke, he started walking toward the farm road, as if expecting them to follow. 'Game starts in a half-hour. I wanted to get a couple of shots of that drain pipe while it's dry.'

'Anything wrong?' Scott said, walking beside him.

'Aw, the friggin' Water District's all over my butt,' Sugar told him. 'They want to lower the lift gates today. How the hell was I supposed to know we'd make the World Series?' He looked around, then said to Ellen, 'Your nephew around? Truck's here, I noticed.'

'Must be here somewhere,' Ellen answered, and she followed along behind them, afraid of how it would look if she didn't. She focused on relaxing, trying unsuccessfully to convince herself that nothing was amiss. In fact, she could feel her heart beating hard in her chest.

'I noticed his license plates the other day,' Sugar said, as they rounded the pump house at the top of the hill. 'From Mass, is he?' He was looking back at Ellen again.

'Neal's mother moved to Greenfield a few years ago,' she told him.

'Is that where he lives now?'

'He lives here,' Scott said, 'for the time being. He's rebuilding our barn.'

'Huh,' Sugar said again, returning his eyes to Ellen.

'He likes to travel,' she said. Is this when she'd have to start lying, she wondered, and how far could she take it? Inside her funeral dress, a drop of sweat slithered down her side.

Momentarily they reached the dam, and Sugar suddenly stopped walking. Staring down at the deep, stony gorge that Ellen had never seen dry, his shoulders sank.

Scott stepped up beside him. 'What's up?'

Below them, on the downstream side of the dam, Neal was crouched with a bucket of mortar, striking the area around the outlet pipe with the tip of his trowel.

'Looks good,' Scott called.

Neal glanced up, the sun in his eyes. 'Let's hope so,' he said. 'I'm green at this.'

'Which way down?' Sugar asked.

Scott walked around the abutment and started climbing down the stony bank, a half-natural and half-constructed staircase of granite blocks. Sugar followed behind, while Ellen remained on the abutment. She looked over the dam to the floor of the pond twenty feet below, where a graceful, serpentine puddle ran along its center.

'This where it was leaking?' she heard Sugar say. She looked over the downstream side again, where Sugar crouched in front of the pipe, running his thumb over the fresh cement.

'I chipped the old cement away and repacked it,' Neal told him. 'With any luck, it'll hold for another fifty years.'

'What do you think?' Scott said.

'You know what I think?' Sugar said. 'Kind of pisses me off, that's what I think.' He lifted the camera to his face and snapped a picture of the pipe, then turned and made his way to the bank.

Scott looked at Neal and shrugged. 'Something wrong?' Scott said as they climbed up to the bank behind Sugar.

Crossing the abutment, then bracing himself on the concrete face of the dam, Sugar took hold of the algae-slick rungs and lowered himself down to the pond bed, then walked directly into about four inches of water, not stopping to take off his softball cleats.

'Only thing wrong,' Sugar said finally, 'is that I already got my ass chewed out once by the old man for not calling him the other day. Now I gotta deal with this.' He went directly to the pipe, which was similarly mended, also recapped. 'You don't remember me sayin don't touch anything here?'

'I thought you meant just for that day,' Neal answered, coming closer.

Sugar bent his knees and took a photo of the pipe straight-on, then looked back at Scott. 'Scotty, I told you.'

Scott scratched his head. 'Yes, you did, but you also told us they needed to release water up at the rez. I guess I figured that meant it was okay to repair the dam.'

'Yeah, no shit,' Sugar said. He looked back at Neal. 'What do you do, just ignore the police in Massachusetts?'

'Come on, Sugar,' Scott said, 'it was an honest mistake.'

Sugar made a throaty noise, a sort of growl, then snapped another picture of the dam. 'Yeah, honest mistake, and I'm the one that catches hell for it.'

'If you want, I can chip that cement out of there so you can get a couple of pictures,' Neal told him.

'Ah.' Sugar scraped at the cement with his thumbnail. 'When did you do this side?'

Neal shrugged. 'Last night. I wanted to give it a couple of days to cure.'

'Beautiful.'

'It's no trouble, I'll chip it out right now,' Neal offered again.

Frightened as she was, Ellen marveled at Neal's demeanor. Even with the multitude of reasons she suspected he had something to hide, she found herself increasingly convinced of his innocence.

Sugar squatted, ran his finger around the inside of the pipe. 'Rusty and all,' he said, 'but not eaten away. See, that's what I mean. Just how the frig was this thing leaking?'

Neal looked at Scott, then Sugar. 'It was the cement that was corroded, not the pipe,' Neal explained.

'Frost heaves, most likely,' Scott suggested. 'The pipe could have seesawed on a rock in the middle of the dam, a tiny bit at a time. You know the way old mortar crumbles.'

'Huh,' Sugar said, and he took another picture. 'So what the hell are those things?'

About seven feet high on the dam, three shiny U-bolts protruded from three fresh circles of concrete, sapced evenly across the dam.

'I put them in yesterday,' Neal told him. 'So next time someone has to release water, they can harness themselves.'

Sugar said nothing, but took a picture of the U-bolts, then stood up, fished a pack of Marlboros out of his pants pocket and tapped one out.

'You know, I got the authority to stop the Water District from lettin down those floodgates,' he said.

Neal glanced up at Ellen and she saw in his eyes a quick but discernible glint of concern. But Sugar kept his eyes on Scott, as he flicked his lighter and lit the cigarette, then blew the smoke out. Waiting for one of them to speak, Ellen realized she'd been holding her breath. She let it out.

Sugar looked at his watch. Then he started climbing up the rungs. Scott climbed up behind him.

'See, I wouldna thought anything about anything,' Sugar said, 'except I got a call from What's-his-name, the medical examiner. Ramsey. He said Randy had a stab wound in his leg, right through his wetsuit.'

Pulling himself onto the top of the abutment, Sugar looked straight at Ellen; she refused to meet his eyes.

'The wound wasn't all that deep,' Sugar continued, turning back to Scott and Neal, as first one then the other mounted the abutment. 'But it came from a serrated blade, like a hunting or fishing knife. Divers use them. But Randy didn't have no knife on him when we pulled up out of there. All he had was that little leather holder there—'

'Sheath,' Neal said.

'Yeah, strapped to his leg,' Sugar said. 'But no knife.'

He looked at Scott and said, 'You were down there with Randy. You see a knife?'

Scott shook his head. 'I never saw a knife.' He looked at Neal, who said, 'Nope.'

Then Sugar turned to Ellen, who shrugged the way she might have if he'd been speaking in another language. But a shivering had started in her stomach, and she was unable to stop it. She felt like she was going to vomit.

'How about when you both went down?'

'Maybe he cut himself with the crowbar,' Neal said, giving Sugar a perplexed frown.

'Maybe,' Sugar said. They all walked down the bank and onto the gravel farm road. For a few seconds, no one spoke.

'What time's your game?' Scott said.

'You told me you tried to pull him out by the arm,' Sugar answered, to no one in particular. 'You dislocated both his shoulders, by the way. That's the other thing they found, pulled right out of the sockets.'

Scott raised his hands. 'Christ, Sugar, if we didn't, you'd be asking why we didn't pull harder.'

'Hey, I'm not trying to give anybody a hard time,' Sugar said. 'But, Jeez, one day Ellie wants to arrest the kid for assaulting your daughter, next day you go and hire him, day after that he's dead. Don't forget, I got the old man to answer to when he gets back.'

'Oh, fuck this,' Scott said. 'I hired Randy because we needed a diver, because he was our son-in-law, and because Moreen told me he never did a thing to hurt her. But that's a whole other story. Ellie thinks her sheep can do no wrong.'

Sugar looked back at Ellen again.

'And I still think Randy kicked Moreen and put her in the hospital,' Ellen said. 'Does that make me a murder suspect?'

'Doesn't make anybody a suspect,' Sugar said. 'Far as I'm concerned, this was an accidental drowning. I guess the question I forgot to ask the other day is how long it was between the time Randy went down with the crowbar and the time that you went down after him?'

He looked over at Scott as they walked, then back at Neal.

Scott shrugged. 'I don't know exactly. Ten, fifteen minutes?'

'Give or take,' Neal said.

'So you didn't go down there with Randy when he was trying to get the cap off,' Sugar said. 'I mean, Randy was already stuck when you went down.'

'Yeah, alright?' Scott replied, bristling.

Sugar nodded. He looked at his watch and started walking faster. ''Course, now we got that stab wound – on the dorsal part of his thigh, which the medical examiner says is where you get defense wounds, like if you're fighting somebody. I'm just sayin, you know? Red flags I gotta follow up on. You got this, you got that, you got your daughter's hysterectomy.'

Now Scott stopped walking, and he looked back at Ellen with a hard scowl. 'What hysterectomy?'

'I'll tell you later,' she said, walking past him.

Sugar turned and eyed Scott carefully while he took a final drag on his cigarette. 'That's probably best left to the two of you,' he said, keeping stride with Ellen. 'Anyway, I gotta boogie. If I'm not on that pitcher's mound in ten minutes, we forfeit the tournament.' He flipped his cigarette on the gravel road as he pulled abreast of Neal.

'So, Greenfield Massachusetts, huh?'

'Yeah, my mother moved there when I was twelve,' Neal replied, 'after my father passed away.'

'Huh. So what the frig were you doing looking in somebody's window in Virginia Beach?'

Ellen looked at Sugar, then at Neal, wondering what they were talking about.

'I was going to steal a car,' Neal answered with a bit of a smile, 'but I wasn't too smart about it.'

'Yeah, no shit. Fifteen years old, your family lives in Greenfield, Mass, and you're down in Virginia Beach by yourself?'

'I ran away from home,' Neal said. 'I was headed for Disney World. Tell you what. You go down to Virginia Beach in the middle of the winter and hold out your thumb for eight hours, you'd commandeer a friggin car at gunpoint – "Step out of the vehicle, Ma'am. Police business." '

Scott laughed. Even Sugar chuckled a little. 'I might just,' he said. 'I might just.'

Ellen traded a smile with him. She figured it was the first time in Neal's life he'd used the word 'friggin'.

Sugar got in his cruiser, looked at his watch again and started the engine. 'I don't know what I'm gonna do about the Water District,' he said to Scott. 'Have to think about it. Maybe I'll have 'em release the water, maybe I'll wait for Dad to get back tomorrow and see what he thinks.'

'Do whatever you need to,' Scott said. 'It's Ellie that's gonna have to haul water for her sheep, not you or me.'

'I hear you,' Sugar replied, and he sped out of the dooryard with his blue light flashing.

Scott did not speak to Ellen right away. He opened the liquor cabinet and mixed himself a strong whiskey and ginger ale. By the time Ellen had changed out of her funeral dress and was headed out to do chores, Scott was mixing another one. He caught up to her in the lamb's pasture, where she was filling the trough with grain.

'Moreen asked me not to tell you about the hysterectomy,' she said without turning to look at him. 'So I didn't.'

'Funny that Neal knew about it.'

'Neal drove her to the hospital. He was there when they told me.' Without turning to look at him, she went into the shed and grabbed two water buckets, which she carried to the faucet on the side of the house. Scott followed, and watched her as she filled the pails. Standing there, not speaking, they could hear hammering: Neal inside the barn, down underneath the new addition, building a set of stairs.

'Husband and wife really shouldn't keep secrets from each other,' Scott said.

Ellen turned, saw that he had two drinks in his hands. She gave a short, bitter laugh and carried the full buckets back to the pasture, while Scott walked alongside her. 'Ellie, what the hell is going on with you?'

She sighed. 'I told you, Moreen didn't want you to know.'

'I'm talking about you. You've been hating me ever since Neal showed up here.'

'This isn't a good time,' Ellen said, opening the fence and walking through.

'All because of something that happened twelve years ago.'

'It has nothing to do with that.'

'Twelve goddamn years ago. And I've about killed myself ever since, tryin to make it up to you.'

She set one pail on the ground, spilling water over the rim, then splashed the other pail into the water trough. 'I forgave you, Scott.'

'Then what is it? I'm sorry if the economy went to hell, I'm sorry I lost my business, I'm sorry I can't build you a fucking barn, I'm sorry I didn't finish high school, I'm sorry I'm not twenty-four years old again.'

Ellen glared at him as she lifted the other pail. 'Neal talks to me.'

'I talk to you.'

'He *listens* to me.'

Scott turned away from her and took a drink, while she spilled the other pail into the trough. He looked toward the barn, where Neal was still hammering, then he turned back again and realigned her in his vision. 'You never forgave me,' he said. 'You never came close. You disappeared is what you did, with all your fuckin sheep and your weaving. You disappeared from me, and you disappeared from Moreen.'

'Get away from me,' she said, pushing past him.

'All for your precious sheep,' he persisted. 'Well, it was one of your sheep that hurt Moreen. It wasn't Randy, and you know it.'

She wheeled around and stared at him long enough that his face began to disassemble. The dead brown eyes, the pink mounds of his cheeks and receding hair . . . could have been anyone.

Then his chest seemed to collapse in a sigh, and he turned away from her, shaking his head.

'Don't listen to me,' he said. 'My nerves are shot.' He heaved another sigh and turned back to her, holding out a drink. 'Here, you want this?'

'I'm not drinking with you anymore,' she said, and walked back to the house.

As much as she wanted to go into the barn and tell Neal to pack his things and leave, she knew she needed to cool off. The truth was – and she was dimly conscious of this – she did not want a conversation that might illuminate her own culpability in Randy's death.

When she stepped into the kitchen, she saw her answering machine blinking. It was Maddy, in three separate messages. The first one said, 'Call me, please.' The second said, 'I know you're there. I have to talk to you.' The third: 'You need to pick up.' Then, after a moment's silence, 'Goddamn you.'

Ellen locked the back door and went upstairs to call Maddy from her bedroom.

'We have to talk,' Maddy told her.

'We can talk,' Ellen replied, trying to sound innocent.

'Is he there?'

'Is who here?'

'You know what I'm talking about. Does he know?'

'Maddy, what are you talking about?'

'You know goddamned well. I lied to the police for you.'

Ellen sat on the bed, telephone to her ear, and she felt a tremor start in her chest.

'Ellie, I'm scared shitless over here. Now you tell me. Does Neal know that Randy wrote on my hand?'

'No.'

'What did Scott say?'

'About?'

'About that.'

Ellen hesitated. 'Nothing.'

'Scott doesn't know anything about this, does he?'

Ellen didn't know what to say, so she said nothing, just stood there at the window shaking, watching Neal hammering at her symmetrical new barn.

'You come over here,' Maddy said. 'So help me God, you come over here. And don't tell him where you're going. *Don't you tell him.*'

Maddy lived in York Harbor, in a cottage that was surrounded on three sides by Victorian mansions. It was dark when Ellen pulled up to the curb in her pickup truck, yet none of Maddy's window lights were lit . . . which was strange, because her new BMW was parked at the foot of her short, hedge-lined driveway. Ellen walked up to the door and knocked softly. She waited, smelling the beach roses that wafted over the salty air. She knocked again, louder, then turned and looked at the inn across the street, where someone was watching her from a second-floor window. She was about to knock one more time when she remembered that Maddy's house key was on her key ring. She pulled the keys out of her jeans pocket and held them up to the moonlit sky until she was able to identify Maddy's.

'Come down to the beach.'

'*Jesus—*'

Maddy stepped around the corner of the cottage. 'Come on,' she said, heading for the road. At the end of her driveway, she turned left. Ellen followed, neither of them speaking as they walked past the houses to the end of the road and took the flagstone path beside the tennis courts. When they got to Harbor Beach, where waves broke noisily over smooth, potato-sized rocks, Maddy stopped.

'I told the police that the word Randy wrote on my hand yesterday was "Moreen".'

'Yeah, so?'

'We both know what he wrote, so don't bullshit me,' Maddy said. 'It was the last thing he said to anybody in this lifetime: '*Murder*.'

'And you believe him.'

'I lied to the police,' Maddy hissed. 'That makes me an accessory – and in this state, accessory is the same as murder.'

They studied one another in the moonlight. Then Maddy broke away from Ellen again and headed to the left, toward the cliff walk, a three hundred-year-old trail that cut between the old Victorian houses and the rocky bluff overlooking the ocean. Ellen caught up to her when the path narrowed and turned uphill.

'In the first place, Randy's death was accidental,' Ellen told her.

'Not according to Randy.'

'Oh, come on, you know what a whiner he was. So he screws up, what's he gonna do, take the responsibility himself? No, he's gonna blame somebody. "*They murdered me.*" '

'I'm touched by your sympathy.'

'Look, Randy was an abusive prick and I'll be honest, I'm glad Moreen is free of him. But he was not murdered. The fact is, he should never have been working on that dam by himself.'

As the path led through the middle of a thicket of beach roses, Maddy ducked and disappeared amid the bushes. Ellen followed, holding her cap with one hand and protecting her eyes with the other. They emerged on the moonlit face of the bluff, thirty feet off the rocks below, and looked out over the water. Across the cove from them window lights of a condominium wavered like snakes. Below them, the waves exploded, sending up a bright, steady mist.

Maddy said quietly, 'El, you've got to listen to me. You're into something way over your head.'

'No, you listen,' Ellen shot back. 'I've done nothing wrong.'

'I'm not talking about you. I'm talking about your sociopathic nephew.'

'He's Scott's nephew. And you don't know what you're talking about.'

The women stared at one another again, until Maddy turned away. 'Let's go back down,' she said, looking nervously behind her.

Ellen took the lead, bending low into the dark tunnel of roses. Maddy stayed close behind, holding onto the back of Ellen's T-shirt. When then they were in the moonlight again, they carefully descended the sharp-edged rocks of the path to the weathered stones of the beach.

'In case you've forgotten,' Maddy said, 'this is the same young man whose father killed himself the day you caught Scott in bed with his mother.'

'That was a lifetime ago,' Ellen said. 'Besides, Neal doesn't even know about that.'

'Oh no? Exactly what do you think brought him back after all these years?'

'Maddy, you're being paranoid.'

'And you may be involved in your son-in-law's murder.'

Exasperated, Ellen stopped walking. 'I don't know why I keep telling you. No one was murdered.'

'Then it's just a coincidence that Neal came to live with you.'

'What coincidence?' Ellen said. 'He knows how to build a barn.'

'And I suppose he knows all about sheep.'

'He worked on a sheep farm when he was younger. What are you saying? He's been planning this since he was fourteen?'

'Most likely since he was twelve.'

Even as Ellen smirked and started walking down to the water, she couldn't help but hear the echo of that number: twelve. Maddy came alongside her and they followed the shoreline for fifty feet or so, staying just back from the waves that chased after their feet.

'I need to ask you something,' Ellen said. 'You talked to Randy.'

'Once. He ended up coming to see me.'

Ellen took hold of Maddy's arm and stopped again. 'Did he tell you?'

'Tell me what?'

'If he kicked Moreen.'

'Of course he didn't tell me. He denied it.'

'Well, what do you think?'

Maddy shook her head. 'Ellie, I don't know.'

They stared at one another, straight-faced, until Maddy sighed and looked around nervously. 'I'm going to tell you something because you're my best friend and because, technically, it's not betraying confidentiality.'

Ellen waited.

'Moreen's started counseling with me. It's something I wouldn't ordinarily do, get involved with the family members of a friend but Mo seemed desperate – and broke. That's all I'm going to say. But you probably knew that.'

'How would I know that? Moreen doesn't talk to me, in case you haven't noticed. Oh, she smiles, she kisses me, she says she loves me. But always from a mile away.'

'Kind of the way you were with your mother?' As soon as the words came out, Maddy touched Ellen's wrist. 'I didn't say that.' She turned, gave Ellen's wrist a tug, and they began walking again, along the beach.

'Look,' Maddy said, 'Mo's a very bright kid.'

'Also very self-destructive,' Ellen replied.

'When she was six, she walked into your barn and found her uncle hanging from a beam,' Maddy said. 'A trauma like that is bound to have repercussions. Did you ever talk to her about it?'

'I didn't think I should push her,' Ellen answered, wondering how true that was.

Maddy hesitated. 'Maybe it's something she'll talk to me about.'

Ellen felt a hollow pang in her chest, something akin to jealousy. She turned to face the ocean.

Maddy took her long braid in her hand and stroked it softly. 'El, you know she's not coming home,' she said. 'Even if she wanted to, I'd discourage her.'

Ellen bristled and gave her a look. 'She's my daughter.'

'Ellie, she hates that house.'

'She hates *me*. And you're using this!'

Maddy squared herself to Ellen. 'What am I using?'

Ellen would not meet her eyes. Maddy took gentle hold of her arms. Ellen had all she could do to keep from pulling away.

'You know, El, it's possible that the person Moreen hates is herself, not you. You just happen to be the closest thing she's got.'

'Hates herself why? Why won't she tell me?'

'Maybe she feels she's protecting you from something.'

'Protecting me?' Ellen sneered. 'From what?'

'I don't know. Maybe we'll find that out.'

Ellen looked out at the ocean again, and let out a voluminous sigh.

'El?'

Ellen turned her head.

'Look, I don't know exactly what happened at the pond the other day,' Maddy told her. 'And I don't know what's going on between you and Neal—'

'*Nothing is going on*—'

Maddy squeezed her arms, stopping her. 'And I'm not sure I even want to know,' she said. 'Just promise me you'll be careful.'

Ellen met her eyes with brittle defiance.

'I'm serious. We're not sneaking a joint in your bedroom now, we're not climbing out your window to party with the college boys. You're really starting to scare me.'

Ellen stiffened, looked off down the beach. 'Are we done?'

Beside them a wave collapsed with a startling roar.

When Ellen got home, Neal was around the right side of the barn, standing in the glare of his truck's headlights, nailing siding boards to the new addition. The left-hand shed was already sided. Ellen pulled her pickup truck close to the porch and went in the house quickly, avoiding him.

She found Scott asleep on the living room floor, his electric guitar slung across his chest, the old amplifier humming loudly. She flicked the amp off and lifted his guitar off him.

'Where'd you go?' he asked, jerking awake, sitting upright and looking suspiciously around the living room.

'For a ride,' she answered.

He rolled to his knees, picked himself slowly to his feet and started up the stairs. 'You coming up?'

'Later.'

The knock on Wes Westerback's front door was so timid that Wes didn't hear it over the television until his wife Polly came in and tapped the footrest of his recliner. They had driven home from the lake after spending most of the day fishing, and he was dog tired. Sugar was also asleep, sprawled on the couch in his softball uniform, an empty Budweiser can and bag of potato chips on the carpet in front of him. He hadn't even taken off his cleats.

'Someone's at the door,' Polly said. She was a fairly heavy and friendly woman who enjoyed coffee and cigarettes and usually had one or both going.

Wes levered the recliner upright and fixed the glasses on his face. 'Must have closed my eyes,' he said.

'Me too,' Sugar said.

'Don't know how anyone could sleep with this TV so loud,' Polly said, cigarette smoke exhausting from her mouth. An old John Wayne western was on, and the Indians were whooping. She turned the volume down a little, then made her way to the front door.

'I can get it,' Wes said, pushing himself up. Polly had hip trouble, and he didn't like to see her do any more than she had to. But she was there already, opening the door.

Seeing the small bleach-haired girl with the rings through her eyebrow and nose, and the nervous way she kept checking behind her, Polly turned to Wes.

'I think she wants you.'

CHAPTER TWELVE

Ellen waited until she heard Scott snoring, then she went up and took off her clothes in the dark. She didn't bother closing her eyes. She knew there would be no sleeping for her. The way the moon shone through the window screen onto her white bedspread, like a spotlight, the way the terrible silence outside pressed in around the room, while Scott snored obliviously . . .

She had participated in Randy's murder – she could no longer deny this. Even if she hadn't been directly involved, she had encouraged it, and she'd helped set it in motion.

No, there would be no sleeping tonight. Not with her secrets.

How long would it be before Sugar Westerback would return with his father, or with other investigators? And how long could Maddy withstand the gnawing guilt of her own involvement?

Scott let out a snort and stopped snoring, and the night became perfectly quiet. And terrifying. To Ellen, the silence was a dry pond bed, a dam laid bare, it was evidence exposed, like old mortar deliberately chiseled away, granite stones gouged, chunks of cement clustered high on a bank downstream where chunks of cement couldn't have ended up unless they'd been carved out of the dam when the stream was still flowing.

A single sheep's bell tinkled as Ellen's thoughts raced on (fiber evidence, flesh under fingernails, DNA in wrong places). Then she heard the jangling of another bell, and another. With a start, she thought of the coyote and sat up in bed. But it was a curious rustling of trees that came through the screen, a strange concentration of wind that grew stronger until the bells of her sheep became a jubilation and even their drumming hoof beats were overpowered by this incredible rushing of sound.

Ellen got out of bed and went to the window, pulled back the shade. Looking down, she suddenly understood what was causing this tumult: Water. Tons of it, cold and clean, cascading down through the woods, uprooting brush and unseating boulders, demolishing banks, capturing frogs and lizards and chipmunks in its furious mouth. The gates had been opened at the reservoir.

In the moonlight she could see the wide contrail of mist charging down through the trees, then all at once the river exploded off the granite chute into the deep gorge of her pond, the roar thundering back off the woods. She saw a wall of mist rising straight in the air above the dam. She saw Neal silhouetted on the crest of the hill, kneeling out of his blanket to witness the flood, his smooth shoulders surrounded by moonlit, rising mist. On and on the water pounded, and Ellen's heart pounded the same way. She could smell the water, she could feel it misting through the screen and brushing over her face and breasts, cooling her, freeing her.

Yes, and freeing Moreen.

She realized this with dazzling clarity: Randy had enslaved Moreen with pregnancy, imprisoned her with marriage. He had beaten her and terrorized her, and he would have continued. But now Moreen was free. That was all that mattered.

Whatever had been done to ensure that, in this long, exuberant moment, Ellen knew without question that it was precisely the right thing.

She raised her face and breathed deeply. The river roared through the woods, pulsed riotously up the banks, dislodging rocks, destroying evidence, the moon transforming the rising mist into a fiery opalescence. Ellen stepped to her closet, opened the door and took her flannel nightshirt off the hook, slipped it over her head and went quietly downstairs.

She padded through the house in darkness, the squeaking of the floorboards underfoot covered by the surging flood outside. She pushed open the screen door and walked onto the porch. The noise was louder out here, astoundingly so. Mist mounded over the valley. She could feel its wetness in her eyes, on her cheeks and arms, as she seemed to glide across the dooryard, and then she was opening the pasture gate and walking through, the grass cool and moist under her feet. She could see Neal plainly at the crest of the hill, up on his knees, staring down at the flood as if transfixed.

She came up behind him and set her hand gently on the muscular space between his neck and shoulder. He took a quick breath as if she'd startled him, then reached his left arm around her legs and drew her against him, laid his cheek on her hip. He took a deep breath, as the river surged into the gorge, pounding against the dam, pounding and pounding.

She looked down at him. His nakedness had not occurred to her until now, that his blanket had fallen down to his thighs. He looked up at her and said, 'I killed him, Ellen.' His voice, too loud, resonated through her hip.

'Shhh,' she said, not necessarily to quiet but to soothe him. He held her with both hands, his face against her stomach, the cool locks of his hair sliding between her fingers, his warm hands rising slowly up the backs of her legs. 'It's good,' she said, as his hands slid up the backs of her thighs, onto her buttocks.

Now she reached to stop him, saying, 'Neal,' but his hands continued up the small of her back, lifting her nightshirt, the cool air sweeping around her thighs, the water pounding all around them. He raised his face.

'Neal—'

'I killed him,' he said again. Then, taking her by the waist, he gently pulled her down to her knees, while her own hands melted down his neck to his chest, meaning to stop this, absolutely to stop, but now with the heat rising off him and the moon in his eyes, his hands, so warm and able, slipped around the front of her and cupped her full breasts, and she lost her breath as she lost her will, and he moved his lips onto hers.

They kissed, and she turned her head away, gasping as quietly as she could, 'We can't do this.'

'Oh, Ellen, how long,' he breathed in her ear, 'has it been since anyone wanted you this bad?'

And they kissed again, completely covered by the mist and roar of the flood, his liberating fingers exploring first her ribs, then her breasts and nipples until she raised her face, raised her arms, and her night shirt pulled into the air and now she was fully naked with him and falling safely into his arms, his hand moving over her hip, inside her thigh—

'Wait,' she breathed, pushing him off forcefully enough so that when he fell back he pulled her forward into his lap. 'Neal—' She caught her breath, this dark part of him standing thick and urgent only inches from her face, utterly distracted by its size, its hardness, its smoothness. The head was not a mushroom-topped thing like Scott's, but muscular, tapered, rounded. She could almost feel its warmth in her hand, though she was not yet touching it. Nor would she.

She sat up again, and he sat up with her, his fingers lightly tracing her temple to her chin, as if studying her face.

'I've got to go back,' she said, taking hold of his hand. 'But I need to ask you something.'

'Ask me what?' He turned his face and leaned in close, kissing her jaw, her mouth. She broke off breathlessly.

'How you did it,' she breathed. 'Without Scott knowing.'

He took her face in both his hands and turned her toward him, then kissed her softly, his lips full and warm. Their tongues touched, but barely.

'If I told you that,' he said, 'you'd no longer be protected.'

'I'm not protected now,' she told him. 'I've already lied to the police.'

'Lied how?'

The way his eyes searched hers, or maybe the way his head was angled—

'I feel like I've been lying to everybody,' she said, keeping her eyes on his but seeing Randy's finger moving in Maddy's palm. 'I feel like I killed him myself.'

'Ellen, should I be worried?'

He kept watching her, and she moved her hand across his thigh, the soft cover of his body hair sliding through her fingers, his heat rising around her wrist.

'Should I?' she replied.

Keeping his eyes, her hand descended to the center of his heat, and she closed her fingers firmly around him. She hadn't planned to, so she was startled at the first touch: his thickness, his heat. Closing her eyes, she leaned in closer and kissed his chest, ran her tongue over each of his tender nipples. She heard him gasp as she explored him with her other hand. His balls were a compact part of the package, his sac compressed and rounded, and she cupped it gently in her left hand, feeling the heat of his abdomen against her ear, breathing him in, his incredible warmth and musk. He made another sound. She squeezed his shaft, milking a bead of oil out of the top. She ran her thumb up through the liquid, then ran her thumb back down, lubricating his glans. She heard him sigh deep in his chest. She felt her own nether lips opening, beckoning wetly, hungrily.

She took his solid buttock in her left hand and lowered her mouth to his abdomen, kissing him, tasting him, unbelievably moving her mouth closer until she felt the softness of her lips touch the softness of his head. With her hand she squeezed him, and another drop of oil emerged. She moved her tongue to taste it, and now she was powerless to do anything but suck him softly into her lips.

Her mind was gone. The sound of his low moan spurred her on. She felt his fingers comb lusciously through her hair, then his hands gripped her shoulders, her underarms, while all around them water thundered down the gorge. Then her eyes rose to meet his as she devoured him, amazed at what she was doing. His hands moved down her sides, and he clutched at her breasts. He moaned again and she felt him swell inside her mouth. A hot sweetness hit her tongue. It was insane. It was wrong, she knew this without question, so terribly, deliciously wrong, the way she wanted him inside her now, desperately needed him filling her, flooding her. She wanted their minds together, their hearts together, she wanted to be totally consumed—

And she knew she had to stop.

She sat up abruptly and started to turn, but he captured her, his left hand going under her arm, his right hand under her buttock, and he lifted her naked into his arms. 'Neal,' she said with a laugh, and he stopped her protestations with his mouth. Barely aware that he was walking, she tasted his tongue, she sucked on his tongue, she played her own tongue inside his mouth, while she absently watched the gable of her house dip below the hill, and then she felt him opening the gate at the bottom of the pasture.

'What are we doing?' she whispered, feeling suddenly confused, with the mist swirling round her head and the flood pounding in her ears, then they were sinking into the wet grass, and they were kissing and she had him in her hand again, her mind flying apart. She couldn't remember the last time Scott had kissed her this passionately. In fact, she knew she'd never been kissed like this, and she knew there was no longer any question about stopping, no possibility. She guided him, and she gaped up at him as she felt him move inside her.

Her mouth sprang open as if to scream, but her throat closed. He seemed to grow larger as he went deeper, and he kept going in, slowly, incredibly, until it seemed she could feel him moving up her spine. He took her breasts in his hands, tenderly squeezed her nipples between his fingers and thumbs. She felt strangled, staring up at the mindless moon, having no mind herself but this one enormous, magnificent sensation of their union, and then, incredibly, he was moving out. Her mouth opened wider in protest, she felt a pressure grow behind her eyes, that if she didn't scream her face would explode, he was moving that slow, much too slowly . . .

'*Ohhh!*' she yelled and immediately buried her shout in his shoulder, biting his solid, slippery arm, clutching his hard buttocks and pulling him into her again, taking him in until their bodies molded perfectly together. She strained, she ground her pelvis into him. She arched her back. 'Oh *God*, this is wrong,' she whispered, and she reached for his shoulders, to stop him, but his hands moved under her hips and he lifted her, sliding, along his hard stomach and lowered her again, filling her so effortlessly, so completely, again and again and again.

The two of them moved like that, brilliance upon brilliance, their overheated bodies emerging through seventy-five feet of cold vegetation, the scene glowing with the indistinct lines and shadows typical of older night-vision scopes.

Up on the wooded hill the pair looked down. One wore goggles strapped to his head, a binocular eyepiece that transformed to a telescope. The other, the larger of the two, watched through more traditional Nite Site binoculars.

'I say now,' Gator said.

'Later,' Rooftop replied firmly, 'when he's alone.'

Gator started to stand, but Rooftop stood first and grabbed Gator's neck in a way – his thumb hooked around the larynx – that made it clear to Gator that if he went for his pocket, he'd end up swallowing his Adam's apple.

'*I said wait.*'

'*God!*' Ellen cried. She gripped his hard buttocks, dug her fingernails in, as every muscle in his body turned rigid and huge. She felt him expand inside her, she felt an astonishing heat. His mouth opened at his ear. She heard him strain for a breath.

'*Stay still,*' he gasped.

Mindlessly full of him, it was impossible for Ellen to comply. His breath in her ear drove her on. Her own muscles surging, she pulled him into her as deep as he'd go. A shout caught in her throat. He covered her open mouth with his hand, and she tasted him, the salt of his skin, and that's where her mind stopped, at one with his taste, with her flooding, the flooding of the river, everything gushing out of control. Her teeth bore down on his palm, and all at once the massing of energy exploded inside her, like a deluge of sparks, a swarming of ice crystals. She rose over him, gazing down, transfixed, unable to breathe, this orgasm going on endlessly, deliciously, as if they were creatures made entirely of raging muscle who needed no oxygen, no light, no sustenance. Mindless, sightless, they stared into one another, deeply, endlessly—

'*Oh stop!*' she cried, and she sprang off him, rolled onto the grass, realizing for the first time that they were on the bank above the pond.

'*Shh—*'

She held out her hand to keep him back.

'*Don't be frightened.*' He was on his knees, alert.

She looked back, afraid Scott was coming down. 'What?' she whispered, shaking.

He stared up into the woods across the pond. 'Probably the rogue,' he said softly. 'The coyote.'

'What do you mean?' She rose to her feet. He touched her thigh cautiously.

'We probably spooked him,' he whispered. 'I don't think animals have ever seen behavior like that.'

Suddenly sober, Ellen could feel his semen running hotly out of her, down her thigh. Her breasts were engorged, electric. 'God,' she said, her legs trembling beneath her. 'I must be out of my mind.'

Behind her, the pond was already full and flooding noisily over the dam. Tree branches and whole bushes clung to the safety cable. Others washed over. She was astounded by what she had done, and, suddenly conscious of her nudity, she felt a riveting bolt of fear, sensing the enormity of her sins. Or perhaps she glimpsed the possibility that Maddy could have been right about Neal. She folded her arms tightly across her breasts.

Neal rose to his feet beside her, still peering off into the dark woods. 'Ellen, walk back to the house,' he said quietly.

Heart thumping, she gave him a look. He returned an urgent nod, and she did as he instructed, walked down off the bank and across the farm road to the pasture gate, completely naked, feeling as though hundreds of hidden eyes were following her, wanting desperately to run but refusing to give in to the fear. When she turned back, Neal was nowhere in sight.

She started to run.

CHAPTER THIRTEEN

Ellen locked the back door when she got inside. She took a short, frightening shower with the bathroom door also locked, then tiptoed upstairs wrapped in a bath towel. She slipped into bed naked and closed her eyes, but she did not sleep. She didn't dare. Her conscious thoughts were more nightmarish than anything sleep might concoct.

Murder.

Adultery.

Incest.

The reality stared down on her starkly. There were clues, there were witnesses, and now, apparently, there were watchers.

She thought of the woods above the pond, where she had seen Neal working. If you want to lead someone, make a road, he had said.

Actually, the road was little more than a trail, and the way the trail wound through the woods, it looked no different than any other animal path, taking seemingly random turns around trees and brush and rocks, as if generations of coyote and fox and raccoons had worn the route to the stream above the gorge.

In fact, with the night fully penetrating the woods, there was no other way for the men to come. And they came eagerly, the bed of pine needles softening their footsteps – not that they were in danger of being heard, anyway, over the noise of the pond filling. The path led them downhill at an advantageous angle, permitting advance behind a cover of foliage while allowing a constant view of the pasture from between branches. Through their night scopes, they could see the green shimmer of someone sleeping on the pasture hill, tucked inside his blankets.

The plan was simple: Recover the money stolen from Ray

LaFlamme and make the guilty parties wish they'd never been born. In case things got out of hand, Gator had secreted a silenced .22 Ruger Mark II in the back of his jeans.

The one complication with this plan was that Rooftop, suspecting Ray LaFlamme had ordered Gator to kill him and everyone else in the house, had slipped a bullet-proof vest under his hooded sweatshirt and a .45 Smith and Weston in the rear pocket of his work pants—

—both of which, to Gator's Nite Sites, appeared as stark impressions against the warmth of Rooftop's body.

So, as the pair made their quiet way through the woods and down to the stream, they never lost sight of one another for more than a second or two, nor did their right hands ever stray far from their weapons. Gator didn't know exactly what Rooftop had in mind, but the concealed piece didn't bother him half as much as the flask of rum the giant kept raising to his mouth.

When Rooftop made his final approach down to the granite bank of the stream, the path dumped him directly behind a large block of ledge with a V-shaped top – perfect for surveillance. However, even as he crouched behind the ledge, Rooftop kept his head turned back and his Nite Sites trained on Gator, who snickered like a chipmunk as he made his way down the path. As soon as he ducked beside Rooftop, the giant rose up and moved around the ledge, stepping down into the black current, continually looking back at Gator's grinning face as he slogged on, knee-deep, five paces to the middle of the stream, where the rounded top of a huge boulder rose out of the water.

Working carefully around to the left, upstream side of the boulder, Rooftop stumbled and caught the top of the granite to keep from falling. As soon as he regained his balance, he looked back at Gator, whose right hand was suddenly hidden behind his leg. Gator grinned. 'You be careful out there,' he called in a whispered drawl.

Holding the boulder with his left hand, Rooftop came back around the front of the rock, all the while keeping his eye on his partner, keeping his eye on Gator's hidden hand. Now, moving around to the pond side of the boulder, he stumbled again, feeling the floor under his feet suddenly fall away. He leaned in closer to the rock and sidled steadily around it, until finally the boulder separated the two men. Then he quickly navigated the remaining ten feet to the opposite bank and backed himself up onto the rocks, aiming his long green face at Gator.

As the kid furtively tucked his pistol back in his pocket, through his goggles, he watched Rooftop's green hand move down to his hip, then bring the flask up to his mouth. The giant's fingers were shaking.

Gator snickered, then slipped into the current and plodded through the water. Reaching the boulder that split the stream, a thrill of goosebumps raced up his lean sides. Not only was he now protected by the rock, but he knew Rooftop well enough to know that, even rummed up, the giant would never fire first, never risk murdering Ray LaFlamme's relative – especially since it was Rooftop who was responsible for the missing money in the first place. And there he was, sitting up bigger than life on the open bank.

Gator pulled the .22 into the night. He almost laughed, thinking about what Rooftop apparently didn't know: that .22 shells are little enough to penetrate the fabric of a bulletproof vest.

He touched the silencer to the right side of the rock. If he was lucky, the size of his shells wouldn't matter. He'd place his first shot straight in that big target of a face and prevent Rooftop from firing the .45 and alerting anyone else. He raised his eye slowly from behind the rock, looking for the edge of Rooftop's green aura . . . and there it was: the bony top of Rooftop's crown, shining like the moon.

Gator felt a jerk of adrenalin and he stepped out to the side ready to fire. But then Rooftop wasn't even looking at him. He was twisted around on the bank, training his Nite Sites on the pasture. Gator lowered the .22 behind his knee. Fine. He'd get even closer – close enough to drill one clean through the giant's eye as soon as he turned around.

Holding his left hand on the pond side of the rock, he stepped ahead, finding the granite bed solid and free from obstruction. Except that halfway around, the bottom suddenly dropped steeply into the pond, and Gator stumbled, his right arm rising for balance, his .22 out in the open.

Rooftop swung the .45 around, aimed dead at Gator's heart.

Gator fell against the boulder and aimed at Rooftop's face.

Rooftop stretched his arm as far as he could, as if his bullet might reach Gator's chest before Gator's bullet perforated his own forehead.

Gator grinned.

They stood in that position for a number of seconds, without speaking, until Gator said, quietly, 'Man, you should see your fat face.'

Neither of them budged. Several more seconds passed. Then Gator slowly spread both arms out to the sides, his .22 aimed out over the dam.

'You drunk enough to drop me in cold blood, Jackson? I seriously don't think so.'

Rooftop kept his weapon trained on Gator's chest.

Finally, Gator shoved the .22 into the pocket behind his hip. When he brought his hands around in front of him again, he showed Rooftop his unoccupied fingers.

'You gonna let me cross over now?'

Rooftop took a big breath. Let it out. Then he nodded his head. But he did not lower his .45.

Gator snickered as he proceeded ahead, keeping his left leg pressed against the base of the rock – and his eyes riveted on Rooftop's shining hand, watching for the slightest twitch. When he felt a sudden, tug at his right boot, he figured he'd been snagged by a submerged branch carried in by the flood. But when he went to move his foot, he found himself firmly caught. And the instant he reached his hand underwater, his leg was yanked violently from under him and he plunged feet-first down into the pond, propelled fast and deep.

He drew his gun, ready to fire. But without a good breath in his lungs he also pulled hard for the surface with his free hand – to no avail. Something was hauling him down. Then his foot hit something hard, and his forward motion stopped. He lashed out with the pistol, and his silencer struck concrete – the dam, he realized. His ankle twisted hard against it.

The pressure in his ears told him he was down deep. His lungs cried for oxygen. He reached for his trouser cuff and found that what had snared him was a steel cable, maybe a quarter inch in diameter. The cable ended in a tuna hook, which had pierced both his cuff and the top of his leather boot. The cable led through a steel U-bolt in the face of the dam and then back out again, pulling in the direction from which he'd come, the U-bolt acting as a pulley. His attacker could have been twenty feet away.

With complete and sudden terror, Gator understood his predicament. He dropped his gun and grabbed onto the tuna hook with both hands. He pulled up on it, trying to tear it out of his boot, but the barb would not let go, no matter which way he pushed or pulled. Now his lungs shrieked for oxygen.

He unbuckled his belt, tore open his trousers and pulled them down. Logic failing him, he turned the pants leg inside-out over the tops of his boots and tried to swim out of them, but his right boot was married fast to the U-bolt. It didn't matter. All he could do, all he could think to do, was to break for the surface. Bright lights were flashing behind his eyes, his head was spinning crazily. With his free foot he stood on top of the U-bolt, then he stretched every muscle, stretched every inch of his strong young bones, pulling higher and higher, until finally his fingertips broke into the air. He felt the water dancing past his knuckles on its way over the dam. He reached higher, he dug his fingers into the concrete, watching his bright green hands as if they belonged to someone else, someone groping for life. He felt a rush of excitement. He felt air on his fingernails and thought wildly that air on his fingers was enough. Then he saw another flash behind his eyes, an expanding, blinding orb, and his mind gave over totally to instinct. He opened his mouth and let the water fall in. It felt so cool and light at first, like a bright summer wind. With great relief, he breathed all of it in.

In Ellen's dream, she is in her garden, picking cucumbers. The day has ended with a pleasant calm, swallows darting about in the sky, peepers just beginning their evening song. She is making a salad for Scott and Neal. As she steps through her thicket of cucumbers, her foot sinks into a soft depression in the soil. She parts the fat cucumber leaves to get a better look, when she's startled by a most unusual frog, big and brown and bulbous-eyed. In fact, he looks startled himself, as if she's caught the frog doing something wrong basking on the edge of this cool dark hole. His wide mouth clamps down tight, his eyes stare up at her like two black pearls. Ellen makes a kissing sound and reaches her thumb to pat his head, but he darts away – and this is the strange thing. He doesn't jump. He glides, almost as if he's on wheels, *gliding* around the rim of the hole and then down in. When Ellen parts the spinach for a closer look, she is the one who jumps, repulsed at her discovery. This is not a gliding frog at all, but a coarse, black snake. The frog is in its mouth, half swallowed.

'*Jesus Christ*,' Scott mutters in his sleep, and Ellen, waking, realizes she has kicked him.

Outside, bells were ringing.

She turned her head, squinted at the clock and saw that it was ten past two. Scott snored once, loudly, sleeping again. She could tell by the depth of his snoring that he had taken his sleeping pills. She'd seen the bottle on the bathroom sink.

She stepped out of bed and went to the window. She pulled back the shade and looked for Neal down in the pasture, but couldn't see a thing outside except the black wooded hill standing up against the night sky. But the bells kept ringing. She thought of the trail he had made up in the woods – *if you want to lead someone somewhere . . .*

She leaned over Scott and took the flashlight off his night stand, took her bathrobe off the bedpost and went out the door, headed down the stairs, through the dark living room and kitchen. She was afraid to turn on the lights, she didn't know why. Her whole body shivered.

In the dark, she went out onto the porch and across the dooryard. The night was quiet, except for her sheep. Even the waterfall had settled to its normal whisper. Leaving her flashlight off, she opened the pasture gate and wove her way silently through the agitated sheep. As she approached his sleeping form at the crest of the hill, she knew something was wrong. Catching her breath, she crouched down and gently laid her hand on the blanket. The body was soft, but lifeless. Simultaneously, a hand clamped down on her mouth.

'*Shh.*'

She knew it was Neal. His grip was gentle, but his arm against her cheek was soaking wet.

'*Go back to the house*,' he whispered close in her ear. She could feel wetness soaking through her bathrobe into her back.

She turned to him, and saw he was wearing a pair of goggles over his eyes – if that's what they were. He was also bare-chested, and he held a long pistol in his hand. Her stomach dropped. He laid his finger on her lips, then leaned in to her and whispered again. '*Lock the doors when you get inside. Go*.'

She left him there, padding back across the pasture in the dark, wondering who else was here, who was watching her tripping past her sheep. Opening the gate, she ran barefoot across the gravel to the porch and up into the kitchen, where she locked the door and pulled the windows shut and locked them. She left the lights off. Her chest pounded. Her mind raced with options: Wake Scott. Call the police. Get Scott's gun and go back out to help Neal. Lock the front door.

She felt her way past the cookstove and stepped into the living room, a sweet, fresh breeze blowing the scent of roses through. She realized too late: The door was already open—

She turned to run, and an arm clamped around her chest, under her arms, yanking her powerfully off her feet.

'Don't say anything,' the low voice whispered. With both hands, she took hold of his massive, hairless forearm, and he carried her back into the kitchen. She could barely breathe.

'I don't mean to hurt you, Mrs Chambers,' he said, releasing some pressure.

Now Ellen knew who it was holding her. 'Rooftop, is that you?'

'The devil's out there,' he answered. 'You've got to call him off.'

Above the sound of his wheezing, she could hear Scott snoring upstairs. She thought about yelling for him, but was afraid of what would happen if he came charging down.

'What do you want?' she gasped.

'I got nothing against you,' Rooftop said. 'I got nothing against anyone. I just need to get back to my van.'

She could smell alcohol on his breath. She could feel him shaking. In fact, they were both shaking.

'Rooftop, I don't know what you think I did – or what any of us did.'

Something dug into her ribs. 'Just go to the window and call him, tell him I want to leave.' He turned her around and together they shuffled toward the window.

'*Don't call.*' Neal's voice rose quietly from the darkness behind them, the living room.

Rooftop's arm hardened around Ellen's throat. 'I've got a gun,' he said. The pistol lay cold against her cheek.

'As do I,' Neal said. 'So be careful, Mister Paradise. What you feel against your kidney might be a little wet, but it's perfectly functional. With one twitch of my finger, I can paralyze you faster than you can blink – and I will. You're an intruder, which makes you fair game.'

Ellen heard Rooftop's wheezing intensify.

'Now I'm going to take the gun from your hand. I don't want to startle you.'

Ellen felt the cold steel lifted from her face, then she ducked out from under Rooftop's arm and backed to the counter.

'Are you okay?' Neal said.

'I guess,' she answered. 'Can I turn on the light?'

'No, I can see. Rooftop, I can see like a cat with these goggles your buddy gave me. I can see that little tic on your temple.'

'Should I call the police?' Ellen said. She could hear Scott snoring fitfully upstairs.

'Hold on,' Neal told her. Then, to Rooftop, he said softly, 'Put your hands on the table.' With his foot, he slid a chair back. Against the relative lightness of the window, Ellen could see him run his hand down Rooftop's hip. 'That's quite a little militia you had there,' he said as he frisked the giant. 'Hands behind your head.'

Rooftop complied, and Neal, a full head shorter and a hundred pounds lighter, pulled something from Rooftop's pocket.

'What's this?' he said.

'Rum,' Rooftop answered.

'Rum, you say.' Neal tossed the flask on the table. 'I'm going to ask you some questions now, and the Geneva Accord does not apply. You lie to me, I'll take you outside and shoot you. Understand?'

'Neal—'

'I wasn't going to hurt anyone here,' Rooftop said.

'What did I say about lying to me?'

'I don't lie,' Rooftop said. 'There's money missing.'

'What money?' Ellen said.

'The money that was in Randy's Jeep.'

'What's he talking about?' she said to Neal.

'You think I stole that money, or somebody here stole it,' Neal said. 'Is that why you and your buddy came in the night with loaded weapons?'

Ellen's heart dropped. Gator had been here.

'It's a bad situation,' Rooftop said.

'I don't particularly like the insinuation that we're thieves.'

'Neal, you've made your point. Let him go.'

Neal sighed. 'See, this is something my aunt and I disagree on. My aunt believes in turning the other cheek. I'm just the opposite, sort of the New Testament – Old Testament dichotomy. Do you know what I mean?'

Rooftop breathed in and out.

'There were just the two of you, right?' Ellen said. 'You and Gator?'

'Yes,' Rooftop said. 'But now I need to go.'

'From what I saw out there tonight,' Neal said, 'there didn't seem to be a whole lot of trust between you and Gator.'

Rooftop did not answer.

'Does Gator have a wife?' Neal asked. 'Girlfriend somewhere?'

'He's got people down in Louisiana. They think he's dead.'

'Maybe Gator took the money, and he's gone back to his family. You think so?'

Rooftop wheezed, in and out.

'How about you? You got anyone expecting you home tonight?'

'My family's passed on.'

Neal reached around Rooftop's body and picked up the flask from the table, swished it around.

'See, I thought you gave the stuff up,' Neal said.

The giant stood there quietly with his hands behind his neck, his head near the ceiling.

'Proverbs,' Neal said. ' "Give strong drink unto him that is ready to perish." Mister Paradise, are you ready to perish?'

Ellen placed her hand on Neal's sopping shoulder. 'Neal, I mean it. Let him go.'

'You need to know that Mister LaFlamme isn't going to give up on this,' Rooftop said. 'He's bound to get his money back, and he doesn't care who gets hurt. For my own self, I'm bound to protect certain people.'

'Certain people . . . you mean Moreen?'

Once again, the only sound in the house was Scott's deep snoring.

'Neal,' Ellen said softly.

'Okay, I'm going to set you free,' Neal said to Rooftop. 'You've been good to Moreen, and I know that you intend to do the right thing. But first' – with his teeth he unscrewed the cap of the flask – 'I want you to finish this.' He reached the flask up to Rooftop's hands. 'Take it and drink it down,' he said. 'Ellen, do you have any more rum in the house?'

'Just whiskey and tequila,' she answered.

'Would you get him the whiskey, please?'

She hesitated.

'I'm letting him go,' Neal told her. 'Just get it.'

'Excuse me,' Rooftop said.

'Down the hatch,' Neal said. 'Do you think I'm playing games?'

While Rooftop drank, Ellen went to the cupboard and lifted the heavy bottle down, then brought it over. 'Neal, I want to know what's going on,' she said.

'Take the cap off, please,' he said to her. She did as he asked, then set the bottle on the table. 'Pick up the bottle, Mister Paradise.'

Rooftop stood stiffly. Neal slid the silencer underneath his sweatshirt.

'Pick it up,' he said again. 'I want to hear you swallow.'

In the darkness, Ellen could make out Rooftop raising the whiskey bottle to his mouth. She heard the bubbling of liquid as it ran down his throat.

'More,' Neal said.

Rooftop took several more gulps, his Adam's apple pumping loudly, until finally he sputtered and coughed.

Neal took the bottle from him and set it on the table. 'Where's your van?'

'Up on the fire road, other side of the hill.'

'Let's go, I'll walk you down to the stream.'

'I'm coming with you,' Ellen said.

Neal turned toward her. She thought he was going to argue, but he didn't. She stepped past him and unlocked the door, and Rooftop and Neal went out. Ellen followed with the flashlight.

'You gonna give me back my gun?' Rooftop said, as he stumbled down the porch steps. 'I need my gun.'

'You'll be better off without it,' Neal told him, keeping his own gun aimed at the giant's lower back.

Ellen pulled up beside them and shone the flashlight beam in front of Rooftop's feet.

'Next time I see Moreen, I'll tell her you were asking about her,' Neal told him as they walked past the pump house.

'Yeah, big damn joke,' Rooftop muttered. By the time they reached the dam, his boots were slapping the gravel road. 'You see

Moreen, tell her you stole my damn gun,' he said. 'That's what you can tell her.'

'Forget your gun,' Neal told him. 'Man your size doesn't need a gun.'

'Little prick.'

They took a few more steps, until Rooftop tripped over his feet and almost fell. Then he stopped and turned toward Neal, his long chin seeming to melt to his chest. 'I'd like to know what the hell you're doing here,' he said.

Ellen moved in between them, to head off another confrontation. 'Neal, where do you want to cross?'

'Shut the hell up while I'm making a point,' Rooftop slurred.

'I might as well shoot him right here,' Neal said.

'Here,' Rooftop turned around. 'Here's my damn back.'

'Rooftop, just go home,' Ellen told him.

Rooftop snorted groggily. 'Yeah, home.' To Ellen's relief, the giant turned and resumed walking, following the farm road alongside the water until they reached the end of the pond, where the stream entered.

'This is where you cross over,' Neal told him.

Rooftop stopped. He turned, stumbling again as he did so, then glared down at Neal, his big head bobbing. Ellen could hear his labored breathing.

'I'm gonna tell you for the last time,' he said. 'I need my gun. I do not intend any harm to the good people.'

'I'm going to shoot you if you don't leave,' Neal said.

The giant stared drunkenly through the darkness.

'You can sleep in your van if you can't drive,' Ellen told him.

'Yeah, sleep,' he said with a sneer, then he stumbled up the rocks to the top of the bank. 'You tell Moreen for me—' As he slowly turned his body to face her, his knees collapsed beneath him, and he fell hard on the rocks and rolled down the other side. Ellen heard the shallow splash and climbed up the bank to help him. Neal climbed with her, but held her back.

'He's going to drown,' she said.

'He's a professional diver,' Neal said. 'Isn't that right, Roof?'

Rooftop staggered up out of the current only to fall a second time. He caught hold of the boulder in the middle of the stream and pulled himself up, then turned and peered straight into Ellen's flashlight beam, his thick lenses reflecting the light like twin mirrors.

It made Ellen think of a crocodile deciding whether or not to attack. She was glad that Neal was beside her, glad he had the gun.

'Just tell her for me,' Rooftop said. 'Tell Moreen.'

'Tell her what?'

Rooftop stared some more, then he scowled painfully, as if he wanted to cry. Ellen kept her light on him until finally he turned and slogged away from them. Reaching the opposite bank, he pulled himself up a birch sapling, gave one more look back at the light, then turned and started trudging up the hill.

'He can't drive like that,' Ellen said, as they listened to footsteps crashing through the woods.

'He'll be fine.'

Soon the rustle of uneven footsteps diminished to silence, lost in the noise of the waterfall. Ellen shut off the flashlight.

'Look up,' Neal said, touching her back. 'You can see the stars.'

Indeed, the mist had subsided, and a black, glittering sky shone down on them.

'The stars have nothing to do with me,' she said, turning away from him. 'Neal, you need to answer some questions.'

'I'll try.'

'What did you do to Gator?'

'I let him go,' he told her.

'Was that him in the pasture, under the blanket?' she asked calmly. She didn't want to know, but she needed to.

'It was one of the lambs,' Neal answered. 'A decoy. I knew they'd be coming.'

She stood there, unable to absorb all this. 'Neal, what money?'

He looked toward the house. 'Don't ever tell Scott I told you this.'

She waited for him to continue.

'They worked for the loan shark – Randy, Rooftop and Gator.'

'Randy?' She stared at Neal through the darkness, her mind grasping at bits of memory, trying to piece them together.

'The bank loan Scott got last week, he owed most of it to the shylock,' Neal continued.

'I knew that.'

'Well, he gave the money to Randy, and apparently Randy never delivered it to the boss. Now it's missing.'

Ellen felt a low rumble in her stomach. 'So Scott knew that Randy worked for this criminal?'

'Randy and Rooftop were the collection men. Which is how Randy first met Mo, when they came here looking for a late payment.'

Ellen turned away from him and started walking toward the house. Neal caught the sleeve of her bathrobe, gently stopping her.

'Ellen, you don't know any of this.'

'*Why?*'

'Because it would give you motivation.'

'For what?'

'Randy's death.'

Ellen stood there stunned. Her mind refused to work.

'Neal, did you take that money?'

He shook his head, looking into her eyes. 'No, I didn't,' he said, and she believed him.

The clock radio turned silently, from 2:48 to 2:49. Sugar Westerback rolled from his right side to his left, scratching at a fierce itching in his palm as he drifted out of sleep in the dark. He heard the mosquito pass close to his ear and he swiped it away. But in a few seconds it was back again, and when it landed on his cheek, he slapped himself.

Awake now, he turned over onto his back, fluffed up his pillow and tucked the sheet under his chin. He could hear an army of other mosquitoes bumping up against his window screen, whining crazily, trying to get in at him. He scratched and scratched at his palm. He could hear peepers singing off in the woods. He wondered what they were saying to each other.

'*Hey, these mosquitoes taste good.*'

'*Yeah, I've had a dozen already.*'

He wondered if the mosquitoes could hear the frogs, if that's why they were so desperate to get through the window screen. '*Come on, buddy, open up. The frogs are murdering us.*'

He scratched at his palm some more.

Outside, some distance in the woods, an owl hooted into the night.

Sugar stopped scratching.

His fingernail remained in place, poised in his hand, as he whispered the word in quiet amazement.

'*Murder.*'

CHAPTER FOURTEEN

Rooftop Paradise fell to his knees again as the doors came open. He freed his hands from the handles and reached inside the panel truck. There was a long, plywood box built inside the left rear quarter. He threw open the lid, and his hand dropped into the box. Pulled out his weight belt with a loud clatter, as each eight-pound lead weight followed the previous one out of the box and onto the floor of the van. When the entire length of belt was free, Rooftop dragged it across the bumper and it fell heavily onto his hip. Eyes closed, he gathered the whole belt in his arms and pulled himself to his feet. He fell backwards. As much as his body cried for sleep, he refused to submit. Not tonight.

He got up again and made his way to his door, then climbed onto the soft vinyl seat, hitting his chin on the steering wheel and his head on the ceiling. He felt for the ignition key, pushed in the clutch and started the van.

He pulled his headlights on. The woods lit up a bright, sleeping green. Staring at it all, Rooftop realized he'd never really seen the beauty of the woods before. He started to sleep, but he revved the engine to wake himself, and the wheels rolled out of their mossy ruts. He'd forgotten how far in he had backed – with his boat attached. Maybe a quarter-mile, maybe more. Didn't matter. The gas tank was full, and he had a few hours before morning light. In fact, he was already moving, hauling his big Boston Whaler down that beautiful green tunnel toward the end of his life, watching tree after tree turn gracefully past him, saluting him, scratching at his roof to keep him awake, white and black birches, white pine, red oak, rock maple, red maple, red pine . . .

Just after one o'clock the bartender of the Belle Atlantic Restaurant served last call. The kitchen had closed at midnight and only one waitress and a busboy remained, waiting for a party of four to leave. Upstairs, in Ray LaFlamme's money room, the dining room manager had just finished the day's receipts and stood by the door while LaFlamme put half the cash in his safe. On his way home the manager would deposit the rest of the cash, plus the credit receipts and checks, in the night deposit box at Saco First Federal. When the safe was closed, LaFlamme and the manager rode the elevator down to the ground floor office. In the meantime, the bartender went out to the parking lot and started LaFlamme's bulletproof Eldorado, then drove it around to the kitchen door. He did so every night, armed with a .377. At that point the manager, who was also armed, escorted the boss out to his car. Both men would remain in the parking lot until LaFlamme was on his way home. Then they would go back inside, get rid of the stragglers and lock the restaurant for the night.

Ray LaFlamme lived four miles from his restaurant. His home, a nineteenth-century captain's mansion, sat on a gently sloping hill overlooking Saco Bay. These days the place looked more like a fortress than a captain's home, protected by an eight-foot-high stone wall and inner steel fence that was wired to alarm systems in both the master bedroom and the guardhouse. By land, the only way into the property was through the front gate that stood at the end of a quarter-mile private road. The gate was made of two eight-foot-high wrought iron sections that slid open from the center, each section rolling on tracks behind the stone wall. The brick guardhouse, which sat directly behind the gate, had three small bedrooms, a bathroom, kitchen, living room and armory.

When Ray LaFlamme arrived home, Herbie Handcream was on watch. From his window, Herbie opened the gate and gave LaFlamme a fingerless wave as the old man drove past. LaFlamme continued up the drive and pulled his Cadillac into his garage and the door closed behind him. When he walked into his kitchen he found that his wife Catherine had left a cheese croissant and cup of mussel stew on the counter. He heated the stew in the microwave and ate at the kitchen table while he watched the end of a Ray Milland movie on a 14-inch television. After he'd finished his food, he lost interest in the movie, so he turned off the TV and went to bed.

The Boston Whaler sailed due north on Route One, tacking left, tacking right, as Rooftop fluttered from dream to wakefulness and back again, the rain blowing lightly past his ear, wetting the left lens of his glasses. The towns were sound asleep, which was good. His windshield wipers clocked hypnotically, while Rooftop stretched his eyes wide open, then squeezed them shut. He banged the graduation march on his steering wheel and chewed on coffee beans to stay awake. The taste was terribly bitter but strong enough to do the job – some gourmet brand, rainforest mocha nut, something that cost ten dollars a bag. Rooftop hadn't realized the coffee wasn't ground until he'd pulled back on the road. So now he chewed on the beans while he drove, handfuls at a time, and it wasn't long before he found himself pulling into Biddeford.

With his gun, he wouldn't have had to be so sneaky. Herbie Handcream would be in the guardhouse. Seeing Rooftop driving in at this hour – hauling his Boston Whaler, no less – Herbie wouldn't know what to think, but he'd open the gate, thinking Rooftop had brought him LaFlamme's money, of course never suspecting that Rooftop would shoot him in the face. Then the giant would go inside the guardhouse and kill Marcel. He'd grab the keys to the mansion and go kill the old man. After that, he'd throw all three guys in his boat and head out of Kennebunkport five or six miles, where the Army kept an undersea dump in a hundred-fifty feet of water, and he'd weight the bodies down and toss them overboard. Then who knows? If he had a shell left for himself, maybe he'd lash himself to his motor – 125-horse Johnson – unclamp it from the transom and blow his own big head off, give the fish a real feast.

Only thing was, now without a gun, he'd have to improvise. Not that easy when you're drunk as a skunk. He turned off Route One onto a side round, hauling his boat under a canopy of oaks and maples, until he came to a fruit stand, then he turned right, then left and left again, negotiating the panel truck along a narrow, winding road until he came to LaFlamme's sign, PRIVATE – ABSOLUTELY NO TRESPASSING, and there, at the gate, he stopped. The rain falling on his roof sounded like applause.

The guardhouse was positioned just to the left of the wide drive. A bay window jutted out a foot from the side of the building, with a small counter positioned below the window and a pair of floodlights above, much like a bank's drive-up window.

Rooftop flashed his high beams, then saw Herbie Handcream's

head jerk up behind the glass. He saw Herbie stare out at him, then heard the snap of a loudspeaker embedded in the stone wall.

'What the fuck do you want?' Herbie said.

'I got Mister LaFlamme's money,' Rooftop answered.

' "Wha-wha-wha," ' Herbie mimicked. 'Speak up, moron.'

Rooftop stared back at him through the rain until his eyes started to cross. 'I brought the damn money,' he enunciated.

The gate slid open, and Rooftop drove in until Herbie held up his good hand. Rooftop slammed on the brakes and the Boston Whaler slammed against its trailer hitch. Rooftop stared at Herbie, who slid the glass aside, slid the screen aside and stuck his head through the window, looking back. 'You gotta pull up. You got your boat on, and I can't close the gates.'

Rooftop kept staring.

'You're stickin out, asshole. Pull up.'

'I need to see the boss,' Rooftop said.

Herbie squinted past Rooftop, into the empty front seat. 'Where's fuckin Gator? He's supposed to relieve me in two hours.'

'He's on his way,' Rooftop answered. 'Tell Mister LaFlamme to come out so I can give him his money.'

Herbie peered through Rooftop's thick lenses. 'Whaddaya, tanked? Just give me the fuckin money.'

Rooftop leaned across the front seat and opened his glove box. He reached in and pulled out a fat pink Dunkin Donuts bag, held it up for Herbie to see.

'Yeah, good,' Herbie said. 'Put it up here and go home. I'll have Ray call you in the morning.'

'I want to give the money to Mister LaFlamme personally,' Rooftop insisted. 'I don't trust you minor bums.'

Herbie smirked. He bent down, out of sight, then appeared at the window again, his good hand down where Rooftop couldn't see it. 'Big boy, put the money on the counter and back on outta here.'

'Go ahead and shoot me,' Rooftop said. 'You don't even know what's in the bag. Yeah, kill me. Then go explain a bag of doughnuts to Mister LaFlamme.'

He tossed the bag on the floor of the van, then grabbed another fistful of coffee beans and tossed them in his mouth, started chewing. A gust of rain washed his windshield.

Herbie expanded his chest, blew a big sigh. Then he swung away from the window. At the same time, Rooftop stepped out of the panel truck. His legs stiffened underneath him, and he almost fell, but he made his way around to the guardhouse door.

Inside the house he heard Herbie say, 'Hey.' Rooftop imagined the little man thumping on Marcel's bedroom door with his elbow. 'Hey, Sleepin Beauty.'

Rooftop stepped in front of the guardhouse window, where he saw a telephone sitting on Herbie's desk, a large bottle of Rolaids and a couple of Maine State Lottery tickets. Herbie came back over, pushed the leather desk chair aside and picked up the telephone. 'Ray ain't gonna like this one friggin bit,' he warned. 'If you got the money, just bring it inside.'

Rooftop leaned heavily on the counter. Fat raindrops patted the top of his head.

Herbie pushed a button on the phone, then grabbed a pen and started tapping it on the desk. 'Marcel, don't go back to sleep in there,' he hollered, and was answered by a low, muffled curse.

A squawk over the telephone made Herbie wince. He listened for a second, then said, 'Yeah, Ray, we got your money here. I know, it's . . . No, Rooftop. No, he's here now. He says he has to give it to you in person.'

'Outside,' Rooftop said.

Herbie looked at him.

'I give it to him outside,' Rooftop repeated. 'Out in the open, not in the house.'

'Ray says just give us the money here. We'll bring it to him in the morning.'

'To heck with him,' Rooftop said. 'I'll buy myself a plane ticket to Argentina and spend the money myself.'

'You hear that?' Herbie said in the phone, then he hung up and looked up at Rooftop. 'Ray says okay. Just hold your fuckin horses. We'll drive you up to the house.'

'Nope. We walk.'

'You on drugs? It's a fuckin typhoon out there!'

Rooftop turned carefully and stepped to the corner of the building, where he watched the screen door bang open. Herbie stepped out, wearing a green rubbery poncho and yellow leather moccasins.

'Big man, big balls,' he said. 'I'd watch your mouth around Ray LaFlamme, or you'll be eatin those balls for breakfast.'

'Where's the other bum?' Rooftop said.

Herbie turned and yelled at the door, 'It ain't exactly dry out here!'

Marcel grumbled something in response.

Now Rooftop stepped out from the corner, spreading his black, knee-high fishing boots carefully on the flagstone walkway.

Herbie, seeing the weight belt he wore loosely around his waist, and the way Rooftop held his big hands around the buckle, said, 'What the fuck are you supposed to be, some kinda fuckin Argentina cowboy, with the fuckin kangaroos?'

Then the door swung open and Marcel emerged, wearing a white T-shirt and jockeys, and a dark felt hat on his head. A small, bright pistol in his hand was aimed in the vicinity of Rooftop's knees. 'Okay, Fuckinsky, what?' he said, raindrops pelting off his brim.

Evidently, the rather slow turn of Rooftop's shoulders did not alert him until the weight belt snapped out of the darkness six inches from his ear. Then it was too late. The square-cornered slab of lead at the end of the belt weighed only eight pounds, but it was propelled by a whipping force of nine identical weights distributed along on a nylon belt 60 inches long – not to mention the 300 pounds of drunken rage driving it home.

The lead hit the back of Marcel's head with enough force to launch the big man clear off his toes and out of his hat. The weight belt never stopped in its trajectory, but kept whistling around Rooftop's head.

'Hey, Roofy!' Herbie said, and his arm shot up to his face, but the belt passed through his phantom hand and knocked him in a wild backward flip. Sprawled in the grass with the weapon still in his hand, Marcel drew his muscular arms alongside his ribs, wanting to push himself up. But the weight belt continued in its orbit and drove straight down, no fewer than six lead weights smashing down the length of Marcel's spine to the back of his skull. The big bodyguard flattened in the wet grass, one last ripple of energy traveling down the fat of his back. Herbie was already dead, a two-inch-wide fissure cracked in the center of his forehead like a third thick eyebrow, but Rooftop clobbered him once more, straight down over the top of his head, as though he were swinging a splitting maul.

Then, fastening the belt around his waist again, Rooftop picked up both bodies and dumped them in his boat, then opened the panel truck door and took out the Dunkin Donuts bag. He turned.

Out in front of Ray LaFlamme's mansion stood a life-sized statue of Jesus Christ absolving the property. The statue was brightly lit by a pair of in-ground floodlights. Rain hitting the lights danced like sparks. Lining up Jesus in his vision, Rooftop marched up the rain-soaked asphalt and across the lawn. When he reached the statue, he stepped beside it and turned toward the house, the rain beating off his forehead and glasses. The floodlights blinded him, so he closed his eyes. When he opened them again, Ray LaFlamme was standing on the other side of his screen door in a red satin robe.

'I've got your money,' Rooftop called, raising the dripping doughnut bag.

'Okay, where are my boys?'

'Back there.'

The old man stuck his hand in the pocket of his robe. 'Rupert, be good and bring me the money.'

'You'll have to come out and get it, Ray LaFlamme.'

The old man blinked his eyes a few times. Raindrops jumped up and down off the roof above his head. 'So they stayed back there, did they?'

'They don't like the rain.'

'Neither do I,' LaFlamme said. He stared intently through the screen.

'How much is there?'

'I didn't count it up,' Rooftop replied.

'Okay, open the bag and let me see the money, so I know you're not up to any sort of trick.'

Rooftop set the doughnut bag in the palm of his hand and unfolded the top. LaFlamme opened the screen door and stepped halfway out, keeping his hand in his pocket. Rooftop stuck his hand in the bag and pulled out three bills, tossing them into a rain-filled sea breeze. The currency flipped and tumbled over the wet grass.

'Roofy, don't let it blow to the neighbors,' LaFlamme said.

Rooftop folded the top of the bag down and tossed it toward the veranda, but only halfway. It landed on the lawn with a wet splat.

LaFlamme drew his pistol, gave the giant a long look, then stepped down into the rain, the slender, silvery barrel in his hand sparkling with the rain and reflections. 'I know you're a good boy,' he said, as he walked out on the lawn, 'but you're acting too funny.'

Keeping the pistol aimed at Rooftop, he picked up the doughnut bag and hesitated curiously, bouncing the bag to gauge its weight. Then he unrolled the top and let the bag open.

The curse caught in his throat as the first swipe of Rooftop's weight belt shattered his ribs, the whip-end cracking against the middle of his back, sending him and three jelly doughnuts tumbling onto the wet lawn. The old man flopped over on his side underneath the Christ statue, one arm crossed over his chest, as though protecting himself. His other arm lay beneath him. His knees twisted uselessly to the side.

Rooftop came and stood over him, his weight belt slung to the ground. 'I did not choose this path,' he said, and he was about to say more, but he saw the silver barrel under LaFlamme's arm, aimed point-blank at his long, flat face. He stared into it, waiting to be shot.

'Oh, God bless,' the old man gasped, 'I'm all numb, I can't feel my body.' His head was shaking, like someone with mild Parkinson's, and his pistol was still aimed at Rooftop. Yet the old man seemed to be smiling. 'Rupert,' he breathed.

Rooftop leaned in closer, until he could see right down inside the small barrel.

'Rupert,' LaFlamme whispered again.

Rooftop looked directly into the old man's eyes.

'I'm talking to God now, Rupert.'

Then, slowly, Rooftop straightened. He lifted the end of his weight belt in two hands. Then he stepped back, swung his arms in a powerful arc, swiping the belt over his head like a bullwhip. The ground shook at the impact, and water splashed up from under LaFlamme's body.

Then Rooftop was driving on Route One, the rain blowing in his windows, warm and salt-smelling, buffeting the panel truck, shaking the boat behind him. He dozed as he drove, eating jelly doughnuts and chewing coffee beans by the mouthful, his body pleading for sleep. He dozed even as he stood in the rain, winching his boat down the trailer at the public landing. He brought the bag of coffee beans into the boat with him and kept eating them as he plowed through three-foot standing waves at the mouth of the river, bounding headlong into a rose-colored horizon, feeling the black land backing away from him for the last time.

The motor sang, despite the weight: three dead bodies and a

cement statue of Jesus Christ lying on the deck. Rooftop stood at the console staring at his compass, but it made no sense. He set his course and closed his eyes.

When he heard a car horn, he grabbed the wheel, expecting to be on the highway, but it was a lobster boat flashing its running lights, some father and son trading time for distance, out to beat the dawn. Rooftop turned on his lights in response, then fell asleep again.

When he awoke, the rain had stopped. The low horizon glowed brightly, pink-streaked gray. The ocean rolled big and dark.

Realizing he had missed the dump, probably by miles, Rooftop cut the engine to an idle and sat there quietly, bobbing in the swells. The Christ statue rocked on the deck, from elbow to elbow. With a length of yellow nylon rope, Rooftop tied Herbie Handcream to Marcel, then tied Marcel to Mr LaFlamme, then tied Mr LaFlamme to the two hundred-pound concrete block he used as a mooring. He removed the pistol from LaFlamme's pocket and tossed it overboard. Then he went to the console and opened the side door, took out the bag of doughnuts. He pulled out the last one, a honey-glazed, and stuffed the bag in the pocket of LaFlamme's robe. Then he ate the doughnut.

Next he removed the hatch door from the left side of the boat, leaving the deck level with the ocean's surface – his diving platform – and he heaved the concrete mooring over the side. The three bodies jumped in after it, one by one.

Rooftop stepped over the statue and returned to the cockpit, opened the throttle and headed further out to sea. Sea water splashed in the open hatch, lapping up the blood. As the boat bounded over the swells, Rooftop dozed again and dreamt that he was swimming with giant sea turtles.

When he woke up, he cut the throttle and turned off the key, stopping the engine. He went back to the stern and cut another length of nylon rope, then threw his fishing knife into the ocean. He lifted the Jesus statue upright and walked it to the very edge of the diving platform, then tied one end of the rope around its outstretched arm. He picked up his weight belt from the deck and buckled it around his waist. Then he returned to the console and took out Marcel's handgun, the .380. He checked the clip as he returned to his diving platform, where he sat beside the statue, facing out to sea. Waves rocked the boat. The statue wobbled heavily beside him. Rooftop set the gun in his lap while he tied the other end of the rope around his weight belt, imagining those great slow turtles again.

Then he picked up the pistol and leaned his long body over his knees, taking up the slack in the rope between himself and Jesus. The boat splashed up and down. He took a deep breath of the cool, salty air, then blew it out, then pressed the muzzle to his forehead. As he slid his thumb inside the trigger guard, he looked into the water one last time.

Then he closed his eyes and asked Jesus to forgive him.

CHAPTER FIFTEEN

When the window blinds began to gray with the dawn, the radio music started. Ellen kept her eyes closed and listened to Scott slap the clock quiet, then get out of bed. Hearing the sound of his bureau drawer opening and closing, the simple jingling of his belt buckle, she wondered if he knew, or even suspected, everything she was guilty of. She could barely believe it herself, the things she had done. She listened to Scott go downstairs and eat breakfast, same as he did any other day. She heard the back door close, then his voice outside.

'Jesus, man, don't you ever sleep?'

' "He that will not work," ' Neal recited in response, ' "neither let him eat." Thessalonians three, verse ten.'

'Yeah, well, "All work and no play kinda sucks." Scott Chambers, chapter one, verse one.'

Ellen stepped out of bed and looked through the screen, saw Neal walking around the front of the barn in his black sweater and corduroys, carrying a small, fixed-pane window in his arms.

'Looks like it's gonna be a wet one,' he said. 'I want to get these windows in.'

Hearing his voice, Ellen felt a stirring deep in her abdomen, but resisted it, disgusted with herself. She watched Scott slide into his old Mercedes and drive off. She watched Neal fit the window into the wall of the addition.

In ten days he had refashioned the barn into a beautiful thing. Its front doors were slightly narrower than they had been, but arched at the top, lending the building a sense of grace and symmetry it never had, as did the attachment of the two additions and the centering of the silo, which rose off the roof's peak. Ten days. If Neal was serious about finishing the job in twelve – and she knew he was – tomorrow he would be done and gone. As far as she knew, the only thing left to do was install the windows in both additions, twenty-four in all.

Imagining his absence, a keen sense of relief washed over Ellen, yet standing there naked, watching him work, Ellen felt the stirring grow inside her again, like a low, tantalizing hum. She turned away from the window. Opening her dresser drawer, she took out a pair of cotton underpants and stepped into them. No more french-cuts. No more tank tops, halter tops. She found a clean gray sports bra and put it on. Nor would she swim with him anymore. She put on a black T-shirt and an army-green muslin skirt, slipped on her clogs and went downstairs.

She started the coffee-maker, then went into the bathroom to wash her face and brush her teeth. She heard the scream of the circular saw outside. The sky looked darker. She was sure it would rain. So she'd stay inside and wash the kitchen floor. Maybe she'd finish her tapestry today. She uncapped the deodorant, reached it under her T-shirt and rubbed it under her arms. Time to shave, she thought, but she didn't want to take the time. She heard hammering again and pulled the bathroom window down, but left it open an inch or two. Neal was inside the barn, she couldn't see where. She saw two raindrops paint long diagonal lines on the window glass, as a low black sky moved over the pond, sealing off three beams of sunlight, one by one. Then more lines graced the window, as the smell of rain came richly through the screen. She couldn't believe what she had done.

With both hands, she gathered her hair behind her ears, then opened the vanity drawer, where she kept her barrettes and elastics. Instead of an elastic, she took out a pair of scissors. As long and thick as her hair was, it took her less than ten minutes to cut it all within an inch of her skull. As the summer rain fell down her window, great, warm sheets of auburn hair slid down her arms and calves and mounded around her ankles. When she was done, feeling amazingly lighter, Ellen went into the kitchen and got a trash bag, then came back and stuffed the hair inside.

Then she went back into the kitchen and took a coffee mug down from the cupboard. All at once the rain hitting the porch roof sounded like a stampede. She looked out the window and saw Neal's shadowy form come running toward her through the wall of water; she heard his footsteps pounding on the porch. When he came in the door, she went to the counter and poured her coffee, keeping her back to him.

'Looks like rain,' he said with a glint.

She didn't respond. Against her wishes, her heart was hammering.

He walked closer to her and said, 'I've read that when a good person commits a crime of passion, disfigurement is one of the signs of guilt that investigators look for.' He stepped closer. 'But you've done exactly the opposite.'

She raised a hand to deflect him and said, 'You need to get out of here.' Although it wasn't how she'd intended to tell him, it was exactly what she meant to say.

'One more day, and I'll be through,' he replied quietly.

Ellen turned, saw how the rain had wet his hair and face. He pulled his wet sweater over his head and tossed it across the room, onto the washing machine. She turned away.

'I've never hated myself before,' she said. 'I don't want to give myself any more reasons to start.'

His hand touched the cool back of her neck, brushed a severed strand of hair away. 'You are so incredibly beautiful,' he said, standing so close she could smell the rain on his arm. 'Ellen, do you have any idea what it's like to kiss you? Just to kiss you?'

She pushed his hand away. 'For God's sake, Neal, you're my nephew.'

'You know that's not true,' he replied. He put his hands firmly on her shoulders, and the rain seemed to beat harder on the roof, mimicking her heart. It was like sorcery, the way his touch seduced her.

'Ellen, do you remember the picture of the barn I showed you when I first came here?'

She sighed.

'There's also a house. And sixty acres of the greenest farmland you've ever seen. It belongs to me.'

She looked out the window, the gray rain streaking down the eaves, splashing off the gravel dooryard. What was he saying to her?

'I invested my inheritance,' he continued. 'I have all the money we'd ever need. You wouldn't have to teach unless you wanted to.'

She stared down at the water on the floor, his boot prints. She took a breath, hesitated a second, then said, 'Neal, how did you know Mo was getting married?'

She looked back at him, and he laughed a little. 'Why is that important?'

'How did you know?' she persisted.

A playful glint crossed his eyes. 'I've been stalking you,' he said.

She waited.

'You're serious?'

She turned to face him.

He shrugged. 'I was feeling nostalgic one day. Lonely, I guess. I called the hardware store to talk to Scott. Somebody there answered the phone and said he was out making wedding arrangements. It was a week away, so I decided to surprise you. Why?'

She closed her eyes, massaged her brow. 'You need to leave,' she said, stepping away from him.

'Ellen, if I left the barn without windows, people would wonder – especially this soon after Randy's death. Besides, who's going to fix your hair?'

She shook her head, refusing to smile. 'Just go outside,' she told him. 'Work in the barn. I've got to think.'

He sighed. 'Okay if I take a cold shower first?'

'Take whatever kind of shower you want.'

She could feel him standing behind her, could feel the change in air pressure when he finally turned and walked into the bathroom. She brushed her fingers briskly across her skull, feeling the cool bristle of hair snap through her fingers. She retrieved her mug of coffee from the counter and brought it to the table, where she sat and looked out the window. While the rain trampled the roof and washed down the eaves in sheets, she heard the clink of Neal's belt buckle hit the bathroom floor. Then the shower came on.

Against her will, she pictured him lathering his arms and chest. She put it out of her mind, but couldn't quite suppress the memory of his warmth the night before, the incredible, solid thickness of him. She breathed deeply to regain control of her mind, and she recalled the precise smell of him, so she leaned toward the window to smell the rain. She heard the water pump shut off. As she sipped her coffee, she imagined herself living with him hidden in the hills of Vermont, where no one knew anything about them, or the things they had done. It was ridiculous, the way her mind worked against her. When she heard the bathroom door open she said, 'Neal, I'm scared.'

'Scared of what?'

'Everything. You, me, the money that's missing. What if Mo's got the money, or Scott?'

She turned, saw him standing outside the bathroom door, holding a brown bath towel around his waist.

She turned away, then listened to him walk softly across the room and stand beside her. She could feel the heat coming off his body. She looked up at him, and he leveled his dark eyes at her.

'Ellen, I promise you,' he said. 'There is nothing to worry about.' He made it so easy to believe him. She felt his hand brush softly on her head, then move down the back of her neck. She took a deep breath and let it out in a sigh, radiating in his tender touch, as the rain continued slapping at the gravel outside, drumming on the roof.

'What worries me,' he said, 'is how I'm going to live without you.'

Under the slightest pressure of his hand, she let her cheek lay against his warm side, and they stayed like that for a number of seconds, not speaking, while she watched his chest expand and contract with his breathing, and water droplets roll down the rippled muscles of his stomach and through the fine black hair under his navel. She could feel the humidity rising off him. She could hear herself breathing harder, could hear the drumming of her heart. All the while she told herself to get up, get away from him, but this other notion was already in her head, deep in her gut and gnawing at her resolve: the two of them alone all day, closed inside the house, warm and dry and out of the rain.

How had she allowed this to happen? she wondered. It was as if another person lived inside her, with powerful needs and a will not her own. As she watched, her hand left her coffee mug and came to rest on his stomach, firm, wet and warm. She watched herself brush the water slowly down his abdomen, breathing huskily at the sight of him rising out of the terrycloth. She squeezed her thighs together, feeling a wetness starting, as his rough hand began caressing her cheek. While a distant voice screamed at her to stop, her fingers tucked quietly under the terrycloth, into that rich black jungle of hair—

The telephone rang, and she jumped out of her chair, almost knocking him over.

'Ellen, let it ring,' he said, moving in front of her.

Her heart pounded. Everything inside her trembled. They watched each other fervently, while the telephone kept ringing. Then her answering machine picked up.

'Go get dressed,' she said, pushing off him. 'Finish my barn.'

She went around him to the counter and grabbed the phone from its cradle. The machine cut off. She took a breath, tried to relax her chest as she said Hello.

'They know,' Maddy told her.

Ellen's heart thumped against her chest.

'What are you talking about?'

'The police know what Randy wrote in my hand. They just left here.'

She felt Neal come up behind her, press his hardness against her, his rough hand sliding around her hip, up under her T-shirt, electrifying her.

'Wait,' Ellen said, turning away from him, holding up her hand to keep him back. 'Did you tell them?'

'Tell them what he wrote? El, they already knew. One of them was there when it happened.'

Ellen heard a car slowing down out at the road. She walked to the living room doorway, ducked her head and saw the blue roof attachment gliding past the window. She wheeled back into the kitchen and pushed Neal toward the bathroom, staring hard at him.

'They're here. Maddy, what did you say?'

'I told them I thought Randy wrote "Moreen" in my hand. And they patronized me. But they *know* what he wrote.'

Ellen grabbed Neal's wet sweater off the washing machine, opened the bathroom door and threw it in. Her legs were shaking.

'Ellie, they're not interested in you.'

'Is that what they said?' Ellen was practically yelling now. She returned to the table and sat down in front of her coffee mug, trying to appear as if nothing were wrong. She smoothed her skirt with her hand.

'It's Neal they want,' Maddy said. 'Stop protecting him.'

Ellen took a deep breath, reached across the table and shut the window. Her whole body tingled.

'Listen to me,' Maddy said, 'I'm risking my goddamned life while I'm waiting for you to come to your senses. Do you know what it's like to be here alone every night, waiting for that doorknob to turn?' Maddy's voice dropped suddenly. 'You told him, didn't you?'

'What?'

'You told Neal that Randy wrote in my hand, I know you did.'

'Maddy, you need to get a grip—'

'Don't you fucking tell me to get a grip. He's already made it impossible for you to go to the police without implicating yourself. Ellen Chambers, don't let him get you in any deeper. He needs to be put away.'

The cruiser pulled up to the porch. Sugar Westerback was driving, his father Wes riding shotgun. Their side windows were rolled up and rain-spattered, and she was sure they couldn't see her inside. The wipers and headlights went off, then the engine.

'I've got to go,' Ellen said, her voice shivering. 'But it's really important that I find Moreen.'

Maddy said nothing.

'Maddy, just tell me where she is. Someone might be after her.'

'Jesus Christ, don't you get it?'

'*What?*'

'You're living with him.'

Ellen shut her off, slammed the phone on the table and watched out the window as the car doors opened and the men stepped out, Sugar wearing his police uniform, Wes dressed in a khaki shirt and trousers, an outfit a game warden might wear. Ellen raised her coffee mug to her mouth. 'The police are here,' she called casually.

Inside the bathroom, the shower came on.

'Did you hear me?'

Footsteps clomped up the porch steps. Ellen tried to slow her breathing as she got up from her chair. She wondered how flushed her face looked. She scratched her fingers roughly across her scalp as she opened the screened door. Then she stood in the doorway so as not to invite them in.

The men climbed slowly up the steps, despite the rain, Sugar staying close behind his father.

'Hi,' Ellen said as innocently as she could. She felt like she had a light bulb glowing between her legs.

'Hope it's not too early,' Wes told her.

'Just watching the rain,' she said. 'What's up?'

The two men stopped on the porch where the roof protected them from the deluge, both staring unabashedly at her shorn skull.

'Not a whole lot,' Wes said. 'I heard about the trouble this weekend. Sorry I was away.'

'I don't begrudge you a break, Wes.'

'We just need to tie a couple of things down,' he said. 'I wondered if I could talk to your nephew, ask him a thing or two about the incident. Inside, is he?'

Ellen knew she couldn't hesitate, yet in the moment she couldn't think of a way to deflect them.

'He's taking a shower,' she said. 'Want to come in?' She offered the door to them.

'If it's no trouble,' Wes said, stepping inside on the small throw rug. Sugar squeezed in behind him, although he was looking back at the barn.

Ellen walked to the cupboards, pretending nothing was wrong. 'Can I get you coffee?'

'None for me,' Wes replied.

'I wouldn't mind,' Sugar said.

'Just take a sec,' Ellen told them, taking a mug down, wondering if she was seeming too hospitable. Skirting the counter, she knocked at the bathroom door. 'Neal, are you almost done? The Westerbacks are here, and they want to talk to you.'

'Be right out,' he said.

'He got caught in the rain,' Ellen explained as she poured Sugar's coffee.

'Just a couple of questions,' Wes said, looking up from the floor, where a pair of small puddles faced the kitchen chair she'd been sitting in. The telephone was there on the table, beside her coffee mug.

'Milk and sugar?' she said, wondering if they could hear the pounding of her heart.

'Yes, please,' Sugar answered.

'Have a seat,' Ellen told them as she opened the cupboard and took down the sugar bowl, along with a box of shortbread cookies. When she turned back, both men were looking down at the puddles.

'Neal?' she called.

'Coming,' he said.

She brought the mug of coffee and sugar bowl to the table and set them down, then moved her mug to the end of the table, away from the puddles.

'Watch out for the water,' Wes said, as Sugar sat in Ellen's chair, his shoes spreading the puddles around.

'That's okay,' Sugar said. 'Vibram soles.'

Wes pulled a small notepad from his shirt pocket, the one Sugar had used during his interview, and he put it on the table along with two pencils. 'You'd better get that ear looked at,' he said to his son, whose lobe was inflamed around his silver stud. Sugar's eyebrows went up and down, terminating the fatherly advice.

The bathroom door opened, and Neal came out wearing only his jeans, his wet sweater bunched in his hand.

'I don't have anything dry,' he said to Ellen. He glanced up at the policemen. 'I was trying to put in the last few windows before the rain.'

'Not a problem,' Sugar told him.

'I'll get you something of Scott's,' Ellen said, taking the sweater from him. She went upstairs where she hung the heavy wool across the footboard of the bed, then found a Patriots sweatshirt in Scott's bureau.

When she came back down, the three men were talking about Neal's father, a subject Ellen had always steered clear of. It amazed her, how easily Neal could be conversant, leaning back against the counter, bare-chested, sipping a cup of black coffee, smiling and agreeing, while Wes went on about how much Jonathan had done for the community. Neither of them mentioned the fact that Wes had been the one who responded to Moreen's 911 call twelve years ago and found Jonathan's body hanging from the barn's center beam – or that it had taken him twenty minutes to reach the farm because he'd been casting for stripers down at Cape Neddick.

She gave Neal the sweatshirt and he pulled it over his head. It was blue and hooded and loose-fitting, and she thought it made him look like a monk or a prize fighter.

'Now, I read your statements at the time of the accident,' Wes began, thumbing back through the pages of the notebook.

'I should've done separate interviews,' Sugar explained, staring at Ellen's hair while he scratched at his own.

'Next time you'll know,' Wes told him. As Ellen sat down again, Wes pulled a small tape recorder out of his shirt pocket and set it on the table. 'You mind if I use this?' he asked. 'Saves a lot of writing.'

Ellen shrugged. 'Of course not.'

He switched on the machine and faced it toward Ellen, then looked up at Neal. 'We had a visitor last night.'

'Out of her mind on something,' Sugar interjected.

Wes turned his attention to Neal. 'She told us that you had a little altercation with Randy a while back, at the wedding.'

Hearing this for the first time, Ellen looked over at Neal as nonchalantly as she could manage.

'Hardly an altercation,' he said, sipping his coffee. 'We were drinking, words were exchanged, you know how it goes.'

'You and Randy and that other one,' Sugar said, sliding his finger across the table toward his notepad. 'The southern kid.'

'I remember talking to Randy, can't say I remember anyone else,' Neal told him with a perplexed frown. 'You did say this girl was out of her mind.'

Ellen glanced at Neal, her misgivings flooding through her. She sipped her lukewarm coffee so the Westerbacks wouldn't see her agitation.

'What was your trouble with Randy?' Wes said.

Neal smiled at the older man's persistence. 'I don't know what the girl told you,' he said. 'I suggested to Randy that he start showing a little more respect for the family.'

Sugar nodded. 'That checks with her story. But she said you were all set to get physical. Matter of fact, I myself saw Randy coming out of the barn. He had a bloody finger, which he said he got from the barn, old nail or something.'

Neal laughed a little. 'I don't know how Randy got cut. We shook hands. That's as physical as it got.'

The older man turned to Ellen. 'You didn't see the altercation, did you?'

Ellen took a chance. 'Neal told me he had a discussion with Randy at the wedding,' she lied. 'From everything I saw, they got along fine afterward.'

Wes nodded thoughtfully, studying her. 'You still believe Randy was the cause of Moreen's injuries?'

'I know he was the cause,' she told him. 'I hope that doesn't make you think that it was anything more than Randy's own carelessness that got him killed.'

'I don't make you out to be a killer,' Wes told her. 'It sounds like you did everything you could to get Randy free once he was stuck.'

'We all did,' Ellen said.

Neal put his coffee mug down on the counter. 'What we needed was a fire truck to pump out the pond,' he said. 'But the trucks were all at the parade.'

Wes looked over at Neal. Ellen stared straight ahead, afraid to move her eyes, wondering why he had said that.

'I know you probably went over this already, but maybe you could tell me one more time,' the old man said to Neal. 'How long was it before you went down to check on Randy?'

Neal shook his head. 'Scott went down to check, I'd say fifteen or twenty minutes after Randy went down with the crowbar. When he came up and said Randy was in trouble, we both went down and tried to pull him out, but we couldn't budge him. That's when Scott ran up to the house to call for help.'

'And you don't have any idea how Randy's leg got cut?'

'Thigh,' Sugar said, pointing to a spot on his own leg.

'Maybe when he was trying to pry the cover off the pipe,' Neal suggested.

Ellen felt Wes's eyes on her. She glanced over at him, and he gave her a fatherly smile. 'Did your friend call you this morning?' His eyes dropped to the telephone on the table.

'Madeleine Sterling,' Sugar said. 'She was down at the pond that day.'

'We asked her not to call you,' Wes said, 'but she wouldn't be much of a friend if she didn't.'

'I guess she's not much of a friend,' Ellen lied, trying to seem unconcerned. 'I haven't heard from Maddy in a day or two.'

'So you don't know what she told us, about Randy—?'

Sugar picked a cookie out of the box and started toward his mouth, then he stopped and balanced it on the rim of his coffee mug. 'You know how Randy was writing in her hand,' he said, 'just before he drowned there – remember how you said he probably wrote the word "Moreen"?'

Ellen lifted her mug and sipped casually, though she knew that Neal's eyes, and probably Wes's too, were probing her.

'Well, I got a little different theory,' Sugar said. He leaned his elbows on the table. 'It didn't kick in at the time. He starts writing, and your friend says "M," then "U," then "R" – then you told her it must've been an O – for Moreen – and I figured, "Yeah, that makes sense," you know?' He sounded like he'd had too much caffeine.

'I don't understand,' Ellen asked them. 'Maddy said he wrote Moreen's name.'

Sugar pretended to write in his palm. ' "Moreen"? "Murder"?

Big difference.' He looked over at Neal, who shrugged.

'First I've heard of it,' he said.

Wes kept his eyes on Ellen. 'Probably we ought to talk to Ellie alone,' he said, glancing over at Neal. 'Mind?'

'Not at all,' Neal replied, pushing back from the table. 'You need me, I'll be out in the barn.' He made fleeting eye contact with Ellen, a slight, reassuring glance, then walked out the door.

Wes turned in his chair and watched him as he walked down the steps and headed toward the barn. 'Building's comin along,' he said.

'Neal's done a good job,' Ellen replied.

'Interesting look to it,' Sugar said.

Wes returned his attention to Ellen again. 'You know, I can't honestly say what I'd do if I thought my daughter was living with someone who was a danger, and the law wasn't protecting her. Maybe resort to my own devices.'

Ellen looked at him. 'You might. I didn't. And I don't like your insinuation.'

Wes gave her a patient smile. 'We're not looking at you,' he said. 'But what do you think of the chances that Neal had it in for Randy?'

'Zero.'

'Except that Randy and Neal already had words,' Sugar said.

'We told you there was no problem between them,' Ellen said, showing some impatience. 'Besides, Scott and Neal were together the whole time at the dam. There's no way Neal could have done anything to Randy without Scott knowing.'

'Didn't you say Scott came up to the house to get you?'

'Randy was already caught in the pipe then. Obviously.' It struck Ellen how serious the conversation had become all of a sudden. Wes was studying her, the paternal sparkle gone from his eye.

'They could've been in on it together,' Sugar said, popping another cookie into his mouth.

Ellen kept her eyes on Wes. 'Scott liked Randy,' she said. 'When I wanted Randy arrested, Scott defended him. As a matter of fact, he was just about to take Randy in as a business partner.'

'Coulda been a setup.' Sugar said, chewing.

'Wes, that's ridiculous and you know it.'

The older man shrugged. 'People oftentimes don't want to believe anything bad about someone they love,' he said. He watched

Ellen while he drummed his fingers on the table for a second or two. Then he stopped and folded his hands around the tape recorder. 'I've known Scotty since he was a youngster,' he said. 'I've seen him get into scrapes, and I've seen him get out of 'em. I watched him build up his business, and I watched him lose it. And you're right. I don't see him doing anything like this. But how well do you know your nephew?'

'Well enough to know that he's not a murderer.'

Wes sat back, examining his thumbnail. 'He did have some trouble when he was a boy. Not only here, but over in Mass. I talked to the Greenfield police this morning.' His voice had quieted somewhat.

'Oh, come on,' Ellen said. 'Who didn't get into trouble when they were young?' She tried to sound confident, but now she wondered what kind of trouble the old man was referring to.

Wes let out a troubled sigh, and Ellen thought he was going to stand. Instead, he clicked the tape recorder off. He leaned his arms on the table and looked over at her.

'I don't mean to scare you, Ellie, and God knows you folks don't need another expense. But I've got to say, I think Scotty might think about hiring himself a lawyer on this.'

Ellen felt her stomach tighten.

Wes took a deep breath, let out a sigh, then put his hands on the table and pushed himself to his feet. 'Is he at the gun shop today?'

'As far as I know.'

'Okay if I take a couple for the road?' Sugar said, standing, stuffing his hand in the cookie box.

'Help yourself,' Ellen answered. 'Wes, I need to ask you a favor.'

'We'll do what we can.'

'Does Moreen need to know about this?'

'About—'

'That you're asking questions about Randy's drowning.'

Wes took a breath and let it out reflectively. 'Sooner or later somebody might need to talk to her, Ellie.'

'Listen, if Moreen even thought there was a chance that Randy's death was anything but an accident, she'd never forgive us. I'm serious. I don't know what's going on with her, but she's finally getting some help. Wes, I don't want to lose her.'

The old man nodded. 'We'll do what we can,' he said again. 'But we may end up shooting this whole thing over to the state police, and you know I can't speak for them.'

Sugar slipped in the water getting up. He caught the edge of the table to keep from falling.

'Careful,' his father told him.

'Kill myself one of these days,' Sugar said, as the men left the house.

When the policemen drove away, Ellen watched Neal come across the dooryard, wanting to see some sign of awareness that he'd just implicated Scott – or that he'd kept his fight with Randy from her. But all she saw was Neal's confident stare as he climbed the stairs.

'What are you doing?' she demanded, suddenly feeling terribly vulnerable.

'Making a road for them.'

'That leads straight to Scott.'

'And away from us. Scott's innocent. He's believable.'

Above their heads, the rain slammed down on the porch roof. Neal smiled at her. 'Ellen, stop torturing yourself. There's not a trace of hard evidence that can possibly implicate us.'

She kept her eyes on him. 'But now I have to wonder,' she said, 'if Randy's death had more to do with your getting revenge than protecting Moreen.'

'Does it matter? Moreen is safe. Randy is out of her life.'

Ellen stared at him, struggling to keep her composure.

'I did what I did for you,' Neal said calmly. 'I have no remorse for Randy.'

'Maybe that's the difference between you and me,' she replied.

He gave her a look long with skepticism. 'Tell me honestly, Ellen: You didn't get the slightest bit of satisfaction watching him die?'

'It made me sick.'

He kept her eyes for another second or two, then turned and walked back out into the rain. She pursued him, banging the door open, wanting to finish this, but words wouldn't come.

CHAPTER SIXTEEN

Mainely Hardware came into town with a flourish: mass mailings, radio commercials, and a full-page ad in every newspaper within thirty miles. GRAND OPENING SALE, announced the orange banner that stretched across the quiet village street. A new electric sign jutted out from the old brick building where the wooden *Destin Hardware* sign had hung for fifteen years. The new sign shone garishly, even in the daytime, the little dancing handyman smiling down on the sidewalk, which was crammed with merchandise: wheelbarrows, riding lawnmowers, gas grills, plastic trellises.

'Times are changing,' Wes said as they drove by.

'Scotty don't care,' Sugar said. 'Bound to get more business out on the highway.'

'Just what the world needs, more guns,' Wes said. 'Let's go have a look.'

Sugar glanced over at his father.

'Now? I thought you were givin' him a chance to talk to a lawyer before he talked to us.'

'Why would I do that?'

Sugar said, 'You told the wife Scotty ought to get a lawyer.'

Wes smiled. 'See, police work's like a game of poker sometimes. Little bluff here, little bluff there. You never want to show what you're up to.'

'You really think something funny happened over there?'

'Either that or some pretty good coincidences.'

'If we're talkin' murder, maybe we oughta turn it over to the big-hats.' Sugar looked over at his father.

'Keep your eye on the road.'

'I know.'

★ ★ ★

The transformation from tire store to gun shop took longer and cost more money than Scott had anticipated. It took a week to clean up the tires, oil drums, and assorted brake parts that had been stored in the building. The landfill fee came to almost two thousand dollars.

Then, while he had the showroom painted and carpeting laid, he began hauling over the contents of Tommy Spampinato's shop – unsold weapons and ammunition, an assortment of oak cabinets, shotgun racks, glass display cases (Tommy threw in a stuffed black bear and four deer heads). On Wednesday Scott paid a couple of carpenters to build plywood counters and shelves. And he hired a bulldozer to start building his skeet and trap ranges outside. On Thursday and Friday the carpenters turned the garage into a shooting range. First they built a long plywood counter, three feet high, and separated it into six four-foot bays, with plywood dividers between each to deflect ejected casings. Above each bay they hung simple pulley clotheslines from which targets hung at the end of the range. To prevent ricochets, Scott had taken up the steel floor plates from around the garage and propped them up near the back wall, angled down forty-five degrees to deflect rounds into the mechanics' pits, which he'd half-filled with sand.

On Friday the first shipment of guns arrived, thirty thousand-dollars' worth, and Scott bought a half-page ad in the Portland and Portsmouth Sunday papers.

NOW OPEN FOR BUSINESS
30% OFF ALL FIREARMS
CHAMBERS AND SON
GUN AND FIRING RANGE

When Scott saw the Westerbacks walk into the store, he was arranging boxes of shells in a display case. He caught Wes's eye, then turned away defiantly, while a bulldozer labored outside, reshaping the gravel pit.

'Nice-looking store,' Wes said.

'It's gettin there,' Scott said. Off to the right, behind a heavy door, came the muffled sound of gunshots. 'Guy tryin out a forty-five back there.'

Wes walked over to the counter. 'You got somewhere quiet we can talk?'

'Now what,' Scott said, staying put. 'Come on, Wes, you busted me over twenty years ago for growing a little weed. You think that qualifies me for murder?'

'I think you'd protect your daughter,' Wes replied. 'Father's bound to protect his child.'

'Maybe I would have, if I thought Randy hurt her.'

A rapid seven-shot volley interrupted them.

Sugar said, 'Scotty, you know that friend of Ellie's, Madeleine Sterling?'

Scott swiped the air.

'She told us that Randy wrote something in her hand when he was stuck in the drain pipe.'

'He wrote Moreen's name,' Scott said, contorting his face. 'Sugar, you were there.'

'Except "Moreen" don't start with M-U,' Sugar said. 'Not when I went to school.'

'The way we spell it, Moreen starts with M-O. It's a type of wool.'

'Scotty, the woman said "M-U," not "M-O." You know what I think? I think what Randy wrote was "murder", and Madeleine Sterling sure acts like she's covering up for somebody.'

Scott shook his head. 'That woman is crazy as a shithouse rat, just like she's always been.'

'Believe me, Scotty, I'd like to put this one right to bed,' Wes said. 'But we got other problems too.'

'Red flags,' Sugar said.

'Ellie's claim that Randy kicked Moreen.'

'That'd be motive,' Sugar said.

'Which never happened,' replied Scott.

'Not to mention the stab wound in Randy's leg.'

'What, we stabbed him in the leg now? It's not enough we drowned him, now we stabbed him in the leg.'

'Never mind that the fire trucks that could've saved him were all off at the parade.'

'*Oh, bullshit!*' Scott yelled. 'Those trucks are in the parade every goddamned year!'

'Now there's no need—'

'Ah, fuck you!'

'Hey, hey! Don't be—'

'It's all bullshit—'

'Hey, Scotty—'

Wes turned to Sugar, holding his hand down to keep him cool.

'Scotty, just don't swear at him,' Sugar said.

'Fuck you too, Sugar. You know me better than that.'

'Just watch your language, that's all I'm saying.' Sugar's glance met with his father's, then separated. 'Anyway, I was there,' he said to Scott. 'I know *you* probably weren't involved.'

'Hey, thanks a shitload.'

'Fact of the matter is,' Wes said, 'it's your nephew Neal we're looking at.'

'I was with Neal right from the start,' Scott told them both. 'We stayed together up top while Randy went down. When he didn't come up after ten minutes, I'm the one who went down after him. Then Neal came down with me and we tried to pull him out.'

'But you don't know how he got stabbed? I can understand the cut on his shoulder – hesitation wound, it's called. You see them in suicides. But the cut in the thigh, that sure looks like a defensive wound, like he'd been in a fight.'

Scott shrugged. 'I told you what I know. Hey, the guy's drowning, he's got a knife in his hand, the way they flail around—?'

'I can see that,' Sugar allowed. 'But where's the knife?'

'Scotty, we're probably gonna have to drain the pond again,' Wes said.

'Drain the fucking pond,' Scott told them. 'Do whatever you want to do. Just don't talk to my daughter about this. You make her think we had anything to do with Randy drowning, I'll have the both of you in court so fast it'll make your head spin. I mean it.'

'Like I told Ellie, we've got no plans to question Moreen right now,' the older man said. He glanced over at Sugar, then lowered his head, rubbing his palms together nervously as if he had something more to say.

'Scotty, I don't really know a gentle way to put this,' he began, looking up again.

'You worried about upsetting me?'

Wes pressed his lips together. 'You think there's any chance that Ellie and Neal—'

'What, Ellie killed Randy?' Scott smirked. 'You guys really are fishing.'

'I didn't mean that exactly,' Wes said.

Sugar gave his father a curious look as the old man scratched at the back of his head.

'Scotty, do you have any idea why both Neal and Ellie would make it a point to tell me that both your fire trucks were busy at the parade?'

'What are you talking about?'

'Well, where you're the fire chief, I'm assuming you knew—'

Scott cut in. 'What do you mean, "they made it a point"?'

'Trying to be delicate here,' Wes said. He lowered his voice to a croak. 'You ever hear of something called "female midlife crisis"?'

The lines on Scott's forehead deepened.

Sugar's eyes remained riveted on his father.

'Let's put it this way,' Wes said. 'Suppose the tables were turned, and every day of the week Ellie left you at home with a pretty young woman, say, twenty-five or so. You work together hand-in-hand, you talk together, you swim in the pond when it gets hot, maybe have a drink or two in the afternoon. What time do you usually get home at night?'

'Wes, she's his friggin aunt.' Scott spread his arms in disbelief. 'Wes!'

The old man held up his hand. 'I don't mean to offend, embarrass, whatever, but oftentimes a husband's the last to know.'

Scott held his head. 'He's our nephew. Jesus, Wes, what kind of people do you think we are?'

'Well, I'm sure you're right, Scotty. It's just funny that both of 'em made it a point to tell us that you were the first one to go down after Randy, and then like I said about the fire trucks.' The old man shrugged his shoulders.

For a second or two, while gunshots knocked at the side doors, Scott just shook his head adamantly.

Wes turned to his son. 'You got anything else you wanted to add?'

Sugar looked at him, dumbfounded. 'Not to that.'

'You guys,' Scott said, still shaking his head. 'I think you both need a long vacation.'

'You got that right,' Sugar said.

'You know us old cops,' Wes added. 'We see trouble around every corner.'

'I guess,' Scott said. 'Ellie and Neal?' He waved off the idea with both hands.

★ ★ ★

Driving away in the cruiser, Sugar said to his father, 'You really think there's something goin' on there?'

Wes shrugged. 'Who knows? Sometimes this work is a little like a game of solitaire.'

'Always some card game.'

Wes chuckled. 'You know how it is when you get stuck and no matter how hard you stare at that deck you just can't make a play—?'

'I bin there.'

'Well, best thing to do at that point is shuffle up the deck once or twice, then deal again. See if those cards look any different to you.'

'Yeah, that's called cheatin'.'

'It is indeed. In cards.'

Sugar thought for a minute. Then he chuckled too. 'I guess we just shuffled 'em up pretty good.'

'Yes we did.'

Ellen stood under the clothesline, facing the barn, white bed sheets flapping around her shoulders in the clearing breeze. Several minutes ago, when she had come outside with the laundry, the hammering in the barn had stopped. She had ignored the silence then, but now as she looked for Neal inside the long, shed-roofed addition, eleven brand-new windows winked back at her. The twelfth window opening gaped darkly, the last unfinished piece of the barn, and that's where she focused her gaze.

'I know where she is,' the voice said.

Ellen jumped. Behind her, Neal pushed between the sheets and bath towels.

'Moreen?' she asked, bending nonchalantly for her laundry basket. 'Where?'

He waited until she straightened and looked at him. Then he held her eyes intently with his own.

'My father's house.'

They drove up Main Street, along the east side of the commons, then turned down Oak Street, where Ellen pulled over at the entrance of the deserted cemetery. They got out of her truck and walked through the iron gate, where weathered gravestones rose out of lush, wet grass that looked like it hadn't been mown in weeks.

Neal led the way alongside the whitewashed stockade fence until they were behind the church and their feet were soaked. Then he lifted up on the door in the fence and pulled it back on its one remaining hinge. The door croaked as it opened.

'Go ahead,' Neal told her.

Ellen looked into the church grounds, to make sure they weren't being watched from the parsonage, the rear corner of which was visible on the other side of the church – the downstairs living room and an upstairs bedroom. The Wings lived there now, Al and Louise and three of their five children. Al, a former church deacon, had taken residence in the parsonage in exchange for maintaining the property after Jonathan's death. Judging by the condition of the buildings and grounds, it was an arrangement that benefitted the Wings much more than the church. Neglected clapboards on both buildings showed graying grain beneath the scant film of paint. Roofs needed repair. Two window panes were broken and patched with cardboard and duct tape.

'Go on,' Neal said, ushering Ellen through the stockade door and following close behind. As soon as they'd taken five or six steps across the deep lawn, the parsonage was obscured by the corner of the steeple.

Centered at the rear of the church, three stone steps led down to a black wooden door set in the stone foundation. Neal went down the steps past Ellen, taking a screwdriver out of his back pocket.

'Mo and I used to do this all the time,' he said quietly, sticking the screwdriver between the jamb and the latch. 'For the communion grape juice.'

He looked back with a glint as the door swung open. Ellen glanced nervously over her shoulder, then followed him in. He closed the door behind them, and they stood together in the darkness at the head of a long corridor. Ellen heard him sniff. At the same time, she detected the faint smell of smoke – cigarettes, candles. Then a small penlight came on in Neal's hand. He wrapped his hand gently around her shoulder, as he directed the beam to the gritty floor in front of her feet. 'Go ahead,' he told her.

'I'll follow you,' she whispered.

He stepped out ahead of her, and they went creeping along behind the light beam, opening doors on both sides of the corridor, until they came to an interior room where the smoke smelled stronger. They went in, Neal shining his penlight at a long, rectangular table that had a mound of melted wax in its center. In a corner of the room, an empty potato chip bag lay on the floor beside an overturned, mostly empty liter bottle of Coke and another puddle of candle wax.

Coke and potato chips. 'It's her,' Ellen said. She lifted the bottle but was unable to detect the warmth of a recent hand. When she pushed her thumb into the soft wax, however, she felt heat.

Neal touched her shoulder, then gestured with the penlight to the door. She followed him out into the corridor where, a few feet ahead, he turned right into an intersecting corridor.

'Moreen?' Ellen called as they walked on, bypassing other rooms. At the very end of the corridor, Neal opened a blue door and stepped down a concrete step to a concrete floor. Ellen waited nervously in the doorway while he shone the light around the small, dingy room.

To his immediate right, a wooden bin holding between two and three feet of coal stretched about twelve feet to the back wall. In the rear left corner stood an ancient black furnace, separated from the coal bin by a massive brick chimney.

'She's not in here,' Ellen said quietly, but Neal went further into the room and shone his light on the narrow, soot-gray plaster wall between the chimney and the coal bin. 'What are you doing?' she asked, but when she saw him reach his hand up into the dark bay between two floor joists, she knew. It was the Indian tunnel, the secret, underground passage that connected the cellars of the church and parsonage. Ellen stepped down into the room just as Neal tugged at something with his finger, and the narrow wall jumped a bit. Now he squeezed his fingers between the chimney and the exposed edge of the wall and swung the wall out, revealing an arched, brick opening that reminded Ellen more of an oven than a passageway. Holding the wall open, he looked back at her, as if expecting her to step inside.

'I'm not going in there,' she told him. He didn't argue. He simply turned away from her, ducked his head and stepped into the tunnel, taking the light with him.

'Neal?'

The wall swung shut. He stopped it with his heel. Ellen came closer and got her fingers inside, pulled it open again. The entire tunnel was arched and very small, two feet wide and only five feet high, if that. Because the floor was natural bedrock, it rose in places, lowering the ceiling even more.

'She's not in here,' Ellen said, hanging back.

In response, Neal aimed the light beam at a loosely rolled sleeping bag just ahead of him. Ellen felt a weakness in her legs, a slight shivering.

'Christ, Mo,' she said, and she ducked in, pushing her hip against the door to keep it from swinging shut.

'Is it hers?' Neal asked.

Ellen turned her head toward the opening and took a deep breath, preferring the ashen air of the boiler room to the sour, under-earth chill inside the tunnel.

'Wait a minute,' she said, taking another breath to calm herself. Then she hunched her shoulders and moved in. When the wall shut behind her, she closed her eyes for a second, to stop the slight panic from muddling her mind. Then, taking the penlight from Neal, she stooped and picked up the sleeping bag, uncovering Mo's backpack and boom box.

She shook her head, exasperated, then raised the light and saw that fifteen feet ahead of them the tunnel bent to the right.

'Maybe she's up around the corner,' Neal suggested.

'She's not,' Ellen replied, wanting only to get out of there.

'She could be hiding in my cellar,' Neal said.

Ellen looked back at him in the darkness. It was the second time he'd referred to the buildings as his or his father's.

'Only one way to find out,' Neal prodded.

Aware that he was goading her, Ellen stepped over the sleeping bag and moved along, tossing the light beam out ahead of her while she did her best to ignore the spider webs that collected on the bill of her cap. Coming to the bend, she ducked around the corner and saw that the tunnel stretched out another forty feet, to the end. Here, underground between the church and parsonage, she suddenly felt like she couldn't breathe. She started to turn back, but Neal was right behind her.

'Don't stop,' he said.

'Neal—'

'We're almost there.'

'Are you enjoying this?' she snapped, swinging away from him and proceeding on. At the tunnel's end, a single, wide pine board, she reached up into the cobwebs and found a small iron ring lying flat on the sill. She managed to stick her thumb into the ring and pull up on it. The door popped open on the right, only an inch, but the bright daylight angling in startled her. Ellen peered out into the cellar of the parsonage, the dusty casement window shining at her from the top of a stone foundation. She heard a noise above them: the ring of silverware against dinner plates.

Neal laid a hand on her shoulder, reached around her and pushed the door open wider, exposing the black oil tank on their left, the wooden stairs off to the right, the spider webs that draped like insulation from ceiling timbers.

'Are you claustrophobic?' he said quietly.

She grabbed his arm, squeezed it to quiet him. 'I don't like to be closed in,' she whispered.

'That's often called claustrophobia,' he teased.

'She's not here,' Ellen whispered. 'Let's go.'

A sudden voice called, 'Hey, didn't you make a pie this afternoon?'

Ellen jumped. Neal wrapped his arm around her chest to steady her. 'Shh,' he said in her ear. His hand dropped down to her breast. She grabbed his wrist, moved his hand back up.

'I thought you were gonna make a strawberry pie.' It was Al Wing, up in the kitchen. They heard a chair scrape against the ceiling, then a woman's muffled voice. Ellen could feel her heart pounding against Neal's forearm. He took the penlight from her hand, then stepped around her, out into the cellar. She grabbed the back of his sweatshirt. 'Mo's not here,' she whispered. 'Let's go.'

'Well Jeez Louise,' Al Wing said, raising his voice. 'If I'da known I was supposed to get the strawberries, somebody should've told me. I'm not a mind reader, you know.'

Neal reached back and took hold of Ellen's hand. He pulled her arm gently, but she twisted out of his grasp, remaining in the mouth of the tunnel. 'Neal, I mean it.'

'I want to make love to you,' he said softly. He stared at her, as footsteps crossed overhead.

'A simple matter of communication,' Al Wing said, his voice becoming much clearer.

'I'm going,' Ellen whispered. 'Give me the light.'

He shook his head at her as he backed toward the stairway.

'Neal, I want the light,' she said, stepping down onto the hard-packed cellar floor.

Holding her eyes with a dark, seductive look, he continued backing away. 'Come on, El. It's driving me crazy, I can't think of anything else.'

She gave him an incredulous look. 'Here?' she said, as she pursued him.

'Yeah, on the stairs,' he replied, staring as though trying to understand her resistance.

'Well, excuse me for trying to catch a little friggin fish to put in the freezer!' Al Wing yelled above them, and Neal blurted a laugh, shattering the silence.

Now they stood perfectly still, eyeing one another as the house hovered silently around them. Ellen looked up the stairs, listening for the latch of the door at the top, prepared to turn and run back into the tunnel, light or no light. A sudden bang of a cupboard door shot goosebumps down her arms.

'Great!' Al Wing shouted. 'Now we're out of Oreos?'

Neal smiled at her, though the darkness in his eyes hadn't changed a bit. 'Tell me what's the matter,' he said.

'Just give me the light.'

He held the penlight away from her, teasing, but the grin had left his face. 'Tell me,' he said.

'I said no!' She pushed him hard enough to make his eyes flash. Then she spun away and ducked into the tunnel without the penlight, rushing off into the darkness.

They didn't speak on the drive home, until Ellen pulled into Destin Plaza, saying, 'I've got to drop off some work at Wool 'n' Things.' Because it was after five and the store was closed, she drove around the rear of the plaza and parked beside the dumpster.

'I'll be out in a minute,' she said, stepping out of the truck and lifting the bag of wall-hangings from the back, five small seascape tapestries for which Ingrid would pay her twenty dollars apiece. Ellen unlocked the back door with the key Ingrid had given her when she'd relocated to the Plaza twenty years earlier.

Returning to the truck, Ellen shifted into gear and pulled around the front of the building, then drove across the parking lot, trying to ignore the fact that Neal was sitting with his back against the passenger door, staring at her.

'Can you not do that?' she said finally.

'Do what?'

'Leering. I teach school in this town.'

'I'm not leering. I'm admiring your haircut.'

'I'm wearing a hat.'

'Okay, I lied. Actually, I'm thinking that this is my last night with you and wondering if you're even going to kiss me goodbye.'

'No, I'm not,' Ellen said. 'But since it is your last night, I thought we'd pick up some tuna steaks to barbecue for dinner.'

'Tuna steaks.'

'Yeah.' She gave him a firm look.

'I'll continue leering, if you don't mind.'

Without humoring him, Ellen stopped the truck near the Beecham Supermarket on the other side of the plaza, far enough away from the other parked cars to avoid running into anyone she might know. She turned off the key and pulled three twenty-dollar bills from her pocket. 'Would you get the fish? I need to pick something up at the drug store. And buy a couple of lemons and some barbecue sauce. We also need paper towels and a jug of milk. And Scott's out of pickles – kosher dills. Spears, not whole.'

Neal kept staring.

'No?' she said.

'Put your money away,' he told her, and he popped open the door. 'Fish, lemon, barbecue sauce, milk and paper towels, right?'

'Do you mind? And kosher dills, for Scott.'

As soon as he got out of the truck and started walking to the store, Ellen pulled the truck over to the pharmacy. She hurried inside and bought the first thing she saw – Rolaids – then hurried back outside.

Keeping her eye on the supermarket next door, she went to the public telephone in front of the pharmacy. She used her calling card and dialed Massachusetts directory assistance, asked for the Greenfield Police Department. When a Corporal Philbrook answered the phone, Ellen identified herself as Sergeant Beecham, with the Destin Police. 'Chief Westerback called you a day or two ago, asking about a Neal Chambers,' she said.

'I remember,' the corporal told her. 'I spoke with your Chief.'

'He wanted me to follow up,' Ellen said. Shielding her eyes from the lowering sun, she watched the people entering and leaving the supermarket. 'What we're interested in,' she continued, 'is any anecdotal information you might have on Mister Chambers.

Maybe incidents you remember, or crimes where he might've been a suspect—?'

'That's your boy,' the corporal said. 'He was only in town for a couple of years, you understand. Then he went away to school and never came back – someplace in Maine, I believe – after DYS cut him loose.'

'DYS?'

'Yeah, Department of Youth Services,' he said, as if Ellen should have known. 'They had him in Springfield, locked up in a twenty-day assessment unit.'

'For what?'

'Jeez, you name it. Fires mostly, a couple of pet mutilations. Trouble is, we could never make any of the charges stick. When his mother lawyered up, like I said, DYS had to cut him loose. At least they convinced her to send him out of town. I think it was Maine he went, maybe Vermont.'

'We were led to believe the state placed him in a boarding school after his mother was hospitalized with a nervous condition.'

'Nope. Best of my knowledge, the mother was never hospitalized. Even if she had been, the state wouldn't have had the authority to send him out of state. Technically, the boy never did a thing wrong. But I'll tell you this, if you could build a case against someone on the basis of how much quieter things got after he left—'

'*All set?*'

Ellen turned. Neal was standing behind her, holding two grocery bags in his arms.

'Okay,' she said in the phone. 'I'll see you when you get home.'

She hung up and tried to read Neal's face in the fleeting glance they exchanged, as she took one of his bags and started walking to the truck. 'I didn't see you come out of the store.'

'I went through to the pharmacy,' he explained. 'Who was that?'

'Scott,' she said, walking around to the driver's side, to avoid his eyes. 'I called him at the shop. He loves tuna.'

'Is he going to join us?'

'He said he's busy, but he'll try.'

When Ellen pulled into the dooryard, Scott's Mercedes was already there. Her heart fell.

'Wow, he really does love tuna,' Neal said, giving her a look.

It was the way the car was angled toward corner of the barn, like he'd almost run into it. Ellen knew he'd been drinking; she also knew the Westerbacks had been to see him. Before she turned off the engine, she heard a volley of gunshots. She gave Neal a quick, ominous look.

He shrugged and opened his door. The gunfire stopped. 'Over there,' he said.

Standing beside the pump house, Scott appeared to be loading a handgun. When he spotted them, he turned away, raised his arm and fired six rounds toward the pond. With each shot, Ellen could see flames spewing from the muzzle. She got out of the truck.

'Thirty-eight special,' Neal said.

When Scott finished shooting, he turned back and stared at them.

'How's it going?' Neal called.

Scott bent down and grabbed a handful of shells, popped open the cylinder and began feeding the revolver.

Ellen glanced at Neal. *Something's wrong*. The look Neal returned was thick with arousal. He started walking toward Scott.

'Neal?' she warned softly, but he kept walking. Ellen followed, trying to clear her face of emotion.

While Scott watched them coming toward him, he raised a half-liter bottle of whiskey to his lips and drank, then set the bottle down beside his feet. Then he turned and fired another volley, each loud shot churning Ellen's stomach. She blocked her ears as she got closer, trying to read meaning in Scott's actions, at the same time deflecting Neal's backward glance with a look of her own: *He knows*.

'That for me?' Scott said to her when he stopped shooting. She realized he was talking about her haircut.

'No, me,' she answered. 'I couldn't stand it long anymore. Ready for grilled tuna?' Even her tone of voice was a lie. 'We've been out looking for Mo.'

'I liked it long,' Scott said as he bent and picked through the spilled box of shells at his feet, then reloaded the small revolver. Off beyond the pump house, about a hundred feet away, he had propped an eight-foot sheet of plywood and drawn a figure of a man in black marker.

'We think she's been camping out in the old church,' Neal said.

Scott turned to him, snapping the cylinder back in place. 'Hey, you wanna knock off a few rounds?'

Neal regarded the .38 for a moment and, with a shrug, took it into his hands. 'Colt Detective Special,' he said, obviously feigning admiration. But perhaps it wasn't obvious to Scott. The way Ellen felt, everything was obvious, every gesture transparent. 'We shooting anyone in particular?'

Scott looked off at the target with a murderous smile and said, 'I haven't decided yet.'

The revolver was black, with a blue sheen, and no bigger than Neal's hand, from hammer to muzzle. He wrapped his palm around the grip, gave Ellen a reckless look. 'Block your ears,' he said as he straightened his arm.

Scott turned his back on him, bent for his bottle and brought it to his mouth, all the while studying Ellen fatefully. He didn't flinch when Neal started firing the handgun. Neither did Ellen shrink from his gaze, although she pressed the heels of her hands against her ears and winced with each shot.

When Neal had emptied the cylinder, Scott held out his hand and Neal dropped the revolver in it.

'Your turn, El,' Scott said, his stare on her intensifying. 'Can I still call you El? I mean, you haven't changed your name, have you?'

She stared back at him, bright with anger.

He persisted. 'No?'

'I'm going to light the grill. I'll let you know when dinner's ready,' she said, leaving them both, walking up the gravel drive but wanting to run to her truck and drive out to the highway and keep driving. As she reached the porch, the sound of pistol shots pounded like fists on her back, and she could no longer resist the fear. She ran up the steps, tore open the screen door. The telephone was ringing. She picked it up.

'*Asphyxia*,' said Maddy.

Ellen walked away from the window.

'Did you hear me?'

'Maddy, I can't talk to you now.' Unnerved at how dark the kitchen was, nevertheless, Ellen left the light off, not wanting the house to seem inviting.

'How did Randy die?' her friend demanded.

'You know how.' Ellen paced across the floor, legs shaking. Six rapid gunshots slapped off the clapboards. Then it was silent.

'He drowned,' Maddy said. '*Asphyxia*.'

Footsteps clomped up the steps. Ellen felt the kitchen shake. Neal opened the door and stepped inside, giving her a long, fervent look.

'Hold on a minute,' she said to Maddy, and covered the phone with her hand, waiting for Neal to leave. But he remained at the door, staring seductively, while outside the windows another volley of shots pounded a rhythm in sync with her heart.

She stared at him. He crossed the kitchen to the refrigerator, opened the door and grabbed a bottle of Pabst, held it up to Ellen as if offering it – or maybe he was toasting her. She turned away and heard the screen door slam. When she saw him walk down the porch steps, Ellen carried the phone through the living room. 'Tell Mo I need to talk to her,' she said to Maddy as she climbed the stairs.

'Moreen's fine. Listen to me—'

'Don't tell me Moreen is fine. She's my daughter, and I want to talk to her.'

'What about your mother?' Maddy persisted.

'What about her?'

'How did she die?'

'You know how.'

'She choked to death on a piece of candy,' Maddy said.

Ellen went into her bedroom and shut the door, pulled the shade down over the window, then peeked through the side to watch Neal walking toward the pump house. She turned away from the window.

'And Scott's parents went through the ice in Carrier Pond. They drowned.'

'Maddy, some drunk ran them off the road.'

'Some drunk who was never caught. The car was stolen, with no fingerprints but the owner's. They were robbed of their breath, all of them – just like Neal's father.'

Three gunshots rang out. The bedroom reverberated.

'Even his own mother—'

'Neal's mother committed suicide,' Ellen interrupted. 'She stuck her head in the oven and gassed herself.'

'Right. Also called asphyxiation.'

Ellen scratched her fingers across her hair. 'Look, I can't talk now.'

'I just talked to Jeff Hamill,' Maddy said. 'He was the school psychologist when Neal went to grammar school here.'

'I know who he is.'

'He hasn't seen Neal in fifteen years or more, but he said the kid was a textbook example of severe conduct disorder.'

'Which is?'

'Which *does*.'

The window shade jumped with a puff of wind. Ellen's heart hammered.

'Ellen, he's a born fucking sociopath.'

'Those were Hamill's words?'

'His words? He said he'd never met a ten-year-old who scared the shit out of him the way Neal Chambers did.'

Ellen breathed a loud, exasperated sigh.

'Ellen Chambers, listen to me. You might think this is just some kind of kinky affair—'

'Maddy, you're obsessing about this. You're paranoid—'

She heard a click in the phone and thought Maddy had hung up on her. 'Christ,' she breathed, knowing she'd have to call back and apologize.

'Just tell your house guest this paranoid lady's bought herself a gun,' Maddy said, still on the line. 'Drop it in a conversation where it seems appropriate.'

Ellen frowned.

'El, are you there?'

'Hold on.'

Ellen returned to the window, pulled back the shade and looked out over the pump house, the pasture and barn. She saw Scott's Mercedes parked in the dooryard, she saw Neal's pickup truck beside her own, but neither Scott nor Neal was anywhere in sight – and the shooting had stopped some time ago.

'Ellie, what's the matter?'

'Hold on.'

She took the phone with her and went out the bedroom door. The hallway seemed much darker than it had only minutes before.

She went to the head of the stairs and called down softly. 'Hello?'

'You're scaring me,' Maddy said. 'What's going on?'

'I'll call you back.'

Ellen switched off the phone and started down the stairs.

'Scott?' she called, a tremor tightening her voice. 'Neal?'

She walked through the living room and was about to step into the kitchen, when her heart jumped. She turned.

Scott was sitting on his desk, the bottle of whiskey in his hand, the telephone and revolver sitting side-by-side at his elbow.

'The cops stopped by my shop a while ago,' he told her. 'Wes and Sugar Westerback.' He nodded his head as he watched her, dangerously passive.

'Is Neal outside?' she asked.

Scott laughed quietly. 'Don't you want to know what they wanted?'

She looked at him fearfully as he raised the whiskey bottle to his lips again. She turned and hurried through the kitchen, threw open the screen door, looked left and right, then spotted Neal walking out of the barn with his sleeping bag rolled under his arm, his tool belt flung over his shoulder. He pitched the things in the back of his truck, as though he were leaving, but then he went around to his passenger door and opened it. 'You'd better come with me,' he said.

She heard Scott's footsteps behind her. Her heart pounded.

'Ellen, come on,' Neal told her.

The screen door banged open behind her. Ellen turned, saw Scott standing crookedly with the .38 in one hand, his whiskey bottle in the other. She felt the railing post dig into her back. Scott took a step forward, and the door slammed shut behind him. He chuckled a little.

'This been going on awhile?'

'Scott, you need to put that away,' Ellen told him, trying to make eye contact. 'You've had too much to drink.'

He glared at her, then he looked out at Neal. 'So, did I tell you two about the cops coming by the shop today? I started to tell you.'

'Scott, please, would you give me the gun?' She moved cautiously toward him.

'Somehow,' he said. 'Somehow—' He waved the gun out toward Neal and fired a deafening blast.

'*Stop it!*' Ellen cried, as a chip flew from a barn board two feet above Neal's head. Seeing that Neal was unhurt, she turned back to Scott and stepped in front of him, in front of his gun, her chest pounding crazily.

Scott's eyes brightened. 'Somehow,' he said, 'the cops think that I had something to do with Randy drowning.'

'They were here,' Ellen told him. 'They questioned us too.'

'Us, huh?' He started nodding again.

'Ellen, come with me,' Neal called to her. He was standing against his truck with his arms folded, in full view of Scott, who walked past Ellen to the head of the steps.

'Don't do this,' Ellen said to him, reaching again for the revolver. Scott pulled it away from her and laid it up beside his ear.

'Neal, just go,' she said.

'I'm not leaving you here with him.'

'That's good,' Scott said. 'Because before anyone goes anywhere, we've got a number of things to talk about, the three of us.'

Ellen looked back, saw Neal stick his hands in his pockets and start walking toward them.

'Neal, get out of here!'

She stepped in front of Scott again, ready to grab the pistol if he moved it off his shoulder.

Neal stopped within spitting distance of the porch, staring at Scott with a sharp glint in his eye. 'You have something to say to me, Uncle?'

Scott glared down at his nephew. Ellen could hear him breathing.

'Neal, I want you to go,' she said, as calmly as she could.

'Oh, turn my back on him?'

'I took you in,' Scott said to Neal. 'You ate my food, you slept in my house—'

'I wouldn't sleep under the same roof as you,' Neal told him.

A chill of nausea swept through Ellen. She looked at Scott and saw sobriety tug at his drunkenness.

'Scott, please' she said, 'let me talk to him.'

'Talk all you want. Go with him, for all I care. Ellie, what the Christ are you doing to me?'

'Give me the gun.' She held out her hand.

'You want the gun?' He shouted at Neal. '*You* want the gun?'

He dropped his arm, aiming straight at Neal's chest.

'Scott, don't!'

She saw Scott's eyes glaze over, as he breathed noisily through his nose. Then he stepped back to his left, found the deck chair with his leg and sat down hard. He tossed the revolver on the glass tabletop, slammed the bottle down beside it. 'Go talk.'

Ellen checked him for a second, then turned back toward Neal.

'I'm staying here with Scott,' she told him. 'You need to leave.'

'Is that really the way you feel?'

She looked back at Scott again, who seemed to be chuckling to himself. Then she walked down the steps, passing Neal and going to his pickup truck, where she got in the open passenger door. Neal kept his eyes on Scott for another few seconds, then turned and walked around to the driver's side. When he got in and shut the door, Ellen looked straight at him.

'You want to know how I feel?' she said. 'I'm scared to death.'

'Scared of what?'

'Why did you pretend you didn't know about what happened between your mother and Scott?'

He stared straight out the windshield. 'Why bring up the past?'

'Because I think you're obsessed with revenge, that's why. And I want to know why you ever came here.'

Neal turned to Ellen, his dark eyes gleaming. ' "Obsessed with revenge." Interesting choice of words. To be honest, I never knew exactly what happened the day my father died – until now.' For the moment, Neal's eyes left hers. Then they returned. 'Tell me this: Did you ever forgive my mother?'

Ellen watched him adamantly. 'Yes, I did.'

'And you forgave Scott?'

She looked off toward her house, where Scott was slumped in the deck chair, sullenly watching them. 'It took a long time,' she said, 'but yeah, I forgave him.'

Neal laughed. 'If that were true, *Aunt Ellen*, we wouldn't be sitting here having this conversation.'

Her stomach clenched. She glared, wanting to lash at him with her fist. Instead, she pushed the door open and got out of the truck.

He started the engine. She closed the door, then looked in the open window at him.

'When does it stop, Neal?'

'When does what stop?'

'Your *justice*! When does it stop?'

The way he smiled, she could tell he'd been waiting a long time for that question.

'When all the twelves are in line,' he said, raising the clutch and backing away from her.

She kept her eyes on him while he stopped and shifted, then started to drive away. 'That's childish, cryptic bullshit!' she yelled.

He gave her a smile as he drove slowly out of the yard.

'Asshole!'

Then he pulled out on the road and was gone. Through the dust of his departure, Ellen turned back to the barn, all the bright new windows gazing blindly out at the pasture.

'How does it feel, Ellie? Feel pretty good?'

She looked over at Scott sitting on the porch with his gun and whiskey bottle on the table.

'I've got to admit,' he said, 'I never saw it coming.'

Bristling with fear, Ellen came toward him, climbed the steps and went into the kitchen. She threw open the cupboard, pulled down her bottle of tequila and spun the cap off . . . then stopped. She bowed her head and heaved a deep, shivering sigh. She slid the bottle to the back of the counter, then went over to the table and leaned on it heavily with both hands, feeling the heat from her chest rising up over her face. *When all the twelves are in line.* Neal's words came back to her. She looked out the window at Scott sitting with his back to her, his arms folded, the bottle of whiskey and revolver standing in front of him. Her heart would not stop pounding.

She spun off the table, punched out the door and grabbed his .38 off the table, taking the box of shells with her trailing hand.

'Honeymoon over?' Scott said.

She went down the steps and marched to her truck, intending to leave, go anywhere, maybe to Maddy's, just leave. She threw the door open and slid inside, then leaned across the seat and popped open the glove compartment, stuffed the revolver and shells in.

That's when she heard the cars turn in, and she stared up at her rearview mirror as they passed behind her – the blue Destin Police cruiser in front, followed by a dull black Dodge Colt.

'Here it comes,' she heard Scott say. 'Here comes the knife in the back.'

Stealthily, she closed the glove box, then sat up and checked her face in the mirror, her jagged hair, her wild, dilated eyes. She took as deep a breath as she could manage and stepped out of the truck. The Westerbacks got out of their cruiser at the same time.

'Comin' or goin'?' Wes said to her. He seemed slower and heavier than he had in the morning, but no less animated, as he approached the porch.

Caught without an answer, Ellen pretended not to hear. 'I didn't expect you back so soon,' she said, climbing the steps beside him while she glanced back at the man in the station wagon.

'Business must be good,' Wes said to Scott when he'd stepped onto the porch. 'You haven't been home this early since you were in high school.'

Ellie had learned to be wary when Wes acted that friendly.

'I figured if you guys were gonna be throwin my butt in jail, I might as well enjoy a couple of hours of freedom,' Scott answered.

'Actually,' Sugar said, 'this doesn't have anything to do with what we were talkin about before.'

While they talked, Ellen watched a man get out of the Dodge Colt. He was maybe five-nine, dressed in a moderately wrinkled tan suit over a white shirt and black tie, and he approached the porch in a distinctly businesslike way. He looked to be forty, his face was round and his brow and beard heavy, his lips unusually wide and pulled down at the corners in a permanent frown. He reminded her of a Neanderthal.

'Detective Dave Gallagher,' Wes said, introducing the man. 'Dave's with the State Police.'

'Beautiful farm,' the detective said, his frown unchanged.

'This is a personal call then?' Scott remarked. 'If so, beer's in the fridge.'

Gallagher rested his shoe on the bottom step of the porch, a brown wingtip, impeccably polished. 'I'd like to ask you some questions, if you've got a minute or two.'

'Fire away,' Scott told him. 'Whatever's wrong, we must've done it.'

Ellen noticed the worried glance Wes cast toward Scott. As much as the old man liked to play close to the vest, his feelings for Scott showed through.

Gallagher checked a small notepad in his hand. 'Mister Chambers, could you account for your whereabouts, say, from one until seven o'clock this morning?'

'At one this morning I was in bed,' Scott replied.

'And you have someone who can verify that—?'

Scott looked at Ellen and said, 'Would you like to verify that, dear?'

Ellen looked at the detective. 'We were in bed. Why?'

'Is there anybody else who can vouch for your whereabouts?'

'Neal around?' Wes asked Scott. 'I don't see his truck.'

'Neal is your nephew?' Gallagher consulted his notepad.

'Scott's nephew,' Ellen said. She saw Sugar's less-than-furtive glance at his father. 'He's been staying with us for a few days, rebuilding our barn.'

'Sleeping here?'

'That's right.'

'And he slept here last night?'

'Yeah.'

The detective wrote in the notepad. 'Mister Chambers, could you describe your relationship with a man named Raymond LaFlamme?'

Scott looked at Ellen as if she had asked the question. 'I borrowed money from him, and I paid him back. Why?'

'How about Randy Cross?'

Scott lounged deeper in his chair. 'What, these guys didn't tell you?'

'I'm conducting a separate investigation,' Gallagher said pleasantly.

'Randy Cross was married to our daughter,' Scott said. 'He drowned in our pond. He caught his arm in the drain pipe and we couldn't get him out.'

'Neal was the other one who went down in the water,' Sugar said. 'The nephew.'

Gallagher kept his attention on Scott. 'You had a business relationship with Randy, as well?'

'He was coming to work for me in my gun shop. I was going to make him a partner eventually.'

'I was referring to your relationship with him in his capacity as Ray LaFlamme's employee.'

Scott looked at Wes again. 'Am I permitted to ask what the hell he's doing here?'

'I don't see why not.'

'Address your comments to me, please, Mister Chambers,' Gallagher said.

'Okay.' Scott stared over the table at him. 'What the hell are you doing here?'

Gallagher nodded without a trace of emotion. 'If you'll answer a couple more questions, I'll tell you what you need to know, okay?'

Wes gave Ellen a cautious peek. His meaning was clear.

'Detective, should we have a lawyer present?' she asked.

'That's up to you and your husband,' Gallagher answered cordially, with a glance at Wes. 'I like to keep things informal. However, if you'd like, we can drive to the police station and continue our discussion there. You could have your attorney meet us.'

'I don't need a goddamn lawyer,' Scott said. 'Randy was one of LaFlamme's part-timers. I gave Randy the money I owed the old man.'

'How much was that?'

'A lot.'

Gallagher's pen waited on his notepad.

'Around a hundred fifty thousand.'

'And Randy drowned here the day after you paid him the money, is that correct?'

'Exactly,' Scott intoned.

'Your son-in-law drove a Jeep Cherokee, is that also correct?' Gallagher said.

'That is also correct, sir.'

Wes interrupted. 'You folks expect Neal back anytime soon?'

'Was the Jeep parked here during the time Randy was caught in the dam, as well as afterwards, while the pond was being drained?'

'Hey, last I knew, there was nothing illegal about borrowing money from a man and paying him back.'

'Yeah, but Scotty, they're all missing, LaFlamme and his bodyguards,' Sugar said. 'So's the money.'

Scott looked directly at Sugar. Ellen looked at him too. As did Wes and the detective.

'Excuse me,' Gallagher said, 'could I have a word with the two officers?'

When the Westerbacks walked off the porch, and Gallagher accompanied them to their police car, Ellen saw a white lollipop stick stuck to the seat of Gallagher's slacks, and she wondered if the detective's children looked like neanderthals too. After a minute of tense conversation, Wes and Sugar got in the cruiser and drove off, and Gallagher returned to the porch, where he stood a few feet away from the rail with his arms folded.

'Mister Chambers,' he said, 'Ray LaFlamme and some of his employees turned up missing this morning. Your name is on a receipt that was discovered in Mister LaFlamme's office. The receipt was signed by Randy Cross, but we don't believe Randy ever delivered the money to LaFlamme.'

'Okay, Lieutenant, Sergeant, whoever you are,' Scott said, pulling himself upright in his chair. 'You want to know if I drowned my daughter's husband and took my money back, right? The answer is, "A, I love my daughter, and B, I'm not a fucking murderer or an idiot." If you're asking whether I had anything to do with LaFlamme and his people disappearing, I already told you: I was in bed all night.'

Gallagher's mouth straightened, from cheek to cheek. 'How about your nephew, Neal?'

Scott looked over at Ellen.

'He was here all night,' she said.

'If both of you were in bed all night, how do you know for certain what Neal did after you fell asleep?'

Ellen felt her husband's eyes linger.

'Scott goes to bed before I do,' she said, the heat rising to her face. 'Neal and I stayed up until two o-clock, talking. When I got up at six, he was already working on the barn.'

'So who's to say he didn't go out for a drive between two and six in the morning?'

'I didn't sleep very well,' Ellen said. 'I would've heard him.'

Gallagher looked over his notes again.

'I've read the police report, including the complaint that Randy physically abused your daughter—'

'Which he did not,' Scott interjected.

'Together with the knife wound and certain other information,' Gallagher continued, 'I wanted you to know that we'll be opening our own investigation into your son-in-law's drowning.'

He stuck his hand inside his lapel, then approached the porch and set two business cards on the rail. 'I'd like you to stay in touch with me if you hear anything or maybe think of anything that might help. I'd also like to ask that, until the investigation's over, you'll notify me before going out of state.'

Scott snorted. 'I'll tell you right now, if I'm your chief suspect, your investigation's a long way from over.'

Gallagher's mouth widened again. 'I'll be in touch,' he said.

The knocking was incessant – knock and scrape, knock and scrape, knock and scrape – as slowly the tops of two scrawny pine trees came into focus, outlined by a flat, slate-blue sky and three dim stars winking down.

Rooftop shivered with the cold. He rolled to his left and saw Jesus lying beside him, one-armed. The absolving limb lay on the deck between the console and the pilot seat, attached by a long yellow rope to Rooftop's weight belt.

Rooftop sat up slowly and looked around, saw that his boat had run aground in a wooded cove, although he had no idea where he was or how long he had slept. He realized that the pistol was no longer in his hand, which was crinkled and pink. He looked around the cove for houses but saw only rocks and bristly evergreens, a low, dark ocean and high, darkening sky.

He wasn't totally sure if he was alive, indeed, if this was the same earth he had intended to leave. If it was, he knew that he was not the same man who had left it.

He eased his body to the edge of the platform and lowered himself down onto the rocks. Then he swung the boat around and walked it out till he was waist-deep. He pulled himself back onto the deck, raised himself to his feet, and walked quietly to the console. He started the motor, then shifted into forward and headed out for deeper water, to get his bearings.

CHAPTER SEVENTEEN

Ellen drove straight to the church, barely able to think. She parked her truck behind the high school and walked briskly across the green commons, keeping her head down, except to look for Mo's black Cherokee. It was just after eight, and overcast; street lights on both sides of the commons cast Ellen's faint shadow left and right in the grass. She carried a small disposable flashlight and flathead screwdriver in her hand and a scrap of grocery receipt and pen in the pockets of her jeans. If Moreen wasn't in the church, Ellen would leave a note, warning her that police were looking for Randy's missing money – and that Neal knew her whereabouts.

As she turned down Oak Street, outside the range of the street lights, she tried to assure herself that if Neal had been responsible for the disappearance of Ray LaFlamme and his men, it was because he was protecting Moreen, as he had been when he killed Randy.

Then why was she running through the cemetery?

Squeezing through the stockade gate, she hurried across the overgrown church grounds and down the cement steps, then jammed her screwdriver in the door jamb and pried open the door, the way Neal had shown her. Closing the door behind her, she flicked on her flashlight in the darkness, illuminating the long corridor. The church hovered over her in a deep silence.

'Mo?' she called quietly. Her echo made the damp walls shimmer with life. 'Honey, I have to talk to you.'

She stood and listened but heard nothing, so she walked briskly down the corridor, then turned right at the main intersection and continued to the end. Inside the boiler room, she walked past the coal bin, squeezed in beside the huge chimney, reached up and pulled back the iron ring. She felt the latch give, and the right side of the wall swung out an inch from the bin. She pulled it open and ducked into the arched brick tunnel, shining the light out ahead of her, at Moreen's things – sleeping bag, backpack, boom box.

Kneeling, Ellen gathered up the sleeping bag and backpack, but gave up on the boom box when she found the handle was broken. She turned back to the tunnel door, reached for the latch and pulled, then ducked out of the tunnel, into a pair of open arms.

'*What are you doing?*' cried Moreen.

'Mo—?' she gasped.

'*Mom, I don't want you here!*'

'Come on,' Ellen said, walking ahead. 'We're going home.'

'Mom,' Moreen cried, pursuing her. 'I need my things.'

'You can't stay here,' Ellen said. 'Neal knows where you are, and I don't trust him.'

Reaching the back entrance, she slapped the thumb-latch with the flashlight, pulled open the door and walked up the steps, grateful for the open air.

'Would you stop?' Moreen persisted, following her outside. 'I'm not going with you.'

Ellen pushed through the stockade gate and turned, Mo's backpack and sleeping bag stuffed in her arms. 'Listen to me,' she said quietly. 'The police came to our house. Did you take some money from Randy's Jeep?'

'Why are you asking me that?'

'Because the men who were looking for the money are missing. The police think they were murdered.'

'I don't know anything about that money.'

'Then what are you hiding from?' Ellen pleaded.

'You!' Moreen glared wildly, then ripped the backpack from Ellen's hands and headed off through the cemetery.

'Mo, wait,' Ellen called, but Moreen started to run, quickly dissolving into the shadows of gravestones and oak trees. A dog started barking. Then another. Ellen lowered her head and walked to her truck with Mo's sleeping bag, never once looking back to see if she was being followed.

Maple trees turned fat, green circles in her headlights, two boys labored to peddle their mountain bikes up Ramsey Hill, a white Corvette squealed out of the convenience store in front of her, but Ellen barely noticed any of it. She was thinking of a Saturday morning a long time ago, trying to remember exactly when Moreen had stopped coming into her bedroom in the mornings. She wondered if it was a gradual thing, or if it had happened suddently at the time of Jonathan's suicide. It must have been a gradual thing, Ellen told herself, or she would have noticed.

On this particular morning – it must have been a Saturday, she was sure, because Scott had left early for work but she didn't have to get up – she did anyway and was stripping the sheets off the bed, when she felt like she was being watched. She turned and saw Mo standing in her doorway wearing her plastic Dracula teeth, which means it would've been around Halloween that year, a week or two after Scott's affair – and Jonathan's death.

'Oo, you scared me,' Ellen said. 'Coming in?'

But Mo just stood there sleepily. Her hair was redder then, as Ellen remembered. In fact, she had on her purple flannel nightie.

'Did you have a nightmare?' Ellen asked her.

Moreen continued looking in. It wasn't exactly a sleepy stare; it was more a scowl, a sober, worried look, and Ellen was afraid it had to do with Jonathan's hanging. 'Mo, lamb, is everything okay?'

Now Ellen remembered the way they stood there watching one another; the way Moreen's vampire teeth clicked, the way her eyes moved, as though she were figuring something out for herself; finally the way Mo sighed, then nodded her head

'You sure?'

What Ellen remembered most clearly is how relieved she felt when Mo turned out of her doorway and went quietly away.

When Ellen got home, the empty bottle of Harwood's was on the kitchen counter, along with two empty bottles of ginger ale. She stepped into the living room, where Scott sat in his recliner, the remote control in his right hand. Television channels blinked rapidly by.

'Can we talk?' she said.

His eyes didn't leave the television. 'Not a whole lot to say,' he told her. 'I guess I got what I deserved.'

She walked past him and sat on the couch, so she could at least see his face. 'I found Mo,' she said, wanting to allay any suspicions that she'd gone after Neal. 'She won't come home. She won't even talk to me.'

Scott ignored her.

'The only one she'll talk to is Maddy.'

The channel-surfing stopped. Scott muted the volume and looked straight at Ellen.

'What's she talking to that dizzy bitch about?'

'Mo's in therapy. Anything she says is confidential. Maddy thinks she's protecting me from something, she won't say what.'

With a sour laugh, Scott turned his head, glared at the dark window.

Ellen leaned forward on the couch. 'Scott, I have to tell you something.'

'Hey, load it on.'

'When Randy got caught in the dam—'

'Yup.'

'—I don't think it was an accident.'

Scott chuckled to himself.

Ellen sighed. 'Scott, Neal told me he was going to do it.'

Scott turned slowly toward her, a deep scowl on his brow, while a Pepsi commercial played silently between them.

Ellen shook her head helplessly. 'When he told you the dam was leaking, it wasn't. Neal was setting the whole thing up. To kill Randy.'

Scott sat back in the recliner. Slowly, a broad, closed-mouth smile dawned on his face, and his eyes shut. 'Ellie, why are you telling me this?'

'Because I'm going to turn him in.'

Scott's eyes opened again, gravely. 'And, what, tell the cops you knew what he was up to all along? You want Moreen to find out?'

'Of course not. But I'm afraid, Scott. I think Neal set everything up right from the start.'

Scott paused for what seemed like a full minute. Then he grinned again, broadly dismissive. 'I think you're right,' he said. 'But you can't go to the cops.'

'I don't know how else to stop him.'

Scott chuckled again, a soft, bitter sound. He paused thoughtfully, then shook his head with a bright look of defeat.

'You can't go to the cops,' he explained, 'because I was the one who helped push Randy's arm in the pipe.'

A fast silence settled over the room, broken only by the whisper of the waterfall and the hum of the television. Ellen stared at her husband, wanting desperately to see some sign that he was lying, perhaps to taste a little revenge of his own.

'Neal told me all about Randy kicking Mo,' Scott continued. 'He told me about the hysterectomy and he said that I wasn't supposed to know. He told me not to let on. With you ranting and raving, if there was any suspicion, the cops would look at you. When they saw you were innocent, they'd write it off as an accident.'

'Neal said the same thing about you,' Ellen said.

'That's why I stuck up for Randy,' Scott said. 'That's the only reason I offered to take him into the business with me.'

Even as she marveled at the precision with which Neal had manipulated them, she felt a wave of sickness engulf her. She held her breath until it passed. 'Scott, did you take the money?'

'Oh, of course I did, dear,' Scott said, his sarcasm weighted with a rancor that she feared would never go away. 'I gave Randy a hundred-fifty thousand bucks and I had him sign a receipt, then I murdered him and took my money back. How dumb do you think I am?'

She stared at him, feeling her rising blood color her face.

'Nope, Neal got his revenge, all right. A few days' work, a little slap and tickle, and he drives into the sunset with a cool one-fifty. And we go away for murder.' Scott laughed again, almost as if he admired Neal's cunning. 'See now? That's why you can't go to the cops.'

'But what if Neal's not finished with us?'

Scott turned back to the television, hiked up the volume and resumed changing channels. 'Believe me, Neal won't be back,' he said with fierce satisfaction. 'He got everything he came for.'

Ellen took a quick breath to respond, but held the poisoned air in her lungs.

Scott reclined his corduroy chair almost flat. The channels kept changing.

'Scott—'

'Just don't tell me you're sorry,' he told her.

Ellen tended her sheep the next day, tended her gardens and worked on her tapestries. Scott went to work early in the morning without saying goodbye and he came home well after midnight, smelling of whiskey. In bed they lay together like mannequins, staring up at the darkness until Scott started to snore. Finally, when it was well past four o'clock, Ellen rose from the bed, electric with energy.

She gathered her sweatshirt and jeans off the floor, went down to the bathroom to put them on. When she was dressed, she started the coffee maker and wrote a note to Scott. *I'll be gone for a day or two. Please try to find Mo and feed and water the sheep. Be careful.* She brushed her teeth, washed her face and filled her thermos with coffee. Then she fit her cap on her head, grabbed a box of Cheerios from the pantry, snatched the photo of Neal's barn off the refrigerator and went out to her truck. Up above the hill, the sky was already glowing yellow behind the treetops. She opened the glove compartment, reached her hand inside to feel the cold steel of Scott's .38, then she started the engine.

Before she drove away, she went back in the kitchen, picked up the pen and added to her note: *Love, Ellen*. She wondered if her handwriting looked forced.

CHAPTER EIGHTEEN

Ellen got into St Johnsbury at three in the afternoon, by which time she was hungry and deeply tired. She stopped at a McDonald's, where she used the bathroom and washed her face with cold water, then she pulled up to the drive-through, ordered a salad and a large black coffee. While she waited for her food, she studied the map the helicopter pilot had drawn for her, and she ate while she drove, continuing north on Route 91 until she left the highway in Barton, heading west. According to the pilot, who sprayed for farmers all over the state and had recognized the unusually-shaped barn, she was looking for Route 14. In ten minutes she found it and turned south.

Of course Neal knew she was coming. Where else would she go? The road he'd made for her led directly to this place. She thought of the revolver in the glove compartment and felt a weak jolt of panic, which fell instantly to dread.

When the blacktop narrowed, crowded in by thick woods on either side, she drove for another five minutes until she crossed over a bridge. A sign on the abutment said BLACK RIVER. She checked her odometer and went another half mile, where she saw a mostly hidden dirt road that rose straight into the woods on her right. She turned in, and the road curved around a gigantic boulder, then pitched uphill. As she shifted into low and started up, the gravel giving way to shale, she wondered why she had come.

Did she expect an explanation at gunpoint? A confession? An apology? Yes, all of that, though she knew she'd never get it.

So could she shoot him?

Before she had time to answer herself, the vista yawned open up before her. She hit the brakes.

It was a painting, a dreamer's farm, cradled in a basin of the richest greens and surrounded by ancient, round-topped hills that seemed to pile one on top of the next, far into the graying distance. By the looks of the pasture, the farm had been unattended for years. Unmown grass, three feet high, waved gently in the cool of the late afternoon, flavored with buttercups. Small yellow butterflies hopped along the tops of the flowers all the way to the tree line, where birch and pine saplings crept in from the woods.

Nestled in the center of the basin, the white farmhouse and barn stood side-by-side facing east, seeming to pay tribute to the hills. The barn was identical to Ellen's, with its arched windows and high white silo rising off the peak. In fact, from her vantage point, Ellen could easily see the resemblance to a church.

There was no truck in the dooryard, nor any sign of any human habitation. No highway sounds, no planes passing overhead. Except for the ubiquitous chirring of insects, everything was perfectly remote.

Ellen lifted off the brake and let the white truck roll quietly down the hill, her approach seemingly unnoticed amidst the elaborate workings of the field. When she stopped her truck in front of the house, the sun was already down behind the barn. She could feel a bright chill in the air, a harbinger of clear August nights, wide open windows. But night approaching made her think of sleep, and the thought of sleeping in Neal's house made her shudder.

Opening her door and stepping out of the truck, four dark windows stared out of the house at her, each one hung with lace curtains. She considered taking her revolver, but decided against that. In a way, she wished Neal would just open the door and come out, so they could have the conversation. In another, she prayed he wasn't there.

'Neal?'

The old shingles absorbed her voice like rainwater. She looked for footprints in the gravel but saw no clear impressions. Nor was there any sign that anyone had been there recently. A pair of power lines came down the drive, attached to old leaning poles, but no phone line accompanied them.

Ellen walked to the porch, climbed the three stairs and pulled the screen door open. She knocked on the inside door, peering through the glass into the kitchen, then turned the doorknob.

'Okay, I'm here,' she called as the door opened. But the building hovered in silence.

Almost certain that she was alone, Ellen let the screen door close quietly behind her. The house smelled like it had been left to itself for a long time, the scent of unused cupboards, of a damp cellar penetrating the floorboards. Yet the kitchen looked perfectly clean, and this made Ellen nervous. Corners of the ceiling were free of cobwebs; the old pine floor looked freshly waxed.

If he wasn't here now, it was clear that he'd been here recently – and he'd be back. The only question was how long he'd make her wait.

She opened the refrigerator, found it empty. She opened a cupboard and saw a stack of white china plates on the bottom shelf, cups and saucers on top, all neatly arranged. In the cupboard beside it, juice glasses and drinking glasses stood in perfectly aligned rows. She ran her finger over the counter, picked up no dust. She bent and threw the lower cupboard doors open, one after the other, each one empty.

'Neal?'

Her shout raced through the empty house. She walked into the next room, a small parlor that contained an overstuffed burgundy-colored sofa and a Boston rocker. On the opposite wall was a stairway, painted salmon-pink. She turned on the lamp and walked up, each tread creaking loudly underfoot. As she suspected, she found two neat bedrooms upstairs, each with beds made.

She walked down to the kitchen again and opened a white door over a set of brown cellar stairs, old but freshly painted. She flipped the light switch and the red dirt floor lit up below. She refused to be afraid. Hiding in a cellar like some troll was not Neal's style. If he was here on the farm, Ellen knew he would have already made his presence known. Then what was the point in going down? None, she told herself, but what was the point in not? She descended the treads as casually as if the cellar were her own, and when she reached the floor she saw the furnace, the water heater and pump, exactly as she'd expected. But when she turned to go back upstairs, the door above her moved. Her chest clenched with fear and she ran, taking the stairs in a blinding panic and throwing doors open, practically running down the porch steps. Light was dying outside, the surrounding greenery darkening. She ran to her pickup truck, intending to leave. But the barn . . .

Standing beside her truck, then stepping away from it, she walked to the arched front doors, curious about how exactly he had replicated the barn where his father had died. She pulled the doors open and caught her breath.

Not a speck of sawdust, no sprig of hay, not even a boot print. Yet everything was exact, from the roof rafters to the hayloft to the twelve stalls that lined the left and right shed walls, even to the heavy, hooked chain hanging from the low center beam. Lumber was crisp and sweet-smelling as the day it had been milled.

'Neal, if you're here, we have to talk!'

The barn swallowed her shout. Once again Ellen's rational voice told her to get in her truck and drive away as fast as she could. But she listened to the voice of her heart, which told her that a connection had been forged between them. Even if their love-making had been pretense, she knew they'd been joined at the heart the day Neal's father had killed himself.

She walked out of the barn and gently latched the doors, then went back inside the farmhouse, stopping first at her truck to get the box of Cheerios. Inside the kitchen she set a chair against the door, facing the rest of the house, and ate the dry cereal with her hand, until the room had darkened and the empty box fell on the floor.

Then she waited. She set her sneakers flat on the floor. She leaned her elbows on her knees, rested her cheeks in her hands. Above the somnolent buzzing of insects in the field, she listened to a lone cricket chirping over and over. Too early for crickets, she thought sleepily, as she closed her eyes and followed its sound down a warm, dark river . . .

. . . She gasped and was pacing the floor before she was fully awake. The night pressed against the windows, throbbing and chirring as if the entire farm had conspired to make her sleep. She looked at the wall clock, saw that it was twenty past ten. She went to the sink and splashed cold water on her face.

Determined to wait him out, she climbed the stairs and tore the blankets off the bed, then took them outside and crawled into her truck. She locked both doors, then cranked the windows down a half-inch. Took her pistol out of the glove compartment. Laid it on the floor. Curled up under the blankets. Closed her eyes.

Madeleine Sterling kept her pistol under her pillow – not the pillow she slept on, but the one beside it, the one her eight-year-old

Siamese, Cleo, slept on. The weapon was a Wilkinson Sherry, a demure, nine-ounce automatic with a blue trigger and slide, and a black cross-hatched stock. The remainder of the pistol was bright, gold-framed steel that reminded Maddy more of an elegant cigarette lighter than a firearm.

They had gone to bed at eleven fifteen, she and Cleo, after Maddy's nightly ritual: checking the locks on her windows and doors with her pistol in hand, then closing herself in the bedroom, where she looked through her huge walk-in closet and under her bed.

Finally she'd slid between the satin sheets, placed her pistol under Cleo's pillow and turned off the lamp. Although the room was stuffy with the windows closed, and the ocean sounds muted, she was lulled to sleep by the cat's steady purring.

But the instant Cleo stopped purring, Maddy opened her eyes. The room was dark, but she could tell the Siamese was sitting upright; she could see the cat's eyes collecting the dim light from the Venetian blinds like twin black pearls. Maddy lay there, all heart. She did not even breathe. As quietly as she could, she slid her hand along the sheet, under the pillow, under Cleo's weight, until she found her gun. Ordinarily, the cat would have thought it a tease, but Cleo remained intent.

Maddy wrapped her hand around the stock, but she was afraid to take the gun out from under the pillow. Everything inside the room was so incredibly still. She moved her eyes, not her head. But without her contacts or glasses, all she could see were shadows upon shadows and the dark glow of her window blinds across the room. A blacker shadow moved against the blinds, which she tried to convince herself was the hawthorn branch waving outside. But the longer Maddy stared, the more she saw.

In the corner of the room, her clothes tree came to life – as if a human figure were separating from the jerseys and jeans, legs from legs, arms from sleeves. Cleo sat rigidly on the pillow, her weight pressing heavily on the back of Maddy's hand, while the pistol in Maddy's palm grew clammy. Suddenly the cat sprang from the pillow. Maddy heard its feet hit the carpet. She felt the small vibration through the mattress, of the cat moving under the bed.

Now Maddy watched the human shape step in front of the window. And she watched it come closer.

This is real, Maddy told herself, her hand frozen on the pistol. *It's finally, truly happening.*

A gunshot awoke Ellen, and her revolver was in her hand before she opened her eyes. Chest pounding, she raised her head just enough to see out her side window. The sky was solid white. A gust of wind shook her truck, and Ellen heard the bang again: not a gunshot, but the screen door slapping against the jamb.

She set the .38 on the seat and pulled herself upright by the steering wheel. Judging by the activity of the swallows that flitted about the silo, she guessed it was around seven in the morning. But was it Friday or Saturday? The screen door banged again, and she looked over at the porch, half-expecting him to come walking outside. It was Saturday, she determined. And he still wasn't here. She stepped out of the truck and stretched her long bones, feeling surprisingly well-rested.

She went into the house and used the bathroom. Washing her face, she peeked out at her truck through the lace curtain. Swallows continued to dart about the barn roof, undisturbed. She came back into the kitchen and opened the cupboard to get a glass of water. The glasses—

Her heart hammered.

—were rearranged.

Both drinking glasses and the smaller juice glasses were now assembled in two uneven rows – six on the left; five on the right. The meaning was clear. He had left her house on Thursday, his eleventh day, without finishing the shed windows—

—which meant he had returned on Friday.

Ellen swung down from the porch and ran to her truck, started the engine and fishtailed in his dooryard, speeding up the drive, retracing the country roads on instinct. In less than five minutes, just outside of Barton, she pulled up to the gas pumps at a country store and ran inside.

'Do you have a phone?' she asked the elderly man at the cash register.

He raised his brow in a bemused sort of way and, without hurrying, reached below the counter and set an old black telephone in front of her.

'It's long distance, I'll pay you,' Ellen said. 'It's an emergency.'

The man placed a crooked finger on the body of the phone,

pointing to an orange sticker that read POLICE, FIRE, AMBULANCE, DIAL 911.

She dialed her house, desperate to hear Scott answer, but after four rings the message machine came on.

'Could I get a large black coffee to go?' she said to the man. He turned on his stool and pulled a Styrofoam cup out of a slender plastic bag. When Ellen heard the beep, she said, 'Scott, if you're there, pick up.'

Her flesh tingled, imagining Neal sitting in her empty kitchen listening to her frightened voice. The old man poured coffee in the cup and snapped a plastic lid on the top, watching her all the time.

'Scott, find Moreen and keep her away from the house. I'm on my way.'

She pushed down on the cradle, lifted up again, dialed Maine directory assistance and asked for the number of Chambers' Gun Shop. The old man slid a pad of paper to her, set a freshly sharpened pencil on top. 'I need gas,' she told the man. 'Would you fill it?'

While she dialed, he lifted himself off his stool and walked around the counter. To her great relief, Scott answered the phone at his shop. 'Did you find Mo?' she blurted out after his hello.

'How the hell do I know where she is?' He sounded like he'd been drinking already.

'Scott, Neal's after us,' she said. 'He knew that Mo was hiding in the church. He'll find her again.'

'And if Neal is after us, that would be my fault, right?'

'Jesus, this isn't a game!'

'Like I told you, Neal got exactly what he came for,' Scott replied. Then he hung up the phone.

'Scott!' Ellen yelled. She pushed down the cradle and dialed Maddy's number, but got the machine.

'Mad, you've got to find Mo,' Ellen said. 'Tell her not to come to your house, not to go anywhere. Then call the police and have them pick her up. I'll get there as fast as I can. Maddy, you've got to do this.'

Ellen took her coffee off the counter and went outside. The store owner had pumped eleven dollars' worth of gas in her tank. She reached in her jeans pocket, pulled out some bills.

'This should cover everything,' she said, giving him an extra five.

The man moved slowly, pulled the nozzle from her truck and

shut off the pump, while Ellen screwed her gas cap back on. The man looked closely at the money she'd given him, looked at the gas pump, then turned back to her.

'Come back anytime,' he said. 'But I'd think twice about drinking that coffee.'

The owner of the inn across from Maddy's cottage stared down from his ladder as the old maroon Bonneville pulled up to the curb. It was dented along the right side, as though the car had been rolled; two rear windows were covered with duct-taped plastic wrap. 'Great goddamned advertising,' the man muttered, dipping his paintbrush in the can. The girl stepped out of the car, the same young, sloppy broad who'd been coming every other day for the past week.

'She's got a driveway, use it!' he yelled. Never mind that the woman's own little howdy-mister sports car was blocking it for some stupid reason. The girl glanced back, then turned away like she never heard him and walked across the street to the cottage. 'Fine, ignore me, I'll have you towed.' Though best not push it, he thought, she might turn on him. You never knew with these people. In fact, it was hard to tell who was crazier, the nuts who came here all the time or the so-called psychologist they came to see. It wasn't bad enough that his guests had to look at her dark little cottage with so much ivy crawling over it you could barely see the windows, but now with the blinds pulled day and night, and this loony parking on his curb. He heard the girl knock at the front door of the cottage. And knock. And knock.

'Oh, for God's sake,' he said. When she knocked again, he laid his paintbrush on top of the can and turned around to yell, but now she was at the side of the cottage with her face pressed against the window glass, moving her head up and down like a cat.

'That's it,' he said, climbing down. But as he stepped off the ladder, he turned to see the girl racing toward the street. Hard to imagine anyone running that fast, man or woman, especially over a parked car.

'You don't have to kill yourself,' he called to her. 'Just move it away from my curb.'

But she ran right past her car and on up the middle of the street, like a wild woman. Talk about lunatics – the look on her face.

'Goddamned loonies,' he muttered, and ambled off to make the call.

★ ★ ★

The long bands of yellow tape danced in the sea breeze. Ellen sat on the curb across from Maddy's cottage with her cap pulled down, watching the men entering and leaving through the front door, feeling like she might never be able to stand again. She could not come close to fathoming the depth of her guilt.

Down at the bottom of the street, the ocean hummed restlessly, as official-looking vehicles came and went. Already, police cars lined both sides of the street. Two from the York Police Department, one from the York County Sheriff's Department, two cruisers from the Maine State Police, as well as three or four unmarked wagons and SUVs that belonged to the lab men. Mostly Ellen kept her eye on the dull black Dodge Colt that was parked two houses up from Maddy's cottage – beyond sight of even the police tape. The detective sat inside with his back to his door. Moreen sat opposite him, her arms folded.

'Twelve, in what sense?' Wes Westerback asked again. He was sitting on the curb beside Ellen, his notepad balanced on his knee, while Sugar stood facing them both, leaning against the cruiser with his arms folded.

'I don't know, twelve everything,' she explained. 'Twelve-volt battery, twelve-gauge shotgun, twelve months in a year . . .'

'Twelve men on a football team,' Sugar added.

'The dimensions of the barn are in multiples of twelve; he put twelve windows in each side,' she explained. 'He told me he was going to do this.'

'Kill your friend?'

'Not in those words. But I should have known. I *did* know.'

'Ellie, what words did he use?' Wes asked gently. The smell of his spicy aftershave was an odd comfort to her. She took a breath of it.

'I don't know exactly. He said he was going to finish the barn in twelve days.'

'I wouldn't have taken that as a threat.'

'He talks in code. He teaches you the code.'

Wes nodded in a kind way, keeping his eyes on her.

'I think he killed my mother and Scott's parents,' she continued. 'They all died the same way his father did. His mother too. Asphyxiation.'

Sugar pushed himself off the car, giving his father an urgent look. 'Want this on tape?'

Wes shook his head.

'Asphyxiation,' he repeated, nodding thoughtfully. 'I handled your mother's death – and I was first on the scene when Scott's folks drowned, but I never made anything of the coincidence. As far as I recall, nothing appeared suspicious. Just terrible accidents. But you're saying he's taking revenge for his father's hanging himself by asphyxiating the people closest to you and Scotty?'

His tone of voice said he didn't necessarily share her suspicion.

Ellen sighed wearily. 'Neal holds Scott responsible for destroying his family, so he's destroying our family. Is that so hard to believe?'

'Well,' Wes said patiently, gesturing toward Maddy's cottage, 'Madeleine Sterling wasn't family. And she wasn't asphyxiated. She died of a bullet wound, which right now looks like it was self-inflicted.'

Ellen turned away in frustration.

Wes leaned forward on the curb. 'Ellie, did Neal have anything to do with Randy drowning in your pond?'

'No.'

She refused to meet the old man's stare, knowing that she couldn't tell him what she knew about Randy's drowning without implicating Scott in the murder. She pictured Neal and imagined a coyote picking off a flock, working systematically, patiently, from the outside in to the center.

'What worries me,' she said, 'is that Neal has finally shown his hand. Now he's committed. Now he's going to show us how smart he is.'

'How smart is he?' Sugar asked.

She glanced up at him.

'Thank you, officers.'

Ellen turned, saw Detective Gallagher walking down the sidewalk toward them.

'I'd like to ask Mrs Chambers a couple of questions now, if you don't mind,' he said, patting the trunk of the Westerbacks' cruiser, signaling them to leave.

Behind him, Moreen's Bonneville turned out of the road, and Ellen jumped to her feet. 'I told you I wanted to see Moreen when you finished with her.'

'Your daughter's headed home, you can talk to her there,' the detective replied.

Ellen laced him with a glare. 'Moreen doesn't live at home. You just let her get away – and her life is in danger.'

The detective gave her a patronizing, seemingly disinterested frown. 'Who is it you believe is endangering her?'

'The same person who murdered Maddy.'

Showing no emotion, he pulled a notepad from his suit coat pocket. 'From the evidence collected so far, we believe that your friend took her own life.'

'If you're so sure it's a suicide,' Ellen replied, 'why send a homicide detective?'

'I recognized your daughter's name when the call came through,' he explained. 'The decedent was present at the death of your son-in-law – who is also peripherally connected with the missing men from Old Orchard Beach. And now there's your message on Miss Sterling's answering machine this morning. That's a lot of connections.'

'Detective, I think we've got a serial killer on our hands,' Sugar said.

Gallagher ignored him, keeping his eyes on Ellen. 'I assume you're referring to Neal Chambers, your nephew.'

'Neal Chambers killed Maddy,' Ellen told him.

'You're certain of that. How?'

'You need to find my daughter before he does,' Ellen snapped. 'And I want to know what you told her.'

Gallagher nodded thoughtfully. 'Before we get off on a tangent, let's operate under the assumption of available facts and see if we can rule out the possibility of suicide. Tell me about your friend Madeleine. Are you aware of any previous suicide attempts?'

'None,' Ellen said. 'Even if Maddy wanted to kill herself, which she did not, she would never have shot herself in the head.'

'She was vain—?'

'She was particular about her appearance.'

'Was she unhappy with her appearance?'

'Not enough to shoot herself. Besides, if she wanted to kill herself, she had a small pharmacy in her medicine cabinet.'

'Oh? Any illness that you know of?'

'No.'

'Financial difficulties?'

'Maddy had more money than God.'

'Issues of guilt?'

'None.' The way Gallagher glanced up at her, Ellen wondered if she had answered too quickly.

'How about problems with men?'

'Yeah, she was terrified of Neal Chambers.'

'Did he give her some reason to be afraid?'

Now Ellen could feel Wes's eyes on her, too.

'Maddy knew what Neal was up to,' she said.

'What did she know, exactly?'

'That he was here to destroy my family.'

'How was he doing that?'

'He murdered my mother. He murdered Scott's parents. He wants to kill everyone we love.'

Gallagher glanced at the older man, who shrugged slightly.

Ellen expanded her chest. 'Look, is it that hard to make a murder look like suicide?'

'To experienced investigators, frankly, yes,' Gallagher said. 'In this case, the decedent has a single bullet wound to the side of her head. The bullet is the same caliber as her weapon, her weapon is found in her hand, with her prints and no others. There's no sign of a struggle, either on the body, her clothing, or the bed covers. There's nothing disturbed anywhere in the house, although she had cash in plain sight and a significant amount of jewelry in unlocked boxes.'

'Neal Chambers is certainly intelligent enough to place the gun in her hand and clean up after himself. He's not stupid.'

'Okay,' Gallagher said. He paused a moment, as if reluctant to continue, but he went ahead just the same. 'Without getting into details, we can be certain that the decedent was sitting upright in her bed at the time of death, with her reading lamp on. That much we know; it could not have been staged after the fact.'

'He could have killed her, then propped her up.'

Gallagher shook his head. 'Blood dispersion. Your friend was alive and sitting up in bed when the bullet entered her skull.'

Ellen turned away.

'We also know that she kept the firearm under her pillow,' the detective continued. 'And because we can fairly accurately pinpoint the time of death at three fifteen in the morning – two independent reports from neighbors who were awakened by the gunshot – we're able to put together a scenario.'

He paused, as if to give Ellen a chance to stop him; she didn't.

'In order for this to have been a homicide, we must assume that Madeleine was sitting up in bed without trying to defend herself, while this man, whom you say she was terrified of, talked her into handing him her pistol, which he then held an inch from her head and pulled the trigger.' The detective stopped and gave Ellen a look of helplessness, while Ellen sat numbly, trying to force the picture from her mind. 'So far we have no evidence of a struggle.'

'Neal Chambers killed Maddy,' she maintained.

Gallagher shrugged. 'How did he get in? There's no sign of forced entry. The doors and windows were all securely locked. The only way anyone could have gotten into that house is if she let him in herself. You tell me: Would Madeleine have let Neal Chambers in?'

Ellen's hands tented around her mouth. Tears distorted her vision, but she could see Wes scowling at her, as though waiting for her to speak. She knelt up and dug her hand into her jeans pocket, pulled out her key ring. Her voice barely escaped from her mouth.

'I let him in,' she said. 'I have Maddy's house key,' she explained. 'He must have taken it and copied it.'

'Bingo,' said Sugar.

Gallagher folded his lips inward, a speculative expression. He turned to the elder Westerback. 'Excuse me, gentlemen, at this point what we have on our hands is a suicide. As such, the York Police are handling it. If it rises to a homicide investigation, then it falls under state auspices, in which case I will conduct the investigation. Is there a reason the Destin police force is present?'

'We're not here in official capacity,' Wes said.

'Exactly,' Gallagher replied.

'But where Ellen and her family live in our town, we need to learn whatever we can, so we can provide protection if we have to.'

Gallagher furrowed his brow for a moment. Then he turned back to Ellen.

'You and your husband have both told me that on Wednesday morning, between one o'clock and six, when Ray LaFlamme and his bodyguards disappeared, no one left your house, and no one came to your house. There were just you, your husband and Neal on the premises, is that right?'

'Yes,' Ellen replied, without hesitation.

'And you and Scott stayed in bed together until morning.'

'That's right.'

'Where did Neal sleep?'

'Neal always slept outside, either in the pasture or in his truck, if it rained.'

'So it's conceivable he could have left for an hour or two and come back, and you wouldn't have known?'

'It's possible.'

'And you also feel that Neal was responsible for your friend Madeleine's death.'

'I know he did it.'

'As well as the deaths of other relatives.'

'That's right. All of our relatives.'

Gallagher nodded. 'So how is it you're so sure that Neal had nothing to do with your son-in-law's drowning?'

Ellen sat like a stone under the eyes of the men. Gallagher didn't make her answer. He closed his notepad and stuck it in his pocket. 'Is your husband at his shop?'

'This has nothing to do with Scott,' Ellen said.

'Oh, I'm going to talk to your nephew,' he said. 'I'm going to keep talking to all of you. Because regardless of how your friend died, I think there's a definite connection here to your son-in-law's death. And I believe that when we find the missing money, most of our questions will be answered.'

'This is *not* about money,' Ellen said.

'Rule of thumb,' the detective replied. 'Murder's almost always about money, or it's about sex.'

From the corner of her eye, Ellen saw Sugar look in her direction. Gallagher waited, giving her a long invitation to reply. She didn't.

'Make sure you let me know next time you decide to go out of state,' he said, then turned and walked across the street, to the cottage where Maddy had died.

Early the next morning, Ellen was awakened by the sound of the Boston Whaler rolling in. The minute she stepped out of bed and looked out the window, she knew by the silence that the waterfall had stopped. She got dressed and went downstairs, opening her door as Rooftop Paradise ducked around the back of his van with a blue dive bag slung over his shoulder.

'I've been asked by the state police to drain your pond,' he said, glancing at the porch, not necessarily at Ellen. Despite the way he hunched, he looked enormous in his wet suit, about the size of her door.

'It's almost dry season,' she said. 'If you drain the pond now, they'll leave the liftgates open for the rest of the year, and the pond won't have a chance to fill up again. I'll be hauling water till next April.'

'Not my decision,' he said, hoisting his bag on his shoulder. 'It's a small pipe – take a couple of days to drain. Maybe you got some barrels you want to fill now.'

Ellen sighed. What bothered her more than the thought of hauling water all winter was the way he avoided looking at her. No mention of his recent late-night visit, no acknowledgment that anything unusual had happened between them.

'Rooftop,' she said, feeling slightly ridiculous saying his name, 'do you have any idea where I can find Mo? I've called anyone who might know, but no one's seen her – either that or they're just not telling me.'

For a moment he didn't speak. Then he said, 'Moreen doesn't seem to want me in her life.'

'Then you've seen her—?'

Obviously uncomfortable with the conversation, he started walking toward the farm road.

'Can you at least tell me if she's okay?'

'Just fine, according to her,' he replied, continuing on.

'Please?'

He stopped.

'If you see her again, would you please tell her that it's very important that she call me?'

The giant turned and peered at her through his magnifying lenses. 'I don't mean to sound uncaring, Mrs Chambers,' he said, 'but I'd just as soon rather not have any more to do with this family.'

CHAPTER NINETEEN

The remaining days of the week passed slowly, with a kind of silence that seemed to be fed by the drought that had settled over the northeast. Ellen tried to fill the cavernous void of Maddy's death by staying as busy as she could. Meanwhile, Detective Gallagher came and went, asking endless questions about Randy's death, and detectives in blue lab coats crawled all over the dam and stream bed, Ellen made hay alone, mowing, baling, gathering and stacking the bales into the barn. She weeded her garden and planted fall spinach; she froze peas and broccoli. Without the pond to water her sheep, she had to fill four barrels from the reservoir every other day, but other than that, the animals required little of her time. She wormed them, as she did every summer, and she trimmed their hooves.

When she wasn't busy at home, she searched for Moreen. From various sources she heard various stories: Mo was bumming around Portland, living on the streets in Cambridge, she'd been seen at a punk club in Portsmouth. But the sightings were always second-hand or third-hand. The only thing clear was that Mo seemed to be avoiding her.

At home with Scott, the silence was deadening. When they did speak, words were strange, tones indifferent. He told her that Detective Gallagher came to the gun shop every day, but all they talked about was baseball. Although Ellen and Scott continued sleeping in the same bed, they retired and rose at different times. Scott left in the morning without saying goodbye, and he spent his evenings at Stan's, the local sports bar, rarely returning home before midnight.

She spent her own evenings in her spinning room, her revolver on the floor beside her, working on several small pieces for Wool 'n' Things. On Friday afternoon, when she dropped the tapestries off at the shop, she thought it unusual that Ingrid didn't speak to her while she stood at the cash register, figuring Ellen's commission. Ellen wondered if the silence was just her imagination. Then Ingrid looked up and said, 'Dolores, do you have everything you need?'

Ellen turned and spotted Dolores Packard pretending to shop for natural dyes close to the cash register. Ellen knew the woman was philosophically opposed to any dyes she couldn't find at K-Mart, so why had she been standing there? Mrs Packard approached the register, smiling pleasantly, and paid for the things in her basket while she talked to Ingrid about the gorgeous weather as though she'd never seen Ellen before, although Ellen had taught both her sons in high school. When the woman left the store, Ingrid shook her head in disgust.

'This can be a miserable little town,' she said. Nine years earlier, Ingrid had abandoned a ten-year marriage for a relationship with another woman. Ellen remembered the unofficial boycott of the store, and the way her own consignment work had dropped off as a result. Ingrid punched the cash register and the drawer rang open. She counted out thirty-eight dollars and placed it in Ellen's hand.

'You keep your head up,' she said, keeping her hand on Ellen's. 'Don't let the fuckers wear you down.'

Ellen studied her friend, feeling an abrupt chill of reality, realizing that Neal's careful work was only beginning to bear fruit. When she returned home and found a message from Brian Quinn, asking her to come to his real estate office the following Monday, she began to glimpse the size of the orchard he had sown. Quinn was not only a realtor, he was head of the Destin School Board.

The second she sat down in his office, he got up and closed the door, then returned to his chair. 'I wanted to let you know in advance of official notice,' he told her, 'the Board is going to recommend suspension pending outcome of the police investigation.'

He had obviously spoken to the School Board's lawyer. She had never heard anyone use the word 'pending' in a normal conversation. Not that Quinn was a bad person, in fact he was an old friend of Scott's, notwithstanding his history of flirting with Ellen.

'You will continue to be paid until either you return to the classroom or you're terminated. Although officially we need to wait for the investigation to conclude, I believe I speak for all the board members when I say I feel strongly that it's in the very best interest of the children of this town if you'd tender your resignation at this time.'

She stared at him without emotion. 'On what grounds?'

Quinn hesitated, as if contemplating what to say, but Ellen knew the gesture was rehearsed. 'Ellie, officially speaking, you're a public school teacher who's involved in a criminal investigation. Of course, this is America, and you're innocent until proven guilty.'

He made eye contact for the first time, and she knew what was coming.

'Unofficially, it's the extenuating circumstances.'

She squinted at him, wondering if this was going to be as bad as she suspected. Quinn sighed heavily, and she knew it was. 'You know what a small town this is. Even if the rumors going around are totally without merit—'

She felt a trembling in her gut and stood up, pushing her chair back with such force, it slammed against his computer desk. 'Who have you been talking to?'

'Oh, come on, Ellie. Look, gossip is gossip and it doesn't amount to so much smoke, but that's not the point. You know how much newspapers love a story like this, a school teacher involved in a sex scandal, let alone a death investigation—'

'Tell me who you've been talking to.'

'We both know that you can't begin to function as a teacher without the respect of your students.'

Ellen gave him another searing look, then turned and threw open the door.

Quinn stood up, hands open. 'Ellie, this was not my decision. You know I'd do anything in my power to help you.'

Ellen paused, feeling suddenly lightheaded. All she could think of was Moreen – keeping Moreen from hearing the rumours – but she was afraid it was too late.

'You're a fucking weasel, Brian,' she said in a low voice, and she left his office. She did not slam his door. She simply walked out of the building and across the parking lot, feeling as though she was being watched by every window in the village as she stepped into her rusted white pickup truck. She waited until she had pulled out of the parking lot and was beyond sight of Quinn's windows before she started to cry.

★ ★ ★

The last load of sheep pulled out of the dooryard just as Scott drove in. Through the stakes of the truck Ellen could see her favorite ewe Helga huddled with her lambs. She saw Scott follow the truck with his eyes as he opened his car door. She wondered why he was home early and realized someone must have told him what was going on. As he surveyed the scene over the top of his Mercedes door, his gaze settled on the cardboard boxes stacked in the back of her truck. Ellen's head began humming in anticipation of what she had to say.

'I rented an apartment,' she told him. 'Above Nielsen Ford.'

'Yup,' Scott replied, the sum total of his emotional response.

'I'm going to start working part-time for Ingrid.'

'Hey, you're going to live in a car lot, maybe you can get me a deal.' He closed the car door and leaned back against the fender with his arms folded. She could tell that he'd had a couple of drinks with lunch. He shook his head with a regretful laugh. 'Funny thing is, I thought we'd make the perfect match,' he said, 'now that you're no better than I am anymore.'

Ellen got into her truck, closed the door and gave him one last look out her open window.

'Maybe that's why I'm leaving.'

CHAPTER TWENTY

Gradually, as September came and went, and Ellen grew acclimated to her apartment and job – and Detective Gallagher finally stopped calling with questions – she began to consider the possibility that Maddy may indeed have taken her own life, that the deaths of her mother and Scott's parents had been accidents, that Neal had built their barn and rid them of Randy because of family loyalty, and that his leaving had been out of indignation that she'd mistrusted him, rather than any sinister plan.

Even Ingrid tried to convince her that the stresses of Mo's hysterectomy – and then Randy's drowning and Maddy's suicide – could have triggered paranoia in anyone. Furthermore, that Moreen was an intelligent, independent young woman who had been the real victim of the tragedies – and for the moment, at least, had chosen to sort out her life without help from her mother.

Ellen's apartment was roomy for a single person, with a kitchen, living room, bath and two bedrooms, one of which Ellen used as her spinning room. Her entrance was a covered staircase in the rear of the automobile showroom, where the mechanics parked cars waiting to be serviced. She tried to time her comings and goings when the lot was closed, to avoid the stares of the mechanics and the car dealers.

In the same way, when she returned to the farm to harvest vegetables and put them up for the winter, she always went when Scott was at work. One such morning, the first day of October, Ellen dug the last of her potatoes and wheeled them down the barn's bulkhead and into the root cellar Neal had built. The room was deep and narrow, six by twelve, with rock walls and three wooden bins on the back wall. An insulated steel door, wide enough to accommodate Ellen's wheelbarrow, kept the room dry and constantly cool. Because the root cellar was underground and situated on the side of the barn facing the pump house, Neal had run the new water pipes through the wall just above the center bin, then elbowed the pipes up the wall and along the ceiling, and on through the wall into the cellar of the barn.

The digging and storing took Ellen most of the morning. When she was finished, she lifted the planks off the bulkhead stairs and returned to the root cellar to close the door. That's when she saw the calendar.

Destin Hardware
All Your Hardware Needs

Scott had given out the calendars every December. At first, Ellen thought it was just another sign of Neal's efficiency: hanging a calendar in a root cellar to record harvest dates . . . but Ellen had been in the root cellar several times before today, storing carrots, turnips and early potatoes. Why hadn't she seen the calendar before? Of course Scott might have hung it in the past few days . . . but why? Then she noticed the photo of the man fly-fishing in a river and realized it was last year's calendar. Yet none of the pages had been removed.

She pulled the calendar off the door and turned it under the single ceiling light, becoming increasingly aware of the silence around her. If Neal had hung it, what did it mean? Certainly that he had visited Scott's store long before Moreen's wedding. Ellen started folding back the months, expecting to see some cryptic message, but the pages were all unmarked—

—until she came to October. And there it was: a thick red circle around October 2.

'It's his birthday,' Ellen said, slapping at the calendar. 'It's the anniversary of his father's hanging. It's tomorrow, and he's coming. He told us he's coming.'

The detective leaned his elbows on his municipal gray desk, pressed his folded hands to his spacious mouth in a show of rumination.

'Just playing devil's advocate,' he said, 'let's say you're right about your mother and your in-laws, and let's say Neal Chambers has this thing with twelves. The twelfth anniversary was last year. This will be the thirteenth anniversary.' He shrugged his shoulders. 'Why now?'

'Oh come on.'

'I'm not unconvinced,' he said, turning the calendar toward himself. 'I just like to talk things through. Now, how many of the other deaths in your family occurred on October second?'

Ellen sighed. 'Look, if you're not going to help, just say so.'

Gallagher paused. 'Ellen, you're demanding that we find this man in the next twenty-four hours—'

'Fourteen hours,' she said. 'October second starts in fourteen hours.'

Gallagher sighed, conceding the distinction. 'You're talking about a full-bore search, and right now I'm not armed with enough evidence to convince my lieutenant that such a search is warranted.' He looked up at her with a raised, furrowed brow. 'That is, unless you or your husband know something about your son-in-law's drowning that might incriminate Neal.'

'Great, play games,' Ellen said, flipping her hand by her ear. 'Neal Chambers killed my mother and my in-laws. He killed his own mother. He killed my best friend. He's taken everyone Scott and I love, except our daughter – and I'm trying to tell you she's going to be next.'

'Again,' Gallagher said, 'I don't want to seem disparaging, but we still have nothing concrete – I'm saying concrete – that links Neal Chambers to a single death.'

'Me. They're linked to me.'

The detective leaned way back in his desk chair, his hairy fingers raised off the arms. 'Even if your friend Madeleine was murdered – and in three months of investigation, we haven't found a single thing to support that theory – she died in the middle of July from a bullet wound, not October, not asphyxiation.' He lifted his shoulders and brow simultaneously. 'The fact is, and I say this hoping to give you some peace of mind, none of your friends or relatives has died on October second.' He reached forward and placed his hands on the edge of his desk, as if to tell Ellen that their meeting was through.

Ellen breathed deeply, pretending she hadn't read the gesture. She looked down at the calendar, the bright red circle around October 2. The calendar stared back at her.

'Three months,' she said, giving Gallagher an obvious look.

She swung the calendar toward herself and flipped back three pages, then grabbed a black marker off his desk and marked a thick black X through July 14. 'This is when Maddy was murdered,' she said.

He raised his brow at her, a patronizing look.

She placed the marker on the X and counted six weeks forward, through July and August, then began counting aloud as she rapped the marker against the calendar page, 'Seven, eight, nine, ten, eleven . . .'

Flipping the page, her marker landed with a slap . . . on October sixth. Four days past Neal's red circle. Her shoulders fell.

The detective gave Ellen another look, with as much sympathy as his primitive face could probably muster. 'Close,' he said. 'If your friend's death had been four days earlier' – he flipped the pages back to July, put his finger on the tenth – exactly twelve weeks from Neal's birthday, well, maybe I could do some convincing. But from everything you've told me about your nephew—'

'Neal Chambers is my *husband's* nephew.'

Gallagher gave her a look. 'Do you really think Neal Chambers would be four days off?'

Ellen stared at the date. July 10 was the night that she and Neal first made love, she thought, but she didn't say that.

Gallagher got up from his chair and came around to the front of his desk, where he sat on the corner, somehow managing to squeeze one of his large hands in his pocket. The more casual he tried to act, the more awkward he appeared.

'Ellen, I'm not trying to dismiss your fears,' he said. 'Judging from the evidence we've gathered, there's more than a good chance that Neal knows something about your son-in-law's drowning, as well as the disappearance of the men who loaned money to your husband.'

'Look,' Ellen said. 'I'm here. And I'm warning you. My family is in danger.'

Gallagher slid off his desk and went to the door. 'Let me talk to my lieutenant. Maybe we can arrange to put you folks under surveillance for the next day or two, until you feel the threat has passed.'

Ellen slapped his desk. 'You *cannot* protect my family,' she said. 'Neal Chambers has systematically picked off everyone close to us, and he is not going to stop until he's destroyed us all.'

The detective looked down at the floor and let out a tired, contemplative sigh. Then he looked back at Ellen. 'Would you wait here for a minute,' he said, and he walked out of the small office, closing the door behind him.

Ellen stared down at the ink-stained desk. Like the rust from the window bars that stained the sill, the office had the appearance of having been worked too hard for too long. The only sign of life in the room was the pair of small, framed photos on the heater, one of a gangly, blond-haired boy around ten years old, holding a baseball glove beside his head; the other of a smaller boy holding a fat fish in his hands. The smaller boy had a squat build and the dark, heavy brow of his father. Ellen looked closer and saw a white prosthetic thigh showing under his bathing suit. She wondered how the boy had lost his leg; and she wondered why Gallagher had no photo of the boys' mother.

She looked back at his desk, the calendar. She turned the pages ahead to October again and stared at Neal's red-circled birthday – Tuesday, October 2 – then she counted ahead by Tuesdays, flipping the pages through November and into December . . . her finger stiffening on the twelfth week, the shiver climbing her arms.

'Christmas,' she whispered. The day Scott's parents drove into the river and drowned. Twelve weeks, exactly. She rose from her chair. Hearing Gallagher's voice in the next room, too muffled to distinguish, she pounded the wall with the side of her fist. 'Christmas!' she yelled.

She sat down in Gallagher's chair, snatched the black marker and scratched an X through the date. Then she returned to October 2, and she counted backward twelve days. Now the shiver took her entire body. September 20, the date her mother choked to death. Another X.

When all the twelves are in line. Neal's words dropped into her mind as though he were standing right beside her.

She opened the manilla folder marked CHAMBERS and looked at Gallagher's scribbled notes, until she found the name of Neal's mother, April Chambers, and the date of her death: October 14. Twelve upon twelve upon twelve.

She heard the door open behind her and turned to see Detective Gallagher standing there. Ellen stared up at him, almost afraid to speak. The detective blinked his eyes.

'He's coming for Moreen,' she said.

The small green ranch house had been built in 1955, the last property on a dead-end lane that was surrounded by boarded-up summer cottages and separated from the rest of the neighborhood by about five acres of wooded marsh land. The home's owner, a widow who wintered in Florida, left her house vacant nine months of the year, with shades drawn and a timer set to turn lights on at dusk and off again at dawn, to convince prowlers that someone was home.

In fact, someone was. Inside the steam-filled bathroom, Moreen sat naked on the toilet with her eyes closed, emptying her bladder and beating on the sink, singing, 'Oh-ay-oh-ay-oh,' while water poured into the bathtub and the Automatics wailed in her ears:

They're just wasting away,
Hanging out at EJ's,
Living their life day by day by day,
Hoping everything will be okay.
Oh-ay-oh-ay-oh,
Oh-ay-oh-ay-oh.

When the door opened, Moreen kept singing at first – until she saw who it was. Then she threw her Walkman at the door. 'Why are you here?'

A policeman pulled Ellen out of the doorway. 'Cover up,' he told Moreen, averting his eyes. 'You're coming with us.'

When Moreen was dressed, they hustled her into the living room, where her friends – three guys and her friend Keirsted – sat lined up on the couch. Another cop was telling them they were free to get out of town and stay out. Then they were herded outside, where Rooftop Paradise waited, slouched in the dark against the side of his panel truck.

Seeing him, Moreen screamed, 'Bear, what are you doing to me?'

The officer hustled her toward the patrol car and seated her inside.

'Don't hurt her,' Ellen said, getting in beside her daughter.

'Do you actually think you're helping me?' Moreen demanded, with a searing glare.

Ellen closed the door, and they drove quickly away.

By midnight, everyone was protected. Down in the car lot that surrounded Ellen's apartment, two pairs of men kept watch from inside smoked-glass vans that were parked strategically among the cars for sale. Motion sensors had been set up around the perimeter of the lot. Inside the showroom, where security lights routinely burned through the night, nothing stirred. But two men waited behind the counter and another pair sat quietly inside the dark garage. Upstairs, in the kitchen of Ellen's apartment, an officer sat in the dimly lit living room, peeking out the window; another sat in the kitchen, doing the same.

It was Neal Chambers' twenty-fifth birthday, the thirteenth anniversary of his mother's infidelity, his father's suicide. For the next twenty-four hours, the decoys and guards would remain in place, while Moreen and Ellen shared the holding cell in the York Beach Police Station, and Scott stayed in a sixth floor Holiday Inn suite in Portsmouth.

Scott made the most of the situation, playing nickel-dime poker with the cops and eating room-service steaks. While the cops drank coffee, Scott drank highballs until the whiskey was gone, then he went to bed and slept until eleven, at which point he had a huge breakfast sent up, along with another bottle of Crown Royal. Although there was almost no chance that Neal would know Scott was here, let alone infiltrate the security, Detective Gallagher was taking no chances. Outside of the lieutenant and the officers assigned to the detail, nobody knew about the operation, neither the officers' families nor the local police departments.

Internment in the York Beach holding cell was not so pleasant. Ellen and Moreen were locked together in the windowless, cinder-block room, with a twelve-inch television sitting on a wooden chair and an armed woman stationed just outside their door, while another policeman guarded the corridor. Police had instructions that no one arrested in the next twenty-four hours was to be brought to the station but taken straight to the county jail in Alfred or else released. Drunk drivers and casual drug users were to be driven home; dealers, burglars and wife abusers handed over to the State Police.

Everything in the cell was painted light green, from the cinder-block walls and iron bars to the small wooden table and chair, even the iron legs of the two cots. For the first two hours in the cell, Moreen refused to speak. She stalked the floor of the tiny room, drinking cup after cup of black coffee, while Ellen lay under the covers in her jeans and jersey, trying to read a *People* magazine under a borrowed desk lamp, wondering if the words existed by which she could ever begin to make amends with her daughter. With Moreen pacing, Ellen knew enough not to try.

'I can't believe you did this,' Moreen said, finally.

'It was the only way to protect you,' Ellen replied.

'As if I ever needed your protection.'

'Hey!' the policewoman yelled in. 'You start showing your mother some respect, young lady, or I'm liable to come in there and kick your ass.'

'Great,' Moreen muttered, and she paced for another five minutes, then finally shut off Ellen's lamp and got into bed.

The farmhouse was the most heavily guarded site, not only because of the number of ways in, but because of the likelihood that Neal would strike here. Pairs of armed personnel were stationed in the pantry of the house and in the barn's hayloft. Detective Gallagher sat at the top of the stairs with his police radio turned on, keeping an eye on Scott's and Moreen's bedrooms, inside which lay decoys under the covers, each armed with a five-shot .38 Special, in the unlikely event that Neal Chambers might somehow materialize in the room.

At the bottom of the pasture and across the stream, up through the woods at the beginning of a fire access road, two other detectives sat in the back of an unmarked panel truck, their radio left open between the farmhouse, the car lot, the York Beach Police Station and Detective Gallagher at the farmhouse, so all parties could hear each other's conversations. One of the detectives in the van wore headphones. The other sat in a low-slung beach chair eating a tuna sandwich and listening to the perking of the 12-volt coffee pot he'd brought along.

Neither of them heard the shifting of rock dust or saw the black figure stalking their vehicle. In fact, the detective wearing the headphones was just beginning to nod off, and the one eating the sandwich was just pouring coffee into his thermos cup when the light burst through the window.

The man dropped the cup and coffee pot and dived behind the seat, pulling his piece from his shoulder holster in the same move.

'Freeze right there!' the attacker shouted outside the van.

The sleeper, pinned by the light beam, raised his hands in front of his eyes, half in surrender, half in an attempt to block the light or gunshot, whichever came first. But instead of the gunshot, he heard a voice.

'Hold on, you fellas on the job?'

'No, we're rabbit hunters,' said the man with the headphones. 'Who the hell are you?'

In the distance, a siren sang a winding solo.

'Identify yourself,' said the cop behind the seat, 'or I'm gonna shoot right through that fucking light!'

'Whoa! I'm on the job too.'

The inside of the truck darkened as, outside, the flashlight beam lit up a silver shield. 'Destin Police,' Sugar Westerback said. 'I've got the farmhouse under surveillance.'

The man with the headphones reached for the radio, pressed a switch. 'It's okay,' he said into the mike. 'Some local cowboy action.'

'Excuse me?' Sugar said.

'You want to come around to the back,' the detective replied. 'I've got someone on the radio who'd love to speak to you.'

In the York Beach holding cell, Moreen slept until four in the afternoon, while Ellen lay on her cot reading a worn copy of *To Kill a Mockingbird* that the dispatcher's son had left in her car.

When Moreen woke up, the recriminations started all over again.

'Mo, I explained it to you,' Ellen said, handing her a Styrofoam cup of coffee. 'Tomorrow morning we can leave, but until Neal is in custody, you're not safe.'

Moreen looked up at her, meeting her eyes, giving her a smile that was a combination of helplessness and abject curiosity. 'Do you actually think I feel safe with you?' she said. Then she vomited.

Ellen dropped her book.

The guard came to the door.

'Where did you get the coffee?' Ellen asked.

'Right here,' the woman answered. 'I opened a can and made it myself.'

'Call a doctor, please.'

'I don't need a doctor,' Moreen said dizzily. 'I need to leave.' Then she vomited again.

'It's the same coffee you've been drinking,' the guard said. 'We've been drinking it all day. I feel fine. You're all right.'

'Get a doctor!'

Fifteen minutes later a young man came into the cell and took Moreen's temperature and pulse and looked in her eyes, ears and throat. He told Ellen she'd come down with a stomach virus.

'Is something going around?' Ellen asked.

The doctor smiled as he packed his bag. 'Looks like it will be.'

Six hours later and six hundred miles down the coast, in Virginia Beach, a handsome woman was opening her front door.

The black-bearded young man in a red chef's hat smiled. 'Medium combo,' he said, opening the lid of the flat box and displaying his creation. The smell wafted through the screen door.

The woman looked past him at the van parked on the curb. 'I'm afraid you might have the wrong address,' she said apologetically.

The delivery man looked at the slip of paper in his hand. 'Four-sixteen Shore Road?'

'That's our address,' the woman said, perplexed. 'Drew, you didn't order a pizza, did you?'

Her husband, a fit, white-haired man of sixty-two, came up behind her. 'Not me.'

The pizza man eyed the husband curiously.

'Care to use the phone?' the husband said. He was dressed in a blue sweat suit.

'Wouldn't do much good,' the delivery man answered. 'I own the business, and I'm on my way home. You were my last stop.' He gave the husband another protracted scowl, then said, 'Excuse me, but aren't you' – he snapped his fingers – 'I'm terrible with history.'

The woman smiled. 'Oh, boy, you just made his day.'

'The astronaut, right?'

'Drew McDermott,' the man said, folding his arms.

'Drew McDermott, unbelievable.' He gazed through the screen, admiring the older man. Then he said, 'Hey,' and held the box up to the door. 'I'm only gonna throw it away when I get home.'

The woman turned to her husband. 'Want to go off your diet?'

The astronaut rocked his head, deliberating. 'It smells great,' he admitted. 'Okay, let me get my wallet.'

'Don't move a muscle,' the pizza man said, opening the door. 'You sign your autograph on my slip, and we'll call it even.'

While the astronaut and his wife spent the next fifteen minutes – the last of their lives – jerking and gasping and crying for breath on their living room carpet, Moreen lay hunched on her cot shivering and moaning, while Ellen sat beside her all night in the dark, listening intently to her every breath and covering her whenever she kicked her blankets off.

At seven thirty in the morning, Ellen turned on the television, keeping the sound down to keep from waking Mo. The first image she saw was a cartoon man lying prostrate, panting like a dog, while a voice-over explained how cyanide poisoning prevents the oxygen in a person's lungs from bonding with his blood. The image cut to the network's medical expert, who had been providing the voice-over.

'And so,' he continued grimly, 'while the victim can respire up to two hundred-fifty times a minute – and this can take fifteen minutes or more of pure agony – he slowly suffocates.'

Cut to the show's somber host, who thanked the man.

Dissolve to an image of earth as seen from space, then a face superimposed. A name. A date.

'But you're not even sure he was your father,' the detective said, his eyes glassy from sleeplessness, his face black with whiskers.

'It doesn't matter. Neal Chambers believed he was my father. And he died, *he suffocated*, on October second.'

'I want to go,' Moreen said bitterly, sitting on the edge of her cot with her backpack in her lap and her long hair hanging over her face. Gallagher held up his hand, quieting her.

'Neal Chambers was arrested in Virginia Beach when he was fifteen years old,' Ellen told him. 'The police caught him looking in someone's window. Call them, check the records – see whose house it was.'

'You can't keep me here,' Moreen told them, sounding terminally bored.

'Mo, please,' Ellen said, then addressed Gallagher again. 'Call Walpole State Prison, in Massachusetts. There's an inmate there named Michael Landry.'

The detective gave her a questioning frown.

'He's the other man who might be my father,' she explained.

Moreen sighed heavily and flopped back on the mattress. Gallagher held up his hand again, which was possibly his way of letting Ellen know he was not patronizing.

'Believe me,' he told her, 'it's only a matter of time before Neal Chambers ends up in an interrogation room with me. We've added his name to a long list of people wanted for questioning, and every major police department in North America has his profile. However' – the detective moved a bit closer to Ellen's cot – 'as I explained to you, "Wanted for questioning" doesn't carry the same weight as "Wanted for murder".' He shrugged his heavy shoulders. 'So until somebody comes forward with something incriminating, "wanted for questioning" is about as much as we can do. That is, unless you or your husband has thought of anything about your son-in-law's drowning that may have slipped your minds—?'

Ellen heard a squawk from the springs of Moreen's cot. She glared at Gallagher in disbelief. He stared back, with absolute deadness in his eyes.

'No?'

She continued to glare. He reached back for the door.

'I'll be right back,' he said. 'I'm going to check on that prison for you.' He turned and left the cell.

When he closed the door behind him, the silence that remained was suffocating. Ellen sat perfectly still, keeping her eyes on the door as she listened to Moreen's breathing. They remained like that for what seemed to Ellen like several minutes. Finally Moreen sniffed – or she laughed. Ellen turned, saw her lying on the cot, staring at the ceiling, her eyes tearing, her mouth curved in a sort of smile.

'Hon, it's because I went to the police about Randy, that's all. They'd have to wonder about something like that. It's their job.'

Moreen closed her eyes.

Another minute crawled by in tortured silence, until they heard the sound of footsteps outside the door, then the hollow clatter of the lock as the door opened, then shut again. Moreen sat up on the edge of the bed. Gallagher came in. Moreen got up, threw her backpack over her shoulder.

'Michael Landry died a year ago in prison,' the detective announced. 'He was in the weight room, and his barbell fell on his windpipe. The prison physician's report called his death accidental.'

Ellen kept her eyes on the green bars. 'What date?'

'A year ago last night.'

'October second,' Ellen said, fixing her glare at him. 'Is Neal wanted for murder now?'

'I think we can bump the search up a level.'

Moreen walked to the barred door, tried opening it.

Gallagher eyed Moreen for a moment, then he turned back to Ellen.

'Ellen, we're going to find your nephew,' he said with complete assuredness. 'Until we do, we'll have people watching your family at all times.'

'You mean you'll use us as decoys.'

He gave her a stern look. 'If you'd rather, we can relocate the three of you to another state until your nephew's in custody.'

'We have lives,' Ellen asked, keeping her eye on Moreen. 'How long?'

Gallagher shook his head. 'You know I can't answer that. If you choose to remain in town, we'll give you as much privacy as possible. But you can be assured we'll be protecting all of you.'

'Please unlock this,' Moreen said.

'Moreen, you can go home with your mother, or you can go with your father,' Gallagher said. 'Your choice.'

Moreen glared at the wall outside the cell, her eyes sunken and dark. 'I'm eighteen,' she said.

'She's seventeen,' Ellen said.

'Don't you fucking speak for me.'

Gallagher tried to make eye contact. 'Moreen, we can keep you in protective custody until your cousin is apprehended. Is that what you want?'

'Fine.' She slung her pack over her other shoulder and waited.

'Which?'

'Either.'

Gallagher looked at Ellen. 'Do you want her?'

Ellen glared at him. 'Are you ignorant or just totally insensitive? You just insinuated that my husband and I had something to do with the death of her husband. Of course I want her! Do you think she's going to stay with either of us?'

Gallagher studied Ellen for a moment. He turned to Moreen, who stood at the door, looking at the ceiling. When the detective stepped up beside her, they were the same height.

'Moreen, are you going to stay with your mother?'

'Yes,' Moreen said, staring through the bars.

'This isn't the time to be difficult, young lady,' he said. 'Until we find your cousin, we need to know where you're going to be at all times, or we'll lock you up for your own protection. Do you understand me?'

'I understand you.'

He studied her for another long moment, then gave Ellen a look.

'If she runs off, give a call, and we'll grab her up.'

Ellen looked away.

'Door, please,' Gallagher said, and the policewoman came with the key.

Ellen drove inland, towards Destin, with her daughter beside her and an unmarked car following a hundred feet behind. Afraid that Moreen would bolt the first chance she got, Ellen drove through stop signs and took a roundabout, wooded route to her apartment, trying to buy time, though she knew how pointless these maneuvers were.

'Mo, please, I know you're angry at me—'

'I'm not angry.'

'Honey, just tell me you understand the danger.'

'I understand. I just feel shitty.'

'Are you getting your period?'

Moreen slouched in the seat, shivering and pale.

'Do you want to stop somewhere for breakfast?'

Moreen lurched up. 'Pull over,' she gasped, holding her mouth.

Ellen kept her foot on the accelerator.

'*Pull over!*' Moreen cried, grabbing the steering wheel as she spread her legs and gagged painfully, as if she were going to throw up on the floor.

Ellen hit the brake.

Mo gagged again.

'Please don't do this, Mo.'

But Ellen stopped the truck on the shoulder, and when Moreen opened the door, she grabbed her backpack that lay between them. Ellen caught the strap of the backpack and held tight as she popped the clutch, hit the gas. The truck shot forward, and Moreen let go of the pack, tumbling out of the truck.

'Mo!' Ellen cried, stomping the brake. She turned and saw her daughter pick herself off the roadside and stagger back to the door, gazing at Ellen with a glassy smile and blood running from her nose. Behind them the gray sedan came up fast. While Ellen watched, paralyzed, Moreen reached in the open door and seized her pack.

'Love you,' she said, then ran down the embankment into the woods.

Ellen jumped from the truck. 'Moreen, don't!' she cried, but her daughter was already being swallowed by the foliage.

The gray sedan chirped to a stop. Both men jumped out. One ran to Ellen, the other took off after Moreen.

'Don't chase her!' Ellen yelled, knowing it was futile to bring her back. She also knew that they'd never find her. She prayed that Neal wouldn't, either.

CHAPTER TWENTY-ONE

Ellen returned to her life alone, though she felt like she lived in a bell jar. For the first week, every time she passed a window she was aware of binoculars on her, men in vans with smoked windows, detectives pretending to be car salesmen. When she drove to work, cars pulled out of side streets behind her. Men followed her into the pharmacy when she bought sanitary pads, they followed her around the supermarket. Even the Westerbacks, although they'd been officially barred from the case, drove past Wool 'n' Things several times a day when Ellen was working and through the car lot repeatedly while she was home.

Slowly, as the days turned to weeks and the nights grew long and cold, with no sign of Moreen, no sign of Neal, Ellen found herself getting used to living her life on the brink of disaster. Although she knew without doubt that the day would come, that one fiery moment when all their lives would finally be ripped apart – and she always kept her revolver close at hand – eventually she was able to shut the lights off when she went to bed.

As intrusive as the surveillance might have felt, the scrutiny from townspeople was far worse – the cautious glances of the customers who came into the store, the awkward, truncated conversations with old friends and ex-coworkers. In fact, Ingrid remarked one afternoon that she'd never seen such a busy fall.

'You probably never offered a sideshow,' Ellen replied.

On November fifteenth, Detective Gallagher called to tell Ellen what she already suspected. Although the search for Neal had been given top priority all over the country, the surveillance team protecting her and Scott would have to be scaled back slightly. He went on to explain that they would bolster security on certain 'target dates', such as Christmas, but otherwise they'd begin coordinating with the county sheriff's department.

'Are you giving up on Moreen too?' Ellen asked.

'We're not giving up on any of you,' Gallagher answered. 'Fact is, we've talked to a couple of people in Portsmouth who heard she was in the Boston area recently, and we have people there as we speak, following up.'

'What if Neal's already found her?'

The detective shook his head. 'We're doing all we can.'

The next day, three inches of snow fell. Two days later a cold, two-day rain dissolved the snow and heralded in a stretch of thirty-degree, sunless days that left little doubt that a long, gray winter was on its way. A week before Thanksgiving Ingrid began playing Christmas music in the store and staying open till nine. Ellen was glad for the extra hours, not only because she needed the money, but because working kept her away from her empty apartment. She also found comfort in Ingrid's company.

'My first Thanksgiving alone wasn't exactly a picnic,' the older woman said one night.

'I haven't thought much about it,' Ellen answered, as she finished a piece on the tapestry loom, though she knew it was glaringly apparent that she was dreading the holiday.

'Some friends and I get together every year,' Ingrid told her. 'We eat like pigs and drink like fish, and we're all very thankful for the opportunity. Why don't you come with me?'

Ellen smiled as she snugged the shed rod down. 'Thanks. But I don't think I'd be much fun.'

A moment of silence followed, after which Ingrid asked, in a kind way, 'Ellie, why do you stay in Destin?'

Ellen kept working, though she lost her smile. Not that she minded Ingrid's prodding. Indeed, she felt a kinship with the woman, who reminded her of her mother in the way she prized her independence. Unlike her mother, however, Ingrid was also practical and present and strong.

'Where am I supposed to go?' Ellen replied.

'It's your map,' Ingrid answered simply, then went on with her work.

At five thirty the next morning, when only the milk trucks and bread trucks were out, the blue Taurus wobbled down the back streets of Hampton Beach, then pulled into an alley beside a darkened tenement building. In a minute the driver emerged from the alley wearing an oversized black sweatshirt, her face hidden deep inside its hood. She turned the corner onto a deserted boulevard of boarded-up T-shirt and pizza shops.

There were no other cars, no people, no sounds except for the murmur of ocean waves breaking in the distance. Half a block down the street, she came to a door that opened on a narrow set of stairs. She looked behind her, then rang the bell. In a minute a man came down and let her in. He was startlingly thin and wore a rust-colored terrycloth bathrobe that was comically large. Celtic designs were crudely tattooed all over his arms, from his wrists up. Moreen didn't know his age. Some days he looked fifty, some days older. This morning he seemed to have developed some kind of twitch in his eye.

'Come on up,' he said, 'you're gonna love this stuff, which is why I got in touch with you, I mean you're really gonna dig it.'

He was called Speedo not because he took amphetamines – in fact he was a heroin addict – but because he talked so fast, which was usually a sign that he hadn't fixed in too long. Moreen followed him up the stairs, into his apartment. Empty Pepsi cans were strewn everywhere, candy bar wrappers, chewing gum wrappers. A box of Sugar Smacks sat on the table, beside a small white candle that smelled of vanilla.

'Same weight, is that what you want, same weight?' Speedo asked.

'Yeah,' Moreen answered.

He turned his back on her, undid his bathrobe tie and reached into his money belt, pulled out a small plastic bag with a quarter-inch of cream-colored powder in the bottom.

Moreen reached in her jeans pocket, came out with her money.

Speedo sat down at the table. 'Got time for a little sample? On me, I'm not gonna charge you, I want to see the look on your face, you know what I mean? That's my enjoyment.'

Moreen said, 'Whatever.'

He grinned at her with discolored teeth, then stuffed his thin hand down inside the Sugar Smacks box and came out with his works, along with a short length of brown rubber tubing.

Moreen looked around the kitchen. 'Got a bathroom?'

Speedo stared at her, his nose twitching.

'I don't want to wet my pants when I get off,' she told him.

'Yeah, yeah, it's that good – you don't want to wet your pants.' He laughed, rat-a-tat-tat. 'Through that door, first room on the left, she don't wanna wet her pants, I like that.'

Moreen went into the bathroom and urinated, and when she came out again, the syringe lay on the table, all ready. Speedo rattled an empty cellophane packet in his hand.

'I only use brand new, disposable, you know, medical supply, quality control – which is why Randy always came to me. He knew I could be trusted, know what I'm saying? Why take chances?'

He kicked the chair back for her. 'Go 'head, tie off and I'll do you, I already did myself before, just a little before you came, I'll probably do some more later, but first I wanna see the look on your face, go on, tie off.'

Moreen pulled her sweatshirt over her head and dropped it on the floor, then sat in the chair. She unbuttoned her flannel shirt and pulled her arm out. Underneath, she wore a black T-shirt. She picked up the tubing and tied it around her right arm, pulled the end tight with her teeth as she made a fist, flexed it and squeezed, then watched the hungry veins rise to the surface, big and dark. Her eyes watered while Speedo studied the road map with his finger.

'Like I said, this is top-shelf, only the best, only the best,' he said, tapping the vein and watching it swell even more. He held her wrist with his free hand, but he never looked at her face when he sank the needle in. Didn't look at her when he pulled her blood into the solution or pushed it back into her bloodstream. He did peek, however, when she unlooped the tubing and the drug rushed into her brain.

At first, her head went slowly back, a lazy smile taking her lips. In the next instant she met his eyes with her own, stark and protesting. Before Speedo could slide the syringe out of her arm, she tried to stand, but her chair kicked out from under her. Attempting to catch her in his arms, Speedo ended up falling to his knees with her head in his lap.

'Okay, man, I don't need this,' he said, pushing up on her shoulder, searching down her arm for his works. He ran his hand under her back. 'You said you weren't a cop,' he said quietly, though he was not speaking to Moreen. 'And once you say that, I have immunity from prosecution under the Constitution, that's in the Bill of Rights, check it out, man.'

He found the syringe under his own leg and examined it, grateful that the needle hadn't broken off in her arm. He turned Moreen's face toward him.

'I don't know what you had me give her, but she's under, man. I mean you could fuck her six ways to Sunday and she'd never know what hit her.'

He heard the young man's footsteps move out of the darkened hall and into the kitchen. He glanced back over his shoulder.

'Like I said, I don't know what your deal is, but if you're looking for that money . . . I *heard* there was money missing, I *heard* about Ray LaFlamme's money, I mean, Randy and I discussed a certain sum of money which I later assumed to be Mister LaFlamme's, I'm not saying we didn't discuss a sum of money, I just didn't ask where it came from at the time. It's not my business. I'm not the IRS, you know? Just a small businessman. Randy came to me lookin to score big, but I don't keep that kind of weight on hand, then the next thing I knew, he's history, and then LaFlamme's history . . . So they say.'

The stranger slid a wooden chair over behind Speedo. 'Sit down,' he said.

'It's none of my business, like I told you, I don't know nothin about nothin, but if you want my opinion, this girl doesn't have that money, either, just my impression, my general overall impression based on lifestyle, etcetera, etcetera.'

'Sit.'

Speedo did as he was told.

'Not to be uncoöperative but, I mean, but what are we doing here?'

The stranger stripped a length of duct tape from a roll. 'Give me your leg.'

'Okay, this is totally unnecessary,' Speedo objected, starting to stand, but the stranger flashed him a quick, dark look.

'I don't want to be followed,' he said. 'Leg.'

Something in his voice told Speedo that the next few minutes of his life would go a lot easier if he didn't argue. So he sat back down and watched while the stranger bound one leg, then the other, to the front legs of the chair.

'Oh, yeah, like I want any more to do with this happy horseshit, which I know nothin about,' Speedo grumbled.

When the stranger finished with Speedo's legs, he said, 'Hands behind you.'

'Follow you for what? To each his own, that's my golden rule.'

'Put your hands behind you.'

'Seriously, do I look a hero to you?'

'Hands.'

'Fuck.' Speedo took a big breath, wrapped his arms behind the chair.

'Lean forward,' the stranger said, and Speedo complied, immediately feeling the tape securing his skinny arm to the wooden stile, after winding around his forearm, wrist and hand.

'There's such a thing as overdoing it,' Speedo complained, as his other arm was bound. 'You know? I'd like to get up sometime this year—'

His voice was cut off as the stranger reached over his head and stuck a length of tape over his mouth. Speedo grunted an objection when the tape wound around the back of his head and over his mouth again. And he objected strenuously when the third winding covered his nose. In fact he threw his head back, as if to shake the duct tape free, and he made a loud sound in his throat, but the stranger grabbed his hair and went once more around, this time sealing his nose completely.

Then the stranger stepped back and watched.

Speedo stared up in wild indignation. His chair jumped off the floor and fell on its side with a crash. He flipped the chair onto its front and began knocking his forehead off the floor, like someone hammering. He polished the linoleum with his knees, with his shoulder and with his cheek, trying to peel the duct tape away, while the noises from his throat began sounding like the cries of a far-off whale. When he rolled the chair onto its back, his eyes were huge, sprouting tiny veins. His chest and stomach heaved rapidly. Suddenly his eyes closed in a tight grimace, and his chair began rapping at the floor like a jackhammer. When the convulsions stopped, Speedo's eyes opened again, cherry red. That's the way they stayed.

'Come on, I haven't been drunk in years,' Ingrid said, counting the money in her cash register drawer. 'What the hell, we're halfway there now. I'll call a taxi, we'll get chauffeured.'

It was five minutes to five, the day before Thanksgiving, and they were closing early. For lunch, Ingrid had surprised Ellen with a turkey dinner and a bottle of Chardonnay, which they'd shared while they worked.

'Actually, I was looking forward to going home and taking a long, hot bath,' Ellen answered, as she lowered the quilted shade on the storefront window. In fact, she was picturing the telephone, not the tub, and wondering if Ingrid had any idea how much she was hoping Moreen or Scott would call.

She opened the door to the small back room, went in and turned off the cassette player, turned off the coffee maker and brought the coffee pot into the bathroom to wash it out.

'I talked to Priscilla Clancy last night,' Ingrid called. 'Remember her, from the Guild? She moved out to Oregon.'

Ellen flushed the toilet, then turned off the bathroom light. She could hear the wind outside, whipping the dead leaves up against the back door. She checked the back door, to make sure it was locked, then took her jean jacket off the coat rack and walked back into the store.

'Priscilla's in wine country,' Ingrid said, 'raising llamas and sheep – prize Rambouillets. She said she's got too much farm and too much house to manage alone.'

Ellen smiled. 'Not that there's any particular point in telling me this.'

Ingrid shrugged, while she wrote in her accounting book. 'I figured I'd give you something to think about so you're not sitting by the phone for the next two days.'

Ellen laughed a little. Being around Ingrid gave her hope that she might be happy again someday, although on days like this it wasn't always easy to believe.

As if on cue, the telephone rang. Both women looked over at it, as though Ingrid had somehow willed it to happen.

'Can you get it?' the older woman asked, pretending she couldn't be interrupted. But Ellen knew they were both thinking the same thing. She went to the phone casually and let it ring a third time, so as not to seem anxious. Ingrid looked up at her. Ellen picked up. The phone beeped at her.

'Fax,' she said, and pressed the START button. The paper curled out of the back of the machine. Not that it would be unlike Scott to fax her a dinner invitation. Avoid the chance of rejection. The machine beeped off, then cut the paper.

'If it's not obscene, we don't want it,' Ingrid said.

Ellen pulled the paper from the tray, turned it over, saw the dark photo centered on the page. She pulled the paper out and turned it right-side-up. She stared.

'What is it?' Ingrid said.

The ransom is you.

Ellen's legs weakened. She backed against the wall. In the photo, Moreen was sitting on a wooden floor with a blanket wrapped around her shoulders, her eyes downcast.

'Ellie, what?' Although Ingrid was coming closer, her voice sounded miles away.

Pay phone at Gethsemane, 12 minutes. Do not betray me.

Ellen crumpled the paper in her hand, stuffed it in her pocket.

'It's him, isn't it?' Ingrid whispered, coming toward the phone with a fan of dollars crushed in her hand. 'Ellie, call the police.'

'Don't.' Ellen's unfocused scowl stopped the older woman. She bunched her jacket in her hand, felt for her keys in the pocket. 'It's nothing,' she said, wondering if Neal was watching her right now. 'I'm going home, and you're closing the store.'

'*What's going on?*'

'Please. Smile and say goodbye,' Ellen said, heading for the front door. 'Keep cleaning up. I'll call you in an hour.'

'I'm smiling,' Ingrid said, following her. 'But your truck's out back. Ellie, just tell me where you're going.'

'I'll call you,' Ellen told her, throwing the door open and walking off into the darkness.

Ingrid locked the door, then stood there, vibrating. She watched Ellen walk across the parking lot of the plaza toward the pharmacy, illuminated briefly by a car's headlights. Then Ingrid turned and went back to her telephone. She did not lift the receiver, but she angled her trifocals to read the buttons on the front panel, then pushed the one that said FAX MEMORY. Immediately she heard the paper roller shift into gear.

The ransom is you.

Sugar Westerback had just stepped out of his new shower when the 911 call came through. 'Hold on, wait,' he said. 'What pay phone?'

'The only one in the plaza,' Ingrid told him. 'Outside the drug store.'

'Okay. He's calling her when?'

'Ten minutes. But no one's supposed to know.'

'Right.' Sugar stared at his naked reflection in the window, wondering if he should call his father at the Lobster Palace.

'What about the FBI or the state police, shouldn't we notify them?' Ingrid said. 'She's in danger. Her daughter's in danger.'

'I'll take it from here,' Sugar told her. 'You stay put. If you hear anything else, call me on my car phone.'

He gave her the number, then hung up and called Stan's Sports Tavern and asked to speak to Chuck Lyon. Chuck was the right fielder on Sugar's softball team. He was also a cable splicer for the phone company.

'I need a favor quick,' Sugar told him, and explained what he wanted.

'You got a warrant?' Chuck said. 'You need a warrant.'

'You got a driver's license?' Sugar shot back. 'You and I both know I could take that license from you any night of the week, and I will. Now get your ass in gear!'

He hung up and got dressed as fast as he could, finished with a bulletproof vest, then strapped on his shoulder holster, his Desert Eagle .357 magnum. He folded down the visor of his Patriots cap, then walked out to his Bronco, where he dialed the number Chuck had given him. While he waited for his friend to answer, he pulled the Bronco to the head of the driveway, facing the road. The phone kept ringing. He drummed on the steering wheel until he heard it pick up.

'Sugar?' Chuck asked, sounding out of breath.

'Ten-two.'

'Hold on, they're already connected. I'm gonna patch us in. What's that motor noise?'

'My vehicle.'

'Shut it off. Keep quiet.'

Sugar turned the key. In the phone he heard a click, then silence. Then Ellen's voice: 'Neal, please tell me.'

There was a pause.

'Ellen, is anyone else on the line?'

Sugar recognized the male voice as Neal's. He felt his heart accelerate. He looked down the dark country road, first left, then right, all the bare branches clicking at the clouds.

'Just tell me what you did to her,' Ellen persisted, although she sounded timid, as if she were afraid to hear his answer.

'What *I* did?' Neal replied calmly. 'Moreen sold a brand new Jeep. A month later she's living on the street. Her arms are bruised, her friends are junkies, and her husband was a dealer. What *I* did? I may have saved her life. But that's up to you.'

'*Don't play games with me, Neal. Where is she?*'

'Somewhere she can't stick a needle in her arm. I left her enough blankets to keep from freezing and a couple days' supply of food and water so she won't starve.'

'It's Scott you want to hurt,' Ellen told him. 'Scott and me. Not Moreen.'

' "Shall I give my firstborn for my transgression, the fruit of my body for the sin of my soul?" ' Neal recited, his voice radiating a warmth that sent a chill down Sugar's back. 'Ellen, you know I don't want to hurt Moreen. All I want is a chance to see you one last time, so I can ask your forgiveness.'

'I forgive you,' Ellen said icily.

'See me,' Neal told her. 'Grant me your forgiveness, and I'll return Moreen to you and be out of your lives forever.'

The silence on the line bristled.

'Will you deny me three times?' came Neal's voice.

Sugar squeezed the steering wheel, his forearms pumped and ready.

'Where?' Ellen demanded.

'Scott won't be home for another hour or two.'

'I'm not meeting you in the house.'

'Of course not. The barn is far more appropriate.'

Silence.

'When?'

'If you don't mind my overworking a theme—'

'*When?*'

'Twelve minutes.'

'Don't hurt Moreen, Neal. You know she doesn't deserve it. I'll get there as fast as I can.'

'Alone.'

'I won't tell anyone. Please, Neal.'

Sugar heard the click of the phones disconnecting.

'Still there?' Chuck croaked.

'Ten-four.'

'I recorded the conversation for you,' Chuck told him. 'Maybe it'll help you find the girl. You can't use it for evidence, though, or I'm screwed. So are you. Okay?'

Sugar started the Bronco and swung out on the blacktop, pounding through the gears, racing toward the River Road, less than a mile away. 'Chuck, where'd he call from?' he said, switching the phone to SPEAKER.

'Hold it, I'm in the database now.'

'Just tell me where he called from.' Sugar's headlights illuminated the back of a jogger on the road, dressed in red. Bad night to be running, he thought, with a storm coming in. Way too dark.

'Tell you one thing, your guy wasn't too bright staying on the line so long,' Chuck said.

'Oh, he's plenty bright enough,' Sugar replied. 'But he's definitely a donut shy of a dozen.'

Suddenly the jogger stopped running and turned slowly into the Bronco's headlights. Sugar eased up on the accelerator and peered through the windshield until the face came into focus . . . Theresa Arnold, he had dated her in high school. As he pressed the gas pedal and blew past her, he thought maybe he'd give her a call this weekend, see what she was up to.

'Got it,' Chuck said. 'Cell phone.'

'Just my luck,' Sugar said, downshifting to second and swerving onto River Road with a long fanfare of burning rubber.

Approaching the top of the hill, he punched off his headlights and rolled to a stop overlooking the farm. 'Well, well,' Sugar said quietly, peering down at the light coming from the arched hayloft window. He turned off the engine. 'Looks like you got company, kid.'

'Hey, Champ, you want me to call the staties?'

'Negative,' Sugar answered. 'Big-hats'll screw things up. Just give me two or three minutes, then page my dad with my 10-20.'

'Now English.'

'My location. Just tell him "Code thirty-three". You don't have to understand shit, okay? Dad'll know what to do.'

Then Sugar was out the door, darting downhill from tree to tree, his big Desert Eagle tight in his hand. When the trees gave way to open hayfield, he kept his body low and ran as hard as he could. The rising wind helped cover his uneven footfalls.

Vaulting across the farm road, Sugar pulled up behind the pump house and drew his pistol. His chest heaved, his heart pounded.

Steam huffed from his mouth into the raw November night, as he assessed the situation. The light in the barn was the kid's second mistake. The phone call was definitely his first. Raising the pistol beside his ear, Sugar peeked around the side. He scanned the twelve windows of the shed, from back to front, hoping to see movement inside, and that's when he saw the open bulkhead. He pulled his head back. Strike three.

Right about now, his father would be throwing his lobster bib on the table and marching out of the Lobster Palace, elbows pumping out from his sides the way they did when he hurried. Sugar pictured Detective Gallagher and the rest of the staties speeding into the dooryard from all directions, jumping out of their cars with their guns drawn, only to see Sugar Westerback emerge from the barn, pushing the prisoner along before him. 'Someone lookin for this guy?' he'd say.

He took his small flashlight from his vest pocket and swung out from the pump house, then ran low across the hardpacked paddock and pivoted beside the bulkhead, so that his back pressed against the barn between windows, his Desert Eagle ready. Stooping down beside the raised bulkhead door, he moved around to the entrance and peered down into the cellar. He could make out a dim yellowish light coming from the right, but couldn't hear a sound but the wind behind him. Flicking on his flashlight, he shone it on the wooden steps, then ducked low and started down.

The steps were made of new planking, solid and silent under his feet. Reaching the concrete floor, he looked toward the source of yellowish light and saw a new pine stairway coming down from above. The light was upstairs. Sugar swept his flashlight to his left, the beam fluttering along the new wooden posts until it illuminated the tractor and hay baler that were parked at the rear of the barn. Satisfied that he was alone in the cellar, he decided to wait right here until Ellen showed up. Once he heard them talking upstairs, he could make his way up while the kid was distracted.

Then Sugar smelled the kerosene.

At least he thought it was kerosene. He sniffed the air attentively, thinking maybe it was diesel fuel from the tractor. Whatever it was, it had an odd tinge to it, like maybe a note of turpentine. Or pine pitch. And, actually, it seemed to be coming from the right, not from the tractor.

Holding his pistol and flashlight out in front of his chest, Sugar crept over to the stairway, circling around behind the stairs, out of the light. He held his breath and listened for footsteps above him, but the barn remained completely silent, strangely so, which meant either the kid wasn't there yet . . . or else he was waiting at the top of the stairwell.

Sugar braced himself. With both hands, he held the .357 and flashlight together in front of his face. Took a breath. One . . . two . . .

He wheeled around the corner post, aiming up. Strange, now the smell seemed to come from above.

He placed his foot on the first step and pushed himself up. The wood squeaked. Goosebumps broke out all over his arms – seemed to freeze there. He waved the big Desert Eagle out in front of him, keeping his eye at the top of the stairwell. He waited another moment, listening. But nothing stirred. Nothing but the smell wafting down, now more intense than before. He lifted himself to the next step, then climbed two more, feeling his leg shiver each time he set his foot down.

He could see by the low wooden ceiling at the top of the stairwell that the stairs emerged in the barn's new shed-roofed addition, and he knew the kid could be hiding in any one of the stalls that stretched to the back of the barn. In fact, he might be anywhere. Imagining suddenly that Neal was below him, Sugar swung his pistol down at the darkness behind him, and his flashlight whacked off the railing and jumped out of his hand. He watched helplessly as it banged off one step, then hit each successive step in its clamorous descent, until finally it smacked the concrete floor and rolled away from the stairs, glazing the dusty floor with its long, narrow beam.

Sugar stood suspended on the stairway, tingling with goosebumps. In fact, he was beginning to regret having come by himself. Then he noticed that the railing under his hand was wet – no, oily: He lifted his fingers to his nose and smelled: diesel fuel. His belly fluttered.

He concentrated on the .357 in his hand, the trigger under his index finger, and he turned to face the top of the stairs again. Point of no return. Quiet as possible, he resumed climbing. When his head was almost level with the floor joists, he lowered his back and crawled up one more step. Now, with his face close to the oil-soaked treads, he could detect other smells: alcohol, maybe gasoline, maybe paint thinner, a conglomeration of fumes that burned his eyes and told him he really had to get out of there. But he also had to protect Ellen Chambers.

He readied himself, knowing that when he raised his head above the floor, he'd have a clear shot down the shed's walkway and into the top of the first stall, possibly into the open barn. He gripped the ten-inch magnum with both hands. He took a breath . . .

No guts, no glory.

He sprang up—

Then lowered himself again.

Kneeling on the step, heart pounding, he replayed what he'd seen: wires everywhere, buckets and crates and wax-paper milk cartons lined up along the wall. Sugar crouched there as he puzzled it out, ears pricked for any speck of sound around him. Then, very slowly, he raised his head again and stared.

The tops had been cut off the milk cartons. Stretching down the length of the wall that divided the shed from the open barn, there were probably fifty or sixty of them, and he was sure they were filled with fuel. The goose bumps went down his body in a flood. He looked over his right shoulder, at the door to the paddock. A ten-penny nail protruded from the top corner of the door, positioned to connect with a long strand of copper wire if the door opened an inch. Attached to the nail was a shorter length of wire that was buried in the glazing that surrounded the door's window. Not glazing, Sugar realized: Plastique, enough to perforate someone with glass shrapnel, head to waist, if the explosion didn't blow his head right off.

Another copper wire followed the low ceiling in two directions: over Sugar's head and into the main section of the barn; and over the stalls to the rear wall. That's when Neal Chambers' plan became clear to Sugar: total destruction – and escape during the chaos.

Sugar lowered himself down three steps and unclipped his radio from his belt. He flicked it on and whispered: 'Dad? Over.' He released the microphone button and waited for a response.

'Where the hell are you?' Wes replied in a whisper, which either meant he was acknowledging Sugar's code 33, or he was close to the barn himself and afraid to raise his voice.

Sugar continued backing down the stairs, keeping his eyes peeled on the ceiling above the stairwell, watching for any hint of movement. 'Dad, stay away,' he said in a barely audible croak. 'Everything's booby-trapped.'

'Are you in the barn?' His father asked, exasperated.
'That's affirmative,' Sugar answered, glancing over his shoulder into the darkness below him.
'Okay, get out of there.'
'Ten-four that.' As if he needed to be told. In fact, the second his foot hit that cellar floor he was going to bolt for the bulkhead and shoot anyone who tried to stop him. But first: 'Dad, you've got to stop Ellen Chambers from coming.'
'Just get the hell out of there. I'm a few minutes away. Backup's coming.'
'Ten-four.'
Reaching the bottom step, Sugar released his mike button and clipped the radio to his belt. He eyed his flashlight lying halfway to the bulkhead – the red glow of its lens cover – and he planned his move. He took a shallow breath of the dangerous air, then made his break, running full-tilt, snatching the flashlight on the fly, then veering left—
—and stopping quick, spinning around, waving his light at the darkness, as if he were fencing. Then he swiped the light back around to the bulkhead, which was now closed, copper wire and gray plastique affixed to the aluminium doors.
He shuddered with unspent adrenalin, then turned in a circle, painting his meager light beam across the kerosene-soaked posts, when his light landed on a gray door built into the stone wall, no more than ten feet from the bulkhead. In fact, the door looked like it might be another way out. Either that, or a trap.
'Come on, asshole,' he said to the darkness. 'But you better be good.'
Sugar approached the door cautiously, examining the jamb for wires, studying the hinges. It could be the kid's escape route, he thought, which would explain the reason it didn't look booby-trapped.
''Cause I got a nine-shot .357 magnum in my hand,' he continued. 'Fully loaded.'
He reached out and touched the door with the back of his flashlight hand. It felt cold, probably made of steel. He hooked his finger under the latch, snapped it up. 'Yup, you better be real, real good,' he said as he eased the door open so gently that a thread could have stopped it.
Now the cold, sweet stench hit him hard: like he had popped the

lid on a giant can of turpentine. He shone his light through the crack between the door and the jamb and peeked in at a pile of potatoes in a wooden bin. He pushed the door another inch and got a much stronger smell of turpentine, along with a slightly rotten whiff, heavier than bad potatoes should be, more like a dead rat in a wall. He opened the door wider, and that's when he saw the body.

The flashlight stared, along with the magnum.

Encased in a plastic bag, the young man was sprawled face-down, dressed all in black: black sweater, black corduroys, black boots, hands by his sides. Sugar could make out the ear and cheekbone, and he knew without question that the kid was dead. No mistaking death, once you've seen it. But he kept his pistol aimed at the body, just in case.

The words THIS SIDE UP and a bold red arrow were printed on the plastic – probably a refrigerator bag, Sugar guessed – and the opening was folded up at the bottom and sealed with duct-tape. What was weird was the way the bag stuck to the side of the corpse's ear with a strange, reddish translucence. The hand was similarly colored, as though an inch deep in shellac.

Sugar recalled the Californians who killed themselves with bags over their heads and new sneakers, believing they were going to hitch a ride to heaven on the tail of a comet. By the looks of things, with the kerosene and booby-traps, this kid had booked himself a one-way ticket to hell and was looking for fellow passengers.

'Sorry, my friend, not this time,' Sugar said, raising his radio to his mouth and pushing the button down. 'Hey, Dad,' he said. 'Elvis has left the building. Over.'

The radio clicked, and his father said urgently, 'What the hell are you talking about? Are you outta there yet?'

Sugar pressed the button to respond, but his voice was cut off.

Her mind swimming with trepidation, Ellen drove down the hill to her farm. She pulled into the dooryard unceremoniously, the same way she'd pulled in thousands of times when she had lived here, as if nothing were wrong. Indeed, no other vehicle was parked there – but she guarded against taking any relief from that.

She had known this day would come, this moment, and now that it was here, she felt utterly helpless to do anything other than follow the path Neal had prepared for her. She pictured herself wandering through the barn door and seeing Moreen hanging from the beam.

She should have called the police, that's what she kept telling herself, while another voice kept warning her of what Neal had intimated, that any police involvement would cost Moreen her life. Neal didn't lie. Ellen knew that much about him. He considered lying beneath his dignity. But his particular brand of truth was always riddled with layers, his self-righteous sleight-of-hand. Another thing she knew: No matter what words he used, he was not about to abandon his vendetta at this stage.

But what could she do?

Forgive him? Of course she could say the words. But she'd be lying, and they both knew that, without going through the ceremony. Somehow this little drama didn't seem symbolic enough or brilliant enough for Neal's *coup de grâce*. And if there were some significance to the date – the day before Thanksgiving? – Ellen couldn't figure it.

She stepped out of her truck and walked cautiously to the barn. The front doors were opened maybe two inches, wide enough so she could see a dim, vertical line of light in the opening, and, as she got closer, wide enough so she could smell the kerosene. As soon as she pushed the door open another inch, she saw the glint of Neal's eye less than two feet from her face. Startled as she was, she almost didn't recognize him. He'd grown a beard and let his hair grow long.

'Ellen, don't be afraid,' he said, smiling softly. He opened the door another inch and peered out at the night. A fine, icy mist hung in the air.

She looked past him into the barn and saw the milk cartons, the rags piled around posts. Now the smell of kerosene was overpowering, and she knew he was planning to destroy the building.

'Come in,' he said, opening the door wider so she could see the centerpiece of this passion play: a thick rope hanging from the low hanging beam, ending in a noose. Her heart stopped. One of her kitchen chairs stood below the noose, surrounded by a frightening mound of oil-soaked hay, perforated with lengths of two-by-fours criss-crossed with oak timbers.

Reacting to Ellen's expression, Neal's smile turned beatific. 'This is the cup my father has given me,' he said. 'Shall I not drink it?'

Suddenly she wondered: Was he planning to kill himself?

'Neal,' she began, then didn't know how to continue. *He thinks he's Jesus Christ*. His eyes shone fiercely, as though daring her to say he was insane. 'Neal, please tell me what you did with Mo.'

As though he'd been waiting for that question, he lifted a hand in front of his face. A small leather pouch tied by rawhide dangled from his thumb. Then he turned away from her and walked into the center of the barn. She opened the door wider.

'Neal, you don't have to do this.'

She held the door, terrified to go in after him. But having no choice, she stepped inside, and once she did, the door swung shut behind her. She heard a clunk above her and looked up, saw a pair of ropes on pulleys attached to the doors, with plastic pails tied to the ends of the ropes – counterweights, to keep the doors closed. She also saw copper wires and rags and milk cartons attached to the door's frame, and she realized that the hanging pails were probably filled with gasoline. She moved further into the barn, out from under the gently swaying pails.

'Neal, I understand how you feel,' she said. 'And I forgive you.'

He turned his head as she approached his funeral pyre and gave her a placid smile, teeming with contempt. 'You forgive me? For what?'

'I know you murdered my mother,' Ellen continued. 'You killed Scott's parents too. I know the things you've done, and I know why.'

' "Breach for breach," ' he said calmly. ' "Eye for eye, tooth for tooth." '

'*Neal, I forgive you.*'

He stared at her darkly, the glint leaving his eye.

'Is Moreen here?' Ellen said. 'Is she in the barn?'

Holding the pouch by its rawhide tie, he held it out to her again.

Ellen stopped breathing. Did his gesture mean the pouch held the answer to Moreen's whereabouts – or was it her remains? She did not try for surprise, nor was she coy. She reached into her jacket pocket and withdrew the revolver, aimed at the center of his chest.

'I'm not playing this game with you,' she said. 'Tell me what you did with my daughter.'

'Or you'll kill me.' He shook his head at her, the pouch still dangling from his thumb.

She lowered her aim to his stomach. 'You know I'm capable.'

Even as she thumbed the hammer back, his expression did not flag. Rather, he held out his other hand, then spread both his arms wide, offering himself as if he were Jesus on the cross. Then his other hand opened, revealing what might have been a pager. But it wasn't.

'My twelve legions,' he explained. 'Also called a dead man's switch, for the benefit of the Pharisees listening in. Meaning if I drop it, or if my thumb somehow releases this button—'

Ellen narrowed her eyes at him, refusing to avert her aim. 'Nobody is listening in, Neal. No one is here but you and me.'

His smile disappeared. He turned his back on her and climbed up the oil-soaked pyre onto the chair, saying, ' "And ye shall know the truth, and the truth shall make you free." '

'*I have told you the truth!*'

Balancing himself precariously on the chair, he turned to face her again, and the noose brushed his hair. Even though Ellen matched his persistent stare with her own and kept her .38 trained on his stomach, they both knew he held the upper hand: He had Moreen. When her vision twisted with tears, she lowered the gun.

'Neal, don't you think I know how much you were hurt?' she said, exasperated. 'I was hurt too. We've all been hurt. But Moreen had nothing to do with it.'

'Colossians three,' he said. ' "The wrath of God cometh on the children of disobedience." '

'Neal, you're not God. You could at least give her a chance.'

He studied her again, and she hoped he was considering what she had said. Then he tossed the pouch to her feet. The sound of it striking the floor convinced her it was not filled with ashes. When she came forward and picked it up, its contents jangled like heavy coins.

'You don't have time to open it,' he said. 'You need to leave.'

She looked up, saw him pulling the noose down over his head, raising his face to fit the rope under his beard, all the while holding his dead man's switch close to his face. As he pulled the noose tight around his neck, Ellen straightened and raised her revolver again, aiming at his thigh, prepared to fire. 'I've forgiven you, Neal. I've done everything you asked. Now tell me what you did with Moreen.'

He raised a boot on the chair's top, coaxing the chair to wobble, and Ellen started backing away from him. 'I'm not going to watch you, Neal. You're not going to leave me with that. Just stop it!'

'You know this cannot be stopped,' he said, 'or how else could the prophecy be fulfilled, which says this has to be?' He fixed his dark eyes on her, long and sorrowful. 'Ellen?'

Her boot heel hit the door. She reached behind her, found the latch. 'Neal, I need my daughter.'

'Don't forget me.'

'Neal—'

Suddenly her arm was caught from behind, and she was yanked out the door. In the same instant, an explosion sent her hurtling to the ground. Another explosion shook the earth, and she heard the horrible din of men shouting and screaming. Then she was hauled roughly to her feet and dragged along, her boots hitting the ground as the explosions continued clocking off behind her, one after another, while someone chanted, 'Keep going, keep going, keep going.' Ellen couldn't tell how many men were pulling her along while she resisted, trying to get back to the barn.

'*Let me go!*'

'Mrs Chambers—'

It was Gallagher, by himself. He pulled Ellen down on the gravel road behind the pump house, and she threw her elbow at him, trying to escape.

'You're okay,' he said, capturing her arms. 'Keep your head down!'

'*Asshole, he's got Moreen!*'

'I know. Stay down!'

He pulled her back against the pump house door and held her tightly.

With each small explosion, lines of fire radiating from the barn raced serpentine paths across the hayfield and pastures, until the entire farm was networked in flame lines. Ellen saw a man running a crazy path away from the barn, holding his face, and another man, his back and shoulder on fire, writhing in the muddy paddock, while flames crackled out of all twelve shed windows, and flashlights fluttered like moths around the burning farm, silhouettes of men racing in confusion. Ellen watched one of them running toward her, vaulting line after line of flames, scattering the smoke. Wearing a dark windbreaker, he fell to his knees beside Gallagher, barking into a handheld radio, 'Stand by!' Then he looked wildly at the detective. 'We've got to pull back, we're gettin' hammered up there.' In the flickering firelight, Ellen could see blood stringing down his cheek from a gash under his eye. Suddenly sirens rose up amidst the chaos, and the blowing smoke started flashing red.

'Keep everybody back, firefighters, everybody,' Gallagher told him. 'But watch the windows and doors, and watch the foundation – this may be a smokescreen for his escape.'

The officer sprang to his feet and took off running, shouting into his radio. As dozens of men retreated from the barn in what looked like military maneuvers, a floodlight lit up on the farm road about thirty feet in front of Ellen, and another lit up in the dooryard to the right of the house, both aimed through the smoke at the barn.

'*Get those vehicles out to the road!*' someone shouted. Someone else called out, '*Save the house!*'

Huddled against the safe side of the pump house, Ellen realized that the explosions had stopped. Now she could hear the busy murmuring of the fires inside the barn, like elders in conference, and she could hear the droning and shouting of men's voices, the drumming of firefighters' boots as they ran through the burning field with Indian pumps strapped to their backs. Underneath all the commotion, she realized with amazement that Neal was dead.

Suddenly a firefighter burst through the smoke, his boots and trouser cuffs steaming. 'Detective, you need to move!' His voice was nearly obscured by the rushing of grass fires that threatened to close in on them.

'Come on,' Gallagher said, grabbing Ellen's arm. The firefighter took her other arm and, pulling her to her feet, they ran further down the farm road, maybe fifty feet, to the crest of the hill, where they dropped to their knees and turned back. Now the pasture on one side and the hayfield on the other were lit in smoking, flickering yellow-gray.

'There it goes,' Gallagher said, watching the barn.

The fire did not climb the side of the building, but seemed to materialize through the walls in a solid sheet, like some brilliant, shimmering ghost.

'Rainstorm or no rain,' someone said, a firefighter in a long, black coat, 'there won't be nothing but a pile of ash by the time we can get to it. That's one hot son of a gun.'

Even from this safe distance, Ellen felt the incredible heat of the fire. Holding the pouch toward the light, she tugged at the rawhide drawstring.

'Don't open that!' Gallagher snapped, ripping the pouch from her hand. A bright jangle flew from the opening.

'He's got Moreen,' Ellen shot back, lunging at the ground to find what had spilled. Twin flashlight beams cut through the yellow smoke, shining on two silver dollars in the wet hay. She grabbed for them, just as a black shoe came down beside her hand.

'Move!' she snapped, pushing at the leg. A hand gripped her shoulder.

'Did you see my boy in there?'

'You're in my light!' she yelled.

'Look, I need everyone to shut up for a minute. Chief—'

'*My son was in that barn!*'

Ellen looked up, saw that the older man was standing over her, his face streaked black and red in the firelight, his eyes stark.

'My boy Sugar was inside,' he said to her. 'Did you see him?'

Horrified, she stared back at him and shook her head, at the same time understanding the meaning of the pouch: Moreen was lost. She rose to her feet and looked recklessly at the barn. Gallagher positioned himself in front of her, as though to keep her from running back to the burning building.

'Why did you come?' she said.

'Look,' he said, spilling silver dollars from the pouch into his open hand. 'Silver dollars, that's all he gave—'

Gallagher jumped back, and the coins and pouch hit the ground together with a deadening smack. The flashlight beams intersected, then illuminated the fleshy ringlet that smeared the hay: a severed ear, decorated with a single silver stud.

Ellen's heart stopped.

'Jesus,' the trooper said softly, while Ellen stood there shaking, desperately telling herself that the ear could not be her daughter's. She tried to remember what Moreen's ear looked like, and with a flash of relief recalled its multiple rings and studs. Beside her, the old man sank to one knee and reached for the ear, his hand trembling.

'Probably best if we brought that to the lab,' Gallagher said, trying to sound sympathetic even as he wiped his bloody fingers on his handkerchief.

The old man rose again, almost summarily, and peered off at the raging barn, already radiating so much heat that the firefighters and equipment had given up on it and were focusing all their water on the house, which sent thick clouds of steam up its clapboards.

'He's gonna want that sewed back on,' Wes said, setting the ear gently in Gallagher's handkerchief, then staggering slightly toward the valley, where dozens of volunteer firefighters roamed amongst the flames, pumping water at the grass fires. 'Any of you men check down by the pond? Cripes, injury like that could turn anyone around.'

Gallagher wrapped the ear in the handkerchief, then put his hand on the old man's shoulder. 'Chief Westerback, you understand we've got to keep moving on this? I'll call you as soon as we know anything.'

Although their eyes did not meet, Ellen could see that a certain understanding passed between the two men. Gallagher looked over his shoulder and said to someone, 'Officer, help Chief Westerback home, please.'

Wes looked toward the barn once more, his eyes glimmering. Then he expanded his chest, turned and started walking up the gravel road. 'I'll be in my car,' he said. 'Take care of that ear. His mother's gonna want that sewed back on.'

Gallagher turned back to Ellen, who crouched with a trooper on the ground, collecting the spilled contents of the pouch. 'Thirty dollars,' the trooper said with his hands full.

Ellen narrowed her eyes at Gallagher. 'Didn't you know he told me to come alone?'

'This is all he gave you,' the detective answered, indicating the coins. 'It's all he ever intended to give you.'

'He told me to come alone, and he'd tell me what he did with Moreen!' she persisted. 'Don't you understand?'

'We have certain information,' Gallagher said calmly.

'*Information*. So now my daughter's life is in the hands of a caveman.'

The detective turned and stepped away from her.

Ellen heard a commotion and spotted three men walking around the pump house, arguing. She recognized Scott's voice. The other two men were state troopers. Gallagher stepped toward them and barked, 'Let him through!' The men separated, and Scott came running across the blackened, smoldering field, his eyes raging.

'What the hell's going on?'

'Neal's got Mo,' Ellen said. 'He told me to come alone.'

'*Is she okay?*'

'I don't know. Neal's dead. In the barn.'

'Jesus,' Scott breathed, looking off toward the inferno.

'We found the car your daughter was driving,' Gallagher said.

Ellen wheeled. 'Her car, where?'

Gallagher ignored her. 'The Hampton police tagged it this morning,' he explained to Scott, 'parked in an alley by the beach. It belongs to a girl who admitted she loaned it to Moreen. We're also investigating a homicide that occurred in the vicinity of the car. There's a possible connection. If so, then Neal probably kidnapped Moreen two days ago.'

Ellen sucked in a rigid breath. 'You said we'd be protected,' she said. 'So how does he manage to come here and fill that barn full of explosives? How does he get to Moreen before you do?'

'I told you, we identified certain target dates, based on our profile,' Gallagher said, not looking at her. 'November twenty-second wasn't one of them.'

'John F. Kennedy's assassination,' offered a woman trooper who stood next to Ellen.

'That's not it,' Scott said.

Ellen stood stiffly, while the others turned to Scott.

'November twenty-second was my brother's birthday,' he explained.

'Oh yeah, target dates,' Ellen said.

She felt a hand on her arm. The female trooper moved her a couple of steps back. 'I know you're upset,' she said quietly, 'but the detective's got a little boy in the hospital, and he's not doing too good. Why don't you lighten up a little.'

'Our tech people are analyzing the document your nephew faxed,' Gallagher said to Scott, unaware of the trooper's intercession. He turned to Ellen. 'They're listening to tapes of your telephone conversation with Neal, as well as your conversation inside the barn. What I need to know is if he said anything that we missed, maybe in a whispered voice. Or if he made any gestures or facial expressions that might be meaningful.'

Ellen stared at the detective, trying to think. She felt rain hitting her face, or maybe it was spray blowing over from the fire hose. She shook her head helplessly.

'You must have some idea where she is,' Scott said.

'Somewhere she can't stick a needle in her arm,' Ellen answered with an accusatory ring that she did not intend.

'What's that supposed to mean?'

'That's what Neal said to me.'

'It fits,' Gallagher said. 'The victim in Hampton Beach was a heroin dealer. We're canvassing the neighborhood and checking the vacant cottages and shops. There's a possibility Neal locked her up somewhere in the neighborhood.'

'But where?'

'Any of hundreds of cottages,' Gallagher said. 'It's a beach town, everything's closed up for the season.'

Ellen took the fax out of her jacket pocket and unfolded it. The female trooper shone her flashlight on it: Moreen sitting sullenly in the corner of the room.

Scott lowered his face toward the paper. 'She's not tied up. Why wouldn't she leave?'

'It's possible he's got the doors and windows booby-trapped, like he did here.'

'More likely she's out in the water,' a deeper voice said.

Ellen turned, saw Rooftop Paradise towering over them all, dressed in a black firefighter's coat that was open down the front and much too short in the sleeves. The Indian tank strapped over his shoulder looked like a thermos.

'Keep on with your work and let us do our job,' one of the policemen said to him, but Rooftop didn't move.

Gallagher ran his finger across the photo. 'See the construction of the wall behind her – no wallboard, no insulation? That's either a cottage or a hunting camp in some remote location.'

'You don't get light like that in the woods,' Rooftop said. 'That's under the open sky.'

Gallagher turned and looked up at the giant.

'Besides, any beach cottage with an ocean view isn't likely to be this ramshackle,' Rooftop added.

A loud cracking started, then a barrage of shouting, and they turned to see the barn collapsing, its roof parachuting down with a fierce crunch, blowing flames and sparks in all directions. An almost visible wave of heat rolled over them. Ellen thought of Neal with amazement, killing himself that way, but her thoughts quickly returned to Mo.

'How many islands are off the coast?' she asked.

Gallagher hesitated, then said to Scott, 'I just don't know how he'd get her out there.'

'Boat,' Rooftop said.

Ellen turned to Rooftop. 'Are there any islands twelve miles out?'

'For Christ sakes, El, let the men do their job,' Scott told her, then he turned to Gallagher.

'Okay, look, what I can do is notify the Coast Guard,' the detective said. 'I'll have them call around to the boatyards, see if anyone's had a boat stolen. For now, we'll focus our resources on the more plausible scenarios.'

Ellen glanced toward the burning barn and her chest hardened. She turned back to Rooftop. 'Where's your boat?'

'El, don't fucking start.'

She started walking away, then turned back to the giant. 'Are you coming?'

'Twelve miles or twelve nautical miles?' Gary Pope asked, his eyes never leaving the television. 'And twelve miles from where? Shit, my own dock's twelve miles from Ogunquit, Kittery, Berwick, you name it. Everything's twelve miles from lots of places.'

The fisherman was small and wiry, probably in his fifties, with wire-rim bifocals and a thick growth of neatly parted gray hair. Dressed in his green work clothes and black rubber boots, he sank deeper in his leather recliner, eating a boiled hot dog with his fingers. His television sat on top of the refrigerator, tuned to *Wheel of Fortune*. The room smelled strongly of cigarettes. The kitchen table, where Rooftop and Ellen hovered over the nautical chart, was given to piles of bills and receipts, an adding machine, a set of scales, and a boxy two-way radio whose dial danced with silently blinking red lights.

Rooftop placed a transparent plastic ruler on the chart, with the zero line approximately centered in the clustered Isles of Shoals, and he swung an arc westward over the shore, tracing the 12-mile mark with his finger.

'How about Rye Beach?' Rooftop said. 'That's next door to Hampton.' He turned. 'Hey, Gary, we need to know if anyone had a boat stolen in the past couple of days.'

The fisherman let out a sigh. He levered his recliner forward and sprang to his feet, walked over to his radio and flipped a switch.

'Rye Harbor Marina, Rye Harbor Marina, Urchin Matters, switch and answer, channel sixty-eight, over.' He listened for a moment, then flipped the switch again. 'Rye Harbor Master, Urchin Matters, switch and answer, sixty-eight, over.' He stared at the television while he waited for a response. 'Take the B, stupid,' he muttered.

'Okay, Urchin Matters,' the radio squawked.

'Just checkin on something,' Gary continued. 'Anyone down there have their boat stole, past few days? Over.'

'Hold on. Over.'

Ellen and Rooftop exchanged a look, while the radio hissed. Then the squawking resumed.

'Yeah, Urchin Matters, fella named Hughes came in two mornings ago and said his cabin lock was cut. No damage, nothing missing except for a half tank of fuel. Figured some kids took it out for a joyride. Over.'

Gary looked over at Rooftop, who nodded.

'Gotta be some unfulfilled to go joyridin in a lobster boat,' the harbor master said. 'Over.'

'I guess prob'ly,' Gary said into the radio. 'That's that then. Over and out.' He pushed the toggle switch, silencing the radio.

Rooftop eyed Ellen solemnly. 'Just about exact,' he said, holding his ruler on the chart.

A charge of apprehension started Ellen's heart beating.

'Gary, I need you to gas me up,' Rooftop said.

The gray-haired man stared hard at him. 'In this weather, mister, you ain't gonna do a thing but radio the Coast Guard. Besides which, they're not about to go out in a storm themselves, where you don't even know for sure if the girl's out there.'

'I know she's out there,' Ellen said to Gary, pulling a slicker off its hanger. 'I need to borrow your rain gear.'

Rooftop gave her a look, then turned back to Gary. 'You mind if she keeps you company?'

'I'm coming with you,' Ellen told him.

'Too dangerous,' Rooftop said, not even looking at her. 'Gary, gas me up.'

'Do you have some gloves?' Ellen said, pushing her arms into the rubber sleeves.

'You can't come,' Rooftop told her.

'It's my daughter out there,' she said, pulling the zipper to her neck. 'Now hurry up.'

Gary showed her an indulgent frown. 'Well, yes, ma'am.'

★ ★ ★

Rooftop stood at the console and steered the Boston Whaler out of the York River, his red and green bow lights making haloes in the rain. Ellen sat on the pilot seat to his right, holding tight to the side rail. Despite the rain slicker and layers of clothing underneath, the cold spray from the waves and riotous beating of near-frozen rain on her hood made her realize just how much they were at the mercy of the elements.

As they left the safety of the harbor, Rooftop yelled over the howling motor, 'It could get rough,' and they hit the first wave of the open ocean with a startling crunch. With its characteristic tub-shaped design, the 17-foot boat lifted its bow and slapped the water again and again, harder every time, until Ellen felt each impact jar the base of her spine. Soon a green bell buoy rose out of the gray, like a foreboding angel, bobbing and clanging as it passed on their right. Behind them, far back to the left, she heard the owlish hoot of the Cape Neddick foghorn.

She peeked up at Rooftop hunched behind the short windscreen, saw the water blowing off his face as though he were taking a shower.

'How can you see?' she yelled.

'Forty-five minutes!' he yelled back, obviously misunderstanding her.

He wore a miner's lamp strapped around his watch cap, and he angled the beam at the chart that was clamped between the windscreen and wheel. Incredibly, the rain began blowing harder, and the waves grew larger, lifting and lowering the boat in an endless, nauseating rhythm. Despite the windscreen, every time the boat climbed, the waters found their way into Ellen's hood, gloves and sleeves, working a deep chill into her shoulders. Her shivering was more from fear, however, than the cold.

As the boat fought its way further from land, she clutched the side rail and tried to envision Moreen waiting safely indoors, while her uncooperative mind whirled with images of the barn fire, of Sugar's ear, of Neal's spectacular suicide, until she realized that she had lost the sounds of bell buoys clanging, and the foghorn had disappeared far behind them. Now there was only the wind, the rain and this small boat churning laboriously up the sides of mountainous waves, then plummeting down the other. The way the motor screamed to make it to the top, it almost seemed that they were making no forward progress, but just fighting to keep from being driven back to shore.

Once when they descended into a trough Ellen felt water slosh against the backs of her boots, about a foot deep. Terrified, she looked up at Rooftop.

'The bilge pump's working as hard as it can,' he shouted.

As they rode up and over the next wave crest and descended to the bottom, the water piled over her calves, knocking her into the console.

Rooftop lifted her by the elbow. 'She's unsinkable!' he yelled, with more confidence than was his nature, as a wall of water slammed against Ellen's side, knocking her off her thoughts.

'Hold on, we're turning south,' he yelled. 'It's gonna get a little rough.'

Ellen gave him a look, aghast, as the motor churned valiantly, pushing the whaler up toward the black rain. This time, when they started to fall, she felt a weightless chill take her stomach, and she fell back heavily in her seat. Feeling like she was about to vomit, she tried to put it out of her mind.

'How much longer?' she yelled, her stomach swelling like the waves.

'Stay up,' Rooftop yelled back at her.

She pulled herself to her feet, clutching the console rail with her left hand and the grab rail with her right, and she realized she had lost her left glove. Another wave hit the corner of the bow and blew past her shoulder. She burped and tasted the wine she'd drunk in the afternoon. She sank dizzily in her seat, lowered her face and stuffed her cold hand in her pocket. When they plunged into the next trough, the flood splashed full against her chest, knocking her to her knees.

Rooftop raised his fingers to his teeth and pulled his neoprene glove off his hand.

'I don't want that,' Ellen shouted at him.

He slapped the glove against her arm. 'Put it on, my hands are protected!'

Not stopping to figure out what he meant, she took the giant glove and slid her hand inside, grateful for the warmth. The boat plummeted. Her stomach leaped. She caught the grab rail and vomited on the throttle. Bilge water walloped her. She fell against the console and vomited on the dash. Rooftop pulled the chart out of her way. They turned skyward and she fell heavily against him, turned her head away and puked over her knee.

'I'm sorry,' she moaned.

'You get *me* throwing up, you'll know what sorry is,' he replied. 'Hold tight.'

He wrapped a long arm around her just as a hard, cold spray hit her face. Then he reached his other arm in front of her and cut the motor. A jolt of panic shot through Ellen, thinking he was going to throw her overboard. She grabbed for the rail.

'Listen,' he said.

The wind whipped across the froth, as a wave lifted the boat high, then dropped them back down. Ellen felt her stomach roll.

'Waves,' he said.

'No shit.'

'Listen,' he told her.

Ellen listened, but all she could hear was the hum of the bilge pump laboring and the rain slapping off her hood. However, as the next swell passed under them, she heard the whisper of a distant surf crashing against a shore. She looked off toward the sound and thought she saw a small haze of light winking through the fog.

'The White Island lighthouse,' Rooftop said, slowing the motor even more. He switched on his miner's lamp and pressed his face close to the chart, then looked over at the compass. In the light, Ellen could see rain the size of dimes hitting the windscreen.

'Five minutes,' he encouraged, opening the throttle and turning the wheel fully to the left. As they surged ahead, he said, 'Two or three of the islands are inhabited, but they're close to most of the others, so she could've hailed the mail boat. Only a couple of islands are isolated. Just one of them has a shack on it, that I know of: Lunging Island.'

'Lunging? Like lungs?'

'I guess.'

Ellen pulled herself to her feet. 'That's the one.'

Amidst her fear and nausea, Ellen found an empty spot in her mind where she said a short prayer that they would find Moreen on the island, and that she'd be alive. That was all Ellen dared to ask for, certainly more than she felt she deserved.

Rooftop peered over the windscreen, his glasses spilling the rain. 'We want to head for the lee side,' he said. 'There used to be a dock.'

Five minutes later, they found the dock standing in water that was incredibly calm, despite the fury of the storm. Rooftop tied the boat to the posts, and they followed his flashlight beam off the slippery wood and up a trail to puddled bedrock, then to moss. On the island, the fog was every bit as thick as it had been at sea, and Rooftop's flashlight beam did not reach even ten feet in front of them. Luckily, a slight path was worn in the sea grass.

'Mo?' Ellen yelled into the wind. 'Moreen?' She stopped walking for a moment, to listen for a response.

'Just ahead,' Rooftop told her, and they continued for twenty feet or so, before his light landed on a gray-shingled wall, a small window. The shack looked to be about ten feet from corner to corner, and the single window was hung with burlap.

'Mo?'

'Here,' Rooftop said.

The door was solid wood, chipped green paint. Ellen took the doorknob in her hand.

'Maybe you should let me go in first,' Rooftop suggested.

'No,' she said, and she shoved the door open. The wind blew in, and a foul stench blew out. Rooftop moved the flashlight across the floor to a pile of blankets in the corner, with dark hair flowing out of the top and a single black boot sticking out the bottom. Ellen shivered in the doorway. Rooftop steadied her.

'Mo?' she said, her voice shaking.

The moan she heard might have been the wind.

'Mo?'

The blanket twitched.

'Oh God.' Ellen threw herself across the floor and pulled the blanket away from her face. In the light beam, she saw the closed eyes, the tattooed tears. In Ellen's frozen hand, Mo's cheek felt hot.

'Don't touch me,' Moreen complained, jerking the blanket over her head.

'Oh, God, Mo,' Ellen breathed, clutching her daughter tightly. 'Oh God, you're safe—'

'Get *off*!' Moreen said, thrashing out of the blankets so that the back of her hand caught Ellen's frozen cheek and sat her back, momentarily stunned.

Mo squinted against Rooftop's miner's lamp. Her pea-coat was buttoned wrong, her jeans were wet and stank of urine. Her cheeks looked horribly gaunt, her eyes sunken. 'You woke me up,' she said, then crawled back inside her blankets.

Ellen heard Rooftop's sigh. 'I'll radio the Coast Guard,' he said quietly, and walked out into the rain.

CHAPTER TWENTY-TWO

Moreen spent the next thirty-six hours in the Portsmouth hospital, refusing to speak, refusing to eat the hospital food, even refusing the pecan pie Ellen had baked her for Thanksgiving. Her weight had dropped more than twenty pounds, but other than exhaustion and an overall listlessness, doctors found no reason to keep her longer. On Friday evening, at six thirty, while Ellen dozed in the waiting room, she was awakened to the sound of Scott's voice.

'We're going home,' he said to her. 'Mo's coming with me.'

Ellen took a deep breath, a sort of yawn, wondering how long she'd been asleep. Then Mo was in the corridor, behind her father. She glanced in at Ellen, her beautiful brown eyes conveying nothing, then walked out of sight, while the facts assembled in Ellen's mind – Moreen going to live with Scott?

'I'll see you,' he said, and he turned for the door.

Ellen drove home, tense with the chill inside her truck, trying to convince herself that, under the circumstances, things had worked out for the best. Neal was dead. Moreen was alive. Certainly, having Mo living at home with Scott was an improvement on wherever she had been staying. Indeed, if she'd been hooked on heroin, maybe the ordeal had scared some sense into her.

Ellen turned up the heater in the truck and lifted the collar of her jean jacket, but still she could not shake the feeling, this anxiety, that things were profoundly unresolved. Yes, Neal was gone, and that was a relief, but his death did little to balance what he had taken from her. And how was it that Neal, who'd been so calculating, had extracted his vengeance on everyone *except* Scott?

The car lot was closed when she pulled in. The showroom lights glared, and orange-tinged security lights projected hazy rings on hundreds of windshields and hoods. But Ellen's apartment was dark, and she couldn't help feeling nervous. Pulling around the back of the building, she shut off the truck, took her keys from the ignition, then reached in the glove box and took out her revolver and slipped it into her jacket pocket. She got out of her truck and walked quickly to the stairs.

Inside the enclosure that protected her stairway from the elements, she climbed into darkness, keeping her hand on the .38 in her pocket, wishing she had left the stair light on. Reaching the door, she scratched her key over the lock until it found home. She pushed the door open, but didn't go in. Instead, she turned her head and looked down, saw him standing at the bottom of the stairs, a stationary shadow.

'Mrs Chambers?'

'*Jesus—*'

'Ellen, it's Dave Gallagher,' the detective said. 'Sorry to startle you. Can I come up for a sec?' Her hand came out of her pocket. She reached into her kitchen and snapped on the overhead fluorescent light, then went to the gas space heater and dialed up the thermostat. When she turned back, Gallagher was there rapping lightly on the door jamb. She didn't tell him to come in. He did anyway, carrying two manilla envelopes in one of his hands. He was wearing a dark trench coat and a fedora pulled down to his brow. He looked freshly shaven. The combination enhanced his appearance measurably.

'I wanted to apprize you of the results of our investigation,' he said.

'Close the door, please,' she told him, and he did. Then he turned back to her, holding the envelopes in front of him, and told her that while police and fire investigators were still sorting through the ashes of her burned-out barn, their investigation confirmed what they already knew, that Neal had rigged the barn with enough fuel to practically vaporize the building and everything in it, including himself.

Gallagher's cheeks were pink, making Ellen think he'd been waiting in the cold for some time. Either that, or he was embarrassed that she had found Moreen and gotten her to a hospital while he and his troops were still breaking into summer cottages in Hampton Beach. For her part, Ellen felt a little remorse having called him a caveman, especially in light of his son's medical problems. She wondered if the boy had cancer.

He told her that Sugar Westerback's remains had been found in the root cellar, which, although protected from the flames by its steel door, had acted like a giant roasting oven. Nicks on the front of his spine indicated that his throat had been cut.

'I don't need any more details,' Ellen told him finally. She left her jacket and cap on while the room warmed up.

'We also found your nephew's van,' Gallagher said.

'He was my husband's nephew,' Ellen told him, not for the first time.

'The van had been stolen in Pennsylvania four years ago, probably kept in his barn till he needed it. He got the license plates in June, off a car in Portland.'

'How do you know the van was his?'

'He left a couple of detonators behind, his sleeping bag, some carpenter's tools . . . and this.' The detective tried to hand Ellen one of the envelopes. She refused to take it.

'It's a deed to his Vermont property,' Gallagher explained. 'Notarized and signed over to you before his death.'

'I don't want it.'

Gallagher tossed the envelope on the table. 'You're free to sell it. You don't need to decide now.' He set the other envelope on the table, too, this one heavy and bulging. 'This is yours too.'

Hearing the sound it made when he set it down, Ellen didn't need to ask what was inside. 'Keep the money,' she said. 'Don't you have a policemen's ball or something?'

'I'm not allowed to take donations.'

'Take it home and give it to your little boy,' she said. 'How is he?'

Gallagher held up a finger, declining the distraction. 'Mrs Chambers, did Neal ever talk about religion?'

'You mean, did he believe he was Jesus Christ? I think that's obvious.'

Gallagher folded his arms. 'Judas was paid thirty silver coins to betray Jesus,' he explained. 'When the Pharisees came to arrest him—'

'I know. His disciple Peter cut off one of their ears.' Ellen's heart stopped. She turned away from Gallagher to lean heavily on the kitchen table. 'Doesn't it make you wonder?' Ellen asked, taking off her cap and tousling her thickening hair with her fingertips.

'What?'

That maybe Neal also planned for his resurrection—'

The detective frowned, and he shook his head slowly from side to side. Although his eyes were dead-on reassuring, he fell short of convincing her.

'How do you know that was him you found?' she asked. 'Did you do DNA tests? Dental matches? What exactly did you find?'

'We were present when he died,' the detective said. 'You were there. There's no way he got out of that barn.'

'He could have dressed as a fireman and jumped out a window during the explosions.'

The detective shook his head again. 'We had men videotaping that building the entire time. We've reviewed those tapes over and over. You've seen the damage. Even in the cellar, the tractor melted. Nobody – not even Jesus Christ himself – could have survived that fire.'

'Neal Chambers began planning his revenge when he was twelve years old,' Ellen said, tossing her cap on the counter. 'That has been his sole purpose in life. Not love, not friends, not money . . . but revenge against Scott and everyone close to him. Can you give me one reason I should believe Neal would spare the life of the one person he holds most responsible for his father's death?'

'Moreen.'

'What?'

'I think he had feelings for her.'

Ellen shook her head, refusing to be swayed.

'Look, I'm no psychiatrist,' Gallagher said, 'but I do have a master's degree in criminal psychology, and I've been in this business a long time. I believe Neal planned to execute all three of you on his father's birthday. I also think when he got close enough to your family, when he made real human contact, he saw that Moreen had problems of her own – as did you all.'

'You mean he figured we'd kill each other if he gave us enough time?'

The detective leveled his eyes at her. 'I think he lost the will.'

Ellen balked, slightly nonplussed, while she examined the intensity of his stare. She wondered if his telling her about his degree, along with the new wardrobe, had something to do with the caveman remark.

'With what you've been through,' he continued, 'frankly I'd be very surprised if you didn't have feelings of anxiety. But I want you to feel assured that, as far as Neal Chambers is concerned, you have nothing more to worry about.'

'As far as Neal is concerned.'

Gallagher tightened his lips with an air of helplessness. 'Your son-in-law's drowning,' he said. 'I'm afraid that case remains open.'

Ellen blinked her eyes once, indifferently, while she waited for him to continue.

He lifted a sealed plastic bag from his trench coat pocket. Inside was the blackened, serrated knife blade. 'This is most likely the knife that Neal used to murder Sergeant Westerback. It was found in the root cellar, beside the officer's body.'

Ellen kept blinking, but now her heart was pounding. She recognized the blade – Neal must have dug it out of her cucumber patch.

'We're pretty sure it's the same knife that caused the wounds to Randy's thigh and shoulder,' Gallagher said, studying Ellen for a moment.

'And?'

'I never believed Randy's death was accidental,' he explained. 'Too many coincidences, not the least of which being that his death occurred twelve days after he married your daughter . . . all of which points to Neal.' He raised his hat to his hairline. 'Trouble, is, Neal couldn't have pulled it off without an accomplice. Maybe two.'

'In other words, Scott and me.'

'My personal opinion? Society is better off without Randy Cross. And I have no doubt that Moreen is better off without him.'

'So if I ever feel compelled to confess—?'

Gallagher eyed her without humor. 'I take my job very seriously, Mrs Chambers; it's not up to me to dispense mercy. I investigate, I apprehend, I deliver criminal suspects into the justice system.'

She unzipped her jacket, went to the stove and turned the heat down a little.

'With what your family's been through, I could almost guarantee immunity for voluntary information. And considering all the extenuating circumstances, along with your son-in-law's criminal record, I don't know anyone at the DA's Office who'd be ambitious about prosecuting an accomplice.'

'Don't they take their jobs seriously?'

'They have discretion. I don't.'

She gave the detective a look, wanting him to leave. He took the hint and reached behind him for the doorknob. 'You're here alone, aren't you?' he said, opening the door.

'I can take care of myself.'

'I was just going to say, maybe you've got a friend you could stay with for a few days, until you feel better about things.'

'Thanks, but a few days isn't going to change much.'

Gallagher smiled slightly. 'You have a license for that—?' He nodded to the bulge in her pocket.

Ellen waited.

'Just' – he raised his hand – 'get one when you have a chance. Or give the weapon back to your husband. Believe me, you'd be a lot safer without it.' He stepped out on the landing. 'Ellen, if you'd care to call me tomorrow, I'll be happy to put you in touch with someone you could talk to. She works with trauma victims.'

Ellen stepped into the doorway. 'Detective, do you know how sheep defend themselves?' she asked.

Gallagher gave her a look, a shrug.

'Individually, they don't. They can't. They're not strong enough or smart enough.' Ellen took the door from him. 'So they flock. Which means they bunch up. The strongest and fittest of them manage to push their way into the center of the flock, which leaves the oldest and youngest and weakest on the outside, vulnerable to attack.' She ran her hand down the outside of her jacket pocket until she felt the revolver hard against her palm. 'That's how I've lost the rest of my family. I'm not going to lose any more.'

He hesitated in the doorway, as though to reply, but she shut the door before he had a chance, then she locked it.

She kept her jacket on, feeling the weight in her pocket as she walked through the apartment turning on lights. She looked inside her bedroom closet. She looked under her bed. She returned to her kitchen and poured a shot's worth of tequila in a coffee mug and drank it down. Then she called home. The answering machine came on. When she began to speak, Scott picked up and said, 'Yup.'

'How's Mo?' Ellen asked.

'In bed.'

'Has she eaten anything?'

'Sugar Pops.'

'Can I talk to her?'

'I want to let her sleep.'

The flatness of his voice seemed an accusation. Ellen was tempted to tell him she was sorry – but why? It was Scott, not she, who had put them in this position.

'Detective Gallagher just left,' she said.

'Yup. He's been over here for three days, him and the rest of 'em.'

She considered telling him what Gallagher had said about the investigation into Randy's drowning, but didn't want to have the conversation over the phone.

'He told me they have a counselor Moreen can talk to,' she said. 'It won't cost anything.'

'Mo's all right,' Scott said. 'She just needs to get on with her life.'

Ellen resisted this argument, too, knowing it was time to hang up.

'Tell her I'll come over in the morning,' she said.

'Maybe you should give her a few days.'

'No, I'll be over to see her. If you want, I'll come while you're at work.'

'It's not me,' Scott said.

'What do you mean?'

'It's Mo,' he said. 'She'd rather not see you right now.'

Ellen's chest tightened. 'What did you tell her about me?'

'Nothing,' Scott said. 'Maybe Neal talked to her when he took her out to the island.'

Ellen's heart kicked. 'What did he say?'

'I don't know. Mo asked me if I had anything to do with Randy's drowning. I said no.'

'Then she's talking to you.'

'Not a whole lot.'

'So it's only me she wants out of her life. It doesn't matter that I saved her, or that I was the one who tried to save Randy.'

'Look, I don't know what she's thinking.'

Ellen paced to the limit of the phone cord, then stopped. 'Scott, do you think this is fair?'

'What?'

'That she's chosen you.'

'Fair's got nothing to do with it,' he replied. 'Like I said, give her a few days.'

Ellen stood there staring at the side of her gas stove, the blue flames flickering behind the black heater grate. She felt the scowl hardening on her brow.

'Tell Mo I won't bother her,' she said, and she hung up the phone, then turned back to her quiet apartment, feeling more alone than she'd ever felt in her life.

CHAPTER TWENTY-THREE

The next day, Ellen walked into Brian Quinn's real estate office and set the deed on his desk. 'Can you sell this?'

He gave the document a quick look, then regarded her with a curious scowl. 'In Vermont?'

'Can you?'

He shrugged. 'I can contact a realtor up there and get it on the multiple listings.'

'Good. Take your commission and give the rest to Sugar Westerback's parents.'

'No reason I can't do that,' Quinn said amiably, pulling a padded chair close to his desk, showing no sign that he'd blackmailed her into resigning. Gossip was gossip. Business was business.

'Thank you,' she said, and left.

November turned to December, unnoticed. With Christmas season escalating in a blur, Ellen started working seven days a week in the store, sitting at the tapestry loom from ten in the morning till nine at night, while endless streams of faces passed by, some asking questions about her craft, most just staring as they passed by. Through it all, Ellen concentrated on her work, certain that many townspeople blamed her for Sugar Westerback's death; just as certain that they'd all heard about her affair with her nephew and his subsequent, fiery suicide. In fact, she suspected that her notoriety may have had something to do with the unusually fruitful season.

As fast as Ellen could turn out her handicrafts, customers would carry them out of the store – linen hand towels and aprons imported from China, onto which Ellen would embroider a tiny image of Nubble Lighthouse, or a lone pine tree under a full moon, or a bright red lobster. It didn't matter. Her two inches of hand-stitching brought thousands of dollars into the store every week. Although Ellen's own share of the proceeds amounted to far less, she was grateful for the occupation.

On these busy days, it was often close to ten when Ellen got home. She liked it that way. She would read or watch TV for a half-hour, until she got drowsy, then she'd go to bed and fall painlessly to sleep.

For most of the month, Ellen kept her word to Moreen. She neither telephoned her daughter nor visited the farmhouse. On occasion she did stop at the gun shop during her lunch break, to pick up her mail, and then she asked about Moreen, but Scott was stingy with information.

'She's okay,' he'd say.

'Has she decided to go back to school?'

'Not that I know of.'

'Is she looking for a job?'

'Not yet. She pretty much stays in her room.'

While Ellen drove back to work one day, sorting through her mail, she came upon an envelope from Quinn Real Estate. Parking her truck behind the store, she opened the envelope and found a clipping advertising Neal's farm. It was from a Vermont regional newspaper called the *Cold Hollow Express*. The photo showed snow surrounding the house and barn, and bare trees in the background – the same silent place she had visited. With one exception.

Ellen took her keys from the truck, went to the back door and unlocked it, letting herself in. She heard Ingrid in the front of the store, thanking a customer. She came through the door, saw at least ten people wandering the aisles.

Ingrid looked at her and rolled her eyes. 'Two more days of this,' she said.

Ellen walked over to the register. 'Look at this picture,' she said. 'Tell me if you see anything strange.'

Ingrid peered through her trifocals. 'The cross on the silo?' She turned to Ellen, raising her brow. 'Are you thinking of buying it?'

'I need to use the phone,' Ellen answered.

'Help yourself,' Ingrid said with a curious scowl.

Ellen brought the telephone in the back room and dialed Quinn's office. 'The clipping you sent me,' she began.

'Place looks great,' the realtor said. 'We've had some bites.'
'Who took the picture?'
'Of the farm? The listing agent, I imagine.'
'When?'
He paused. 'I can find out for you.'
'Did you notice a cross on the silo?'
'I guess I didn't look that close,' Quinn said. 'Ellie, is there something I can help you with?'
'I'll let you know,' Ellen said, and she hung up, then returned the phone to the front. Judging from the way Ingrid examined her, Ellen knew she must have looked terrified.
'Give me another half-hour?' Ellen asked.
'Ellie, are you okay?'
'I'll be back as soon as I can.'
'That's not what I asked.'

Under the frozen sunlight, the place where Ellen's barn had once stood was nothing but a black, stony cellar hole filled with crystalized mounds of ash and melted machinery. The temperature outside struggled to reach five degrees Fahrenheit, and the forecast predicted minus five by the end of the day. Despite the cold, Ellen could smell the destruction the minute she stepped from her truck.

Even the porch railing and posts of the house had been scorched from the heat of the barn fire. Paint on the clapboards had blistered; soffits had blackened. Ellen climbed the steps and discovered a small, freshly cut spruce lying on the porch, a Christmas tree that Scott had evidently dragged in from the woods but hadn't brought inside. She tried the door and found it unlocked.

She went in, saw a couple of Christmas cards on the table. Hers was on top, the one she'd sent to Mo, the envelope unopened. Other than that, no sign of the holiday. Dishes were piled in the sink and on the counter, a pile of dirty clothes dumped on the floor in front of the washing machine.

Besides the hum of the furnace in the cellar, the house sat quietly. Ellen walked through the kitchen into the living room. Shades were drawn. Two empty plates sat on the coffee table, an empty popcorn bowl on the floor. She crossed the room and started up the stairs.

'Mo, it's me,' she called. She climbed up to the hallway upstairs and turned on the light. More clothes on the floor. 'I need to talk to you,' she said, taking hold of Mo's doorknob. She waited for a response, then opened the door.

It took a couple of moments for Ellen to understand what she was seeing: Moreen sitting at a low table made of plywood set on cinder blocks. Her back to the door, Mo worked closely on a reddish-brown hunk of clay with a sculpting knife.

'Mo?'

'Hi,' Mo sang lightly, not turning around.

Surrounding her feet and lined up along the wall were figures of humans, most with women's features, no larger than fifteen inches tall, each of them grotesquely deformed . . . but every one teeming with life: arms and legs twisting painfully, heads thrown back in agony, eyes staring outward.

'Moreen, did you do these?'

'Mm-hm.'

Ellen stepped closer, stunned, while Mo worked her knife delicately, her fingers white from squeezing the tool.

'Do you like them?'

The sculpted girl stared up accusingly at Ellen, her womb scraped out like a melon, revealing another face growing out of the empty abdominal wall: It was Randy, Ellen realized, his goatee softened, a limpid smile on his closed lips. She scanned the other figures in the room – there were nine or ten of them, each missing body parts, each with extra faces. They were horrifying but undeniably brilliant.

'Mo?' Ellen searched for words. 'Do you understand how wonderful these are?'

Moreen smiled.

'You have every bit of your grandmother's talent,' Ellen said.

Looking closer at the figures, Ellen could see that all the bodies were Moreen's, hollowed out, ravaged. All seemed terribly confined, too, entwined with extra arms and legs not her own, while heads and anguished faces tried to push out of her body, as if other people were imprisoned inside her. In fact, now Ellen thought she recognized Maddy's features in one of the trapped faces. She saw Randy in others. A face that might have been Scott's brother Jonathan stared up sternly from a womb. Yet these faces of death were soft and membranous, their noses small and round: they were the faces of infants, stillborn.

The moment paralyzed Ellen. It was as though she were in the company of a woman with years and experiences far beyond her own. Although Moreen was not yet eighteen, she had lived through widowhood, a hysterectomy, she had survived a kidnapping, she'd been addicted to heroin and beaten back the addiction. The elementary task of living on her own, which Ellen was struggling with – even that, Moreen had already done. It was not hard for Ellen to feel childish in her presence.

'Mo,' Ellen began, 'I need to talk to you. Honey, there's a chance that Neal might be alive.'

Moreen turned her face to the side, still smiling. 'Really?' she said, then returned to her sculpting, her long black hair covering her like a shawl.

Ellen's head throbbed. 'Just for Christmas,' she said, 'I'd like you to go someplace with me.'

'Where?'

'It doesn't matter. We'll get the truck and go find a hotel, just for a day or two.'

Moreen kept working at her clay. 'I'd love to,' she said, 'but I don't want to leave Daddy alone on Christmas.'

He's the one who murdered your husband! Ellen almost screamed. *He's the reason Neal is hunting us down!*

Ellen sighed. 'Moreen, would you stop that, please, and talk to me? Just stop.'

Mo laid her knife on the table and turned to face Ellen, her eyes lit pleasantly, her face devoid of emotion. She placed her hands in her lap.

'Jesus Christ, don't look at me like that,' Ellen told her, the words tumbling recklessly from her mouth. 'And don't tell me you *love* me and you'd *love* to go with me, when you make it clear with everything you do that you only want me out of your life!'

Mo gazed at her for another moment, her expression unmarked, then turned back to her work.

Ellen stepped closer, resisting the urge to touch her.

'Mo, just talk to me, can't you? Tell me what I did to you.'

Moreen leaned closer to her work, her knife ticking like a clock at the small clay mouth.

Turn around, Ellen told herself. *Turn around and leave.*

In the gun shop, she slid the newspaper clipping across the glass case, the neat display of handguns and leather holsters.

'The cross is new,' she said, pulling her hand out of the wool mitten. Her ears stung from the cold outside.

On the other side of the counter, Scott flicked the clipping back to her, refusing the conversation.

'Scott, I think he's still alive,' Ellen said.

'Think what you want,' he replied.

'It's not what I *want* to think.'

He leveled his eyes over the counter. 'I watched them pick through the ashes for two solid days,' he said quietly. 'I saw them take out Sugar Westerback wrapped up like a mummy so he wouldn't fall apart. They took Neal out in a shoe box. What gives you the idea he's not dead?'

'You,' she said, gathering up her newspaper clipping and stuffing it in her jacket pocket. 'You're still alive.'

Ellen heard his stunned silence as she turned and put her mitten back on, then went out the door. She imagined his bowels slackening, and it gave her a small degree of pleasure; her Christmas gift to herself.

When Polly Westerback opened her door, her eyes seemed to fill with worry.

'I'm very sorry to bother you,' Ellen told her. 'I called, but no one answered, and no one's in the office. Is Wes here?'

'He's in having a nap,' the older woman said. 'There's a new man in training, but he's out on a call. When he comes back, I can have him get in touch.' She looked as though she hadn't slept herself.

'It can wait,' Ellen said. 'I'm sorry to bother you.'

She went to shut the door, but the older woman put her hand on the glass, kept it open. 'What with the holidays, Wes isn't having an easy time of it,' she said. 'Just as soon as they find another office space, he's going to retire. This is too much.'

'I'm sorry,' Ellen said again.

'Should I have the new man contact you when he gets back?'

Ellen shook her head. 'That's okay.'

Ellen returned to Wool 'n' Things, sat down at her tapestry loom, and continued turning out gifts. Christmas music played incessantly, customers came and went, talking with Ingrid about the frigid weather and the prices of things, she heard the noises their children made. Everything stayed in the back of her mind. White yarn, red yarn, blue yarn, gray, black and brown. Another lighthouse, another solitary seagull, another lobster.

At six o'clock, as soon as Ingrid went to dinner, Ellen picked up the phone and called the state police, asking for Gallagher.

'I'm sorry, Detective Gallagher is not available,' the dispatcher told her. 'Is there anyone else who could help you?'

'No, just contact the detective, please, and tell him Ellen Chambers needs to speak with him.'

'Mrs Chambers, I'll put you through to the shift commander. Just a moment.'

'I don't want to talk to anyone but Gallagher,' Ellen began, when another voice cut in.

'This is Sergeant Anderson,' the man announced with military crispness. 'I'm familiar with the case. Why don't you tell me the nature of your problem and we'll see what we can do.'

'I need to speak with Detective Gallagher,' Ellen said as calmly as she knew how.

'Detective Gallagher has been out on personal leave for most of the week,' the sergeant replied.

Ellen's mind stopped. 'Is it his son?'

'We're not at liberty to divulge that information. If it'll make you feel better, Mrs Chambers, we can send another detective by.'

She stretched the telephone into the back room and shut the door on the cord, holding the newspaper clipping in her hand. 'Could you just get a message to Detective Gallagher for me? Tell him I received a Christmas card he needs to see.'

The sergeant took a moment to respond. 'This is a difficult time of year for a lot of people,' he began. 'Let me see if I can get someone you can talk to.'

'Look,' Ellen said, her face heating up, 'I don't need to speak to a goddamned counselor—'

'Hello?' The voice called from behind the door, along with a tidy knock.

Ellen opened the door a little. Two elderly women dressed like Eskimos stood there smiling, one of them holding up a pair of lobster pot holders along with her wallet.

'One sec,' Ellen mouthed. She closed the door again and said to the sergeant, 'Are you going to take me seriously?'

'We take all calls very seriously, Mrs Chambers. What we can do is send someone out to see you, we'll assess your situation and take it from there.'

'And while you're assessing the situation,' Ellen said, 'God help you if anything happens to my daughter.'

The sergeant paused. 'Mrs Chambers, that's not the way you want to be speaking to a police officer.'

'Really. How's this? Go fuck yourself.'

Ellen banged open the door, wheeled around the corner, lined up the phone cradle and slammed the phone down, then turned to the startled women.

'Cash or credit?' she said.

Ten minutes later Detective Gallagher phoned the store. 'I have no doubt that Neal nailed the cross to the silo,' he said quietly. 'His father was a church minister who killed himself in your barn. Neal also killed himself in your barn. He obviously saw great significance in symbolism.'

'But I was at that farm,' Ellen said, trying to hold her anxiety down. 'I was there, and that cross was not.'

'You were there when, in August?'

'That's right, the night he murdered Maddy Sterling.'

Gallagher sighed tiredly. 'Neal Chambers died in November. He apparently erected the cross sometime in the intervening months, September or October.'

'Look, this is a riddle, it's a game. To Neal, everything was a game. Let me fax this picture to you.'

She heard him sigh again. 'I'm at home,' he said. 'I don't have a fax machine. I understand what you've told me—'

'The ashes you found – your human remains? That was not Neal. It was a man called Gator. He worked for Ray LaFlamme. He came to the farm one night, and Neal murdered him.'

'Were you a witness to the murder? Did Neal tell you he did it?'

'Are you serious?'

'Ellen, the only way such a premise is plausible is, one, if your nephew could have somehow kept the corpse from decomposing for three months, without detection; and, two, if Neal himself had survived that barn fire. The first variable is extremely unlikely. The second is impossible.'

'You didn't know Neal.'

'Neal is gone,' he said. 'You need to come to grips with that.'

'I *want* him gone.'

She heard Gallagher take another deep breath. She knew he was having difficulty talking. 'Ellen, have you called the person I told you about?'

'I'm sorry I bothered you,' she replied, intending to hang up.

'Ellen.'

'What?'

'It's not a good time to be alone,' he said softly. 'Why don't you try to find a friend you can spend time with for a couple of days. Keep yourself busy.'

'Thanks.'

'I'll be back to work after the holidays,' he said. 'In the meantime, if you just want someone to chat with, I'll leave instructions with dispatch to page me.'

'Thanks,' she said again. This time she meant it.

Hard little snowflakes ricocheted off her windshield as she drove home that night, not enough to make her turn on her wipers. In fact, the temperature was too cold to snow in earnest, already minus two and falling. The steam from Ellen's breath seemed to stick to the glass.

When she pulled into the quiet car lot, hundreds of tiny blue Christmas lights blinked at her from the showroom windows. She drove around to the back of the garage and parked her truck.

Stepping out into the cold, she walked briskly around the building, her hand cupped under the leather bag so she could feel her .38 in the bottom. The night was so quiet, it fairly crackled as she passed through it. In fact, she could hear the distant hum of traffic on the interstate, ten miles away.

Relieved to see the light of her staircase, she hurried up the stairs with her key in her hand, unlocked the door and flipped on the kitchen light. She locked the door behind her, but before taking off her jacket and cap she turned up the gas heater on the side of her stove. Then, keeping her hand inside her purse, she walked through the apartment as she had when she'd first moved in, checking closets, peeking under beds.

Finally satisfied that she was alone, she took off her overclothes but kept her purse slung over her shoulder. To help her sleep, she poured a small glass of tequila, then went into her living room to watch the eleven o'clock news. She set the purse on the floor beside her rocking chair. As she absently watched a report about a Lewiston apartment fire, she sipped the tequila and felt her chest relax by degrees.

Then she began to stare at her tapestry loom. The unfinished masterpiece stared back: Scott's father's milk truck, Scott's mother's loom. Such wholesome endeavors, Ellen thought, such good people . . . yet how could they not have seen how desperately Scott tried to win their approval? And why had they constantly withheld it?

Ellen felt the heaviness grow in her chest, and she knew she should stop drinking, but she also knew she needed to silence her chattering mind, so she drank the tequila down, then walked out to the kitchen and poured another glass. She returned to the living-room with a serrated steak knife.

Standing behind the loom, she carefully pushed the blade through the center of the work and sawed outward to the side, separating warp from weft, sawing up, sawing down, tearing out the colors, freeing the images . . .

A car door closed.

Ellen jumped to the lamp, darkening the room. She dropped to her knees, found her purse and pulled her revolver out, then shut off the TV and hurried down the hallway into the kitchen, where she switched off the overhead light. In the blackness of her apartment, now she tried to listen for footsteps on the stairs, but she heard only the stove's heater fan blowing from across the room. She crept over to it, reaching blindly for the thermostat, knowing she'd burn herself – and she did, twice, before she found the dial and silenced the fan.

Now, rising with her .38 in her hand, she held her breath and listened. But hearing no traitorous creak of stair, she made her way back to the living room, where her two front windows blinked dimly at the front of the room. Positioning herself between them, she inserted two fingers in the Venetian blinds and spread the slats apart.

Beads of snow drifted like dust motes past the arc sodium lamps. Blue Christmas lights winked off the roofs of the vehicles below like hundreds of eyes, row after row. But nothing else moved. She stared intently at the cars, then returned to her dark hallway, running her hand along the wall until she reached her bathroom. Creeping in and sidling along the bathtub to the small window, she peeled back the shade and peered through the corner of the pane at the seven or eight vehicles parked below her, awaiting repair. She thumbed the icy window clear and moved her eyes to the right, over the dumpster to the small pile of wooden pallets.

Behind Ellen, something gulped. She swung the gun around.

The toilet. It gulped again.

Ellen drew a sharp breath, then blew the air out in a shuddering laugh. She lowered the revolver to her knee, then jiggled the flush handle, to stop the leak. Shaking her head at her own nervousness, she walked back to the kitchen and turned the light on, her rational mind returning. Ten below zero, nobody would be out there. Obviously.

She poured herself another glass of tequila, then brought the drink, along with the revolver, into her bedroom. She set them both on her night stand, then sat on the edge of the bed and pulled off her boots, tossing them at the closet, one at a time. She liked the sound of their heels hitting the hollow core door.

With the cold night seeping through the walls, she decided to sleep with her clothes on. Or maybe she was just too tired to take them off. She pushed in under the blankets, took the last sip of tequila, then slid the revolver under her pillow.

She thought of Maddy. She thought of Mo. She was grateful for the alcohol. Under its warm influence, a cross atop a silo no longer seemed threatening. A gulping toilet in the night became nothing more than a plumbing problem. In fact, lying there in her quiet apartment, protected from the icy night outside, it was very easy for Ellen to believe what Gallagher had been trying to tell her all along: that the dangers she had imagined were just the spinnings of her guilt-ridden mind. By degrees, her chest relaxed, her breathing slowed. She reached for the lamp, clicked on the night.

While outside in the frozen dark, her daughter stood at the bottom of the stairway until the cold had worked its way too deeply through her layers of clothes, and she could stand there no longer. Then she turned and walked back to her car, the old blue Taurus, and drove quietly home.

★ ★ ★

Every good thing about me, you know. The bad things arouse you.

This is the conversation Ellen has.

I love your hands, she tells him. I love your *capabilities*.

My capabilities? He laughs a little. Do you love my mind?

Her eyes go distant. I love the relationship between your neck and your shoulder, she tells him, and he smiles.

I love your depth, he replies, teasing her.

She smiles back at him. 'I love the relationship,' she continues, 'between your brow and your jaw.' With her finger, she traces these parts of him as she speaks.

But do you love my mind?

'Your mind scares me,' she confesses. 'What I love is the relationship between your chest and your stomach.' His flesh flows like warm oil under her palm.

'I love the relationship between your foot and your colors,' he says as he kneels at her feet, looking up at her.

She beams curiously. 'My colors?'

'Your colors,' he says again. His voice is soft as a cello breathing, and his hand running down her leg is even softer.

Watching her darkly, he cups her heel in his hand, and she realizes they are both naked. She feels a stirring deep in her abdomen. He dips his hand in a bowl of water, to wash her foot, and she flinches when she feels how cold the water is. He smiles. The muscles of his shoulders flex rhythmically as he works, and the chill rises to her thigh. Her nipples harden.

'I've always loved your hands,' she tells him.

'My hands?' He teases her, knowing that she is really looking at his erection, which stands stiffly beside her ankle. His eyes blacken, captivated, as he runs his cold hand up her thigh. When she opens her legs for him, they both hear the kiss of her vagina opening. He lowers his face, and his beard, soft as a felt cloth, brushes her inner leg. She closes her eyes as she feels his icy fingertips dance down her sides. Her hips ache pleasantly as her thighs open wider.

'I love the relationship,' he breathes, 'of your length and your depth,' his cool words popping off her delicate bud, electrifying her.

'My depth?' she says, with a breathless, luxurious smile.

His mouth descends to her vulva. His hands engulf her breasts, his sudden touch whipping a spasm through her. She arches her back and opens herself wider, and his cool tongue enters. Her nerve endings sparkle. She oils his tongue, and his tongue swells in response. His soft lips press down harder. She moans and tries to warm him more. But his tongue remains cold and moves deeper inside her, incredibly deeper.

'*How are you doing that?*' she asks in shuddering disbelief, his coldness radiating out through her hips.

His black eyes stare over her pubis. Then, with torturous slowness, his tongue slides deeper, steadily thickening, steadily filling her. Her body writhes, behaving without consent. She forgets to breathe. Her stomach is already filled with him, yet he plunges even deeper, far deeper than she's ever dreamed possible, approaching this secret, ecstatic ache at her very core. Her blood rushes, and she starts to shiver, as she feels her orgasm coming, like the rumble of a distant flood.

'*Wait,*' she gasps. All her life she's been vaguely aware of this unreachable place. Now she realizes that he may touch it. And it frightens her, yet she pushes into him. She cannot help herself.

She gasps: '*God, how can you possibly do that?*'

His black eyes gleam. His tongue flickers. And all at once a monstrous wave of energy floods around her chest, surging up through the top of her head and down through the deepest part of her.

My heart! she realizes. *He is actually touching my heart.* She clutches his head, pushes into him, as her orgasm pours on, wave after wave of ecstacy. His soft hair tangles in her fingers.

The chirring of crickets fills her ears, and she realizes they are lying outside in her cucumber patch, immersed in a cool bed of greenery. The waterfall rushes nearby. A flood is roaring through her.

'*Neal, is this really you?*'

Because she knows this cannot be possible. Her orgasm is endless, his hair entwined in her fingers, his cold black eyes staring up through her tangled mound of pubic hair, like the mesmerized eyes of a frog staring out of fat foliage. She feels the fine scratching of cucumber leaves on the backs of her arms. But wait. Not a frog. She feels his tongue flicker again, deep inside her chest. She jumps—

—grabbing for her lamp while he grabs for her ankle, her foot caught in the blankets. The light comes on, piercing her eyes like fangs. She tears her foot free, throws off her blankets, looking for the snake, but she finds her gun, swinging left and right around the room, heart pounding, mind racing, stopping her aim at the black, open doorway . . .

Did she hear a car door again? Toilet gulp? Footsteps in the hall? Did she hear anything but her own heart knocking at her chest?

She shivered with the cold. She saw her breath clouding the air in front of her face.

The gas heater . . . she had turned it off before going to bed, but forgot to turn it back on. She took a deep breath, a long, steaming sigh, and lay back down, tense with the cold. She rested the revolver on her chest, watched it bump up and down, up and down.

Do you love my mind? he had asked her.

I detest your mind, she wished she had said.

She listened to the incredible stillness outside, the night deeply frozen. She looked at her clock: 2:58.

Chilled as she was, the muscles in her abdomen glowed with an ache that told her she'd had an orgasm in her sleep. She felt the cold wetness between her legs.

Do you love my mind?

Off in the distance, she heard the gong of the church bell two miles away. She thought of the silo and the cross. The bell rang again.

I abhor your mind.

Barn with a steeple. Church with a silo.

Ellen sat up in bed. The bell rang a third time. Her stockinged foot slid on the floor, and she almost went down, but she caught the doorknob and swerved out into the hallway. Her shoulder hit the opposite wall, and she ran into the kitchen and slapped on the kitchen light, ripped the phone off the wall.

'State Police,' the woman said. 'What's your emergency?'

'This is Ellen Chambers, I need you to page Detective Gallagher for me,' Ellen said. 'Tell him I know how Neal Chambers survived the fire.'

'Is this an emergency, or can it wait till morning?'

Ellen's heart pounded in her temples. 'Just tell him!' she yelled, then she hung up.

★ ★ ★

The farmhouse was dark when she pulled in. But under a bright, misshapen moon the night was bright enough to see the pump house standing alone in the field, the black, rubble-filled foundation off to its right, the white tire tracks winding down through the blackened field, itself ribbed with a dusting of snow along dark harrow grooves.

Ellen picked up her flashlight from the seat beside her – a $2.99 special that occasionally needed a whack to work – and stepped out of her truck. She wore a flannel shirt and sweatshirt, a wool sweater and her jean jacket, with a wool felt hat pulled down to her eyes and thick wool mittens on her hands. She didn't need a thermometer to know it was below zero: the mucous inside her nose froze solid as soon as she'd stepped out of her apartment.

Everything lay so silent under the stars, it was as if the night could hear her every move. As she walked to the foundation, the burned and frozen grass crunched beneath the film of snow like tiny bones breaking. She heard her knee pop when she crouched to lower herself down the aluminum ladder someone had left inside the foundation. Stepping off the lowest rung, her boot squeaked in the frozen coals.

She swung her flashlight toward the front of the foundation, sliding the light over the blackened rocks. But seeing no stone large enough to hide a passageway, she turned her beam to the right, where the eastern wall was interrupted twice: once by a warped steel door hanging by its top hinge – the root cellar – and, further down, the opening to the bulkhead. Ellen climbed over the frozen ash heaps to the root cellar and shined the light through the angular opening.

She was surprised to see that the destruction inside was not total. In fact, the timbers and plank ceiling, although profoundly charred, still managed to support the weight of the frozen ground above. Even the two copper pipes that ran along the ceiling, although nonexistent in the main foundation, looked fairly sound inside this protected room. On the back wall, where three wooden bins stood side by side on the floor, the frozen mounds of blackness still held the shape of potatoes.

Ellen pulled the door open a few inches, until it stopped, then squeezed inside the room. She approached the potato bins gingerly, nervous that a loud noise might bring the earth-covered ceiling down on top of her. The bins were two feet wide and waist-high, their backs standing flush against the stone wall, their bottoms extending out from the wall at a 45-degree angle. The inch-thick plywood was black and blistered like alligator skin, but still solid. Four inches above the middle bin, the two copper pipes emerged through the rock wall and were elbowed up to the ceiling.

Ellen reached her mittened hand to the potato mound in the left-hand bin, found it had solidified into one charred mass. She pushed and pulled on the mound, but it held fast to the wood. When she tried the same thing with the middle bin, she felt a slight rocking – not in the potato mass, but in the bin itself. She dropped to her knees and aimed her flashlight underneath, looking for an opening in the wall, but the bottom edge of the bin met the concrete floor square. She got to her feet, pulled off her mitten and reached over the top of the bin. Unable to fit her fingers down behind the wood, even into the seams between the rocks, she climbed up into the potatoes and pressed her cheek and flashlight against the rocks, trying to see down. She couldn't. She ran her hand over the cold rocks above the bins, from left to right, searching for a catch or latch of some kind . . . then she found it. A small hollow in the underside of a rock. Poking one finger up inside the notch, she felt a metal ring. A small rush of adrenalin spurred her. She folded her finger through the ring and pulled.

The center bin gave way, dropping her to the hard concrete. As she rolled onto the floor, stunned, the bin swung up again, evidently counter-weighted, and closed neatly into place between the other two bins.

Ignoring the pain in her knee, Ellen retrieved her flashlight and climbed into the potatoes again. This time when she pulled on the ring, she was ready for the ride. As the bin released, she kept one boot on the floor to ease the lid down, all the while shining her light on the exposed opening in the wall.

Judging from its black mouth, the tunnel was only as wide as the bin – two feet – and not much higher. She saw that its floor was made of plywood, as were the walls. From her vantage point, Ellen could not see the ceiling, but assumed it was also plywood: a wooden, two-by-two chute. She thought of the tunnel connecting the church to the parsonage, and knew that Neal had built a secret passage just like it here, only much more confining.

Forgetting her frozen ears and nose, even ignoring the cold in her fingers, Ellen reached into the fallen bin with both hands and pulled the loosened potato mass forward so its weight overhung the bottom, to keep the bin from closing again.

Then she climbed over the top, holding the rock wall to balance herself as she slid her long legs down the back of the bin and into the mouth of the tunnel. Under her weight, the bin tried to close on her, but she pushed back with her shoulders until she was sitting at its base, with her legs squeezed inside the tunnel. Then she slithered in until only her head leaned against the back of the opened bin.

By the slight tug of gravity on her bottom, Ellen could already tell the tunnel had been built on a decline. She also knew that it led straight to the pump house – the copper pipes running down the center of the ceiling told her that. Additionally, she remembered the night Neal had dug the ditch; he had told her he was replacing water pipes. In truth, he had been preparing his vendetta.

She pressed her knees against the walls of the tunnel and aimed the flashlight between her legs, down the length of the tunnel, raising her head slowly to see its end. Hearing the sudden creak behind her, she threw her head back, but too late. The potato bin swung shut, closing off the night with a solid thud.

She reached over her head and pushed, but succeeded only in sliding down the tunnel floor. Pushing herself up close again, she shone her flashlight all around the seams between the tunnel and bin, searching for any glimmer of metal that might be a latch. She pressed her heels against the tunnel floor and pushed the bin with her hands again, but it held fast, and once again she slid away.

'*I'm down in the root cellar!*' she shouted, hoping that if she yelled loud enough, her voice might carry through the water pipes into the house. She stopped and listened for a response, or any sound at all. What she heard, from the foot of the tunnel . . . yes, a quiet humming, almost like the whirring of an electric motor. The water pump, she realized. Someone in the house was awake and running water – probably Scott using the toilet. She rapped her flashlight on the pipes.

'*Scott, I'm down here!*'

She listened again. Only the whirring replied.

Flicking off her flashlight to conserve batteries, Ellen started pulling herself forward to the pump house inchworm-style, using her boot heels, butt and elbows, trying to ignore the terrified voice that said Neal had lured her down here and trapped her in the dark. At least the tunnel was warmer than the air outside, she reasoned. But a strange pungency pervaded the air – the sweet smell of pine pitch, fouled by the stench of death.

Noting the thick glassiness of the plywood floor, she had assumed it was another example of Neal's meticulousness – shellacking the tunnel that he intended to use only once. Then she realized another truth: He had also used the shellac to preserve the body. Yes, he had murdered Gator – she knew that for certain now – and stored his body down here. She remembered Neal reading once that ancient Egyptians had preserved their mummies with pine pitch. In Neal's case, the pitch served a second purpose: fuel to destroy the evidence.

Despite the twinge of satisfaction she felt knowing that she'd been right about Neal, she felt a far more powerful fear knowing for certain that he was still alive. Her boots clunked and squeaked along the shiny floor, her breathing came faster and louder. Then her boot heel splashed.

She stopped moving, confused at first, until the ice water hit her fingers. She jerked on her flashlight, and her heart jumped. She scrambled back a few feet . . . then stared through her legs with a sickening dread.

Less than twenty feet away, the end of the tunnel lay sealed off with cinder blocks that were half-submerged in water . . . which meant the pump house was flooding. Worse, the water was getting deeper, creeping up the tunnel floor.

Her logic ravaged by panic, Ellen banged her flashlight on the water pipes until the light went out. She twisted the lens cap. The light flickered weakly.

'*Somebody!*' she screamed.

She fought for clarity: whether to continue ahead into the water and try to kick the cinder blocks out, or to retreat back to the root cellar and try again to break through the potato bin. Those were her only options, she told herself. If she pushed ahead to the pump house, she knew she would have to go into the water – and there was no guarantee she could break through the cinder blocks. But if she went back to the root cellar and failed to free herself, she would have lost the chance at the pump house.

As she tried to decide, the water bit at her fingers again. She aimed her light at the opening and now saw only six inches of dry cinder block exposed. She knew that the water pump could exert enough pressure to fill the entire tunnel to the top in a matter of minutes. She had to move. She turned off her flashlight and flung it back up the tunnel, to keep it dry. From here on, she would be less like an inchworm, more like some sightless subterranean fish.

She charged forward, amazed when the icy water poured into her boots that cold could hurt so much. Raising herself onto her hands until her knees rubbed the ceiling and her forehead touched the pipes, she crab-walked ahead. When the water hit her wrists, she yelled to alleviate the pain, simultaneously allowing the assault on her buttocks, but she kept moving ahead, finally submerging her back, the icy water tearing at her kidneys.

Screaming, she splashed deeper, until the water wrapped around her ribs and threatened to paralyze her lungs. Then her boot felt resistance, and she knew she had reached the end. She pushed with her toes, she kicked with her heels. The cinder blocks kicked back solidly.

Taking as big a breath as she could, she let her arms collapse, and she plunged completely under water, astonished at the severity of her pain. The aching in her forehead alone was enough to steal her consciousness. She pressed her hands on the ceiling and doubled up her knees. She grabbed hold of the water pipes. Flattening her boots against the cinder blocks, she pounded with her heels until she felt the jolt in her spine, but the cinder blocks refused to budge.

Giving up, Ellen pushed herself back out of the water with a terrified gasp, her frozen heart pounding weakly against her chest, retreating up the ramp until her elbow hit the flashlight at the head of the rising water.

'*Somebody help me!*' she screamed.

She turned on the light, looking around wildly, while the ice water inched steadily toward her heels. Confused as she was, she knew there had to be a latch, some way that Neal had let himself into the pump house. She also knew she had to go back into the water, this time head-first.

Pulling her feet up to her buttocks, she wrapped her arms

around her legs and tried to roll forward onto her knees, jamming her head against the water pipes and pushing off the tunnel's side with her shoulder. She twisted her neck and heard the copper squeak against her cheek. Then it released her, and she fell forward onto about two inches of ice water.

She turned off her flashlight and stuffed it in her pocket, then pulled herself out of her wet jacket and wedged a sleeve up over the water pipes, to keep the flashlight dry.

In total darkness, she bellied forward into the water until it reached her chin. Then she took three panting breaths to fill her lungs . . . and dived ahead with her arms outstretched. Streaking through pure weightless cold, she felt tunnel floor slide under her chest. Brows aching, she frog-legged off the floor and walls until her wrists jammed against the cinder blocks, and, with fingers too numb to feel anything but hard resistance, she vainly searched the sealed opening for a latch, ring, wire, or peg. Then a light came on.

Ellen doubted her eyes at first, thinking this thin glimmer along the upper edge of blackness was just a hallucination. But the light didn't waver. Someone was in the pump house. Desperate for air, she pushed off the concrete, fighting her way backward through the water, lungs flaring, pressing her shoulders up to the pipes until finally the back of her head broke water. She turned her face to the ceiling, gasping the meager air.

She tried to shout, but her voice wouldn't come. Backing further out of the water, she waved one arm wildly over her head until her hand hit her jacket. She stripped her revolver from its pocket and fired two shots at the water, the explosions crushing her eardrums, the powder flashes blinding her.

'*Help me!*' she screamed.

It didn't matter that she was five feet underground, somewhere between the pump house and barn, or that whoever had been in the pump house was looking down into three or four feet of rising water and would already be returning to the house to kill the circuit to the pump.

The water splashed over Ellen's hand again, and she crawled further backwards, until her boot hit the potato bin. Angling the revolver under her arm, she pulled the trigger, and the gun exploded against the wood. With all the fullness of her chest, she screamed.

'SCOTT!'

Her elbow splashed in the water. She fired the gun into the bin again, and screamed louder and longer than she ever had.

'I'M IN THE ROOT CELLAR!'

The water rose up her wrist and knee. She pushed herself upright, pressing her back against the pipes. She heard a voice – or thought she did. She fired the gun again.

'BEHIND THE POTATOES!'

She heard the voice again, muffled, but clear enough to tell it was Scott.

'Reach behind the bin! On the right!'

He yelled again, interrupting her.

'*Shut up!*' she screamed, rapping the wood with the butt of the revolver. 'Find the rock, a hollowed-out rock!'

Suddenly the wall fell forward, Ellen fell with it. She felt the icy bite of the night on her neck and tried to vault over the potatoes, but her legs were too stiff to move. His flashlight beam hit her face.

'Ellie, what the hell are you doing? You almost killed me. And you left the fucking pump house door wide open, so the pipes burst.'

Although Ellen's jaw was too frozen to work, she managed a distinct pair of syllables for him.

'I never went near the pump house,' she told them. 'It's obvious who opened that door – and who shut me in.'

Detective Gallagher nodded his head with a blank stare, a gesture meant to show that he was not patronizing. Indeed, as bedraggled as he looked – his eyes sunken, his cheekbones prominent – he'd be hard-pressed to patronize anyone. He reminded Ellen of pictures she'd seen of prisoners-of-war. A state trooper, dressed in a thick, fur-lined parka, stood behind him, just inside the kitchen door.

Ellen reached her hand out of the blankets, retrieved her coffee mug from the floor and filled her mouth. It was incredible, how good the coffee tasted. She was sitting in a chair in the middle of the room, while a wood fire roared behind her in the cookstove. Underneath the blanket she wore a thermal underpants and shirt. Beside them, the electric dryer tumbled her clothes.

Gallagher turned to Scott. 'Do you remember the last time you went out there, to check on the pump house?'

'I don't know,' Scott answered. 'Three, four weeks, maybe more. When Ellen got rid of her sheep and moved out, I went down to make sure she shut off the water to the barn.'

'Your daughter?'

'What about her?'

'Is there a chance Moreen left the door open?'

Scott shrugged. 'There's been no reason for either of us to go out there.'

'So the door could've been open for weeks, and you wouldn't have noticed—?'

'I suppose so. This is the first time we've had a deep freeze.'

Ellen threw her hands out of her blankets. 'I don't believe this,' she said. 'Scott, did you ever leave that door open? Have you ever forgotten to close the hatch?'

'Hey, the way things are goin, I might've forgotten a lot of things, okay? Half the time I can't remember my own name. It wouldn't surprise me, that's all I'm saying.'

Ellen looked directly at Gallagher. 'Neal Chambers trapped me inside that tunnel. He knew I was coming. He opened those doors so the pipes would freeze. If Scott hadn't come out, I would've drowned in there.'

'And if I'd been a foot to the left, you woulda friggin shot me through the heart. Ellie, what the hell are you doing here?'

'I'm trying to protect Mo!'

'No, you're using Mo,' Moreen said sweetly from the living room doorway. 'You're trying to convince yourself that I need you, as always.'

Her dark eyes glistened angrily, and they lingered – and for some reason, Ellen felt a connection.

'When are you going to understand, Mom? I gave up on you a long time ago.'

Then Scott intervened. 'Don't talk to your mother like that,' he said wearily.

As Ellen searched her eyes, Moreen turned and walked back into the living room.

Ellen turned to Gallagher again. 'Neal Chambers hid in that tunnel while the barn burned down,' she persisted.

'What tunnel?' Scott said, getting louder. 'It's a conduit for the water pipes so we could get at them if we ever had a problem. I told Neal to build it that way.'

'Or did he tell you?'

'As far as his hiding in there during the fire,' Gallagher added with an infuriating calm, 'anyone in that narrow space would have suffocated in a matter of seconds. A fire of that magnitude would have sucked out all the oxygen.'

'What if he had an oxygen mask, a scuba tank?'

Gallagher cocked his head, not that he was considering her suggestion. He was just too tired to argue.

'Conduit, tunnel, call it what you want,' Ellen said, 'Neal kept a human corpse down there, then substituted it for himself during the fire. Do the research.'

Without looking at her, Gallagher said, 'Ellen, I followed up on this Gator character after our last conversation.' He shook his head. 'No record.'

'I talked to him. He attacked me.'

'Detective Gallagher isn't saying he doesn't exist,' the trooper said. 'If you say you saw him—'

'I hit him in the face with a fire extinguisher!'

From upstairs a bang shook the house: Moreen slamming her bedroom door.

Gallagher stood up from his chair and zipped his parka. He looked unsteady on his feet. 'Ellen, after the holidays why don't you come down to the barracks and look at some pictures, maybe we can put a better name to this person.'

'Neal preserved his body with shellac or pine pitch,' Ellen continued, practically yelling. 'It's all over the wood in the tunnel.'

'That's plywood we scrapped from the tire store,' Scott told her, reclining tiredly in the wooden chair. 'It was from their paint room, the walls and floor. We junked it up and Neal brought it back here.'

'All right, who shut the bin?'

'What?'

'When I was inside the tunnel!'

'It could have blown shut. I don't know.'

Gallagher's partner, waiting at the door, shrugged his shoulders. 'Ma'am, there are no footprints out there, except yours and your husband's.'

Ellen rocked her body forward and stood, dropping the blankets to the floor. 'That's right, you've got answers for everything.' Stiff and sore as she was, she brushed past Gallagher and pulled open the clothes dryer. 'So you do nothing,' she said, jerking out her clothes, hot and humid, far from dry. She bundled them at her chest, then hobbled to the table and snatched her keys in her fist. 'Do nothing,' she said again, pushing past the cops.

'Come on, El, where are you going like that?' Scott said. 'It's below freezing out there.'

'What do you care?' she muttered, yanking the door open. Then she snapped her head around. 'When you went out to check the pump house, Scott, didn't you see my truck?'

'What?'

She gave him a long look. 'Maybe it's you that wants me dead.'

'Jesus Christ, Ellie.'

She balked in the doorway, knowing she was being scrutinized, knowing also that she'd just blown whatever scrap of credibility she might have had. She thought to say something – an apology, another fuck you, a simple goodbye – but she walked out into the frozen dawn.

Back at the car lot, blue lights blinking, the eastern sky was brightening. Ellen walked up her stairs, realizing that she was no longer thinking of Neal Chambers, no longer wondering where he might be lurking or when he'd make his move. She was too tired and too cold to be frightened of him. Indeed, right now she was more frightened of her own hysteria. Besides, it was much easier to believe what everyone but her seemed to know, that Neal was dead, which was to say, no longer of this world, no longer walking, thinking, breathing. Obviously. Dead.

Letting herself into her apartment, she dropped her heavy purse on the kitchen table and walked down the hall in semidarkness and turned into her bedroom. She stripped off her wet clothes and frozen socks and got under the covers wearing nothing but her underpants. The sheets were cold, her feet were icy. She lay there stiffly and closed her eyes, waiting for sleep to come. She rolled on her side and hugged herself, trying to warm up. She tried to pretend that Mo was five years old again, snuggling in bed with her. She wanted to feel the warmth of her little body, to hear the soft sound of her voice, to recall the particular smell of Mo's hair. But her imagination was barren, and the bed chilled her. She opened her eyes and stared at the pear-toned window shade and let the tears run down her nose. Off in the kitchen, the heater fan blew. Other than that, nothing stirred.

'Forgive *myself*?' she had once yelled at her mother-in-law. 'The truth about what?'

Now, she suspected, she was starting to learn.

Ingrid closed the store at noon on the day before Christmas, and for once Ellen looked forward to the solitude of her empty apartment so she could finish making Moreen's gift – a black sweater and matching cap she'd started over a month ago. But when she got home, she found the car dealers having a party in the showroom.

As soon as she got upstairs, she opened the bottle of Pinot Noir that Ingrid had given her, from a winery in the same Oregon town where Ingrid's friend owned the sheep farm. Ellen brought the bottle and a glass into the living room, where she settled on her couch under a quilted comforter, and she started knitting, listening to the Christmas music that drifted upstairs through the walls, the occasional bursts of laughter.

After her first glass of wine, she set her knitting in her lap, closed her eyes and fell asleep. When she awoke, it was dark, and she was hungry, so she went in the kitchen and cooked up some spaghetti and sauce, and toasted some garlic bread in her oven. She drank a glass of wine while she cooked, and had another glass while she ate. When she was through, she poured herself a fourth glass and returned to the living room, intending to knit Scott a hat, a way of apologizing for what she'd said to him.

Downstairs a few people were singing 'I'll Be Home for Christmas'.

Ellen could tell the party was winding down, and it made her wish they'd go on all night. What she really wished was that she could be with Scott and Mo in the morning, opening gifts. She imagined sitting on the couch in her bathrobe, with a mug of hot coffee in her hand. She even wanted to hear the Perry Como album that Scott played every year. *The Beach Boys Christmas* album. She wanted to smell turkey roasting, bread baking. She wanted to sit by the tree, reading, while Scott slept in his recliner in front of a football game.

When the singing stopped, Ellen waited for another song. Instead, she heard the sound of doors closing in the parking lot, then car engines starting. This was the hour she dreaded.

She turned on her little television. *It's a Wonderful Life*.

Naturally. Jimmy Stewart balancing along the bridge, ready to jump. Great thing to show people on Christmas Eve, she thought, especially people who don't believe in angels. She clicked through a few more channels, then shut the TV off.

She knelt on the couch and opened the Venetian blinds, looked out on the car lot. Snow was falling, fat, blue-flashing flakes spinning down, not enough to satisfy the skiers, but enough to cover the cars below . . . except for one. The dark station wagon sat at the back corner of the lot, its dull hood and roof melting the snow that landed, its clear windshield fogged on the passenger side. Gallagher.

Ellen put on her jean jacket and walked down the stairs, turning the corner around the garage, and she saw the detective's head move, saw him pull himself up in his seat. As she approached his door, he opened his window.

'You seemed so sure of yourself,' she said. 'I almost believed you.'

'I am sure of myself,' he replied. 'I only came here so you could get a good night's sleep.'

'You're alone?'

His eyes moved uncomfortably.

'Here, I mean, keeping watch.'

'The Lieutenant isn't about to authorize protection from a dead man,' he told her. His thermos mug steamed the windshield.

'Christmas Eve,' Ellen said. 'Kind of a lousy night to spend alone in a parking lot.'

'That's what I get paid for,' he replied, but in the blinking lights, the rigidity of his eyes betrayed a darker countenance.

'If you're going to watch my apartment, you might as well do it upstairs,' she said. 'I have a couch you could sleep on.'

He sipped his coffee, watching straight out his windshield.

'We could probably both use someone to talk to,' she said.

'I don't think we'd have much of a conversation,' he replied, still looking out at the snow. 'Not unless you want to talk to me about how Randy Cross got his arm caught in your dam.'

Ellen stood at his door for another second or two, waiting for him to make eye contact. He didn't. 'Have a good night, Detective,' she said, as his window went up.

Back upstairs, she stared at her half-filled wine glass. She'd drunk plenty, to be sure, but probably not enough to make it through this night without curling up in a tiny, self-pitying knot. She picked up the glass and drank it down, then tossed her knitting aside and went to the kitchen to finish the bottle. She picked up the telephone instead.

'I need to apologize,' she said when Scott answered. 'I didn't mean what I said last night.'

He made a low sound in the phone. It made her think he might be feeling as bad about Christmas as she was. How could he possibly feel about the anniversary of his parents' death?

'How's Mo doing?' she asked.

'Asleep,' he told her. 'We both went to bed an hour ago.'

Ellen looked at the clock, was surprised to see it was past eleven thirty.

'I'm sorry,' she said. 'I just wanted to see when I should bring gifts over for you and Mo.'

'I didn't get anything for you,' Scott told her. 'I don't really know how this is done.'

'Neither do I,' Ellen said. 'I'm not finished with yours anyway. Maybe I'll bring them over tomorrow afternoon. Do you and Mo have plans?'

'I asked her if she wanted to go out for dinner. She didn't really answer me.'

'I could stop by in the morning,' Ellen said, a little too casually.

He gave an equivocating grunt. Not that she expected anything more.

'Scott, I don't know,' she practically blurted . . . then she stopped and started again. 'I don't *understand*,' she clarified, 'what makes people do the things they do.'

'It's a rough time of year,' Scott said.

'I mean me. I always thought . . . at least I thought I knew myself.' She stopped talking again, wishing she had phoned him three glasses of wine earlier. 'But I never would've believed I was capable of some of the things I've done.'

'El, can we do this another time?'

'Wait – I want to ask you something.'

He listened.

'Not that I expect you to answer me,' she said, 'but just, hypothetically . . . Do you think you could ever forgive me? I'm not asking you to. I'm just wondering if you think it's possible.'

While she listened to the silence on the line, she remembered what it was like getting in bed together after setting Christmas gifts under the tree. She imagined crawling into a warm bed with him tonight.

'I don't think so,' he said.

Ellen's mind stopped. She took a slow breath in, then let it out.

'I think you're right,' she told him.

'I know I am.'

She waited for him to continue, but he hung up.

She returned to the living room and drank the rest of her wine, then considered starting on the tequila. But she didn't. She kept knitting his hat.

Of course, he was right.

How could someone in love even imagine forgiving such a betrayal? Of course, one may agree to remain with an unfaithful partner – passing on the stairs, eating meals together, going to movies – believing that in time the wound will heal over.

But how could she believe she had ever forgiven him – truly forgiven him – the way her stomach wrenched every time she heard April's name? The way her mind blanked whenever she climbed the stairs and found her bedroom door closed. The way she could never feel him enter her without imagining the path of his mind.

And probably Neal had been right, that the only reason she'd ever fallen in love with him was to get back at Scott.

Time heals all wounds? No. Scars last. They smile and they kiss and they profess loss of memory. But after thirteen years, how ripe she'd been for revenge. Even now she could not deny the small pang of pleasure she felt, picturing Scott lying in his cold bed, regretting one single day – one hour – that happened so long ago it could have been someone else's life.

Ellen awoke to a sharp knocking on her door. Disoriented by the bright sun shining on her blinds, she got out of bed and went into the kitchen.

'Merry Christmas,' Ingrid said when she opened the door. 'Do you know there's a well-dressed Neanderthal parked outside the building?'

Ellen didn't even try to smile. Her eyes were caked, her face stiff. 'No, but if you start it, I'll sing along,' she answered sullenly, turning to her coffee maker.

'Go get dressed,' Ingrid told her. 'We're having Christmas dinner at my house.'

Before Ellen could decline, Ingrid stepped inside and closed the door. 'You weren't answering your phone, so I called Scott, to see if you were there.'

Ellen brought the coffeepot to the sink.

'No time for coffee,' Ingrid said. 'I've got people coming and a twenty-pound turkey in the oven.'

Ellen gave a half-smile, even as she felt the ache in her throat. 'Really, I can't.'

'They're all women. Most of them make you look like a poster-girl for well-adjustment.'

Filling the coffee maker with water, Ellen took a shaky breath. She wished Ingrid would leave.

'You can't refuse,' Ingrid told her. 'You're at the head of the table this year. It's a spot reserved for anyone who shoots at her husband.'

Ellen turned. The older woman's eyes glinted kindly.

'I shot three times,' Ellen said. She blurted a laugh, and tears broke from her eyes.

Ingrid doubled her fist. 'That's my girl.'

The women drank spiced wines and cider, homemade Christmas ale and a Swedish holiday concoction called glög. A couple of them smoked Cuban cigars out on Ingrid's deck; two or three shared a bowl of Jamaican ganja in the bathroom. Some watched football with the sound muted and remarked on the players' thighs and their potential as seed donors. One of the women, a licensed massage therapist, gave massages in Ingrid's bedroom. Another read tarot cards in the spinning room. Ellen declined the massage, the cigar, the pot and the tarot reading, and she limited herself to a single glass of wine.

At the table, the women loosened their belts, unbuttoned their skirts, and ate for nearly two hours. As Ingrid had promised, she seated Ellen at the head of the table. Ellen was relieved that no one asked why.

After dessert, with flames crackling in the fireplace, they drank gourmet coffee and drew names for a gift exchange – Ingrid had thoughtfully brought along one of Ellen's tapestries from the store so that she'd have something to give. Then they sat on pillows and cushions around the coffee table, or huddled together on the couch, and shared stories. Ellen learned that some of the women were couples, that one woman had an ovarian cyst; another had lost her father on Thanksgiving. When five of the women, members of a 200-voice women's chorus in Portsmouth, squeezed together on the couch and sang a gospel song called, 'I Feel Like Going On', Ellen struggled to hold back her tears. That's when she slipped into Ingrid's bedroom and picked up the telephone. Moreen answered after the fourth ring.

'Hi, hon,' Ellen said. She waited a few seconds for a response. 'Sorry I didn't get your gifts over to you today.'

'Are you all right?' Moreen asked, sounding more annoyed than concerned. But Ellen didn't let that bother her. She felt strong tonight, actually in control of her part of the conversation, without feeling responsible for Mo's part too.

'Better,' Ellen said. 'Thanks for asking. How are you doing?'

Mo paused. 'My expectations are never that high.'

Ellen laughed a little. 'That's one way to do it,' she said. 'Listen, I'll bring your gift over someday this week.'

'Don't worry about it.'

Ellen smiled. 'I miss you, Mo.'

She heard Moreen take a deep breath. 'I've gotta go,' Moreen said.

'Merry Christmas, hon.'

After Ellen replaced the phone in its cradle, the door opened, and Ingrid stepped inside.

'Leaving?'

'My eyes are starting to cross.' Ellen found her jean jacket under the coats on Ingrid's bed. She pulled her cap out of the sleeve and fit it over her head.

'Feel better?'

Ellen nodded. 'Thanks.'

Ingrid waved off the gratitude, then shut the door behind her. 'I have something for you. I'm afraid it's not too classy, but I'm hoping you'll know what to do with it.'

She handed Ellen a simple red card that said GREETINGS. When Ellen opened it, ten hundred-dollar bills slid into her palm.

'I didn't want the others to see it,' Ingrid said. 'A couple of them used to work for me, and I wasn't as generous.'

Ellen's shoulders dropped. She felt a compunction to refuse the money, but the glow she felt – maybe it was what Maddy used to call self-actualization – prevented her from doing anything but folding the bills in half and slipping them into her pocket.

'It's a lot of money for a part-timer,' she said.

'You're worth much more. In case no one's told you lately, you're a kind, intelligent, strong, beautiful and imaginative woman.' Ingrid raised a brow. 'Sometimes too imaginative.'

Ellen smiled. 'Thanks,' she said again. 'But you forgot "rigid".'

'Rigid. Really.'

'As in "unforgiving".'

Ingrid gave her a skeptical look. 'Tell me something,' she said. 'How many times have you forgiven your daughter?'

Before Ellen could recover from the small jolt, Ingrid opened her door. 'Busy day tomorrow. Get a good night's sleep.'

CHAPTER TWENTY-FOUR

On the day after Christmas the store was crowded with people returning gifts or spending their gift money. Thankfully, Ingrid closed at five. Ellen put in her hours, processing exchanges, working at the demonstration loom, weaving small lighthouse and lobster wall-hangings in preparation for tourist season. Ingrid was convinced that people would buy dried dog shit if a lighthouse or lobster were painted on it. Ellen was convinced she was right.

Back in her apartment that night, Ellen found the phone number Ingrid had given her of her friend in Oregon who owned the farm. Although it was eleven o'clock, on the west coast it was only eight. She made the call.

In the morning she gave her notice, and Ingrid grinned. 'When are you leaving?'

Ellen shrugged. 'End of the month?'

'Go next week, if you want,' Ingrid told her. 'Once the after-Christmas rush is over, it's hardly worth opening the doors again till April.'

Ellen took a deep breath.

'Excited?'

'I've never even seen the Pacific Ocean.'

Ingrid put her hands on Ellen's arms and turned her toward the door. 'Go talk to your daughter.'

Moreen was still sleeping at eleven o'clock, when Ellen knocked on her bedroom door.

She groaned tiredly when Ellen walked in and sat on the corner of her bed. 'Merry late Christmas,' she said, setting her sweater and knit hat beside her pillow.

Mo closed her eyes again. In the corner of the room, small arms and legs intertwined in a pile, all her sculptures thrown together.

'Hon, I wanted to talk to you,' Ellen began, already knowing how the conversation would go. 'I think I'm moving.'

Moreen rolled over, facing away from her.

'Do you remember a woman named Priscilla Clancy? She was in the Weavers' Guild with me. She lives in Oregon now, on a farm. She has a guest house that's empty.'

Ellen put her hand on Mo's shoulder. Mo drew her arm back.

'There's a state college in the next town, with a good art department. If they saw your work, I know they'd offer you a scholarship.'

Moreen pulled her blankets over her head. 'Go if you want. I need to sleep.'

Ellen sat for another few moments, then got up. Resisted the temptation to pick Mo's jeans and sweatshirt off the floor. 'Honey, I'd like you to come with me. I hope you'll think about it.'

Moreen didn't answer.

Ellen left the house, drove to the gun shop.

Scott smirked when she'd told him what she was planning.

'What about Mo?' he said.

'I told her I'd like her to come with me.'

'Fat chance of that.' He turned and lifted a long cardboard box – a rifle, Ellen guessed – from a wooden shipping crate. 'Truck gonna make it?'

'I'd probably sell it and rent a van.'

'Yup.'

'Anyway, I wanted to look through the attic and see if there's anything I can take – the old toaster, plates and pans and silverware and things. Is that okay?'

Scott scowled over the counter at her, as though it was just dawning on him that she might be serious. 'Moreen's not going to go with you, you know that. Are you seriously planning to leave her here and go three thousand miles away?'

'Yes, I am,' Ellen replied, a bit surprised at her own conviction.

As the cold week passed, and Ingrid trimmed Ellen's hours back further, Ellen kept herself busy making arrangements for the move, pricing rental vans and gathering kitchenware from the farmhouse attic. She disassembled her looms and spinning wheel and bagged all her raw wool and yarn, boxed everything and stored it in her spinning room at the house. She did everything but set a date.

On the last day of the year, Ingrid took her to dinner at the York Harbor Inn. They split a bottle of good champagne and talked of ordinary things, not Oregon, which Ellen took as Ingrid's not pressuring her. In fact, Ellen still hadn't reserved the van. The subject came up only at the end of dinner, when Ingrid promised to visit someday. Her tone of voice said she was wondering if Ellen was still planning to leave. It made Ellen wonder herself.

Because they'd arrived in separate vehicles, their goodbye in the parking lot was brief.

'Gonna be okay tonight?' Ingrid asked. 'Dick Clark can be murder when you're waiting for the phone to ring.'

'New Year's Eve never did much for me anyway,' Ellen assured her.

'What about tomorrow?'

Ellen rubbed the chill out of her arms. 'Anything but football.'

'Good day for a long drive,' Ingrid said.

'Maybe.'

The blues took Ellen by surprise. Almost as though some internal clock were programmed for holiday depression, she spent the night in front of her television with the remote control in her hand, keenly aware of her solitude, keenly disturbed because of it. Finally dozing off during the eleven o'clock news, she practically flew off the couch when the telephone rang.

'What are you doing?' Scott said. He sounded almost as miserable as she felt.

'It's midnight,' she said, looking at the clock on the kitchen stove.

'I know.'

Neither of them spoke for another moment or two.

'Well, happy New Year,' Ellen said.

'Mo's been in bed since ten,' Scott replied. 'I wish she'd do something, get a job or go back to school.'

'I guess we have to give her time to find her way.'

'I guess. Trouble is, with you leaving, I just don't know what that's gonna do to her.'

Ellen waited him out.

'Have you thought any more about it?'

'Leaving? I think about it a lot,' Ellen told him, wondering about his change in attitude. 'I don't seem to be doing much about it, though.'

'I've been thinking too,' he said. If he was drunk, she couldn't detect it in his voice. 'Remember what you said the other day, about forgiveness?'

'Yeah—?' She couldn't remember the last time they had actually had a conversation.

'I guess I could try.'

Stunned, Ellen leaned heavily on the kitchen counter.

'El, I know you did your best to forgive me after that thing with April.' Scott continued. 'I guess I'd like to think it's not over.'

Hearing his voice in her ear, she nodded. It was about all she could do.

'Then again, I know you well enough to know that once you set your mind on a course, there's not much that can hold you back.'

He stopped talking.

Ellen swallowed hard, to keep her emotions down. 'I think I'm going to go to Oregon, Scott.'

She heard him sigh. 'I understand,' he told her. 'But maybe before you do, you might think about this as something we can get over someday. I mean, maybe it's not possible. But along the lines of whatever – curiosity? – I was wondering if I could take you to dinner next Saturday.'

She closed her eyes. The tears burned. It was ridiculous, how much her heart ached.

'I was thinking of leaving before then,' she said, trying to keep her voice from breaking.

'I know. And if you go, you go. I'm just saying, if you're still around and you want to give dinner a try, that's all I'm saying.'

Ellen breathed a long, heavy sigh. 'I guess another week won't kill me,' she told him.

'El, I've really been missing you.'

'I miss you too,' she said, though she had meant to choose her words more carefully.

For Ellen, the week dragged by. Even though she worked only four hours a day at the store, with hardly any customers those hours seemed endless. To make matters worse, early Friday morning a northeaster blew into town, canceling school and keeping most everyone homebound. The store remained deserted all through the morning, which was fine with Ellen, since Ingrid had called to say she had to tend to her car, which had been vandalized during the night.

As Ellen worked at the loom, the sound system played music that Ingrid had made for the shop, a taped mix of international folk songs by women who sang about sisterhood and the pleasures of country life without men – not Ellen's favorite music, but after six weeks of Christmas carols played on hammered dulcimers and banjos, she considered any change a relief – not that she was paying close attention, anyway.

She was far too occupied with thoughts of Scott and Moreen, wondering if it could be possible for the family ever to live together again, with all they'd been through. Even if it were possible, she wondered if they could continue living in Destin.

As she wove her lighthouse scene, looking out at the snow blanketing the parking lot, images of Oregon passed through her mind with greater frequency. She pictured green vistas of grape vineyards, mountainsides trimmed with tall evergreens, the wide blue Pacific.

Maybe it was time for all of them to move, she thought. She could teach school anywhere. And Scott, with his business experience, would have no trouble finding work. It was Moreen she worried about, wondering how the uprooting might affect her. On the other hand, that far removed from Destin, maybe Mo would find it easier to try on a new personality. Maybe college would inspire her.

The doorbell interrupted her reverie.

'Don't get up,' the man said, not a customer but Douglas, the driver from Spruce Bush Farms. Ingrid liked to stock a couple of shelves of offbeat things, such as dilly beans and canned fiddleheads, herbed oils and gourmet mustards. Douglas visited the shop twice a month to restock the shelves.

'How's the driving?' Ellen asked.

'Terrible,' he said, and he stuck an opened jar under her nose.

She wrinkled her nose at the vinegar kick. 'What is it?'

'It's a new line we're trying: "Widow Jimmy's Famous Frickles." '

'*Frickles?*'

'Pickled french fries. Try one.' He was a roundish man with David Crosby hair, rimless glasses and a bump of a chin. His eyes sparkled when he grinned.

'I don't think so,' Ellen said.

He brought the opened jar to the cash register and set it on the counter beside a small, free-standing promotional display that held six jars. 'We're giving away free samples all over New England, big promotional campaign.' He set a box of toothpicks beside the jar.

'Pickled french fries?'

'They're not as bad as they sound. The story's great. Apparently, this woman's husband came up with the recipe, but then he disappeared and all he left her was a barn full of these things. It looked like she was going to lose the farm, but one morning she opened the door and there was a Dunkin Donuts bag on her porch with a hundred grand inside, no name, no explanation. Just the cash – a hundred thousand dollars. She put a bundle into marketing, and now she's making money hand-over-fist.' He shook his head while he popped a Frickle in his mouth and started to chew. 'Who said this was a crazy world?'

He picked up the carton and headed down the food aisle.

'Speaking of which,' he said over his shoulder, 'are you trying to drive yourself nuts in here?'

'What do you mean?'

He stuck his head out of the aisle with a distasteful squint. 'For two solid months I've put up with that Christmas shit. Enough already.' He waved a hand at the loudspeaker mounted in the corner of the ceiling, as the song sailed through the store: '*. . . three French hens, two turtle doves, and a partridge in a pear tree.*'

Ellen laughed. 'I don't even hear it anymore.'

'I can tell. But really, once is bad enough.'

Ellen looked curiously at him.

' "The Twelve Days of Christmas," ' he explained. 'The song just ended – then started up again. Come on, the holidays are over. Let the dead rest.'

Ellen scowled. She got up from the loom and walked around the counter, opened the door to the small back room. On a shelf beside the desk, the tape player was running, as usual. Then she noticed a trail of small puddles leading in from the back door. She stepped over the puddles, turned the knob and pulled the heavy door open. The blizzard was blowing diagonally out of the colorless sky, the dumpster and woods obscured by whiteness. She checked the knob on the outside of the door – still locked.

'Is everything okay?' the driver said from the doorway, startling her.

Ellen closed the door, then looked at him for a moment. 'Yeah,' she replied. She went to the tape player and pushed STOP. The shop became perfectly quiet, except for the snow ticking at the door. The driver eyed her curiously.

'What's the date today?' she asked him.

'The sixth,' he said. 'Why?'

'January sixth,' she confirmed.

He nodded his head. 'If you're a fan of Shakespeare's, also called Twelfth Night.'

Ellen scowled at him, a surge of weakness playing at her knees.

'The twelfth day after Christmas,' he explained. 'I assumed that's why you were playing that god-awful song.'

'Twelve days,' she breathed, pushing past him into the front of the store, where she turned to the cuckoo clock behind the cash register.

Eleven forty-five.

'Twelve hours,' she whispered.

The man picked up his empty carton, seeming to study her. 'Gotta go, I'm running almost two hours late,' he said.

Twelve years, twelve months, twelve weeks . . .

She tried to clear the terror from her face, even as her mind raced: *Neal is here*. No, he'd *been* here. Now he was on his way to find Scott and Moreen.

'See you in a couple of weeks?' the driver said, still watching her.

'Yeah,' Ellen said.

He headed down the main aisle, pushed the door open, then turned to give her one more look. 'Have a good one,' he said, then he walked out. Ellen watched him fade into the storm.

Then she grabbed the telephone – but what could she say to convince anyone? In a moment it didn't matter. The phone was dead. She dropped it and ran into the back room, to the desk, reached into her pocketbook, felt around. Her revolver was gone.

Ripping her jacket from the hook, she pulled the coat tree to the floor, then threw the back door open and charged out into the storm. Her truck was parked about fifty feet away, on the other side of the dumpster. She got in, started the engine and turned on the windshield wipers, but the snow was too heavy to clear, so she jumped out and swiped the snow with her arm until the wipers started moving.

She ducked back in the cab and shifted into gear, turned her defrosters high, punched her emergency flashers, then tore off across the parking lot. At the turn, her truck skated a half circle and slammed backward into the snowbank the plows had made.

'*Shit!*' Ellen yelled, restarting the engine and popping the clutch. The truck fishtailed wildly, then slid headlong through the lot and into the road, narrowly avoiding a furniture truck which swerved to miss her. She hit a patch of road sand and shot ahead, straight through the stop light.

The clock on her dash said 11:50. Even on a good day, the drive to her house took ten minutes. Fortunately, the plows had been out all morning, and the road wasn't bad. She passed one car, then another, then swung back into her lane just as a sand truck turned toward her, blasting its horn.

She concentrated on her breathing. Drop the diaphragm. Fill the belly, fill the chest. Full breath in, full breath out.

Clear the mind. *Think*. Cassette tapes are usually forty-five minutes to a side. Which meant Neal couldn't be more than forty-five minutes ahead of her. More likely a half-hour or less. But how long did it take to kill someone?

Twelve years, twelve months, twelve weeks, twelve days, twelve hours: all the twelves in line, at last. It was what Neal had been planning since his twelfth birthday—

—and now he had her gun.

11:51.

And she had nine minutes to stop him.

Moreen would still be in bed – she rarely got up before noon. Scott would have come home for lunch a half-hour ago. Ellen's only hope was that Neal would wait for her, wanting them all together.

She pressed the accelerator down. At the intersection with the Reservoir Road, she swerved left through the stop sign and forced a jet-black Altima into the ditch. She never slowed.

11:55.

She reached into the glove compartment, felt around for something she could use as a weapon, found a Phillips screwdriver about four inches long. She would not hesitate to kill him with it. She pictured herself driving it into his chest, his throat. Whatever it took. She jammed it in her jacket pocket as she made the turn onto River Road.

She knew Scott would have a gun in the house – unless he got rid of it when Moreen moved back home. It didn't matter. Neal would never give him a chance to use it. He'd find a way to take them by surprise.

Her keys—

Of course, Neal had copied her keys – the same way he'd let himself into Maddy's house and into the store. Yes, he'd let himself in the front door while Scott was in the kitchen with the portable television on, having his lunch.

Then Ellen would steal into the house the same way. She hit her brakes, skidded to a stop at the top of the hill. Her white farmhouse below was completely obscured by the blizzard, and for a moment she felt that gave her an advantage.

11:58.

Except that Neal knew she was coming. He had begun constructing this particular road another lifetime ago, and today Ellen had no choice but to follow. With a sinking fear, she also realized that nothing she could do to stop him would have escaped his consideration.

She slammed into low and her white truck jumped over the crest of the white hill and surged straight down. She pumped the brakes as she approached her driveway. The back end of the truck drifted rightward on the ice, she downshifted into second, then hit the gas and plowed into the snowbank beside her driveway, the impact pitching her into the horn. So much for surprises.

11:59.

She kicked her door open and fell out into the snowbank, dropping her screwdriver. She picked it up and ran into the dooryard, the snow freezing her wrist. The blizzard was blowing down harder, making it difficult to see more than a few feet ahead, but she could make out Scott's Mercedes parked there, the recently-cleared windshield, the dark hood melting the snow as it landed. A fresh set of footprints led from the car to the porch. No other tracks were visible.

Clutching the screwdriver close to her chest, Ellen followed the tracks onto the porch and tried the door, found it unlocked. She pushed it open, looked inside. The kitchen was quiet. She looked up at the clock on the wall, the second hand sweeping up to twelve.

'Scott?' she called, and a fierce chill went through her. '*Moreen!*'

She heard the muffled hum of the noontime fire horn from off in the village. She jerked her head toward the clock as the second-hand passed over twelve and silently continued rounding the numbers. Ellen backed against the counter, braced for the attack.

'*Scott?*'

The sound of her voice slapping off the bare walls sent goose-bumps down her sides. Reaching behind her, she quietly pulled out the drawer, where she found a steak knife. She set her screwdriver on the counter.

She thought of the pantry, of Neal lurking that close to her, and she sidled along the counter until most of the small room came into view, empty.

A gust of snowflakes tapped at the windows. She looked back at the clock, the second hand sweeping up to 12:01.

Twelve minutes . . . Of course. He would draw this out till the last second. *All the twelves in line.*

She walked into the living room, the steak knife tight in her hand. The stairway rose silently, white storm-light coming in the windows, projecting the soft shadows of the banister up the white wall.

'Scott?'

She listened for a response above her, but heard only the wind rattling at the windows . . . and she remembered another time, years ago, when she stood here calling his name.

'Moreen, answer me!' she yelled. Beside her, the VCR blinked from 12:01 to 12:02. On the other side of her—

She stopped.

A Bible lay open on the coffee table, a black circle scrawled around a passage. She bent closer to see: '*And ye shall know the truth, and the truth shall make you free.*'

She batted the book on the floor, then crossed to the stairs, transferring the knife to her left hand as she took hold of the railing, climbing steadily, knowing her bedroom door would be closed and terrified of opening it, wondering what she would find this time.

She remembered perfectly the image of Scott and April getting dressed beside the bed, the look in their eyes when she opened the door . . . now she pictured Scott and Moreen lying on the same bed, corpses silently staring.

A tread squawked under her foot and she stopped, nearly paralyzed. But why wait? He knows she's coming. He knows she can't refuse. She climbed the last two steps and stepped around the corner into the hallway. All three doors were shut, as if each held back a secret.

Her hand reached out, took hold of Scott's bedroom doorknob.

Neal, we only want to help you.

Yeah. With a steak knife in her hand, that kind of truth would not set anyone free.

She turned the doorknob and pushed. Her head hummed, her heart pounded. The door swung open. The room stared back at her. The bed was disheveled, sheets discolored where he slept. Underpants tossed in the corner with his socks; pocket change scattered on the night table and floor; closet door opened on his permanent press shirts, his thirty-dollar neckties. A strange feeling washed over Ellen, something akin to relief. *I don't miss this*, she thought.

Was that the truth Neal wanted?

Scott, living without you the past three months has been the loneliest time of my life. I never imagined anyone could feel such emptiness. But the truth is, I don't miss you.

Maybe it was true, Ellen thought, but not entirely.

Yes, I do miss you. But I don't believe we ever loved each other, not the way love ought to be. Even when we had sex, I felt like you were having sex with my breasts. I was never part of it.

She opened her own closet, still hung with the skirts and blouses she had no more need of – polite clothing of a woman who would never dream of having sex with her nephew, murdering her son-in-law . . .

When I said I forgave you, Scott, I think what I really meant was that I was afraid to leave you. Or maybe I was afraid you'd kill yourself, like your brother did. Maybe I was afraid of what people would think of me.

On Scott's night stand, the clock-radio whirred.

12:06.

Six minutes to save their lives. Ellen went to his bureau and opened the drawers, searched under T-shirts and sweatpants for a weapon she knew wasn't there. She wheeled and hurried out into the hallway, holding the knife out ahead of her as she crossed to Moreen's room and threw the door open. Her heart leaped. Then it fell. Clay body parts littered the room.

Ellen knew it was Moreen's doing, not Neal's, destroying all that was beautiful about herself.

Moreen, every time you came home with a new tattoo or another piece of hardware through your flesh, I felt like you were disfiguring me.

Or is that me being self-centered again?

The disembodied faces – Moreen's faces – glared up at her, screaming in a silent rage.

Ellen stepped over the clothes, the smashed, twisting limbs, and crossed to the closet, wondering if she'd find Mo's body hanging inside. But there was only the collision of tattered jerseys and T-shirts, obscenity-scrawled and stinking of body odor.

How's this: When we were together in public, I was embarrassed that people would know you were my daughter. Sometimes when you were out at night past your curfew, and I was afraid for you, sometimes I wondered how my life would be if you never came home at all.

Ellen felt the tremor building deep in her gut.

Maybe I was glad when you lost the baby. Maybe in my heart I knew that Neal was lying about Randy kicking you. Maybe I helped murder your husband because I was angry at you.

Was that the truth he wanted?

'Moreen, answer me!' Ellen shouted.

Her Betty Boop clock turned to 12:10.

Ellen left the room, turned in the hall and pushed open the door to her spinning room. Filled with boxes and bags, useless fragments, it made Ellen wonder if the house was as empty as it seemed, indeed, if this was all her imagination again.

No. It was Neal who had left the Bible for her. He was here.

A scream spun Ellen into the hall, heart leaping. But it was only Moreen's alarm clock sounding, from the bedroom. Then she heard Scott's radio come on. '*If everybody had an ocean, across the USA . . .*' Steak knife in hand, Ellen hurried down the stairs (the VCR blinking 12:12, 12:12, 12:12, the stove alarm jangling), burst into the kitchen, turned off the stove timer. She looked up at the clock on the wall, its second hand twitching . . . seven . . . eight . . . nine . . . all the twelves. Finally. All lining up.

Ellen backed against the front door, the knife flashing in front of her. Then a deep, distant roll of thunder shook the floor, rattling the dishes in the cupboard. Then silence.

Ellen opened the door and looked out into the falling snow. Just the wind in the woods, a deep, steady blowing. Squinting into whiteness, she stepped to the edge of the porch, where the falling snow was able to reach her. The only footprints she could see were Scott's and her own, coming into the house. How could they not be inside? Unless—

She turned left and walked to the end of the porch, moving faster as the answer became apparent. And there they were, tracking down beside the house and across the dooryard, three sets of prints. They had gone out the front door.

Ellen made a frightened sound, her voice swallowed by the rush of wind that seemed to be intensifying . . . except the snow continued falling straight down.

There was no wind.

That's when Ellen realized what was making the sound, and her heart leaped.

She started to run.

A gray ghost sat in the vice, the same unfinished fly that had been staring at Wes Westerback for a week now, with his magnifying light hovering over it. Wes himself reclined in his desk chair, watching the snow tumble down past the glass doors, not listening to the telephone ringing, or the scanner chattering, or the vacuum cleaner that rolled back and forth on the floor over his head, not wondering about the explosion he'd heard, not even thinking about his dead son Sugar. What occupied his mind was watching the bluejays and squirrels battle for a handful of sunflower seeds in the snow – and feeling heartbroken about it. Not the most healthy way for any man to spend his days, let alone a police chief. Wes knew this. But nothing else seemed to hold his attention. Not even the trout fly.

On the seventh ring, Wes picked up his phone and said, 'Yup.'

'Wes, it's Dave Mercurio, up at the Water District.'

'Yeah, Dave.'

'I don't know what the hell's going on, but I think some goddamned kids blew up the dam.'

Wes didn't say anything for a second. Outside the glass door, a squirrel dived off a spruce branch and caught the bird feeder in mid-air, kicking seeds out of the tray as it swung.

'You think?' Wes said.

'We're losing half the goddamned reservoir, Wes. The valley's gonna flood. I don't know what we can do to stop it. I got divers coming, but it's not just the liftgate. Half the friggin' dam's blown to smithereens.'

Wes inhaled deeply, then let out a long sigh. He watched the squirrel jump off the feeder into the snow and scurry about grabbing his booty. He thought he was going to cry.

'Gotta be kids,' Mercurio said. 'They're all home from school today.'

Wes exhaled another sigh. 'Dave, do me a favor and call the State Police. They'll handle it. Anyone lives along the river, you'd best get 'em evacuated to the high school. Call Hawkins, the Superintendent, and have him open up the school, turn on the heat and get the cooks in. He'll know what to do.'

'I'll make the call, Wes, but who's gonna to listen to a Water District engineer?'

'Tell them you're a sergeant with the Destin Police,' Wes told him. 'I just deputized you.'

Ellen ran as fast as she could through the snow, but she kept sinking in the previous tracks and falling to her knees. When she reached the pump house she stopped. Through the falling snow she recognized Neal's silhouette, sitting ghostly on the middle of the dam. She could tell by the turn of his shoulders that he was watching her. She stepped out beside the cinder-block building and marched down the hill toward him. He had made it impossible for her to do anything but.

'*Where is my family?*' she screamed at him, slipping as she climbed up the bank to the dam. His hair had grown even longer and his beard was black and full. His eyes gleamed meaningfully through the snow.

When she stepped to the edge of the abutment, she saw her family fifteen feet below her, shackled to the dam: Moreen on the left, Scott on the right, six feet apart, their left arms raised above their heads, handcuffed to the U-rings that Neal had embedded seven feet high in the concrete. Dangling there on the frozen, rocky floor of the pond, they looked like frozen marionettes. Between them, a single handcuff dangled down from the U-ring. Ellen knew it was hers.

Turning to Neal, she shouted, 'How do you blame Moreen for what your father did to himself?' She saw the revolver in his hand, resting on his knee. It was her gun, but he was not aiming it at her, nor at anything in particular. He just kept staring.

Moreen had her pea-coat on, along with a wool cap. She wore heavy wool mittens on both hands, even the one that was handcuffed. Scott, however, was dressed in a pin-striped shirt and blue polyester V-neck sweater. His left arm hugged his chest, he looked sick, and he shivered painfully. Then Ellen noticed red drops in the snow by his left shoe.

She reached out and caught the highest rung in the dam, then started climbing down with the knife clutched in her hand, shivering more from fear than the cold. When her boots hit the icy rocks at the bottom, she leaned on the dam for balance as she made her way to Moreen.

'Hon, are you okay?' she asked, reaching up and sawing at the handcuff chain. The blade barely scratched the steel.

Moreen didn't answer, but stared off at the distant rushing of sound, the gathering flood.

Ellen looked up to the top of the dam. 'Is this what you've lived for?' she yelled. 'This is it?'

Neal looked impassively over the safety cable. 'Not the best time to be patronizing, Aunt Ellen. Who knows? Maybe today I'll do things your way. Maybe I'll forgive everybody.' He showed her something small and silvery in his fingers. A key?

While snowflakes lit harmlessly on her eyelashes, Ellen could feel the rumbling in her feet. She looked off at the narrow gorge out ahead of her. All she could see above the steep granite walls was the white sky and the tips of three or four scrawny red pines.

'Neal, just let them go. No one wants to hurt you.'

He leaned forward and aimed the revolver down at the top of Moreen's head. 'That's your last lie, Ellen.'

'*No!*' She dropped the steak knife down into the rocks.

Still he kept his pistol aimed at Moreen. 'Ellen, I need you to fasten the center handcuff to your left wrist.'

Ellen stared up at him, knowing it was pointless to try and dissuade him. 'Don't hurt Moreen,' she said. 'Just don't.' Reaching up, she took the open cuff in her right hand and snapped it around her left wrist. The icy steel bit into her flesh. 'Okay,' she called up to him. 'Now, please, let Moreen go.'

He smiled down imperiously. 'James five, sixteen,' he said. ' "Confess your faults to one another, that ye may be healed." '

'Confess what?'

'The truth,' he said. 'The truth shall set you free.'

'What do you want us to say, Neal?'

Lowering the pistol, he said, 'Why not start at the beginning?'

'*I don't understand!*'

'Ellen, we don't have time to waste. Think back. There was a hurricane.'

As the rushing sound intensified out beyond the gorge, she heard a distant crack in the woods, maybe a half-mile away, and she imagined the flood waters crashing through the trees, tearing up everything in its path.

'I was teaching,' she said. 'I came home from school early, to make sure the sheep were safe.'

'That's the only reason you came home?'

'That's the reason. I went upstairs and found your mother in our bedroom.'

She looked over at Scott, who gazed grimly at the icy walls of the gorge that surrounded them.

'And what was my mother doing in your bedroom, Ellen?'

'She was with Scott, getting dressed.'

'Sounds innocent enough,' Neal said. He raised his face into the falling snow, as if he were listening to the far-off rushing of the flood.

'They'd had sex, alright?'

'Okay,' Neal said. 'What did you do then?'

'I left them there.'

'And?'

'I drove to your house.'

'Yes, you did. Why?'

'I didn't know what else to do.'

'So you went to my house and what?'

'I told your father.'

'Told him what?'

'That they slept together.'

'Something wrong with sleeping?'

Ellen closed her eyes. 'That they had sex!'

He waited.

'That's it,' she said. 'Then you came home from school. You know the rest.'

As the rumble under her feet grew stronger, Ellen looked over at Scott, who was gazing up at the head of the gorge, as if inviting the deluge.

'So that's everything?' Neal asked.

'That's what happened,' Ellen told him. 'That's the truth.'

'Your truth,' Neal replied. 'Now do you want to know what actually happened that day? I came home from school expecting a birthday party, but when I walked in the door, you were there. My mother was hysterical and my father was leaving the house. And you left with him. The next thing I knew, my father was dead, and *nobody—*'

Neal aimed the revolver down at Scott; Ellen caught her breath.

'Nobody ever had the common courtesy to tell me *why*.'

'You were twelve years old,' Scott said weakly, not realizing he was in Neal's sights. 'How the hell could you understand what was going on?'

'Scott,' Ellen said, trying to quiet him.

'Uncle Scotty?' Neal asked calmly.

Scott looked up, saw the revolver aiming down. He pulled hard on the chain, trying to protect his face. 'Jesus Christ, do you think I didn't regret it?' he shouted. 'Every day! Do you think your mother never regretted it?'

Neal gazed down over the cable at him, the white, snow-filled sky outlining his head and shoulders.

'He's telling you the truth,' Ellen called, her voice shaking badly. 'How could you expect your mother to tell you something like that?'

Neal reached the key over the dam as if he was about to drop it down to Ellen. 'Come on, Ellen, the truth shall set you free.'

Ellen whipped her own face skyward. 'Quit the pretense, Neal! You came here to indulge yourself with a few more deaths. Just get it over with.'

'Would you rather let your daughter die than tell her what she has a right to know?'

'Moreen is not part of this!'

'Moreen is the reason I'm giving you a chance!'

Ellen turned to her daughter – the beautiful eyes, the tattooed teardrops, the fixed hard scowl on her face.

'You want the truth, Neal?' Ellen shouted up at him. 'When I thought I was falling in love with you, I was having my revenge against Scott. It meant nothing else.'

'Good,' he yelled. 'So you had sex with your nephew as an expression of resentment.'

'That's right.'

'See, that's the way it's done, folks. Come on, Ellen, you're almost there. Tell Mo about Randy.'

'I've told her! I hated what he was doing to her.'

'That's right,' Neal mocked. 'Hate the sin, not the sinner.'

'*Grow up!*' Ellen yelled. She turned to Moreen. 'When I saw Randy hurt you, I told Neal I felt like killing him. I didn't mean it. But I said it.'

Moreen stared placidly ahead, the rumble above them sounding like a battery of earth-moving machines tearing through the woods.

'All right, look,' Neal said, exasperated. 'I murdered Randy, I think everybody is aware of that. I swam down behind him and pushed his arm into the outlet pipe. Okay? *This isn't that hard, folks.*'

Ellen turned back to Moreen, who refused to meet her eyes. 'Maybe I did mean what I said,' she continued. 'Maybe I knew Neal would do it, I really don't know. And it doesn't matter. I could've stopped him, but I didn't.'

Moreen looked down, showing no expression beyond her shivering. Rocks around her boots shook off their cover of snow.

'Ellen, up here.'

Ellen raised her eyes, and Neal dropped the key. She panicked and flashed out her right hand as the glitter fell down through the snowflakes. She felt the key sting her palm, and she slapped it against her chest. Carefully she cupped her hand around it.

'Don't drop it,' Neal said. 'It's the only one.'

Ellen squeezed the key between her thumb and fingers, then stretched up toward Moreen's handcuff.

'It's yours, not Moreen's,' Neal told her. 'Mo's going to have to set herself free.'

The destruction intensified in the air. Ellen visualized ice chunks tumbling down the hillside, deadwood snapping into splinters. She imagined it all pouring into the gorge on top of them.

'*Neal, please! Let her go!*'

'Moreen, do you see your mother's dilemma?' Neal called down. 'See, she's so torn apart with guilt, she'd rather die than free herself.'

Angrily, Ellen reached up and stuck the key in the cuff that held her. She gave it a twist, and the steel snapped open. Her arm fell and her foot slid off the rock. She stumbled against the dam.

'What's worse,' Neal continued, 'she doesn't know if she's just an overprotective mom or an accessory to murder. Because she doesn't know if it was Randy who hurt you, or her ram.'

Moreen's dark eyes lost focus. For the first time since she was a little girl, Ellen thought she looked frightened.

Neal held out another key in his fingers. 'Come on, Moreen, was it Randy or the ram?'

'It's okay,' Ellen said to her, touching her daughter's cold cheek.

Mo's eyes narrowed. Her jaw clenched. She turned her face to Ellen and said, 'I did it.'

'Speak up,' Neal called down.

Moreen ignored him, focusing her eyes on Ellen, tight with anger. 'I used your barbell. I dropped it on myself. Then I let Bucky out.'

Ellen stared at her daughter, desperately wanting Moreen to take back what she'd said – to tell her anything else, but the persistence of Mo's glare told her all she needed to know. Regret gone to resentment, shame to pride, the eyes said it all: She'd been a junkie carrying a junkie in her womb. In one fleeting act, she had spared her baby and punished herself and everyone around her. Ellen put her hand behind Moreen's head and gripped her as gently as she knew how. She kissed her cheek. 'It's okay, Hon.' She felt too cold to cry, but hot tears burned her eyes. 'It's okay,' she whispered.

'Hold out your hand,' Neal called.

Ellen looked up. The key was already falling. Desperately, she reached out, and it bounced off her arm and clinked off the rocks. Ellen dropped to her knees and pinched it out of a crevice. Then she stood and reached for Moreen's wrist. Despite her shaking, she maneuvered the tiny key into the lock, and the handcuff snapped apart. She caught Moreen's arm and turned her toward the rungs, shouting to Neal: '*Don't you hurt her!*'

'She's free to go,' Neal yelled back against the roar above them, while Moreen pulled herself stiffly away from her mother and started climbing the rungs up the face of the dam. 'Of course, she might want to stick around and help her dad, who we all know has a little trouble owning up to things.'

'All right!' Scott blurted, shivering furiously. 'I was involved, too. In the Randy thing.'

Moreen pulled herself to the top of the dam, but stopped there, looking down at her father.

'Mo, get out of here,' Ellen yelled at her.

'I think she's waiting for Dad to come clean,' Neal said. 'Come on, Uncle.'

Scott looked up at Moreen. 'He told me that Randy kicked you, Honey. He told me about the hysterectomy. I was only trying to protect you.'

He lifted his face expectantly, but Neal only pulled the blanket off his shoulders and threw it over to Moreen, who climbed onto the abutment to retrieve it.

'What the hell do you want from me?' Scott shouted wildly. 'Okay, I held Randy's legs while Neal pushed his arm into the pipe. Jesus.' He looked up angrily.

'That's a start,' Neal called.

'Neal, he made a mistake,' Ellen shouted over the tumult bearing down. 'Your mother made a mistake. It was thirteen years ago. Maybe she wasn't as strong as you, maybe she needed someone to love. Maybe your father beat her down with that religion the same way he beat you.'

'And maybe I helped kill my father, as my mother was so fond of saying.'

'Maybe you did.'

Neal smiled. Then he calmly aimed the revolver down and fired. Stone dust and snow exploded from a rock inches in front of Scott. 'I did *not* kill my father,' Neal said. 'It was my *mother* and your *husband* who killed my father.' He fired the .38 twice more to punctuate his words.

'You know that's not true!' Ellen shouted., 'They don't deserve to die for having sex!'

'For committing adultery,' Neal countered, ' "*they shall both of them die*." Deuteronomy twenty-two.'

He fired the .38 again, and Scott jerked his arm, rattling the chain. The way his eyes blinked told Ellen he hadn't been hit.

'Moreen, take my truck and get out of here!' Ellen called, but Mo stood over them, wrapped in the blanket, watching.

'Come on, Scott. My aunt seems to be convinced that I'm the

one who killed Madeleine Sterling.'

'Oh, no,' Scott cried. 'No way, man.'

'Daddy, just say whatever he wants,' Moreen cried, staring out of the blanket.

'Don't say anything that's not true, Scott,' Neal said. 'Come on, now. Who shot Maddy?'

'I don't know anything about that!'

Neal leaned over the safety cable and, with both hands, aimed the revolver down at Scott's head.

'Last chance, Uncle.'

Scott's head lolled back as if he'd intended to look up at Neal, but he just hung there by his wrist while he hugged himself with his free hand. Then he closed his eyes.

'I went over to talk to her,' he said. 'That's all.' He turned his head and gazed imploringly at Ellen, the words from his mouth sounding increasingly distant. 'She was crazy. You know how she got. She was feeling guilty, I don't know. She had the gun to her head, I tried to talk her out of it.'

Ellen stared at her husband. Her mind had stopped working. She no longer heard the roar in the sky or the clicking of rocks all around her, nor even the sudden hiss of headwaters. But when Scott's eyes snapped up to the top of the gorge, Ellen looked up to see the monstrous flood head explode over the gorge like an avalanche, as tons of muddy water surged down the falls in a boiling, snowy froth, thundering down the high granite walls. When the full force of the waters hit, Ellen was slammed into Scott, who howled in pain as he swung from his shackle, the water astonishingly icy and immediately thigh-high, rollicking with ice chunks. Ellen held onto Scott, trying to lift him, to keep the handcuff from cutting into his wrist. But, pummeled herself, she reached up and caught the open handcuff beside him.

'Scott, look up here!' Neal shouted down.

Grimacing, Scott raised his face hopefully, as Neal whipped his hand over his shoulder. Clutching the hanging handcuff beside her husband, Ellen watched the silvery glitter as it arced through the blizzard and disappeared in the waterfall.

'*He told you the truth!*' Ellen screamed, slapping the dam, though deep inside she knew the truth was far from told.

'Do you believe that Maddy shot herself in the head?' Neal shouted down at her.

As the flood thundered into the gorge, he stared down at her for a second or two, and she stared back, while the half-frozen deluge pressed her against the concrete.

Neal set the revolver on top of the dam, then stood and pulled his sweatshirt over his head. Underneath, he wore a diver's dry suit and a weight harness strapped like suspenders over his shoulders. Picking up the revolver, he walked off the dam toward Moreen.

'Mo, run!' Ellen screamed.

But Moreen remained on the edge of the diving rock, staring out of the hooded blanket, as Neal bent at the abutment and started climbing down the rungs to the water. Five feet above the surface, he dropped and splashed feet-first beside Ellen. The roiling water engulfed him at first, and she thought to go for his gun, but he immediately gained his footing and thrust the revolver straight at her. Hanging on the handcuff, she stiffened, waiting to be shot.

'Take it,' Neal said, slapping the revolver in her free hand.

She regarded him skeptically, even as she fit her frozen fingers around the grip and aimed the gun at him.

'You be the judge,' he told her. 'You can shoot me if you want. Or shoot his handcuff chain. Your choice. You've got one bullet left.'

She slid her finger into the trigger guard, as a chunk of ice slammed against her hip; she hardly felt the sting.

'If you kill me,' Neal told her, 'you'll be rid of both of us. It's up to you, Ellen. Forgiveness or revenge.'

'Ellen, hurry,' Scott groaned, jangling his wrist.

'He's right,' Neal said. 'If this water gets much deeper, you won't last five minutes before hypothermia kills you both.'

Tightening her hand around the open handcuff, she kicked herself closer to Scott, reached out and pressed the muzzle against the middle link of his handcuff chain.

'But I don't think we've heard the reason Maddy was murdered. Have we, Uncle Scott?'

Ignoring the comment, Ellen thumbed the hammer back. She angled the barrel slightly up, hoping to prevent a ricochet or spray of shrapnel, but the water rocked her so badly she was afraid she might miss entirely.

'Turn your head,' she said to Scott. 'Close your eyes.'

'It wasn't because Maddy was going to tell the cops about Randy. Let's face it, the police knew Randy's death was no accident.'

Ellen touched her finger to the trigger. Although she could still feel the water climbing up her waist, she was already growing numb to its cold.

'Just shoot it,' Scott whispered, his jaw barely able to move.

'Maybe Maddy had some other information that Scott wanted to be kept secret. Didn't I hear that Mo was seeing your friend on a professional basis?'

A wave of intense shivering attacked Ellen's arm, and the muzzle of her .38 scraped off Scott's handcuff chain.

'El?'

'Like maybe something Moreen saw when she was young – too young to know what to do about it.'

As the frigid waters pounded her side, Ellen looked back at Moreen standing high on the diving rock, staring out of her blanket.

'El, shoot it,' Scott sputtered. 'He's insane.'

'I guess it's up to you, Mo,' Neal called. 'Can you tell us what you saw that day?'

Up on the high rock, Moreen seemed to be entranced, the way she raised her beautiful, ornamented face into the falling snow, the way her head shook almost imperceptibly, back and forth.

'See, she's telling you!' Scott cried. 'She never saw a thing!'

'Oh, yes,' Moreen said, and now she looked directly at her father. 'I did see. Daddy—'

To Ellen, it seemed like the entire world had spun off its axis. For that moment, she did not feel the iciness that paralyzed her body. For that moment, nothing existed except Scott and his desperate denial.

'I heard you out in the barn fighting with Uncle Jon,' Mo continued. 'Yes, you were. He was yelling and you were yelling. I was scared, so I went in the house and hid in the pantry. Then you came into the kitchen and got a chair, and you went back out again.'

Shaking and gray-complected, Scott tried to smile, as he shook his head and repeated, as though he were drunk, 'Nope. Nope. Nope.'

'I ran out the door, and you ran after me. You caught me in the pasture and said if I ever told anyone you'd been there, the police would take you away and we'd never see you again.'

Scott turned to Ellen, the icy water assailing his chest. 'He was trying to kill me.'

Face the truth, Thelma had told her. *If you want to save Moreen.*

'You stretched out his necktie when you strangled him,' Neal said. 'So you tied it to the chainfall. Then you hoisted him up and dropped the chair under him.'

Ellen fixed her frozen gaze on her husband, but he wouldn't meet her eyes.

'He was the town preacher!' Scott cried, throwing his face out of the water. 'I was a high school dropout with a brand new Mercedes! Who the hell was gonna believe me? That I killed him in self-defence?'

Ellen stared at this man, her husband, as if she were seeing him for the first time – his downcast eyes, the incredible sadness in his own gaze.

'You could have told me,' she said to him. 'Scott, didn't you know I would have understood?'

'*Lie!*'

The invective echoed off the hill, as a wave of ice water splashed down Ellen's jacket. She peered up through the snow, immobilized.

'*You never understood a thing!*'

Ellen hung suspended, her vision filled with the image of her daughter standing high on the rock, the little girl who had once stood speechless in her doorway . . . a grown woman now, a perfect stranger.

The world went white.

'Mom, save him!'

Ellen felt like she'd lost consciousness. She looked at Scott hanging heavily from the handcuff, while a floating plate of ice played against his armpit. He had stopped shivering. His eyes stared down at the water, nearly shut.

Ellen heard a splash behind her and turned to see Neal holding the handcuff Mo had hung from. He was only an arm's length away. Afraid he'd try to take the revolver from her, she raised it beside her ear.

'We're running out of time, Aunt Ellen,' he said quietly. 'Forgiveness or revenge?'

Matching his electric stare with her own, she shook her head at him. Then she turned back to Scott, reached the .38 to the handcuff, pressing the muzzle firmly against the chain. As she was about to fire, however, the handcuff shook free of the gun.

'Scott, hold still,' she gasped, trying to follow the chain with the weapon.

But he shook his arm again, a reckless flash of confidence shining in his eye. In other circumstances, Ellen would have thought him playfully drunk – in this circumstance he was telling her something: Use the last bullet on Neal.

The ice water splashed against her chin as she shook her head.

He scowled at her, telling her to get on with it.

She scowled back at him.

Then he gave her a strange, forced smile. And before she could question him, he dropped his face into the water. She saw his back lurch powerfully, as a great cough of bubbles exploded around his ears.

'*Scott!*'

She started in after him, but Neal's arm locked around her throat, and his other hand grabbed for the revolver. She drove her left elbow into his ribs and Neal ripped her hand from the cuff, hauling her under water into a skull-crushing freeze, wrenching her arm back until it felt like her shoulder would rip from its socket.

She threw her skull at him, got her chin up over his shoulder and bit down on his ear. He jerked his head into her nose, throwing her off. She swung the gun around. He caught it in his hand. She squeezed the trigger, and her ears shattered with the blast. She dropped the .38 and sprang for the sky, blindly catching the open handcuff and pulling herself up, but Neal caught her ankle and kept her under water. She held tight to the cuff, even as he tried to drag her back down. But he wasn't anchored, and she was, and she reached her other hand up and caught the U-bolt, pulling for the light with every last fiber of her strength, while he climbed her body like he was climbing a rope, crawling up her legs and hips, her stomach and chest. With the bright sky dancing only inches above her mouth, every morsel of Ellen's being screamed for a taste of air. But then Neal captured her hand that held the U-bolt, and he wrapped his legs around her waist. Now, while she beat at his face with the handcuff, he concentrated on tearing her hand free with his teeth. Suddenly she felt a fierce sharpness in the knuckle of her index finger, an incredible pressure at its base. She looked up and saw her finger in his mouth, then she heard the snap of her bone breaking. Pain flared behind her eyes and she lost hold of the U-bolt – but not the handcuff.

She slammed it over his wrist. The chain snapped taut as he tried to yank free. With all her strength, Ellen jammed his wrist against the dam until she felt the handcuff catch, then she broke free.

Splashing into the air, she ripped an agonizing breath into her lungs as she pulled for the ladder. But, hearing a groan behind her, she turned.

'Mo!'

Her daughter's dark eyes stared out of the water, her dark hair spread across the surface. Ellen could tell that she was holding onto Scott, shivering helplessly.

'Mo,' Ellen gasped, reaching back for her. 'He's gone, Mo. Hurry.'

Grabbing her daughter under the arms, Ellen pulled, and Mo's hand came out of the water, losing hold of her father. She moaned defiantly and tried to fight. Then her eyes flared in fear.

Ellen turned, saw Neal's head rise above the surface right beside her, eyes open, dark and glinting. She pulled Moreen back, grabbing onto the U-bolt just under the surface, the one Scott was shackled to. The ladder rungs were less than ten feet away, but they couldn't reach them without going through Neal. Neither could they go around him, lacking the strength to swim against the current, even though the waterfall pouring into the gorge seemed, strangely, to have subsided.

'Honey, stay awake,' Ellen said, giving Mo a shake, although she struggled to stay conscious herself. Moreen could do little more than hang shivering in her arm.

As the water rocked quietly around his nose, Neal reached his face out of the water, pursed his lips and made a long, steady hissing sound, sucking a volume of icy air into his lungs. His bloody hand came out like a serpent, and he brushed the hair from his eyes, pink water streaming down his face. Then he turned the hand toward Ellen, showing her the crimson, gulping hole in his palm.

'Now do you understand?' he declaimed. 'Now do you understand my life?'

Easily within grasp of the hand, Ellen held tight to Moreen, while she curled her wrist around the U-bolt, fixing herself to the dam. Then, with a fearsome shudder, she nodded her head compliantly. 'Yes, I understand,' she gasped.

Raising his mouth out of the water again, Neal refilled his lungs with a windy whistle, his eyes sparkling with validation.

'I understand perfectly, Neal,' she said, and she matched his glint with one of her own. 'You didn't get your birthday party.'

In that one frozen moment, as Neal's eye lost its light, Ellen's boot shot out of the water. Numb as she was, she nevertheless felt a solid impact, the cartilage of his nose snapping under her heel.

She leaped ahead, grabbing the U-bolt that held his handcuff and pulling Moreen over the top of him. Catching hold of the last U-bolt, she shoved Moreen toward the ladder. 'Mo, swim!' she gasped.

As Mo's hand came weakly out of the water, reaching for the rungs, Ellen heard the splash behind her, saw the bloody hand arc past her face. Moreen's head was yanked back.

Ellen lunged, caught his wrist in her hand. She felt Moreen's hands there too, fighting to free her hair from his fingers. Clutching the U-bolt, Ellen wrapped her arm around Neal's elbow and tried to pull him to the surface, but he was too strong. When he started pulling Mo's head deeper, Ellen felt the U-bolt slipping through her frozen fingers. Then she lost it, and she grabbed desperately for the hanging handcuff, felt its chain scrape the web of her hand until her thumb hooked its base. With every bit of her remaining strength, she focused on her right elbow, refusing to lose her daughter. She pulled right. He pulled left. Her biceps flared. Her chest ached. She heard her own groans straining in her ears as she tried to bring her arms together. Incredibly, she felt Mo's head bump against her chin, and there was Neal's bloody hand hard against her breast.

Seeing her chance, Ellen jabbed the handcuff at his wrist. He deflected her attack effortlessly, snapping his hand around, gathering more of Mo's hair. Then he started dragging her away. Ellen screamed and attacked his wrist with the handcuff again, but struck the heel of his hand, the base of his thumb, the side of his fingers. Then he stopped pulling. Holding his position with his wrist just out of her reach, he shone his black eyes at her from behind the veil of Mo's floating hair, his grim, self-satisfied grin.

Holding his eyes with her own, she shook her head intently at him, then snapped her own hand around, sinking the hook of the open handcuff through his bullet hole. Reflexively, his fingers sprang open, trying to shake the manacle out of his hand, but Ellen slammed the cuff into the dam, engaging the lock. He shook his hand violently, and Mo's head shook too. Desperate for air, Ellen fought to free her, when suddenly she was knocked roughly aside. Fighting back through an explosion of bubbles, she grasped for Moreen, but grasped at only water. Then, in amazement, she watched her daughter ascend into the air.

Ellen burst up into the snowstorm with a furious gasp. She heard Moreen coughing, saw her rising up the rungs, caught in the arm of Rooftop Paradise.

The giant looked down at Ellen. 'Can you get out?'

Ellen wrapped her arm around a ladder rung. Breathlessly, she tried to nod her head, but it took all her strength just to hang on. She hugged the rung.

'I'll be right back,' Rooftop told her, climbing.

Amazed to be alive, Ellen clutched the iron and watched her other arm come stiffly out of the water and reach for a higher rung. She felt firmness under her boot and strained to straighten her leg, trembling weakly as she tried to push herself up. Then she stopped, to gather strength. Every movement ached deeply, even though the surface of her body felt numb. She stared at the gray concrete in front of her eyes, trying to grasp the reality of Scott's death. But Moreen was safe, she told herself, and that was more than she had hoped for.

Shivering desperately, she began to notice the silence around her. In fact, it seemed the entire world had become quiet, offering up no sound but the bright trickle of waters melting down the sides of the gorge. Then she heard the burst of bubbles behind her. Her heart jumped and she clutched at the rungs, steeling herself against another attack. But then she realized it was Neal exhaling his last breath. And then she wanted nothing more than to forget the sound forever. She closed her eyes. She listened to the silence. She began to drift.

When the arm wrapped around her chest, she cried out.

'I've got you,' Rooftop said softly, and she felt herself pulling upwards, watching the dam falling swiftly past her face, her boots bouncing off the rungs as she rose. At the top of the dam he carried her to the snow-covered embankment, where Moreen sat on the blanket, wrapped in Rooftop's fur-lined parka. Mo's face was white, her lips as blue as her teardrop tattoos. Shivering intently, she looked out over the gorge.

'There's an ice jam up at the Rez, so the water's stopped for now,' Rooftop explained, setting Ellen down on the blanket beside her. 'I'm going to run Moreen up to the house and call for an ambulance. Then I'll come back for you.' He lifted Moreen effortlessly into his arms, taking care that the parka stayed on her.

'Get Mo warmed up,' Ellen said, 'I can make it back myself.' (Although she was surprised that her frozen jaw even moved.)

'I've got to come back anyway,' he said. 'Cover up.'

He lifted a corner of the blanket over her shoulder, and Ellen caught it in her frozen hand, huddling inside, closing her eyes, still trying to fathom everything that had happened. Then she heard the bubbles again. She turned, her body tingling.

'You got bolt-cutters up at the house?' Rooftop asked her. 'I shoved a little emergency tank in his mouth, but it's only good for five minutes or so. I'm going to have to cut him out of there.'

Ellen stared up at him.

'Maybe I've got something in my truck,' he said. 'Hang on, I'll be right back.'

As he walked briskly away with Moreen in his arms, Ellen rolled to her shoulder and pressed the heel of her hand in the snow. She bent her leg, painfully, leaned her elbow in her knee and pushed herself upward until, incredibly, she felt her frozen body rising. Holding the blanket around her like a shawl, she straightened her back and, more painfully, her knees, then took her first unsteady step toward the dam, her stiff legs aching inside her heavy, hardening jeans.

She heard the bubbles again.

She took two more steps until she stood at the point where the abutment narrowed to the top of the curved dam. Gathering all her strength, she stepped up. To her left, a bed of snow-covered granite lay at the bottom of a twenty-foot drop; to her right, the surface of the pond lay six feet below, floating with ice chunks and driftwood, silent and still, except for a small pocket of turbulence over the spot where Neal was shackled.

Ellen took another step onto the dam, feeling the slight resistance of the safety cable against the right side of her shin. Carefully, she brought her other foot even with it, steadying herself. Out near the opposite bank, she could see the pale image of Scott's hand dangling under the water. Closer to her, she could see Neal looking skyward, a white tank the size of a liter bottle jutting sideways from his mouth.

Lashed with his back to the dam, his upturned eyes seemed to track her movements as she shuffled further out onto the dam, until she was directly above him. In the distance she heard a siren start, and she knew he would be rescued soon.

As though reading her mind, Neal blinked once, calmly. Then a small flurry of bubbles jostled up, laughing as they broke the surface. When the water cleared, she saw his eyes again, glinting triumphantly up at her.

She stared back, horrified, almost mesmerized, wishing she had the strength to jump in the water and tear the tank from his mouth. Then she saw Neal's eyes dart to the side.

'Is that him?' came a man's voice from the riverbank.

Ellen turned slowly. Wes Westerback came stepping onto the dam from the wooded bank, carrying a long, black rifle strapped to his shoulder. Wearing a red hunting jacket and snow-frosted crusher, his cheeks were bright, his eyes dull.

'Can you make it back to the house?' he asked her.

She looked down again, saw Neal's eyes move from Wes to her. She nodded her head.

Suddenly Neal's elbows began flapping, and his body jerked, looking like a fat bass fighting a line. When Ellen heard the quick, hard catch of a shell being chambered, Neal's struggling ceased. His eyes targeted Wes, widening in a scowl of protest. A scowl of warning. Then his eyes sprang back to Ellen.

'Ellie, go look after your daughter.'

Gazing at Neal for another second, she took a breath, then turned her eyes away. She heard Neal's bubbles again, breaking furiously on the water, but she ignored him, keeping her eyes hard on the dam as she turned her body and began shuffling stiffly along, listening to the siren wailing from the top of the hill. Stepping off the dam onto the abutment, she followed Rooftop's big boot prints down over the bank to the farm road. As she started uphill, she heard the first rifle shot, a hard, flat slap that died in the surrounding snow. She did not flinch, nor did she stop walking. But before she'd taken two more steps, she heard the second shot.

She saw Rooftop run out beside the pump house and peer down through the whiteness. Then he started running again, his long black legs looking like sticks as he lifted one after the other out of the snow. Reaching Ellen, he bent to lift her.

'Police are on their way,' he said, wheezing thickly. 'Let's get you up to the house.'

She shook her head in protest, even as she felt herself falling. He caught her.

'Okay?' he asked, bending tentatively for her legs. She leaned back on his arm and closed her eyes, letting him lift her.

The ache of thawing was the worst pain Ellen had ever felt. She stepped in her bathtub fully clothed and turned on the shower. Even though the water was barely lukewarm, it gnawed like fire at the deepest part of her body. She moaned, withstanding the ache, but stopped when she heard a knock.

'Mrs Chambers, the EMTs are here.' It was Rooftop, outside the door.

'I'll be right out,' she answered.

She stripped off her frozen jean jacket and dropped it in the tub. Gradually, as she was able to make the water warmer, she removed the rest of her clothes and let the water work on her. When she was through, she shut off the shower and slid the plastic curtain back.

A thick, green bath towel sat folded on the corner of the sink, along with her bra, jersey, a flannel shirt and sweater, a pair of cotton underpants and loose-fitting jeans and heavy wool socks. She wondered if Mo had put them there for her, hoped she had. Stepping out of the tub, she noted with some relief the fiery redness of her skin, hoping it meant she hadn't gotten frostbite, although even the touch of the towel on her arm sent a fierce, burning pain through her.

When she opened the bathroom door, two men and a woman in blue, fleece-lined jackets were sitting at the kitchen table. The ambulance crew, Ellen guessed. A state trooper stood by the door, watching out the window. Moreen sat close to the cookstove with her hair wrapped in a towel and her dark eyes downcast. Rooftop sat on the floor in front of the chair, rubbing her stockinged feet tenderly in his hands.

Ellen went over to her. 'You okay, Hon?' She touched Mo's head. 'I love you, Mo.'

'We'd like to run you and your daughter to the hospital, Mrs Chambers,' one of the EMTs said, 'if you're ready.'

Ellen turned to respond and saw Wes Westerback through the

window. He was sitting on the porch stairs with his rifle laid across his knees. Detective Gallagher was coming up the farm road from the pond with a broad-shouldered young trooper beside him.

'Give me a minute,' Ellen said, and she went to the door.

'Put something on,' one of the EMTs told her. She ignored him and opened the door. Wes turned around. His eyes stared softly, his jaw clenched tight.

Seeing Ellen, Gallagher slowed his pace about fifteen feet from the porch. He was wearing his dark brown trench coat and matching fedora, but he was not wearing them well. Regarding Ellen tentatively, he put his hand to his brim, as though holding his hat against the wind. Ellen imagined he was thinking of a way to deflect the blame for his mistakes, or maybe improvise an apology. She was wrong.

'Condolences on your loss,' he said stiffly, speaking louder than usual. 'Is that Neal down there with your husband?'

'It's Neal,' she said. 'Is he dead?'

Gallagher nodded. 'As far as we can see, he has a gunshot wound in the head, maybe two.' The detective took three steps closer. 'Do you mind if I come inside and talk with you and your daughter?'

Ellen took a deep, shivering breath. 'Neal shot Scott in the foot, then handcuffed him to the dam. He tried to handcuff Moreen and me, but we fought him.' The words steamed from her mouth.

'Who's "we?" '

'I fought him,' Ellen said. 'Me alone.'

Gallagher gave her a nod, pulling a pad and pen from his pocket, as a gust of snow blew across his shoulders.

'When we fought for the gun, I shot him in the hand. Then I handcuffed him to the dam.'

'Shot him with—?'

'The gun's at the bottom of the pond. Are you going to write this down?'

Gallagher looked down at Wes, then back to Ellen. 'Mrs Chambers, I only have a few questions. You shouldn't be out here.'

'Moreen and I are going to the hospital now, Detective,' Ellen said. 'Am I under arrest?'

'Not at all. Chief Westerback already told me that he fired the shot that killed your nephew. I just need a more thorough statement from you and your daughter. Nothing that couldn't wait a day or two.'

Ellen shook her head. 'I don't want you talking to Mo. Not today, tomorrow, not ever. She's been through enough.'

The detective's eyes left hers, hung suspended for a moment or two in the snow. Then he put his hands, along with his notepad, in his pockets. The young trooper standing at his side seemed to be studying him.

'Detective Gallagher,' Wes interrupted. He labored to stand up, taking his rifle off his lap. 'Would you mind picking me up at my house?'

'What for?'

Wes came off the porch and handed Gallagher his rifle. 'I'd like to drop off my vehicle, save my wife from having to come over here to get it.'

Holding the old man's weapon, Gallagher's eyes wandered down Wes's wool trousers to his rubber-bottomed boots, then back up again. Then he turned his head toward the trooper and said, 'Go ahead and warm up your car, we're not going to be long.'

The trooper nodded and left them. When he was out of earshot, Gallagher turned back to Wes. 'Chief, why would I be picking you up?'

Wes stood, stone-faced.

Gallagher looked back toward the trooper's patrol car. 'Unless someone tells me differently,' he said, avoiding eye contact with the older man, 'my report's going to say that when you fired your rifle into the water, you were aiming for the handcuff, trying to break Neal Chambers free.'

Ellen watched the detective carefully, curiously, as he returned the rifle to the older man.

'Bullets do unpredictable things when they hit the water,' Gallagher said, 'even high-velocity shells. That's what I'll be writing in my report.' He shoved his hands in his pockets and looked off toward the pond.

'Under the circumstances,' he said, turning toward Ellen with a halting glance, 'I also wanted you to know that I'll be closing the book on the diving accident that claimed your daughter's husband.'

The detective touched his brim again. She didn't know if he was protecting his hat from the wind or if he expected thanks. She didn't feel especially thankful, so she said nothing.

Gallagher pulled up his collar. He gave her one more look, then he put his hands in his pockets and walked to his car.

EPILOGUE

Ellen popped awake in the dark, heart pounding. The green light lay flat on her eyelids, then went black again. Her pillow was wet with perspiration. But she was safe, she told herself. Moreen was safe. She tried to relax her breathing. She tried to convince herself.

She had hoped the nightmares would stop once she got out of Maine. But even at the edge of this desert, two thousand miles away, she'd been jolted by some snap of silence. Not that it surprised her. She hadn't had a full night's sleep since the flood, alerted to every tick from the water pipes, each creak of roof rafters objecting to the cold. Sometimes she'd wake with a shout, and then she'd lie in the dark trying to rid her mind of images – Neal's black eyes blinking up out of the water, the handcuff through his hand; the supreme confidence of Scott's last smile. More often, it was her body's memories she'd need to exorcize – Neal's fingers from her flesh, or hers from his; his taste from her tongue, his weight from her thighs.

The green light came on. The green light went off again, the Green Oasis Motor Inn flashing its seven-second greeting over the highway. In a strange way, the light was a comfort. Every time it lit, the room looked the same: the Royal Crown Cola bottle standing atop the TV; the opened suitcase beside it; Moreen sleeping in the other bed; Rooftop spread out on the floor in front of the radiator, his long, noisy breathing drifting just out of sync with the cadence of the motel light. Ellen turned away from the window and closed her eyes, burying her ear in the pillow, covering her other ear with her arm. She tried to focus on her breathing.

For two nights and a day the Boston Whaler had chased the black panel truck across the country, Rooftop driving, Moreen sitting beside him, staring out at the snow fields, while Ellen sat squeezed in the back seat between cardboard boxes and grocery bags. Finally in the desert somewhere in western South Dakota, they pulled off the highway. Moreen had barely said a word for the duration of the trip. Aside from a few obligatory replies, neither had she spoken to Ellen at all since the flood, not even during Scott's funeral.

At least Mo had agreed to the move. Ellen took great encouragement from that and hoped she could get Mo back into counseling once they landed in Oregon. She was also heartened by Mo's relationship with Rooftop. It wasn't difficult to see that they found great comfort in one another's company.

Ellen's eyes opened again. The green motel light came on, lighting the closed bathroom door, the hanging jackets, the boots. Then the room darkened again. On for seven seconds, off for seven seconds. She closed her eyes and tried to close her mind to everything but her own breathing, as she'd learned in yoga.

Full breath in.

Full breath out.

Pause. Peace. Repeat:

Fullness in.

Fullness out.

Pause. Peace. Soon she began slowing her breaths, pacing her respiration to the cycles of the motel light. By degrees, she felt her body relax.

Full breath in when the light comes on.

Full breath out when the light goes out.

Pause. Peace. Repeat:

Full breath in when the light comes on.

Full breath out when the light goes out.

Pause. Peace . . .

But the light stayed off.

Ellen's eyes opened, saw the dark figure standing over her.

'*No!*'

She thrashed out of her blankets. Her wrists were caught. A bright light flashed on. Ellen stared up into the glare, stark and shaking. At first, Moreen appeared to be laughing, the way her shoulders shook.

'Hon?' said Ellen.

All at once Mo let out a pitiful sob. Her arms collapsed, and she fell heavily onto Ellen, shaking so hard that even the bedsprings seemed to cry.

'Honey, it's okay,' Ellen whispered, combing her fingers gently through her daughter's hair. Behind her, Rooftop stood tensed, his body covering the door. Ellen could see his chest expanding, could hear him wheezing. Her own heart was pounding. And it was breaking, the way Moreen nestled in the warmth of her body like she had when she was five years old, the way she pushed her grown-up hand under her mother's arm.

Ellen pulled the blankets over her, steadily stroking her hair as Moreen's tears fell down her neck. They lay like this for a minute or more.

Then Rooftop turned the room light off.

'It's okay,' Ellen whispered again and again, even as her own tears ran from her eyes.

Moreen cried and cried until only weariness quieted her. When she finally fell asleep, Ellen held onto her, fit her warm head in the hollow of her neck, her warm breast under her arm. A welling of happiness rose inside her, a great warmth of joy, and she knew she wouldn't be able to sleep, but she didn't care. She looked over toward the window and saw Rooftop sitting tall in the dark, his back against the door. The way his glasses reflected the green light in slow, silent intervals – Ellen was reminded of a lighthouse on the coast.

He would sit there like that until morning, keeping watch. Ellen would lie there, gazing at the ceiling until it paled with the desert light. And Moreen would sleep peacefully. In the morning they would emerge from the room and continue their journey together.

UNDONE

For Glenna

PROLOGUE

He was aware of nothing at first. Then eight tiny beeps sounded from his wristwatch, and his heart started, a faint beating. He heard the swish of blood in his ears. He become aware of light on his eyelids. He heard Noel speak his name, like a sweet, faraway song.

'Bobby?'

Bobby Swift lay, surrounded by velvet crepe, inside the finest mahogany casket at Wicker's Funeral Home. He took a breath that was nearly imperceptible. He knew that Eliot Wicker was standing there too. He heard the lanky funeral director say, with no emotion, 'Here he comes.'

He felt the cold inside him like the frost in a hard winter ground. He wanted to tell them he was freezing, but his jaw wouldn't work, nor were his lungs able to push a single sound through his vocal cords.

'Temperature's down,' Wicker said, bending so close that his breath felt hot on Bobby's neck.

A second shadow moved in from the left: Noel. 'Should I get a blanket?'

'Here he comes,' Wicker said again.

Cold! Bobby tried to say the word.

'Bobby?' Noel's voice sounded near, and now her hands were under his neck, hot. His heart thumped, and a fierce chill jolted him.

'He's having convulsions!'

'He's shivering,' Wicker replied. 'Go up and run a bath, lukewarm.'

Bobby watched as Noel's shadow pulled away, and then Wicker moved in, hot hands on Bobby's ears. 'You're too cold, Bob!' he said in a loud voice. 'I'm going to carry you upstairs.'

Bobby tried to make himself heavy. The thought of Eliot Wicker carrying him anywhere was a sour one, but he could do little to prevent it. He could not even stop his own shaking. The undertaker's hands went underneath him inside the casket. He heard Wicker grunt, repositioning himself, and suddenly Bobby was lifted in the air, slung over Wicker's bony shoulder. He watched the backs of Wicker's boot heels take the stairs. He muttered an objection.

'Hold on,' Wicker said, straining. When they reached a landing and went around a corner, Bobby heard Noel call from upstairs. Wicker's reedy response carried through Bobby's chest: 'I got him.' Bobby reached for the wall, not wanting Noel to see him helpless like this.

'Put me down,' he slurred.

'Be another second, Bob.'

'Now,' Bobby told him, and then there was brightness, gleaming white floor tiles. He heard the rushing of water, and suddenly he plunged into a great aching steam, a crushing pain. He let out a cry and exploded out of the water, clutching the towel rack. 'You're gonna kill me for real!' he cried, fighting to stand, pulling himself up to the showerhead. The water thundered out of the faucet, splashing off his shirt. His entire body shivered. His heart pounded. Humiliations compounding, here he was urinating into his waterlogged pants.

All at once he surrendered, his convulsions peaking in a single violent shudder, a loud, quavering moan. He lay his face against the shower tiles. Another tremor followed like an aftershock, another moan.

'It might be hypothermia,' Noel said.

Bobby hit the drain release with his foot, watched the vortex start between his legs. He heard Wicker croak, 'He's okay, get him a towel.'

Pain subsiding, Bobby reached down and made the water warmer, lifted his face against it. Standing in the cascade, he opened his eyes, turned to Noel and grinned. 'How'd I do?'

She turned away from him and opened the third of a bank of drawers built into Wicker's beige bathroom wall, retrieving a thick brown towel. Bobby watched the backs of her long legs through the shower, the muscles of her thighs. She was barefoot. As she turned back to him, she used a corner of the towel to wipe the water that dripped down her own neck.

'You were dead,' she replied.

Noel Swift was the most beautiful woman, without a doubt, that Gravity or any other Maine town had ever seen, a rare cosmopolitan out here in the sticks. Her eyes, which were the startling green of emeralds, seemed to shine when she was aroused, and they were shining now. Her lower lip was heavy, dark with lipstick; her orange hair lay in a sheet beside her right eye, a wet strand tangled on her cheek. Today, on what was otherwise a typical Wednesday in May, she was wearing a cream-colored muslin dress that ended near the tops of her thighs. Bobby loved her wholly, longed for her constantly, even though she was already his. He wanted to pull her into the shower with him – and would have if Eliot Wicker weren't standing there. He had an urge to, anyway, just to spite the undertaker.

Then Wicker reached in and turned off the shower. 'Not clinically dead,' he said. 'But passable to the naked eye.'

Bobby peeled his shirt off his back, balled it up and tossed it in the sink. 'Be the richest dead man alive,' he said, giving Noel a look as he unbuckled his belt – 'clinical or not.' At thirty-three, he had the physique of a swimmer and the dark good looks of a movie star, topped off by a disarming laugh that came so easily and so often that laughing seemed a part of his normal speech. For an edge, he'd had a red rose tattooed on the back of his right hand. 'You got something dry?' he said to the undertaker. 'I don't want to catch a cold for my funeral.' He stared at Wicker and laughed, then turned to Noel, grinning. She returned a look of her own: shining. He dropped his pants.

Downstairs in the casket selection room, Bobby knelt beside his casket, dressed in Wicker's bathrobe. He worked his hands under the velvet and snugged the Velcro strap around one of the oxygen tanks. There were two – slender green tanks lashed to either side at the head of the casket – and, concealed by the closed lower lid, a pair of eighty-pound scuba tanks fitted with a T-bar connector. Bobby's legs would rest on top of the scuba tanks.

'If I gotta be tilted for the show,' he said, adjusting an oxygen tank, 'this one digs into my side, makes it harder to concentrate.' He added, 'At least I won't have to worry about falling asleep. Could you see that, I start to snore?' He looked at Wicker and laughed hard. In another basement room, the undertaker's clothes dryer hummed.

'Do you really have to bury him?' Noel asked, strolling an adjacent aisle of showcase caskets. Her concern warmed Bobby, even though he knew what Wicker's response would be.

'Oh yeah, like the pallbearers aren't going to know the casket's empty.'

'You could bury bricks. Or rice.'

Wicker shook his head. 'Not a possibility. Once the organ music starts, this box won't be alone till it's underground.' He knocked on the mahogany with one knuckle. It made a solid sound. 'Call it off now,' he said. It was a clear threat, not without mocking.

Bobby stood, put his arm around Noel, his hand on her warm hip. 'I did forty-five minutes today—'

'Forty-three,' said Wicker.

'Tomorrow I'll do an hour for the doc, no sweat. Fire up that heating pad and I bet I go two by showtime.'

'You're gonna be underground five.' Wicker again.

'And we got three hours of air in the tanks, normal breathing. Tranced out, I can stretch it to six, eight hours, no sweat.' Bobby turned again to Noel, spoke reassuringly. 'You got plenty of time to dig me up, Babe. But then you're going to have to do something to get me warm.' He looked at Wicker and laughed as he ran his hand up her side. Wicker averted his eyes. 'Seriously, though' – Bobby was still talking to Noel but now he was watching Wicker – 'you'll have a couple of hours to dig me out.'

Wicker said: 'You're up on the west end of the cemetery – all gravel. She could dig it with a spoon.'

Bobby nodded, giving Noel's side another squeeze, reassuring her. But at the edge of his mind, something was agitating him. 'Come on,' he said. 'Let's give the man his down payment and hit the road.'

They went through a door into the burgundy-carpeted office, where Noel's green silk purse was slung over the arm of a velvet couch. It was a comfortable room, softly lit and noticeably, forcefully, quiet. Framed prints of snow-covered city streets hung on the walls, intermingled with Wicker's funereal certificates. Noel opened her purse and withdrew a bulging white envelope, lifted the flap and slid a stack of twenties and fifties onto the desk. Wicker checked the window behind him.

'Make me look good,' Bobby said, 'and there'll be a bonus for you.' He grinned at Wicker.

The undertaker's gray eyes, half-closed, met Bobby's with a measure of acrimony. Eliot Wicker was an efficient funeral director. His chapel was sweet smelling, and his recorded organ music always understated. But the man was no artist, and on the rare occasion that a mourner remarked how good a client looked, anyone in town would know it was a conspicuous lie. Of course Bobby could have gone closed casket all the way, except it wouldn't have been Bobby. He wanted to know, in his next life, just what he had pulled off.

But tonight, as Noel drove home through the quiet town, something was bothering Bobby, something more than the risk. He couldn't put his finger on it. After they had driven a mile, he said to Noel, 'Call Sal. I mean, if anything gets screwed up.'

Noel drove silently for a few seconds. 'Did you tell him?'

'No. I'm just saying, if something goes wrong, call Sal.'

'Nothing's going to go wrong.'

'I'm just thinking here – you get a flat tire on the way to the cemetery, you throw out your back digging me up, somebody finds the shovel in the woods. Anything happens, you can call Sal. He's the reason we came here in the first place.'

'We came here because the locals still don't seal up their dead in concrete vaults. Nothing's going to go wrong.'

Bobby let a few moments pass.

'I don't see any other way to get at the money. The IRS is watching me, the Treasury Department is watching me, the people from the Resolution Trust. The bank wants their money back, they got their loan officer in prison. He gets out, he's gonna come looking for his share . . . or he's gonna send someone. So they hear I'm dead, they'll all have a drink and a lousy night, and then get on with their lives, right?' Bobby laughed. Noel didn't.

He opened the window, let the chill night air swirl through the car. The peeping of tree frogs came and went as they passed a bog.

'I feel important,' he said. He put his hand on her inner thigh. Her legs closed. Houses they passed were dark. He took his hand off her leg, turned in his seat and faced her. He said with a grin, 'You're nervous.'

Seconds passed. Then her legs opened again and she said to him, 'Bobby, I'd rather be stuck in this horrible little town for the rest of my life than have anything happen to you.' She returned the accusation: 'You're nervous.'

He gave a shrug. 'This isn't like jumping from a plane. Up there its wide open, you're in control.' He paused and let the vision grow. 'But this . . . you do get edgy when that lid comes down.' He laughed a little, nervously.

'Call it off,' she told him. 'We're paying the bills with what we earn from the store.'

'I *will* miss Blueberry Blossom Day,' he said, giving her a laugh.

'You'll miss Sal Erickson.' She continued watching the road, her back rigid.

'Babe, I didn't say anything to him. My point is, if anything comes up, we can trust Sal Erickson—'

'We trust *no one*.' She responded so fast that her words overlapped his. And the silence that followed set those words in the air between them as if they'd been solid.

No one.

And she was right. Who in the world could keep a two-million-dollar secret?

1

'No one can forgive me but my baby.'

—Tom Waits

'*Sal?*'

Salvatore Erickson was awakened by the harsh whisper, the beam of light brushing his face.

'*Sally—*'

Someone at the window with a flashlight. Sal sat up fast, heart thumping.

'*Come on down.*'

Sal caught his breath. 'Bobby – Jesus—'

Beside Sal, Iris stirred.

'It's Bobby,' Sal said to her. He tucked the sheet under her chin.

'Bobby?'

She groped the nightstand for her glasses.

'I'm on the ladder,' Bobby explained.

Sal kissed Iris's thumb. 'He's on the ladder. Go back to sleep.'

'Come on down for a minute,' Bobby said.

'It's one-thirty, Ace. We gotta work tomorrow.'

'That's okay, come on down.' Bobby was gone from the window before Sal could object again.

With a labored sigh, Sal folded the covers back and set his feet on the carpet, grabbed his underpants and corduroy trousers off the bedpost.

'Sal?' said Iris.

'It's okay, I'll only be a second.'

Stepping onto the floor and into his pants, Sal heard the sleepy plod of Davey's feet outside his room. The landing light came on, and then his fair beanpole of a girl was standing in the doorway. 'I heard talking,' she said in a breath, squinting against the light.

Iris smiled. 'Oh, love.'

'How come Daddy's getting dressed?'

'Hurry back to bed, hon,' Sal told her. 'Mommy has to get a good night's sleep. She's got a final exam tomorrow night after work.'

'Tonight,' Iris corrected. 'It's already today. And I'll be delivering a baby, too, when Trudy decides she's ready.'

Dazed, Davey looked in at her mother. 'I'll go back to bed so you can study.' Joking.

'How about a hug first?' Sal said, pulling a sweatshirt over his head.

In a single motion Davey swept across the bedroom floor and wrapped her arms around him, delicate limbs that seemed to grow longer every week. Sal moaned sleepily, lifting Davey to give her a kiss. 'You're getting so big,' he said, as he set her on the bed beside Iris. 'Give Mommy a kiss now and then hurry back to bed.' He touched Davey's hair.

'See you in the morning,' she told him, extending a lazy arm.

'See you in the morning,' he returned. Then to Iris he said, 'I'll be right back.' As he turned to leave, his sweatshirt snagged. He reached back, found Iris's hand there. He removed her fingers gently, lifted her hand to his mouth and gave it a kiss. 'Don't worry, okay?' he said, then leaned over to kiss her mouth before he left the room.

Holding her daughter in bed, Iris listened to her husband go down the same worn stairs she had climbed for the first eighteen years of her own life. After a few seconds she heard the kitchen light click on. Then the familiar squeal of the kitchen door.

'Hey,' Davey whispered. 'You gonna let me go so I can get back to bed?'

Iris smiled, unclasped her hands from around Davey and kissed her cheek. Davey rolled off the bed and glided silently from the room.

Another summer coming, Iris thought, steeling herself.

Outside, the night bristled with spring – the clean chill of the air, peepers chirring off in the distance, the smell of worm-perforated soil. Sal came out quietly, pulling his corduroy sportcoat over his sweatshirt. 'Kinda late, ain't it, Ace?' he whispered to Bobby.

Sal was thirty-four, a year older than Bobby. They had grown up together outside of Providence. Like Bobby (whose maternal grandfather, Sordillo, had come from Italy), Sal was dark-eyed and dark-haired, his mother's Italian blood easily overpowering his father's Scandinavian. In fact, the only legacy Sal carried of his Swedish father (besides the surname) was his strong Nordic jaw.

'Come on,' Bobby said. Dressed in his leather jacket and black jeans, he started across the road.

Sal held back. 'What's up?' he whispered.

'Nothing, I gotta talk to you.'

'Yeah, don't wake up One-Eye,' Sal whispered. The mongrel belonged to Iris's father and brother, Otis and Jerry Royal, who lived in the small blue house across the road. The old dog had spent his life chained to the ramshackle garage that was attached to the house, presumably to keep thieves away from Jerry's collection of car parts and appliances that littered the property, or the blue gospel bus parked on the knoll, or the chickens that roamed free (one of whom, long since deceased, had given the dog its name). Roused, old One-Eye could bark for hours.

'Come on, let's go down to the falls,' Bobby said.

'Talk here,' Sal answered, but Bobby was already crossing the road, leaving Sal little choice but to follow. They joined the worn path at the left corner of the Royals' lot and started following it through the scrub field, when they heard the sudden snap of One-Eye's chain. Sal caught Bobby's arm.

'Stay still,' he whispered.

The dog, blinded by the 200-watt floodlight over his head, stretched his short chain, sniffing the air.

Bobby reached down with his hand, felt around in the grass and came up with a rock in his hand. 'Don't screw around,' Sal told him. 'They're crazy in there. They've got guns.'

Bobby laughed softly, drew his fist behind his ear.

'No,' Sal whispered, too late.

The rock arced into the night, shot like a meteor through the zone of floodlight before rejoining the darkness again, and then in the gospel bus, window glass jangled.

The dog spun, sprang at his chain, barking.

'Come on,' Bobby said, and the two men hurried along the path, their footsteps covered not only by the barking and chain-snapping but by the sudden, gravel-throated shouts from inside the house.

'SHUT UP! YOU SHUT UP, GODDAMMIT!' A light came on in the back of the house. Bobby laughed as he ran. One-Eye's barking grew more frantic. A door slammed. 'SHUT UP! HEY! HEY! *HEY!*'

As Bobby and Sal reached the river, a gunshot sounded. The barking ceased abruptly even as the gunshot echoed off the trees, leaving the night air suddenly full of other dogs barking in the village, while Otis and Jerry Royal howled at one another inside the house. Amidst all the noise, Sal and Bobby veered away from the open river and headed right, into the woods toward the fishing pool.

They made their way through fifty feet of sparse, second-growth pine, where two of Jerry's old station wagons lay, not yet overgrown, Bobby aiming his tiny penlight beam in front of him, breaking through low, dead branches to what promised to be a moonlit riverbank.

However, the nearer they got to the river, the heavier the mist grew. By the time they reached the bank, it was like walking into a heavy cloud. The moon was a mere smudge above them, while all around sang the full, keening chorus of peeping frogs, the river whispering off to their left. Bobby slowed up, handed the penlight to Sal and said, 'Here, you know the way.'

Sal shone the penlight into the fog (for what little good it did) and led the way down to the bank.

'I think he shot his dog,' Bobby said aloud, and he laughed.

'Shh.'

Sal stopped at his fishing rock, a flat granite slab overlooking a shallow bog. Bobby put a hand on his back. 'Low tide,' Sal whispered, 'watch your step. It's not deep, but the bottom's like quicksand.'

They were at the head of the reversing falls, the phenomenon for which the town of Gravity was named. Every high tide, the river gradually slowed and deepened and then turned back on itself, the estuary waters washing inland, creating small, noisy rapids over the rocky incline just below them. When that happened, the reversing river overflowed its banks and transformed the bog they were standing on into a wide, waist-deep fishing pool.

Now the tide was low, and that was fortunate. Because at low tide rocks and tussocks rose out of the water, making the bog traversable.

Sal shone the penlight against the mist, looking for his first step. 'Ready?' he said, and he left his fishing rock, landing on a wide, firm tussock. He got his balance, made room for Bobby and shone the light down at his foot. Bobby stepped, landing right behind him. He took hold of Sal's arm to keep from falling.

Off to their right they heard a car pass on the road, obviously in response to the gunshot and the shouting. They could hear traces of men's voices.

'Nice of us to give the locals something to do,' Bobby croaked, chuckling. 'Fuckin crazy Jerry, I think he shot his dog.'

'Shh.'

Sal looked for the next step, a high flat rock. He saw it, barely, and was about to step off when Bobby grabbed him.

'*Jesus!*'

Sal reeled with his free arm to keep from falling.

'*Jesus Christ!*' Bobby said again. In response, the peepers stopped trilling.

'Shh! What're you doing?'

Bobby snatched the penlight from Sal and shone it behind them. The beam was barely two feet long. Up in the village, dogs continued barking.

'*There's a body.*'

'What body?'

Bobby moved the penlight through the fog, illuminating a couple of plastic bottles floating under the bank. 'I'm not shittin you, Sally.' His voice was a whisper. 'I saw the ass cheek in the moonlight. Over there.'

'Ass cheek in the moonlight—?'

'Stickin out of the water. Ass and thigh.' Bobby leaned over the tussock and followed his shivering penlight beam until the light stopped on something. Sal held Bobby's leather jacket to keep him from falling.

'That?' Sal said. 'That's a milk jug. A plastic milk jug.'

'That wasn't it, Sally.' Bobby moved the light back, over a plastic bag, a slab of light blue Styrofoam, a plastic soda bottle. The pool had a habit of collecting whatever litter hadn't been carried to the ocean when the river reversed. The stuff backed up and then settled in the cove after the pool retreated with the next tide.

'That?' Sal took Bobby's hand, guided the beam to their right. 'That's a kickball, a kid's broken kickball.'

Unconvinced, Bobby pulled back to the left, moving the light through the fog. 'You know what they say about this place, Sally, how the Indians used to see things all the time. Spirits down here.'

Sal snickered. He'd never seen Bobby this shaken over anything. Bobby Swift, who'd raced motorcycles in high school, test-piloted F18s in the navy and then opened a sky-diving school when he got out – Bobby Swift afraid of ghosts?

'Right out there,' Bobby whispered. 'It's gone now.'

'The ass cheek of a ghost—?'

'Buttock and thigh. Fuck you, I know what I saw.'

Abruptly leaving the tussock, Bobby stepped down into the water and went slogging noisily for the bank.

'Hold up, I can't see,' Sal called in a whisper, but it was clear that Bobby wasn't stopping. Without the aid of the light, Sal had little choice but to step off the rock and follow, a dozen ankle-deep, foot-sucking, methane-releasing steps, until the bank rose firm and dry, and the river narrowed to their left and was loud again. Bobby waited on the path, his penlight a faint yellow dot in the mist.

When Sal climbed up alongside, his sneakers sloshed like sponges and smelled like raw sewage. 'Make sure you come get me next time you feel like talking to someone,' he said, taking the penlight from Bobby and following the path upstream. Bobby stayed two paces behind, the noise of the river easily outdoing their footsteps. Momentarily the peepers resumed behind them, and the two men were swallowed by their song, by the river sounds, the night and the mist. As the bridge began to emerge ahead, vaguely silhouetted by the lone streetlight in the village, the trees on the bank receded, giving way to piles of disused concrete supports, rusted tentacles of rebar twisting out of their sides. Beside the bridge a worn path led up to the road just below Bobby's store. Sal headed for the path. On the bridge above, a car rumbled past.

'Hold up,' Bobby told him, 'let's catch our breath, wait'll things settle down.' He sat down on a block of concrete.

Sal came back a few steps, crouched on the ground beside the concrete. He could smell Bobby's boots.

Bobby lowered his head and laughed softly. 'You hear 'em back there?' he said. 'Fuckin Jerry, man, you got some dangerous relatives.' He looked at Sal through the darkness and gave another laugh, high-pitched, nervous.

'What's up, Ace?' Sal said. It was what they used to say to each other when they were both drinking. He pushed to his feet and took a seat beside Bobby.

'I don't know. It's good to have somebody you can do this shit with. It's important.'

Sal couldn't remember a time when he had seen Bobby so serious.

'Everybody needs one person they can trust completely,' Bobby told him. 'You know what I'm saying? I mean trust with your life. Your wife, friend, I don't care. One person.'

Since Sal had quit drinking, he'd found such alcohol-fueled conversations exasperating. 'You've gotta trust yourself,' he replied, even though he knew it wasn't what Bobby wanted to hear.

'Come on, Sally, who do you trust?' Bobby stared at Sal through the darkness. 'I mean, completely. Implicitly.'

'Completely? Myself.' Sal knew by Bobby's persistent stare that he wouldn't settle for that answer. So he said, 'My wife, alright? I trust Iris.'

'Trust her with your life,' Bobby said, staring.

'Yeah.'

'With your life.'

'Yeah, why not?'

'Well.' Bobby, head lowered, nodding, resigned. 'I guess that's the way it's supposed to be.' He rubbed his palms on his pants, which meant the conversation was over, then he slid off the concrete onto his feet. 'Whaddya say, Ace? Let's go join the search party.'

When they emerged at the foot of the bridge, they walked a few feet down to the stop sign. On the road to their right, Sal's road, three men were walking toward them with a flashlight. A ways beyond the men, the blue light from the constable's car was flashing in front of the Royals' house, and silhouettes of more men crossed back and forth in front of the car's headlights. Bobby pinched a Camel from his shirt pocket and lit it with a lighter, then called to the men as they approached, 'See anything down your end?'

'Hey, Bobby!' one of them answered. It was Jerry Royal, carrying a flashlight in one hand and a 16-ounce Pabst in the other. His flashlight beam found Sal's eyes, remained there longer than necessary. Although the two men were brothers-in-law, Sal and Jerry hadn't spoken since Sal and Iris had moved from Providence eight years earlier and taken over the family house, which the town was about to confiscate for back taxes.

Jerry said to Bobby, 'We ain't seen a thing on our end. How 'bout you, down here?' (With Jerry, the word *here* had two syllables: *hee-ah.*) 'Anyways, whoever it was cost me a dog.'

'He shoots his own dog,' one of Jerry's companions said. 'I still can't believe that.'

'So?' Jerry replied lightly. 'Weren't my fault.'

His flashlight beam returned to Sal, moved down his corduroy trousers to his muddy sneakers. Then, with his other hand, Jerry dropped his empty beer can into the grass behind him. When his hand returned to his front, he was brandishing a small snub-nosed revolver. Sal felt a rushing through his chest, a tensing of muscles. He tried not to show it.

'Got my shotgun confiscated,' Jerry said. 'Imagine the town constable scared of a little honest justice?' His flashlight beam moved over the asphalt to Bobby's black boots, which were also mud-caked.

Bobby covered smoothly. 'We checked down the river, Jerry. No sign of 'em there.' He dropped his cigarette on the road, scuffed it out, then said to Sal, 'Well, Ace, we did our part. Guess I'll go in and get some sleep.' He turned his eyes up the hill to his store, where a light was on upstairs. 'Then again, it looks like Noel's awake. Maybe I won't be sleepin after all.' He looked straight at Sal and gave a laugh.

'I like the sounda that,' Jerry said, sticking the pistol back in the waistband of his jeans.

Bobby took Sal by the arm, led him aside. 'You be good,' he said. He gave a squeeze and then started for home.

Bemused by Bobby's good-bye, by the entire episode, Sal stood for a minute with the other men and watched Bobby walk over the bridge. Then Sal turned and started walking down his own road.

'Take 'er easy, Bobby,' Jerry called. The other men bade similar good-byes – to Bobby. It was a fact of Sal's life with Bobby, from childhood on: Bobby fit, Sal didn't. Heading toward the car lights and commotion in front of his house, Sal put his hands in his jacket pockets, felt a chill on his neck and thought of his hat, the old tweed touring cap that he'd lost the summer before. When he reached his house, Otis Royal was still in the road raising a ruckus with the constable while a rough semicircle of men looked on.

Sal stayed to the left, out of the light, and cut quietly across his front lawn to his back door. In the kitchen, in the dark, he took off his sneakers and socks, took off his sportcoat and laid it over a wooden chair, then made his way up the stairs. In his bedroom, he pulled his sweatshirt over his head and draped it over the bedpost. He undid his belt and stepped out of his trousers and underpants, hung the trousers over his sweatshirt. He could hear by Iris's breathing that she was awake, waiting for him. He nestled beside her under the covers, found her face with his hands and kissed her on the mouth.

'We should really start spending more time with your family,' he said.

She made a sound in her throat. 'Did they shoot at you?'

'I wasn't the one barking.'

She sighed.

'Don't worry, okay?' He kissed her again.

The seconds passed silently, until she said: 'Bobby's going to get you killed someday.'

His hand, chilled from the outdoors, went underneath her T-shirt and found her warm breast. She curled away from him. He pursued her.

'Sal, we have to get up in three hours.'

He pulled the blankets over her shoulder, then massaged the back of her neck with his thumbs until he could feel her muscles relaxing and hear by her breathing that she was starting to fall asleep.

Outside the house, the episode ended in stages. Car doors opened and closed, car engines started, revved, then died away. Up and down the road, house lights blinked off one by one until once again the singing of peepers and the whisper of the river were the only sounds in the long bright night.

Sal lay there, his fingers tenderly working Iris's muscles, hearing all of it, hearing none of it. He was thinking about Bobby and the way he had said good-bye. Most of all he was thinking about their conversation under the bridge.

'Who do you trust?' Bobby had asked him. Sal knew the answer Bobby was looking for – he'd known it at the time too. There was something Bobby had come to tell him, some reason Bobby was asking for his confidence, and Sal had withheld it.

Silently, he lifted the covers and slipped out of bed, took his bathrobe from the bedpost and padded out of the room, putting it on. Feeling his way down the dark stairs and around the corner of the living room, he turned on the light over the kitchen table and picked up the telephone.

It was only after he began dialing Bobby's number that he thought of the hour and hung up again, telling himself that he'd go see Bobby after work. In days to come, when he thought of Bobby Swift, he'd remember this night. He'd remember the conversation under the bridge, the phone call he'd almost made, and how he had let Bobby down.

2

Gravity, Maine, boasted a population of one thousand people, give or take – more in the summer, fewer in the winter. The town supported an elementary school, a health clinic, a volunteer fire department and a grange. Roads were narrow in winter and buckled with frost heaves in spring. Blueberry fields comprised a good deal of the land in town, certainly most of the farmland, but blueberries didn't make money anymore, not for the family growers. Gravity was a poor town, by national standards, as it always had been. Houses were old, barns patiently caving in, boats in need of painting. But by Maine standards, people were not wanting. Nearly half the adults in town had jobs; the other half were unemployed or self-employed (mostly as fishermen, lobstermen, clammers) and did enough business to get by, same as townsfolk had done for decades.

The Gravity Superette was a two-and-a-half-story, white-shingled building built across from the firehouse in the village, just above the river. Bobby and Noel Swift had bought the old store with the profits from the sale of their Boston condo, and in three years (which was two years longer than Noel had planned to stay) Bobby had turned the mom-and-pop into an enviable business, all the while biding his time. Nurturing the Plan.

The Superette was the center of town life. If you needed gasoline, kerosene, groceries, beer, wine or liquor, fishing or hunting gear, work clothes, plumbing or electrical supplies, hardware or rental videotapes – you could find it at the Superette. The town's fire phone was located there. A lunch counter and six fountain stools ensured that mealtimes were lively with men's gossip and local politics. Although Bobby's fish chowder was the biggest seller, according to Herb True (whose wife Bonnie worked at the store) it wasn't the chowder that kept the fountain stools occupied but the fact that Noel Swift served it. Herb liked to say that Noel probably caused more unplanned births in town than the pope.

Bobby and Noel lived upstairs from the store, in a spacious apartment that Noel had decorated entirely in African. Tribal ritual masks hung on the walls, animal icons peered down from shelves and corners, and every window was surrounded by lush green jungly plants – an oasis of high life in this poor fishing town. Down behind the building, facing the garage (and surrounded by woods on the other three sides), was Noel's in-ground swimming pool; word was that in the summertime she swam naked every night after the store closed, although no one actually claimed to have seen her – no one whose word was good, anyway. The basement was Bobby's – the garage where he kept his Corvette and his Harley, the workshop where he kept his tools, and the small gym where he died.

At noon on Friday, after lunch, Noel drove to Bangor to buy paint for the bathroom. She didn't kiss Bobby when she left because she never did; although today Bobby would have liked that. At 3:30, after high school let out, Erica and Chad came to work as they always did, and Bobby went downstairs and changed into his gym clothes. He usually kept the thermostat off, but today he needed a cold sweat, so he turned it up to eighty.

At 4:00 Eliot Wicker came in for his afternoon coffee. At 4:30 Noel called from a Bangor hardware store and asked for Bobby. He's not answering the phone in the apartment, she told Chad, maybe he's down in the gym.

The baby-faced, broad-shouldered boy – Chad was captain of the school football team and a churchgoing Baptist – hurried downstairs and knocked on the gym door. He called Bobby's name. When he got no answer, he pushed the door open and saw his boss on the carpet beside his exercise bike, one foot stuck in the stirrup, his face contorted in pain. In the first instant, Chad was dumbstruck. Then he ran to the bike and dropped to his knees, knocking into Bobby's arm, and struggled to pull Bobby's foot out of the stirrup, hoping the stuck foot was the extent of his problem. 'Bobby, you okay?' he said.

But Bobby's arm was clammy to the touch, his eyes slack and unfocused.

'Bobby?'

Chad took Bobby by the shoulders and shook him. Bobby's head flopped lifelessly.

'Wait a minute!' Chad blurted, and he looked wildly around the room. 'Wait a minute!' he said again, then ran out the door, glancing hard off the frame.

Now Bobby relaxed, let every molecule of his body fall into a calm of keen concentration. Chad was a smart boy. He'd call the emergency number posted on the store phone. After 4:30 on Fridays, Walt Moody was the only doctor at the clinic. The young man had twice in the past half-year listened through a stethoscope while Bobby made his heart turn somersaults. Both times he had rushed Bobby to Downeast Memorial, where the disorder was diagnosed as cardiac arrythmia; and so it was charted at the Gravity clinic. Bobby's history listed a grandfather who had died of heart failure before his fortieth birthday – a fiction, but part of the official record, nonetheless. With such a background, and a God-fearing football captain as a witness, there'd be no cause for suspicion, no reason for the insurance companies to request an autopsy. Doc Moody, who was known to tremble in the presence of death, would gladly stand aside for Eliot Wicker, who was already on his way downstairs. Without complications, Bobby knew that he'd be on his way to the funeral home in a half hour.

Bobby let go of his body, let go of his mind and went deep into himself. This was not sleep, but *focus*, pure and total, the way he had been taught by the Brahman, the way he had trained for the past four years. He let his bladder empty into his sweatpants. He *became* his heart, *became* his lungs, and he brought himself to rest, quelling his body's panic with masterful control, so that even when his heart began slowing and his lungs shutting down, he could hear the undertaker's throaty voice rising above the rumble of footsteps coming down the stairs. 'No one allowed,' Wicker was saying, 'No one allowed.' Bobby was at once totally aware and totally unaware of it all.

* * *

Sal Erickson's headaches were nothing new, but today he had a beauty. The annual Blueberry Blossom Pageant was Sunday night, and his only schoolwide rehearsal had been a disaster. Children didn't know how to line up on the stage, they didn't know words to the songs, and their singing was brutal. It was the same every year with these shows: kids acting up, stressed-out teachers buzzing around him, *Mrs Bonnevill's class has the best songs again this year, Mrs Perkins never did it this way*, day after day, week after week, a thirty-four-year-old man spending the best years of his life corralling little kids onto a rickety gym stage, the same man who, ten years earlier, had toured Europe as a featured soloist in Woody Herman's Thundering Herd, whom *Downbeat* had called 'one of the brightest young trombone players in the east,' Mr Sal Erickson, ladies and gentlemen, now performing a little number about pussy willows, pufferbellies and flying fucking unicorns.

When Sal got home after school, the cat was on the counter drinking milk that Davey had spilled, and Davey was sprawled on the living room floor watching cartoons. Sal took off his corduroy jacket and tossed it on the couch.

'Tough day?' he said.

She took her hand out from under her chin and rocked it a little, never taking her eyes off the television.

'Take me fishing?' she said.

'You talking to Bugs Bunny or me?'

She wiggled her skinny butt at him.

'I gotta make supper, hon. Mom's got her big test tonight. Besides, I bet you didn't weed the peas like I asked you.' Davey wiggled her butt again. 'Or practice your piano.'

He went into the bathroom and stepped out of his trousers, hung them on the towel rack, then took his black sweatpants out of the hamper and put them on. Sal had been a good athlete in school. He still had an athletic body, able and well-proportioned. In fact, with his thick neck and coarse, cropped black hair, he looked more like a football player than he had a musician – or a music teacher, as he had come to acknowledge himself. He unbuttoned his shirt, pulled it over his T-shirt and pitched it in the hamper, then went into the kitchen to find his sneakers.

'I'll take you fishing tomorrow morning,' he called to Davey as he laced up, 'but you gotta do your piano and peas.' He stepped out the back door, where he saw Jerry Royal across the road, working over a smoking trash barrel. It was where Jerry incinerated his oily rags and trash and the occasional chicken that got flattened in the road. Jerry was stirring the fire with a charred piece of two-by-four that was also on fire, by the looks of it. By the stench, Sal guessed that Jerry was burning the dog he had shot the night before.

Aware that his brother-in-law was staring at him through the smoke, Sal turned right, toward the village, checked his watch and started jogging. Actually, what Sal did couldn't be called jogging. From the start it was a flat-out, lung-singing sprint. A straight half mile in 2:10. 'Like someone was after him,' their neighbor Martha Abraham would tell people at the post office.

Sal's lungs were already burning as he blew past Mrs Abraham's house, past the lone apple tree in her field. He pumped hard, his lungs stretching beyond their limit, his heart pounding in his chest. Then he pushed even harder, certain that he had never run as fast, chasing his own elongated shadow up the frost-heaved asphalt. He could hear Thelonius Monk in the whistling through his teeth. *Little Rootie Tootie*. Yeah, they're chasing me now, Mrs Abraham.

Behind him he heard a car coming fast. He thought wildly that he could keep pace with it, and he opened up even more, incredibly, until he felt as if his heart might explode – and then the vehicle passed him. It was the undertaker's black Suburban, Eliot Wicker heading to the Superette for his afternoon coffee.

At the junction of the Village Road Sal slowed to a jog, to a walk, then bent at the waist, panting. He checked his watch. Two ten, a new record. He walked a wide arc in the road, hands on his hips. His face burned, and his lungs replaced air like a two-stroke engine. Off ahead of him, the sun sat low above the trees, a warm, smiling peach, while the surrounding sky had become the kind of promising blue that only happens in spring. Sal felt good about that, felt good about noticing it. A lone peeper began chirping down at the river, getting a start on the evening. Sal felt good about that too. Six months since he'd quit drinking, to the day. He felt strong, every day stronger.

He and Iris were getting along better than ever. Davey was happy and healthy and doing aces at school. His Sunday concert, he knew, would go fine. In fact, the only unsettledness in his life, as he saw it, was whatever he had left hanging with Bobby the night before – and now, while he had a few minutes, he was going to take care of that. Heading up the hill to Bobby's store, he sprang into a run, bolting straight up the middle of the grated bridge, pushing with everything he had left.

'No one allowed,' Wicker sang, his spindly arms outstretched to the stairway walls. Sal pulled on the undertaker's shoulder, trying to push past. 'No one allowed!' Wicker said again, shaking him off. But on the landing Sal shoved past Wicker as if the man were a turnstile.

'You can't go down there!' Wicker told him, as Sal took the remaining stairs two at a time, then swung around the half partition and charged through the door that led into Bobby's gym.

'It's his heart!' Chad called from behind Wicker.

Sal flew into the room, crouched over Bobby. 'Call a doctor! Did somebody call a doctor?' he shouted.

'You either!' Wicker said, banging into the small room, attempting to close the door on Chad.

Sal lifted Bobby's head into his hands and spoke into his face, as if he were waking his friend from a nap. *'Bobby?'* The hair that hung over Bobby's neck was wet. His skin was chilled. *'Come on, Bobby!'*

'Let me in there, leave him alone!' Wicker snapped, slapping his hand down on Sal's shoulder, his fingernails digging into Sal's skin.

Sal disregarded him. He slid his leg under Bobby's neck to keep his head from falling. With his left hand he raised Bobby's shoulder, cradling him. 'Bobby, you come on now!' he cried. With his right fist, he thumped Bobby's chest.

Bobby gasped. His eyes gaped. His body stiffened, trembled for a second and then fell limp, even though his eyes held their same stark surprise.

'Get him off!' Wicker yelled, wrapping his arm around Sal's neck and pulling back.

Now another pair of arms grabbed Sal from behind. 'Mr Erickson!'

It was Chad, much stronger than Eliot Wicker. Together they hauled Sal back across the carpet, Bobby sliding with him.

'Let him go!' Wicker strained, locking his arm around Sal's arm and pulling back. 'You probably killed him yourself!'

'No, he's coming out of it!' Sal shouted, not relenting. He reached to pound Bobby's chest again, but with Chad wresting his arm back, he managed only a glancing blow. And then he lost Bobby, as Chad drove him back against the door. 'Mr Erickson, you gotta stop!' he said.

'*Somebody call a doctor!*'

'I called the ambulance!' Chad said.

'It doesn't matter!' Wicker shouted. '*He's dead!*'

The words stunned Sal. For the moment he lay against the door, motionless, looking over Chad's shoulder, while Wicker knelt beside the sprawled body, holding Bobby's wrist between his thumb and first two fingers, his other hand on Bobby's heart, his ear pressed to Bobby's open mouth. The picture of concentration. After a few seconds, the undertaker raised his head and took a deep breath. He looked over at Sal and gave a shrug, his teeth clenched hopelessly.

'I'm sorry,' he said, bringing all his funereal compassion to bear. 'He's gone.'

'No, he breathed,' Sal asserted, Chad still pinning him against the door, digging the sides of his sneakers into the carpet.

Wicker shook his head with a patronizing smile. 'Reflexes,' he explained. 'You knocked the wind out of a dead man.'

Sal didn't get home until ten that night. When he walked in the living room, Davey was sitting in the rocking chair, wrapped in a quilt and watching TV. Iris, already back from school, was asleep on the couch, her notebooks and textbooks and pager spread on the coffee table and floor. Sal lifted Davey off the chair. As he carried her up the stairs, she said sleepily, 'Where were you?'

'Something came up,' Sal told her. He carried her into her bedroom and put her in bed, tucked her in.

'Mommy had to get Melissa to stay with me while she went to take her test,' Davey said to him, giving him a worried look.

'I know,' he said. They kissed lightly on the lips, then Sal shut off her raccoon lamp and started downstairs.

'See you in the morning,' she sighed.

'See you in the morning.'

Downstairs he kissed Iris awake. She opened her eyes placidly, then adjusted her specs and held up her middle finger for him. He kissed the finger. 'How was your test?'

She held the finger in place.

'I get the message.'

'Just making sure,' she said.

She looked at him curiously. Her soft eyes sharpened and her finger went slack.

His words fell like wood. 'Bobby died.'

She drew a quick breath. 'Bobby Swift?'

'He had a heart attack, working out.'

Iris raised herself on her elbow, eyes glistening. She took another breath, let it out. She reached for Sal's arm, took a fistful of his shirt and pulled him down on top of her. He kept a knee on the floor.

'Are you okay?' she asked him.

'Yeah,' he answered, with some surprise. Actually he *was* okay; stunned, maybe, but not distraught, as he thought he'd be. (As he thought he *should* be.) He had already stopped wondering if there was any psychic significance to Bobby's late-night visit the night before, or to the way Bobby had said good-bye. He started to kiss Iris again and, without planning to, opened his mouth and found her tongue with his own. He took hold of her small breast, took her nipple between his thumb and finger. Her body rose into his. She took his hand and broke the kiss.

'We don't want to do this now.'

Involuntarily, he drew a long breath, thinking he might finally cry. But he didn't. He ran his hand up under her cotton jersey, found her nipple hardened, and he manipulated it again.

She took his hand. 'Sal, we wouldn't be any good.'

'I don't know about that,' he answered.

He thought he should feel some shame for the way he wanted her now, but now he felt so grateful to have her. They went into the bathroom and brushed their teeth together, then climbed the stairs with only the moon through the window below lighting their way. Once in bed, they had tumultuous sex for an hour, their first in weeks.

3

Bobby came to in Wicker's black Suburban, zippered in a white body bag. As he had done the night before, he once again broke into uncontrollable shivering. His wet sweatpants didn't help. He rattled the plastic bag, clattered the collapsible stretcher and then heard Wicker shout at him to keep still. When they got to the funeral home, Wicker wheeled him on the stretcher into the laundry room, where he unbagged Bobby and wrapped him in an electric blanket. Despite its low heat, the acclimation was just as painful as when he'd been dropped into the bathtub.

But it was nothing compared to the boredom that followed – the seemingly endless thirty-six hours closed in that laundry room, lying on a pile of wool blankets reading *Money* magazines and ten years' worth of *American Funeral Director*, or periodically going into the toilet enclave and masturbating, imagining Noel.

The confinement was brutal. But Wicker had threatened to expose the whole scam if Bobby so much as opened the laundry door, and Wicker was nervous enough to do it. He had kept Bobby awake for most of the first night, clearing his throat upstairs, a meticulous, continuous dislodging of phlegm. The more Bobby tried to ignore it, the more aware of it he became, so that his own sleep was fitful at best – and he needed to be rested.

The only respite from the boredom was an hour on Saturday morning, when Sal came with Noel to choose the casket. Hearing Sal's voice through the wall, Bobby was saddened to think that he was losing his best friend. At the same time, he was revisited by the unsettling suspicion that something was slipping his mind, and he wished more than ever that he had included Sal in the Plan.

When the voices came closer, Bobby cupped his ear to the wall and heard Sal say something about the teachers' retirement fund – offering to help pay for the funeral. And Noel refusing.

'Just send me the bill,' Sal said to Wicker.

'If Mrs Swift is comfortable with that,' Wicker replied.

'Send me the bill,' Sal said again.

Noel was wrong. Sal they could trust. And, after all, things *could* get screwed up. Noel could get in an accident driving to the cemetery. Kids could be up at the cemetery raising hell. With Sal as backup, they'd be able to handle it.

'If there's anything else I can help you with,' Bobby heard Wicker say, getting rid of them. Bobby slid to the door. He could do it now. He could open the door and—

'We make this as easy as we possibly can for the bereaved,' Wicker continued. Bobby could hear their footsteps moving past. The thought of telling Sal what he was pulling—

He took hold of the doorknob.

Now or never. Include Sal. Sneak up behind him, scare the shit out of him, take a picture of the look on his face and laugh like hell.

A door closed, and Wicker's voice went away. 'Times like these . . .'

Yeah, tell Sal. And then leave him here.

Another door closed, the voices becoming thin tones through the wood paneling.

Because if Sal knew that Bobby was alive, he wouldn't be able to leave it like that. Not for the rest of his life. Someday, maybe ten or twenty years from now, when he thought it was safe, Sal was bound to find a pay phone somewhere. Or take an innocent Cayman vacation. If suspicion ever arose, if the government got more proficient at tracking down every missing pebble in their mountain range of defaulted savings and loans, all they'd have to do is take a look at Sal. Question him on the wrong day, threaten to separate him from his family.

Noel was right. The Plan was perfect. He winced to think how close he had come to blowing it. All his life Bobby had thrived on risk and fear, had burned it like fuel. But it had never worried him like this.

Maybe it was because he had never had to rely on anyone else.

And now his life depended on Noel. So ... The Plan was perfect. The Plan was in motion, and, besides, it was too late to turn back.

For the rest of the day – and all through that long second night – Bobby lay sprawled on the heap of blankets, withstanding the odor of detergent, listening to the footsteps pacing above him (and the incessant throat-clearing), going over it again and again.

The shovel and pitchfork were waiting in the woods near his plot. The rental car was reserved at Bangor International Airport (in the name of Dale Newman, who had also reserved a hotel room at the Logan Airport Hilton in Boston). Once closed inside the casket, Bobby would open the tanks in succession: the scuba tanks first, then the oxygen tanks. He would set his watch alarm each time he opened a valve in order to rouse himself when it was time to start a new tank. Sometime before the third alarm sounded, Noel would be there digging him out. She'd awaken him with a whisper. She'd have a suitcase of new clothes (they'd leave his burial outfit in the grave). In the suitcase would also be scissors, hair dye, tortoiseshell glasses and his new wallet, along with Dale Newman's plane ticket, passport and birth certificate – courtesy of a Brookline counterfeiter Noel had met in her modelling days. In the new wallet was Dale Newman's driver's license and an identification card issued by the Atlantic National Bank and Trust, where two million dollars waited in an offshore Cayman account shared by Bobby Swift and Dale Newman. Now that Bobby Swift had passed on, the account belonged solely to Mr Newman. New man indeed. He'd make his first withdrawal Monday morning. Buy a bicycle and some diving gear and start his new life.

When the life insurance settlement came in – twenty-five thousand, not enough to cause suspicion – Noel would take a vacation, leave the store in Herb and Bonnie's hands and go on a cruise out of Tampa. She would write back that she'd met a wealthy man on the boat and fallen in love. She'd hand over the store to Bonnie True, lock, stock and videotape, and then disappear.

From then on, the Newmans would be islanders. Their leased condo stood two doors from the water. Once they won approval as Cayman residents, they'd buy beachfront, invest the rest in conservative mutual funds and live fat and free for the rest cf their lives. They'd ride bicycles with straw baskets on the handlebars, they'd dive everyday down the bottomless reefs. What else was there to do on Grand Cayman but scuba dive, bask, feast and hide your money? They'd eat fresh fruits and fishes, drink rum punch and fall asleep every night in each other's arms, listening to the hush of the surf, knowing they were safe in the vast, warm hold of the Atlantic. Except

the coughing—

Except for Eliot Wicker.

That was it.

Noel's words came to Bobby with a cold slap: *We trust no one.* A single vision chilled him: shiny black wingtips scuffing through beach sand.

At five o'clock on the morning he was to be buried, Bobby Swift opened the laundry door and came into Wicker's office with his penlight. He stole through the embalming room, through the casket selection room and into the chapel, where his own mahogany casket sat up in front of fifteen rows of chairs. Only the viewing lid was open, as it would remain during the funeral. The room was windowless, airless.

He opened another door and crept into the arrangements office, where ivory dawn light lined the venetian blinds. He moved to the window and quietly parted two slats. The sky was softly lit. Brighter was the white sign on the front lawn – WICKER'S FUNERAL HOME – as was the parking lot; the double lights on the single pole swarmed with insects. Why any funeral director needed to advertise, why he needed to light an empty parking lot—

But of course Eliot Wicker wasn't advertising – or helping customers park their cars. He was afraid of the dark, plain and simple. He was afraid, and he would break, Bobby was sure of it now. Once Wicker's share of the money was spent and all he had left was his gnawing envy and that throat-clearing fear – he'd spill it all. Maybe to some out-of-town therapist, maybe to his mother, maybe he'd go straight to the police, or he'd gas himself in his spotless Suburban and leave a note. Whichever way Wicker wanted it, there'd come the day when the black shoes would appear at Bobby's beach blanket, double-knit cuffs fat with sand.

He pictured Noel being led off the beach in handcuffs. He pictured himself killing Eliot Wicker.

Pistol shot to the head, knife through the heart – he allowed the notion to grow. He even caught himself trying to justify it: Wicker was greedy and heartless, and the world would be a better place without him. But that wasn't the point, and Bobby knew it. Murder was murder, and Eliot Wicker was standing between this dead man and a lifetime of bliss. It could be quick, it could be done tonight, after the resurrection, before Bobby left for Boston. Noel would never need to know.

Murder.

And who better to commit the crime than a dead man? Bobby waited for some pang of remorse, but none came, even as he turned back into the building (wiping doorknobs with his shirt-sleeve) and slipped into the embalming room, where he pulled on a pair of latex gloves and went quietly opening drawers until he found the two things he was looking for: a tiny screwdriver and the weapon. He didn't know the object's real purpose, but it was assuredly built to do the deed – a hollow steel shaft, sixteen inches long and pointed at the tip. A touch of irony – the word SLAUGHTER was engraved on its side.

Murder.

He crept back to the chapel and hid the thing in his casket, under the velvet, under the scuba tanks, beside the six-volt lantern battery that would power his heating pad.

Then he went back to the arrangements office, lit brighter with the dawn. There was a black plastic panel of four switches on the wall. They were labeled MUSIC, SIGN, PARKING, CHAPEL. Penlight in his mouth, Bobby unscrewed the panel cover, saw the red wire he wanted and leveraged it off the terminal with a spark. He looked out the blinds and saw the parking lot lights extinguished, then tucked the wire back in the box and replaced the panel. He returned the little screwdriver to its place in the embalming room and headed back to the laundry room, where he continued his preparations. In the enclave, up by the ceiling, there was a small casement window. Bobby stood on the toilet seat, reached up behind the venetian blinds and unlocked it, then he settled back on his bed of blankets to sleep. Murder, indeed.

The notion made him slightly more nervous than his burial, and now he found himself clearing his own throat. He heard Wicker's cough like an answering call, and he answered back noisily, wondering with a quiet yet persistent laugh if the undertaker was stretched out on his bed, staring at the ceiling, thinking the very same thing: that there was almost nothing a dead man couldn't do.

Rest Awhile, the hillside cemetery was named. Grass was thick here, and trees crowned with a lofty iridescence. Sunday morning, Blueberry Blossom Day, the day of Bobby Swift's funeral, Sal's school concert. The walking calmed Sal.

Watching Iris and Davey stroll ahead, Davey touching each windsmoothed tablet as they walked, Sal was touched by the similarities of mother and daughter: the shiny, oaken, pageboy hair; the slight, agile bodies. They even walked the same, upright, with short tentative steps, like sprinters saving something. It was here that Sal and Iris sought to smooth over whatever crags Bobby's death had cut in Davey's young philosophy.

For his part, Sal was handling it judiciously – although he remained unable to thoroughly absorb the simple fact: Bobby was dead. Over the two days, he'd found himself repeating it – Bobby is dead. Bobby is dead. But it wasn't sinking in, even when he'd revisit the experience: Bonnie True's watery eyes when Wicker wheeled the body out the garage door; the way the regulars sat at the counter, back-to, bitterly reviewing the warning signs they had missed; or the smart, fatalistic look Noel had given him when she had arrived, and the way she'd hugged him, seeming to be offering comfort rather than accepting it.

'Remember when Thelonius died?' Iris's voice broke the silence. 'And we buried him out back, with his little gravestone?' With the black clip of a pager stuck to her pocket (one of her midwifery mothers from Oyster Cove was due today), she reminded Sal of a tour group leader, the way she seemed to glide over the lawn, conducting this family lesson in mortality.

'Is Thelonius in heaven?' Davey asked.

'Imagine,' Sal said, 'a heaven full of cats.'

With a backward glance at him, Iris answered Davey: 'If you

think about it, cemeteries are really for those of us who are alive, so we can remember the people and pets we loved.' Iris seemed unmindful that the other members of her family, Otis and Jerry Royal, were at the top of the hill, digging Bobby's grave. Sounds of their arguing wafted down the hill.

'Is that where they're burying Bobby?' Davey asked, looking up. 'Way up there by himself?'

'Mm-hmm.'

Sal wondered, as he often had (as many townspeople had), how Iris and Davey could have come from the same gene matter that invested Iris's father and brother.

'I know where my grandmother is,' Davey said abruptly, breaking away from Iris.

'We really don't have time, love.'

'Daddy showed me once,' she said, venturing deeper into the cemetery.

Iris looked back at Sal, who called to Davey, 'Come on, hon, we've got to get you to Kristin's.' But Davey had already found the marker in the ground.

'I found her, Mommy. Leonna Royal.'

Sal climbed the terrace, walked to Davey's side and rested his hand on her head.

'She's got killed in the bus crash, right?'

'Yup.'

'But how come there are no flowers?' Davey looked back at Iris. 'You said cemeteries were to remember the people we love.'

Iris joined them, her arms folded. She glanced back to see her father at the top of the hill, leaning on his shovel, looking down at her. 'Sometimes people don't have good memories,' she said.

Davey scowled. 'Was she mean?'

'Not mean, just sort of – hollow.'

'*Hollow—?*'

'Empty,' Iris attempted, 'unforgiving ... love, I really don't remember.' She turned toward the road, caught a breeze in her face. She held her hand out. 'Time to go,' she said. Davey took hold and they started back toward the gate. Sal hung back to give them time.

It was the blue gospel bus, the dented shrine that sat on the knoll beside her father's house. Sal had learned some of the story from Iris, more from Bobby. The Royals had been returning from a gospel jubilee in New Brunswick. There was a photo in a scrapbook at the town house, autographed. Iris, who was eight, played mandolin. Her father played fiddle, her mother played guitar. Jerry, at fifteen, was the grinning star of the band, slapping a big upright bass, THE ROYAL FAMILY decaled in white letters on its face. GOSPEL TROUBADOURS.

The kids were asleep when the bus left the road, Otis too drunk to manage a curve. The bus rolled only once; in fact, the vehicle escaped with minimal damage. But inside, the Royals and their equipment were tossed about like bingo pills. Only Iris, tucked into bed, was not seriously hurt. Jerry broke his leg; Otis fractured his skull, broke both wrists and several ribs, and was unconscious for two days; Leonna, who had just put Iris to bed, broke her neck and died instantly.

'I'd be sad if you were killed in the accident,' Davey said to her mother, then deadpanned with a backward look at Sal. 'Then again, I guess I wouldn't be here to be sad.'

'Clown,' he said, catching up to her and wrapping an arm around her neck. She grabbed his hand and pulled it around her shoulder.

'Anyway,' she said to him, 'I still don't see why I can't go to Bobby's funeral. How old were you when you went to your brother's funeral?'

'Are you still playin that old song?'

'Mm-hmm.'

'I didn't go to my brother's funeral,' he told her.

'How come?'

Sal shrugged his shoulders. 'I wasn't invited.'

Davey looked up at him. He shrugged again. She sighed, her eyes wandering over the ground.

'What's up, hon?' he said, pulling her against him.

Davey shook her head, scowling. 'I really miss Bobby,' she said in a small voice, no longer clowning. Sal lifted her off the ground, put his cheek against hers and resumed walking. She wrapped her arms around his neck, her legs around his waist. He heard her sniff. Bobby is dead, he said to himself. *Bobby is dead.* But all he could feel was the warmth of Davey's face on his, the warmth of the sun on his back and the wonderful quiet of the morning.

'What the hell did she send this monkey suit for?' Bobby complained. He and Noel had argued about the tweed suit ever since she'd brought it home for him a year ago, in preparation for the funeral.

'Close your eyes,' Wicker told him.

Bobby lay on the embalming table, dressed in tweed slacks and a sleeveless T-shirt, his face stiff with foundation. Wicker had spent almost ten minutes working on his hair, bent over him, sighing, grunting, holding his breath. The service was two hours away.

'Close,' Wicker said again. Bobby did, and the undertaker rubbed his thumbs on Bobby's eyelids. When he finished, Bobby opened his eyes and saw him screwing the cover on a large white jar. EYE SHADOW, the label said.

'Wait a minute,' Bobby told him. 'Gimme a mirror.'

'Be quiet. You've got to have color.'

'I've got color, I'm alive. Just give me a fucking mirror.'

'I don't have a fucking mirror.' Wicker turned and picked up a small bottle from his tray. 'This is for your lips,' he said.

'No way, no lipstick,' Bobby told him.

But as Wicker unscrewed the brush applicator, it was clear that he wouldn't be swayed. 'It's not lipstick anyway, keep quiet.'

Bobby grabbed his hand. ZIPLIP, the label said.

'It's to keep your mouth shut,' Wicker told him. There was some satisfaction in his voice as he brushed the vaporous liquid on Bobby's lips. 'Close,' he said. 'Breathe through your nose.'

Fortunately, Bobby's nostrils were clear, and the fumes from the glue cleared them more, but that still didn't quell the slight panic he felt. He snapped his lips apart. 'Am I gonna be able to get this stuff off?'

A door closed in the next room. Wicker's hand shot out, clenched Bobby's jaw. The grip was firm; the hand trembled. Footsteps approached loudly. Bobby closed his eyes. The door opened. A voice said, 'I come over early, Eliot. Think we might need more chairs.' *Chayuhs*. It was Jerry Royal, the odd job man.

Bobby heard satisfaction in Wicker's response: 'I don't think we'll get that many today.'

There was a protracted silence then, and Bobby knew that Jerry's eyes were on him. Under Wicker's perfumed hand, Bobby's teeth dug into his lip. 'Awful young,' the voice said.

'Jerry,' Wicker replied, 'knock, okay?'

'No problem.'

The door closed. Wicker's hand left Bobby's mouth, and Bobby tried his lips. The cement had set. Wicker began to hum as he unscrewed another jar. When Bobby opened his eyes, he saw Wicker's two fingertips, smeared with red, coming down to his face.

'Oops,' the undertaker said happily, as he began making small circles on Bobby's cheeks. ROUGE, the jar said.

Bobby grabbed his hand. It wasn't to stop him, as Wicker thought when he first tried to pull away. It was a handshake, a pact. A grip of faith in another human being. Bobby's eyes, burning from glue fumes, locked onto Wicker's. His fingers locked around Wicker's hand, held it strong.

The undertaker twisted out of Bobby's grasp. '*Okay*,' he whispered.

It was at this moment that Bobby knew for sure that he would return tonight to kill this man. He hoped he wouldn't enjoy it.

Sal avoided looking at Bobby's casket as they made their way into the cool chapel. Likewise, he avoided Noel, who stood surrounded by flowers and mourners in the front corner of the room.

There was no question that she was as striking a widow as Gravity had ever seen. Her dress was camp, a black lacy tribute to the '40s, the sleeves a membranous skin that hugged her wrists to the heels of her black lace gloves. She accepted sympathy straight-backed, almost defiantly, presenting the rich façade that no townsperson had ever come close to penetrating.

Taking a seat at the end of a row of folding chairs, Sal kept his eyes on his own fingers in his lap. Sitting this quietly, he felt the tremor playing deep inside him, as he knew it would. He tried to ignore it by concentrating on the recorded organ music, the soft talking.

He had been to only one funeral in his life, his grandmother's, when he was too young to be impressed. Although he was ten when his younger brother Anthony drowned, his parents went to the service without him. And then neither of them ever again mentioned Anthony's name in his presence.

The boys had been walking through the woods near their house when Anthony walked out on a section of frozen river. Sal had told him not to, but Anthony laughed at him and went out further. That's the way Sal remembered it, anyway. When Anthony broke through, it was only up to his waist, and Sal laughed right back at him – at the way Anthony's mouth and eyes flared from the cold – but then Anthony slid under. He was wearing a red hooded sweatshirt, and Sal watched the color travel beneath the ice, limp as a flag. Sal screamed Anthony's name, he stood helpless for a second or more. Then he ran down through the trees thirty feet or so to a spot downriver where the banks widened and the ice opened up in the middle. He got there before Anthony did. The ice, which grew in around the rocks along the bank, was maybe a half-inch thick. But where the river deepened and the channel got stronger, the ice thinned to a film and then gave way to moving black water. Sal made his way out to the furthest rock and, as he did, Anthony emerged in the open – facedown, hands dragging the bottom. Sal stretched his arm as far as he could. He leaned his hand on the film of ice until it broke through. But his little brother floated past, out of reach, and once again started to slide under the ice. Sal screamed at him to stop. He shifted his body on the rock and kicked his heels through the ice, intending to go in after Anthony.

But the river was dark and frigid, and it poured into Sal's boots like fire, trying to pull him under too. So he sat there with his legs in the water, clutching the rock while he watched his brother disappear for good.

For a number of seconds, or a number of minutes, he sat motionless, letting the icy river tug at his feet. He was stunned by the cold, by the clean, bright silence of winter. In fact, it amazed him how peaceful the woods and river seemed, with Anthony tumbling away under the ice and his own senseless legs dangling in the river. Finally he lowered himself off the rock until his feet hit the bottom and the water reached his waist. Holding the rock dearly, he lowered the rest of his body in, dropping to his knees and letting the icy river pour over his neck and head. He came up screaming again because it hurt so much, and because that's all he could do. Scream and run for home, the frozen survivor.

It was a mile downriver that Anthony finally stopped, snagged by a half-submerged shopping cart behind the town pizza place. The boys' Italian mother didn't speak a word for almost a year but sat in her living room and watched television hour after hour. Sal's father, a Swedish stonemason who had never talked much anyway, began spending his evenings in the cellar, where he carved duck decoys and listened to Lutheran radio broadcasts from Chicago. Sal – ten years old, eleven years old – stayed outdoors as long it was light, playing pickup sports in the neighborhood. At night, when he came inside, he would shut himself in his room and practice his trombone. When the family ate together, it was in silence. The morning his mother finally spoke, it was to a glass of orange juice that Sal had knocked off the table. 'Sock it to me,' she said.

Sal felt inside his sportcoat pocket for the pills. The Librium had been part of his detox therapy the previous winter. Before leaving the house for the cemetery, he had stashed three or four in his pocket. Not that he was craving a drink, but a raw unsettledness had been growing in him since Bobby's death, like a caffeine overload. He reasoned that it was stress. First Bobby's death and now the funeral, not to mention his school show later in the evening. No reasoning about it – an icy vodka martini danced on the fringes of every thought. He let the pills slide through his fingers and removed his hand from his pocket. He'd gone six months without needing one; he didn't want to start now.

Without meaning to, he looked up and saw Bobby. The pink, mannequin face. Lying there in a coat and tie. Christ, Bobby hated neckties. Leashes, he'd called them.

When I die, Bobby had said once, *I want my body to be dropped on the White House lawn from twenty thousand feet. No chute. Bam!*

During a press conference, the president up there, a note around my neck saying, 'Bullshit.'

Sal's chest jumped with a laugh, thinking of the way Bobby had laughed when he'd said that. He shifted in his chair, noticed Eliot Wicker in the corner of the room, standing stiffly beside the minister, his hands folded solemnly in front of him while his eyes darted around the room, eliciting nothing but a cold, indifferent greed, just the kind of man to escort you from the world.

By now the mourners were crowding in both doors, while Jerry Royal, stuffed into a light blue leisure suit, pushed up the aisles carrying more chairs.

Now Sal could hear weeping, and he looked to his right, where a broad-backed teenage boy was hugging a sobbing girl with a blotchy face. It was Chad and Erica, from the Superette. Chad seemed to be holding the girl up. That touched Sal.

Still, he wasn't close to tears himself. He figured – not for the first time – that this too was due to his alcoholism. Here he had just lost his best friend – his only friend – and he felt nothing so much as the low, steady drumming of his vodka god.

As the minister asked everyone to stand for a prayer, Sal slipped his hand in his pocket, pulled out a Librium and stuck it in his dry mouth, forced it down.

It was late afternoon when they buried Bobby. Sal and Iris stood together in front of the casket. Noel and the minister stood beside them, casting long shadows. The sound of an occasional car passing on the road below was audible only during the silent meditation, and then only when the wind stopped.

Sal spotted Iris's father waiting under an oak tree with a shovel and pitchfork in a wheelbarrow. Otis was a fat man, white-haired and pink-faced, wearing a white T-shirt that showed his pinkish gut. He was making noise with his tools, probably because Iris was there.

It was over quickly. The minister blessed Bobby and blessed the mourners, and the townspeople filed past, some stopping to lay a flower on the casket. Sal, subdued by the Librium, stood at the grave until the last person left.

Noel came up behind him and took his arm, and then she took

Iris's arm and worked her way between them both. 'You guys are coming over, aren't you? Help me get through this?' Iris started to say that, no, she had a baby to deliver in Oyster Cove, when Noel abruptly let go of Sal's arm and turned Iris toward the cars. 'Keep walking,' she said.

Sal saw the reason. Otis was coming toward them, his tools clattering in the wheelbarrow, his round gut bouncing like a sack of feed. Sal was impressed, but not altogether surprised, by how deftly Noel had read the situation. He noticed Eliot Wicker standing by a black limousine, holding the back door open, watching the women. Wicker cleared his throat pointedly. Noel turned, then gently released Iris and said to Sal, 'I'm supposed to ride in the limo. I'll see you there.'

When his wristwatch started to beep, Bobby started his heart. He drew a shallow breath through his nose as he rose slowly to consciousness. His eyes opened to blackness. Close to his face he could hear the dull, uneven rhythm of gravel piling onto the coffin. Another sound – his scuba tank sputtering – meant he had stretched a half hour of air to an hour and a half, right on schedule. His body began to shake, but not as badly as it had in the past two days. The heating pad helped. In fact, the lower part of his back burned from it. By contrast, the backs of his legs were cold from the scuba tanks. He allowed himself a deeper breath, and that's when he remembered that his lips were sealed. He quelled a slight panic, focused on calming himself and was able to breathe easier.

He wanted to move the heating pad but found his arms pinned against the oxygen tanks; likewise his knees, propped on the scuba tanks, were pressed against the casket lid. Once again he had to calm himself, concentrating deeply, to quiet his heart before it had a chance to beat any faster.

He guessed the dirt on the casket was a few inches deep by the muffled sound of its falling. In this total darkness he could picture the Royals up above in the sunlight, father and son shoveling furiously so they could brag at the store later how they made thirty bucks an hour, cash-money, and that's no horseshit.

Bobby shifted his right shoulder a bit, appeased himself with that small movement, and then reached between his legs for the T-bar connector, which linked the diving tanks. He opened the left-hand valve a half turn until he heard hissing, then backed off a bit. He noticed that his shivering had already subsided, and he was glad for that, glad for the heating pad.

He raised his hip an inch and managed to withdraw the penlight from his pants pocket. Flicked it on, and his heart took a thump. The velvet was inches from his face. He felt terribly closed in, felt his nostrils constrict. He tried to separate his lips with his fingers, but they were sealed tight. He wanted to wet them with his tongue, but his mouth was dry. He reached down and opened the valve a little more, then lay back to calm himself with logic. Yes, he was underground, but less deep, actually, than most people's basements. He was comfortable, relatively so. In four hours Noel would be there, opening the lid. And they would be wealthy and free.

When he felt calm again and able to breathe easily, he checked his watch to make sure the alarm was set for another two hours. He calculated his pulse. Then he reached down and turned the air to a bare whisper. He flicked off the penlight, tucked it into his shirt pocket and set his mind to relaxing every muscle. Simultaneously, he focused on his heart. The sound of dirt hitting the casket was dying now, replaced by his own blood slowing, like a wind dying, like a gentle surf sizzling off island sand. He was lying under a dome of blue sky, the burning on his back was sunshine, and the waves grew so quiet that he finally strained to hear anything at all, until what he heard was—

a snore.

He snapped awake, heart pounding. He had nearly fallen asleep. He pinched his stomach. Hard. *The one thing he could not do was fall asleep*. Sleeping, he'd miss his alarm. Sleeping, he'd suck his oxygen dry. Sleeping, he might never wake up. He thought of how Eliot Wicker's coughing had kept him up for two nights, and his hands tingled. He reached down and opened the valve again, let the compressed air breathe freely into the casket. Taking in two big lungfuls to clear his head, he replayed the murder once more, to heighten his senses. He sinks his thumb into Wicker's throat, he sees those expressionless eyes flare, hears the startled, strangled gulp as he thrusts the weapon straight into Wicker's heart. *An embalming tool*. That's what he'd taken from the mortuary, now he could feel its blunt end against his butt. That's why the thing was hollow, for pumping embalming fluid into corpses, or for draining body fluids out. So tonight he would embalm the embalmer.

When his own heart was once again pumping normally and his brain was sharp, Bobby felt for the valve and turned it down. Confidently in control again, he focused on his respiration, his circulation, and he slowed them both, shutting down completely, silencing his mind, becoming keenly aware of nothing.

When the first tray of finger sandwiches was empty, Noel sent Chad down to the walk-in cooler for more. The store had closed at three for the funeral and would remain closed to the public for the next two days. However, beer and wine were available to anyone who showed up for the reception. As it turned out, so many townspeople came to pay their respects that most of the men ended up down in the parking lot, sitting on tailgates, smoking cigarettes and drinking the free beer. Jerry Royal, already back from the cemetery, was busy needling the clam-diggers. 'Forty-five dollars an hour, cash money,' he told them every so often. 'Your plumber don't even make that.'

Upstairs, Noel's kitchen counter was lined with bottles of wine and liquor. To avoid temptation, Sal stayed in the long corridor that connected the kitchen to the living room, drinking seltzer and watching as the number of guests increased, passing from one end of the apartment to the other and eventually overflowing into both ends of the corridor, trapping him in the middle. Had Noel not asked him to stay, he certainly would have gone home. But home alone, he reasoned, he would only be nervously counting the hours until his school concert. Besides, the Librium he had taken at the funeral was making the reception bearable. Mostly he passed the time looking through the long bookcase that stood against the wall, housing Noel's showpiece books that had outlived their time on her coffee table: books about whales and witches, erotic massage, Zen Buddhism, rain forests, American Indians, American women, angels. Beside the bookcase, a short hallway off the left wall led to the bedroom and bathroom, which people began using with more frequency.

At one point, while Sal was thumbing through a book on French impressionism, a couple stopped and the man said he understood that Sal had once played with Woody Herman. Before Sal could respond, the man's wife said, 'McHale's Navy?' to which the man replied, 'No, that's Ernest Borgnine. We're talking music, dear,' to which the woman responded pointedly that she didn't have time for music, and the couple went away in opposite directions.

Sal pulled out a thin paperback, its bright red spine block-lettered SABOTAGE! The cover read, A GUIDE TO RADICAL ENVIRONMENTAL ACTIVISM. Inside were pages crammed with typewriter type and crude drawings of mechanisms for immobilizing logging equipment, or recipes for concocting explosives from fertilizer and sawdust. Sal was reading about brewing a delayed-ignition fire starter using swimming pool cleaner and hair cream when a hand touched his arm, a black glove. 'Thoughtful custom,' Noel said quietly. 'Your husband dies and everybody comes over and drinks all your liquor.' The glove, intricately laced, held a champagne glass by the stem, but it wasn't champagne she was drinking. Sal could smell the vodka martini on her breath.

'That's not Dom Perrignon,' he said to her.

'I needed something stronger today. Does it bother you? I probably shouldn't have brought it over.'

'I'm okay,' he told her, actually impressed at how the Librium seemed to deaden his craving for the drink. 'How're you doing?'

She gave him a dead-on look that said she'd rather be anywhere than here. 'You'll stay to the end, won't you?' she said.

He looked at his watch. 'My show's in two hours,' he answered, and he felt a twinge of anxiety.

'Situational ethics?' a voice interrupted. Eliot Wicker.

Sal didn't know what the mortician was talking about until Wicker took hold of Sal's book and tilted it up, reading, 'A guide to destroying the destroyers.'

'They're recipes,' Noel explained, 'for fucking up bulldozers and burning down billboards.'

Wicker gave her a patronizing look. Dressed in a white shirt and black bow tie, he sipped champagne from a wide-brimmed, stemmed glass. 'More like recipes for killing off the human race so that genetically inferior species can prolong their imminent extinction,' he said.

Roundly ignoring him, Noel turned and walked down the corridor toward the living room, exiting before Wicker had finished the sentence.

'I love women, don't get me wrong,' Wicker said quietly to Sal, 'but something in the cognitive reasoning department—' He raised his brow in a show of futility, took another drink from his glass, then launched into a racial interpretation of Darwinian theory that would have given Hitler insomnia. It wasn't long before Sal pinched another Librium into his mouth. He considered dropping one in Wicker's champagne, wondering if the undertaker was always this agitated after a burial, or if Wicker considered the confrontation that had occurred between them in Bobby's gym a sort of bonding experience. In Sal's mind the feelings lingered that Wicker could have done more to save Bobby's life. Now the man was recounting some of the more ironic deaths of his other clients – and there were many.

While Wicker talked, Sal lost track of time. When he looked at his watch, it was 6:00 and Wicker was still talking. Thinking that the second Librium wasn't working, Sal dropped another while he pretended to cough.

'... tractor rolled over him three times, veritably pinning him against the very same apple tree that his father had planted for him when he was a baby – exactly sixty-two years to the day, as God is my witness ...'

Sal smiled pleasantly, actually felt quite pleasantly numb, drifting in and out of attention while Wicker pontificated about taxes, welfare, crime and capital punishment.

Just before 7:00, Noel appeared, stepped between the men and led Sal aside. Handing him a half-filled vodka martini, she pressed against him so only he could hear and said, 'I've got to get out of here. Can you take away everybody's drinks and tell them to hit the road?'

Sal nodded. Looked at his watch. 'I've gotta go myself,' he said.

She brushed the side of his neck with her lips and whispered,

'Are you having fun talking to the undertaker?'

In response, Sal looked straight at her, brought the martini to his mouth and tossed it down.

Staring at him darkly, Noel gave a hint of a smile.

The heat took his breath away.

4

Once again Blueberry Blossom Night had fallen in Gravity, Maine. The moon shone full and bright in the sky, the night air scented with springtime pollens and grasses. At the school, cars and pickup trucks overflowed the parking lot into the road. In the east, sporadic firecrackers sounded where bingo was getting underway at the Baptist church and a contra dance was about to begin at the Jolly Hollow Grange. There and all over town, young Gravity men were working at prodigious volumes of beer in preparation for the annual outhouse burning. Word was, the fire would be outside the Superette this year, in memory of Bobby Swift.

Alston Bouchard, the town constable, was out cruising the roads in his yellow Subaru wagon, ostensibly to prevent the immolation. But the town's older men (who had long since burned their last outhouse) knew what Bouchard was up to. He'd let the boys outsmart him tonight, same as every year. He'd be a fool not to, and everybody knew – the smarter ones, anyway – that Bouchard was no fool. Laid back, maybe. Lazy, some said. But he had outfoxed enough of them in his twenty years on the job that at least they knew he had a brain.

At just before 8:00, when her apartment was finally empty, Noel walked down her back stairs into the garage. She flipped a switch on the wall, and the garage door opened behind her. She walked quickly to her Volvo and opened the door. As she was about to climb inside, a voice startled her.

'Don't shut me in.'

Jerry Royal, lumbering through the door of Bobby's gym.

'God, Jerry,' Noel said, her hand on her chest. 'I thought everybody had left.'

'Noel, I feel just awful,' Jerry said, approaching her.

She stood behind her car door. 'I'll be okay, Jerry.'

'No, that too, but I mean about using the toilet in there. We were outside yakkin and I had to go, and it wasn't something I could do in the bushes, if you know what I mean, and I knew Bobby had a toilet down here, but then when I'm in there I'm thinkin, where he, you know, and I'm on his toilet, I shoulda found someplace else, whatever—'

'Jerry, it's okay, really.'

'I know. You're being brave. But you oughta know: Bobby was a friend to everybody, rich, poor, whatever. Matter of fact, just tonight we were up there discussin about getting a statue made, settin it up there by the firehouse.'

Noel smiled. 'He'd appreciate that, Jerry.' She lowered herself onto the car seat, waiting for him to leave. He took the door from her, leaned over the top.

'No,' he said, close enough so that she could smell the beer and cigarettes on his breath, 'I just wanna say that, *whatever*, you ever need anything, *ever!* 'Cause I know you're gonna find another man, no problem there . . .'

He moved around to the edge of her door. She took hold of the armrest, to close it, but he wouldn't let go.

'You know what I'm sayin,' he told her. 'So, where you off to?'

'Just – nowhere.' She looked at her watch. 'I need to take a ride, to clear my head.'

'No, but if you need company—'

Noel smiled at him. 'Thanks, Jerry, I'd rather be by myself.'

Without warning, he leaned in and smothered her in a one-armed hug. As big as he was, her face ended up at his armpit. At first it didn't seem like he was going to let go, but she managed to slip his clutch.

'So, okay,' he said as she shut the door. She started the engine and quickly shifted into reverse. While she backed out of the garage, he hurried around behind the car and backpedaled toward the swimming pool, directing her. 'You got it, you got it, you got it . . .'

She shifted into first.

'Go for it,' he told her, 'I'll get the door.' But she was already closing it with the remote control attached to her visor. 'Okay, you got that thing,' he said, as she drove up her driveway and headed for the cemetery.

In the school gymnasium, the town's children were herded, one classroom at a time, onto the old stage, while teachers assembled them onto three risers, smiling gamely while cameras flashed over and over, while parents carried on scores of conversations in the audience, sometimes from two and three rows apart. As usual, many of the fathers refused to sit in the seats, preferring to mill around the gym door in T-shirts and caps, discussing work and local politics as their children sang. For Sal, it was bearable tonight. No, tonight it was a genuine kick.

Only Mrs Abraham, the accompanist, seemed distracted, worrying over the talking, the out-of-tune piano, the astounding cacophony of the children's singing. But she was new in town, unaccustomed. During the applause for the second-grade finale, a particularly jarring 'This Land is Your Land,' Sal crouched at the edge of the stage and said to her, 'Don't worry, no one listens anyway.'

Then, rising effortlessly – demonstrating his impeccable balance – he strode across the stage to wait for the next class. He noticed the school principal, Avery Bingstream, slender and straight-backed in his brown business suit and big square glasses, standing in the side aisle, beaming. Sal considered going to the microphone and asking for a round of applause for the principal but decided against it. He ducked around the curtain, reached behind an empty paint can, found his mug and took a drink. The Russian vodka shone through the Librium like a midnight sun on snow: frigid, bright and blinding.

In darkness and silence that were absolute, Bobby's penlight came on. He shivered from the cold. He saw burgundy velvet. He stared. He was wet with perspiration, panting hard, forcing air in and out of a nose that was badly clogged. With some effort he bent his elbow and looked at his watch. 8:15. His heart surged. His alarm had gone off over an hour ago and he had slept through it. His nose breathing accelerated, but he couldn't catch his breath.

There was no oxygen left in the casket, he realized. He opened both valves on the scuba tanks, heard nothing. He wondered how he had awakened at all.

He reached around under his left arm, fit his hand under the velvet to unfasten the Velcro strap, and rolled one of the slender oxygen tanks up onto his chest. He twisted its valve until he heard the faintest hissing. He took a breath through his nose. Another.

Now he concentrated on calming himself. Noel would be opening the lid in an hour and a half. He had the two E-sized tanks left – pure oxygen. Each held about twenty minutes' worth, normal breathing. With slow breathing, he could double that. Tranced out he could make the air last three to four hours – as long as he didn't sleep again.

His toes felt icy, his legs asleep. He wanted to take off a shoe and warm his feet with his hand, but his knees were pressed against the coffin lid by the scuba tanks (which were worthless now – worse than worthless, they took up space). His cold feet might as well have been a mile away.

More distracting, his nostrils were neatly shut. Once again he tried to open his mouth with his fingers, but the cement held fast. With both hands he took hold of his lips and gave a quick pull, ripping some skin. His eyes teared from the sting, but his lips remained welded. He realized he'd have to separate the lips somehow. He thought of the embalming tool he had stashed for Wicker. He lifted his right hip, reached a hand under the velvet and brought the cold instrument up. He laid the penlight on his chest while he directed the point of the thing into the center of his pursed lips. The tip was icy. He opened his teeth inside his mouth so he wouldn't strike them, and then with a painful grunt, he pushed. His eyes stung. He shut them tight. He leaned into the tool until he felt more skin tear, but still he failed to break through. Suddenly, as if to surprise himself, he gave a short, hard thrust. The shout came out his nose, muffled instantly inside the casket. The oxygen tank rolled off his chest. The shaft had seared through his lips, and the tip sliced the underside of his tongue. He withdrew the instrument, tasted blood seeping in his throat. To his relief, he was able to draw a whistle through his mouth. It burned.

He cupped the tank in the crook of his elbow and, under his

penlight beam, set his watch alarm for an hour and a half, certain that he wouldn't need it, confident that Noel would be there rousing him from his trance. He pictured the look on her face when he opened his eyes, the feeling of her hands helping to lift him out. In all the world, he thought, no one had ever loved a woman the way he loved Noel.

He brought the oxygen valve close to his face and looked at his reflection in the chrome plating. A twinge of fear gripped him. Wicker had made him a death mask of white, then compensated with a powdery pink. Twin circles of rouge dotted Bobby's cheeks, and his lips were deeper red, darkened with a puddle of blood in his blowhole, which bubbled with each little breath. Worse, his eyebrows were lined, his scowl wrinkles caked, eyelids shaded blue. He thought of Noel seeing him like that, of Sal, and everybody else in town. This is how Bobby Swift would be remembered, like a fucking transvestite—? He felt the bottom of his rib cage with his middle finger, then ran his thumb up his chest until he felt his heartbeat. He gauged the distance between the two and calculated the angle. That's how he'd kill Wicker, under and up.

He should have told Sal, he thought again. He could always count on Sal. They were like brothers, best friends since childhood. Of course he could count on Noel too. After all, he had trusted her with his life. And why not? Encased as he was inside this tight, black tomb, he allowed no thought of mistrusting her.

In his imagination a picture appeared: Noel working above him with her shovel. He wondered if he could really see her, if their minds were that finely attuned. He tried to listen for her but heard only the whisper of oxygen.

He closed the valve down until he could barely hear the air flowing, and then he held the canister in his hand like a baby's bottle, aiming its breath of air at his little mouth. He shut off his penlight and commanded his muscles to relax. He slowed his heart. He cut his breathing in stages...

Noel, he thought... Noel would take care of him.

She had a way of always getting the best seats at a show, the best table in a restaurant. It was that certain tone she took with maître d's and ushers, something of a promise in the look she gave them, a promise she had no intention of keeping. She did lie, after all, when it suited her. In small ways.

Without intending to, Bobby imagined the sensation of breaking out of the casket into the crushing, suffocating blackness around him, where the weight of the earth on top was equaled by the pressure of gravity below, so that, with only seconds of air in the lungs, completely disoriented, you claw against the blackness and end up burrowing deeper...

Bobby's chest heaved. He cleared his mind. Total silence. Lying in the relative comfort of his casket, he oriented himself: up from down.

A picture of Eliot Wicker intruded on him, tall and toothy, hair perfectly combed and parted, asleep in his bed. The undertaker would awaken with a start when Bobby shined the light in his face; say something like *What the hell are you doing here?* And Bobby in his tortoiseshell glasses and brown hair would reply, 'Saying good-bye,' and then squeeze that scrawny white throat in one hand, and with the other, *PLUNGE* – under and up, under and up—

Bobby caught his heart racing again. He forced Wicker out of his mind completely. He listened for Noel's digging again and actually thought he could hear her now, standing above him. He pictured her face and felt the onset of a beautiful peace. The next time he opened his eyes, he knew she'd be there, the pale moon over her shoulder, her warm hands on his face. Pale moon over her shoulder, warm hands on his face. Warm hands on his face.

Eliot Wicker had just kicked back in his recliner to watch the Red Sox, when a sudden loud knocking threw him to his feet. Pacing through the kitchen, he could only believe that something was wrong. He imagined it was Noel. He eased the door open with a lazy, ominous look. But it was Alston Bouchard standing in the yellow breezeway light.

'Hello, Alston!' he said, acting aboundingly happy to see the constable. He turned and headed back inside. 'Come in, you want coffee?'

'Nope,' answered Bouchard, catching the door.

Leaving him standing in the kitchen, Wicker went into the

living room and turned off the TV, then rejoined Bouchard again in the kitchen. 'I hate the Red Sox,' he said. 'You?'

'Not especially,' answered the constable. Alston Bouchard was a dark, uncomfortable man who seemed to add darkness to himself as a way to hide. A black John Deere cap covered black hair that grew densely behind his ears, and his marbled black beard covered the rest of his face and neck except for his dark, humorless eyes, which were themselves covered by the thick lenses of his black-rimmed glasses. He rarely spoke, rarely smiled; mostly he'd just stand in a room, watching, listening, making people wonder what wrong thing they might have done, though that was never his intention.

'So,' Wicker said, 'busy day.' He did not hide the nervousness well, and he knew it. Looking Bouchard square in the face, he might as well have said, *Look, I'm completely natural.*

Bouchard put his hands in his pockets. 'Too bad about—'

'—Bobby, you know it. Town's gonna miss him.' Wicker swung his long leg over a bar stool and then started to cough. 'Sit down, Alston, you want to sit down?' The constable remained standing. Wicker coughed harder. 'Fuckin postnasal drip.'

Bouchard moved a couple of steps toward Wicker's bulletin board, a patchwork of bills and business cards beside the wall phone. 'Nope,' he said. 'I'll set when I get home.' He had a deep voice, deeper than even his considerable bulk suggested, but he spoke softly, as if he had learned to do so to avoid frightening people.

Wicker wondered if anything incriminating was on his bulletin board. He wondered what Bouchard was doing there. He decided that it was natural to ask. 'So, what, Alston, my landfill permit's expired again?'

'Just' – Bouchard jerked his thumb toward the window – 'you know your lights are out?'

Lights—? Wicker stared at Bouchard while his mind raced, trying to understand how lights might implicate him. 'What lights?'

'Parking lot,' Bouchard explained. 'Your sign too.'

'Maybe a circuit breaker, I don't know.' Wicker swung off his stool and looked out the window toward the road. Was he acting defensive? By Bouchard's silence, he guessed he was. So what? Defensive, for him, was natural. Besides, any other night of the week he would've wanted the man out of his house. He moved toward the door, meaning for Bouchard to follow. 'I'll look into it, Alston. Was there anything else? I'm kinda watching that game.'

Bouchard shook his head. 'Just thought you might want to know about . . .' The constable had a habit of ending sentences with a gesture rather than words. He aimed a thumb at the door, meaning the lights. 'The boys are gonna be out rammin' tonight. They can be . . .'

'Yeah, they do get wild.' Wicker opened the door and stepped out into his breezeway, holding the door for Bouchard. 'They get their outhouse yet?' he asked, offering the constable a little small talk for the road. He could see that his parking lot was indeed dark.

'Not yet,' Bouchard said, finally joining Wicker in the breezeway.

'Oh, well, harmless enough, I suppose.' It was an exit remark, which Bouchard failed to read.

'I imagine one of these days someone'll miss 'em,' Bouchard said.

'Who? Miss who?'

'The outhouses, I mean. Where so many have indoor plumbing now.' Small talk was awkward for the constable. He hesitated at the breezeway door, took off his cap and combed his fingers carefully through the few long strands of hair that covered his head. He replaced his cap, pulled it down and asked, unexpectedly, 'You planning on staying in tonight?'

'What, I can't stay home?'

'Nope,' Bouchard said, 'you can.' He walked a few steps down the walk and then turned around the corner of the house, heading for the parking lot.

Wicker called after him, 'I mean, Christ, Alston, a man should be able to stay in his house on Blueberry Blossom Night without someone making a federal crime out of it.'

Just as the oxygen began to sputter, Bobby's watch alarm beeped. He came to, found his penlight and switched it on. Looked at the time. 9:30. He listened for Noel digging above him, but all he could hear was the sputtering. He closed the valve to silence the tank, then held his breath to listen. She was there, he knew she was. He turned off the light, thinking the darkness would help him hear. But total silence pressed in around him. He flicked the light on again, looked at his watch. 9:32.

He'd gone an hour and a half on twenty minutes of oxygen, right on schedule. With one more tank, even without trancing, they'd have plenty of leeway in case the digging was a little hard or she'd been delayed. Obviously she'd been delayed. 9:33.

He pushed the spent tank down his chest, beside his leg. It made a bright ring against the empty scuba tank. Pulling the other tank up from beside him, he felt a pleasant relief at the shoulder room he had now. He opened the valve, heard the oxygen hiss out. He backed off again, then pulled a deep, calming breath through the little hole in his lips. Closed his eyes and listened for Noel. Even if she were digging down, he thought, two feet above the lid, he wouldn't necessarily hear, soil being such a good insulator. She could have been six inches away from him. He flicked on his light again and checked his watch. 9:35.

He shut off the penlight, closed his eyes and opened the valve once again, proceeded to slow his heart. He turned his thoughts to the island, the long, wide, sunlit beach. Lying there on a blanket with Noel. She'd raise a finger and the waiter would come down with another margarita.

He thought of the horse in their living room – the bronze-plate sculpture she had bought from the Boston importer. Four hundred dollars, she had told Bobby it cost. They'd lived with the thing for a month before he found out she had actually charged twenty-eight hundred bucks to his Visa account.

So she did actually lie, even to him, on occasion. When it suited her. But he'd never considered that kind of brazenness anything but endearing. He liked street smarts in a woman, especially in a woman like Noel. Even now, as he felt himself drifting off, he snickered a little, the way that bronze horse stood in his living room with that little smile on its face, while he was down here picturing it.

* * *

While the audience talked on, the third graders stood on the risers and waited for Sal to return to the microphone. He was in control now, completely and confidently so. Striding out from the curtain, perfectly balanced, he reached for the microphone and his fist struck the stand, making an explosion in the gym. Seeing the mike leap from its holder, he flashed out a hand and snatched the mike from the air, then brought it to his mouth as if the move had been choreographed.

'Ladies and gentlemen,' he began. He heard a little laughter and acknowledged it with a warm Mediterranean smile (Tony Bennett eyes, Iris used to say about his crinkled smile). He glanced back at Davey. She knew. No, she didn't. He gave her a wink. She fidgeted. The audience grew louder.

'Okay, folks,' he said, 'let's quiet down.'

The talking subsided a bit. Microphone in hand, Sal felt like Jerry Lewis – all he needed was the tuxedo and cigarette. He looked around the audience, spotted Iris. Gave her the smile. Thought of dedicating the show to Bobby, decided against it. Thought about talking to the crowd about the pleasure of actually *listening* to music for a change, but decided against that. 'Erie Canal,' he said finally, 'Erie Canal,' and replaced the mike in its stand.

He looked behind him at the third graders, then turned to Mrs Abraham and counted off the song. She played the intro, and the children began to sing about the mule named Sal, and Sal laughed at that. But by the end of the first verse, their voices were already at war with one another. 'Low bridge' sounded like the mule might have been trying to cough up a slug of barbed wire. Standing in front of them, Sal bent his knees and made a pulling gesture, as if he were helping the animal dislodge the obstruction, but his pantomime was lost on the crowd.

Then, afraid they might think he was making fun of the children, he said into the mike, 'Very nice,' which the audience took as a cue to applaud, which in turn caused the nervous accompanist to think he was abandoning the whole thing and stop playing. 'No, keep – keep—' Sal wheeled his hand and Mrs Abraham resumed dutifully. The problem was, by now the singing had also stopped, and the audience talking started up again. Mrs Abraham's eyes, hard on Sal, gelled with fear.

That's when Sal got the idea that would change his life. He said to her, 'Keep playing,' and then said to the audience, jokingly, 'You quiet down.' They did. All the while, he held out his hand to the children, keeping them from singing. When the last line of the intro came around, he nodded to the singers and said, 'Hum it this time, you know how to hum?' They grinned at him, their lips clamped. He tossed his hand and they began, their voices sailing over the noisy gym like a swarm of happy bees.

'Don't stop,' Sal told them. 'Don't stop,' he said to Mrs Abraham, and then he made for the wings.

Noel climbed the terraces close to the tree line, shaded from the light of the full moon. She had left her Volvo in the woods just below the cemetery, on a gravel turnoff to the river, where it wouldn't be seen. The contra dance and bingo game were in full swing on the east side of town – she could hear distant sounds of cars and firecrackers. This part of town was quiet, however, with the town's children and their parents all ensconced in the school gym. Not a single car passed.

All along the hillside the polished gravestones reflected the moonlight, winking at Noel as she walked, their shadows sharp on the flat grass. When she left the tree line for Bobby's lone grave, a car did pass below, soundlessly, just a trailing of taillights over her shoulder. She walked around Bobby's plot and headed for the forked limb of a tall maple, then pushed into the woods on its right.

She switched on her flashlight and aimed the beam ahead of her, at three birch trees. Everything else was darkness. She stepped carefully over a small deadfall that Bobby had laid in the way, then deflected some pine branches with her shoulder. In the spot of her light stood a lichen-encrusted wall of rock, too wide to be seen in its entirety. At the near end of the boulder she reached down and pulled aside a couple of pine boughs and then lifted the shovel and pitchfork, their handles aligned, wrapped in a dark wool blanket. Evidence of her crime. Gripping the bundle tightly so it wouldn't make a sound, she turned back and pressed for the moonlight.

* * *

In the gym, the audience watched in rapt silence as the third graders finished humming the fifth chorus of 'Erie Canal' and then began an sixth. A couple of fathers paced nervously by the door. Several had already left the building and were smoking cigarettes in the parking lot. Mrs Abraham, still accompanying the song, kept her smile up, but it had hardened considerably.

All at once the gymnasium was shattered by the blare of a trombone, a bluesy fanfare, as Sal strode in stage left, doubling the hummers' melody on his instrument. There rose a small outburst of applause and laughter, mixed with a low, indignant cheer. The hummers grew louder. Sal stopped for a moment, looked out in the crowd, then shut his eyes and played a scorching Dixieland counterpoint on his horn, cakewalking around their tune; capsizing it.

'Don't give up,' he told the kids as he approached the microphone, waving the piano on to another chorus. He drew a voluminous breath, tossed his head back and blew a dissonant squall, blew it loud and long until his face grew red and veins bulged at his temples. His heart pounded. It had been so long since he'd played – really played.

'What are you doing?' Mrs Abraham sang at him, still smiling, struggling to keep the song in motion. Sal ignored her. He looked back at the risers and saw Davey stiffen, her eyes glistening. He closed his own eyes again, raised his face and let go with a long, plaintive wail. He was saying to Davey, *These are tears, honey*. He blew another one, let it arc and sail over the room . . . for the rest of the town. Hell, everyone knew Bobby. They'd know what Sal was feeling. He almost lost his footing then, staggered back a step – but he did not fall. *Balance*, ladies and gentlemen. Sal Erickson is in complete control. Then another one for Bobby, a long, strident blast to shake him from the clouds. Sal shook it, gritty as you please, then shuffled it into a raunchy, strutting blues. Bobby's Song. He played it loud, played it fat and slow.

He became dimly aware that he was soloing. The piano had stopped at some point, he didn't know when. The children had stopped humming too. He opened his eyes and saw parents and teachers escorting the kids off both sides of the stage. Christ, they were tiptoeing, some of them. Sal wailed on, soaring, gone, pure and total. In a small part of his mind he could see the exit doors bottlenecked with townspeople, Philistines escaping the fire, but all turning back for that one last look. He could see Iris's white uniform for an instant, and the back of Davey. Too late for losers, he was gone. And now some smart-ass pulling the curtain closed in front of him – like that was going to stop him. He glanced into the shadows and saw Charlie Walker at the ropes, the custodian. He made a move toward Walker, and the old man retreated.

Behind the curtain now, Sal continued blowing. Jazz, people! Monk, Diz, Bird, Miles, Satch. *Jazz!* When his slide found the break in the velvet, he followed it through and almost stepped off the stage into the seats. He teetered for a moment, but he didn't fall – not a chance. *Balance, baby.* And suddenly the gym was practically empty, just the fat men in T-shirts milling around the perimeter like dogs, waiting for him to fall. Not a chance. For them he stood on the very edge of the stage and rocked back and forth. For them he reached into his animal brain, gave them something gristled and warlike to chew on.

And, right on cue, here came Avery Bingstream, the principal, striding up the center aisle in his gray suit, watching his shoes. There was a careless bounce in his step, which meant that he hadn't thought this thing through. Sal matched his footsteps with his horn. Then the stage went dark and the houselights started blinking off, a row at a time – that son of a bitch Walker again. Sal started to turn, but then Bingstream was already mounting the stage stairs. The timing was off. The rhythm was building. Sal took it up a key, warned Bingstream back with a growl. The principal kept coming.

Sal stepped back, into the curtain. Spread his legs for balance. His music was industrial now, he wished somebody was recording it. Ornette meets Igor, right? On the top step the principal stopped; straightened his glasses. Picked up the microphone and replaced it in the stand, giving Sal his most placid smile. But Sal could read the flurry of lines behind those big square glasses: uncertainty and fear. He shook a fierce glissando at the man.

'Well,' Bingstream said, working off a shrug, 'I guess it's—'

Centurion hoedown, right in his face.

'—time to go home, put the feet up, have a rest.' The principal reached his hand out slowly, as if he were disarming Sal.

Sal warned him back with an eyebrow, pumping the slide back and forth, back and forth, but then Bingstream caught the slide in his hand. The note exploded from the bell as the slide pulled out of the instrument. The surprised, gravity-stricken principal, reeling with his trophy, caught the mike stand with his other hand, hugged it like a crooner as he back-dived off the stage and hit the floor below with an amplified WOOF! A folding chair spun on one leg then crashed. The mike stand rolled away. Bingstream sat up fast, but then just remained there clutching the trombone slide, staring at his shins.

Sal closed his eyes and leaned back against the curtain, which failed to support him – he didn't fall, though. Never fall. He felt the warm velvet sliding up his back, massaging his shoulders. *Balance*, ladies and gents, he had it in spades.

But someone is laughing in the dark – the bronze horse is snickering like crazy. The penlight makes a faint, beige dot. Bobby makes a whistle when he laughs. He's sweating, whistling like a locomotive in a runaway laughing panic, and the horse can't breathe. Bobby can't find his consciousness, that's the trouble, he's stuck in this idiot dream! Or is he even asleep? The velvet crepe is moist, burgundy, a delicate floral pattern in front of his eyes. The whole world is cold, extremely cold, and he's wet with perspiration. His throat is dry. He's whistling, in and out, faster and faster. It's because there's no more air. It's because his nose is clogged and he has only a blowhole for a mouth. It's because he's a fish out of water! He whistles faster when he pictures this. He flips like a fish, *sees* himself as a fish. He laughs at this, whistles like a fish. The oxygen tank is laughing too, sputtering madly. Empty or full, he can't decide.

Or else it's the shower that's hissing. He's standing, fully clothed, in Eliot Wicker's shower, and Noel turns away from him to get him a towel.

Too much oxygen – that's the problem. He shuts down the valve. That's right, save what's left. The tank gets quiet. But he's still whistling up a storm, panting like a horse. Sea horse. Sea horse metabolism – his little lungs are on fire. He puts his knees up to the velvet, and it gives. He thinks he's pushing the casket lid open. He thinks he's up on the hilltop, free. But it's his muscles, not the lid, giving out. Then he hears her digging.

Noel.

He makes a little sea horse squeak in his throat that embarrasses him – and he hopes she hasn't heard. His knees are pumping together furiously, the way a sea horse swims. Or are they? He can't tell. No, he's lying perfectly still, *thinking* about swimming. Don't panic! It's his inner voice. Bobby Swift is telling the sea-horse-man to think. *Think.* He listens to the oxygen tank again but hears only his own rapid back-and-forth whistling, like someone sawing wood, like those little ornamental woodcutters, dutifully driven by the wind; though Bobby's lungs are sawing at nothing. His chest is collapsing. He thinks the tank is dead – can't remember if he closed it down. The penlight flares. He shakes the oxygen tank like a deodorant can, the valve cracks his jaw, his knuckles brush the low ceiling, he listens again, hears his own sputtering whistle, then he remembers—

The other oxygen tank, *the other tank*! It wasn't completely empty when he changed over, still time left, party time, party time. He reaches for it, but it's not there.

'It might be hypothermia.'

It's Noel's voice he hears, but then he's not sure. His head is swimming in voices, whispers. 'He's okay,' Wicker says. 'Get him a towel.' Bobby feels for the tank. The penlight rolls off his chest onto the floor, glows brilliantly. The casket is floodlit. He tingles in waves. He snugs his body down, butt against the T-bar, knees against the soft lid, his body is swimming on its own now. He feels for the tank, his body doubled up, his knees jammed against the side of the coffin, and the valve is in his hand suddenly, it's been there all along, he thinks it's a handful of change at first, to put in his pocket, but see he knows he's hallucinating. He's a bronze horse stuck in its shipping crate, he laughs at the thought, snickers through his blowhole, can't whistle any faster, but he does. He's a bird, he's a peeper. He opens the valve, and it whispers:

Noel.

She turns away from him, opens the third drawer and pulls out a thick brown towel. She's barefoot, and when she turns back she's wiping the water off her own neck, her green eyes are shining, shining. 'You were dead,' she tells him.

He kisses at the valve, forces the cold steel against his burning lips and sucks the oxygen deep into his lungs until his head glows inside. *Noel*, he thinks, a prayer. He takes her in, fills his lungs, fills his bloodstream, and then the whisper goes away. He opens the valve until all sound stops, turns it both ways, but there's no whisper left. He sees stars. Stars everywhere. And suddenly he realizes that everything is perfect.

Everything is fine. Because Bobby Swift is master of his heart. And one breath of oxygen is all he needs. He rolls onto his back to relax. Master of his heart. His back is arched, his lungs are filled. No, it's his face – his face is expanding like a balloon. His heart is beating jungle drums in his chest.

And then he feels a kick, a terrible beat – a belch of pure white light. And Bobby Swift's last thought is clear as the full brilliant sun going off in his head.

Noel knew where Eliot Wicker kept his bath towels.

5

'I don't care,' Eliot Wicker said into the phone. 'I've got to see you.'

Pressing the telephone to her ear with her shoulder, she tipped the suitcase upside down, spilling Bobby's summer clothes onto the bed.

'Noel, I'm a nervous wreck over here by myself.'

'Don't be,' she said.

'After what we did?'

Shirts and trousers, she reached into each pocket and ran her fingers along the linings. The plane ticket was gone. So was his wallet.

'Come on,' Wicker said. 'No one'll see me. I'll leave in the morning before it gets light.'

Had Bobby stashed them in the casket and forgotten to tell her? Or made some last-minute arrangements with Wicker? Impossible.

'Okay, you come over here then,' the undertaker said. 'Come in the middle of the night, I don't care. You've got a key. What the hell are you doing, Noel? Say something to me.'

A moment passed, then she said softly, 'Don't call me anymore.' And hung up.

Sal marched past his house a second time. He couldn't go in, not yet anyway, certainly not with the bottle in his hand. Iris had vowed that if he ever drank again, their marriage was through. That was six months ago. The way he felt right now, the night so full of promise, what did another broken marriage matter in the whole magnificent, spiraling cycle? He lifted his face and smelled the river, the red oak, the white pine, the bracket fungi, the whole awakening world. He heard a car horn far in the distance, barking dogs and the paper-thin sounds of music. The night pulsated with rhythms, a thick heartbeat rising up from the earth, a long, seductive breathing above. The spring was fully upon the town, and Sal was certain that in his entire life he had never felt half this good. He unscrewed the cap and finished the vodka, then set the empty bottle gently in the mailbox at the foot of his driveway.

Tires squealed. He looked up. Headlights flashed as a pickup truck bore down on him from the village. He stared into the lights as it came, transfixed, until the truck went fishtailing past him, boys whooping out the windows. Which meant the outhouse raid was about to begin. He waved, shook a confederate fist above his head.

And here came the blue flashing of Alston Bouchard's dashboard light. The truck had been an obvious decoy, meant to lure the constable away. But he came on anyway, the dour Acadian, not quite fast enough in his old Subaru. The annual rebellion. Raise hell one night a year, mind your manners the rest. Yes, Sal thought, it was a wonderful town.

He was tempted to go down to the store and raise a little hell himself. And before he knew it, he was doing just that, springing up the road, his lungs effortlessly exchanging air with the cold, moonlit night, blowing past the sleeping houses like a phantom, and then he was turning up the Village Road, jogging over the iron grate bridge, pumping up the hill until he reached the store, where he circled the parking lot to catch his breath.

'Hey, there!' *They-uh*. It was Jerry Royal, coming up from the right corner of the building, where the driveway went down. 'Hear ol' Mister Music got into the sauce but good tonight.' Jerry laughed – a cartoonish guffaw. He was zipping his fly.

'What the hell, it's Blueberry Blossom Night,' Sal replied. 'How are you doin?'

'Oh, I dunno, 'bout as happy as a bastard on Father's Day, I guess.' In eight years, since Sal and Iris had moved to Maine, it was the most the two men had spoken.

'So, whatchu doin out past your bedtime?' Jerry continued. 'The old lady won't let you back in the house?' At this Jerry belted out another gutful of laughter. 'Join the club. She won't let me in that house, either! Me *or* the old man, and he's been dry ten years.' He chortled again, then drained his beer and crushed the can flat in his fist, tossed it into the road.

A window raised above their heads. 'Come on up,' Noel said through the screen. 'We'll get some coffee into you.' Both men knew that she was addressing Sal, not Jerry.

'That's an invitation I wouldn't deliberate on long,' Jerry remarked quietly, then added, with some remorse, 'I shouldna said that, under the circumstances.'

All at once a truck came squealing up from the River Road, blowing its horn as it crossed the bridge. It slowed, approaching the store, then stopped, revving its engine. 'That's my taxi,' Jerry said, and he skipped onto the running board, slapped the roof and the truck sped away. The night became remarkably quiet then, just the river singing off to the right, the river and the peepers.

'I could use the company,' Noel said. Her silhouette was softened by the screen. 'Go around to the garage. I'll let you in.'

Noel's driveway led down along the right side of the building, then turned around the back, where there was a set of double garage doors and, to their right, a window-paneled entry door.

When Sal got down there, the garage was dark. The only light came from the stairway, which was concealed behind a partial partition on the right-hand wall. He looked in the door window but saw only his own reflection against the sky. Suddenly the door opened and she was there, barefoot, dressed in red spandex leggings and a plain black T-shirt. She turned without saying anything and made for the stairs. As Sal followed her up, he became fixated on her buttocks. Although he wasn't especially attracted to women's backsides, Noel's was singularly stunning: high, round and compact, cheeks that strutted in front of his face all the way up two flights.

As they reached the top, Noel reached back and patted herself. 'Good for the derrière,' she said.

'I can see,' Sal replied, teasing. She waved her hand, a playful slap meant to miss him. It was their customary, innocent flirting and nothing more. Of course, Sal was completely faithful to Iris; and he would never have touched Bobby's wife. But he had occasionally fantasized about Noel, wondering how far she'd take it. He'd always been the one to back off.

The kitchen already looked like a single woman's kitchen – no tools on the counter, no boots by the door. The bottles and trays of food from the reception were gone. Except for the flowers, there was no evidence that Bobby had ever lived – or died – here. But then Sal couldn't have expected differently; Noel was not a sentimental person. He liked that about her, certain that most women in her spot would have felt obliged to wear their sadness like an overcoat so people wouldn't think them heartless.

She opened a cupboard and stretched high to reach something, her bright red legs lithe and long. He remembered her saying once that when she was a girl she liked to wrestle with boys. He bet she didn't often lose.

She took down a canister and measured fresh coffee beans into a small electric grinder, then sank the plug into the outlet, all the while giving Sal an icy stare. The grinder screamed as she pressed its top. Still she never took her eyes off him, and it became an effort of growing pleasure to hold her gaze with his own. Was she teasing him? Testing him? Suddenly the screaming stopped.

'What's that look?' she asked.

'What look?' he replied.

Noel turned to the door. Footsteps came out of nowhere, and before either could react, the door flew open and Eliot Wicker stepped in. Sal looked at Noel, her face a sheet of neutrality. Wicker, in turn, looked at Sal, fairly dumbstruck. Then he turned back to Noel and said, 'I thought I'd look in on you, make sure you're okay. It's part of my job.' His eyes fell to her legs.

'I'm fine,' she said impassively. Her lipstick, Sal noticed, was not the bright red he thought she usually wore, but a browner tone, more like the red of a medium roast.

Wicker appeared short of breath, and his face glistened with perspiration. 'I heard they were on their way over here tonight, with this outhouse business. I wanted to make sure it didn't get out of hand.'

Sal saw that Noel's blank expression hadn't changed. Then he realized why she was silent – and he felt embarrassed at being found there, as if he were making a play for his best friend's widow. He moved toward the door and said, covering, 'Noel, anytime you feel like talking, Iris and I are always there, you know that.'

She gave him an odd, bemused smile, while Wicker opened the door for him, looked him over in a way that made Sal stop on the threshold.

'You got a problem?' Sal said.

The undertaker folded his arms and replied, with utter disregard, 'No problem in particular.'

Sal nodded. He could see the man wasn't too bright, the type that got shafted as a boy because of his deficiencies and now spent his life getting even with the world. He held Wicker's listless stare for another second or two, then said, 'My mistake.'

'Hey,' Wicker answered. He pointed a finger at Sal, a sporting gesture, then shut the door behind him.

Wicker stared at the door. He listened to the footsteps as Sal walked down the stairs. When he heard the basement door close far below, he pushed the lock on the apartment door, then turned and brushed past Noel, walked down the hall to the living room and looked out. In a moment he saw Sal, under the streetlight, walking down the road toward the bridge.

'What's he, got another woman waiting for him down there?' Wicker asked, hearing Noel enter the room behind him. 'Move away from the window,' she said.

Wicker stepped aside and lowered the venetian blinds, taking his time doing it.

'Do you know anything about Bobby's wallet?' she said. 'Or his plane ticket?'

'What exactly am I supposed to know?' he answered.

'Do you?' she shot at him.

He turned around and stared at her, eyes half-open, appearing disinterested, as he always did. 'No, I don't,' he said. 'Do you know I almost killed myself coming over here?'

'And?'

He held up his right hand, scraped raw. 'I almost fell down the bridge embankment. Goddamn Grand Central Station out there.'

Noel looked at him with disbelief. 'Jesus, don't you understand?' She stopped, turned up her palms and said, '*Murder.*'

'Don't worry, Noel, nobody saw me. But I do think I deserve to know what that guy was doing here.'

She threw a finger toward the window. 'That guy saw you here.'

'So what was he doing?' Wicker stared at her, thinking his persistence seductive.

She shut her eyes.

'Alright, maybe I'm overreacting. I *am* overreacting, okay? But I think it's best to straighten these things out at the outset of a relationship. Do we want to see other people or not? My vote is no.'

She crossed to the floor lamp and turned it off, so that only yellow light from the hallway entered the room. 'I'm leaving,' she told him.

'Come on. Where are you going this time of night?'

'Leaving. Going away.'

He paused to take this in and determined quickly that it was part of their argument.

'I guess I've just got to get used to it,' he said. 'God knows how many guys are going to be coming onto you now that they think you're alone.'

Noel turned and walked around him, stopped beside the bronze horse. She took a breath, then turned to face him, fingers folded in front of her, businesslike. 'Eliot, your money is at the Prince First Federal in Nassau. On the first of October I'll give you the account number, just as we planned.'

He took another moment to respond. 'I said I was sorry, okay? I was out of line. I know you weren't up to any hanky-panky, come on.'

She narrowed her eyes. 'I was going to fuck him,' she said, 'until you came.'

His breath left him in a sort of laugh. But he wasn't smiling, just staring at her with those sleepy eyes.

'Eliot, go.'

With his long fingers he scratched his long stomach. 'Okay, you want to move, we'll move. Anywhere. That's the beauty of my business.'

She stood rigidly. 'Listen to me,' she said. 'All we are, all we've ever been, is business partners. Now go.'

He laughed, a self-assured snicker. 'Sorry, not after the other night . . . you can't tell me that.'

'The other night,' she said, 'was business.'

'Some business.' He attempted a smile, reached out and took hold of her arms.

A car pulled into the lot below; they heard a country song, a burst of laughter. She twisted out of his grasp. 'Listen,' she said, 'you repulse me, do you understand? You're shallow and bitter, you speak like bad television. And you're going to get us caught.'

Stunned, he continued staring at her. The smile died on his lips. Now it looked like he was about to cry.

'Give me your hand,' he said, his voice shaking. She began to object but he grabbed it, pressed her palm to his chest. 'Can you feel that?'

She could. His heart was beating.

He glared at her, his translucent eyes for once fully exposed, and she thought for a moment that he was going to hit her. He whispered, 'I *killed* for you, goddammit, and I would die for you. But there's one thing I will not do!' His voice was rising again.

'Shhh,' she said, her own voice starting to shake.

'*I will not let you go!*'

He could see that he was beginning to scare her, and it boosted his confidence.

'Noel, I'll say it simply. Life without you would not be worth living – and secrets would not be worth keeping.'

A silence fell over the room. Noel, looking down, gently wrested her hand from his heart. She spoke quietly. 'You're not being clear, Eliot. What is it you're trying to say?' Another truck pulled into the lot down below, male voices laughing and loud.

'I'm saying that if you leave me, I don't care anymore. I'll expose us, I don't care. Noel, you've got to give me a chance.'

She took a quick breath, but spoke deliberately, almost lightly. 'Eliot, when you say "expose," what exactly do you mean?'

'Expose,' he said, and a volley of firecrackers rang out. 'Tell.'

'So you'll tell.'

He leered at her, giving her a taste of his newfound power.

She backed up a step. 'And they'll dig up Bobby's grave,' she said. 'They'll find his body, they'll find oxygen tanks, scuba tanks, a heating pad and flashlight. And it will become abundantly clear that Eliot Wicker knew he was burying a living man.'

Wicker nodded confidently. 'You got it.'

She closed her eyes slowly, and when they opened again they were cold and steady. Wicker was still nodding, but now he was beginning to pay attention too.

'Think,' she said. 'Was I there when Bobby died? Did I bury him? Can you think of a single shred of evidence in that casket, or anywhere, that could implicate me?' Her face became a mask of innocence.

Wicker stared.

She said, 'Bobby planned this whole thing with you so he could get away from me.'

'Alright, why did I double-cross him, then? What was in it for me?'

'Me.'

He attempted a laugh, but his eyes betrayed him.

'You had a thing for me. Isn't it obvious? Running up at midnight. And now we have a witness. You just won't leave me alone.'

He gave a small laugh that was meant to ridicule her, but it was a pitiful sound.

'Do you actually think a jury could believe that any woman would leave Bobby Swift for you?'

Wicker remained stationary, even as his insides collapsed. He felt himself swaying.

'For me,' she continued, 'life with you would not be worth living. So go right ahead, Eliot. *Expose*.'

She held him in her triumphant gaze and he stared back at her, numbed. More voices sounded below them. The undertaker turned mechanically and took hold of the doorknob.

'I don't think you want to go out the front,' she said.

A volley of firecrackers rang out, followed by a chorus of whooping. Wicker paused, then swept dizzily past her and marched down the hall toward the kitchen. She heard the back door open and close again, quietly. Now a glow appeared on the front blinds, a soft, flickering orange. Outside, horns started blowing and boys started whooping. Flames crackled. Noel opened the slats and looked down. In the middle of the intersection, the outhouse shot flames into the sky like a giant candle, belching thick, asphalt smoke off its slanted roof. Suddenly the country boys scattered to their pickup trucks, and in seconds they were gone, escaping in two directions. From the left, Alston Bouchard pulled up in his Subaru wagon, blue dash-light flashing. He circled around in the parking lot and then parked across from the store, on the other side of the flaming outhouse. He turned off his lights and his engine and then just sat there, to wait out the fire, while horns sounded gleefully in the distance.

Noel stepped away from the window. Another Blueberry Blossom Night had ended in Gravity. For Noel Swift, she thought with great relief, it would be the last.

Eliot Wicker's shoulders ached before he was two feet deep. But he was driven – worlds beyond heartsick – fueled by a white-hot rage. He didn't know exactly what he'd do about Noel Swift, but he sure as hell wasn't going to let her dump him. Not without the fight of her life. So he stood in the moonlight and stabbed the earth with his spade, again and again, piling dirt on the tarp he had dragged up from the toolshed.

He had been bluffing, of course, when he'd threatened to expose their crimes. But he feared she wasn't bluffing at all. For down in that casket there was more than enough evidence to screw him up, but good: oxygen tanks, flashlight, heating pad. It would be obvious that he had cooked something up with Bobby Swift. So, after tonight, let her talk. See where it would get her. They'd open the casket and find – *voilà* – Bobby's Swift's corpse and nothing else. So let her talk.

Wearing his navy blue windbreaker and brand-new jeans – *which he'd bought just for her!* – he had marched two miles from his home to the cemetery, actually running half that distance by necessity, darting from cover to cover so he wouldn't be caught in a clearing, should a car pass. But now it was well after one and the town was fast asleep. The entire way over here, he'd seen only two cars, a couple of diehards going home.

Originally he had considered sneaking the body back to his morgue for a proper embalming, but he decided it was too chancy. Anyway, there was no need. If they ever did exhume the body, Noel's story would be blown at first sight. *Where's the oxygen tanks, lady? Where's the scuba tanks?* She'd be instantly discredited, and they'd close the casket and be done with it. Granted, the corpse would be profoundly decayed, but no one expected Wicker's work to be perfect.

By the time he had dug little more than three feet down, he was shoveling with one knee on the ground, barely able to fill the spade. Distasteful as it seemed, he was forced to step down into the grave, where he kept digging until finally he stabbed the casket lid with the toe of his shovel, eight or ten inches down. 'Fuck you,' he grumbled to himself as he scraped the dirt off the polished, arched wood. 'Fuck the both of you.' His hasty plan was to free the viewing lid only, hoping to accomplish his mission without having to open the whole thing. So he stood in the lower half of the grave and pulled the dirt toward him, mounding it under his feet, each shovel clearing more of the upper lid. When enough wood was exposed, he knelt in the dirt and reached down for the latches. Strangely, he found them already turned.

A rotten suspicion weltered up inside him. He straightened his back, got his fingers around the edge of the lid and pulled with every molecule of strength he could muster, straining until the lid turned up in his hands. He swung it open, spilling dirt down his sleeves. When he looked down, his heart walloped inside his chest. The body!

Bobby Swift was gone—

'SHIT!' Wicker cried, even before be began to understand the implications. He ducked down in the grave, hoping no one had heard his shout.

Gone—

The thought sent a hard chill through him. Gone where? No man could burrow his way out of a closed casket six feet underground. Not even Bobby Swift. Then what if – Wicker visualized this with a shudder – what if Bobby had broken his way out, started crawling into the earth and died there? It was a horrible thought, but one that had to be true. Wicker felt along the dirt wall, looking for a hole, expecting to find – what, Bobby's foot? – when he heard a sound.

He fell back and whipped his gun out of his windbreaker pocket, a Colt .38 semiautomatic. He quietly pulled back the slide, chambering a round, then he rose to the surface, moving his aim in a slow circle. Out in the night, everything lay still. The moon poured a wide, stark light over the cemetery below. The woods that wrapped around behind him remained perfectly quiet. He could even hear the river, nearly a mile away.

Pocketing the Colt, he turned his flashlight back on, then stepped down inside the casket, reaching his toe beneath the lower lid. He could feel the scuba tanks and both oxygen tanks, all covered with a dusting of dirt. Everything in place except the corpse—

That's when it hit him:

She had dug him up after all! Or else she had hired someone to. Wicker's breathing intensified. His face filled with pressure. Bobby Swift, alive! Probably far away by now – Cancun, Belize – Wicker was sure it wasn't Grand Cayman. No, they were too smart for that. Wherever Bobby was, Wicker knew damn sure that Noel was getting ready to join him.

And Eliot Wicker – once again, folks – Eliot Wicker gets screwed.

Oh, he wanted her now. Those icy green eyes, that crooked, haughty mouth, he wanted her worse than ever. And what could he do about it? He squeezed a handful of dirt so hard that his arm trembled. Here she had him sitting asshole-deep in an empty grave, surrounded by the evidence that could put him away for life. And for what? The crime of stupidity, of desperate, stupid love.

But she wouldn't get away with it, no way. He didn't know exactly what he would do, but he did know this: he would get her somehow, no matter what the cost to himself. He lifted one of the oxygen tanks out of the casket, flung it onto the turf above with a hollow ting. The other tank he hurled over his shoulder into the sky so high he could feel the impact through the earth when it came down.

Even if it meant he'd lose his license, he didn't care. If he had to do years of hard time, she'd pay. Oh, how he wanted the day to come when he'd be standing on the free side of a bulletproof pane, telephone in hand. What would he say? Something simple. Fuck you. Yeah, the big fuck you. Twenty-five rotting years in some hellish asylum, and he'd visit her every day just to say it. Fuck you, baby.

He struggled with the twin scuba tanks, got them up over his head and heaved with all his might. They made a ring when they hit the ground, which was a remotely satisfying sound. He bent down, felt under the closed lid for anything else, and found – luckily – the dead penlight. He threw that into the sky as far as he could, heard it snicker through the trees. Lying bitch. Next he snagged the heating pad, followed its double wires to the battery, bundled the whole thing and threw it so far into the sky he never even heard it land. He imagined it coming down over the cemetery like a parachute. He imagined Bobby Swift, prison pants down by his ankles, being buggered up the ass by some grizzly 300-pound Colombian drug lord. You too, Bobby. The casket would be clean.

Clean as his own alibi: The man was never buried, he'd say – if it came to that. Simple. Bobby Swift had tricked everybody. Otis and Jerry Royal had lowered an empty coffin into the ground; they were too drunk to notice, that's what he'd say. As for his failure to embalm Bobby—

He'd have to think about that one.

He got down on his knees with his flashlight and swept his hand around in the loose dirt, feeling for anything else, when something pierced the palm of his hand.

'*Bitch!*' he spat, blaming Noel for this, too, and then pulled the thing out of the dirt. A trocar – his embalming tool.

He shone the light on its dirt-encrusted tip, trying to make sense of the thing, when one of the oxygen tanks rolled back into the grave and glanced sharply off his head, knocking him onto his hands. He pressed his forearm to his head, the pain throbbing over his entire skull. And this, finally, was more than Eliot Wicker could stand. He threw his face into the air and—

Somebody was standing over him, at the edge of the grave, holding the other oxygen tank.

Wicker's first thought was to explain himself. 'I'm just reconfirming,' he said.

His second thought was to get at his Colt. In a flash he went for his pocket and brought out the gun, but then the oxygen tank came whistling down. There wasn't time to duck. Its impact on Wicker's head made a vicious PING. It was the last sound the undertaker would ever hear, if he ever heard it at all.

6

Sal opened his eyes when he heard the door close. A heaviness rolled over him like faraway thunder, the drone of an engine: the school bus driving away. He realized he was lying in front of the living room couch. A cushion lay on his side . . .

'Iris?'

He heard the refrigerator close. He sat up, and the heaviness in his head thickened. Then the back door closed. Dizzily, still dressed, he tossed the cushion off him, got to his feet and went into the kitchen, opened the door. She was getting in her car.

'Why didn't you wake me up?' he said. 'I'm late.'

The look she gave him was short, but long with sober resolution. She started the engine and backed out of the driveway. A sickening fear shot through him as he watched her drive away.

Numbed, Sal tried to remember the previous night; failing that, the previous day: Bobby's funeral, Noel's reception ... His conversation with Eliot Wicker faded in a Librium haze. His show? He knew it was useless to try.

'Just like this when we found it,' Jerry Royal said.

Alston Bouchard stood beside him, looking down at the cemetery plot. Otis, Jerry's father, sat sidesaddle on the riding lawn mower beside them both, his stomach sacking over his lap. A swath of mown grass stopped abruptly beside Bobby Swift's grave site, where squares of sod fit neatly together – except for one square, pushed up at its corner. But that wasn't what bothered the men. It was the blue-black barrel of a pistol that poked up, aimed at the sky. Otis leaned forward and pulled the sod back, and they could see that the pistol protruded from the earth to the trigger, which was squeezed in the firing position by a dark, greenish-red index finger with a manicured nail.

'Prob'ly rubber,' Jerry said, picking at the finger.

'Jerry,' Bouchard told him, 'maybe you best not…'

'Jumped the bejesus outta me, that thing,' Otis declared. Dressed in a sleeveless T-shirt that was stained with his sweat, Otis was testimony to the overwarm day.

'Somebody's idea of a practical joke,' Jerry said. 'No doubt.' Bigger than his father but not yet as heavy, Jerry was nonetheless obvious progeny. 'Like I said, tamp it down, let the sleepin dog lay.' He set the heel of his shoe on the pistol, attempting to push it down.

'I don't think you ought to do that,' Bouchard told him. He crouched down to get a closer look, picked a bullet casing out of the dirt, then peeled the sod back and found five more in a cluster.

'Thirty-eight,' Jerry said. 'I already checked.'

'Looks like he was trying to get somebody's attention,' Otis said.

'Either that or duck-huntin,' Jerry added, looking for a laugh.

'You boys move anything?' the constable asked.

'Just like this when he found it,' Jerry said again.

Bouchard sniffed the casing. It was around 6:30 in the early evening, a hazy, oversized sun melting over the western hills. The Royals had waited until late afternoon before mowing, hoping for a cooling breeze, but it never happened. The air sat over the town, dead heavy.

'Want us to dig it up, Alston?' Otis asked. 'While we're on the clock.'

'Too hot for that shit,' Jerry answered.

'I don't think yet,' Bouchard said. 'Either you boys talk to Eliot Wicker today?'

'Not me,' Jerry replied, and Otis grunted the same, as he scratched under his arm, then wiped his hand on his belly. 'Awful warm, Alston, you don't need us anymore.'

'I don't.'

'Want to leave the lawn mower, for evidence?'

'Leave it.'

'Okay then.'

As father and son lumbered from the grave to their new Chevy pickup, Jerry's black shotgun hanging in the rear window, Bouchard called out to them, 'You got a shovel here—?'

'Down the shed,' Jerry told him.

Bouchard rose to his feet, said, 'I'd appreciate it if you boys would keep this to yourselves. It'd likely upset her.'

'No doubt,' Jerry said, sliding into the truck. As they drove down the hill and turned out of the cemetery, the man who had arrested both of them countless times over the years stepped away from Bobby Swift's grave and looked up at a branch of an old maple tree, where something peculiar was hanging.

'They'll believe you,' Sal said again, but he was getting nowhere.

Iris, her back to him, poured a glass of water from the kitchen tap and drank it, fortifying her resignation. It was almost seven and still ninety degrees outside; even hotter inside. Still in uniform, Iris was just back from work.

'I need to take care of Davey,' she said, 'and I need to take care of myself. You need to take care of yourself.' Her words were laced with a maddening indifference, as if she were talking to a stranger – or firing an employee. She stuck her glass under the tap for more water.

He started to respond, but then he stopped. He wanted to tell her that he didn't know how it had happened, but he knew that anything he could think to say would be futile. More maddening, he actually didn't know what he had done. That he had gotten drunk was obvious – he remembered the first sip at Noel's reception. He remembered making another drink in her kitchen once everyone had left. After that, between the Librium and the vodka, the wall was up and there was no penetrating it.

'Iris, are you sure about this?'

He was speaking matter-of-factly, showing that he could be resigned too, hoping that she would rescind. But she stood with her back to him, unyielding.

'It was a bad night,' he said. 'It was the Librium, it was Bobby's funeral, it was a mistake.'

She sighed. 'It was no mistake, Sal. You knew what you were doing before you took the first drink. You knew what the outcome would be.' She turned and looked directly at him, her sea gray eyes steady behind her lenses. 'I want you to leave,' she said.

He took a deep breath of the stilted air, feeling like the oxygen had been sucked from the house.

'That's it, then,' he said.

Her expression didn't change.

'What are we going to tell Davey?'

'I don't know yet.'

He went to the counter, picked up his car keys.

Iris didn't budge.

'I know that was the deal – I agreed to it,' he said. 'But we need to be realistic for a minute. If you don't go to that school board meeting with me, I'll lose my job, and then you and Davey end up passing out food stamps at the store like the rest of your family.'

She turned away from him again, stared out the window – a reaction at least, but he cursed himself for saying it. He went to touch her, to put his hand on her shoulder, and then he saw what she was looking at: Davey, in the garden, weeding peas.

By the time Sal and Iris reached the school, word of green hand and the pistol had spread around town. The story was, teenagers had stolen a mannequin's arm from the Bangor Mall and buried it in Bobby Swift's grave, along with a stolen .38. In the school library, George Web was relating the tale to the other board members, but he stopped when Sal and Iris entered the room.

The couple was asked to sit in small wooden chairs on one side of a long library table. Despite the heat, Sal wore his usual corduroy jacket over a gray jersey. Iris wore her uniform. The five school board members sat behind the table along with the principal, Avery Bingstream, whose left arm was set in a white plaster cast and sling. Sal guessed that he was the cause. A mediator from the Maine Teachers Association, a young man sweating liberally in a three piece suit, sat at the head of the table, symbolically between the two factions. As the meeting went on, he removed the coat, then the vest, and then his tie, apologizing each time.

'What you are telling us, then, Mrs Erickson, is that Salvatore was, in fact, under the effects of antianxiety medication—?' This was Helen Swan, a retired psychiatrist from New Haven and head of Gravity's school board. White-haired and unadorned in a meticulous way, Helen was a former summer resident who had settled in town permanently four years ago to be near her son and granddaughter.

'Librium,' Iris confirmed, her hands in her lap. 'Sal was under a lot of stress with Bobby's death. We had the bottle in our medicine cabinet – sometimes I need help sleeping.' With the proper self-effacement, Iris covered her lie with a smile for the woman.

'I see,' Helen Swan replied tentatively.

'That's understandable, with stress,' George Web piped in. 'Tough thing when you lose a friend.' George was the only man on the board, a subsistence-level carpenter and blueberry farmer and the member with the most seniority. Sal knew he could count on George's opposing Helen Swan on any matter.

'I told him to take two or three,' Iris added, embellishing her story. 'I didn't know he'd have such a reaction.'

Sal looked down at her clenched fingers, and he felt a sudden longing, like it was years ago and they were united against the world. He did not want to believe he could lose her. He took hold of her hand, which became lifeless in his.

'The truth is,' he said, 'Iris warned me not to take them before the concert. I didn't think it would be a problem.'

He looked up to see Helen Swan holding a coffee mug. 'MY FAVORITE TEACHER' was printed on it, a Father's Day gift to him from Davey. The woman peeled cellophane off its top. Neither Avery Bingstream nor any of the board members needed to see what was inside. Neither did they watch Sal. They kept their eyes on Iris, who twisted her hand out of Sal's. The mediator shifted in his chair.

'It was backstage,' Helen said.

Sal's stomach clenched. He knew what the mug meant. Helen tipped it forward, offered it to him. He did nothing. She slid the mug to the mediator. 'People in the audience saw him drinking from it.'

The young man dipped his finger into the liquid and touched it to his tongue. He sniffed at it and then cleared his throat. 'Vodka?' he asked. No one responded. 'Mr Erickson, would you care to say something on your behalf?'

Sal shook his head no.

'Mrs Erickson, is there anything you'd like to add, or change, regarding your testimony?'

The panelists waited quietly. Avery Bingstream ran his plaster cast across five or six inches of the wooden table, making a dry, scraping sound. The fan in the doorway grew louder. Sal felt the heat surge over him. Beside him, Iris stared straight ahead, almost entranced, humiliated beyond words.

'Please, let's not prolong this,' Mrs Swan said. 'Unless anyone has anything to add, I believe the board is prepared to vote on dismissal.' The other members nodded uncomfortably.

Sal stood up. 'I'll save you the trouble,' he said, pushing his chair neatly under the desk. 'I'll hand in my resignation in the morning.'

Helen Swan looked briefly at the other members, then replied, 'I'm afraid you don't have that option, Mr Erickson.'

Alston Bouchard worked alone. Protocol dictated that he call the state police, but he wanted to know what he was reporting before making the call – he didn't want to be the brunt of a Blueberry Blossom Night prank. By the time he discovered that the hand was indeed attached to an arm, he had also uncovered the head, the hair, and then the face, of Eliot Wicker – but then he noticed a leather belt wrapped around the dead man's neck and the tops of two shiny tanks behind his shoulders . . . so he continued digging.

It was dogged, drenching work. He kept a gallon of water on the ground beside him and assuaged his thirst every few minutes. With each shovel of dirt, perspiration poured off his nose and streamed down his glasses, rippling his vision. Now it was almost eight and darkening, and he was down to Wicker's jeans, far enough to see that it was Wicker's own belt that held the scuba tanks to his back – and that whoever had buried him had also taken the time to poke a flashlight out of his fly.

The local undertaker dead and buried with scuba tanks, a shining erection and a gun. And a missing corpse. Some prank.

The constable stopped digging. He took off his glasses and splashed water on his face, and then he looked out over the horizon. An hour earlier, orange-tinged cumulus clouds had begun billowing straight up in the western sky. As the sun had disappeared, the air had settled to a standstill, birds had stopped singing, and now an ominous quiet hovered over the hill. Thunderstorms had been predicted, but Alston Bouchard didn't need a weatherman to tell him that. Heat like this – in May? – could only mean one thing. When the first rumble crawled across the western sky, he decided to make the call.

Sal drove past their house, past the village, and then turned onto the Townhouse Road. He drove down along the blueberry barrens until they were within sight of the cemetery, and there he pulled over and shut off the engine. The sky, darkening in the west, fluttered with lightning. He waited for Iris to begin, knowing it was useless to apologize.

She didn't speak right away but waited while thunder grumbled across the horizon. Then she sat longer.

Looking absently at the lone man working up at the top of the cemetery, Sal gave no thought to the fact that the man seemed to be digging at Bobby's grave. Rather, he was beginning to finally understand that his life was over, difficult as it was to fathom how it had ended so fast: his marriage, his family, his career.

He had met Iris in the spring ten years earlier, the night the Thundering Herd played the Ellsworth Auditorium. After the concert Sal and the drummer went to a Bar Harbor pub, where a hot local dance band was playing. Iris, two years into nursing school, was there with two friends and phony IDs. She told Sal later that she was attracted to him not because he walked up to the stage with his trombone and roared through an incredible five-chorus solo that brought the crowd – and the band – to a frenzy, but because of the way he slunk back to his seat when it was over; because of his darkness; because of the way he seemed to be hiding inside his tweed cap and overlarge corduroy jacket. His manner didn't fit the ferocity of his music, and she'd told him that she wanted some time to figure him out.

After they had learned more about each other, Iris would say they were attracted to one another by a bond of childhood tragedies. But the real reason she was attracted to him – and they had each grown to see this independently – was because of the drink. Back at his table, two vodka martinis were sent to him, and he'd downed each with a tip of the glass to his benefactors. The second was from Iris, and he'd looked twice.

Now, as they sat listening to the thunder, her indifference was astonishing. He had, with a single act, become just like the other men in her life, her father and her brother: Gone.

'When we get home,' she told him, 'you'll need to pack some things. I don't know where you're going to stay—'

'I'll find a room in town,' he said.

'On the weekend you can come back for whatever else you need, and we'll work out the arrangements. If we can't agree, we'll have to get lawyers.'

She looked out the windshield, finished. Just like that. Like they were scheduling a brake job for one of their cars. A flurry of lightning lit her face, and the night seemed to grow instantly darker. Five or six thick raindrops splattered against the windshield, while a distant roll of thunder went on and on. She refused to even look at him.

He had managed to stay dry for five years after coming to Maine – until Bobby and Noel came to town. It was that first summer, three years ago, when he took a part-time job at the store during his school vacation. That's when he started again. Closing time, they'd have a drink or two, he and Bobby and Noel, and as the summer wore on, he began staying later and later. In July he found himself in the county jail one morning after he and Bobby had torn up an Ellsworth tavern (that's what they'd told him, anyway). Somehow Bobby – who had instigated the brawl – managed to keep it out of the papers, but that didn't smooth things between Sal and Iris. In August, to help Sal sober up, the two men canoed up the 100-mile Allagash waterway in northern Maine, dry. It was an eight-day trip, during which Sal was constantly haunted with vodka cravings – and Bobby, who didn't have the addiction, stayed awake with him every night, talking and tending the campfire. When Sal returned home, he promised Iris that he'd never drink again, and he kept his promise – until the next summer, when he went to work at the store again (over Iris's objections) and fell quickly into another ten-week binge. Some nights he didn't come home at all, nor would he remember where he had been or what he had done. Iris, depressed and angry, told him she had had enough. So he and Bobby canoed the Allagash again at the end of August – but this time Sal wasn't able to kick, and his drinking continued into the school year. In November he checked into a Bangor detox ward for six weeks. Upon his return, she promised him that if he ever drank again, she would divorce him. He agreed to the terms. Now she was keeping her promise.

He started the car, punched the shift into first and started to pull onto the road, when headlights flashed in his rearview mirror. He kicked the brakes as a police car swerved around him, red brake lights glaring through the rain-spattered windshield. The cruiser turned into the cemetery, taillights making their way up the terraces.

Impassively, Iris reached over and flipped on the wipers. 'Davey's home alone,' she said. 'She doesn't like the thunder.'

Back home, Sal sat at the kitchen table while Iris put Davey to bed. When he heard Iris's footsteps cross the landing, he went up. He wanted to pretend nothing was wrong, but Davey was on to him. As they kissed goodnight, she clasped her fingers around the back of his neck and wouldn't let go. 'Come on, hon,' he told her, separating her fingers, 'get to sleep now.' He shut off her raccoon lamp and started to close her door.

'Love you,' she told him.

'Love you too.'

He crossed the landing and went into his bedroom, closed the door behind him. His suitcase lay opened on the bed beside a neat stack of his clothes. Iris was folding his handkerchiefs and laying them in.

'I'll do that,' he said to her. Then the door opened behind him.

'Daddy, I almost forgot,' Davey said, looking in. Seeing the suitcase, she sang, 'Are we going on vacation?'

'Honey, what is it?' Sal said.

'Just – Noel Swift called when you guys were out. I didn't write it down because there was too much, but she said to tell you to come over because she's got something for you, and this time you won't get interrupted.'

A stillness overtook the room.

'Honey, go back to bed now,' Sal told her, then added the lie: 'See you in the morning.'

She pouted.

'Go ahead.'

'See you in the morning,' she muttered, and left the room.

Sal picked up a couple of shirts, folded them and stuffed them in the suitcase. Iris busied herself in the closet, rattling hangers. Outside the walls, thunder murmured. Inside, the silence escalated. Sal picked up a pair of corduroys, folded them and set them in beside the shirts, then grabbed a handful of jockey shorts from his bureau drawer and bunched them on top.

'Did you even wait for the funeral?' Iris said finally.

'Don't start that,' Sal shot back, 'you know there's nothing going on between Noel and me, you resent her because she's an *out-a-statuh*'—

—'obviously enjoy her flirting'—

—'like maybe I resent having to live in your stupid hick town!'

—'Your choice, Sal, your decision'—

—'No, your choice. Your ultimatum! I gave up a career for you'—

—'You got fired from every band'—

—'*Downbeat* called me the best'—

—'*Downbeat* didn't have to put up with your drinking'—

—'Yeah, well I wasn't a drunk till I married you.'

Slamming the suitcase shut and latching it, pulling the suitcase off the bed, he sought to leave her with that. But she followed him out the room to the top of the stairs as he went down.

'My whole life I've put up with drunks,' she told him.

'That's right,' he replied, and he stopped at the bottom to give her a last look. '*You came looking for me!*'

The Superette was closed when Sal drove by, and Noel's apartment was dark. He hadn't intended to stop, but he could see by the faint glow in the storefront window that a light was on in the stockroom, which meant that Noel was back there working. And since she, after all, had just lost her husband – and now that he was in need of a sympathetic ear himself – he pulled down her driveway.

Fully dark now as he stepped out of his car, the night weighed down heavily, while miles above, monstrous clouds tossed electric bolts back and forth, toying. Although the brief rain had stopped for the moment, the water in Noel's swimming pool swayed plaintively, as if sharing some secret relationship with the storm.

Thinking the door would be locked, Sal tried it anyway and it opened. The garage was blessedly cool, and pitch-black. He closed the door, reached out his hands and felt his way around Noel's Volvo. He could hear soft music upstairs, a saxophone and trumpet. Coltrane and Miles, from *Kind of Blue*, Bobby's favorite. Sal had never heard Noel play it before. She prefered world music, pan-global, whatever she called it. Drumming on goatskin, tribal chanting, stomping in the dust.

From the darkness he called hello, but only the saxophone responded. He made his way around the half partition and started up the stairs, climbing noisily, not wanting to startle her with his sudden appearance. After a few steps he arrived at a landing and had to turn right, feeling his way up the stairs with the toes of his sneakers and the handrail. With every step the air grew warmer, and then he emerged on the second floor, where the music was louder and a line of dim light leaked under the stockroom door. Sal took hold of the knob and pushed the door open, and he felt a rush of stifling heat.

He was in the stockroom, a wide-open, dusky, cardboard-smelling, windowless area filled with unshelved merchandise. He looked down a straight avenue created by two rows of cardboard boxes on wooden pallets. Similar aisles stretched toward the store on his left and right. Somewhere to the right of the center of the room, a soft spot of light shone on the wood ceiling. The saxophone sounded from that direction too, sailing over the low, arduous hum of the industrial-sized floor fan that Bobby had kept back there.

'Hello,' he called. The music quieted suddenly, and then he heard her voice.

'How did you get in?' she said.

'Through the garage. The door was unlocked.'

He entered the wide main aisle just as she stepped into the light about halfway down, between two pallets of boxes. She seemed to study him as he approached her, almost as if she didn't believe him. She was barefoot and barelegged under a short denim skirt and lazy beige tank top. Her tangle of orange hair, lit from the right, shone like fire. She held a tumbler in her hand, full of ice.

When he had almost reached her, she looked down at her drink self-consciously and gave an apologetic shrug. 'It's murder up here,' she said. 'There's no air.' Her arms were shiny with perspiration.

'It is hot,' he agreed. As they came together he stopped short of giving her a hug, feeling uncomfortable about touching her, the way she was dressed, the fact that they were up here alone. Seeming to sense his discomfort, she turned away from him and walked around a tall stack of cardboard cartons to her desk, a wide cherry affair covered with invoices, receipts and an accounting book. On the corner of the desk stood a pewter ice bucket; floating in the ice, a pint bottle of Stoli.

'I hope you don't mind,' she said. 'Should I hide it from you?'

Sal shook his head, and a drop of perspiration ran down his cheek. He wiped it with the back of his hand. 'I'm okay,' he said.

She gave him a sort of smile. 'You look great,' she replied. If sarcasm could be seductive, she had it down.

'It's the heat,' he replied. 'Or I'm in shock – I don't know – everything's out of whack.'

She swung the desk chair around for him, then slid herself back on a carton of vegetable oil. In the same motion she reached back to turn off the floor fan, briefly exposing a side of her breast, a smooth, white softness. 'I'd rather have the heat than the noise,' she told him.

He sat facing her with his back to the desk. 'Iris and I—' he began, but then he felt like he was blurting.

Her green eyes sharpened on him.

'We had an agreement...' He raised his fingers off his thighs, helplessly. 'And I blew it. So I'm gone.'

She gave him an odd look: even though her eyes narrowed with concern, her burnished lips turned into a slight smile. It was a feature of knowing Noel, that her mouth was often at cross-purposes with her eyes. She took another sip of her drink, ice cubes chiming against the crystal. A bright green circle graced the front of her tank top, the orange word BOTSWANA scrawled across it. 'Give her time,' she suggested.

'You don't know Iris. Once she shuts the door on someone' – he shook his head – 'it never opens again.'

Raising her glass, she gave him a slightly ironic look, a toast.

'So you're homeless, and I'm a widow.' She tipped the glass to her mouth and drank it down, spilling some of the vodka down her chin. She pulled up the neckline of her top to wipe her chin, lifting a breast against the thin fabric. 'Under the circumstances,' she said, 'I must say you don't look too broken up.'

'Yeah, huh?' He thought of saying the same thing to her.

She slid off the oil carton and leaned over his lap to get at the ice bucket, bracing herself with a hand on his thigh. 'I mean, six months without a drink, Sally, what exactly is the problem?' Her tank top fell away from her chest as she dropped a couple more ice cubes into her tumbler. A warm aroma rose from her body.

'Want me to get that?' he asked, turning his face away.

Retrieving the bottle, she uncapped it and began pouring. He could hear the liquid singing into the tumbler behind his ear, the ice cracking. He could smell the vodka. And Noel, leaning over him again to put the bottle back on ice, now he could smell the keen bite of her underarm.

'I should probably hit the road,' he said.

'I'll prove it to you,' she told him, straightening. Her leg remained pressed against his.

'Prove what?'

The glass rose between them, so close to his face that he could barely bring it into focus. She swirled the drink in little circles.

'That it's just a matter of perspective.' With that, she put the rim to her mouth. Staring at him, she slowly tipped the glass. The ice shifted. Her dark lips thickened and opened as she sucked the vodka into her mouth.

He lifted his hands. 'Uh, that's enough perspective for me,' he said with a nervous laugh. He moved his leg, wanting to get up, wanting to leave.

But her eyes narrowed, a challenging stare. And now, leaning into him, practically straddling his knee, she started moving the glass toward him. 'Hm?'

He felt his heart beating. But, resisting, he took hold of the glass and put his other hand on her hip, intending to move her back.

'Really, Noel, this is not good. I've got to go.'

She twisted the glass out of his hand and bore down on him with it. 'Uh-uh,' she scolded, like a mother administering medicine.

'Come on,' he laughed, weakening. 'You know I can't do this.' He turned his face to the side, but she found his mouth with the rim of the glass. 'Noel, stop, really—'

She gave him a flaccid smile and said simply, 'Tell me why.' Staring at him.

He stared back, heart thumping. She tipped the glass slightly, and the vodka touched his lip. Icy cold. Deadly. He kept his lips closed as he murmured an objection. She seemed aroused herself, almost hypnotized, the way she looked at him.

Then suddenly she stopped. A lightness came over her. 'See?' she said. 'Could an alcoholic resist that?' She smiled warmly at Sal as she began to lower the glass, and it was a powerful relief. But now he couldn't resist sucking a tiny stream of it.

'No, no,' she scolded, but she kept the tumbler at his lips, tipped.

The sensation was heart-stopping – the taste, the heat, the iciness; her smell, her heat on his leg. As he sucked a little more of it in, he gazed up at her, and now she was tipping the glass higher, watching him and making a humming sound, a soothing, motherly sound. Christ, it was like she was nursing him, and he became aware that she was moving her pelvis against his knee. It was far more than he could hope to resist. His mouth opened and he was drinking—

He pushed to his feet, pushing the glass away and sliding out from beneath her. She fell back against a stack of cartons. He didn't care. He just needed to get out of there.

'I can't do this,' he told her, backing away.

Standing there, disheveled, she looked stung.

'I can't,' he said again. 'Besides, I've got to go find a place to live.' He backed toward the main aisle of cartons. 'Are you gonna be okay?'

She didn't answer, just kept staring at him.

'Noel, I really have to go,' he said. 'I'll call you in the morning.' He turned to leave.

As if on cue, the telephone rang. Sal stopped, thinking it might be Iris, calling to take him back. Or Davey.

The phone rang again, but Noel paid no attention to it, just kept staring at him.

He said, 'Probably someone wondering if the store's going to open tomorrow.'

It rang again.

Noel looked at the telephone. Its second red button was flashing. 'No, that's upstairs,' she said. She leaned over the desk and pushed the button down.

'I've gotta go anyway.'

She raised a finger, stopping him, then picked up the phone. Her voice became instantly businesslike when she said hello. Then she scowled as she listened. 'Who were you trying to call?' she asked, then listened again, becoming more distracted. She hung up, then picked up the glass of vodka and walked past him, turned the corner around a pile of cartons.

He stayed where he was and waited a few seconds, but she didn't return. He called her name, but all he heard in response was Miles's soft and steady trumpet over an undertone of faraway thunder.

He followed where she had gone, around a pallet of stacked cartons to the main aisle that led into the store. He walked to the swinging door, looked through its window. 'Noel?'

He pushed on the door and emerged behind the meat counter. Inside, the store was a shade darker than the stockroom, and every bit as warm. Outside the two front windows (the only windows on this entire level), heat lightning continued to flutter, tossing shadows around. In that flickering light, Sal saw the glass of vodka on the lunch counter to his right. But no sign of Noel.

'Who called?' he asked.

When she answered, her voice came from one of the grocery aisles on the left. 'You didn't know I was an addict,' she said.

'What?'

She emerged from the aisles near the front of the store, lit for an instant by the flashing sky. 'Chocolate,' she said.

'Come on, chocolate.'

'The imported stuff,' she continued. 'Back before I knew you. I ate so much of it that I stopped eating everything else to keep from getting fat.'

'Noel, I doubt you were ever fat.'

She came toward him, slowly unwrapping a small package, six inches long. 'I couldn't get enough,' she said. 'The darkest, richest, most intoxicating chocolate I could get my hands on. Finally they put me in the hospital and got me into a twelve-step program.'

'I'm familiar with it.' He slid back onto a fountain stool three seats from where she had left the vodka, turned his back to the counter.

As she drew nearer, he could see that what she had in her hand was indeed a dark, thick bar of chocolate, about a half pound. 'They told me I could never eat it again. No candy, no cookies, no ice cream. Nothing. It's been five years and I haven't had a taste.'

'I'd say you were addicted,' he agreed.

'But I'm not like you. See, I don't isolate myself. I don't hide from it. I *surround* myself with it, the most expensive, the most intense chocolate I can find.' Standing in front of him, she waved the bar under his nose; its heady fragrance made him salivate. 'This is Caracas chocolate from Venezuela – I get it from an importer in Boston. There's a couple of people in Bar Harbor who buy it from me, they'll pay anything.' Now she began sniffing the chocolate, moaning as she did. Even in the dark, Sal could see that her eyes were losing focus. She seemed to float on her feet; her hip brushed his leg.

He turned on his stool away from her. He said, 'So why tempt yourself?'

She breathed a laugh. 'Temptation?' She reached around him, retrieved the glass of vodka and slid it along the counter until it touched his elbow. Then she stretched a knee up onto the stool beside him. 'That's what keeps us alive, Sally. Pure, uncut...' She pulled herself onto the counter, the backs of her legs squeaking on the Formica. Then she swung her body sideways until she was leaning back against the dessert display case in front of his face, her left hip touching his vodka glass. She gave the glass a nudge. 'Temptation.'

Demonstrating, she brought the bar of chocolate to her nose and inhaled deeply. 'God,' she breathed, 'I can actually feel my endorphins flowing.'

And he could already feel the vodka he had sipped, could taste it all around his mouth, could feel it flowing through his blood, working on his brain and body. 'At this point in my life,' he said, 'temptation is the one thing I don't need.'

He looked up at her and saw a dark smudge beside her lip where the chocolate had melted. She made a low sound in her chest, and her right leg reflexively rose in front of him, her silken inner thigh. He took a quick breath. Goose bumps danced up his sides.

'Sally, I'm serious,' she said. 'See how much you can take.'

Her voice was so soft, so weak, he wondered if he'd heard it at all. A bright light filled the store suddenly, turned shadows across the walls and then was gone – a pickup truck driving past, humming over the bridge, then turning left on the River Road. Noel hardly noticed. She was trembling, pulling the chocolate bar down her neck, actually painting it on her skin. She moaned loudly and then laughed, running the chocolate back over her cheek until it was at her mouth again, teasing her open lips. 'Go ahead,' she said, breathing harder. 'What've you got to lose?'

The ice cubes rattled inside his tumbler. He realized the glass was in his hand. His erection pressed against his trousers. What did he have to lose? Indeed.

'Sal?' She blurted his name suddenly, and with alarm. 'Oh God, Sal, I can't' – and all at once those dark lips closed around the end of the bar, the chocolate going softly inside.

'Noel, wait—'

Her knee kicked up, knocked against his wrist, splashing icy vodka over his hand, and then she turned away from him, lying on her side so that he could see the white cheeks of her buttocks, her dark panties pulled tight inside the cleavage. He could hear her lips working against the chocolate, could hear her swallowing as she murmured. He put a hand on her hip to stop her, and she moaned louder, opening that leg toward him. And now, in spite of himself, he was drinking the icy vodka, swallowing steadily – it was all he could do – and when the glass was empty he lowered his cold mouth to her humid thigh, pulling her roughly onto her back.

She made a noise – a protest – but her mouth was full and her sound was garbled. With his hand he opened her leg wider and then discovered her own hand there, three fingers working feverishly at herself. He pulled her hand away, took hold of the chocolate-sticky crotch of her silk panties and pulled them aside, her warm, liquid vulva squishing against his knuckles, then with his left hand he pulled her hips along the counter and lowered his own mouth to her flaccid lips, and God, the taste of her and Jesus, he looked up and beheld her there, propped against the display case, eyes closed, enraptured, her mouth working at that dark mass of chocolate, all the while roaring this loud, murderous ecstasy, and now Sal is reaching his left hand up under her top, up the length of her muscular, clammy stomach until he feels the firm swell of a breast, her nipple standing strong and hard, and he takes it between his thumb and forefinger and squeezes to soften it, and it makes her hips rise up, makes her clutch his head with her chocolate hand and grind her pubic bone into his jawbone, and now he's freeing his arm from her clothes, crawling up on the countertop, pulling her body beneath his own, and he's trying to kiss her dark bittersweet mouth, competing with her chocolate bar, and now they're both moaning in tongues of chocolate and saliva and it's like they're trying to swallow one another, and he's reaching under her, pulling her panties inside out – when more headlights flash across the store – and then they're falling off the counter—

He tries to catch her, tries to get his foot down and succeeds just enough so that when they hit the rubber mat they keep from separating. Their new bed is a cold cradle of hard rubber points, but he feels only an ecstatic sting on his side as he pulls her beneath him, and she squirms like a cat, delighting in the sparks, then wrestles him beneath her, working his trousers to his knees. He tried to toe them off the rest of the way, but she won't allow it, she's on him that fast, freeing his member from his underpants, her chocolate lips sucking down over the head and shaft, her fingers climbing his chest, nails singing his skin, and now he takes her under the arms and lifts her in the air, and her wet legs slide open around his hips, searching until they find what they want, precisely, perfectly – and then she stops—

poised...

He gasps.

Lightning flutters across the ceiling...

With a slowness that's the most exquisite torture, she lowers herself over him – an inch – just enough so that only his glans slips inside. And she stops again. Looking down at him hungrily, dark hair pasted over her forehead, dark lips in a lopsided near-smile, chocolate-smeared, engorged, slackly apart . . . she begins swallowing him inside her with a deliberateness that's reptilian. Staring. Staring. Shining.

There's no warning. The rush is immediate, tingling, overwhelming. He explodes, reaching for her, clutching the cheeks of her buttocks, spreading her apart and forcing himself deeper, entering her completely, pushing deeper still, ejaculating in colossal, heart-bursting spasms – three times, four times, five times, six times – straining as if every vein and artery is going to burst – until she cries out – seven times, eight times – the ceiling above them turning red . . . redder . . .

A car engine!

'Somebody's here—'

The knocking was tentative but persistent. Noel rose to her knees, twisted her denim skirt around, then wiped the chocolate from her face and neck with a towel that hung by the sink. Sal, on his back, hips raised, tried to zip his trousers over his erection.

'Stay down,' she whispered, and then she was gone, staying low, escaping down the length of the counter into the darkness.

From the stockroom he heard the music come on again – the same as before, Coltrane and Evans, smoky sax over a meditative piano – and then her bare feet padding back into the store, past the length of the counter. He heard the click of tumblers as she unlocked the door.

'Alston,' she said. Alston Bouchard. Sal wondered if the constable had seen his car down in back. After all his other transgressions, he did not need to be found here.

'Sorry I didn't hear you,' Noel said. 'It's so hot back there. I had the fan on, and the music.'

Sal saw her underwear on the floor beside him. He picked up the panties and bundled them softly in his hand as he heard Bouchard say, 'There's something I wanted to . . .' A period of silence passed, and then the constable added, 'Should I come in, or do you want to . . .' The man was more nervous than anybody his size had a right to be.

'No,' she said, 'come in, Alston, if you don't mind the dark. I'd put the lights on, but people would think we're open, and I've never been good at saying no.' The door hushed closed. 'Are Ellis's cows loose?' she asked. 'You're not usually out and about this late.'

Bouchard, his voice suddenly present, said, 'That was you I called then.'

'Oh,' she said, 'so that was you.'

'I thought I recognized your voice.'

'That's funny, because I thought it was you, too. But I didn't know why you'd be calling at this hour and not saying who it was. Would you like a Coke, Alston?'

'No, I'd have to pay' – Sal heard Bouchard slap the glass candy case that the cash register sat on – 'and where you've been closed, and the register's off . . .' More silence. Then, 'I guess you got two lines then,' he said. 'A separate phone line for your apartment upstairs.'

'The apartment, mm-hm. Do you want to sit, Alston? It seems like you're leading up to something.'

'No, I'll set when I get home. But you remember which line I called? The store or . . .'

Sal remembered. It was her upstairs line. But Noel seemed to have forgotten. 'I'm not sure, to tell you the truth. I just picked up when it rang.'

'Where?'

'In back.'

Bouchard cleared his throat. 'I don't suppose it'd be permissible if . . .' Sal could picture the apologetic turn of Bouchard's hand. 'The button'd still be pushed down prob'ly. I don't mean to be . . .'

'Alston, do you want to see my phone?'

'Well, not if—'

'It's just a little strange that you'd ask. But come on.'

Their footsteps moved through the store, the swinging door, and then their voices diminished into the stockroom. Presently Sal heard them returning, Bouchard saying, 'You didn't call anyone after I called you?'

The door swung open and they walked into the store again,

stopping on the other side of the counter. 'Alston, this is all a little weird. You're not here because there's trouble with the phone lines.' Her tone was unabashedly patronizing.

Bouchard said, 'You'd just as well take a seat, Mrs Swift.'

'Alston, please just tell me what it is you have to say.'

'I'd still feel better,' he replied uncomfortably, 'if you'd set.'

Sal heard the small wheeze of a fountain stool as Noel complied. He could hear the constable breathing through his nose. 'Alston, what is it?'

'You know Eliot Wicker—'

'Of course.'

'Well, his body turned up today.' Bouchard made a soft grunt, or a cough, and then added, 'Passed on.'

There was a beat of silence. Then Sal heard Noel say, with no discernible emotion, 'Alston, that's terrible. Eliot, dead? How?'

'Won't know for sure until the autopsy. Got the medical examiner up there now. Killed, you'd have to say, by the looks of it.'

More silence. Sal heard Noel slide off the stool.

'Mrs Swift, I wouldn't get up just yet.'

'I'm okay, Alston.' She was walking toward the front door. 'Killed, like murdered?'

'I guess you were the last person he called.'

'Did he call me?'

Bouchard cleared his throat again. 'I went over there, to his place. When I pushed the redial button on his phone, it rang over here. That's how you happened to answer when I...'

'And you recognized my voice,' Noel said. 'That's very clever, Alston. I wouldn't have thought of that.'

'Just trying to...'

'But how did he – how was he—'

'Hard to say. But you don't recall him calling over here?'

Another period of silence. Sal heard a few deliberative footsteps. 'Did Eliot Wicker call me?' Noel said. 'Well, certainly for the funeral arrangements.'

'No, this would've been last night, after the funeral, after your reception. Otis Royal told me that Eliot called him about nine and told him to get the cemetery mowed today. The grass. So that means that Wicker had to call you afterwards. Sometime after nine.'

'God, let me think who I talked to . . . after the reception. What I'm thinking, Alston, is that if he had tried to call me and my line was busy, my number would still be the last one his telephone remembers, wouldn't it?'

'I believe so.'

'Because, Alston, I'm sure I didn't talk to him last night. I mean, I don't know why he would want to call, unless to check up on me after the funeral. Maybe it's customary. Maybe he dialed my number by mistake and then hung up before the phone rang.'

'Maybe.'

'The phone company has records, don't they?'

'Not local calls,' Bouchard said. Then he cleared his throat again. 'I know you're closed up, Mrs Swift, but my flashlight died tonight, the batteries, 'course I'd pay you first thing in the morning, if it's not . . .'

'No trouble at all.'

He heard Bouchard walk toward the front of the store, stop, and then come back. 'Four ninety-seven, I think it says.'

'Pay me tomorrow, don't worry,' she said.

Sal heard the constable take a deep breath. 'Mrs Swift,' he said with palpable discomfort, 'I've just got two more things—'

'Oh, Alston, could it wait?'

'I'm just going to tell you both things before I go, once you set.'

Sal heard Noel sit down again, with a sigh. It was a nervous sound, cut with irritation. 'Alston, what?'

'Eliot Wicker's body,' Bouchard said carefully, 'was in your husband's grave. And your husband's body is missing.'

For a few moments neither of them spoke. Sal recalled the clipped conversation among the school board as he and Iris had entered; and later, the police car rushing into the cemetery.

'So,' Noel began, and then she stopped. 'Alston, I don't understand. Bobby's body – missing where?'

'These are the things I'm trying to determine. Like why he might have wanted you.'

'Who?'

'Eliot Wicker, I mean.'

'But I told you, I didn't talk to him.'

Sal didn't like the constable's insensitivity, or the way he seemed to be pressing her.

'But why he was trying to call you,' he said, and then the front door opened and he started to leave, his voice moving away. 'I'm just trying to figure these things...'

Noel stopped him. 'Alston, you must have some idea where Bobby is. His body—?' Sal could hear peepers singing down at the river.

'You didn't expect him to come here for anything.'

'Eliot? No, I told you that. But what was there – I mean, besides Eliot – in the grave? Just ... Eliot?'

Bouchard hesitated. Sal heard him breathing through his nose. 'Funny thing. Not *funny*, just...'

'Alston – What?'

A beat. Then: 'Well, the circumstances.'

'God.'

'Investigators are there now, medical examiner, whatnot, going over the crime scene. Probably a detective will be down to see you in the morning.'

'Thank you, Alston.' Sal heard the door close. Then open again.

'Mrs Swift, I should tell you also...' The constable sighed uncomfortably. 'The police notify insurance companies in a case like this, with unusual circumstances. Anything unusual they don't like to pay, not until things get resolved.'

There was a pause. Then Noel responded, 'I can understand that.'

'But you let me know if there's anything you think of...'

'I will, Alston. Thank you.'

Sal heard the door close again, and a moment later the car door closed and the engine started. Noel walked back toward the stockroom. 'Stay down,' she said. Red lights from Bouchard's taillights appeared, then the brighter red of his brake lights, and then he was gone, just the sound of his car going away.

Sal buttoned his trousers and made his way into the stockroom and down the aisle, where he found Noel standing by her desk, lost in thought. Miles's trumpet, barely audible, was picking out a deliberate, sultry melody. The fan was humming. Sal wasn't sure whether to touch her or not. He realized that he still had her red panties in his hand, and he didn't know what to do with them. What was equally on his mind was Eliot Wicker's death and Bobby's missing body. And the half bottle of Stoli on the desk – and how badly he wanted another drink.

'You have to go,' she said, turning toward him. Seeing her panties in his hand, she took them from him and set them on the desk. When she turned back to him again, it was with an odd, vulnerable look that he'd never seen from her before.

'Are you gonna be okay?' he asked her.

She shook her head, looking like she was about to cry. 'Oh, Sal, I don't know what you think of me,' she said, 'that maybe I should go around in a veil, that I'm selfish, I'm self-centered, I'm vain . . . I don't know what you think of me.' She breathed a sigh that seemed filled with self-abomination. 'You were his best friend,' she said. 'I know he told you.'

'Told me. What?'

'He told you everything. He trusted you.' Noel's eyes were all over Sal. 'The other night, when you were out together?'

Sal shook his head dumbly.

She looked away. 'Sal, I was leaving him.'

He stared at her, searching for words, but none came.

She met his eyes again and nodded her head, confirming what she had said. 'We were getting divorced.'

Shaking his head in disbelief, Sal leaned back against the support post. 'He didn't tell me.'

And there it was. He could have helped Bobby. He realized that now. Under the bridge that night – *Sally, who do you trust?* It was what Bobby had come to tell him, that she was leaving him.

'Are you okay?' she asked.

'Yeah,' he answered, though it was a blatant lie.

'Come on,' she said, leading him around the wall of boxes. At the main aisle, they walked through the semidarkness to the back of the stockroom, where Sal had entered. Noel opened the door and turned on the stairwell light, and they descended the stairs in silence. At the landing they turned down a few more stairs until they emerged in the back of the garage, where the air was cooler and the room flickered with lightning from outside.

Noel refrained from turning on the overhead fluorescents. The stairwell shed enough light so that when they turned around the partition they could see the cars: Noel's black Volvo; Bobby's black Corvette on the other side. His old black Harley leaning on its kickstand behind the cars. The sight of the bike hit Sal like a dull shock, almost as if the machine were waiting for Bobby to return.

Noel seemed to sense it. 'He loved that thing,' she said, walking over to it, running her hand over the seat. Sal walked behind her. Another flash of lightning lit the room – flickered on and on, not wanting to die. She turned to him. 'He'd want you to have it,' she said, and she pressed a single key into Sal's hand. He looked at the key, took a sudden, reflexive breath. Moving away from her, he walked to the entry door, saying, 'I'll come back for it tomorrow.'

'Sal?'

He opened the door. She caught it.

'Sal, wait.'

He stood there shaking his head. 'I should never have come over here tonight,' he said.

'Take this,' she told him. He turned around and saw her taking a leather riding jacket off a hook. Bobby's. She draped the jacket over his arm. The leather was heavy. Its smell was Bobby's smell, and Sal felt another tug of sadness, of shame. 'Take it,' she said. 'It's going to storm tonight, and you may be sleeping in your car.'

He took the jacket from her and then saw the Stoli bottle in her other hand. 'You might need this too,' she said. 'It could be a long night.'

He shook his head. 'I don't need that,' he told her, as a long, distant thunder rolled overhead.

They looked out the door into the darkness. They could hear big drops of rain splashing lazily in her swimming pool. She took hold of his T-shirt, raised her face and kissed him on the mouth. He broke the kiss, his mind racing with misgiving. She kept hold of him.

'Sal?' she said softly.

He met her eyes longer than he had intended.

'Bobby's gone,' she said, and then he stepped out into the night.

7

The northwest corner of the cemetery was awash with lights: car headlights, portable floodlights, camera flashes – so much light that the lightning in the sky, which was becoming more frequent, might have gone unnoticed if not for the accompanying thunder.

TV news reporters and cameramen, along with print journalists, rimmed the yellow police tape that surrounded the empty grave, interviewing a large, steel-haired man in a cheap checkered blazer, a machine of a man. Inside the restricted area, two evidence techs in light blue lab jackets worked under a pair of tripod floods powered by the tall silver van parked nearby, the mobile crime lab. One man worked inside the grave; the other worked above, sifting the dirt through a wood-framed screen. Off to the side sat the mahogany casket, along with the scuba tanks and an assortment of grocery bags, pillboxes and tins.

The coroner's vehicle, a green Bronco emblazoned with the words STATE OF MAINE, was backed close to the grave with its liftback opened enough to allow the cameras a shot of the stuffed white plastic bag in the back, the undertaker's body. On the gravel drive to the left of the grave, parked behind the crime van, were two state police cruisers and a new, highly polished black Cherokee. A dozen other vehicles lined the road behind them, on down the hillside.

Alston Bouchard registered all of this as he wound up the terraces in his yellow Subaru wagon. When he spotted a space in the line of cars too small for a car to fit, he drove his car through and pulled onto the lawn. Some heads turned. He shut off his lights and engine.

The detective being interviewed was Murdoch, the troop sergeant from CID 3, out of Orono. Bouchard knew enough about Murdoch to know that he was here for the cameras. Somebody else would be leading the investigation. Bouchard's eyes caught another detective crossing to the grave site, a man in his thirties with dark hair and a neat mustache. A couple inches over six feet, he was dressed in a well-fitting beige suit, and he carried an instrument slung over his shoulder, a plastic box of some sort, same color as the suit. A computer, Bouchard guessed, or tape recorder.

The downpour started suddenly, as if the miles of clouds overhead had all opened at once. The rain was blinding. A floodlight flickered with surprise, the sergeant turned abruptly and marched off toward the cars, and the newspeople scurried for their vehicles. Activity at the grave hastened too. The two lab men quickly unfurled a blue tarpaulin over the hole, a trooper threw another tarp over the casket, and the lab men hurried their bags and boxes of evidence into the silver van.

The well-dressed detective who seemed to be in charge was in no such hurry. Pulling a blue poncho over his suit and hunching over the plastic box he wore (but otherwise ignoring the rain), he swung a leg over the barricade and went in close to the casket, raised a corner of the tarp, squatted down and ran his hand along its lid.

A trooper approached the detective then and pointed toward Bouchard's car. He was the on-duty officer who had initially responded to Bouchard's call, a young, close-shaven mastiff named Lemieux. Spotting the constable, the well-dressed detective rose to his feet and, with a casual stride, came over through the rain. Bouchard thought he saw a smile under the man's mustache as he opened the passenger door and bent to look in. A lightning bolt scratched the sky, followed by a whack of thunder. The detective didn't wince. The rain, incredibly, began falling harder.

'Detective Shepherd, state police,' he said. 'You are?'

'I made the call.'

Shepherd's smile broadened. 'The town constable.' He took a small notebook off the passenger seat and tossed it on the dash, then sat inside Bouchard's car. As he shut the car door, he opened his poncho, exposing the plastic box he wore. He released the strap, set the thing on his knees and flipped open its monitor lid. It beeped. A computer.

'Alston Bouchard,' the detective read. 'Mister Bouchard, are you aware that you single-handedly managed to contaminate this entire crime scene?'

Bouchard looked out at the tarpaulin fluttering against the wind. The trooper, Lemieux, had already chewed him out for digging up the body. But that was a sharp reprimand, from one ex-marine to another. It was deserved, and Bouchard had accepted it, despite the trooper's youth (and despite the fact that it was Desert Storm lecturing Vietnam). Shepherd's admonishment, on the other hand, was laced with civility, harder to take.

'For future reference,' the detective continued, 'keep this in mind: Every time you go someplace, you leave part of yourself. By the same token, when you return, you always bring something back.' Shepherd raised his eyebrows, studied Bouchard a moment to see if he understood, and then proceeded to take the constable's statement and enter it into the computer: the missing body, the found body, the heating pad hanging from the tree limb, the dead batteries inside the heating pad (Hi-Crown brand – which were stamped with the same expiration date as the Hi-Crown batteries that the Superette carried). Bouchard gave the detective the new pack. He told the detective that he had last seen Eliot Wicker on the night of Bobby Swift's funeral, and that the last telephone call made from Wicker's house was to Noel Swift's apartment. When Bouchard explained about checking the redial function on Wicker's telephone, Shepherd stopped typing.

'Mister Bouchard, under what authority did you enter the premises of the deceased?'

'He was dead, and I'm the constable.'

Shepherd sat for a moment. Then he turned to look at Bouchard, who elaborated: 'I discovered a basement window which was unlocked. I thought there might be an intruder. So I went in.'

Shepherd shook his head. 'I see. And what besides the telephone did you contaminate at that scene?'

Bouchard, still holding the steering wheel, raised both index fingers. 'I used a handkerchief.'

'A list, please. You touched—'

'Telephone, with a handkerchief.'

'Telephone.' Shepherd entered the information.

'Doorknobs in the bedroom, bathroom. Toilet seat and flush handle in the bathroom. Downstairs in the funeral home, doorknobs, light switches, screwdriver...'

Shepherd drew a tight breath through his nose. 'Why the toilet seat and flush handle?'

'Just...' Bouchard's thumbs flicked out.

'You were looking for what? Blood? Hair? Semen?'

'I had to relieve myself.'

Shepherd stopped typing again. 'You continued utilizing a handkerchief?'

'Not on myself.'

Shepherd raised his face, uncertain if this nearsighted bear beside him was joking. 'Mister Bouchard, is there anything I should know about what you found in Mr Wicker's house?'

'His parking lot lights were off,' Bouchard answered. 'I found a wire in the wall switch disconnected.'

'What do you mean, disconnected?'

Bouchard looked at the detective. 'It had come apart.'

'I mean, did the wire become disconnected because of an electrical malfunction? Or is it your opinion that somebody disconnected it?'

Bouchard flicked his thick wrist. 'Ripped off, I'd say. Being that the terminal screw was tight and there were a couple of broken strands still fastened to it, I'd say somebody...' He snapped his wrist again.

'Motivation?'

'To make the parking lot dark.'

Shepherd paused. The rain beating against the windshield turned briefly to hail, then back to rain again, ice flakes washing down. Through the glass Bouchard could see Trooper Lemieux approaching Shepherd's door with something in his hand. The trooper knocked once on the window, rain splashing off his huge shoulders. Shepherd rolled the window down. 'Anything else?' Still addressing Bouchard.

'About a half hour ago I visited Noel Swift – the widow of the dead man whose body is missing – to find out why Eliot Wicker might have called her. She said he didn't call.'

Shepherd turned to Lemieux, seemingly unaware that the grim young ex-marine was now being pelted with hail.

'Sir, we found this in the woods.' He held the penlight in a handkerchief. 'The batteries are dead.'

'Depth?' Shepherd said.

'Sir?'

'In the woods. How deep?'

'On the surface. On the ground.'

'We're not communicating, Trooper. How far into the woods from the edge of the lawn?'

The hail came down harder. The trooper shouted as if to keep from shivering. 'No more than fifteen feet. No less than twelve.'

Shepherd folded down the top of his computer, then he opened the car door. 'Constable, you've been a big help.' Pulling the poncho over his head and hunching over his computer, he ducked out the door, then turned back and added, 'But do me a favor. Leave the investigative work to the detectives, and I promise we'll be out of your town before you know it.' He threw the door shut, then he and the trooper headed for the silver van.

Bouchard leaned over, rolled down the passenger window and called out. 'The batteries in the flashlight—'

The trooper turned.

'Hi-Crown?'

Chain lightning webbed the sky, followed by a series of thunder. The trooper said something to Shepherd that appeared to be affirmative. Shepherd raised a hand, a wave.

'We'll sign you up at the academy, Constable.'

Noel waited until Sal drove away, and then she locked the door. Standing there in the dark, an undeniable heaviness had descended over the building, a disquieting silence. Sal had told her that the door had been unlocked when he'd arrived. Yet it was always kept locked. Had she unlocked it earlier when she went out? A fear came over her, a fear of carelessness, of things gone wrong. It made her feel terribly small in this dark little corner of the garage.

Bobby—

Had he escaped? Smashed out of his coffin and then burrowed

his way up? She listened to the room around her . . . much too quiet down here, even with the rain and wind and thunder. Had he gotten out somehow and taken his revenge on Wicker? She looked around the dark garage, from his low Corvette over to the door of his workshop and gym, to the stairway partition, keeping her hand on the doorknob, ready to run out into the night if any shadow should jump. And then she stopped herself, forced the fear from her mind and formed a singular, comforting image: Bobby underground, closed in the casket, packed with almost five feet of earth on top of him. Tons of solid blackness. He could not have escaped.

Then where was his body? (And who had killed Eliot Wicker?)

Unless *someone else* had dug Bobby up. Wicker? No, Bobby would never have schemed with the likes of him . . .

Sal—

No, if Bobby had confided in Sal, and Sal knew Bobby was alive, he never would have made love to her. Unless—

An image invaded her thoughts: Bobby, teeth filled with gravel, laughing maniacally, clawing his blind way to the surface.

No! She needed to relax, to calm her mind.

Despite the heat, she thought of soaking in a hot, deep bath. And that's what she resolved to do, all she would allow herself to think about as she turned from the door and made her way around the partition, climbed up the stairs to the second-floor landing, where she stepped once again into the overwarm stockroom.

Turning off the stairwell light and then barring the heavy door behind her, she headed down the center aisle of cartons toward the green-lit ceiling, making the right turn to her desk. There was a wide oak door just beyond the desk that opened on her private stairway, and that was her singular focus now: her stairway, her apartment, her bath.

She unlocked the door and opened it, then flicked on the wall switch, lighting the lavish stairway from high above. Noel's staircase was undoubtedly the most expensive piece of carpentry in town: eighteen treads made of thick African zebrawood, four feet wide and highly polished. Railings of ebony gleamed like black glass as the stairway curved gracefully around to the left. The walls were papered in a rich jungle motif, a pattern of lush fern and fanleaf over smoky yellow.

After a year and a half in Maine, when Bobby still hadn't instigated the Plan, he had hired carpenters from Bangor to build the staircase for her – at a quarter the cost of the entire property. It was unabashed extravagance. After all, they already had two sets of stairs in the building: one in back (which wound two flights from the garage to the apartment's kitchen) and another in front (which led from behind the counter up to the living room). Noel's private staircase was her price for Bobby's procrastination. After a fourteen-hour workday in the store, hearing about this one's arthritis, this one's divorce, that one's delinquent twins – Noel would enter her staircase, shut the door behind her, and her world would be instantly transformed: rich, comfortable and quiet.

Now it was too quiet. Or not quiet enough. She held her breath, trying to *hear* – what? A breath not her own, the tick of a floor board, the rustle of a sleeve. But all she could hear was the humming of the condenser motors from the back of the store and the rain beating all around the building, crawling up the shingles. The steady collapsing of thunder could have been the footsteps of someone trudging across the floor above her, undead.

'Don't.'

She said it aloud to herself, and her own small voice chilled her. *Bobby was dead.* She had been there at the cemetery, removing the evidence at the same time she should have been digging him up. There wouldn't have been enough time for anyone to dig him up after she'd left. Neither had there been enough time before she had arrived – not under cover of darkness.

Bobby was dead.

She pulled the stairway door closed behind her, turned the small lock in the center of the knob. She took a calming breath, then turned and looked up her zebra staircase, let its wild opulence soak into her. Holding the railing, she climbed slowly around to the top, thankful to see her sturdy apartment door closed. Yes, she was alone. *Bobby was dead.* There was no one but her in the building. She took the key out of her skirt pocket and unlocked the door. Pushed it open.

The hallway was dark, as it should have been. She could smell the flowers, but that didn't help. She reached around the jamb and flipped the switch, lighting the long corridor that connected the living room on her right to the kitchen on her left; the light also creeping a ways into the short hall that stretched out ahead of her to the bathroom and her bedroom.

Up here the rain on the roof sounded like the low buzzing of bees. She closed the door behind her, locked it, then turned left and went past the study into the kitchen. Even before she flicked on the overhead light she could see that the room appeared as she had left it this morning – her juice glass on the dish drainer, upside down. She checked the back door and found that it, too, was locked. As she had left it.

She went back down the hall to the living room. Crossed to the front windows and lowered the venetian blinds, then turned on the floor lamp. She checked the front door. Locked.

Back down the hallway, she turned into the wing that led into her bedroom, stopped to flick on the bathroom light and peek in. Her logic returning, she went to the bathtub and turned the faucet, dialed the control to hot. As water pounded in the tub, she walked into her bedroom, made her way to her bedside lamp and turned it on. Going to the window, she pulled down the blinds, then took her green silk chemise off the vanity chair. She glanced in the mirror, checking the reflection of the room behind her, the doorway – as if someone might be standing there.

She realized it was tiredness that made her imagination act this way. She was exhausted – and wanted only to slide into her bath and quiet her overworked mind. She needed clarity.

She pulled off her top and tossed it into her straw laundry basket. She pinched the emerald studs off her ears and placed them on her vanity, then unzipped her denim skirt and dropped it to her ankles—

That's when she remembered her panties – she had left them on the desk in the stockroom. She thought of Bonnie True finding them in the morning and realized that she'd have to go back down and retrieve them.

She opened Bobby's dresser drawer and found his .22 revolver, the weapon he'd worn on his belt when he first opened the store. Then, pistol in hand, she went back down the corridor and opened the door to her staircase.

Her nakedness made her feel vulnerable, but the gun overcame that. Not that she was in danger, she told herself. It was playacting. So she turned on the overhead chandelier and aimed the pistol at the blind curve ahead of her, the maddening swirl of black-white-black, green on green. Playacting, she told herself, she would fire at the first thing that moved. The pounding of the bath water behind her diminished to a whisper as she descended the cool treads to the door. She turned the lock, pushed the door open.

Her shadow fell onto a wall of cardboard boxes in front of her. For a few moments she stood motionless in the doorway, her gun pointing out, her finger on the trigger ... listening. The desk was located behind the boxes. Beyond the boxes, the rest of the stockroom hovered darkly, quietly. Hang the fear, she had the gun. Brazenly, she stepped out of the stairwell and walked around the boxes. Reaching the desk, she felt in the dark for the lamp, slid her hand along its base until she found the brass switch, and turned it on. Her heart jumped. Green light in her face, blackness all around...

...her panties were gone.

Goose bumps skittered up her arms. She picked up the lamp, held out her gun and turned a circle, tossing light around. She hoped to see the red silk on the floor – but there was too much darkness, too much quiet. She felt a fierce constriction, as if the world were suddenly pressing in all around her, and she was suddenly petrified of being there alone, sandwiched between two dark, wide-open floors. Dropping the lamp on the desk, she turned back toward the stairs, clutching the gun. In a blur she was back inside her staircase and the door was locked. Standing there with a foot on the bottom tread, pressing the pistol against her forehead, she hoped the cold steel would revive her logic. Then she remembered her bath and hurried up the stairs into the corridor, locking the stairway door behind her.

She walked across the hall into the wing, turned into the bathroom. The thick steam from the bath was brightened by the overhead light. She swatted the air with the pistol, exciting the vapor while she made her way to the tub, where she reached in and turned off the water. Standing in the cloud, with her naked back to the door, she searched her mind and tried to account for each moment. Maybe she hadn't left her underpants on the desk. Perhaps she had grabbed them on her way upstairs and simply forgotten in the confusion. After the news from Bouchard, anything was possible. A heavy boom shook the house – she spun around with the gun, facing the door. Then caught her breath. Only thunder.

Forgoing her bath, she walked out of the steam, closed the door behind her and made her way to her bedroom. Sleep, she told herself, pulling the bedcovers down. Sleep was what she needed. Still clutching the pistol, she closed the door and dragged over her vanity chair to prop under the doorknob, then balanced a delicate teardrop perfume bottle on top of the chair so it would fall if the door were disturbed. She got into bed and switched off the light. Then, in the dark, she turned onto her side, laid her head on the pillow and aimed the pistol at the door.

Detective Shepherd drove home to his empty Bangor condo under a violent drumming, a stampeding on the roof of his Cherokee. Lightning strobed continuously in the night, laying stark the lone houses and rocky fields along Route 1A. He reached over beside him, felt the heating pad on the seat. It was warm.

He had left Trooper Lemieux guarding the grave site overnight and another trooper keeping watch at Wicker's Funeral Home. The crime lab boys from Augusta – Percy and Esterbrook – had taken a motel room in Ellsworth. Murdoch, the troop sergeant, had given interviews to the media and then gone home. Two years from retirement, Murdoch had said that he wanted to take an active role in this case, which meant that he smelled good press, maybe a promotion and fatter pension. Murdoch.

Shepherd tossed the facts over in his mind. A missing body. An undertaker murdered and planted in the missing man's grave, holding a gun, wearing scuba tanks. An embalming tool found in the casket...

The detective's mind spiraled outward: dead penlight in the woods, dead heating pad hanging from a maple tree – same dead batteries: Hi-Crown, from the missing dead man's store, same expiration date. With new batteries, the penlight shone bright and the heating pad was plenty warm. He didn't ask himself why the things had been discarded. This early in the investigation, premature reasoning could get you lost.

Shepherd, who had the highest solve rate in his troop, concerned himself with facts. Fact: one good penlight found in the woods, twenty to twenty-five feet from the grave, batteries dead. Fact: one hunter's heating pad hanging from a maple branch ten feet high, ten feet from the grave, batteries dead.

With facts, you didn't need reason. Facts created their own reason. Given enough facts, the truth would narrow and steepen, like the lines on a statistician's chart. Enough facts, and the truth would tell itself.

King's Boarding House was a sprawling, three-story wooden structure (originally a farmhouse, later a nursing home), now a last refuge situated on a road that led out of Ellsworth's municipal district but not far enough to escape the slight congestion of the town. Over the century that had passed since the building's construction, a small neighborhood had pressed in around it, ramshackle and poor.

Now in its old age, its tin roofs spilling the rain, the heavy old building looked like it was weeping in the night. A wooden fence on the left separated it from the tenement building next door. On the right, a chain-link fence contained a cinder-block auto body shop whose back lot was packed with junkers. A glaring security lamp on a freestanding wooden pole threw bluish light across the bone-white face of the boarding house, saturating it with a moonlike wash and harsh shadows.

Sal pulled into the boarding house lot, swung right, nose to the wire fence. Only one other car was parked there. He stepped out into the downpour, grabbed the leather jacket off the passenger seat – and then he felt the bottle in the pocket. Noel had left it for him. Stuffing the jacket under his arm, he opened the back door and out pulled his suitcase, then walked to the front porch.

The woman who finally answered the doorbell looked to be in her eighties, wearing a bathrobe and knit sleeping cap. Peering out the screen door, she popped the door open and handed Sal a key. 'Twenty-one E,' she said. 'Right rear. See me in the morning.'

He found the door on the right side of the building, back corner, out of range of the auto body security light. When he unlocked the exterior door, he entered a wallpapered stairwell that was overwarm and lit by a 100-watt bulb inside an antique wall fixture. Two white doors were situated on opposite sides of the stairwell. One had a black iron numeral 11 screwed to it; the other had a 12. Sal climbed the stairs and found an identical landing, with white doors numbered 21 and 22. He chose the one on the right, 21, looked for a lock, found none. He turned the glossy black knob and the door opened.

It was a kitchenette apartment with a studio couch against the right-hand wall. On the near side of the couch, a lamp stood on a low end table. Sal stepped in and found the lamp switch, turned it on, lighting the room. A black telephone and Bible shared the table with the lamp. He noticed a blonde wooden table in the corner of the room, on the other side of the couch. One wooden chair was pushed under the table. The only two windows in the room occupied the same wall, on either side of the couch. The windows were open six inches and propped on adjustable screens that did little to ventilate the room. In the terrible heat, the place smelled like its horsehair plaster had absorbed a century of piss, perspiration and medicinal vapors.

On the left-hand wall was a four-by-four closet made from birch paneling; beside it, a white three-drawer bureau. The closet had no door or curtain, just a pole with a single shelf above it. There was no television in the room, no radio. One framed picture hung on the wall above the couch – a sailing ship in a storm. On the far wall were two doorways. The one on the right led into a closet-sized kitchen, the one on the left, into a small bathroom.

Sal closed the door behind him, felt for a lock but found none. He carried his suitcase and jacket to the bureau, set both on top (hearing the knock of the vodka bottle), then went into the bathroom and urinated. He stripped off his wet clothes and hung them over two door hooks. Standing there undressed, sticky with chocolate and sweat, he could smell Noel on himself, and it made his heart beat. At the same time, a terrible longing was growing inside him, for Iris, for Davey. Images piled up: the cigarette-burned table, Davey practicing her piano, Iris curled on the couch studying...

He stepped into the shower, dialed the water to hot, as if to scald Noel's scent off of him. When he had dried off, he wandered back intothe main room and found himself at the bureau, picking up Bobby's jacket, his hand going in the pocket.

Sally, who do you trust?

He lifted the bottle out, gazed at the orange-bordered label. So she had stuck it in the pocket anyway. He thought of Eliot Wicker, murdered. Bobby's body, stolen. Now he felt even more jittery, wished he had a TV or a book, to occupy his mind. He put the bottle down.

He walked over to the couch and sat, then stood up again; lifted the front of the couch until a hinged metal frame unfolded in three sections, covered with a thin mattress. A sheet and thin wool blanket were already wrapped tightly around it. As if he could sleep. More than anything, he realized, he needed to talk to Iris. Everything had happened so fast. He sat on the bed and lifted the receiver off the telephone, then set the phone down again.

He went back to the bureau and uncapped the bottle, imagined the vodka flowing through its clear neck and into his mouth. But instead of drinking, he brought the bottle to the window, pushed up the sash. The adjustable screen fell out and fluttered to the ground. He reached the bottle out the window and flung it. He heard a hard smash in the auto body junkyard.

Next he reached behind him, grabbed the Bible off the night table. PLACED BY THE GIDEONS, it said. He turned to the window and threw the book too, heard its good pages flutter as it left his hand. On the same impulse, he grabbed the telephone, swung around and chucked it into the night, but the wire snapped against the windowsill, and he heard the phone knock against the shingles below him.

He shut the window on the wire. Stood there feeling tense and hot. Ran his hands through his coarse hair and took a deep breath, let it out. Weather the storm. In the morning he'd buy a newspaper and look for a job, an apartment. He returned to the bureau and unlatched his suitcase, intending to put his clothes into the drawers. But something—

It confused him at first, slick and black and serpentine, the way it draped across his underpants. He took one end in his hand and lifted it. Delicate, long, and lacy – a black silk glove. He brought it to his nose, smelled it. Noel's.

He remembered the funeral, the way the black lace had hugged her forearm. But how the glove had gotten into his suitcase . . . He lifted it until he felt some resistance; that's when he saw that its fingers had been stuffed into the fly of his jockeys. He thought at first that Noel had put it there for him, like she had left him the bottle – but then he realized that she couldn't have. He had packed the suitcase at home and left it out in his car while he was upstairs with her. He pulled the glove out of the fly, his mind too dulled to make sense of it. When the smell of her perfume came to him again, he stopped wondering altogether. He brought the glove to his bed and shut off the lamp, then lay down uncovered in the dark, holding the glove on his chest, listening to the rain beating on the roof, the thunder playing off in the distance, unable to lose that brutal, gnawing emptiness, yet all the while basking in the glow of her scent.

Eliot Wicker was Gravity's first murder victim in forty years, and he not only made the front page of the *Ellsworth American* and every other newspaper in the state, but he was also the lead story on the morning news.

From the minute the Superette opened, the store filled with the cigarette smoke and chatter of men whose numbers rose and fell like the tides, conferring about Wicker's death, Bobby's disappearance, and the police interviews that were going on in town.

Sal sat near the end of the counter, working on his third cup of black coffee. Wearing his usual brown corduroy jacket over a plain black sweatshirt, he didn't quite fit in with the regulars, but that was nothing new. He staked his spot anyway and watched the people who came and went, looking for that one loaded glance that might tell him who had gotten into his car and slipped the glove in his suitcase.

Newspaper writers and news teams from two Bangor TV stations had been in and out since the store opened, talking to Bonnie True, asking for Noel, conducting interviews with anyone who would talk to them. Photographers stopped by periodically to take pictures outside the store and ask questions or directions to the cemetery or to Eliot Wicker's funeral home.

Detectives had already taken statements from a number of

people – Wicker's neighbors and business associates, and anyone who frequented the Superette lunch counter in the afternoon, when Wicker took his tea. By nine in the morning Gravity, Maine, was teeming with intrigue, although not everyone was happy about it.

'Christ a'mighty,' complained Arthur Button (whose nickname was Belly), his 300 pounds sprawled over a fountain stool. 'Just because you're neighbor to a man don't mean you wanna kill him.'

'Don't feel bad,' Jerry Royal said, making a noisy entrance, 'I'm out of a job.'

A number of eyes fell on Jerry, who looked unusually spiffy this morning, wearing green double knit pants and a blue striped shirt with a wide white collar, remnants of vagrant leisure suits. On top of it all, his hair, which normally resembled animal fur, was combed straight down to his eyebrows. With a tip of his nose, he signaled Bonnie for his coffee.

'Looks like ol' Mister Royal's set to go dancin today,' Belly said to him. The two men had been archrivals since third grade, and they missed no opportunity to taunt one another.

'I just got the third degree, that's all, which I passed it with flyin colors,' Jerry replied. 'They're workin on the old man now.' Waiting for his coffee, Jerry rubbed the counter clean with his shirtsleeve, looked over at Sal with a twinkle. 'There he is,' he said, apparently feeling some camaraderie with anyone in trouble.

Sal slid his empty mug forward on the counter, caught Bonnie's eye. He was thinking that the caffeine might help relieve the temptation he felt to grab a bottle and go back to his room. Actually, he had too much to do. For starters, he planned to get Bobby's motorcycle and take a long ride down to Augusta, where he would close out his teacher's retirement account; last he knew, he had about eighteen thousand dollars accumulated. If there was a waiting period, he'd get a cash advance on his Visa card. He'd keep some for spending money, job-hunting funds – the bulk he'd give to Iris.

'Motive, means and opportunity,' the man next to him said. Sal had never seen him before. A salesman, by the shirt and tie, by the build. Pod-shaped and slovenly, the man did paperwork while he ate, his elbows sprawled all over the counter. 'A competent detective'd break this case in a day,' he added with his mouth full, then turned to Sal and lowered his voice. 'You seen the *wife?*'

'She's out back with the insurance man,' Belly answered.

The salesman muttered to Sal through the side of his mouth, 'There's a surprise.'

Sal gave the guy a look, and he noticed Alston Bouchard standing by the door. The constable looked away as if he had been watching Sal. Sal recalled Bouchard's visit the night before, wondered for a moment if it was Bouchard who had put Noel's glove in his suitcase.

'Yeah, well, I got another theory,' said Belly Button, but no one paid attention until he lowered his voice and stole a furtive look at the stockroom door. 'You all knew Bobby,' he said. 'What if – I'm speculatin, of course – but what if Bobby was never actually dead? What if he's pullin a fast one?'

The others at the counter looked over at Belly while a country song came on the radio.

'Oh, I just imagine,' Jerry Royal said, riding him. 'How in the hell do you fit that big fat head of yours so far up your ass?' The others chortled.

'Laugh all you want,' Belly said. 'We're talking about Bobby Swift. I wouldn't put it past him.'

Behind the meat counter, the stockroom door swung open and Noel came through. A white-haired man, small and well-dressed, followed her into the store, and she walked briskly ahead, as if she were trying to get away from him. 'Certainly the last thing we want at this time is to complicate your misery,' the man was saying.

As she led him past the lunch counter to the front door, Detective Shepherd opened the door from the other side. 'So you call just as soon as you hear anything,' the insurance man said. 'Okay then?'

Noel did not respond, but focused her attention on Shepherd, and the older man turned awkwardly to leave. Shepherd let him walk under his arm.

'You must be Mrs Swift,' he said. The detective's sympathetic smile froze under the look she returned. What he failed to realize – what most men failed to realize – was that Noel Swift looked at nearly all men the same way. Whether they were fat, balding, arrogant, shy, too young, too old, too smart, too stupid, rich, or not so rich – her eyes bathed them, from head to toe and back again. For most men it was the sort of insomnia-provoking look they hadn't seen from a woman since they were twenty-five.

'Ask away,' Jerry said to the detective. 'Got half the town here now, you might get lucky.'

Shepherd ignored him.

'Any leads, Detective?' Belly Button asked.

'Just gathering facts at this point.' Shepherd gave the store a quick once-over, briefly running his eyes across Sal's. 'Is there someplace we could talk?' he said to Noel.

Without a word, she led him between the lunch counter and the candy case, then opened the door to the front stairs. Holding the door while he went up ahead of her, she glanced back and then went through. It was the kind of fleeting look that nobody in the place would have noticed, except Sal – full and right on target. He slid off his counter stool, stood and pulled two dollars from his pocket.

'If you're here for the motorcycle,' Bonnie said to him, and then nodded at the stockroom door, 'go on back, you know the way down.'

Sal tossed the bills on the counter. When he checked behind him, he saw that Alston Bouchard was watching him again.

Before Noel had unlocked her apartment door, the detective began his folksy interview: 'Smells like good coffee down there. I understand Eliot Wicker was a regular customer.'

'There are five or six of them,' she answered, pushing the door open and letting him in. Shepherd squinted at the brightness, the morning sun shining through the front windows, lighting the jungle of vegetation in the room.

Noel stood behind him, her arms folded. As much as she had to hide, she felt relieved in a way to have the detective up here with her.

'This'll only take a minute,' he said. 'I just need to verify some facts.' He gestured to the couch and said, 'May I?' She nodded, and he walked over and sat down, set his computer on the coffee table beside a glass vase of red tulips.

He withdrew from his suit pocket a small photo in a plasticine holder and held it out to her. 'Ever see him in your store?' he asked.

Noel came over and took it from him, a picture of a man who could have been anyone.

'Who is he?' she said.

Shepherd smiled pleasantly. 'Actually, I was hoping you could tell me.'

She handed back the photo. 'Detective Shepherd, do you suspect that I murdered Eliot Wicker?'

He scowled. 'Why would you ask that?' he asked, taking the plasticine by the edges and slipping it back in his pocket.

'You just fingerprinted me.' Her eyes remained on his, unflinching.

Shepherd winced. He had an expressive face, and he used it well. He took a breath as if to speak, then paused as Noel turned away from him, went to the front window and parted the curtains, allowing the full sunlight in.

He turned on the couch to face her. 'I want to be clear,' he began. 'We never suspect anyone until we've assembled and analyzed a preponderance of incriminating facts. At the same time, we cannot overlook anyone as a possibility: you, your customers, even your own town constable—'

'He suspects me.'

Shepherd smiled. 'To the novice, first clues can be difficult to forget.'

'Is that a computer?' she asked.

Shepherd opened the lid, and the monitor lit. He punched a couple of keys. 'Actually, it's a simple program I wrote myself. I feed it information, and it cross-references. If I want to check a name, or a word – like "batteries," for example' – he entered the word – 'see, two references already.' He looked up at her.

She looked right back at him. 'So it's a computer,' she repeated.

He smiled again.

He was single, she could tell by the careful way his dark mustache was groomed – a little overdone on looks. When he was younger he'd probably managed to bed every man-crazy girl who'd ever laid eyes on him, and some who weren't so crazy. But something in his face told her that his confidence had been uprooted. She turned away from him again, looked out the front window, down onto her parking lot.

'Mrs Swift, do you recall if Eliot Wicker telephoned you the night he was murdered? Speaking of first clues.'

Noel sighed, kept her back to him. 'Mr Wicker did not telephone me, despite what our local constable cares to believe.'

'I'll put down no. And, again, Mister Bouchard has nothing to do with this investigation. Were you home that night, to the best of your recollection?'

'Yes.'

'Was there anybody here with you who could verify that?'

Her face turned quickly, sideswiped by the sun.

Shepherd nodded contritely. 'Sorry,' he said. 'Sometimes my mouth works faster than my brain.'

He'd been hurt recently, Noel guessed, by a woman who had outgrown him.

'Did your husband have anybody who was mad at him, someone who might want to humiliate him?'

Noel shook her head. On a table under the window, beside a vase of gladiolas, stood a four-by-six photo in a plain silver frame. She picked up the picture and reached it halfway to Shepherd. He stretched his arm over the back of the couch to retrieve it.

'Everybody loved Bobby,' she said. 'That's him on the right.'

Shepherd examined the photo, a picture of Bobby and Sal standing beside an overturned wooden canoe, their arms around each other.

'Brothers?' Shepherd asked.

'Hm? No, that's Bobby's best friend, Sal Erickson. Sal lives in town.'

'He was downstairs at the counter when I came in.'

'Mm-hm.'

Shepherd looked at the picture, shook his head sadly. 'So young. How old was Bobby?'

'Thirty-three.'

'If you don't mind, I'd like to borrow this. It may help to identify your husband . . . if the body turns up.'

Noel said nothing.

Shepherd laid the frame beside his computer. Hesitated a second, then said, 'I have to ask, I apologize. Any infidelities, either of you? Wondering who might want to embarrass him.'

Noel shook her head.

'What about Eliot Wicker – any enemies that you know of?'

She shrugged. 'One, apparently.' She turned to the window again and looked down at the lot, where Alston Bouchard was still talking to the insurance man.

'Your insurance agent?'

Noel turned. Shepherd's mustache straightened. 'We bump into each other from time to time. He probably came to tell you that they're withholding payment until the case is solved.'

'That's right.'

Shepherd showed her his sympathetic smile again. 'Insurance companies are wonderful, in theory.'

She watched him carefully. His identity was wrapped up in his work, she concluded. He was dangerous.

'While we're on the subject, do you know offhand how much Bobby's policy was worth? Again, I hate to ask, but we have to in cases like this.'

Noel turned back to the window. 'In cases like this?'

'I hate to ask.'

Down on the lot, the insurance man drove away, and Bouchard looked up at the window. 'Twenty-five thousand dollars,' she said, turning back to Shepherd.

A minute pause betrayed the detective's surprise. Typing the figure in his computer, he said, 'That's not very much.'

'Not enough for murder,' she answered, looking straight at him.

They videotaped everything. While Shepherd went through the kitchen, entering fact after fact into his computer, the detectives and lab men from Augusta pored over every inch of Eliot Wicker's home and business. With powders and lifters, they dusted doorknobs, drawer handles and tools. With a laser light and Luminol, they went over the upstairs floors and utensils, looking for blood that was both fresh and Wicker's type. The feeling was that Wicker may have been murdered at home by somebody he was familiar with, then transported to the cemetery later.

But no one said that, at least not to Shepherd. They were here to gather facts, not conjectures. Facts: the torn wire in the switch box, the scuba tanks strapped to Wicker's back, the penlight and heating pad, the dead batteries. Every piece of evidence labeled and boxed in the crime van, along with the plasticine envelope Noel had handled and similar envelopes that bore the fingerprints of everyone else Shepherd had interviewed so far.

The detective looked through the refrigerator, through the cupboards, through the dishwasher – and there he found something curious: a pair of champagne glasses, side by side. He removed them with his handkerchief. He recalled seeing an unfinished bottle of champagne in the refrigerator; he carefully took the bottle out and pulled the cork to check for carbonation. He put his nose to the lip and sniffed.

That's when Sergeant Murdoch came in from the dining room, smoking a cigarette. 'Wait'll you're off duty,' he said.

'Wicker lived alone,' Shepherd answered. 'Two champagne glasses suggests he had company.'

Murdoch snorted. 'You're the boss.' He ran the back of his hand across four black garments that hung on the wall. 'Snappy dressers, these morticians,' he said, poking a brown cap.

The only thing worse than having the sergeant along when you were leading an investigation was working for him every other day of the week. A twenty-year veteran of Chicago's finest, Murdoch had taken an early retirement in 1975 after receiving his second suspension for excessive force, and then moved to Maine, where he was hired as a sergeant because of his vast experience. From then on, there wasn't a detective in the CID who didn't look forward to the day that Sergeant Murdoch earned his second pension.

'I want to take an active role in this one,' he had told Shepherd. 'But I won't interfere. You're the primary. You give the orders, I'll do what I'm told.'

In the hour since he had arrived, Murdoch had spent his time second-guessing Shepherd at every turn, second-guessing the lab men and generally hindering the investigation. 'Ask me, we're wasting time here,' he said to the detective now as he washed his cigarette down the kitchen sink. 'We should be out canvassing the townspeople, stimulating that little-known truth serum they call adrenaline.'

As Shepherd filled out an evidence tag and boxed the champagne glasses, the basement door opened, and Alston Bouchard came through, accompanied by Percy, the lab's fingerprint man. The constable had a grocery bag in his hand.

'Grizzly Adams,' Murdoch murmured, loud enough for Bouchard to hear.

While they watched, the constable walked over to the breakfast island, turned the bag upside down on the countertop, then lifted the bag, unveiling a can of Sprucewood Brewery pale ale, upside-down.

'Good morning, Constable,' Shepherd said, handing the fingerprint tags to Murdoch for his initials. 'I see you have a can of beer.'

'It's from the back of the cooler,' Bouchard explained. 'In the store. I'd be interested to know if the fingerprints on it match the prints on the batteries or the diving tanks.'

Murdoch folded his arms in front of his chest, looked off at nobody in particular. 'This must be the local gendarme who was so much help at the crime scene.'

Bouchard said, 'Bobby Swift stocked the beer cooler, and Sprucewood doesn't sell that fast. The cans in back would still have his fingerprints.'

Shepherd took his pen from behind his ear and pulled the beer can toward himself. 'Bobby Swift's fingerprints. What are you conjecturing, Constable?'

Before Bouchard could answer – if he intended to at all – another of the lab men, Esterbrook, entered the kitchen from the hall. Tall and bent like an iced sapling, he wore latex gloves and a lab jacket, and he carried a slender green tank. 'This was under the bed,' he said, holding the tank carefully, as if it were some freakish infant.

'Green's oxygen,' Percy said. 'Probably did some welding.'

'Yeah, right, under his bed,' Murdoch answered.

Puzzled, Esterbrook said, 'It's full. Brand-new.'

'Any markings?' Shepherd asked. 'Company name?'

Percy shook his head.

'See if he's got any welding equipment downstairs.'

'He wasn't . . .' Bouchard said. His thick wrist rotated back and forth. 'A welder.'

'I didn't see any torches or rods,' Esterbrook said. 'We've been all around.'

'It was under his bed!' Murdoch told them, flabbergasted. 'Who welds in their bedroom? Jesus Christ, you country boys – he got off on it! *Think!'*

Sal logged almost three hundred miles on Bobby's Harley that first day, drove down to Augusta on Route 3, then up to Bangor on 95, across to Ellsworth and back to Gravity. It was a beautiful piece of machinery, a 1984 FXRT, basic black and chrome, tough and gutsy. With his inexperience and the frost heaves on the country roads, Sal took it slow going down. But coming back on the highway he averaged seventy-five, passing every car he encountered. At that speed the cold wind numbed his face, but Bobby's thick jacket kept his blood warm. He wore sunglasses more for the insects than the brightness. Racing across the spruce and birch plains, assailed by the season's first blackflies and every emerging springtime fragrance, he felt energized for the first time in days, momentarily liberated from his vodka cravings.

He got back into town in the late afternoon, drove slowly through the village, past the store and the firehouse and on to the health center, a facility housed in a former Baptist church.

Iris, standing behind the glassed-in counter, wearing a dark blue sweater over her uniform, didn't look up until Sal was halfway across the waiting room, and then she looked longer than she had intended. Other people in the waiting room seemed interested too. Gone was Sal's customary corduroy sportcoat, replaced by the leather jacket. In place of his corduroy slacks, he wore stiff black jeans and black, square-toed workboots. His hair was windblown from riding, his face dark and windburned. He didn't remove his shades until he reached the window.

'I didn't think you'd want me to come to the house,' he said, keeping his voice down. 'I brought something for you.'

'Sal, could we not do this here?' she replied. Her voice was as neutral as could be.

'It was that Librium,' he told her, just as matter-of-factly. 'I never would've taken a drink the other night if it wasn't for that.'

Iris looked past him. 'Eleanor?' she said, and an elderly woman rose out of her chair. 'Through that door, dear. Doctor Moody will see you.'

After the woman had walked out of the waiting room, Iris looked back at Sal, losing her smile.

'You're not going to give me a break, are you?' he said.

She replied evenly, 'Sal, I told you what I want.'

'You want me gone.'

She did not reply.

'Okay,' he said. He pulled a folded bank check out of his pocket, slid it through the opening in the glass. 'It's sixteen thousand dollars, my retirement, minus a couple of thousand to hold me over till I find a job.'

The check remained between them, untouched.

'Take it. I've got a call in to the teacher's placement office. They're sending me a list of openings.'

She sighed, lowered her voice. 'We can talk about this on Sunday, when you come to get your things.' As she spoke, the phone rang, then stopped ringing, and presently a young woman in a white blouse and blue plaid skirt opened a door behind Iris. 'Mrs Potter, wondering about her mammogram,' she said.

'The lab hasn't called yet,' Iris told her. 'I'll check with them in a few minutes and get back to her.' She turned back to Sal, unflinching.

He looked through the glass at her. 'Iris, I'm not drinking,' he said. 'I'm over that.'

The way she looked at him, the way she sighed. She looked around behind her, then turned back to him. 'Sal, I went to the courthouse in Ellsworth this morning. I picked up the forms to start the proceedings.'

She avoided the word 'divorce,' but his heart fell anyway. He stood there nodding, knowing he should get out of there, when he heard the door open behind him and saw Iris's attention shift, her eyes brighten. He turned numbly to see Davey coming into the clinic, wearing her Gravity Bears T-shirt and oversized baseball cap, carrying her softball glove. When she saw Sal, she stared. The knees of her jeans were streaked with dirt, and her face was smudged.

Sal managed a smile, found his voice. 'Get a hit today?' He put his fists together.

She shrugged.

'You can sit down, love, I'll be a few more minutes,' Iris told her. 'We're going grocery shopping,' she said to Sal.

God, he wanted to go with them.

Davey walked to a section of the waiting room where there were toys on the carpet and a rack of children's books and magazines.

'Did you win?' Sal asked.

She nodded, not looking at him.

'Thata girl.' Feeling like a stranger.

He turned back to Iris, nudged the check through the opening in the window. 'Take it.'

Iris drew her hands back. 'Sal—'

He leaned closer to her and whispered, 'Do you know the things I've lost?' he said. 'Take the money. It means nothing to me.'

He turned away, back to Davey, who sat in a small plastic chair, her eyes pasted on a book. Sal could tell she wasn't reading. He noticed a man walk past the window over her shoulder. Sal recognized him, the detective who was investigating Eliot Wicker's murder. Sal went over to Davey and knelt in front of her, but she remained inside her book. He put his hands on her knees, rubbed the dirt off her jeans.

'I slid like you showed me,' she said, still not looking at him. Her voice was incredibly small, and it broke his heart.

'Oh,' he said in a low, hushed tone, 'I'm proud of you, honey.'

She lowered the book. Looked straight at him. 'Daddy, I want you to come home,' she said, utterly unconvinced that there could be any reason why they should be separated. It was inevitable, Sal knew, this confrontation, but he wasn't prepared just now.

'Honey—' He looked back as the detective came through the front door, glancing over. When Sal turned back to Davey, her eyes were full. He heard the detective at the check-in counter talking to Iris. He took Davey's hands in his, wiped dirt off her palm. 'Hug,' he said, but she wouldn't comply. He noticed, out in the parking lot, the yellow Subaru wagon beside his Harley, Alston Bouchard sitting behind the wheel, watching the clinic.

'Take me fishing,' Davey said.

'You want to go fishing?'

Her head went up and down.

Looking back, Sal saw the detective walking through a door to the examination rooms. He wondered why. He reached his hands under Davey's arms and picked her up out of her chair as he rose to his feet. She seemed heavier than he remembered.

'Okay, I'll take you fishing,' he said. He looked outside again, Bouchard still there. 'I can't today because you're going with Mommy. But this weekend, Sunday, I'll take you down the pool. We'll catch us a stringer full of schoolies. Maybe a big Atlantic salmon.'

Davey heaved a sigh.

'Can I have a hug now?' he said.

She looked at him, her gray eyes glassy, a cheek already tear-stained, and he felt his heart plummet. He lifted the cap off her head, and she buried his face against him. He heard her book drop on the floor behind him. He spread the fingers of one hand across her back, from shoulder blade to shoulder blade. He could feel muscles there, strong, durable cords he had never noticed before. All the muscles she would need. She would grow up without him.

Inside the small examination room, Detective Shepherd entered three new facts into his computer. 'You were the attending physician who signed Bobby Swift's death certificate?' he asked Doc Moody.

'That's correct,' the young doctor said. In his early thirties and overworked like everyone else at the understaffed clinic, he was an hour behind schedule and due to go home in a half hour. He washed his hands while he talked and didn't offer Shepherd a seat.

'And you recommended that no autopsy be done.'

'An autopsy wasn't necessary, in my judgment. It was clearly an M.I. Mr Swift had a bad heart. He knew it, we knew it. Everybody in town knew it. And he continued to smoke a pack and a half a day.'

'You examined the body and you have no question he was dead.'

Doc Moody looked over at the detective. 'Of course not,' he said.

Shepherd nodded. 'A routine examination then. Nothing out of the ordinary?'

Moody pulled a paper cup from its dispenser and filled it with water. 'Detective, I hope you understand. Our office manager and head nurse has recently decided to become a single parent, she wants to leave at five o'clock this afternoon, and she means business.' He gave Shepherd the sort of smile that a doctor can afford and then said, 'The examination was by the book.' He drank the water down, then crumpled his cup and dropped it in the wastebasket. 'Anything else?'

Shepherd looked over the monitor screen. 'Not today,' he said. He turned off the computer and closed the lid, then returned the doctor's smile. 'See, I promised it'd be painless.'

8

The parking lot was dark. A moonlit fog had risen up from the river and drifted across the bridge, and for the past two hours peepers down at the river had blanketed the night with their shrill song. At nine o'clock Noel had shut off her parking lot light and dimmed the inside lights. Now it was quarter past. Sal sat on his motorcycle watching through the front window, waiting for Bonnie to leave – but the woman didn't seem to be in any hurry, standing there in her robin's egg uniform, talking to nobody while she scraped the grill clean.

And here sat Sal astride his Harley like some dark prince of the night, the collar of his leather jacket up around his ears. He hadn't shaved in a day, and the shadow of his beard darkened him even more. He steadied the beast between his legs as he watched Noel come into view from one of the grocery aisles, wearing this cool, sleeveless melon green top over a short khaki skirt. She turned to speak to Bonnie—

'Can you drive?'

The voice deep in Sal's ear, he wheeled around. In the dark he could see only the wink of eyeglasses: Alston Bouchard – whose hand went to Sal's chest, just enough to ward off a rash response. The question remained. Could he drive?

'Why? You need a ride?'

'No, my car's over the firehouse. I just want you to get home safe.' Bouchard's thick lenses reflected the window light.

'I appreciate your concern,' Sal said to him. He got off his motorcycle, heeled down its kickstand and sat back against the seat. 'But I wasn't going home just yet.'

Bouchard peered at Sal through those glasses. He made a noise with his tongue, like he was cleaning his teeth. 'If I were you,' he said, 'I'd try to be realistic about the things I was risking.'

Sal studied the constable, as much as he could see him, and then the door opened and Bonnie came through. Stepping outside, she said goodnight to Noel and then turned to Sal and grabbed at her chest.

'Oh my dear God!'

'Bonnie, what?' Noel came to the door, a Pyrex coffee pot in her hand. When she saw Sal, her eyes sharpened – not conspicuously – more the way a cat becomes alert when something moves in the grass.

Bonnie left the doorway and walked across the parking lot, giving Sal one more look. 'Skulkin out here in the dark with his jacket on, you'll give someone heart failure,' she muttered. Reaching the hardtop, she turned right and then walked into the darkness. Bonnie and Herb True lived on the other side of the firehouse.

Bouchard turned to Noel. 'Didn't mean to startle you,' he said. 'I had a question, if you . . .' His hands moved inside his pockets.

Noel remained in the doorway, her bare legs set apart under her skirt. 'Guys, I'm so tired,' she said. 'Can it wait till morning?'

'It can wait,' Bouchard answered. 'But you remember the other night, after the funeral—?' He rocked from one foot to the other, as if he were about to turn and walk away – and then he sauntered over in front of her. 'Afterwards you had that little get-together upstairs . . .'

'I remember.'

'After everyone left, did you stay here or . . .' His pockets jumped.

She sighed. 'Alston, it's nice that you're trying to help, but wouldn't it be more effective if you worked with the police?'

Bouchard pulled a small notepad out of his pocket. 'Well, they go home every day at three-thirty, and I was just—'

'Really, I covered all of that with the detective this morning—'

'—wondering whether you stayed home the rest of the night, or maybe you went out for a drive . . .'

She closed her eyes. 'I told you, I have given all that information—'

'—being the night Eliot Wicker was killed—'

'*What are you accusing me of?*' She swung the coffee pot against the door frame, smashing it, then threw the handle at his feet. Sal pushed himself off his motorcycle. Bouchard stepped back. 'Not accusing, really, not trying to . . .'

Sal came over to Noel. 'I don't think he's accusing you—'

'*Everybody in this town is accusing me!*' she said, wheeling on him. '*You can't see that?*'

Bouchard backed toward the road. 'Anyway, you're upset and I'll let you alone now, but I'd think about' – he made a fist and turned it – 'locking your doors, at least until these things get . . .' He backed into the darkness the same way Bonnie had gone, and then his footsteps went sifting through the road sand.

'Accusing you of what?' Sal said to her.

She wouldn't look at him. He touched her arm again. She took a breath. Sal could tell she was listening to Bouchard's footsteps, and then so was he, relieved that the constable was gone. Presently a car door closed in the firehouse lot. The engine started and the headlights came on, then the small station wagon circled in the lot and came toward them. It passed the store slowly, hummed over the bridge. At the end of the road, it turned right. Sal waited until the sound of Bouchard's engine had faded.

'Accusing you of what?' he asked her again.

'Come out of the light,' Noel said, leading Sal past the windows, to the shadows where his motorcycle was parked. And there her hands went into his jacket pockets.

'What are people accusing you of?' he said, as he peered over her shoulder. His eyes sharpened. Down at the bridge—

'Sal, what?'

He stepped away from her.

Someone in the fog – a shape – sitting on the bridge rail.

'Wait a minute,' he told her, and he began walking toward the road, staring down at the fog.

'Where are you going?'

The figure seemed to stand, and then—

'Hey!'

Sal broke into a run, but now he wasn't sure what he was seeing, with the fog and the darkness and the vegetation surrounding the bridge. The closer to the bridge he got, the clearer he could see the bridge railing and only the bridge railing. Whoever had been there (if Sal had actually seen anybody) was gone.

He stopped at the head of the bridge and listened for footsteps running over pavement but heard only the loud river rushing below. He walked onto the steel grid work, looking out toward the end of the road, the streetlight on the corner, the window lights of the facing house. Nothing moved. No dogs barked. In fact, it occurred to Sal that, despite the river noise below his feet, the night had become noticeably quiet.

The peepers. Down on the river, the peepers had stopped. Someone was down there.

He ran to the end of the bridge, swung around the low abutment and lowered himself down the steep, rocky furrow. He caught hold of a bunch of grass so he wouldn't fall, but when his foot could find nothing but a steep slide of gravel, he let go of the grass and slid the rest of the way on his hands and soles of his boots.

At the bottom, he stood perfectly quiet, turned his head to face downriver. He listened for footsteps, peered into the darkness for movement, but all he could hear was the river gurgling beside him like low laughter. All he could see were the hard, square shapes of the old bridge support standing out of the ground fog in front of him. He took two or three steps, until he came to the slab of concrete on which he and Bobby had sat the night before Bobby died. He stopped there, sensing something. A smell of fungus hit him, the dark odor of decay that misted up out of the rushing water. But it was more than the smell.

Something was happening.

He could feel it, a pressure mounting around his ears as if someone were creeping up behind him. He turned quickly, but saw no movement in the darkness. And now he wondered if the figure he had seen on the bridge was the thing Bobby had seen in the bog – or perhaps the thing the Passamaquoddies told about – how men were lured to the reversing falls and then haunted by their transgressions.

I trust Iris, he had told Bobby that night. *I trust myself*.

Motionless, he stared into the darkness, barely breathing. And then his eye caught a movement, a ghostly mist feathering its way up the river, coming steadily toward him…

He turned his head, saw the bridge looming solid and black above him, then looked downriver again, as the river mist softly blew apart.

Sally, who do you trust?

He turned and scrambled up the bank, clutched the bridge support and pulled himself to his knees, started to get to his feet—

—Someone standing in the fog above him, a stiff, tense shadow.

'Sal?'

Noel spoke his name softly, but her urgency was unmistakable. 'Sal, you're scaring me. What's wrong?'

'Nothing,' he said, standing, putting his arm around her and leading her quickly over the grating. 'Nothing, it's my imagination,' he told her as they began mounting the hill. He thought of telling her about the glove in his suitcase but decided against it.

They walked into her parking lot again, keeping to the shadows. 'Sal, did you see something?' she said.

'I don't think so,' he answered. 'But I don't want you staying here alone tonight.'

'I'm having a security system installed tomorrow and all the locks changed.'

'Good,' he said, 'but tonight I think you should come with me.'

She stopped walking. When she spoke, it was in a frail voice, almost a whisper. 'Sally,' she said, 'I'm so scared.'

He turned to look at her and then they were kissing, her arms going around him. His heart started up, his breathing became charged. It was unreasonable, almost unreal, he thought, that he could be doing this or feeling like this while the rest of his life was falling apart, but with her lips against his, the heat of her body radiating through his leather jacket, the heat of her legs through his jeans, he felt overcome.

'I'll take my car,' she said, breaking the kiss, and even her breath on his neck stirred him. 'I don't want anyone to see you bringing me back here in the morning.'

In the next minute they were walking together through the store, through the stockroom, turning off lights, locking doors behind them, hurrying down the stairs into her garage. Noel turned the overhead lights on, the stairway lights off. She opened the garage door with an electric switch on the wall, then slid into her Volvo. Sal got in the passenger side. She started the car and backed out, then turned on the headlights as she activated the remote switch that lowered the garage door. He watched her legs move as she clutched and shifted into first, the Volvo crawling up the incline beside the building until they were in her parking lot again. She stopped her car beside his Harley.

'I'll follow you,' she said.

'It's right in town,' he told her, opening his door. 'Turn right at the river, at the lights—'

Her breath caught sharply, stopping him.

'Noel, what?' Seeing her eyes riveted on her rearview mirror, he turned.

OHW

The letters were backward on the rear window, finger-streaked through a film of dust, catching the moonlight.

'God,' Noel breathed.

'Hold on,' Sal told her, climbing out of the car, 'it's nothing,' and he went around the back to wipe the window with his hand. 'Probably some kids in a parking lot somewhere—'

On the trunk, more words were smeared:

WANTS A CHOCOLATE KISS

'What is it?' she asked.

Sal stared, felt his legs weaken. 'Nothing,' he said again, even as he rubbed the trunk and window clean with his arm. He went back to the door. 'We're both a little shell-shocked,' he said. He locked the door before he shut it.

He swung a leg over his motorcycle and turned the key, gave the engine more throttle than it needed, feeling the shivering in his hands, trying to put out of his mind that on the other side of that storefront window was enough alcohol to stop his shivering for good, to warm him, to let him smile, to make him feel human again.

Noel followed him closely all the way to Ellsworth, making it hard for Sal to see anything but her headlights in his mirrors. When they had almost reached the boarding house, he waved her into the parking lot of the body shop so her car wouldn't be seen by the landlady (or anyone else), and then they walked quickly to the rear of his building. While he worked in the dark to insert his key in the lock, Noel kept her back to him, watching the street out in front, the starkly lit junkyard to her left, listening for any trace of furtive sound.

Sal threw the door open and they went into the bright stairwell, closed the door behind them. Noel gazed at the wallpaper, the light fixture, the enamel-white doors, and said quietly, 'You live in a museum.'

'You don't have to whisper, we're the only ones in the wing,' he said.

'I feel better whispering.'

'Up here,' he told her, and they took the creaking treads as softly as they could. At the landing, he went to his door and turned the black knob.

'There's no lock?' she said as he pushed the door open.

'The downstairs door locks,' he answered, going in. 'Wait here.'

With only the junkyard light through his windows lighting the room, he made his way to the bathroom, flicked on the light and looked inside, checked the space on the other side of the tub. 'If you need the john,' he said, coming back out and crossing to the opposite wall, verifying in a glance that the kitchen was empty.

'Somebody could be in one of the other apartments,' she said.

He smiled slightly, picked up one of the pair of wooden chairs from his table and carried it back to the entry door, wedged the top of the chair under the doorknob. 'We're safe now,' he said, joking, though his humor fell short of assuring even himself.

Behind him he heard the clatter of her lowering the window blinds. He walked around the bed to the other window, lowered those blinds too.

He took off his jacket. 'Listen,' he said quietly, 'who do you think had it in for Eliot Wicker?'

'Oh, Sal, I'd rather not discuss this now,' she told him.

He turned to toss the jacket on the bed and found her standing in front of him. Her arms went around his waist, her hands forced inside the back of his jeans. She kissed him open-mouthed, her fingertips clutching at his buttocks. His heart already drumming, Sal dropped the jacket on the floor. It was her fragrance, her wit, her confidence, her size and shape, the way she moved, the way she stood, the way she looked at him, the amount of pressure she exerted in holding him, the smell of her breath, the smell of her skin, the movement of her tongue, the way she pressed her body into his. And now they were about to sleep together, the two of them, warm and alone and naked through the long, dark night.

At the same time, Sal's head thrummed with misgiving: that in deepening his relationship with Noel, he was further distancing himself from Iris and Davey; that whoever had planted Noel's glove in his suitcase and written on her car window might well be the same one who had murdered Eliot Wicker. Equally unsettling was this vague notion that he knew something about Eliot Wicker that his mind was hiding from him, like a lost memory or a forgotten dream. It was almost as if he could solve the mystery if he could get his mind to cooperate. Pervading all these uncertainties was his alcohol craving, which by now had grown incessant, almost physical, like a buzzing inside him that he could not stop. As Noel's fingers worked around the front of his leather belt, she lifted her face to his.

'Stop thinking,' she told him.

He smiled. 'I don't think I can,' he said.

She pulled the belt through the buckle with a soft slap. As she stared at him, the leather came snakelike out of his jeans, one loop at a time. 'Then I'll have to make you,' she said, pushing him gently onto the bed.

Sal's chest jumped with a silent laugh as she crawled on top of him, laying him back.

'Wait, Noel,' he said. 'Hold on a minute—'

'I said stop thinking.'

'It's not that,' he told her, and then he breathed a sigh. 'I just don't know if I can do this sober.'

With his belt in her hands, she pushed his sweatshirt up to his chest, then bent to kiss his stomach, ran her lips up to his chest, sucked tenderly on his nipple. She stopped and looked up at him. Then, sitting up, she pulled her silk top up her stomach, past her breasts, over her head. Barechested, she looked down on him, eyes shining. Her nipples were dark and swollen. 'You don't think you can get drunk on me?' she asked.

Her hands flexed quickly, snapping the belt tightly between them.

He started to laugh. 'Noel, wait—'

She stretched the leather to his throat, pinning his head to the mattress. He took hold of her wrists.

'I don't think I heard you,' she said.

He turned his head slightly, to free his windpipe. She repositioned herself, staring down at him with the slightest of smiles, like he was something she had captured.

She lowered her face to his. 'You don't think I can get you loaded?' she breathed, the belt cutting into his throat. She bent lower and touched his upper lip with the tip of her tongue.

He felt his face engorging as his heart pumped harder.

'Let go,' she breathed into his mouth. 'Let go of my wrists.' He felt her warmth moving slowly down his stomach. His erection throbbed, reached past the band of his shorts.

Leering at him, she slid her legs further down his body, smooth and humid, until the head of his erection was immersed fully in her heat. That's where she stopped. When she spoke again, her voice was little more than breathing: 'I said let go, Sally. You have to trust me.'

Watching her eyes, he made his fingers open. The belt tightened on his throat.

'Put your hands down.'

Her shining, throbbing eyes. The studied expression on her face. He lowered his elbows to the bed.

'All the way.'

Feeling like his face was going to burst, his hands slid to her thighs.

All at once she released the belt and plunged into him, her tongue entering his mouth, his tongue finding hers. He pulled her roughly over him, pulled her against him until she gasped, and then he rolled on top of her, all the while tearing at her underpants, throwing her skirt to her waist until she was fully, blissfully open, and then needing to open her more, to delve into the deepest part of her, to drink her in.

Their sex was breakneck and explosive, and over in minutes. As they lay there entwined, breathless in the dusky stillness of the room, Noel freed herself, then slithered across his body until their eyes were aligned, and their mouths, her hair draping like a curtain around his face. 'Now,' she said to him, 'tell me you're not wrecked.'

Detective Shepherd was roused by his telephone. He stabbed in the dark to stop its ringing until he was awake enough to remember that there was no one else to awaken. He wasn't surprised to hear Murdoch on the other end.

'Are you screwing someone at the lab?' the sergeant said.

'What?' Four-thirty. Shepherd figured that someone had been murdered. But it wasn't his on-call week.

'We got your prints.'

Shepherd turned on the lamp. 'My prints – what do you mean, the Wicker case?'

'You must be blowing someone in Augusta. They stayed late, faxed in around ten last night. Dispatch just called me.'

'What prints? Where are you?' Shepherd grabbed the notepad he kept beside his bed; his pen. Time, date—

'The fingerprints on the beer can match the prints on the scuba tanks,' Murdoch answered. 'Plus they match the small oxygen tank we found under the bed, and the embalming tool, and every one of the batteries you sent down.'

'Wait a minute.' Shepherd stopped writing while he absorbed this. 'Bobby Swift, the missing corpse – his prints were on the beer can – on the scuba tanks too?'

'Yeah, and not only his. The undertaker's prints are on most of those same things – tanks, flashlight, embalming tool. Not the beer can, not the batteries.'

'But everything else.' Shepherd stepped off the wide bed and walked into the living room. 'Bobby Swift and Eliot Wicker,' he said. He lifted his computer out of his leather satchel, felt his heartbeat accelerating.

'Plus,' Murdoch said, 'they got Wicker's prints on one of those champagne glasses.'

'Yeah?' Shepherd returned to his bedroom, sat on the edge of the mattress and flipped open the lid of his computer. 'And Bobby Swift's on the other glass—?'

'Uh-uh.'

Shepherd stopped. 'Say that again.'

'Negative. Bobby Swift's prints aren't on the other glass – or the champagne bottle.'

'So whose prints are they?'

Murdoch didn't answer.

'Sarge, whose fingerprints are on the other glass?'

'What's your computer tell you?'

Shepherd sighed.

'Unidentified,' Murdoch said. 'No match.'

'Where are you?' Shepherd asked.

'In my car. I'll wait for you. Looks like we'll have to make some good old-fashioned human contact today.'

In the long, dead dark of morning, Sal opened his eyes. Flat on his back, not fully awake, he felt satiated and numb, completely at peace... But something about the silence, or the air pressure around his head, or the lack of air pressure – he knew that something had awakened him. He lay perfectly still, listening in the perfect darkness, the perfect stillness, and he became aware that someone was standing next to him, trying to remain just as still. Sal's heart started to beat. His urge to lunge into the darkness was tempered by a fear strong enough to keep him from even shifting his eyes. He did not alter his breathing. He knew precisely his situation: He was in his boarding room. Noel was in bed beside him. He was on the left side of the bed with his head toward the wall, and the lamp, which he wanted for a weapon, was on the other side of Noel. He listened for her breathing. He listened but could not hear her, could not hear a thing except the silent hum of pressure. Even outside the windows the town lay silent. He stopped his breath on an inhale, as subtly as he could. That's when he heard it – the bare rustle of cloth. He sprang out of the blankets, lurching across the bed for the lamp, flicking it on, lifting it by the base—

Noel—

Standing naked, holding his black jeans under her arm, his wallet in her hand. She squinted against the brightness, her orange hair scattered around her eyes. She pulled the jeans in front of her body, covering herself.

'What are you doing?' he whispered.

'What are you doing? You look like you want to kill me.'

He let out his breath. 'I must've had a nightmare,' he told her.

She pushed the wallet back in his jeans pocket. 'I stepped on your buckle coming back from the bathroom,' she said. 'When I picked up your pants, the wallet fell out.'

He stared; his belt was not in the pants.

'Or your zipper,' she said. 'I stepped on something sharp. Do you think I was stealing your money?'

'Of course not. Something woke me—'

'Hmm?' Her eyes sharpened. She let his jeans fall to the floor so she was completely uncovered. He stared. She lifted a knee onto the bed, stretched her other leg over his stomach. Straddling him, she lifted the lamp out of his hands, then slid up his chest to replace the lamp on the table. 'If you don't believe me'—

—'I believe you'—

—'maybe you'd better search me,' she said, and the room turned dark.

A locksmith from a company called Blue Fin Security Systems was already working on the front door of the Superette when the detectives came in. It was 6:50 in the morning. Besides Bonnie True, who was emptying the dishwasher, and her husband Herb, who was reading the morning paper while he waited for the coffee to finish perking, the locksmith was the only one in the store.

'I didn't think you boys hit the streets till eight,' Herb said to the detectives, 'when the donuts come in.'

'We wanted to catch Mrs Swift before she got too busy,' Shepherd replied.

'Won't catch her here,' Bonnie told them. 'She didn't spend the night on the premises. She's got 'em riggin the place with alarms and new locks from top to bottom, and I doubt she'll spend another night here till you people get things straightened out. I don't blame her. If it was me—'

'Where is she?' Murdoch interrupted. He bit a filter cigarette out of a pack of Winstons, crumpled the pack and dropped it on the counter.

Bonnie eyed the sergeant. 'Like I was about to say, it's none of my business. I only work for the woman.' She picked up the piece of trash and dropped it in a basket behind the counter.

Shepherd looked at his watch. 'I'm going to call,' he told Murdoch.

'We got a phone back here you're welcomed to,' Bonnie said to Shepherd, 'the white one. Red's the fire phone, we like to keep it free in case—'

'We've got a phone,' Murdoch said, pushing the door open. Shepherd gave Bonnie a smile as he left the store, but she didn't smile back.

So orange. She rises, and the sheet slips down her back. The early morning air through the screen sends a chill across his chest as she rides him, dazzling – *orange* – their stomachs sliding together in their mixed perspiration. He is seeing her naked in the daylight for the first time, over and over, though they've been going at this for hours. Her breasts are white and slightly upturned, perfectly smooth. Her areolae are chestnut brown and goose-bumped, her nipples standing out pink and tender, stretching like buds to the dawn light... But her hair, *that orange*, fired by this sudden slice of sunlight. On and on she moves in this slow, steady union, while he tries to maintain his senses through the depths of his sexual inebriation: the exquisite warmth inside her, her acrid-sweet and secret smell; the smacking of their skin separating; the taste of her inner flesh still on his tongue, the deep, intoxicating fullness of her...

On and on she moves, her deep green eyes pinned on him, her mouth a slack, goading smile – like she's aroused by his oblivion. When she comes, he watches with a deeply subdued fascination. First she loses the smile; then her look becomes ravenous. Slowly she rises up, her back straightening, arching. Her puckered, hooded navel catches a pale shadow. And then one eye flashes sunlight, and it startles him – one ice-green jewel flashing over and over, orange hair wildly flaming, as she closes around him – *GREEN-ORANGE-GREEN-ORANGE-GREEN-ORANGE-GREEN*

From his Cherokee, Shepherd called his friend Phil Harwood in Augusta. The two men had gone through the police academy together and become close friends, competitive skirt-chasers, until Harwood got married and then spent a couple of years at the university to get his chemistry degree. Although the men never saw each other outside of work anymore, Harwood was still a valuable comrade at the crime lab, where evidence was backed up sometimes two and three weeks. Shepherd could usually get his stuff bumped to the front of the line if he asked. Like he had yesterday.

'Did I wake you up?' he said when Harwood answered. The car phone was on speaker while he booted up his computer.

'How are you?' Harwood replied, a measure of concern detectable in his voice. Murdoch smirked, looked out his side window.

'Going through some changes,' Shepherd said. 'Hey, thanks for getting the stuff done so quick.'

'I got more. Not official yet, but you're gonna like it. You know the corpse you dug up?'

'Wicker, right? The undertaker?'

'They'll be notifying you from the morgue that Mr Wicker died from suffocation – they found dirt in his mouth, trachea and lungs, even some in his stomach – he looked like he was trying to eat his way out.'

'Pleasant thought,' Shepherd said.

'It also appears that he was knocked unconscious just before he was buried.'

'Okay, that's what we thought,' Shepherd said, searching for his WICKER file. There followed a dramatic pause on Harwood's end, which Shepherd liked the sound of. 'What else, Phil, you got something?'

'The oxygen tank.'

'Yeah, what about it?'

'Just what I said. That's what he was brained with.'

'No kidding.'

'That's what I make of it. The same kind of tank you sent down.'

'Phil, not the one I sent down?'

'I don't think so. The green paint we took off his hair is an exact chemical match. But we would have seen a corresponding mark on the tank, some kind of hair imprint – and we didn't. This tank's shiny and new. Never been used for anything. Which means there must be another oxygen tank out there. Are you aware of another tank?'

Shepherd typed the information into his computer.

'Wait a minute,' the sergeant interrupted, 'what about the scuba tanks? This is Murdoch.'

'Scuba tanks? Why? They're a different color. Different paint altogether.'

'Alright, so we rule 'em out.'

'There's got to be another oxygen tank,' Harwood said. 'E-size, same kind as I've got here. That's what he was hit with.'

'Okay,' Shepherd said, 'so I'm looking for another oxygen tank. Phil, any way of determining where it was purchased?'

'Yellow Pages. Start calling. You have to sign for oxygen; even welders do. You got a name or two, anybody look good?'

'Yeah, maybe,' Shepherd said, then he thanked his friend and hung up. ROBERT SWIFT was the name he entered in his computer. For some reason, he also thought of Alston Bouchard at that moment, and he felt a twinge of anger, or something close to it.

Walt Moody opened his examination room door with his elbow while he glanced over his first patient's chart.

'Mrs Daoust,' he started to say, but then he saw Detective Shepherd sitting on his examination table in a beige jacket, his computer resting on his lap.

The doctor double-checked his chart.

'I told Mrs Daoust you'd be detained a minute,' Shepherd told him.

That's when the doctor understood the nature of the detective's visit. He raised his brow in question, not quite able to muster the level of informality he wanted.

Shepherd gave him a smile. 'Bobby Swift,' he said. 'I'm referring to your signature on his death certificate. I've got you down saying your examination was by the book.'

The young doctor blinked his eyes three times. Shepherd closed the door.

Murdoch bent low so his face filled the window. 'Would you be Mrs Erickson, by any chance?' he said through the opening in the glass.

Iris regarded him curiously. She assumed he was a detective, having seen him come in with Shepherd.

'Your husband,' Murdoch said, 'Salvator-ee? Somebody said he was a close personal friend of Robert and Noel Swift's.'

Iris studied the man. He had a large, unfriendly face and an intrusive manner that seemed to cloud the entire room. She noticed that a boy and his mother were sitting by the door, her eight o'clock, waiting to check in. The boy was coughing.

'Is there something I can help you with?' she said, straightening.

'That'd be your best bet,' Murdoch answered. 'I thought maybe you could tell us where we might find your husband this morning.'

'Excuse me,' Iris said, stepping to the side where she could see the boy's mother. 'Just bring him in the back,' she said. 'I'll weigh him in a sec.'

After the woman and boy had gone through the door, Iris told the sergeant quietly, 'My husband and I were recently separated.'

'Huh,' said Murdoch. 'See, that would be an answer if I had inquired about your marital status. But what I asked is where we might find him this morning. Actually, we need to speak with Noel Swift, and we thought your husband, being a close personal friend, might know where she spent the night.' His mouth opened again as if to say more, but then Iris realized that he was smiling.

The orgasm fires over and over. Like flames dancing under her skin, he's burning from the inside out. But he can't get at her with his arms shackled down, and she's not even close to stopping. She rides him resolutely, rising, rising, shaking him, knuckles hard on his collar bone—

'Hey!'

'Mr Erickson—'

'*What—*'

The man was pushing him down, another man holding his arms.

'Take it easy! *Take it easy!*'

Both on top of him – one was massive, gray-haired flattop,

cheap checkered blazer, cigarette breath. 'Relax, Blacky, we got a couple of questions, *I said relax!*'

'Mr Erickson?'

The other one – younger, better dressed, dark mustache – Sal recognized Shepherd from the store, the clinic.

'Don't get cute,' the bulldog warned, releasing pressure from Sal's neck.

Sal sat up fast. 'What the fuck,' he said. 'Did I wake up in Mexico or what?' He looked around the room at the empty bathroom and kitchen, saw the chair returned to the table. Noel was gone, near as he could tell.

Flattop turned to the window and snapped the blinds up, flooding the room with sunshine. 'Your landlady let us in down below,' he said. 'You didn't answer your door, we thought you might need help.'

'Mr Erickson—?'

'What, for chrissake?'

Shepherd showed Sal his shield. 'I'm Detective Shepherd. This is Sergeant Murdoch. A couple of questions, if you don't mind.'

'Even if you do mind,' said Murdoch. He picked Sal's jeans and T-shirt off the floor and pitched them at Sal's chest. 'Somebody said you were a friend of Bobby Swift's. Maybe you can tell us where to find him.'

Sal stared at the sergeant. 'What?' he said.

'*What?*' the sergeant mocked. 'You heard me.'

Sal stepped out of bed and into the pants. 'You think I dug him up?' He snatched his T-shirt off the bed and pulled it over his head.

Murdoch stepped closer, squared his shoulders to Sal. 'Somebody told us you two were out gallivantin the night before he supposedly went to that big general store in the sky.'

'I don't know what you're talking about,' Sal told him. 'Bobby's dead. Back off.'

Shepherd bent down next to the bed, picked up Sal's wallet and handed it to him. 'We're actually looking for Mrs Swift,' he said, 'Noel. Thought maybe you could help us.'

Sal said nothing as he stuffed the wallet in his back pocket. He wondered why Noel had gone without saying good-bye.

'Whaddya, need a drink?' Murdoch said. 'Somebody said you got a problem.'

Sal looked him over. Than he sat on the edge of the bed again, and he shook his head. 'This is one crack investigation team, no shit. You want the person who killed Eliot Wicker and stole Bobby's body, right? You got no other suspects, so you start harassing the woman, the widow.'

'Mr Erickson—?' Shepherd pulled a wooden chair over, sat on the edge holding a small, plasticine-covered photo out to Sal. Before Sal could take it, Murdoch stepped between the two men, hovering over Sal. 'Maybe we don't think she comes across as your typical grieving widow, wise guy—'

Shepherd stood, palmed the sergeant's shoulder. 'Sorry to bother you, Mr Erickson. Sarge?'

Murdoch, however, was neither apologetic nor retreating. 'Like maybe we think there's something fishy when a man in his thirties supposedly drops dead and gets buried with no autopsy.'

'Yeah, yeah.'

'Sarge?' Shepherd took hold of the sergeant's arm, spoke calmly. 'That's enough.'

Murdoch knew it too, because he suddenly stopped talking and just nodded his head up and down at Sal, pink-cheeked.

Shepherd put the photo back in his pocket. 'So you don't know Noel's whereabouts?' he asked Sal.

'That's what I said,' Sal answered, still glaring at Murdoch.

'Come on, Sarge.'

'Wait a minute,' Sal told them, and then he addressed Shepherd. 'What the hell is he saying about Bobby?'

Murdoch reached inside his blazer, then stepped close to Sal and stuck a card in his T-shirt pocket. 'The name's Murdoch, Greaseball, and I'll tell you what I'm saying. From now on, I'm gonna be lookin up your asshole every move you make.' He flexed his thick neck a couple of times, then straightened and led Shepherd out the door.

Outside a Shop 'n Save in Bangor, Noel made a long-distance call to Worcester. She wore dark sunglasses to hide her eyes and a hooded green sweatshirt over a kerchief to cover her hair. When the man answered the phone, she told him she was Brenda and gave him a phone number to call. She hung up, walked quickly to her car and drove out to the road, checked the lot behind her, checked left and right to make sure she hadn't been followed, then headed west on Broadway. After a mile she pulled into the small parking lot of a Trustworthy hardware store. She parked near the pay phone at the corner of the store, then waited in the car, surveying her surroundings. Only two vehicles sat in the lot, an old pickup truck and a maroon Toyota wagon, mid-'80s. Momentarily the telephone rang. She got out of the car and picked up. 'It's Brenda,' she said.

'Go ahead, Brenda.'

She turned her back to the brick wall so she could watch the parking lot. 'Does September thirty ring a bell?' she said.

The man on the other end paused for five full seconds, then said, 'Excuse me with that tone of voice, I know my business. Is there something you want to alter regarding that date, or did you wish to cancel at this time?'

She pulled the phone cable to its limit trying to see around the front of the store, but it didn't reach far enough. 'Are you saying that one of your representatives wasn't here prematurely?'

'That is correct, Brenda.'

'Are you sure?'

'Hey, I haven't even put anyone on it yet, okay?'

Noel heard a door close, and then a man who looked to be in his seventies came around the corner carrying eight feet of plastic rain gutter under his arm. He walked past her and went to the pickup truck in the lot, set the gutter in the back.

Noel smiled. 'I need to cancel then. Somebody evidently got there first.'

Another pause. 'Happens,' the phone voice said.

The old man got in his truck and started it.

'We're all square, then?'

'That's correct. Your deposit covers eventualities such as this. So, maybe another time.'

'Another time,' she began, watching the truck pull out of the lot. 'Would it be possible to get same-day service?'

'Same day,' the man said. 'You realize in that case we have an escalating risk factor on our end, meaning the fee slides up a little, not much. Got a name, place of business, place of residence? Fax over a photo, we could begin the preliminary research.'

From Noel's right, a fortyish man in a knit cap rode silently around the front of the store on a mountain bike, braked at the curb by the phone. She smiled again. 'I'll let you know if I need you,' she said, and hung up the phone.

When the detectives returned to the barracks, Murdoch went over the day's log, checked in with the dispatcher and then went home. Shepherd got an egg salad sandwich and a black coffee from the vending machines and spent the rest of the afternoon with a stack of telephone books, calling every oxygen supplier in the state, asking the managers to go through their records for a two-year period and look for the names of Robert Swift or Eliot Wicker. Most of the people he talked to promised to have the records searched by the end of the following day; the others said they'd run it through their computers and call back within the hour if they found anything. Nobody called back. While Shepherd waited, he telephoned Alston Bouchard, but the constable didn't answer. He tried Noel Swift repeatedly, and Bonnie told him repeatedly that Noel still hadn't returned to the store. At six o'clock Shepherd shut off his computer and drove home.

The detective wasn't the only one trying to reach Noel. Sal had called her too, nearly every hour since morning, and he had visited the store three times. He was concerned about her disappearance, and concerned about the things the detectives had said. But it was more than that. With Iris and Davey and Bobby all suddenly gone from his life, his concern for Noel had turned to a steady fear, that he might lose her too.

At eight-twenty, when she still wasn't back and there was barely enough skylight left so he could see the road without his headlight, Sal rode slowly past Wicker's Funeral Home, checked his mirrors, then leaned the Harley hard into the turnoff and killed the engine. He dismounted the bike and pushed it into the brush so it was hidden from the road, took a penlight from his saddlebag and jammed it into his jacket pocket, then hiked up the hill through the woods.

At the rear corner of Wicker's property, which was surrounded by woods on three sides, Sal emerged from an orderly stand of white pine. The large white house sat giftwrapped with yellow police tape on a knoll facing the road. An attached four-car garage made an ell off the back, lining the left side of the driveway and parking lot.

Sal made his way to the rear of the breezeway, which connected the ell to the house. Colors had diminished with the daylight, and now everything lay quiet in the dusk. Sal had no intention of finessing the break-in. Pulling the police tape over his shoulder, he ducked under, then punched his elbow through a windowpane. The leather protected his arm.

He didn't know what he was looking for. All he knew was that somebody had murdered Eliot Wicker, and the police had made Noel their chief suspect. Wicker's was a good place to start.

What Sal knew about Wicker was what everybody knew – that the man had made a country fortune snatching up property from the estates of his recently deceased clients. So that's what Sal intended to search: Wicker's real estate files. He left the lights off, using his penlight to navigate through the house, eventually making his way downstairs, where he opened doors until he found the burgundy-carpeted office.

With his penlight in his teeth, he want through the Rolodex on the desk, but found mostly vendors: chemical companies, casket and headstone makers, a number of clergy, surveyors and attorneys. He turned his search to the file cabinet, where folders were arranged alphabetically – accounts of the deceased in the bottom two drawers, real estate files in the top two. He flipped through every file in all four drawers, one at a time, as the two casement windows at the ceiling slowly darkened over and his second set of penlight batteries died.

When he finished, he left the building through a door downstairs that opened onto the parking lot, feeling more perplexed than before he had come. Wicker had buried more than four hundred people in his years in town, and bought or sold nearly as much property. Almost anyone in Gravity could have murdered him with some degree of justification.

At 9:20, after Noel had returned to the store and Bonnie had finally left for home, the telephone rang. Noel turned off the outside lights, checked that the red alarm light was lit, then went behind the counter to answer. It was Sal calling.

'I'm at a gas station,' he said. 'They still haven't fixed my phone.'

'I was just going up to bed,' she told him.

There was a pause. 'I didn't know what happened to you this morning.'

'I needed to get away,' she said.

'I woke up and you were gone. I was a little concerned.'

Neither of them spoke for a moment.

'So,' Sal said, 'are we still friends?'

'If that's what you want to call it,' she answered.

'I was wondering' – another pause. 'Do you know if Bobby ever got involved in any of Eliot Wicker's real estate deals?'

For a second Noel kept silent. 'Why?'

'I don't know, I'm just – wondering. Listen, I don't particularly want to be alone tonight.'

'Oh, God, I know how you feel, Sal. But I really have to sleep. I didn't get much last night. Sleep, I mean,' she added dryly.

He laughed a little. 'Sure you're alright there?'

'They've been up here all day,' she said. 'They wired all the windows and doors. I'll sleep with a gun.'

'Yeah. Me too.'

'Mmm,' she purred, and she hung up. Then, turning on the light switch to the front stairway, turning off the store fluorescents, Noel opened the door and climbed the front stairs. It wasn't her usual way up, but tonight she didn't feel like going through the stockroom with its maze of shadowy passageways and cartons and corners. Unlocking the door at the top landing with her new key, she entered her living room and closed the door behind her, set the new double locks – latch bolt, dead bolt – then turned for the lamp and—

—Jerry Royal was there. Reclining in her small wicker couch, a hardy grin on his face. Noel was startled by his appearance; but it was his assurance that scared her – an expression foreign to Jerry. He was drunk, she concluded, and here to rape her. But something else told her it was more than that. He turned on the reading lamp beside him.

'Din mean to scare you, Noel,' he said. His hair was wetted and combed down to his eyebrows, like molded plastic. He wore clean white overalls and no shirt, showing off his pink, rounded shoulders. With a red neckerchief tied around his neck, he looked as dapper as she'd ever seen him. What worried her more was the piece of paper he held in his hand. She guessed it was the source of his confidence.

'Jeez, you look like you seen a ghost,' he said.

'Jerry, you can't just come up here,' she replied. She wanted to show him ire, not fear.

'You're right, I can't no more.' He opened his hand and dangled a set of keys – Bobby's keys. 'So I bin up here all day, waitin. Anybody ever teach you to vacuum under your bed?' He dropped the keys on the coffee table in front of him.

Noel gazed placidly at him. 'Where did you get those?'

Jerry's craggy, weather-beaten smile bored into her. 'I heard you down there the other night,' he said.

'I'm going to call the police,' she told him, and she walked alongside a wooden curio of tribal artifacts, beyond his reach, then turned down the hallway.

'"To whom it may concern,"' he began reading, '"I, Gerald Christian Royal" – formal touch, make it legal – "do testify that on May the twenty-fifth I was working at the Wicker Funeral Home in Gravity, Maine, and I heard" – that should be *overheard*, but what the fuck – "I heard Mr Eliot Wicker having a conversation with Mr Robert Swift when Robert Swift was supposed to be dead" – right to the point, see?'

Jerry paused; Noel's footsteps stopped in the hall. 'I guess that got her attention. Anyway – "I heard Robert Swift ask, 'What did she send this monkey suit for?' And Eliot Wicker said to keep his mouth shut because he was putting on the lip sealer, which seals the lips of the deceased. Only thing was, Bobby Swift was not deceased."'

Jerry looked up from his paper at the empty room and said, 'You callin 'em?' He smiled to himself, then found his place and resumed. '"So I and Otis Royal, my father, who personally don't know anything but that Robert Swift was dead like he supposed to be, dug the grave at Rest Awhile Cemetery, and after the funeral we set the casket in and filled in the hole like we always do. But I had my suspicions. I figured there was only one reason a man would let anyone bury him alive – to collect the life insurance, which they would split three ways – husband, wife and undertaker. I myself figured we could split it four ways.

'"So after the funeral, Noel Swift had a party, and when it got over I saw her getting into her Volvo car, which she told me she was going for a drive. So after she left I let myself back in with a set of spare keys that I borrowed from Robert Swift's workshop.

'"Up in the bedroom closet I found a suitcase packed with the clothes of Robert Swift, along with an airplane ticket and some other things, which I removed for the purpose of negotiating with husband and wife when they got back home. But then a half hour later Noel Swift drove back home alone, which wasn't enough time to dig up a grave. And that's when I thought of the other reason somebody might bury her husband. To get rid of him and collect the insurance herself."'

Reclining on the couch, Jerry looked up from his paper and saw Noel watching him from the doorway. He gave her a cocky wag of his head. 'I bet never in a million years you thought you'd get caught by someone like me.' His lips flattened clownishly.

She brought the .22 up from behind her hip, aimed dead at that mouth.

'Whoa, copy, copy' – Jerry covered his face with one arm while he held the paper out to the side – 'just a Xerox copy, I thought I made that clear.' He gave a little nervous hoot. 'Jeezum, lady, you are a dangerous little thing. Slow down.'

But Noel kept the pistol aimed directly at those wet, elastic lips, certain that its report wouldn't sound any different to neighbors than a book falling (if anyone were awake to hear it at all).

'I got the original hid away someplace, which I'm not tellin you where, except it's in an envelope that says, "*To be opened in case Gerald C. Royal shows up missing or dead.*"' He gave a little head movement, conveying a reckless pride. 'Don't think I'm gonna underestimate you, girl. I've watched you work.'

Noel glared at him, wanting so badly to pull the trigger, as if by doing so she could be rid of this idiot complication. But she knew that she had to keep her head.

'Where is he?' she demanded. 'Where's Bobby?'

'Who, *Dale Newman*?' Jerry widened his eyes, demonstrating his knowledge, his power. 'You got me.'

'You killed Eliot Wicker,' she said.

He snorted, ridiculing her. 'Oh, as if,' he said. 'Right here I was, in this very house that night, with you. I saw Wicker come here, and I saw him go away again, some friggin ugly too. Whatever happened down there at that cemetery, I don't know any more'n you.'

She neither budged from the doorway nor lowered her gun. 'What do you want from me?' she said.

'Well' – his face jutting as if the answer should have been obvious – 'a little respect, for starters.'

Noel's expression didn't change.

'Meaning you could point that gun away from my head, bein as how, if you think about it, I got a gun pointed at you that'll take your own head off down to your knees, whether I'm dead or alive, personally speaking.'

But her revolver remained trained on his face. 'Tell me what you want,' she repeated.

He rocked his head back and forth to show that the conversation would not proceed until she had acceded to his first request.

She did so, finally, lowering the gun. But her icy glare persisted. 'I don't have any money,' she told him.

'Yeah, I heard. Friggin insurance companies, they got you comin and goin. Here I thought I was going to be a rich man, drive around town, "Hi, how y'doin?" Same with you, right?'

She sank to the floor, sliding down the corner of the curio. 'Jerry, just tell me what you want,' she said.

His protracted silence was all the answer she needed.

She looked up and saw it clearly in his face, that look of undisguised greed that men get when they imagine a woman is helpless. And then it began. He placed his letter on the coffee table and his voice took on a country-western softness. 'I got a little warm up here the other night, listening to you two down there, with all that chocolate business.' He put his hand deep inside a pocket of his overalls, moved it around, then slowly withdrew her red panties.

A wave of nausea gripped Noel. She raised the pistol again, squinted at him, catlike. 'I'd die first,' she said.

'*Daow!*' he said – an emphatic *no* – as he slid off the couch and sank to his hands and knees, the panties in his fist. 'Like in Cinderella, I'm Prince What's-his-name, come to put these back on you, see if they fit.' He started crawling toward her, his back huge and rounded, his pink shoulders flexing like a lion's. 'I got it all figured out,' he said.

She leaned back against the curio, pulled her knees underneath her, the revolver in both hands, aimed at the top of his head. As he came closer, his breathing became part of his voice.

'My word, look at them straps, *strings* is all you got there, strings holdin up them little titties.' That ragged grin again. 'Come on, Noel,' he said. 'You know you don't wanna kill me.'

Her head began to hum.

'Not with what I got on you.'

Jerry's right hand moved blindly through the air, he took hold of the pistol and lowered it to the floor. 'That's right,' he moaned, and then his raspy fingers slid the entire length of her arm to her shoulder, then headed south down her shoulder strap. 'Now let's just see what you're packin,' he breathed, his dry knuckles grazing the side of her breast.

Suddenly mindless, Noel lurched up, yanked the pistol from under her hip, and drove its muzzle straight against Jerry's cheekbone, under his eye.

Before he could pull his hand out of her top, she pulled the trigger, she couldn't stop herself, his head jerked back, but she stayed with him, on her knees now, forcing the barrel against his face, pulling the trigger again and again, the hammer making a lifeless clank,

a dead ring,

a toy sound—

He clutched her wrist, wrenched her arm powerfully so the back of her hand slammed against a shelf. With his other hand, Jerry fingered the small cut she had made on his cheek.

'Jeezum, Noel, take my fuckin eye out, why don't you!'

A quality in his voice told her that his pain was not only physical. His feelings had been hurt.

'It's not like I was friggin askin to marry you.' He let go of her wrist and felt under his eye. 'Jeez, you gotta think, girl. Number one, I been up here all day. You gotta *know* I'da took the shells outta that gun very first thing. I ain't dumb. Number two, you kill me, it's all over, the old man finds my letter, you spend the rest of your life in prison. Number three' – he fingered his cheekbone again, checking for blood – 'I'm gonna let this one go, but in the future, anything you do to me, I'll do back to you twice as bad. *Twice as bad.* Is that clear?' *Clee-uh.* He jabbed the floor with his finger. 'Now I got knowledge about something, and now the insurance part's all frigged up, and I deserve to get something outta this.'

Glaring at him, clenched with rage, Noel kept her voice remarkably even. 'And what you want is to rape me. Raping me is your life's ambition.'

'Well, maybe once, until you see how much fun it is.' He gave her a gawking, expectant look, waiting for a smile, but it didn't happen.

'You okay?'

She closed her eyes.

'You don't want to look at me, don't wanna talk, whatever, okay.'

She opened her eyes, gazed up at him.

A slow, bruised grin came over his face. 'That's more like it,' he said.

She sprang suddenly, swinging the revolver across her chest. He turned his head, but too late. The cylinder caught him above the ear, made a vicious pop.

'*Geee!*' he cried, pressing his head to his shoulder. As the gun came back the other way, the muzzle sideswiping his nose, he grabbed her throat, squeezing hard enough to slam her shoulders to the floor. With his other hand he tore the gun away from her and wrapped it in his fist like some primitive tool. He cocked his arm by his ear as if he were going to pulverize her face with the butt.

She glared up at him, eyes viciously narrowed.

'Go ahead, asshole,' she whispered. 'Make one fucking mark on me.'

Jerry's eyes opened wide, his lips puckered. He checked behind him for the hallway. Then he looked down at her again and two drops of blood fell from his nose onto her neck. He wiped his nose with the back of his hand. Repulsed, Noel nevertheless kept her steely eyes on him.

Jerry began bobbing his head. 'Don't worry,' he said. Still clutching her throat, he set the gun on the floor and slid it to the far wall. 'Don't worry,' he said again, 'you're gonna wish you didn't do that.' He released his grip on her throat by pushing himself to his feet. ''Cause tomorrow we're takin this up a notch, you and me.' He gave her a punctuation look, then backed into the hallway, where he turned and lumbered off between the walls to the kitchen, checking his wounds as he went. When he reached the kitchen, he turned back one more time and pointed at her. 'Fuckin feminist,' he said, 'you're in for one big surprise.'

9

Sal stood near the back of the store, looking over the videotape selection while he waited for the crowd to disperse. At ten to eight, when a couple of men paid for their coffee and headed off to work, it seemed like the others were getting set to go too.

That's when Jerry Royal walked in. He was carrying a brown bag, folded down tight. When he caught sight of Sal, the two men looked each other over – Sal in his black leather and boots, Jerry wearing magenta jeans and a green rayon shirt with a wide white collar. Although Jerry's raccoon hair was once again carefully combed, this morning a purple half-moon cupped his swollen left eye. He turned away from Sal and took a seat at the counter, between Herb True and Belly Button.

'Who'd you have a disagreement with?' Herb asked.

'Transmission,' Jerry answered.

His father Otis, at the end of the counter, said with low disapproval, 'Look of those dancin clothes, I'd guess a woman did the transmittin.'

'Ol' Mister Pink Pants,' Belly Button added with a chuckle.

Before Jerry could respond, Noel came through the stockroom door, carrying a small cardboard box of chewing gum. 'I'll start with a coffee this morning,' Jerry said to her. 'You can put it on my tab.'

Noel ignored him.

Sal came to the head of the grocery aisle hoping to catch Noel's eye, but she walked the length of the counter without looking his way either. Jerry seemed particularly interested in Noel's faded hiphugger jeans, tight in the thighs, worn through the knees, flared and flayed at the ankles.

'What's in the bag?' Belly Button asked him.

'Nothin'at concerns you.'

'Pink pants,' Belly said again.

'You don't know your friggin colors,' Jerry answered, still watching Noel.

The bell on the door sounded, and Sal turned to see Alston Bouchard coming in. The Superette fell quiet, except for the creak of floorboards under the constable's feet.

'Coffee, Alston?' Noel asked.

'Just five on gas.'

'Coffee down here,' Jerry said, 'in case you forgot.'

Bouchard looked over at him, his gaze passing briefly over Sal and the other men, then returning to Noel as he flipped open the wallet. He dug out a ten and set it on the counter. As she rang it in, he said, 'Man named Dale Newman been in?'

Noel took a five out of the cash tray and held it out for Bouchard. 'Not that I know of.' To the others, she said, 'Dale Newman?'

The men at the counter looked at one another. Jerry nudged Herb. 'Ask what he looks like.'

Bouchard looked over at Jerry, then returned to Noel. 'No picture,' he said. He pulled a card out of his shirt pocket, light green, folded in half. He unfolded the card in front of Noel. 'Just this plane ticket. Looks like Mr Newman missed his flight Monday morning. Grand Cayman Island, his destination.'

Bouchard looked over at Sal again – at least that's the way it appeared to Sal – difficult though it was to see Bouchard's eyes through the glare on his glasses.

'I guess we can't help you,' Noel said, crouching behind the cash register to straighten something inside the candy case. Bouchard stepped back and looked through the glass.

'Monday being the day after Bobby's funeral, he was supposed to fly out of Logan Airport in Boston – Dale Newman, I mean. Maybe someone stopped by you didn't recognize—?' Bouchard knocked twice on the glass, self-consciously.

'Those detectives been in yet?' Jerry said. 'They'll prob'ly want to see that ticket.' He leaned over the counter, trying to get a look at Noel, almost like he was needling her. Sal wondered if it was because she hadn't brought him his coffee.

She stood up behind the candy counter, glanced back at Jerry as if she wondered the same thing. 'Alston, I know you're trying to help,' she said, 'but could you please work with the others?' The look she gave Bouchard conveyed more affection than she was used to showing.

He folded the ticket and tucked it away in his wallet. 'Just thought I'd check,' he said, turning for the door. 'Whoever this is, he missed his plane.'

Jerry said to Sal, 'Where'd he find the ticket, he say?'

Bouchard looked back at Jerry, not answering, then he opened the door.

Sal pushed off his stool, stepped back from the counter. 'Mr Bouchard,' he said. The other men at the counter turned to Sal. The constable stopped, the door in his hand.

'Mr Bouchard, you didn't say where you found that plane ticket.'

Bouchard nodded. 'I know I didn't,' he said, and he left.

As soon as the door closed, Noel slid the candy case shut, pitched the empty carton in the basket and walked the length of the counter, heading toward the stockroom. 'Jerry,' she said, pushing through the swinging door, 'do you have a minute? I need you to look at my car. It's skipping.'

Jerry cocked his head, as if deliberating. Then he dismounted the stool and patted down his hair. He tucked his paper bag under his arm, looked over at Sal and said, 'I guess I got the time.'

'We're not showing a Dale Newman in the whole state,' the woman said over the phone.

'Is it possible the name is unlisted?' Sal asked her. Pen in hand, he looked over Davey's social studies test on the kitchen table, the word EXCELLENT red-penciled at the top of the paper.

'Even if it were unlisted, it would still appear on the screen,' the operator told him.

Sal thanked the woman and hung up the phone. He went to the counter and filed through a stack of bills until he found one from the electric company. He dialed the number listed. Waiting for the phone to ring, he noticed Davey's bathrobe hung on the bathroom doorknob, quilted, pink roses on blue. He turned away before the pang gnawed deeper. When the receptionist answered, he explained that the wrong electric bill had ended up in his envelope. 'I got Dale

Newman's,' he said. 'If you give me his address, I'll mail it to him.'

'His address should be on the bill,' she replied, 'right under the name.'

'It's smudged,' Sal said.

The woman asked him to wait a minute. A few seconds later she was back on the phone. 'We don't show a Dale Newman anywhere in the state. Are you sure you're reading it right? D as in dolphin?'

Sal hung up and then checked the Yellow Pages, under AIRLINES.

'Don't talk,' Noel said. 'Just listen.'

Jerry shrugged his shoulders. 'No problem there.' He stood at the bottom of the stairs in the garage, holding his paper bag under his folded arms.

'Get in,' she said.

'Yes, m'am.'

He stepped around her and ducked into the passenger side of her Volvo, found the lever under his seat and pushed the seat all the way back, stretching his legs. Noel got in the driver's side, started the car and let it idle fast.

She looked directly at him. 'Are you totally stupid?'

'I don't know,' he said. 'Am I?'

'Did you give that plane ticket to Bouchard?'

'I left it someplace where I thought he might find it. Like I promised, Noel, you take it up a notch, I take it up two. Now you wanna keep playin games, you best know I got enough to put you away for life.' He slipped his fingers inside the bag and pulled out a slim white box wrapped in cellophane. He nudged it toward her. 'Fanny Farmer,' he said.

She did not look at the chocolates. 'Jerry,' she said, 'you are risking your life – and mine – just to have sex with me.'

He shrugged. 'Not riskin *my* life.'

'Oh, yes, you are,' she answered solemnly, giving each word its full, ominous weight. 'Believe me, you are risking your life.'

Jerry gave it a moment's thought. 'So, you're risking your life *not* to have sex with me. I'd say that makes you the fool.' He set the box of chocolates on the dashboard in front of her. 'Mixed assortment,' he pointed out. There was a certain arousal in his eyes, slightly tempered by the knowledge that the garage was filling with carbon monoxide.

'Jerry, think about it.'

'Don't worry, I do.'

'Jerry, your *life*. Sex is not worth losing your life over.'

He snickered. 'Yeah. Maybe not your life, it ain't. Maybe Queen Elizabeth or what's-her-name, the president's wife, maybe not theirs. But hey, lady, look at my life. Whaddu I got to lose? A bunch of chickens and a new Chevy truck which you can't take that where I'm goin anyways. And you tell me gettin inside these hippie pants ain't worth a life like that?' He almost touched the low waist of her jeans but stopped short.

She turned away.

'That's not all I want, anyway,' he continued. 'I expect breakfast, lunch, dinner, whatnot, on the house, anytime I come in. Gas for my truck, free videos . . . I figure that's fair.'

Noel closed her eyes. 'I can't believe this,' she whispered.

'I bet you can't,' he said. 'And here you prob'ly thought you were just about the slickest thing ever took a breath of air in this town. And I'm supposed to be so stupid. Well, now look where I got you, smarty.'

Noel looked away from him again, stared out her window into the garage, kept silent for a time. At last her chest heaved with a long sigh of surrender.

'Huh?'

She turned to face him, her eyes welled with defeat, and Jerry's heart nearly stopped. He regarded her recklessly.

'Not here,' she said. 'And not now.'

'You name the time and place, lady, I'll be there.'

She said, 'First I want you to tell me exactly what happened at the cemetery that night.'

'I already told you,' he said, 'I didn't have nothin to do with it, swear to God. For all I know, you and Bobby had it all planned to put the screws right back on Wicker.'

Noel stared at him.

'Give me the evil eye all you want, Noel, I'll tell you this: If Bobby's out there playin games, you best keep him way away from me. 'Cause that letter I wrote'll finish him in a heartbeat, same as you, I don't care what island you run to. And that goes for that other one you been cockteasin, my brother-in-law. Anyway, how do I know the two of you didn't cook up this whole thing from the start, and doublecross everybody?'

Noel's expression never changed. Keeping her eyes glued to Jerry, she said: 'I want you to stay away from Sal Erickson.'

Jerry studied her. 'Sounds like you got some plans for him yourself.'

Noel's eyes narrowed on Jerry so suddenly, so fiercely, that his hand reflexively went to the door handle.

'I said stay away from him.'

The black lab sat on the roadside, whining, as Shepherd peeled the prints off the mailbox. 'You're positive the ticket was inside,' the detective said. 'Folded like that?'

'Seven-thirty I found it,' Bouchard answered, 'when I got my mail.' He patted the dog, quieting him. His long house trailer sat across the road, twenty feet back from the tar. Behind the trailer a long, rocky hill rose, divided up the center by a pair of well-worn tire tracks. To the right of the road, the hill was white with blueberry blossoms that would be this year's crop; to the left, black with char from the biyearly torching.

'And something told you to take that plane ticket out, hold it in your hand, and bring it to the store to show your friends,' Murdoch said, standing off to the side drinking coffee from a thermos cup.

'The flight was the morning after Bobby Swift's funeral,' Bouchard answered. 'I thought it might be connected.'

Shepherd checked his watch. 'A lot of things happened the day after Bobby Swift's funeral,' he said.

'A lot of things happen every day,' Murdoch added. 'Doesn't mean they're linked up.'

'It was one way,' Bouchard said.

Shepherd looked over at him.

'The ticket,' Bouchard explained. 'Meaning he wasn't coming back.'

Murdoch, unimpressed, tossed the last of his coffee on the asphalt, splashing the dog. 'I'll be in the car,' he said. As he crossed the road toward the trailer, the lab barked at him.

'Katahdin, hush.'

Shepherd finished labeling his hinge-lifter, slipped it in his jacket pocket and started walking across the road. Bouchard and the dog walked behind him.

'You found Bobby Swift's fingerprints on those scuba tanks,' Bouchard said. If it was a question, it didn't sound like one. 'Eliot Wicker's too,' he added, 'if I'm not too far off.'

Shepherd stopped walking, turned and faced the constable, stared at him long enough to put both men on edge.

'Mr Bouchard, I don't know how that plane ticket ended up in your mailbox,' Shepherd said, 'or whether it means anything at all. But I would rather not see you again in connection with this investigation.'

With that, the detective turned away and walked to his Cherokee, where he ducked in behind the steering wheel and started the engine. Bouchard came a couple of steps closer. 'That coffin,' he said, 'the shape, I mean, inside – I'm guessing it was tore up some—?'

Shepherd shifted into reverse and backed around, ready to drive out. 'I may have to arrest you,' he said. 'I really may have to lock you up.' He began to pull out when a motorcycle came around the curve, cut in front of him and stopped. Shepherd hit the brakes just short of colliding with it.

Murdoch, recognizing Sal on the Harley, shifted heavily in his seat, muttering.

Sal clutched the bike around to Shepherd's window, shut it off. 'Dale Newman canceled his flight Sunday night at eight-fifteen,' he said to the detectives. 'I called Delta Airlines.'

'Night of the funeral,' Bouchard added from the other side of the vehicle.

'The original fucking Hardy Boys,' Murdoch said.

Sal took a piece of notepaper out of his jacket pocket. 'I couldn't get an address on him,' he continued. 'There was no refund because he didn't give enough notice. But I found out he bought the ticket through a travel agency' – he showed Shepherd the paper – 'Beliveau's, in Portland. He paid cash, last June the twenty-fourth.' Sal folded up the paper and offered it to Shepherd.

For a second or two, both detectives just stared at Sal from inside the Cherokee. Then Shepherd reached his hand out and took the paper.

'I'm just trying to find out what happened here,' Sal said. 'Maybe then you'll leave the woman alone.'

Murdoch opened his door, pushed himself out of the Cherokee so one foot was in the yard. He looked over the hood at Sal. 'Only thing you're gonna find out is how goddamn fast we lock you up next time you interfere in this investigation.' He kept on talking, but the rest of his words were drowned out when Sal started the Harley again, goosed the throttle and rode off.

Sal headed east from Bouchard's, veered right onto a dirt road that led through more blackened blueberry barrens, and then opened it up. Chased by a trail of sunlit dust, he let the wind beat his face while he tried to piece together the information: Somebody had murdered Eliot Wicker the night of Bobby's funeral. And somebody had stolen Bobby's body. And now a plane ticket turns up in town, belonging to Dale Newman, who should have been on his way to Grand Cayman Island the day after Bobby's funeral. Like everything's connected, everything's a clue. Sal tried to remember faces at the funeral, at the burial, at the reception in Noel's apartment, strange faces, but there were still many people who lived in Gravity that he didn't know. Almost anyone there could have been Dale Newman, and he wouldn't have known the difference. And even if this Dale Newman were involved, even if he murdered Eliot Wicker and buried him in Bobby's grave, then why would he have removed Bobby's body?

In Sal's mind, nothing connected – not that his concentration was peak. In fact, he could think of nothing without Noel invading his thoughts, so when the dirt road rejoined asphalt he doubled back toward town and drove directly to the Superette, unmindful that the store was busy with lunch customers. He went inside and saw Noel making change at the cash register. He never took his eyes off her as he approached the register.

'Got a minute?' he said to her. He knew that the men beside him were watching; wondered if they could read the look that he and Noel exchanged.

'I'm busy right now,' she said, feigning disinterest.

'I just got pulled over,' he lied. 'The police want to see the bike registration. I told them I'd get it from you and bring it to the station.'

Noel gave him a momentary look. 'I'll check the desk out back. Bonnie, can you manage for a few minutes?' She walked past Bonnie, who was tending the grill, giving no indication that Bonnie's answer would have made any difference. 'Through here,' she said to Sal, throwing the stockroom door open.

He went in behind the meat counter, caught the door and followed Noel down the dusky aisle between walls of cardboard boxes, gazing at her confident stride. At the first intersection, she turned left around a pallet stacked high with cartons of paper towels. He turned with her, caught her arm, and immediately their mouths came together. He held her neck, the back of her head; she ran her hands inside his open jacket to the back of his jeans; he ran his hands down her sides to the inch of her bare waist at the top of her hips; she kissed his neck; he closed his eyes until the only thing that existed were these two bodies, these two minds, these mouths and their own labored breathing. They circled on the floor as if they were dancing, until she backed into her desk and knocked the telephone off the hook. Roused, they broke the kiss, still holding each other. 'What are we doing?' she breathed.

'Come for a ride,' he answered.

She shook her head, pushed his arms down. 'I can't,' she said, slipping his grasp. She bent to pick up the receiver. 'I have to get back in there, and you have to leave.'

Catching her by the hips, his hands slid up her sides, pulling her back and turning her to face him. 'Hire me,' he said. 'I'll live in the garage.'

Laughing, she looked down at the tail of his shirt that had come untucked. She pressed her body closer to his. 'You can't go out there like this,' she said. With the back of her hand, she pushed his shirt inside his jeans, down inside the waistband of his briefs, where her thumb brushed the face of his erection.

He gasped. She pulled her hand out slowly. 'Someone's going to see us,' she said. Looking toward the store, they could see the small, bright window of the swinging door.

'It's dark in here,' he said, holding her arms.

'Oh,' she shuddered, 'but we don't have time.'

'The way I feel, it won't take long.' Grinning, he reached down, found the button on her hiphuggers. She twisted her hips, laughing.

'God, have you always been this bad?'

He pulled her roughly back to him. 'Come on, we'll drive up the coast, rent a little place on the water.'

'Sal, we can't. The locals are ready to lynch me as it is.'

'Take your car. I'll meet you. I've gotta talk to you.'

She slipped away from him, backing toward the store, eyeing him with a fiercely seductive grin. 'Talk to me?'

'I found Dale Newman,' he told her.

She stopped, her smile frozen, her head cocked.

'The guy who lost the plane ticket,' he explained.

Facing him, she said nothing for a moment while her smile disappeared. She looked wounded – or angry – he couldn't tell.

'I found out where he bought the ticket,' Sal said to her.

She took a step toward him and then stopped, far enough so the distance was meaningful. 'Sal, don't you understand?' she said to him. 'Can't you see I am suffocating here? Everyplace I go, that's all I hear: Eliot Wicker, Bobby Swift, and somebody asking me where *I* was, what *I* was doing, who *I* was with. Sal, I feel like somebody's out there trying to make it look like I'm involved—'

'That's why I checked,' he said. 'I want it to stop. I want to find out what happened to Bobby.'

Eyes narrowed, she stepped closer. 'No,' she said, almost as if she were warning him. 'Sal, you need to stay out of this.' She reached out, put her hands in his jacket pockets and drew him in, drew the jacket around her. 'Sally, you're my escape, my way out of this insanity.' She lifted her face, lightly touching his body with her own, brushing his neck with her lips. 'And I don't ever want to lose you.'

And then she said nothing more, and neither did he, because the thought of losing her was far more than he could bear. So, holding her against him, hearing the low drone of conversations from the store, the clatter of silverware, the drone of country music too distant to distinguish, his lips parted against the side of her hair, breathing her fragrance in . . . and he whispered a vow: 'I'm never going to lose you.'

* * *

When the detectives returned to the barracks, Shepherd shut himself inside an interrogation room with his computer and proceeded to telephone every one of the oxygen suppliers he had contacted the day before, with a new name to check: Dale Newman. After an hour of phone conversations and no luck, he heard the door open, and a shadow fell across his desk.

'A one-way ticket to an island somewhere, and you change horses.' Murdoch leaning in the doorway. 'Don't you think it's a little suspicious that somebody gave it to us?'

Shepherd stopped dialing. 'I think it's connected.'

'And the murderer signed his real name for the oxygen tanks.'

'He signed some name. Sarge, you up for a little research?'

Murdoch turned his head to the side, unresponsive. Shepherd opened a manila folder, pulled out the photo of Bobby Swift and Sal Erickson and slid it to the edge of his desk. Murdoch stepped to the desk, turned the picture to face him. 'Fuckin greaseballs,' he said. 'I thought I left this shit back in Chicago.'

'I want facts on Bobby Swift,' Shepherd told him. 'Where he was born, where he went to school, who he worked for, what his hobbies were – everything he did after he learned to walk.'

The sergeant lowered his head; scratched at a spot on his crown with his little finger, same spot he always scratched when he wanted to show his skepticism.

'I want to get the lab boys back too,' Shepherd continued. 'I want a search warrant for the store, the apartment upstairs, the basement, garage and motor vehicles. The dumpster outside. I'm working up a list. We're looking for shoes – his or hers – so we can analyze any soil residue against the cemetery sample. We're looking for oxygen or scuba tanks or any other breathing apparatus, and I want to check the trash for discarded clothing.'

Murdoch snorted a laugh, shaking his head. 'No wonder it takes you guys so long,' he said. 'Analyze this, analyze that, Jesus Christ, find one speck of dust and analyze it a million different ways. Now you want a goddamn autobiography on this guy. That's what I mean, you go too far with this penny-ante stuff.'

Shepherd lowered the phone. 'Am I the primary on this case or not?'

'Your job isn't to tippy-toe around like you're Andy of fucking

Mayberry. Your job is to tear-ass through that town, scaring the shit out of as many people as you can until you make some sonovabitch talk!'

Shepherd hung up the phone, swiveled his chair to face the sergeant. 'Am I the primary?'

'If I say you are.'

'Am I the primary?'

The telephone buzzed. Shepherd picked up, snapped, *'What?'*

It was the receptionist from a Mid-Maine Supply in Belfast, about an hour down the coast. She'd just finished a computer search of their files and thought she'd found what Shepherd was looking for. He typed the information into his notebook computer as she spoke, then thanked the woman and hung up.

'What was that?'

Shepherd kept typing. 'Two oxygen tanks, size E, signed out last spring, May thirteen. The scuba tanks too. Same place, same date, same name.'

'Yeah?'

Shepherd said coolly, 'Dale Newman.'

'So, good. We find the asshole, we interrogate the shit out of him, we get a confession.'

Shepherd picked up the photo and held it out to Murdoch. 'I told you, Sarge, as long as I'm calling the shots, you're looking for Bobby Swift.'

The police tape was still in place, the back door window still broken. Sal reached through the hole and let himself in. If there had been any neighbors, his penlight beam would have been obvious. The house was dark, and there were no blinds on the windows. He knew he'd be arrested if he were caught here – and Noel would be furious with him – but the detectives seemed intent on hounding her until something better came up. Like maybe Dale Newman.

He went to the wall phone first, shone his light on a clipboard hanging beside it, a list of computer-printed phone numbers in alphabetical order. No Dale Newman listed, but Sal wasn't surprised. He figured that whatever connection existed between Eliot Wicker and Dale Newman – if any – he'd find it in the business files downstairs. He turned with his penlight toward the basement door—

Something stopped him.

He drew the light beam to his left, to a plain maple board attached to the wall, fitted with wooden pegs. A black nylon jacket hung from it. Sal ran the penlight beam to the left: black sportcoat; black hooded sweatshirt. Unused peg. Another peg ... then—

A touring cap. He leaned toward the cap with the light, and the floor popped, startling him. He could feel his heart beating. Brown tweed. He reached out, lifted the cap off the peg ... knew even before he turned it over and shined the light inside. PALMARY HATTERS, PROVIDENCE.

His.

He fit the cap on his head. Perfectly. He'd bought it ten years earlier when he was playing with Woody, wore it on stage, off stage, wore it all the time – until sometime last summer, sometime during the blur ... when he had lost it ...

—at Eliot Wicker's?

He heard a sound—

Bobby—

He wheeled around, the white door reflecting his penlight beam. He flicked the light off. Replayed the sound in his head, a sound that had no reason to be there. It had come from downstairs – a single muffled knock, like a door closing.

He stood in the blackness. For the first time he allowed the real possibility that Bobby was alive. If Bobby were alive, that would explain Wicker's murder. It would certainly explain how Bobby's body was missing. It would explain the glove in Sal's suitcase, the message on Noel's car window. A feeling rose up inside Sal, dark and aberrant, the likes of which he'd never known.

The sound came again, a soft drumming, almost as if it were calling him, daring him. He reached out and found the doorknob, turned it slowly so as not to disturb the latch. Deep inside, a voice counseled him to leave the dead man's house, go back through the woods, get on his motorcycle and go somewhere far away from town until he could make sense of all this—

but then the door was opening in his hand.

Feeling a movement of air rising over him, he listened again, wondering if the noise had been a mouse or a squirrel – or simply his afflicted imagination. But then he heard it again, plainer: a hard, dull knock, too heavy for a rodent. He determined that it was not directly below, but in one of Wicker's back rooms downstairs. He kept the penlight off. Holding the handrail, he descended the stairs slowly, silently. When he could feel the hard floor under his boot sole, he stopped again. The knocking seemed to come from his left, muffled enough so he could tell it was behind at least one wall. He turned on the penlight again, swept the beam quickly around the small room to ensure he was alone. He was. Only the furnace and water heater shared the space with him. He crept to the door that led into Wicker's office.

Standing at the door, he listened again to the noise – more of a rustling now – and guessed that it was coming not from this next room but from one further off. He doused the penlight anyway and turned the knob, pulled the door open. More darkness. But now the rustling sounded closer – and heavier – almost like someone was struggling.

Sal turned on his penlight, shot the beam left and right, lighting the plush burgundy carpet in front of his feet. He raised the beam to his left until he could see, twenty feet away, another door. He padded past the desk and file cabinets, his footsteps absorbed by the carpet. The nearer he got to the door, the clearer the rustling became. He took hold of the knob. Shut off the penlight. Stood in darkness, listening to the sounds. Point of no return, he said to himself, as if by going through the door, he was wandering into his own inexorable destruction—

—as if he hadn't opened that door already, some time ago. Now, finally, inevitably, he was going through.

The door hushed open and the noises stopped. He braced himself, lowered his shoulder, tensed his muscles. There was an odor in the room – carpeting, furniture—

A sudden loud knock startled him – and the rustling resumed, sounding like someone or something was trapped behind a wall. Then the noise stopped again. Sal stood in the thick of blackness, not moving. The room around him seemed to hold its breath, listening. Sal himself stopped breathing. He was afraid to even turn his head for fear that his collar would brush his neck. Then the knocking started again, seemingly oblivious to his presence, and in the knocking he could now detect a dull metallic ring.

He braced his thumb on the penlight switch, took a breath, readied himself. He turned on the light. The beam reflected off the end of a cherry casket ten feet in front of him. Sal swung the light around, saw three more caskets, each with its viewing lid opened, elevated knee-high on a platform that ran down the middle of the room, covered with burgundy cloaking. The rustling continued from the left, unmindful of his presence. He aimed his light in that direction, where more caskets were displayed along the wall, piggybacked on two levels, a row on the floor, another on a carpeted ledge. Under Sal's weak beam he could make out only one casket at a time, so he began crossing to the left, moving the light slowly ahead of him: buffed aluminum, red cherry wood, mahogany and lacquered pine, each viewing lid raised to reveal lush velvet and satin: white, deep blue, peach...

His light beam stopped on one casket just as the knocking started again. Dark, glossy mahogany. He stared. The casket was closed. Someone was inside.

He didn't stop to wonder who, or why, or whether he was in danger. He walked directly to the casket, took hold of the viewing lid, threw it up—

A light in his eyes blinded him, a hand from inside reached up, caught his wrist, pulled down powerfully. Sal pulled back, losing his penlight but twisting out of the grasp. In the same motion he grabbed the viewing lid with both hands and slammed it down, pressed it down with all his weight and muscle, heart pounding, while he tried to regain his bearings in the darkness, tried to calculate his way back through this series of rooms to the outside door.

Then, from inside the box, he heard a voice. 'Looks like I got your flashlight here...'

Bouchard—?

Sal released his weight from the casket, and the lid slowly lifted, throwing a spot of light at the ceiling. The light shifted as the constable grabbed the casket rails and pushed his shoulders up out of the viewing area, his torso following, sharply silhouetted. Something rang as he worked his hips out. Sal could see that a green cylindrical tank had fallen against a similar tank. Further inside the casket, where Bouchard's legs had been, Sal could make out a pair of scuba tanks. The light shifted again, and then in one extended motion, Alston Bouchard managed to push the rest of his body out, stepping onto the floor.

'If I'm not wrong,' the constable said, 'you were here yesterday too.' He walked past Sal, closed the door, and the room suddenly glared in light. As Sal's eyes adjusted, Bouchard's hand turned the dimmer switch to a glow. No windows, Sal realized, the light was safe. But was he?

Bouchard tipped his John Deere cap and wiped his forehead with his sleeve. His cheeks were pink and moist, his glasses fogged.

'Somebody might think you're trying to cover something up,' he said to Sal, somewhat winded.

Sal would have laughed if not for the cap on his own head, and if the constable had not been blocking the door. 'They might wonder a tiny bit about you too,' he said.

Bouchard took off his glasses, wiped them on his shirt and gazed blindly at the floor until he replaced them. He walked past Sal to the casket, bent to retrieve the penlight from inside. Sal watched him carefully.

'Then again, it wouldn't make sense, you covering something up. Not when you just left your fingerprints all over.' He tossed the penlight to Sal, who one-handed it. 'My guess is you're here looking for information on Dale Newman, to keep Noel Swift out of trouble.' He gave Sal a long, magnified look.

'Whatever you say.'

'Then I'd say you're headed for your own trouble, quite a bit more of it than you suspect.'

Sal's chest jerked with a laugh. He was trying to show the constable disdain, but he knew it wasn't convincing.

Staring at him, Bouchard threw the lid closed. 'You'd best pay attention,' he said. 'A murder's been committed. Evidence turns up. Here, here, here' – Bouchard made a fist, thumped it three times on the polished wood – 'evidence incriminating one particular person.'

Sal folded his arms to watch, humoring the constable.

'See, what I'm afraid of – what if that particular person – the suspect – was to die in an accident ... or maybe commit suicide and leave a note?'

Sal nodded. 'I'll be sure to tell Noel you're concerned about her.'

Bouchard peered at him, his black eyes bulging. The fist opened, his short fingers spread apart. 'I'm saying, with enough evidence left behind and the suspect suddenly deceased—'

'Then the case is closed,' Sal said. 'The cops and the taxpayers catch a break, and everybody goes on their merry way.'

'Case closed,' the constable agreed. 'Only what if the suspect wasn't the guilty one? What if it was all a setup?'

Something about Bouchard's steadfast stare made Sal suddenly wary. He stared back, a spark of fear kindling. 'Are you telling me that Noel's life is in danger—?'

Bouchard shook his head. He spoke evenly. 'I'm talking about you.'

Sal raised his face.

'You got somewhere to go?' Bouchard said to him.

'What are you talking about?'

'Somewhere out of state, a good distance from her. That woman's a danger to you.'

Sal held the constable's stare another second. Then he smirked again, took his penlight out of his pocket and switched it on. He turned for the door. 'If you need me,' he said, 'I'll be around.'

'Mr Erickson—'

Sal turned the doorknob, with no intention of staying for more.

'Eventually somebody's going to want to know what you and Eliot Wicker were doing together in her apartment that night Mr Wicker got himself murdered.'

Sal froze, tried not to show it. Night of the funeral, night of his show ... that's where his memory stopped.

'I just don't know what you're going to tell them.'

Sal did not turn around to see if Bouchard was bluffing. He pulled his cap down snug on his head as he left the room.

'I'll tell them they're full of shit,' he said. 'Same as you.'

At nine-thirty Iris tucked Davey into bed – Sal's side – and lay with her through the tears. What Iris told her was that Daddy loves you, but Daddy has a problem, and sometimes he hurts people without meaning to. 'Daddy didn't hurt me,' Davey told her. 'You're the one that hurt me. You made him leave.'

That's the way they left it. When Iris awoke it was ten o'clock and Davey was asleep on her arm. She turned back the blanket, fit her hand under Davey's legs and brought her close, then lifted her off the mattress and carried her out of the room, across the landing and into her own room.

Now as she laid Davey in bed, a motorcycle passed the house. Davey's eyes opened, and her head snapped up. She stared, stark with fear.

'It's okay, love,' Iris whispered, kissing her forehead, pulling the covers to her chin. 'Everything's okay.'

Sal headed east, toward the coast. He didn't know where he was going. Not home, not to his room, not to Noel's – not just yet. Maybe down to Oyster Cove, maybe he'd stop at the fish pier and call her from the pay phone. And what would he say, that he'd been to Wicker's again? That he'd found his cap there? That Bouchard had told him to stay away from her, that his life was in danger? Or maybe he'd ask her directly whether he and Wicker had been in her apartment that night.

He veered right onto the Oyster Cove Road, where, a mile along, he noticed headlights in his mirror, following some distance behind. At the top of a long hill he opened it up, accelerated down the other side of the hill, then really goosed it going up the next, the Harley feeling weightless, pushing him back on the seat. His cap, stuffed in his jacket pocket, pressed against his ribs. But how it had ended up at Wicker's—

It would have been last summer, when he was drinking hard – June, July, August – the months had vanished from his memory, swallowed by that impenetrable darkness (like the night Wicker was murdered). Still, if he had befriended Wicker during that time, or had just stopped by his house with Bobby one night, it stood to reason that he could have left his cap there.

Soaring over the top of another rise, he spotted the headlights in his rearview again, gaining on him. He opened the throttle and shot down a long, winding decline, leaning hard against the curve, until near the bottom of the hill a yellow sign flew out of the lilacs: YIELD. Considering the late hour, Sal expected no traffic, thinking to join the main road on the fly. But he glanced over and saw headlights coming in from the left, seconds from where the two roads joined. He released the gas and squeezed the brake gently to create a moment's delay, but the brake lever snapped to his throttle grip, and the Harley sailed toward impact. He stomped his foot brake, his rear wheel locked, screeched, skated out to the left—

and he was falling, incredibly, falling into the path of the headlights, still holding on to the handlebars, laying the Harley down at fifty as if he and the bike were executing a perfect hook slide, sparks showering his hips and chest, the screeching of chrome over asphalt barely enough to drown out the screech of truck tires, as the headlights came at him, thoughtfully turned to low beam, GMC proudly affixed to the pickup's grill, Sal contemplating in this long swelling sequence that he was about to be crushed, and wondering just as clearly, *Who is doing this to me?*

When all motion finally ceased, Sal lay on his side in the oncoming lane, still holding the throttle, and his engine was quiet. The front of the motorcycle protruded under the middle of the pickup truck, which was also at rest, its own front wheel up on a bank, its rear wheel touching Sal's front tire.

A man looked down at him from the truck window. 'You okay, Bud?'

'Is he okay?' a woman asked from inside the truck.

At that moment, the pickup and the man both became illuminated. Thick white beard. Leather cap. Sal turned his head, relieved that he could do so, and saw the car that had been following him stopped on the facing road. A skinny kid with long, stringy hair stood between the headlights, emergency flashers. 'Is he okay?' the kid said.

The truck driver opened his door and stepped out, his truck lifting an inch or two as he did so. 'Let's get you out of the road,' he said. 'Can you move?'

'Somebody call nine-eleven,' the woman passenger said.

'Turn on the flashers,' the man told her.

Sal raised himself onto his elbow. He felt a burning in his thigh, but he realized – gratefully – that his motorcycle had not fallen on top of him. He bent the leg, pulled it underneath him and raised himself to his knee. The leg trembled.

'Man, you are one lucky son of a bitch,' said the driver.

'Nice thing to say after you nearly killed the man,' said his wife.

'I had the right of way,' the driver replied.

'It was my fault,' Sal said. 'My front brake gave out.' He leaned on the bike to push himself up, then stood there unable to stop his shaking, looking down at himself in the orange flashing lights, amazed that the only damage seemed to be to the shoulder of his jacket. The leather was scraped dull – he scratched tiny pebbles out of it. His jeans were also torn along the outside of his thigh, where he could see raw red skin.

'You are one lucky son of a bitch,' the driver said again.

Indeed. Sal bent for the handlebars and hauled the bike out from under the truck, then strained to hoist it upright. The driver helped, pulling up on the seat. 'Don't look too bad,' he said. 'Got a peg snapped off, saddlebag ground down. Other than that—'

'Fluid,' the kid said. Sal looked over. The kid rose to his feet behind his car. 'There's a blotch of it over here.' He showed his hand, red in the taillights, then sniffed it. 'Brake fluid.'

'Right down here,' the truck driver said, feeling along the Harley's front wheel. 'See, your bleeder's loose. I can turn it with my fingers.'

Sal looked down.

'You ain't noticed your front brakes getting low?'

Sal shook his head.

'No shit, it's opened right up wide.' Now the driver looked up at Sal. 'Bleeders don't usually open up on their own,' he said. 'Not like this.'

The man's ominous tone sent a dull jolt through Sal.

'I don't know, man. You been sleepin in the wrong bed somewhere?'

'Complaint,' said Jerry Royal, signaling the waitress with a sluggish finger. His head was killing him. Worse than that, he felt like a flatlander, dressed like he was. Friggin blue shoes. He squashed out his cigarette and lit another.

Undone

Outside the window, nothing moved, everything was dark. The last window lights from the tenements across the street had gone out hours ago. Cars had long since stopped passing while he sat there waiting for her. Now he was the last customer in the place.

Noel had promised to meet him at eleven-thirty – not in town; not even in Ellsworth, where she was afraid they might be recognized – but fifty miles away, in Bangor, in this nowhere hotel, the Blue BelAir, off in some lost part of the city by the river.

Fuckin room had set him back forty-five dollars. Not to mention the new clothes he had bought at the L.L. Bean's outlet in Ellsworth. A hundred bucks to look like the store mannequin: turtleneck jersey with wide purple and white stripes. At L. L. Bean they didn't call it purple and white; they called it eggplant and oyster. They could have called them grape jam and chicken; he felt goddamned foolish dressed like that. White pants they called stone, with an elasticized waistband. And *reef runners* on his feet – soft nylon things with thin rubber soles, bright blue and black – they looked like friggin ballet slippers! But at thirty-two bucks, hey, compared to what they wanted for leather?

Fuckin buffalo wings was another seven bucks. *Buffalo wings*. Thirty more on rum Cokes, which left him a five dollar bill, no gas in his truck and an hour's drive back to town. Four or five times he had climbed the stairs up to his room to see whether Noel was there; more often had checked at the lobby to see if she'd left a message for him, but there was not a word. And she had warned him not to call her. He did anyway, eventually – he called her – and he kept trying for over an hour, but all he got was a busy signal.

'The buffalo wings was bad,' he told the waitress when she finally made it over, 'what little there was of 'em. They gimme a wicked friggin headache.'

The girl had straight blonde hair and no makeup, the face of a ten-year-old, with freckles and full breasts. College girl from the university. He gave her a sorry look, imagining that she had her own room at the hotel and that she'd take him there and nurse him. Christ, the top two buttons of her blouse were already undone. Askin for it, that type. As horny as he'd made himself waiting for Noel, he was just the man to give it to her. He stretched his reef runners under the corner of the table so she could see. Mr L. L. Bean.

'I'm sorry you didn't like them,' she said. 'Would you like something else?'

He touched her ankle with his toe, and she moved her foot. 'Now that you ask,' he said, his voice sort of low in his throat, 'I might need a place to lay down later.' He was thinking that if she refused him, he might follow her home anyway.

'Did you want to speak to the manager, sir?'

'What for? I ain't gay. I mean you.'

She turned and walked to the bar, where she said something to the bartender, who looked over. Jerry put his hands on the table to push it away and almost tipped it over. He saved the table, but his glass tumbled onto the soft carpet, and two or three ice cubes skated away.

'Don't worry, I'm leavin,' he said. 'Long's you don't expect me to pay for buffalo parts that's about to poison me to death.'

Sal shut off the ignition as he turned onto the Village Road. He let the momentum carry him onto the bridge, where he eased on his foot brake and stopped, set his feet apart on the grating and balanced the bike between his legs. The river whispered below him, peepers chorusing off to his left. He looked up the hill at her building, darkened except for the two front windows in her upstairs apartment, wondering whether to go up there and ask her about what Bouchard had said – that he and Wicker had been together up there that night. And now Bouchard's telling him that someone was trying to pin Wicker's murder on *him?* He wondered, and not for the first time, if Bouchard himself had planted the cap, loosened the bleeder.

or Bobby

He decided to stay on the bridge for awhile, until her lights went out – and if he saw her pass by the window, he would go up. He would not ask about Wicker, not tell her about finding his cap or about his brakes failing. Not tonight anyway. He sat and watched her windows. Not a car passed. Five minutes went by, maybe ten, with no sign of her.

A chill rose off the water. Downriver, peepers sang anxiously.

He lifted his collar, pulled his cap out of his pocket and fit it on his head. *Evidence turns up*, Bouchard had said.

He looked behind him into the darkness, thinking he had heard movement in the trees. But the river was too loud to distinguish any furtive sound. The river. Something about the river bothered him – its persistence, maybe – or indifference—

Evidence turns up.

Sins come back.

That's how the Passamaquoddies had put it. *Sins come back.* The legend was well known in town. In the spring of the year, when the river was still deathly cold, a young man would make his way to the reversing falls. He would sit alone on the sandbar between the river and the pool all night and wait. During the fifteen minutes when the incoming tidal waters made their noisy way over the rocks, defying gravity, the man would take off his clothes, walk into the water and lie on his back in the middle of the flow. It was believed that his past sins would ride in on the tidal waters and wash over him. If his transgressions were few, and if he were truly repentant, the spirits of his ancestors would protect him: he would survive the ordeal and emerge from the river absolved. But if his sins were many, or severe, in the morning his body would be found face-down in the pool.

Now the river rushed under Sal's feet, tearing into the black woods, and an acrid mist rose up through the grating, surrounding him. Downstream, peepers screamed. Above his head, a battery of clouds attacked the moon, further darkening the night. And then his uncooperative mind circled a darker notion. What if—

All at once the peepers stopped.

Someone was down there, down at the pool. Sal's fingers tensed on his handgrips. As he listened, the sound of the river washing over rocks began to sound like soft, secret laughter.

Sins come back.

The fear climbed into Sal's chest, and without another thought, he kicked the starter, engaged the gears, then pulled away, not looking back.

Everything was dark when Jerry left the hotel, everything black and still, as if the entire world were asleep. What he felt like doing was driving straight back to town, waking that smart bitch up and teaching her a good thing or two about keeping her word. But now, with her new locks on the doors and the whole building rigged with alarms – and Alston Bouchard and the detectives and god-knew-who-else keeping their eye on her – fat chance.

So now what? Randy as a three-balled bull in a henhouse, he walked alongside the brick building, looking over at the dark tenements across the street and wondering which one of those groundfloor windows opened onto a girl sleeping by herself.

He turned around the back of the building where the parking lot was even darker. Streetlights out too. Stupid fucking hotel with a pitch-black parking lot. He had gone to the front desk to get his money back for the room, but even that was closed up. So now what? Having forgotten where in the parking lot he had left his truck, he had to navigate his way around the other vehicles by lining up their shapes with the reflection of streetlights from across the wide river.

No one around. No lights for the customers. Good place to get hurt, Jerry thought. Generate a little income. But then they'd say he was drunk – which he was. The bartender and waitress would testify to that. So, fuck 'em, he'd sue their asses too. Plump little thing dressed like that. Prancing around, waving her college butt in the air like a little white-tailed deer, bending over at the tables, giving everyone the tittie show.

Did you want to speak to the manager, sir?

Good place to get hurt, alright. It felt like the night was poised for it, the way his soft new shoes Indian-whispered over the asphalt. Very good place.

He found his truck where he'd left it four hours ago – when the lights were on and he had felt a whole lot better about things, all showered and shaved and dressed in his flatlander clothes – which no one in a million years would ever guess was him. He opened his door and pushed in behind the steering wheel, facing the hotel. Only the lounge windows were lit downstairs, however dimly. Bambi probably counting her five dollars in tips. Everything else was dark and done for the night.

It wouldn't be long, he thought. She'd come out feeling her way in the dark. See what she thinks of Mr L. L. Bean now, ripping off those college girl panties and stuffing them in that sassy little mouth while he teaches her something about customer service.

He stuck his key in the ignition, turned to accessory power. '*Ring of Fire*,' by Johnny Cash, was on the radio. Country Gold. Jerry turned it up a little, to let her hear it when she came out, imagining it'd get her curious and she'd come over to investigate. A little louder, actually, in case she puts up a fight. He rolled down his window, slouched back, folded his arms, leaned the back of his head against the back window and set his eyes on the corner of the building, watching, waiting. His head against the window?

That's when he realized: his gun – his shotgun was gone!

The truck suddenly rocked, and before Jerry could wonder why, an oak log smashed through the glass behind him and struck the side of his face. Falling forward into the steering wheel, Jerry recoiled and started to turn, when the same log smashed through the window again, two gloved hands following in the shower of glass. Jerry tried to duck, but in the same instant he felt a fierce constriction around his throat. His head snapped back into the broken window. Stiff shards snapped against the top of his head. But his throat! He gagged, groped for the constriction and felt absolutely nothing except the fabric of his turtleneck jersey.

He reached behind his neck, felt the gloved hands, hard as knots, twisting around each other. That's when he found the wire, tight and thick, like fence wire. He realized he was being killed. He shot his elbow back, it struck the cab. He wanted to fit his head back through the broken window, to relieve the pressure, but whoever held the wire was pulling much too hard, and he couldn't bend his head to get it through.

Then he was aware of something hard and cold pressing against his cheekbone – someone standing outside his door. The man spoke in a low, almost comforting voice through Jerry's open window. 'Okay, my friend,' he said, 'you've got ten seconds to save your life, and I'll tell you how.'

Friend? Jerry made a gagging sound down in his throat below the wire to show that he understood. The man reached in across Jerry's chest, turned the radio louder, Johnny Cash boomin on 'bout how it burns, burns, burns. Fuckin' A.

'I can either shoot you right here through the ear, or my colleague behind you can give this piano cord one more good twist, which is the way we prefer it. Less noisy, no mess. You, on the other hand, would probably rather take the slug. Less pain and suffering.'

The man in the back of Jerry's truck gave a sharp grunt, the wire tightened unbelievably, the knuckles digging into the nape of Jerry's neck. Jerry's butt came off the seat. His legs straightened and his feet pressed the brake to the floor. He picked at the wire with his fingers, but as thick as his turtleneck was, he couldn't get his nails under it.

'Of course, we could also let you go. I'm guessing that's the option you'd prefer, am I correct?'

Jerry made a clipped, strangling sound, his eyes swelling, ready to blow.

'That's what I thought. Okay then, I'm going to ask you one question. Accordingly, you'll have one chance to answer.'

'*And only one*,' said the man in the back of the truck, his mouth practically touching Jerry's ear, his voice higher-pitched and much less comforting.

'Ready for your question?'

Jerry stomped the brake twice.

'Now, we know that you recently wrote a letter; and, furthermore, that you are now using that letter for the purpose of blackmail. See, we all know that for a fact. But what only you know, and what we *need* to know, is exactly where you hid that letter. So now you tell us.'

'And then we'll let you go,' said the voice in his ear.

Again Jerry stomped twice.

'I think he's going to tell us,' said the man with the gun.

'Hands on the wheel,' said the man with the wire.

'Put your hands on the wheel,' repeated the man with the gun.

Jerry reached out, took hold of the steering wheel, his throat wrung with wire, his face bulging.

'Now my colleague is going to release a little tension from your throat in order for you to give us your answer,' said the gunman.

'However,' added the wireman, 'if you give the wrong answer, or if you take your hands off the wheel or otherwise piss us off, I'm gonna slice through your freakin neck like a piece of provolone. And then he's going to shoot you through the eyes.'

'Are you ready to give us your answer?'

Jerry stomped the brake three times.

'I think he's ready.'

'Okay then,' said the wireman, and he shoved his fists alongside Jerry's neck, releasing the garrote from his neck. Jerry sucked in a harsh whistle of wind, and it caught in his throat, choking him.

'That happens,' said the gunman. 'Take your time.'

Jerry gagged, felt almost like he was going to be sick. The muzzle of the pistol poked his ear.

'Okay, friend, now tell us where you hid that letter.'

Jerry gasped, shut his eyes.

'Tell us now.'

Jerry strained for a breath, filled his lungs. 'Friggin liars,' he whispered. 'You won't kill me unless I *do* tell you!'

Immediately the fists punched into the back of his head again, and the wire snapped against his throat – except this time the wire caught his skin above the turtleneck material, above his Adam's apple, and Jerry rose off his seat, strangling. His fingers went to his neck, trying to pick at the garrote.

'Hands on the wheel!'

Incredibly, the wire tightened, slicing into his flesh. Jerry's knees pummeled the bottom of the dash.

'*On the wheel!*'

Obediently, Jerry grabbed the steering wheel, pulling and pushing on it so hard that its shape began to change. For several seconds while he strangled, nobody spoke, except for Johnny Cash, that is, boomin and burnin, until all of a sudden the radio went quiet.

Then the softer, more reasoned voice of the gunman. 'Okay, my friend. Now I'll have to introduce a rider to our first rule, and that is, if you don't answer our question correctly this time, then you will be tortured until you do.'

'Tell him about the eyes,' said Wireman.

'Now, you called us liars, and I have to say I take personal umbrage at that remark. I gave you my word as a gentleman, and

I give you my word again: You tell us where you hid that letter, and we will let you go.'

'Tell him about the eyes,' Wireman said again.

Jerry made a choking sound deep in his diaphragm.

Wireman pushed his face into the broken rear window, close to Jerry's ear. 'See the way your eyes are poking out right now,' he said, 'like a couple of ripe olives? If I wanted to, I could just dig in with my thumbnail and pop that one right out.'

Jerry could not even blink. Now Gunman leaned further in the side window. The muzzle of his pistol pressed hard against Jerry's cheekbone.

'Okay, Jerry, tell us where you hid the letter.'

'The eyes go first,' said Wireman. 'Then the ears, the tongue – we snip them off with pruning shears – then your thumbs. And that fuckin hurts.'

'Jerry, tell us where you put that letter and we'll let you go. Now, we know it's not in your truck, because we've been all through your truck.'

'So then we deduced that you must have hidden the letter in your house. Is that right? Is that where the letter is?'

Jerry forced a grunt, stamped on the brake.

'Was that a yes, in your house?' asked Gunman. 'Loosen up,' he said to Wireman, and the wire suddenly relaxed, peeling out of Jerry's flesh, the man's fists separating behind Jerry's neck and pushing up under the ears, giving the wire an inch of slack.

Jerry made a strangling sound as he gasped for air.

'Just shake your fucking head,' Wireman said. 'Did you say yes, it's in the house?'

Jerry took another breath, let it out noisily. He lowered his head.

'Wait a minute, he's trying to talk,' Gunman said to his partner.

Jerry took another breath, then raised his face, sat up straight.

'*Pigfucker!*' he rasped, and then with a grunt, he lurched forward, caught the wire against his turtleneck, and pulled against the steering wheel as hard as he could, throwing his big shoulders powerfully forward, dragging Wireman's arms through the rear window clean to the shoulders. In the same motion, Jerry grabbed the wrist that held the gun and pulled the gunman's arm deep into the truck. Then, jerking back again, he created enough slack in the wire to grab it with his right hand, and before Wireman could uncoil the wire from his gloved hands, Jerry pushed the wire forward with all his might, hauling Wireman's head and shoulders through the broken window until Gunman's pistol and Wireman's face were touching.

'*Look out!*' shouted Wireman. Jerry slammed the gun barrel down on his temple, hard enough to make him grunt, but not hard enough to knock him out. Adrenaline surged. Gunman's left fist came searching through the open window, punching at Jerry's face, and Jerry warded off the blows with his left shoulder, while Wireman desperately worked his wrists, trying to unwind the wire. To slow down Gunman, Jerry forced his pistol hand up against the windshield, making it necessary for Gunman to cross his punches over, effectively disarming him. To slow down Wireman, Jerry kicked his right knee up and caught the man's jaw, making a loud *clack*. Wireman cursed, seemed to get stronger. His wrist swiveled and suddenly came free of the wire. Just as fast, Jerry let go of the wire, got his hand around Wireman's neck, thumb hard in his gullet. Wireman threw his left elbow back, connected with Jerry's chest. Jerry retaliated by shoving Wireman's face straight down as his knee came straight up, caught him square. Wireman's head snapped back, as if off its hinges. Jerry kicked again, needlessly – the man was out – but Jerry's knee connected anyway and his foot kicked the dash, the keys gouging his toe knuckle through his nylon shoes. The shoes showed him the way out.

Leaning hard to his left, still clutching Gunman's gun hand and Wireman's neck, Jerry angled his foot upward so the key pressed into his toes. While Gunman continued to throw rapid but powerless punches, Jerry squeezed his first two toes together, caught the tip of the key and twisted his foot, leaned hard to the right, taking Gunman's arm and Wireman's head with him.

The engine turned, started. Jerry reached his left foot to the gas pedal and stomped it. The engine roared. He banged into gear with Wireman's face, and the truck shot forward. Gunman cried out, became an anchor, his body turning backwards. Jerry suddenly let the gun hand fall away as he grabbed the wheel and cut left. The truck jumped. Jerry braked. A gurgling scream came from behind him. Shifting with his knee, Jerry banged into reverse and kicked the gas. The truck shot back, met instant resistance. Jerry braked again. The cry strangled under the truck. Deftly, Jerry toed the accelerator and brake in tandem, and the back of his truck climbed.

Still holding Wireman by the throat, Jerry jammed the gearshift into park and threw his door open. Wireman, emitting a pinched, squeaking sound, started moving an arm. Jerry rammed his head into the doorjamb; Wireman's body once again fell limp. Jerry staggered out, hauling the unconscious man behind him, knees and toes tearing through the broken rear window, then bouncing out the door and onto the pavement. Gunman, pinned face-down under the rear wheel, moaned painfully. Jerry spotted the man's pistol lying on the asphalt beside him. He gave it a kick, sent it spinning underneath a van beside them. Then he dropped Wireman in a heap.

Gunman groaned. 'Oh, man, get it off. I can't feel my legs.'

Jerry bent over him. 'This is a brand new Chevy half-ton,' he rasped.

Gunman breathed loudly.

'Now you best tell me what you did with my shotgun, or next I'm gonna drive it straight over the top of your head.'

'Oh, listen,' Gunman whispered, 'we only wanted to shake you up a little—'

At Jerry's feet, Wireman stirred, sounded like a dog whimpering in his sleep. He pulled his knees up, looked like he was thinking about crawling under the truck. Jerry placed his reef runner on his hip, pushing him over onto his side.

'And you,' he said, 'trying to cut off my head—'

He bent down, grabbed Wireman behind his knees, turning the short man onto his back.

'Oh,' Wireman said, protecting his head with both arms.

It was a wrestling move. Jerry had seen it hundreds of times before, never had a chance to use it himself. Now, locking Wireman's knees in his arms, lifting the man's hips off the pavement, he jerked back and turned to his left, sweeping the man's head and shoulders into the air.

'Oh,' Wireman moaned.

Jerry, leaning back, swinging Wireman by the legs, made a full revolution and then stepped toward his truck. The sudden bang of skull against tailgate stopped his motion. He dropped the man in a motionless pile behind the truck.

'I swear,' Gunman said, 'we were gonna let you go.'

Jerry reached over the side rail, felt among the logs, chain saw, gas can, toolbox, empty beer cans, until he found his shotgun. He lifted it out.

'Honest to God, we never killed anybody in our life—'

Jerry slammed the shotgun butt down between the man's shoulder blades.

'*Huh!*' Gunman said.

Jerry leaned into his truck and set the shotgun in its rack, where it belonged. 'You tell her she's paying for the damage to my truck,' he rasped as he stepped in behind the wheel and Gunman groaned. 'And another thing,' he said, shutting his door. 'Tell her I get the friggin hint.' He punched into drive, hit the accelerator and heard a vicious screech, leaving one strip of rubber on his way out.

At midnight Iris finished folding the laundry and turned off the television. The days without Sal were full and hectic and long – endless, with work and study and house chores and tending to Davey. Evenings were the worst, after Davey went to bed, closed up in her hollow, unforgiving house with no other adult to talk to. So she did homework until after midnight, when she was finally tired enough to sleep, and then she went into the bathroom, where she washed and brushed, and finally she climbed up to her bedroom. She took off her jeans and hung them in the closet; took off her jersey and her bra and was setting her alarm clock when she became aware that a low rumbling had just stopped outside the house. When she heard the squeal of the kitchen door, she pulled on her nightshirt and hurried out of her room onto the landing. By the time she had reached the stairs, Sal was down at the bottom, looking up. Iris's finger went to her lips, silencing him before he could speak. She tiptoed across the landing and pulled Davey's door closed, then went down the stairs, feeling self-conscious about her bare legs. She walked around him into the kitchen, directly to the door, intending to see him out. She did not want a conversation.

'I know it's late,' Sal said to her.

'We'll have to figure something out,' she told him, opening the door. 'You can't just come over because you have a key.'

'Iris, I need to ask you—'

'Can it wait till Sunday?'

'I need to ask you.'

'Shh,' she said. The sharpness of his voice, the look on his face. Iris stiffened.

He folded his arms, looked awkward doing so, as if he didn't know what to say now that he had her attention; or else he didn't know how to stand in his own kitchen anymore. 'I found my hat,' he said. 'Remember I couldn't find my hat?'

The wall clock whirred between them. She looked at him. *Ask.*

'What I wanted to say – I'm trying to remember – Eliot Wicker, was I a friend of his or – an acquaintance – like maybe back in the summer? I'm a little blocked.'

'I don't know what you did last summer.'

He nodded contritely. 'The other night – after my show – do you know what time I came home?'

She sighed. 'Sal, the end of this conversation is you promising to never drink again and asking to come back – and me having to refuse.' She punctuated her statement with her eyes, so soft and gray behind her specs, yet so unyielding.

He shook his head staunchly. 'Iris, I have not been drinking,' he said. 'I'm telling you, I'm over that.'

'Are you over *her?*' Iris glared for an instant, then shut her eyes, wishing she could erase that. Unable, she took a stiff breath, let it out and moved to the door. 'You have to go.'

'Iris, I need to know,' he said. 'I need to know this.'

Her eyes suddenly focused beyond him. He knew that Davey was there. He turned and saw her staring from the bottom of the stairs.

Iris moved quickly. 'Love, please go back up to bed. Daddy will come see you on Sunday.'

But Davey was not retreating. Iris turned on the stairway light, then bent and grazed Davey's head with her lips, saying to her, 'Daddy's just leaving now.'

'Go ahead, hon,' Sal said. 'Day after tomorrow.' Managing a smile, he made a casting motion.

Davey continued to stare, adamant.

He went to her, stepped around Iris and let Davey's hair slide through his fingers. He leaned over and kissed her on the cheek, then knelt beside her and put his arms around her warm back and held her. He wanted to tell her, too, that he was sober and that he would remain so. But the look Davey gave him made him feel like his chest was collapsing. 'Day after tomorrow,' he said again—

All at once Davey's face shone brilliantly, and a colossal boom rocked the house.

Iris cried out. Davey sat hard on the stairs. 'Jesus!' Sal said, capturing his daughter in his arms, covering her.

'It's on fire,' Iris said.

Sal looked back. Through the lace curtains at the bottom of the stairs, he could see that the garage attached to her father's house across the street was fully engulfed.

'I'll call the fire department!' Sal said, releasing Davey and pushing past Iris, turning the corner into the kitchen.

Iris pulled the curtains back and stared. Already the right side of the house was ignited, flames jumping up the sky blue shingles.

In the kitchen, Sal turned on the table light and hit the FIRE button on the automatic dialer. The phone rang three times before it was answered.

'Fire department,' the sleepy voice answered on the other end. Noel.

'It's Sal.'

'Hi. You're on the fire phone, you know.'

'There's a fire,' he said. 'My father-in-law's house, across the street. Royals'.'

There was a pause, and then Noel asked dryly, 'Where are you?'

He tried to decipher her tone. Concerned? Curious? No, she sounded almost casual. He glanced back and saw Iris in the doorway, watching him. The window curtain flickered wildly behind her.

'It's going up fast,' he said into the phone. 'Hurry up, I'm going over to try to get them out.'

'Be careful,' Noel told him, and he hung up. The siren began wailing in the village before he was out the door.

In the living room, Davey moved back to the third step. Iris came and stood in front of her, watching out the window as Sal ran across the street toward the conflagration. Chickens, dancing in the driveway, scattered from him as he bounded through them, shielding his face from the heat. Thirty feet from the house, he was driven back.

Already the fire had worked its way to the front door. The window on the right was pulsing in flames, and black smoke shot out the peak vents both left and right.

Iris could feel the heat through the window glass. And now, beneath the wailing of the firehouse siren and the hard crackling of flames, she detected a dull, steady pounding, like someone beating a drum out of rhythm.

In seconds, flames were surging out all the windows, black smoke pumping into the sky, her father's house roaring like a waterfall. Above the roar, she could hear high-pitched squealing, loud popping, glass breaking. To the right of the house, Sal stripped off his leather jacket. Holding it in front of his face, he seemed to wade into the flames.

'Mommy?' Davey cried.

Iris peered into the fire, trying to see where he had gone, trying to see also if her father or brother had escaped. But all she saw was the white chest freezer on the knoll in back, lit up brilliantly, the blue gospel bus just beyond, the random trail of junk cars and snow-mobiles dancing in the firelight. Besides the scurrying chickens, there was no sign of life, not even Sal; just the flames eating up the shingles, slapping at the eaves in a solid sheet, hollowing out the house. Already its flimsy skeleton was evident, compliantly holding up the flames. In the village the siren wailed on. Iris realized that the pounding had stopped.

'Mommy, I'm afraid,' Davey said.

Iris hardened herself with rationalization: If they had gotten out, they were saved; if not, they were already dead. There was nothing she could do. 'Feel,' she said.

Davey reached out and touched the window glass, then pulled her hand away, giving her mother a look of horror. All at once, as they both watched, the garage across the street fell in with mocking slowness, taking with it the attached right wall of the tinder house. The roof dropped four feet at the corner, nodding. Waves of sparks bellowed into the sky.

'I want Daddy to come back,' Davey said, her voice shaking.

The siren of a fire engine suddenly distinguished itself from the firehouse alarm and the crackling of flames. Headlights cut through the smoke.

'Here they come,' Iris said as the fire truck pulled up, red lights flashing.

'I don't see Daddy.'

A smaller fire truck came up behind. Iris watched a man jump out and grab a black coat off the side. Now cars and pickup trucks began converging from both directions, men in black fire coats hauling the fire hose from the bigger truck.

Another siren screamed in from the right, and a rescue van came in behind it, yellow lights flashing. Men ran shouting, pulling on gear, carrying axes, shovels, portable water tanks. Martha Abraham hurried down the road in her bathrobe, taking flash photos with a pocket camera. A man and woman from the rescue van hurried past her with a stretcher. Another man, adjacent to the back corner of the house, began wheeling his arm, hailing the stretcher-bearers.

'I don't see Daddy,' Davey said again.

The shouting suddenly intensified as a diesel engine raced. The men holding the fire hose planted themselves, and a thick cord of water exploded from the hose. The instant the water hit the house, the entire front wall fell in and the roof collapsed in a dense, loud wall of smoke and sparks. Through the rolling black cloud, suddenly Sal appeared, circling around the back of the ruins, laden with a hulking body in his arms.

Davey pressed her face close to the window. 'That's him! That's Daddy!'

As Sal struggled away from the fire, he was pursued by a

concentration of men in fire gear, their faces concealed by breathing masks attached to their helmets. Four of them bore the empty stretcher.

It was her father in Sal's arms, Iris could tell by the shape, and she wondered how Sal could possibly lift him. A uniformed woman hurried alongside Sal, holding a mask to Otis's face.

Davey looked fearfully up at Iris. 'Is he dead?' she asked.

'I don't know,' Iris answered. The deeper truth was – and this hardened her more – she did not actually care.

At the road, Sal transferred Otis to the stretcher. As rescue workers wheeled him into the ambulance, two other men tried to attend to Sal. One was Herb True, the fire chief, who looked like he wanted Sal to get in the ambulance too. The other tried to put a mask to Sal's face. But Sal waved them both off, trudging heavily through the smoke and headlights. Giving up, Herb signaled the ambulance driver. A woman climbed into the back with Otis and closed the door, and the vehicle took off with lights flashing.

Iris watched out the warm window. Sal's face was blackened, and smoke rose off his back and shoulders. He stood there balancing himself on the roadside, and then he looked across the road at his house, at the front window, where his wife and daughter were watching him. Iris closed the curtains.

An hour later, the last three firefighters quietly wound the hose onto the truck. Only the small pumper remained in the Royals' driveway, ostensibly to prevent the fire from reigniting. But with the ground saturated from the recent rain and the barrage of water from the trucks – and nothing left of the structure but the four corner cinder blocks that had been its foundation – there was little chance of a fire spreading. The main reason the men stayed was to wait for Jerry to come home.

At two o'clock he did, a chill wind whipping through the broken glass behind his head, his neck raw and burning from the necklacing he'd received, his brain racing with the plans he had for Noel Swift. Fifty feet from the destruction, he hit the brakes.

His house was gone.

Gaping out his windshield, a wave of light-headedness overtook him. Where he'd once had a home and a bed, a TV and VCR and recliner, now only a heap of black rubble remained, surrounded by his stony, junk-strewn land.

'Oh boy,' he said.

The fire truck's headlights illuminated his bathtub, sink and toilet clustered together in the ashes, gleaming white. His stove and refrigerator. Worthless survivors, like the chickens that wandered in the road, dazed and homeless; the blue gospel bus; the old chest freezer up on the rise—

'Oh boy,' he said again.

He pulled the truck to the foot of his driveway, shifted into park and left the motor idling as he stepped tentatively onto the road. The freezer, up in the new grass, shone in the pumper's headlights as if it were on stage.

'Jerry?' It was Herb True, heading him off.

'Where's my house?' Jerry said.

Herb's voice was unusually somber. 'We got him outta there,' he said, shaking his head sadly.

Blood turned icy in Jerry's arms; his face grew hot.

'They took him to Downeast. Sal Erickson pulled him out. He'd got himself trapped in the bathroom and punched his way through the medicine cabinet. Must've took it for a window. He drove that sucker right through the side of the house, but then he got stuck halfway out. He's burnt up pretty bad.'

Jerry continued walking up his driveway, twenty feet of gravel that led nowhere. He looked up at his freezer again. 'So what am I gonna do now?' he rasped. 'I suppose the power's out.'

'You want,' Herb said, 'we can offload your frozen goods. Probably room at the Superette, if Noel doesn't mind.'

Jerry stared at the freezer for a second. Then he looked straight at Herb.

'Jerry, you got a place to stay?' The voice came from inside the fire truck. Alston Bouchard.

Jerry ignored him, turned and walked down his driveway.

'Jerry, you okay?' Herb called. Jerry didn't answer. He got in his pickup truck, circled around and was driving away even before he shut his door.

'Downeast Memorial!' Herb called to him. 'Check the emergency ward.'

* * *

Sal sat on his bed and ran a B-flat blues scale up and down, turned it into a rough *Misterioso*. His breath was tight, his lungs gnashing each time he drew a breath. He played because he couldn't sleep, he couldn't go home, couldn't talk to Noel, couldn't take a drink ... because he couldn't fathom his own thoughts. So he played on, grateful there were no neighbors to disturb. His face was parched, red and swollen, and his eyes burned so badly that he kept them closed. Even after showering and tossing his clothes out the window, he continued to smell smoke with every breath. But he played on, hoping to remember.

He thought of Avery Bingstream, the school principal, his arm in a cast. Sal was told that he had pitched the principal off the stage and broken his arm. He recalled nothing of it, not a glimpse. Sober, he never would have harmed the man, who was decent and sincere and gentle. But, blinded by vodka, he had assaulted Avery Bingstream with no apparent reason or remorse.

That same night, Eliot Wicker had been bludgeoned and buried alive. And now Bouchard was telling him that he and Wicker had been together an hour or two earlier. So where was the night hiding? Somewhere deep in his memory, walled over by this narcosis, this uncooperative mind.

He set the trombone on the bed, leaned over to the telephone and called Rhode Island directory assistance, got his parents' phone number. He dialed, then lay on his back while he listened to the phone ring.

'It's Sal,' he said when his father answered.

At first there was no response.

'It's Salvatore, I'm up in Maine.'

Another pause. 'How are you?' his father said, although he didn't sound like he wanted to know.

'I've been teaching school. Eight years. What are you doing? You retired?'

'I was just sleeping. It's very late.'

'You still carving decoys?'

Sal waited while the big man cleared his throat. 'Some.'

I saved a man's life tonight, what do you think of that?

'How's Mom?'

No response.

'I want to talk to Mom.'

'I got her in a home.'

In a home. 'I want to talk to her about Anthony – about the day he drowned.'

Another pause.

'There's no point now.'

'No, there is. I want to get something straight.'

'It's in the past—'

'*Yeah?*' The word came out in a laugh. 'Maybe *your* past.'

His father responded, 'We can't change what's in the past.'

'I didn't tell him to go out on the ice, you know. Do you think I did? Do you think I pushed him in?'

'Why don't you call back another time when you're feeling better—'

'No, why don't you tell me what you think I did that day, because my memory's shot, and I'm never gonna feel any better than I do right now. I saved a man's life tonight, Dad, what do you think of that? I'm a goddamn hero tonight.'

The phone clicked dead.

Up in his boarding room, Sal laid his arm over his eyes, still holding the phone. He pictured the old house, his mother standing by the back door, looking out the window; the ruffled, red-checkered curtains, the sunny little porch filled with grocery bags of apples ... and nobody speaking. He reached over and replaced the receiver in its cradle. Chuckled once, bitterly. *In the past*. He turned over, moving slowly at first. Then, in a blur, he lunged across the bed, toppling the night table and telephone, until he was on his feet, his fist arcing toward the wall, the framed print of a four-masted ship in the storm.

Darkness covered the town, a steady, solemn quiet. Up at the village, only the fire station remained lit, one of its garage doors opened on the empty bay, while two cars waited outside for the pumper's return. A hundred feet back, the Superette stood closed and dark.

Even Jerry's truck was quiet as it swung down the driveway. Headlights off, engine off, his tires barely humming. He braked without a sound and then quietly opened the door. Up on the road he heard the fire truck drive past; he watched its lights flutter over the treetops, from left to right.

Smart bitch, she had hired the hit men, and then she'd set the fire, any fool could figure that. Lured him up to Bangor to have him killed and then burnt him out to destroy his blackmail letter. Smart bitch, high time somebody took some of that smart out of her. He stepped quietly onto the driveway and moved to the door in his soft new shoes, with barely a hush. He didn't have her new keys, but a locked door or an alarm wasn't about to stop him now. He took hold of the doorknob—

To his surprise, it clicked open. Smart bitch, so she burnt his letter. Too smart for her own good – she forgot to lock her own door. What did she think, that he was too stupid to figure it out?

The shadow that rose in front of him was about to answer his question when a voice behind him yelled, '*Jerry!*'

Startled, he spun, and a pistol shot fired. Jerry jumped clear. A second shot rang—

'*That's enough!*' the other man yelled, standing beside the door, his back pressed to the wall. 'That's enough!' he yelled again.

A light came on inside the garage, flooding out the open door. The man standing against the wall was Alston Bouchard. '*Don't you shoot me!*' he said.

'Alston, is that you?' Noel's voice, from inside.

'It's me.'

'He was breaking in.'

'I know.'

Jerry lay flat against the garage door, his heart pounding. He ran his hand up his shoulder to the right side of his face, feeling for blood. He had *heard* the bullet zing past his ear.

'Jerry, you alright?' Bouchard asked him.

'*Jerry?*' Noel said, stepping outside. 'Jerry Royal?'

Jerry raised his arm, felt the torn elbow of his new jersey. 'Fuckin A,' he whispered.

'You were breaking in, Jerry,' Bouchard told him. 'She's got a right to protect her property.'

'Jerry, what were you thinking?' Noel said from the doorway, the revolver in her hand. 'I could have killed you.'

Bouchard looked down at him, also waiting for an answer.

Jerry raised himself to his elbows, weighted by a weakness that approached nausea. Oh, she's suckered him good.

'In case you didn't know,' he rasped, 'I just lost my house! What happened to neighbors helpin neighbors?' He pulled himself to a sitting position, where the faint window light illuminated the glistening raw line on his neck, as well as the dried blood on the turtleneck and shoulder of his jersey. Another blotch marked the knee of his right trouser leg. He looked like he'd just finished a session with his chickens.

'Jerry, what happened to your neck?' Bouchard said.

Seeing how far he was from the door, Jerry realized he had jumped a good ten feet in the air. 'Cut myself shaving,' he answered as he struggled to his feet, leaning on the building for support.

Testing his legs, which were still shaky, he looked back at the door. 'Fuckin blue shoes,' he said with some amazement, thinking for the second time tonight that the reef runners had saved his life. He brushed the seat of his trousers and turned to his truck, and that's when he saw the bullet hole in the door. His shoulders dropped.

'Jerry, you really have to be more careful,' Noel said. 'You can't just go opening people's doors.'

Jerry wandered to his vehicle, touched the bullet hole. He looked at his shotgun hanging from his broken back window, considered pulling it out and blasting her Volvo. He would have, too, if Bouchard hadn't been standing there.

'You got somewhere to go?' the constable asked him.

'*Yes.*' Jerry twisted the word into two syllables, even with his raspy voice. 'Won't be the first time I slept in this thing.' He got in his truck and slammed the door; threw his elbow out the open window, then said, 'Alston, where'd you come from, anyways?'

'I was down your place with the fire truck,' Bouchard answered.

'What *used to be* my place,' Jerry corrected him, glaring at a vague area between Bouchard and Noel.

'Followed you down here to see if you had somewhere to spend the night...'

'Yeah, well.' Jerry started the pickup, gunned it some, then gunned it some more just for the barking it made. 'Brand-new truck,' he said, disgusted.

'Jerry, I'm sorry,' Noel said. 'I'll call my insurance company in the morning.'

He hit the gas and pulled the truck straight for her – stopped with a chirp of rubber – jammed into reverse and shot back into the tulips that bordered her swimming pool.

Bouchard started toward him. 'Jerry, you need to calm down.'

Giving Noel another look, Jerry gunned it good, flinging a few pounds of topsoil and whole, flattened flowers into the chlorinated water. When his tires hit the asphalt, they gave a generous screech, and he shot up the hill and was gone.

After the sound of his engine trailed away, Noel breathed a sigh. 'Thank God you were here, Alston. I'm so jittery, I might've killed him.' She looked down at the pistol in her hand as if the thought had just occurred. 'Oh, no, am I in trouble?'

'Nope,' he answered, 'you've got a right to protect your place.'

'He was trying to break in.'

'I saw that.' Bouchard sniffed. 'Funny, though...'

'What?'

'Well, why you'd turn your burglar alarm off.'

'I didn't *turn* it off,' she told him. 'I still don't know how to program it – God, you need a degree in engineering.'

Bouchard stood there, saying nothing. With his hands hidden in his pockets, all dressed in black, it was hard to see him.

'Alston, where's your car?' Noel asked.

'Over the firehouse. But the other thing I'm wondering... Why you were...' He gestured toward the garage, but she couldn't see.

'Excuse me?'

'Downstairs in the dark.'

She folded her arms, the .22 still in her hand. 'Alston—'

'I don't mean to...' He rubbed his hands together, then shoved them back in his pockets. 'It's just that it's late, and all your lights were off...'

'I've become an extremely light sleeper these past few days,' she said. 'I heard the truck pull in and I came down.'

She heard keys jangle in Bouchard's pockets, and she figured he was just about finished. 'Home all night, were you?'

'Alston—'

'It was you that took the fire call—?'

'That's right. Sal Erickson made the call from his house, I answered the fire phone, and then I sounded the alarm. Are you finished interrogating me now?'

For a few moments there was only silence, and she thought he wasn't going to answer her. Then she saw the moonlight glint across his glasses. 'Yup,' he said, and he turned and walked up the hill.

10

Dressed in his new, torn, bloodstained jersey and trousers, and wearing his lucky blue shoes, Jerry Royal sat on his chest freezer and watched while the woman poked through the blackened remains of his garage. She wore a plain blue sweatshirt with no insignia, no badge. Her trousers, however, were uniform: black with shiny black piping. She held a leash in her hand, with a German shepherd on the other end, sniffing at the ashes. They had positioned themselves this way – Jerry on his freezer, the woman and dog in the rubble – for almost two hours. She was big-boned and meticulous. He liked the way her butt filled her trousers.

'Find anything?' he called over, as he had from time to time. This time the woman was bent over, talking to her dog, and she did not hear. Down past her, beyond the slab, Jerry caught sight of Sal walking up the driveway; Jerry shielded his eyes from the sun and made out that his brother-in-law was carrying a cardboard box.

'I brought you some clothes,' Sal said as he came closer.

Jerry gestured to the collection of boxes and bags strewn around the freezer. 'People been bringin me things all morning. Two cases of Coke, you name it, toaster, electric lamp, FM radio – and me without electricity. Christ, I got more fuckin cookies than you wanna know.'

Sal shrugged. 'People like to help.'

Jerry threw his arms up. 'So how 'bout someone bringin me a new house! I mean, cookies, really.' He took the box of clothes from Sal and bounced it in his hands, gauging its weight as if he were making a trade. 'Kind've on the musty side,' he said, then dropped the box down beside the others.

Sal looked at Jerry's bloodstained turtleneck. 'They've been in my garage,' he said. His right hand ached from punching his wall. His face and arms were red from the fire, and his eyes still burned.

'How come you keep 'em out in your garage?' Jerry said. 'You got an attic over there.'

'Iris doesn't like the attic.'

Jerry sniffed. 'She don't like the attic.'

'How's your dad?' Sal asked.

'Perfectly good storage space, but she don't like the attic. So your clothes get musty. That's women for you.'

'What happened to your neck?' Sal asked him.

'Nothing,' Jerry answered, 'I cut myself.' He turned abruptly to the fire investigator. 'Anyways, you can rule me out,' he called. 'I was fifty miles away, up in Bangor with a dozen witnesses, in case you got any ideas.' He gave Sal a small, triumphant nod and said, 'Government woman.'

The woman didn't turn. 'I'm not looking for suspects at this time, Mister Royal, just a point of origin and probable cause. Kaiser seems to think accelerants were involved. It was definitely a hot fire.'

Jerry looked at Sal again. 'You need a uniform to tell that?'

Sal kept his eyes on Jerry's neck.

'She prob'ly told you about last night.'

'Who?'

'Who do you think?' Jerry replied. 'Noel. I go down there to see if I can use her freezer and she takes a shot at me. Pops my friggin truck. Wasn't for Alston, I'd be a dead man right now.'

Still picking through the rubbish, the fire inspector asked, 'Mr Royal, did you work on motors out here?'

'Chain saws, snowmobiles, you name it, I fix it.'

'You used gasoline or some other solvent—?'

Jerry didn't respond.

She stood up, turned to look at him. 'Gasoline to clean with – in uncovered containers?'

'Nope.'

She lifted a blackened coffee can so he could see. 'Like this?'

'Can't prove it by me.'

'It's not a crime,' she said. 'Definitely not smart, but not against the law. Besides, fuel alone does not a fire make. You also need ignition, something to start the flame. Did you have an electric lamp on the workbench, a droplight of some kind?'

'What?'

'You were raising chickens in here, by the looks of it – hatching chicks?'

'I was hatchin 'em out in a box.'

'And you used the droplight to keep them warm—?'

Jerry raised his face.

'It's not the first fire that's started this way, Mr Royal. You have a dog, maybe?'

'Not anymore.'

'They'll get after the chicks, disrupt the light. They could've easily knocked over the can of gasoline. Then again, it could've been anything, raccoon, fisher, cat—'

Jerry leaned forward in disbelief. 'You sayin animals burnt me out?'

'Then again, it could've been one of the chicks themselves.'

'Oh yeah,' Jerry said as he slid off the freezer. 'Some chick alright.' Sal gave him a curious look.

'People are always surprised,' the investigator said. 'That's why we say, "Keep gasoline in covered containers."' She pushed her notepad in her top pocket, over a breast. Just like that. Then she gave her leash a tug, and the dog followed her out of the ruins.

'Well, thank you, Mrs Smoky the Bear,' Jerry muttered, walking toward the blue gospel bus, which sat on a slight rise off to the right.

Sal watched the fire investigator get into her car and drive away. When he turned back to look for Jerry, he saw a green seat fly out of the gospel bus and land on top of two similar seats. Piled around the seats was an assortment of engine parts and several bulging trash bags; a television, a wooden door.

Sal walked to the bus, climbed the two steps and looked inside, down the gray corridor. Ratchet in hand, Jerry was bent over one of four remaining seats, unbolting its base.

'I wanted to ask you,' Sal said.

'I'm right here.'

'Blueberry Blossom Night—'

Jerry stopped working; he turned his head to the side. 'What about it?'

'I'm trying to remember. Did I see you that night?'

Jerry rose to his feet. 'Maybe you did, maybe you didn't. Maybe you tell me.'

Sal shook his head, wondering if the reaction was just Jerry's normal guardedness. 'I can't remember,' Sal told him. Considering the ordeal Jerry had been through over the past twelve hours, Sal decided not to push it any further. 'What about Alston Bouchard?' Sal said.

'What about him?'

'You think he's on the level?'

Jerry bounced the ratchet in his hand. 'The things you can count on in this life: shit happens, women'll fuck you up, and Alston Bouchard is on the level.'

Sal chuckled, although the implications of Bouchard's levelness were less than comforting. 'Just thought I'd ask,' he said, and he backed down a step, preparing to leave.

'Ol' Mr Do-good,' Jerry continued, bending to his task again, 'and look what good it does. Nothin to his name but a fifteen-year-old Jap car that shoulda been scrapped the day it left the boat and a piece of land no bigger than that fallin-apart trailer parked on it.'

'He's got land,' Sal said. 'What about those hills behind him?'

'Not his land,' Jerry said. 'Used to be. Prob'ly a thousand acres that family owned, at least until Alston's mother died.'

'What happened?' Sal said.

'Lost it, I don't know, ten, fifteen years ago. Eliot Wicker took it over.'

Sal stopped his descent, took hold of the railing. 'Wicker took it?'

'Well, bought it, technically. But he bought it right, part in trade for the funeral, part for the back taxes the old lady owed. Hey, those days everybody was losin their blueberry land to the big growers or the developers, take your pick. Wicker had the old house bulldozed down and then put the land up for sale in some New York magazine for a half million dollars, which no one in their right mind's gonna pay that. But he sat on it, every year leased it back to Alston for the berries. That's how he paid for his New York advertising. Charged Alston more than the berries were worth.'

Sal thought back to the business files he had searched at Wicker's house, wondered how he had missed that transaction. 'Was his mother's name Bouchard?'

Jerry shook his head. 'Blackstone. The old lady married again after Alston's father died. Indian fella from Canada, name of Blackstone. Only lasted a couple of years himself. Died of cancer, they said, but most people figure Indian, prob'ly drank himself to death.'

Sal nodded.

'Lotsa stories,' Jerry said, turning back to his work. 'Lotsa stories.'

'Just thought I'd ask,' Sal said, turning out the door.

'No harm in askin,' Jerry answered.

The Silver Bullet was all the advertising the Superette needed. With the mobile crime lab parked in the lot, the store stayed crowded all day, filled with curious townspeople lingering over coffee or ice cream, or stopping for gasoline they didn't need, watching as men in blue lab jackets carried paper bags and boxes out to the van.

It seemed like everyone had a theory, or at least a notion, about the mystery. Now, with Shepherd upstairs questioning Noel for the second time, the lunch counter crowd was busily and quietly reassessing.

The whispered consensus, at least among those who had known Bobby Swift, was that Bobby had pulled off a one-in-a-million scam and was basking in the sun somewhere waiting for Noel to join him.

'Get real,' the potato chip man said. 'It's your classic cover-up job. She poisons him for the insurance, and the undertaker discovers it during the embalming. He tries to blackmail her, she does him in, and then she buries the husband's body out in the blueberry fields to hide the evidence.'

'Really,' Bonnie said as she flipped bacon and burgers, 'don't you people have better things to do?'

'I say it's your classic makeup job,' argued Herb, her husband.

Down the length of the counter, heads turned.

Tamping cherry tobacco in the bowl of his pipe, Herb explained,

'I think Bobby came back to take his revenge for Wicker's makeup job.' The others made noises of approval.

'Not funny,' Bonnie said.

'I don't hear anyone laughing,' Herb replied.

Shepherd prided himself on his interviewing style. He never bullied, never threatened, never accused. He liked to think that he made friends with the people he talked to, even those from whom he secured confessions. Indeed, most of his suspects would eventually grow so rattled over the course of an investigation that they were actually relieved to finally be able to confess to him. He liked it that way. He liked the psychology of it.

Settling his long frame on Noel's couch, he eased into a conversation about the weather, the blackflies, the tourists, as if this were nothing but a social call: 'Once April rolls around, they come from everywhere – Japan, France, Australia – and now the Cayman Islands. You know, until this plane ticket showed up, I didn't even know where the Cayman Islands were.'

Noel sat curled like a cat on the other side of the couch, her green cotton shift pulled tight over her legs, waiting him out.

'From what I hear,' he said, 'Grand Cayman has the best diving in the world.'

Noel unfolded herself from the couch and got to her feet. She stretched, then walked away. 'You like Gnawi?' she asked, crossing to the wall shelves, where she turned on her stereo.

'Hm?'

'The Gnawa people, from Marrakesh.' She punched a couple of buttons and an eruption of drumming started, dark, humid and hypnotic. Noel turned up the bass, moved her knees with the beat. She came back to the couch and stood there, still moving, looking down at Shepherd as a chorus of chanting joined in.

'Detective, we both know scuba tanks were found on Eliot Wicker's body. And you obviously think the plane ticket to Grand Cayman Island is significant. Please don't patronize me.'

He smiled. 'I'll try to be more direct. Was Bobby a scuba diver?'

She bent to sit down again, and her shift fell away from her body, revealing a fleeting view of her breasts. 'Bobby, a skin diver?' She sat cross-legged, pulled a lime green pillow between her legs.

'Maybe before I knew him. He did everything else. Skydived, raced motorcycles. When we got married I made him stop.' A smirk escaped her, self-deprecating. 'I didn't want to lose him.'

That's when he saw it – the eyes – always watch the eyes. And hers had just watered over. He softened his approach, took his fingers off the keyboard and leaned back against the couch arm. 'You never did tell me how you guys met.'

Noel fingered a lock of hair off her cheekbone. 'I didn't think it would cast any light on Eliot Wicker's murder.'

He shrugged. 'Probably not. Just curious.'

'I quit college,' she said, 'and then I started modeling in Boston. His ultralight company contracted with the agency.'

'Hm?' The chanting made it hard to hear.

'Ultralights,' she explained, 'one-person airplanes. You don't see them much anymore.'

'You said you modeled.'

'They put me on the dunes in Truro, in a black leather one-piece and an apple green crash helmet that showed just my eyes. It was Bobby's idea. I think he was after the S-and-M market.' She gave Shepherd a sharp look.

He pretended not to notice. 'So he wrote the ads, he flew the things, I imagine he got down in the trenches and helped put them together too.'

'That sounds like Bobby. But I wouldn't know. I never got involved in his business.'

Shepherd nodded thoughtfully and was about to respond when a loud knock overpowered the drumming.

Noel turned to the door without expression, and before she could get up to answer the knocking, the door opened and Sergeant Murdoch was standing there.

Shepherd rose from the couch, setting his computer on the coffee table. He glanced at her stereo system as he went to the door, wishing the music were softer, or different. 'You got something?' he asked the sergeant.

Murdoch looked around the room.

Shepherd stepped into the stairway with him and pulled the door closed. The drumming seemed to throb against the wood.

'Sounds like you're having a meaningful interview in there,' Murdoch said.

'What've you got?'

'Nothing,' Murdoch answered cryptically.

Shepherd waited.

'Two million bucks.'

Shepherd studied the sergeant, who pulled a narrow pair of reading glasses from inside his blazer. When he had adjusted them on his nose, he withdrew a document from the same pocket and carefully unfolded it, a fax printout.

'Robert Swift,' Murdoch read, 'three-million-dollar business loan from River City Savings and Loan, Fall River, Massachusetts, January third, nineteen eighty-eight. One year later he files for bankruptcy after defaulting on his loan. Brought to trial in nineteen ninety, found guilty of tax fraud and falsifying receipts to obtain the loan. Three years probation and a hundred-twenty hours public service.'

'Yeah? What about the money?'

Murdoch glanced over his reading glasses, then continued. 'Loan officer Charles J. Mariotta, the bank employee who made the loan, convicted on the same charges – falsifying records and tax fraud. But get this – fourteen years in prison.' Murdoch removed the glasses. 'Mariotta's doin time, and there's two million dollars unaccounted for. The government bailed out the bank.'

Shepherd leaned back against the wall, felt the drums beating in synch with his heart.

'Two million bucks,' Murdoch said again, self-congratulating.

Shepherd made a fist, whispered, 'We got him.'

Murdoch took off his glasses and slipped them back inside his blazer. 'I went through Boston and Providence. Providence came through.'

Shepherd took the fax from him. He looked at it a second, then said very quietly, 'I'm not gonna let on to her. I'll ask her a few more questions, then head back to the barracks, start a search in the Caymans for Bobby Swift – or Dale Newman, if that's his alias. He'll never see it coming.'

Murdoch was already shaking his head. 'Nobody gets jack shit outta that place. Boggs even tried Interpol, but they kicked it back. The case isn't *advanced* enough.' Murdoch looked almost happy about it.

'How advanced do they want? We've got enough to charge him and bring him back. The fact that he's even alive is insurance fraud, to begin with. Incontestable.'

Murdoch, still shaking his head. 'We're gonna have to get it from her. She's an accomplice. Got to be.'

Shepherd paused, seeing the challenge in Murdoch's expression. 'What if Dale Newman wasn't Bobby Swift's alias but actually a third accomplice? He didn't use his plane ticket because Swift got rid of him the same night he did the undertaker. I say we try the Cayman people again, find Bobby Swift. He's a sure thing. And that's where the money is.'

Murdoch gave a futile but satisfied shrug. 'It's not our country, not our rules.' He nodded toward the drumming. 'Let's go back in there and double-team her. Tell her what we've got, I'll promise her thirty years in Thomaston, she'll give him up in a minute.'

Shaking his head, Shepherd reached for the door, giving the impression of blocking it. 'She's too smart for that.'

Murdoch snorted. 'Jeez, I hate to offend, but from what I hear, you haven't had much luck with smart women.'

Shepherd gave him an indulgent nod. 'I'll let you know if I need you,' he said.

'It's against the rules to screw it out of 'em, you know.'

Shepherd looked at him, didn't respond.

Murdoch snickered, then said, 'I'm going down for a bite to eat.' He began a slow, cocksure descent down the stairs, then stopped, as Shepherd knew he would. 'Don't get too cute in there,' he said. 'I wouldn't want to have to take over the investigation.'

Noel was standing at the front window when Shepherd came back into the apartment. He closed the door and walked straight to the stereo receiver, turned down the volume.

'Good news?' she said, though she seemed mildly distracted by something outside.

Shepherd returned to the couch, took the computer off the coffee table and returned it to his lap. He folded his hands over the keyboard, looked over to her.

'See, Noel,' he said, 'what's weird about the Caymans – their crazy confidentiality laws. Six hundred banks on those little islands. Twenty-four hundred corporations and trusts, with a mandatory three-year prison sentence for anyone who divulges information about any depositor.'

'Tax haven for the ruling class,' Noel said, returning to the couch and sitting down beside him. 'You'd think we'd wise up.'

'Except in drug cases. Then our two governments have what's called reciprocity, which means they'll cooperate. Murder cases too.'

'This is a murder case,' she said indifferently. 'Call them.'

Shepherd looked at her. He reclined on the couch, folded his arms confidently and didn't take his eyes off her. 'Noel, we found Bobby's two million dollars.'

Her eyes narrowed on him. 'What?'

He laughed effortlessly. 'Come on, Noel, now you're patronizing me.'

Her back straightened. '*What two million dollars?*'

'Noel, you have to admit—'

'*Nothing!*' In a single motion she was on her feet, glaring down at him fiercely. 'You come into my home and my business, degrade me in front of the entire town, and now you tell me that my husband was hiding two million dollars from me – while you sit there so smug and superior so you can watch my reaction—'

'Noel, I don't enjoy this any more than—'

'Do you want a fucking reaction?'

She grabbed a cut-glass vase of tulips off the coffee table and hurled it past his head.

When the upstairs window blew out, Sal was filling his gas tank, waiting for the detectives to leave. Window glass, green water and red tulips rained down the front of the store. Percy the fingerprint man, on his way to the lab van with a cardboard box, ducked under the flying debris, then hurried back inside the store. In a matter of seconds Noel charged out the front door. She headed directly for the gas pumps, pinning Sal with a secretive stare. Over her shoulder she carried a large, red leather handbag. Behind her, the door swung open and Shepherd came out. It was easy to see by the way he followed her that the detective had been the cause of her wrath.

'Ask me if I want to take a ride,' she said to Sal when she reached the gas island. A bottle neck protruded from the top of her bag, its top sealed – Stoli vodka.

As Shepherd came closer, Sal leaned his hand against the gas pump, a barricade to keep the detective away from her.

'Noel, just five minutes more and we'll be through,' the detective was saying.

Now Murdoch came out of the store too, eating a hot dog, sauntering toward the island, looking pleased. 'Everything under control, detective?' he said.

Noel narrowed her eyes at Sal, cuing him. But he concentrated on the pump, stopping the gas at five dollars and replacing the nozzle in its cradle. He screwed on his gas cap, still feeling her stare. He turned and looked at her, full on.

'Would you please get me away from here,' she said to him. She was not asking.

'Get on,' he told her. He flipped open a saddlebag and she stuffed her handbag in.

'Mr Erickson,' Shepherd said, 'where are you heading today?'

Sal took off his leather jacket and handed it to Noel.

'Hey,' Murdoch said, showing Sal the pâté of hot dog and bun on his tongue, 'you were asked a question.'

Noel shoved her arms into the heavy jacket, said to Sal, 'They think Bobby and Eliot Wicker staged Bobby's death. And then Bobby murdered Eliot—'

'Nobody said that,' Shepherd corrected.

'Is that what happened?' Murdoch asked her.

—'and now Bobby's supposedly living on Grand Cayman Island with two million dollars—'

'Could be ten by now, with interest,' Murdoch said. 'You tell us.'

Shepherd held up a hand. 'Hold on,' he told his sergeant, then turned again to Noel and said, 'I do apologize if I offended you—'

Murdoch snorted a laugh.

'—but we have made no such inferences in this case. We are simply following leads and asking pertinent questions, same as you would do in our position.'

Their attention was momentarily drawn to Alston Bouchard,

who came driving into the lot, directly to the island. His black lab was riding shotgun.

'If you're here for gas,' Shepherd told him, 'I suggest you go somewhere else.'

Sal looked over at Bouchard, made eye contact, then swung a boot over the Harley seat and turned the key. 'Let's go,' he said to Noel.

Murdoch moved in from the side, puffing up his chest. 'We'll tell you when she's ready, smart-ass.'

'Noel, it really is in your best interest to cooperate,' Shepherd said. 'Five minutes, no more.' He held up five fingers, gave her a look that was just short of pleading.

Ignoring him, she zipped the leather jacket, then stretched a long bare leg over the Harley, her short skirt notwithstanding, settling in behind Sal, high on the queen seat. Sal pressed the starter and the engine rumbled to life.

'Mr Erickson,' Shepherd said, 'you didn't tell us where you were going.'

Sal checked behind him, ready to pull out.

Murdoch said, 'Yeah, where's that smart mouth of yours now?'

Sal shifted into first, gave the throttle a turn and roared out of the lot, Noel's arms wrapped around his chest.

As the sound of the motorcycle got lost in the bright afternoon, Murdoch turned to Shepherd and said, 'I'll tell you right now, I don't like that greaseball.'

'Hard to tell,' Shepherd replied.

Behind them, Alston Bouchard cleared his throat. 'Bobby Swift you're looking for, if I'm not wrong.'

Paying no attention to him, Shepherd took a felt-tipped marker out of his pocket and inscribed a wide circle on the window of the gas pump, where he had seen Sal lean his hand. 'Make sure nobody touches this,' he said to Murdoch, and then he walked into the store. In a minute, Detective Percy accompanied Shepherd back out to the gas island, carrying a black attaché case. As Bouchard and the detectives looked on, Percy opened his case and brought out a small plastic container the size of a spice tin. He opened the box and carefully poured iron shavings into a cupped piece of paper. As he held the paper up to the pump window and gently blew the fine powder over the glass, Bouchard opened his car door and stepped out, held the visor of his cap to block the sun.

'That casket they buried Bobby Swift in,' he said. 'I imagine if Bobby was still alive, if somebody had dug him up, then that casket'd be in pretty good shape. Inside, I mean.'

Roundly ignoring him, Shepherd watched as Percy waved a small magnetic wand over the face of the gasoline window, and uncommitted iron powder rose, gradually revealing four fingers and a thumb. 'Nice,' Percy said.

Shepherd bent over, picked an evidence tag out of the black case and handed the tag to Murdoch. 'Initial this for him,' he said, walking away. 'I'm going back inside.'

'Detective Shepherd, I'm talking to you,' Bouchard said.

Shepherd turned his head as he continued walking. 'You're interfering in my case, Mr Bouchard—'

'*My town!*' Bouchard declared, pointing a finger at the asphalt under his feet. '*This is my town.*' The depth of his voice stopped Shepherd like a wall, and the detective turned. Or perhaps it was the depth of the constable's conviction. It *was* his town, and he was its protector, and Shepherd understood at that moment that nothing he could do, short of arresting the constable, would alter that fact.

The two men stood ten feet apart, glaring at one another. The fingerprint man stopped writing. Murdoch moved in beside Shepherd, wiping his mouth with his handkerchief. Two or three customers stepped out of the store to watch.

But when Bouchard approached the detective and spoke again, it was too quiet for anyone else to hear. 'You seem to think that Bobby Swift is alive, don't you?'

Just as quietly, Shepherd responded, 'I take it you don't.'

'I believe things'd be considerably quieter if he was,' Bouchard said.

Shepherd nodded again. Pretended to mull it over. 'That's an interesting theory, Constable. Except for one thing: The inside of Bobby Swift's casket is good as new.'

He gave Bouchard a sustained look, then added, 'I know if I lost my life trapped in a casket, fighting for my last breath of oxygen, I might do a little damage.' He turned back to the store and started walking. 'Have a nice day,' he said.

* * *

SUGAR COATED PUFFS OF CORN! Davey brought the bag of yellow cereal into the living room with her and settled into her beanbag chair in front of the television. Some Saturday afternoon movie about a creature that looked like a giant lizard devouring Tokyo pedestrians, although you never actually saw the eating part, you only saw the shadow fall over the person about to be eaten, and then you heard him scream. Other than that, only bowling, golf and a gardening show were on, so she watched the monster movie and ate the sugar puffs out of the bag and tried to keep her mind from wishing that her father was there. When she heard the screen door open, she jumped out of the beanbag and ran into the kitchen, thinking it was he.

But it was her uncle standing between the doors. Uncle Jerry – though she had never called him that, never actually spoken to him at all. She unlocked the inner door before she thought about what she was doing, and then wished that she hadn't.

'Gawd, I didn't expect a grown-up girl,' Jerry said, his blue eyes traveling down to her red sneakers and back up again. 'Look at the size of you!'

'My mother's delivering a baby,' she said to him, staying in the doorway. Davey knew she should have said that her mother was upstairs taking a nap, but she figured it was obvious that her mother's car was gone.

'Anyways,' Jerry said, lowering his voice as if he were about to share a secret with her, 'I bet you don't even recognize me.' He was bending toward her, and his breath smelled strong, like a bunch of onions gone bad. He had a brown bloodstain on his jersey.

'Yes, I do,' she told him.

'Hah? You know your Uncle Jerry? Hey, we're lettin the blackflies in.' She stepped back as he squeezed in, and the screen door shushed closed behind him. He looked around the room, over her head. Blackflies don't come in, she thought.

'Same table,' he said, walking across the kitchen. 'Same chairs, cupboards.' He opened one, swung it back and forth. 'Different squeak.' He had something on the seat of his pants that looked like he had sat on a fat spider; gum or tar.

He walked out of the kitchen toward the living room, stopped at the stairs and looked out the front window, ducking under a heavy, hanging planter pot. 'You see the fire last night?' he said.

Davey nodded. She noticed the charred blue reef runners on his feet. She wondered if she should tell him that she was sorry about his house burning down, the way adults console one another.

He took hold of the rail. 'Yup,' he said, starting up the stairs, the narrow risers creaking under his weight, 'same old everything.' His dialect reminded her of Mr Walker, the school custodian, and Mr Philbrook, one of the older bus drivers. It was a friendly, country sound. But she wasn't sure she liked him going up the stairs like that. She followed a few treads behind.

'My mother'll be home pretty soon,' she said, trying to be hospitable about it.

'My old bedroom too,' he said. 'Prob'ly you got it now.'

The top of the stairs led onto the landing, a scuffed pine floor, wide boards, with knee wall storage on the facing wall; bins for doors. To the left and right of the landing were the two bedrooms, the master bedroom on the left, hers on the right. As Davey mounted the landing, she could see Jerry looking into hers.

'There it is,' he said. 'Right over there, my bed, under the window.'

Davey didn't come any closer. 'I thought that used to be my mother's room.'

'Both of ours. We slept together when we was kids – same bed even, but ol' mother put an end to that just 'bout the time it got interesting.' He turned his head, giving her a strange grin.

'Do you remember your mother?' Davey asked, changing the subject.

Jerry came back onto the landing, looked up at the ceiling, at the square, hatch cover made a gray shiplap boards and a black iron handle. ''Course I do. I was fifteen when she got killed. I almost bought the farm myself that night. Frigged up my leg for life.'

'My mother said she was mean.'

Jerry doubled his chin. 'Mean?' He snorted like a horse. 'That woman didn't have a mean bone in her body. *Mean?* I can't believe your mother said that. Christ, the ol' lady thought the sun rose and set over that girl. Always buyin her new clothes, settin up with her, readin books. I got stuck with the old man. With Mother, you was always safe, no matter what stupid thing you did. Never holler, never hit, never so much as look at you cross-eyed. Mean? I'd say *your* mother's got her memory banks screwed up.' He looked up at the hatch again, and his raw, red-lined throat poked out of his turtleneck. 'I can't believe that one. Mean.' He looked down at Davey, gave her a quick nod of his head. 'Ever go up?'

Davey shrugged.

'What, you never been up?'

A black handle in the ceiling. That's all the attic had ever been. A handle and a warning. Now, the way he was talking, the prospect of going up excited Davey a little. She shook her head.

'Whoa. How about your mother or dad, they ever go up?'

'My mother said it wasn't safe.'

'Well, by the Christ, what kind of horseshit is she feedin you over here?' He reached up and gave the handle a tug. A cloud of dust fell over them like a blizzard, while a gray wooden ladder jumped out of the dark and unfolded noisily from the hatch's underside. Jerry pulled on the ladder, and a second ladder unfolded from it, skreaking as it unfolded a third time, until the whole thing extended to the floor, like steep, narrow stairs. He put his blue shoe on the bottom rung and pushed, and the ladder snapped in place, straightening.

'Really, you never been up?'

Through the dust that continued to cloud the opening, Davey could see only darkness.

Jerry took hold of the rails as if he were about to climb up, then he turned to her. 'What'd she tell you 'bout it?'

Davey shrugged. 'I'd fall through—?'

He grinned, eyes sparkling. 'She said *that*?' He had a boyish, playful nature that Davey kind of liked. 'Well, then' – he swung off the ladder with one arm and put his hand on her lower back – 'you're in for a treat.'

Davey hesitated.

He gave her a dumb look, like a clown trying to be sad.

'Think about it. If it wunt safe, I wouldn't go up myself, and I'm about two hundred somethin pounds heavier'n you.' He nudged her. 'Come on. You got adult supervision.'

Davey knew that he could have tossed her into the attic with the one hand if he wanted to. But his touch was feathery light. And she really liked his shoes. She gave a moment's thought to her dress, that she should be more modest about going up a ladder with a dress on, ahead of a man. But he was her uncle.

'Here you go, little boost-up,' he said, taking her under the arms and lifting her up to the second rung, his hands so big that his fingertips touched one another across her chest. 'Nothin' to be afraid of. Christ, couple years you'll be coming up all the time with your boyfriends.'

Something about that remark unsettled her a little. Maybe it was the way his voice had softened. 'Gaw'head. I'm right behind you.' She took another step until her head was level with the hatch. The first thing she noticed was the smell: dusty and wooden, like the inside of an old cupboard.

'You got a boyfriend yet?' That voice again. Davey felt the ladder sink as he stepped onto it, and she grabbed the rails, startled. 'Prob'ly still too young for that.' He took another step, and the ladder creaked. 'Not you, I mean the boys. Girls develop earlier, they just don't talk about it all over the place like boys do.'

Now she could feel his breath on the back of her leg. 'All girls got thoughts. Nothin to be ashamed of.'

She didn't like him so close, didn't like what he was talking about, didn't like the darkness above her, or him below—

'I want to go down now,' she blurted.

'*Daow!*' he said. 'Turn on the light, the string by your head. Gaw'head, I'm right here.'

Davey reached up, felt the hot air above her head, waved her hand around – and then she felt it, a little bead on the end of the string, it bounced out of her hand, then bounced off her wrist as it swung back again. She caught hold and pulled. The bulb flashed on above her, illuminating the reddish ceiling rafters, reddish chimney and darkness beyond. Davey's face at floor level, she stared up at the room and all its contents: a green carousel clothesline on its side – like a giant spider web – a brown kitchen chair, a dark chest of drawers, a dark bass fiddle leaning on the wall, a white wedding gown on a dress form, a dirty mattress beside it . . .

'Go on up,' he said.

Suddenly the attic felt terribly unsafe – scary – like the kind of place that would harbor ghosts. Davey shrank back, but Jerry held his hand on her bottom, squeezed her a little. 'That's it,' he said softly. 'I got you.'

'I want to go down,' she told him, lowering all her weight onto his hand, willing to fall if she had to. In fact, if she weren't on the ladder, she would have been running away from him as fast as she could.

'Easy does it, sweetheart,' he said. 'You don't want to go up, that's okay.'

He swung back, giving her just enough room to squeeze past him, and she spiderlegged down the ladder, barely touching the treads with her feet. When she reached the landing, she wiped her eyes.

Jerry looked back at her. 'I'm just goin up for a sec,' he said. 'But one thing.'

She looked up at him.

'Swear to keep a secret?' He was hanging off the ladder like an orangutan.

She nodded, barely.

'I'm hidin something up here that only you know about. Swear to keep a secret?'

He reached into his back pocket and pulled out a white envelope so she could see.

'Swear to keep a secret?' he said again.

She nodded again.

'Just in case anything ever happens to me – that means if I turn up missing or dead – then you tell your mother this is up here. There's somebody evil who wants to do something to me. This is my protection.'

He looked down at her in a way that made Davey's insides shiver.

'But if you tell anybody about it *before* I'm dead – then somebody's gonna come over here and do something to you. And your mother too. And anybody else who knows.'

Davey stared, stunned with fear.

'Swear to keep a secret?'

She made a small, dry noise of consent.

'You got to say it.'

'I swear.'

He went up.

* * *

Noel's legs, pink from the wind, pressed in around Sal's hips. Her arms wrapped around his chest. He turned his head and shouted at the wind, 'What two million dollars? What are they talking about?'

'Just go!' she shouted back. 'They're crazy!' He goosed the throttle, and they flew up a long hill.

'Why do they think Bobby's alive?'

'Go!'

Heading down the coast, they tore through quiet towns already populated with license plates from other states: black on white, white on green, yellow on blue: the first wave of tourists, idle retirees up for a taste of the rugged and quaint working coast.

And here came Sal and Noel – he, unshaven in black jeans and T-shirt; she, in black leather over a short cotton shift; both of them sticky with the salt and spring-flowered air, racing down the highway with no destination except getting away. When Sal saw the turnoff to Blue Hill, he took it. Noel leaned with him. It was an aggressive ride, soaring up and down the blueberry hills. Every now and then the ocean would rise in the distance, flat and silvery, broken by strands of islands. Sal felt edgy and unclear, but he was glad to have her holding him.

Coming down a long hill, he shouted, 'They say anything about Bouchard?'

'What about Bouchard?'

'Anything!'

'I don't want to talk about it!' she said, her hands crawling up his chest. 'Let's find an island somewhere – we'll never go back!'

He shouted sideways at the wind: 'What about me? They say anything about me?'

'Just forget it!' she shouted at him.

'Noel, I have to know!'

He pulled back the throttle some more. The speedometer jumped past seventy. They ripped through the wind. 'My brakes let go last night,' he yelled back at her. 'I think somebody opened the bleeders.'

'I think you're paranoid!'

He pulled back the throttle some more, to see what her reaction would be.

She pressed her mouth to his ear. 'Are they okay now?' she said.

'Yeah!'

'Good. Go faster.'

Cresting another hill, the Harley whipped over the top just under eighty. A white Saab suddenly appeared in front of them – with a pickup truck coming at them in the other lane. Sal didn't brake. He leaned left and shot into the oncoming lane, passed the Saab in an instant then swerved back just as the truck tore past, dust flying, horn blaring.

His jaw clenched tight, Sal kept his eyes peeled on the distance. *I think somebody's trying to pin this on me.* But he refrained from saying that to her.

'What happened with Jerry Royal last night?' he yelled.

'He's an imbecile!' she yelled back. 'He tried to break into my garage, and I shot at him.'

'I'll be sure to knock next time I come over.'

They screamed down the hill, the speedometer needle shivering past eighty. Approaching the bottom, he backed off as he leaned into a long leftward curve, then started up another hill. She nuzzled his ear with her warm mouth, her voice like low cooing. 'Let's find the most expensive hotel on the coast,' she said, her breath warming him. 'We'll pretend it's our last night on earth. We'll do things to each other that no one's ever done.'

The Harley dipped left, right, tore through the road sand. He straightened, easing back the throttle.

'We'll be animals,' she breathed. 'We'll be cannibals. We'll devour each other.' Her lips closed around his ear; he felt her tongue move inside. 'We'll feed each other poison. We'll eat orchids till we piss purple.'

Now her fingers were sliding to his belt. He was there already, straining to get out. She unbuckled him, unzipped him, then slid her fingers down the front of his jeans, took a rough hold of him. 'Or maybe we'll find a lovers' leap,' she said.

'You wanna jump?'

Still in his ear, still in his pants, she said, 'No. I think we should throw each other off.'

He opened the throttle as she worked him over . . . 75 . . . 80 . . . 85 . . . all the while finding it more and more difficult to ignore what

Bouchard had told him the night before: *'That woman is a danger to you.'*

Pulling into her driveway, Iris got out of the car and bent to give Davey a kiss. 'Trudy has a baby brother,' she said. 'What are you doing out here, hon?'

Davey shrugged. But the look on her face—

Behind them the screen door opened, and Iris turned. Reflexively, she reared back.

Jerry held up his hands. 'Don't worry, I didn't steal anything, if that's what you're thinkin.'

It took a moment before Iris found her voice. 'Why is he here?' she asked Davey.

'You're not exactly talking about a dog, you know,' Jerry said. 'I come over for some water.' He looked right at Davey, who averted her eyes.

Iris kept a firm hold on Davey's shoulder. Davey squirmed, letting her mother know she was hurting her, but Iris wasn't paying attention.

'The other thing,' Jerry said. 'I'm off the booze now, same as the old man. So, whatever, I guess we can all be family again. I didn't know what you wanted to do about him, the house and all. We got no insurance.'

Iris glared.

'Well, hey. Sorry if almost burnin to death and losin everything we had puts you out.'

'Don't you come over here,' Iris said to him, her voice low in her chest, nearly trembling.

Jerry rocked his head. 'Well, there's a loving daughter for you. A real fine example you set.' He gave Iris a long, distasteful look as he walked past her. Then, at the foot of the driveway, he turned once more. 'And that's another thing – your memory's all frigged up when it comes to Momma. She spoiled you rotten and you know she did. Which is why today you can't keep a man.'

They sat looking out the tall, multipaned window, the only two customers in a cozy dining room with crème fraîche walls and three antique oak tables. The moon, oblong and pale, hung over the ocean like a stopped pendulum. A Beethoven quartet soothed through the inn, buoyed by the hush of breaking waves, créme d'Atlantique spraying over the jagged rocks. Through the flames of a double sided fireplace, Sal could see another couple in the adjacent room. They looked like lawyers or doctors, well-dressed, sitting close, talking intimately, exquisitely secure at their table.

Sal, in his T-shirt, and Noel, in her work dress, sat just as close, their bare arms touching, not saying a word. Bathed in the heat of the applewood fire, they spread chocolate butter on warm baguette and sucked smoked oysters from the half shell. Noel drank sixty-dollar Merlot. Sal drank seltzer with a lime wedge. He had charged three hundred dollars on his Visa card for a corner room upstairs, which they had yet to see. He glanced at Noel.

What two million dollars?

Sucking chocolate butter from her thumb, Noel returned a secret look, as if she knew what he was thinking. But then he was thinking something else.

'You're eating chocolate,' he said.

She answered by sticking her wet thumb into the small crock and bringing it out again, crowned with a wad of silky chocolate. Still watching him, she brought the thumb to her mouth and slowly sucked the chocolate off. 'That's not all I'm eating tonight,' she said.

Their waiter appeared then, a portly, balding man in a white dinner jacket, carrying a second appetizer, a pâté of rabbit, along with a Stoli martini for Sal, straight up.

'I ordered it when you were in the bathroom,' Noel told him, touching his leg under the cloth. 'What I want to do to you up there, you're going to need it.'

'More baguette?' the waiter asked, his continental accent betrayed by a tinge of *mow-ah.*

Moving her fingers up the inner seam of Sal's jeans, Noel slid the basket toward the waiter, who thanked her and started to walk away.

'Wait a minute,' Sal said. The waiter stopped. Still holding Noel's gaze, Sal found his martini and held it up for the man. 'I promised Davey I'd take her fishing tomorrow,' he said, as the waiter took the drink and left the table.

'Fishing,' Noel said dryly. 'I'm hot just thinking about it.'

He smiled a little, distantly, and her eyes narrowed with impatience. 'Sal, where are you?' she said.

He looked at her. 'The night Eliot Wicker was murdered—'

She shook her head slowly, resolutely.

'Noel, I have to know. I was with him that night – in your apartment – wasn't I?'

By her silence, he guessed it was true.

'I have to know.'

As he watched, the candle flame liquefied in her eyes. When she spoke, her voice was almost fearful. *'You can't know,'* she said, and he realized in that long, floating instant that, indeed, Noel was afraid. For him.

His own fear burgeoned, pressed out against his chest. He took a deep breath, then whispered, 'Tell me.'

She checked the door to her right, looked through the flames at the couple in the next room, then turned back to him. 'You were all fucked up,' she said. 'Acting insane.'

He nodded.

'You couldn't go home. I was trying to sober you up.'

'What about Wicker?'

She paused.

'Tell me.'

'I don't know. He just barged in. I thought he was there for me – he'd made a couple of passes at me after the funeral. But—'

'What?'

'The look on his face when he saw you—' Noel lowered her eyes.

Sal took hold of her wrist. 'What kind of look?'

Noel shook her head. 'You said something to him I didn't hear, or I didn't understand – but it meant something, I could see the way you were looking at him. And then you left. Afterwards, Eliot stuck around making small talk, just long enough to watch you walk down the road. Then he left too.'

'That was it?'

She took another drink of wine.

'What time did I leave?'

'Sal, don't ask me any more.'

'Which way did I go?'

She turned toward the fire.

He moved his chair closer to hers. 'Last summer,' he said, 'I was working at the store, spending time with Bobby. We were both drinking too much. Did Wicker ever come over?'

'Every day,' she said, 'for coffee.'

'After hours, I mean.'

'After hours I don't know. You and Bobby didn't always stick around. Why are you looking at me like that? Sal, would you please have a drink and stop—'

'What they said about Bobby – that he faked his death—'

'I don't know!' She tried to pull out of his grasp, but he held tight. In the adjoining room, the other couple looked over. Sal, nonplussed, released her. Most of a minute passed while they sat, not speaking.

'I think I want you to take me home,' she said.

He met her eyes.

'Noel, if you were involved in this,' he said to her, 'would you tell me?'

She responded by matching his steady gaze. 'If I were involved in this,' she replied, 'I would not tell you.'

He stared at her.

'But I'm not involved in this,' she said. Then she leaned into him, opened her mouth and pressed it gently to his. He breathed in her chocolate, her smoked oysters, her apricot, her Merlot, he melted under the assault of her intoxicating tongue. He wanted to consume her, wanted to stop his racing brain, wanted to hold back time. Indeed, he wanted nothing short of oblivion with her. And he had an idea that oblivion wasn't far off.

The blinds drawn, the doors locked, Davey was finally asleep. Iris sat near the top of the stairs, level with the landing, staring at the footprints in the dust, going this way, going that way, like the primitive grounds of some ritualistic dance. Except no music came to mind. No ideas connected. Only the vague, leaden notion that her mother was watching . . . always watching.

'Why did you let him in here?' she had yelled at Davey (and she never yelled at Davey). She didn't even give Davey a chance to explain. *'That's why we have rules!'* She slammed a cupboard door.

It bounced back, and a jar of honey fell onto the counter and broke with a thud, lost its shape slowly.

'He just wanted some water,' Davey said in a small voice.

'You never, *never*—'

Davey stormed up the stairs in tears. Iris paced a few times, slapped the cupboard door again, waiting to discharge, and finally got a trash bag to put the mess in. She was aware that she had overreacted, but she had to make Davey understand. Understand what? The rules. The Ice Queen rules. Steps to take with an alcoholic family. One: she had discarded her husband. Two: she had watched her father burn without a tear. Three: she had turned her brother away when he needed water. All with perfect composure. Screaming at Davey was the sum total of her emotional involvement.

Iris scraped the honey and broken glass off the counter with a spatula, pulled it into the trash bag, tied the bag in a knot and set it by the door, then scrubbed the counter with a warm sponge, scrubbed the woodwork, wiping everything clean. Calm again, intending to go upstairs and apologize to Davey, she had stopped at the landing . . . and that's when she saw the footprints.

Monster footprints, flat-footed prints circling in the dust like the feet of some big, lummoxy, goat-headed creature, while smaller sneaker treads moved tentatively on their toes. A fierce shiver started inside Iris, goose bumps skittering up her sides. Another spasm started her head shaking, a wordless, mindless refusal. It was a relief at first, the head shaking, but then when she wanted to stop, she found she could not. A noise escaped her, like a child's cry. She clamped down on it, terrified of losing control, forced the impulse down, and went crawling through the footprints, smearing them as she went, decimating them with her hands (angel wings, angel wings), keeping it down, blanking her mind, keeping it down, wiping everything clean.

Back in their room, a new fire crackled in the fireplace. Their bed was an antique four-poster, with a green silk canopy and green silk sheets. Two heart-shaped chocolates wrapped in red foil had been left for them, one on each of their pillows. The window was open just enough so they could hear the ocean, the surf charging against the rocks at long, lazy intervals. Sal sat at the foot of the bed, head down, leaning over his knees, listening to the fire, to the waves. Behind him, Noel crawled around the mattress like a cat, coming to him and finally pulling herself up his shoulders, her knees at the small of his back. He could hear her breathing, could hear the flames devouring the birch logs. She ran her fingers upward from his neck into his hair. Her thumbs pressed into the soft spot behind his skull, and then her hands moved warmly down his shoulders and biceps, her fingers finding their way up inside his T-shirt sleeves, her thumbs searching the dark humidity of his underarms. She pressed her face against his back and she moaned, as her hands moved down his chest to his stomach and then rose again inside his shirt.

She kissed his neck above the neckline, ran her palms up the flat of his stomach to his warm chest, softly covered with hair. She raised herself higher, pressed her body hot against his back and kissed his jaw below his ear. The dark shadow of his beard had grown through the day, and he considered how it must have felt against her cheek (like Bobby's face would have felt).

'God, can you stop thinking?' she said, and rolled away from him.

He took a breath and let it out. He looked back at her. Now she was lying on her side, back to him, facing the pillows. He lay down behind her, put his arm around her. Her breathing was slow and steady. He ran his fingertips over her skin, from her ear down to her neck, until goose bumps rose on her. With one finger, he lightly stroked her lips. With his thumb, he lightly traced her jawline. He breathed in her complex aroma. Her chest moved evenly as he caressed her, and then he pulled her shift down to her shoulders until it restrained her arms. Her breathing intensified. His hand went round to her chest, felt heat rising from her shallow cleavage, the top of her dress confining her. With his thumb, he forced the top button through its buttonhole. With his other hand he reached down to her thigh, then up under her dress. He bunched her panties in one hand and pulled them down to her knees. She began to turn, but he stopped her, held her shoulder down while he rose over her. He forced his knee between her legs. Unbuckling his belt, the leather tip flicked the back of her thigh and he heard her catch her breath.

He lowered his face to her ear. 'Is the temptation hard to resist, Noel?' he breathed.

'What?' she said, not moving.

'Those chocolates in front of you.'

Neither of them moved for a few seconds. 'What are you accusing me of?' she said.

Still holding her down, he whispered, 'I did not do this.'

She paused. 'Okay,' she replied, not looking at him.

He leaned down harder, gazing at her perfect ear, her perfect jaw, her supple, white neck – and he was swept with a sudden urge to take her by the throat.

He fell away from her, turned onto his back. Breathing. Listening to her breathe. Listening to the ocean, which sounded more like machinery now than a rhythm of waves.

'What is wrong with you?' she said, an edge to her voice. 'I said I believe you.'

He sat up, pushed himself off the bed. 'I'm going,' he told her, taking his jacket off the chair. 'I'm going fishing with my daughter.'

She snickered.

'Do you want a ride?'

'Go,' she answered. 'Fishing.'

He took his keys off the vanity and went out the door.

Jerry Royal sat at his plywood table, his head thrown back against the window, a six-inch TV throwing bluish light on his face. Half awake, half asleep, he didn't hear the motorcycle pull into his driveway. But the instant his bus door squealed open, he was on his feet. 'Come on in,' he said, registering Sal, 'pull into a chair, my head's asleep.'

It was hot inside the bus. The power company had constructed a temporary pole at the end of the driveway, from which Jerry ran a long orange extension cord. Besides the TV and table lamp, he was powering a four-foot space heater that faced the table.

Jerry rubbed the back of his head briskly, trying to drive some feeling back in. 'Friggin bus,' he said. 'Thirty-whatever years old, prime of life, livin in a friggin gospel bus.'

He sat down again at his table. The plywood was propped on

sawhorses, between the two facing bus seats. The Styrofoam cooler sat in the aisle beside the table. Empty cola cans littered the floor. Sal stepped carefully over the cans, noticed the muzzle of Jerry's shotgun sticking up behind the seat.

'Warm enough in here,' Sal said.

'Day at the beach,' Jerry answered, working his head around. 'She called you, huh?'

'Who?' Sal remained standing.

Jerry searched Sal's face. Than he gestured toward the road with his head. 'I figured my sister called to tell you I was over there today.'

'Nope.'

'Huh,' Jerry said. 'Well, I was. Great state of affairs when a man loses his house and all his worldly possessions and can't even go to his own flesh and blood for help.'

Sal sat down on a corner of the seat opposite Jerry. He rubbed the plywood with his palm, gathering grains of salt. 'I was thinking about that fire you had,' he began.

'Worst thing that ever happened to me.'

'I mean afterwards, why you didn't go over to see Iris last night, instead of Noel Swift.'

Jerry shrugged. 'Shoulda, woulda, coulda, hey. So I misjudged a woman. Wasn't the first time, and it sure the fuck won't be the last. Don't worry, I know where I'm not wanted. Matter of fact, I'm makin a list.'

Sal looked at him for a few seconds, then stood up from the table.

'You look worse than I do,' Jerry said. He reached into his cooler, took out a fresh can of cola and popped it open. 'You oughta try this stuff – caffeine. Keeps you alert.' He slapped at the back of his head. 'Lotta good it did. Friggin pins and needles, my head's still asleep.' He was still slapping his head when Sal left the bus.

11

Sunday morning the sky was white, and the forecast called for rain, yet the Superette was busier than usual. At noon, when Noel walked through the front door carrying her red handbag, Bonnie True was at the cash register selling beer and prewrapped grinders to a couple of fishermen, while Chad worked behind the meat counter preparing more sandwiches, and Erica made ice cream sundaes for the fishermen's sons.

Bonnie thought it peculiar that Noel came in the front rather than from downstairs, especially since everyone in the store could see that she had arrived in the back of a taxi (and she had left the day before on the back of Sal's Harley). 'How are you?' Bonnie said to her, but Noel went in behind the counter and up the stairs without answering. Bonnie gave the fishermen their change, then locked the register. 'Chad, mind the money,' she said, as she opened the door. Climbing to the landing, she spotted Noel sitting at the top of the stairs. 'I've been wondering when it was going to get to you,' Bonnie said.

In the living room, on the wicker couch, Noel bared her soul. Sal had been Bobby's best friend since they were boys, she explained. 'When Bobby died, he was wonderful, he took care of everything. And afterwards, the way he'd call and come over, to make sure I was alright. And then last night . . .' She shook her head, unable to continue.

'Take your time,' Bonnie said.

Noel inhaled shakily, then let it out. 'After the detectives were here—'

'—I know—'

'—With all their questions, I was feeling—'

'—*pent up*. My God, who wouldn't!'

'I needed to get away. And then he was here. He offered me a ride. We ended up on Deer Isle. At the Urchin Inn.'

Bonnie nodded sagely. 'Mm-hmm.'

'I know I should have suspected. I was just so—'

'*Desperate*. You just don't *know* when you're in mourning.'

'He started drinking at dinner, and then after . . .' Noel stopped abruptly and just stared at her fingers, eyes glistening. 'I feel like such a jerk.'

Bonnie stroked her hand. 'Oh, I could see it from the start,' she said, 'the way he's been coming around. Like the friggin fox to the henhouse.'

Sal gathered the fishing rods and boat net from the garage and leaned them against the car. Dandelions blossomed around the tires of his car. He glanced across the street, where Jerry Royal was tending a fire inside his chest freezer, stirring up thick gray smoke with a flattened aluminum curtain rod. Gray clouds were lowering, keeping the smoke from rising.

'Ready, Freddie?' Davey said.

'Hmm?'

'To fish.' Davey opened the plastic bag of seaweed and bloodworms that Sal had brought. Blackflies swarmed around her head. Sal took a small bottle of fly dope out of his fishing vest. 'Hold still,' he told her, while he doused his hand and rubbed it gently behind her ears.

'I hate that smell,' she said.

'They'll be worse by the river.'

The back door opened, and Iris came out carrying a heavy cardboard box, duct-taped shut. She was wearing a flannel shirt and old jeans. She brought the box into the garage without a glance at Sal.

'We'll be back in an hour or two,' he told her, 'if you want to talk then.'

Walking back into the house, Iris gave him a look, not unfriendly but somehow detached, as if she hadn't heard him. Watching after she'd gone, Sal took the fishing rods off his car. 'Ready,' he said, and Davey took the lead across the road, joining the path that ran alongside the Royals' property.

'What are you defrosting over there?' Sal called over to Jerry. Standing in the smoke of his freezer, Jerry raised his nose, a hello.

'I heard your uncle was over yesterday,' Sal said to Davey. She kept her eyes on the path. She didn't mention Jerry's secret letter. Nor did she mention the fact that Iris had been up all night long washing and waxing all the floors in the house.

At the end of the field the path divided; one branch led straight down to the reversing falls, where the state had once maintained a picnic area complete with a barbecue grill, trash barrel and a sign that explained the tidal phenomenon and the Indian legend. The rightward branch, which Sal and Davey took, led through a stand of pines, then down a rocky bank to the fishing pool.

Their timing was perfect. The tide was in, and the pool was wide, dark and deep, the falls having reversed some hours earlier. By September the water here would be filled with spawning Atlantic salmon, the surface a carpet of red backs you could practically walk on. This time of year the pool was a feeding hole for schoolies – striped bass that hunted upriver with the tides.

Sal stepped down to his fishing rock, a wide slab of granite that overhung the pool. He took off his vest and made a cushion on the rock for Davey. Directly to their right, where the pool formed a small cove, river junk accumulated – plastic bottles and bags, hunks of Styrofoam and other floating things – everything that the last few tides had returned upriver and not taken back again. It was Sal's custom to bring a couple of trash bags with him when he came fishing; he'd scoop the stuff into the bags and bring it home to throw away. (Iris would jokingly refer to the debris as his 'plastic fish,' since Sal kept none of the real fish he caught.) Today he hadn't brought the bags.

When Davey was settled on the rock, Sal pulled out her line and set to baiting her hook with a fat, eight-inch worm. Davey turned her head when it started to curl. 'Hold still, hon, so you don't hook me,' Sal told her. When he was through, he released the line and wiped his fingers on the rock. The pretzeling worm swung out over the water, rocked by the counter-swinging of the red and white plastic bobber above it.

'Poor wormy,' Davey said.

Sal reached for her pole again, saying, 'You watch while I cast.'

'No, I want to,' Davey replied, already rearing her pole back, holding on with both hands.

'You don't know how.'

'Yes, Shannon's father showed me last summer. Remember?'

Sal plainly didn't. 'Just watch out for the trees behind us.'

Davey swung the rod two-handed, and the bobber slapped the water about four feet out, sending out wide, concentric waves.

'Want to try again?' Sal said, but Davey turned away from him, watching her bobber as it drifted slowly toward the bottles on their right.

Sal stripped his own line, tied on a rusty rat, then added a splitshot two feet up the line. He knew the whereabouts of all the submerged rocks, where the smart feeders would be hiding – one rock in particular – about thirty feet out. He gauged its location and then cast side-arm, easily. The tiny lead weight kissed the surface about ten feet upcurrent from the center of the pool, sending out narrow rings to the grassy sandbar that formed the opposite bank. The fly hugged the surface for a second, then sank, and Sal's line began drifting. He caught the line in the first joint of his index finger.

By now Davey's bobber was off to the right, in the thick of the bottles and bags and Styrofoam. 'If you leave your line there, hon, you might catch a plastic bass, but that's all.'

Davey gave him a dour look, then returned to her bobber again, apparently satisfied with its position (Iris's independence – he loved it in Davey). 'Maybe I'll catch this tube of hair goop for you,' she said, her bobber bumping up against a floating yellow-and-blue tube. 'Then you can get all dressed up and bring Mommy some flowers and propose to her again.' She started reeling in, trying to hook the tube.

Sal forced a gentle smile. 'I don't think hair goop'll work, hon.'

Suddenly she stopped. 'Daddy, I got one!'

He looked. She lifted her rod in the air so its tip bent down, but it didn't play. Her bobber hung in the air three inches above the cans and bottles, caught. 'Plastic bass!' she cried, as she let the bobber pull back down. Eyes wide, teasing him, she yanked up on the rod, making the bobber tremble, while the cover of river trash rocked in the turbulence she had created.

Then his own fly was hit. He jerked his arm, set the hook. 'Wait a minute, Davey, I got one,' he said. 'Real bass.'

It felt good, the way the underwater tugging shook his wrist. A healthy striper, to be sure, six, maybe seven pounds. He let the fish run toward the river, his drag *wheeing* as the line ran out. He saw that Davey was still holding her line taut beside him.

He glanced down at her. 'Don't force it, hon. I'll help you in a minute.'

Davey returned a terrified stare.

'That's just my drag releasing,' he explained, 'so my line doesn't break.'

But she continued to stare up at him, tears filling her eyes.

'Davey, what is it?'

He looked down her line, past her bobber to the floating litter, where her worm had hooked a piece of tweed – a jacket sleeve—

a green hand—

a rose tattoo—

Bobby.

'All my life,' Sal said to the detective. Then he tipped the bottle to his lips again. 'Since I was thirteen or fourteen, I don't remember. We went to high school together.'

Down in the water, two scuba divers turned cranelike amidst the river debris, their backs flat to the surface, poring over the muddy bottom of the pool. Up in the field behind them, reporters and cameramen had gathered, kept out of sight by crime-scene tape and the two state troopers who had responded to Sal's call. The medical examiner was on his way.

Detective Shepherd, writing in a notepad, leaned his foot on the bare limb of a deadfall that lay alongside the path. Sal faced away from the river, kept his legs spread for balance. Behind him he could hear the river gurgling beyond the pool, where Bobby's body lay face up on the fishing rock beside Davey's rod like some grotesque trophy, still hooked in the cuff. Murdoch walked slowly along the bank, videotaping the scene.

'Then you'd characterize yourself as a close friend,' Shepherd said, keeping his voice low in consideration of the reporters.

'*Best* friend,' Sal replied. 'They moved up here because of me.' He put the bottle to his mouth again and drank slowly, to make the vodka last. As much as he'd already consumed, he still couldn't look at the body. Bobby's arms inside his jacket sleeves had puffed up like knockwurst. But it was the face that got to Sal: green as the pines above him; cheeks bloated like they'd burst; and the lips, partially disintegrated, were pursed in a gruesome whistle.

'And you're absolutely sure that's him?'

Sal snorted.

Down by the water, Murdoch said, 'Just answer the question, tough guy. Yes or no.'

Sal said, without turning, 'It's Bobby Swift. That's the suit he was wearing when he was buried, that's his tattoo. What do you guys need, a name tag?'

Murdoch sauntered up the bank and stopped within reach of Sal. 'Actually, we got a name tag,' he said. 'Wanna see?' He reached a waterlogged wallet in front of Sal's face. When he flipped the wallet open, a white card showed through a fogged plasticine window. 'But it's not Bobby Swift.'

'It says his name is Dale Newman,' Shepherd said.

The name careened through Sal's mind. He turned toward the river, looked down at the body and swayed a bit.

'Nice friend, you don't know his name,' Murdoch said, giving Sal a come-and-get-it grin.

Sal returned a look that said he was more than ready to oblige.

'Which way to the swimmin hole?' a voice called. Behind the men, Dr Franklin Cafferty, deputy medical examiner for the area, came marching over the bank, carrying a black case.

'Down there,' Murdoch told him, and Cafferty charged past them to the corpse, never slowing. The doctor was a paunchy man with thick glasses and white hair combed stiffly over the top of his head. 'Whadda we got,' he called back, 'creature from the black lagoon?'

'Doctor, there are reporters up there,' Shepherd told him.

Snapping on a pair of latex gloves, Cafferty knelt on the rock beside the body. 'Goddamn human blowfish,' he said, just as loud.

'This gentleman's daughter landed him about an hour ago,' Murdoch explained, flipping a glance at Sal.

Shepherd added, 'We think he might've been buried at the local cemetery last week.'

'Ah, the missing corpse, I heard about you.' Cafferty lifted the green face toward his own. Brownish water ran out of the nostrils. 'What were they using for bait?' he said to no one in particular.

Shepherd turned away. 'Doctor, I'd like your opinion on how long he's been dead. Any way of estimating?'

Cafferty shook his head. 'Not until we get him in the lab. I *can* tell you that his body hasn't been in the river any more than twenty-four hours – if that.'

Murdoch folded his arms, gave Shepherd a satisfied look. 'A third accomplice – just like I've been telling you. Had to be three of them.'

Sal stiffened; weaved dizzily, brushing against the sergeant.

'Have another drink,' Murdoch told him, moving down the bank.

'*Foul!*' Cafferty honked. 'Oh, there's some nasty business afoot.'

'Doctor, they can hear you up there.'

Cafferty turned Bobby's bloated face toward the men. 'See, they prettied him up, but that's about it.'

Shepherd took a couple of steps closer. 'What do you mean?'

'You gentlemen ever hear of embalming?' Cafferty squinted up at the detectives, angling his head to focus through his trifocals. 'This man still has his own blood in his veins.'

Up on the path, Sal turned away again. He felt a drop of rain on his arm, and then two more drops, but it meant nothing. The meaning of the doctor's words dangled out of reach.

Murdoch walked down to the doctor. 'That's been my theory all along,' he said. 'The guy fakes dead, they bury him with some oxygen tanks, the undertaker comes back at night and digs him up, and, whammo – now it's the undertaker underground. Perfect crime, right? But then, just when the trusting husband is about to split the country and start a new life—' Murdoch pointed at Shepherd. 'Poison. I'll bet you a ten-spot she slipped him something.'

'You lose!' Cafferty chimed, deriding him. 'Think, man! The lips. The lips!' He sank his index finger knuckle-deep through the hole in Bobby's mouth, then flicked his finger out again with a sickening pop. 'Hah? How long you think Mister Whistle went around like this? You think he drank the poison through a straw?'

The doctor pushed an eyelid open. 'See, you got petchelie here.' He leaned back so Murdoch could see. 'Red-eye, broken blood vessels – a condition consistent with strangling or suffocation. But there's no hemorrhaging around the neck.' He looked back at both detectives. 'I'd say you got yourselves a little insurance scam that went south.'

'Are you saying he died in his casket?' Shepherd said.

'Of course he did. You want my professional estimation? I'd say this poor bastard got taken for a whale of a ride.'

The rain started falling harder.

Cafferty said, 'I'd better wrap him up and take him along. Don't want him getting wet.'

Gesturing toward the divers in the pool, he said to Murdoch, 'I don't know what you expect to find in there. There's no weapon. He was already dead. They just dumped the corpse here to get rid of it.'

Shepherd stared. Standing there in the rain for another second or two, he turned toward the field, and a scowl came over him. 'Son of a bitch,' he said softly.

Murdoch looked over at him.

Sal stood unsteadily on the path. Despite all that he'd drunk – most of the liter in less than two hours – his entire body was wracked with trembling. He spun around and made for the field.

Murdoch called after him, 'Hey, Greaseball, where do you think you're going?'

Sal kept walking.

Iris stood in the rain at the edge of the road, having forgotten why she was there. Davey was upstairs in her bedroom. Sal was on his way to the store. Iris herself was dressed in a flannel shirt. The back of her hand was spattered white. The rain did not affect the spatters. She did not know how long she had been standing here – a few seconds, a minute, or an hour. Looking off toward the village, she could no longer see Sal. Rainwater ran down her face. Her shoulders were drenched.

It was the house, her own hollow house – the reason she was out here. She had felt it as soon as she'd caught sight of Sal marching past – this vague, utterly ridiculous (yet utterly persistent) notion that – somehow – the house was her mother, and it was watching her; the vague fear that she had finally and inescapably been wrenched from her sanity. Yes, everything was perfectly, swimmingly, vague – except her paralysis. Standing here in plain view of every car that drove past, she felt so conspicuous, like a fawn pinned by headlights.

She could not remember why she had come out here, or what she had been doing before. Working? Studying? Cooking dinner? By the paint on her hand, it might have seemed reasonable to assume that she had been painting, but she made no such connection. It was as if her mind had shut down. Rainwater ran down off her nose. A welling rose up in her chest.

She thought of Davey up in her room, turning pages of a book she had read dozens of times. The welling grew. Iris swallowed it, and she swallowed again. She refused to acknowledge the house, hollow, cold and unforgiving. Instead, she watched the rainwater gather in the ditch by the side of the road and go running off toward the village.

Presently, she became aware of a car in front of her, a silver car, idling. She could see the bottom of the car at the top of her vision, but she refused to look up. She could tell that the driver was watching her.

'Mrs Erickson?' A woman's voice.

Iris flinched.

In her mind, she turned and walked calmly back into her house. In reality, she remained stuck in this spot. She couldn't even get her mind to move.

'Mrs Erickson, are you okay?'

Iris heard the car door open, the footsteps approach—

'*Mrs Erickson?*'

—and then the hands on her, first on her arm, then on her back. 'Mrs Erickson, are you alright?' Warm, dry hands.

Iris looked at the woman. She shuddered—

'Helen Swan,' the woman said.

A rich tremor swept through Iris. She let out a low, tremulous sound.

'Is everything okay?'

Iris closed her eyes. The hand on her back, the woman's voice, felt so soothing. 'No,' she whispered. God, her own voice – what a relief to hear it. Goose bumps coursed over her arms, and she realized how cold she was. She spoke again. 'I can't go in my own house.'

'Are you locked out?'

Iris shook her head and almost laughed at herself, but now she was crying. 'I just can't go in.'

'That's okay,' the older woman said, holding her a little more firmly. 'Are you alone?'

Iris took a breath, let it out. 'Davey's inside. My daughter.'

The woman's arm wrapped around her shoulder, turned her gently around. 'Is that Davey in the window?'

Iris looked up, saw Davey's face behind the glass. The relief was overwhelming. Recognition of the woman came to her in a flood. Helen Swan, the school board chairperson who had caught her in a lie, who had fired Sal – Helen Swan, she remembered, was a retired psychologist or psychiatrist from New Jersey who had moved to Maine after her husband had died. And here was stalwart Iris, clutching the woman dearly in her own front yard, with Davey and the hollow house and God knew how many other people watching.

And it felt so good.

'I was painting the ceiling,' Iris told her. 'I think I painted my whole house today.' She laughed in amazement, closing her eyes, tears running with the rain. She wiped her forehead with her arm, and then she cried harder.

'That's okay,' Helen said. 'Let's go in and get you into some dry clothes.' Helen had the most soothing voice; Iris took hold of her arm, and they started walking.

* * *

The Stoli bottle, not quite empty, stood centered on the roof of Murdoch's black Mercury where a police light might have been.

Murdoch batted the bottle onto the side of the road, where the glass shattered. He walked up to Shepherd's Cherokee, bent to look in the window. Inside, Shepherd held his telephone to his ear. 'That son of a bitch,' the detective said, setting the phone back in its cradle. 'He knows.'

''Course he knows,' said Murdoch, his blazer absorbing the rain. 'He's screwin her, of course he knows.'

'Not him,' Shepherd said. 'I mean Bouchard, the constable.'

'Yeah? Knows what?'

Shepherd switched off the phone. 'About Bobby Swift's casket. Why it wasn't torn apart.'

'Because they whacked him before they buried him.'

'No. Those scuba tanks were empty – he was down there breathing. Till he ran out of air.'

Murdoch gave it a moment's thought and then looked in the window. 'I'd say it's time we interviewed your lady friend.'

'Nope.' Shepherd started the engine. 'I think it's time to interrogate her.'

Sal reached the store just ahead of the detectives. Too drunk to run, barely able to walk, his mind spun with fragments: Bobby, buried alive; his green, whistling face; Dale Newman; Eliot Wicker. Sal pulled the front door open and walked in. Jerry, eating beans and franks at the counter, turned a full circle on his fountain stool, watching as Sal strode toward the back. 'She already knows,' he said.

From the register, Bonnie sang, 'She certainly doesn't need to see *you*.'

Sal ignored them both and pushed in behind the meat counter. 'Chad—'

Chad followed after him. 'Mr Erickson, you can't go back here.' Sal banged through the door without slowing, navigating down the middle aisle of cartons until he turned to her desk, then around another stack of cartons, and—

Noel was there.

Sal leaned against a support post to steady himself, while he tried to focus on her, to wring some understanding from the look she was giving him, that slack, knowing smile. He stepped away from the post, spreading his legs for balance.

'I did not do this,' he said, his words emerging slow and deliberate.

Standing in the open doorway, she wore a plain green dress, while zebra-striped stairs rose madly around her head. 'Why do you keep telling me?' she said.

He took a step toward her. 'Because it had to be one of us. You or me.'

She stood there, not answering, seeming to float above him.

Behind him, the voices, the footsteps, came fast.

Noel pulled the door closed behind her, leaned back against it. That look—

Bonnie and Chad appeared first, sweeping around the wall of cartons. 'Here he is,' Bonnie said. The detectives came around them.

Shepherd dropped a hand by his hip, to calm things. 'Do me a favor, folks. Go on back to work now.'

Neither Bonnie nor Chad retreated. Shepherd took a step closer to Noel, ignoring Sal. 'Want to take a ride?' he said.

She smiled disdainfully. 'You're arresting me?'

'Not arresting. Just going somewhere to talk.'

Murdoch stepped toward Sal. 'You got a hearing problem, Greaseball? You were told to leave.'

Slowly Sal turned to face the sergeant, who happily moved in closer. 'What, you got something smart to say to me?' Murdoch said. 'Go find a bottle and crawl back in your hole.'

Their eyes clashed.

Murdoch's mouth opened. He puffed himself up and folded his big arms, his smile curling downward. 'Real bosom buddies,' he said. 'Oh yeah, I can see the way you ran over here – oh yeah, I can see how you're real broke up—'

Sal jumped him, slammed his shoulder into the sergeant's gut and drove him to the door. Unfazed, Murdoch's grin never left his face while he rabbit-punched at Sal's kidneys. But his angle was off, and the blows had no effect. So he leaned his weight down on

Sal's back, wrapped his arms around his chest and pulled up with a grunt, lifting Sal's feet off the floor. The men stumbled in a circle. Cartons toppled.

Now Shepherd came in from the right. 'Get his legs!' Murdoch barked. Like noseguards, the two men captured Sal, hauling him through a wall of boxes, four-foot cartons of toilet paper avalanching down. As the men tumbled, Sal threw an elbow and extricated himself, a perfect fullback scramble. In the same blurring motion he executed a full-force roundhouse right that caught Murdoch squarely on the neck, just below the ear. The big man staggered a few steps back, then went heavily over a box. Sal spun to face Shepherd, expecting another attack.

He didn't see Alston Bouchard beside him until the constable's fist connected with the side of his jaw. Sal's heels and toes pivoted beneath him as he fought for balance. Instinctively he turned and raised his guard. Bouchard's second punch shot under his defense, slammed into his chest like the butt end of an oak log. Sal reeled backward into the support post. Struggling with consciousness, he slumped there, out on his feet.

Shepherd fell upon him instantly, held him against the post as he pulled the cuffs from his pouch. Bouchard was there too, holding Sal under the arms to keep him from falling, as Shepherd snapped a cuff on Sal's wrist.

'He's not resisting now, Detective,' Bouchard said.

'Yeah?' Shepherd pulled the cuffed wrist behind Sal's back, reached for Sal's other arm.

'I mean, I'd just as soon take him with me,' Bouchard continued, 'get him out of your way.'

Shepherd gave the constable a look, wishing they were alone so he could find out exactly what Bouchard knew about the casket.

'He just needs to sleep it off.'

Shepherd also wanted to get Noel out of there before Murdoch came to and could interfere any more. And he certainly didn't want to leave Sal alone with Murdoch.

'You got what you came for,' Bouchard persisted.

Already the sergeant was pulling himself onto the desk chair, however groggily. Shepherd turned to Bouchard again, pulled the cuff off Sal's wrist. 'Before I change my mind,' he said, nodding toward the front door.

As Bouchard led Sal away, Murdoch pushed to his feet, held onto the desk for balance. 'What's this? Where's he going?'

Shepherd waved them off. 'He's not worth it, let him go.'

It was like telling a pit bull to leave fresh kill. 'You gotta be kiddin me, you cut him loose—?'

'You okay?' Shepherd asked.

''Course I'm okay!' Murdoch stepped forward and bent for his handcuffs, missed the first try, rocked back on his feet. 'Goddamn blood pressure medicine.'

Shepherd nodded to Noel, and they began walking toward the aisle. 'Catch your breath, Sarge,' the detective said. 'Have a coffee or something. I'll see you back at the station.'

Noel's interrogation took place in the August Tea House, a Chinese restaurant in Ellsworth. Shepherd chose the restaurant because it was poorly attended and because he knew Murdoch would never find them there. They sat in the rear of the dining room, in a corner booth. Shepherd had given the maître d' a five-dollar tip and asked him not to seat anybody near them. He ordered appetizers for them both while Noel excused herself and went to find the bathroom. When she returned, Shepherd's notebook computer was opened on the table in front of him. He poured a cup of green tea and passed it to her. She ignored it.

'Okay,' he said, 'let's start with Bobby's business.'

'Bobby's business.'

Shepherd punched a couple of keys and looked down at the monitor. 'After Bobby left the navy, he started a skydiving school outside Providence. Sold the business in 1988 to a group of his former students, then started manufacturing and flying ultralight airplanes.' Shepherd looked up from the computer. 'Bobby liked to take chances.'

'A lot of people fly, Detective.'

'But a three-million-dollar business loan – that takes courage. Especially when it's illegal.'

Noel stared across the table, stone-faced. 'I told you, Bobby was his father's son.'

'Meaning—'

'Meaning when it comes to business, the less the woman knows, the better off she is.'

'Yet you strike me as so modern.' Their eyes remained locked.

'Bobby took on the world every day,' she said, 'and he seemed to be winning. That's all I needed to know. I had my own life.'

Shepherd stroked his mustache with the side of his finger. Watching for signs – dry mouth, restlessness, flushed face, preoccupation with the time – he saw none. Not taking his eyes off her, he recited from memory: 'Charles J. Mariotta, the bank officer who okayed Bobby's loan. Mariotta was sentenced to fourteen years in prison. Bobby, who testified against him, got community service and probation. Not to mention over two million dollars that was never recovered.'

'And I've told you I don't know anything about that money.'

She took a sip of her water. Shepherd watched her swallow. Started to push.

'I don't imagine Charles was too happy with the arrangement. Bobby gets a slap on the wrist, Charlie gets fourteen years. Charlie? Chuck?'

She narrowed her eyes.

'Do you know when Charles Mariotta gets out of prison?'

'You said he was sentenced to fourteen years.'

'Next month, after seven years. A reasonable person might assume he'd want to speak with Bobby about that missing money. Dead's a good way to disappear.' He folded his hands on the table as the waitress arrived with their spring rolls, set them down, then went quickly away.

'This is what I think,' Shepherd continued. 'Charlie Mariotta made Bobby Swift a three-million-dollar bank loan to start a business. In exchange for the loan, which wasn't entirely above-board in the first place, Bobby agreed to cut Charlie in on a share of the company's profits – definitely against the law. That much is indisputable.'

'According to you.'

'And a jury and a judge. Noel—'

She refused to acquiesce, even on this point, but Shepherd wasn't waiting.

'Bobby gets his loan, he starts his company, it's the '80s, money's making money, and Bobby gets rich. That's when you come into the story. You meet this daring young millionaire, you fall in love, you get married. Then the economy bottoms out. The business turns sour. You get this idea, this brainstorm.'

Noel sighed.

'You, plural – you and Bobby. First he stashes a couple million bucks in an offshore account, let's say in the Cayman Islands, where it can't be traced.'

'I must say, the story improves with time,' Noel said, picking up a spring roll.

'It's a joint account or trust – maybe a corporation – with two partners, Bobby Swift and Dale Newman. See, *New-man?* I like it when they give you clues. Anyway, the brainstorm: you move to some little backwater town in Maine, strike up a deal with the local undertaker—'

'Too greasy,' Noel said, setting the spring roll down.

'One day in June a man named Dale Newman walks into a supply house in Belfast, picks up a set of scuba tanks and a couple of oxygen tanks. A year later Bobby Swift dies. There's a funeral, and he's buried. Next day, lo and behold, Mr Dale Newman arrives on Cayman Island and begins living the life of Riley. At least that was the plan. Bobby's plan.'

Noel reclined slightly in the booth. Her eyes, candlelit, glinted with ridicule.

Shepherd stole a glance around the dining room and then leaned forward, leveling his gaze. 'You let him die, Noel. You and Wicker were supposed to dig him up, and you let him suffocate down there.'

Now Noel leaned forward and leveled her own gaze. 'Detective, are you aware that you're accusing me of *not* doing something?'

Once again the waitress interrupted them with food, three covered stainless steel bowls balanced on one arm. In turn, she set each one down and uncovered it for their approval. Shepherd thanked her, and she went away.

Noel looked across the table at Shepherd with something akin to pity. 'Please continue, Detective. I'm dying to hear your theory on why I put scuba tanks on Eliot Wicker and buried him alive in

Bobby's grave, with a gun in his hand. Or why I threw a heating pad in a tree—?'

'To make it look like Bobby did it.'

She nodded gravely, with rich sarcasm. 'Bobby would have done that. And then I spread more clues around – I put a plane ticket in Alston Bouchard's mailbox. I dumped my husband's body in the river a quarter-mile from home. Detective, has it crossed your mind that someone might be trying to make me look guilty?'

The candle on their table flickered.

Shepherd shook his head. 'I'll be honest with you,' he said. 'I've thought about this and I've thought about this, and for the life of me, I can't think of a single scenario in which you would not be involved.'

Her eyes flitted past him with a quick glimmer of relief. He turned.

'Detective,' the man behind him said, offering his hand.

'Do you know my attorney?' Noel said. 'Hal Jones, this is Detective Shepherd.'

'We've met,' Shepherd said.

'He was handling my divorce,' she added as she swiped her purse off the seat and slid out of the booth.

Shepherd pushed awkwardly to his feet while his mind grasped for clarity: *divorce?*

'How's it going, Detective?' the lawyer said with a slight, superior smile.

'How are you?' Shepherd replied, trying not to show his anxiety at the turnabout.

Noel started toward the door.

Shepherd grabbed his jacket from the booth. 'Wait a minute, I'll take you home.'

She kept walking.

'I'll take her,' the attorney said. Jones was a heavy man, in his early forties, with thick brown hair, wire glasses and a drooping mustache. He wore a gray suit, twice as rich as anything in Shepherd's wardrobe. 'Listen,' he said, friendly enough, 'from now on, why don't we make sure I'm present if you plan to question my client.'

Shepherd felt disheveled, blindsided. He smoothed his jacket sleeve.

'It's a strange one,' the attorney said with a laugh. 'Noel's been filling me in: the fake death, the missing money, and now her husband's body. Definitely strange.' He picked a cloth napkin off the table and handed it to Shepherd, nodding to a spot of tea on his pocket. 'I'm telling you this as a favor, Detective. Maybe it'll save you some time. She really was divorcing her husband.'

Shepherd rubbed the napkin on his jacket. 'I appreciate that,' he said, not entirely sincere.

'She was determined not to leave empty-handed. The business, the property, future profits of the store, you name it – their savings and investments – half would have gone to her. I have a list of their assets. If Noel Swift had known about two million dollars, believe me, it would've been on that list.'

Shepherd tossed the napkin on the table, then looked back toward the door.

'If anybody had a motivation for a faked death and disappearance, it was Bobby Swift, to keep that money away from Noel.'

Shepherd nodded. Never saw it coming.

When the detective returned home, there were two phone messages for him to call Murdoch at the barracks. 'I'll be waiting,' the sergeant said, sounding displeased. Shepherd telephoned him before he removed his jacket.

'I got a call from your lady's attorney a while ago,' Murdoch said to him. 'Did you have a date with her tonight?'

Shepherd's ears hummed.

'Take her home and screw her or what?'

'I interrogated her. It was time to eat, so we went to a restaurant. You know the way I work.'

'Yeah, meanwhile I'm back at the station with my thumb up my ass, waiting for you.'

'There's a new wrinkle, Sarge. Bobby Swift had reason to hide the money from her. She was divorcing him.'

'I know that,' Murdoch said. 'The lawyer and me had a long talk. For curiosity's sake, I'll tell you something else. She's going on a little vacation the day after tomorrow. A two-week cruise out of Tampa.'

'Shit.'

'Figure she's gonna boogie?'

Shepherd sighed, pulled his computer across the counter and flipped the lid open. 'We'll check it out.'

'Already did. Delta confirmed a round-trip flight from Bangor to Tampa and back again. She's down for ten days on Tampa Bay Cruise Lines.'

'She could connect to the Caymans.'

'Oh, you don't think she'd do that,' Murdoch said.

Shepherd waited, typing the words DELTA, TAMPA BAY.

'I had it checked out,' the sergeant continued. 'The boat doesn't go there, and nobody by the name of Noel Swift or Noel anybody is flying Cayman Airways in the next two weeks.'

'How about Dale Newman?'

Murdoch chuckled softly. 'Jeez, you know, I thought of that too.'

'So?'

'So nothing. No Dale Newman, no Newman Dale. What I need to know is whether or not you have anything to keep her here, solid enough to convince the A.G.'s office.'

Shepherd told him, 'I don't have it.'

'That's what I thought,' Murdoch said. 'So write up what you do have and leave it on my desk in the morning.'

'Wait a minute—' Shepherd looked up from the computer. 'What are you saying? You're not taking over this case—?'

'Can't be helped.'

'Sarge, I'm almost there. Look, you're right about the third accomplice. No way around it. Maybe it's her, maybe it's not. We've got to get through the Caymans, to see the names on that account. It's clearly a murder case, they'll waive their confidentiality laws.'

'I'll take that under advisement,' Murdoch replied. Shepherd could hear the nasty smile in his voice, and that's when he realized—

Murdoch had planned this from the start, taking over in the final round. High-visibility case, possible promotion before retirement, something to fatten his second pension.

'You're not taking over this case,' Shepherd said again.

'Sorry, it's not my decision,' Murdoch replied. 'It's Boggs. You embarrassed the lieutenant. The media's all over him, and he wants this put to rest. See, once again, *Andy of Mayberry* has led you astray.'

Murdoch hung up the telephone and pressed back in his chair, his upper body stiffened by the cumbersome brace that fixed his neck to his shoulders. He lifted the remote control off his desk, aimed it at the VCR that sat on a cart in front of his desk, and thumbed the button that said SLOW. The television screen flickered on a scene. A black sportscoat hanging on a wall. Slowly the angle panned across the dark fabric to a black hooded sweatshirt; then up the sweatshirt until Eliot Wicker's wooden coat rack was visible, a plain flat board attached to a white plaster wall. Continuing rightward to an unused wooden peg ... and then to the cap, black against the white wall. PAUSE. The image froze on the cap.

Murdoch leaned forward, reached over his desk to the television and turned up the brightness until the black lightened to brown, and a tweed pattern became apparent. He slid the photo under the desk lamp, the picture of Bobby Swift and Sal Erickson, shoved a magnifying glass over it and moved his shoulders until one face rose out of the frame, looking out from under the cap.

Sal opened his eyes, tried again to raise his arm, but it was caught. He tried to shake it free, heard a jangle – and then something dug into his wrist – something cold. He reached with his free hand, found that he was attached to the iron bed frame—

Handcuffed.

'Hey – *Hey!*'

Outside the door a light came on, dimly illuminating the room. Footsteps approached, and then another light came on, much brighter, and a figure appeared in the doorway. Alston Bouchard. A big black dog beside him.

'What the hell is this?' Sal said.

'You've got to get sober,' the dark man answered in a low voice.

A throbbing pain flared through Sal's jaw, rifled across his head. A blur of recollection, nothing clear. (The green hand rising out of the pool . . . Noel rising in front of the zebra stairs . . .)

'Go back to sleep, best thing.'

'Where is she? I need to talk to her.'

'Home, I'd imagine, this hour.'

Sal jangled his wrist again. He sat up on the mattress and pulled against the cuff. 'What are you doing? Get me off this thing!'

The dog started to bark, rapid-fire explosions. 'Katahdin, stop,' Bouchard said, and the dog whined. Sal dragged the handcuff up the frame until it snagged. He rolled off the bed and planted his feet on the floor.

Bouchard closed the door, pulled a wooden chair over in front of it and sat down. The black dog pressed against his knee, whining nervously. 'You've got to get sober,' he said again. 'There's a pan on the floor for you. Don't step in it.'

'I'll tear this goddamn bed apart!'

Bouchard replied, without emotion, 'You'll try, prob'ly.'

Sal rose to his feet, toppling the mattress and blankets, lifting the bed frame halfway up the wall.

'Get some sleep,' Bouchard said to Sal, 'best thing.'

Sal jerked his arm, and the bed frame jumped off the floor and came down again.

'I'd appreciate it if you wouldn't tear apart my room,' Bouchard told him.

Sal stood there defiantly, sweat-soaked. The windows were closed, the room airless. He fixed Bouchard in his vision. 'I got the hat,' he said. 'My hat that you left at Wicker's.'

Bouchard leaned forward and tossed the blanket over the mattress. 'I saw your hat at Wicker's,' he said. 'I didn't put it there. You didn't either. I've got a good idea who did.'

Sal watched him warily.

'Get some sleep,' Bouchard told him again. 'We'll talk in the morning.' He reached for the lamp on the bureau and turned it off.

Sal stood in the darkness for another minute, then lowered the bed frame to the floor, slumping to his knees on the mattress. He exhaled heavily. 'You can't keep me here,' he said.

'Got to,' Bouchard replied.

* * *

Jerry peered through the garage window as he leaned on the service bell. Shortly, a light emerged from the stairway, and then Noel came down, wearing a long dark sweatshirt that reached to the middle of her thighs. Jerry moved over to the entrance door and pressed his face against the window. He shone a flashlight on Noel as she came closer, on her legs. When she opened the door, she stepped back, making room for him to enter the garage. He checked her hands before he did, made sure they were empty.

'Busy day,' he said, 'down the falls.'

She shut the door behind him. 'Come out of the light,' she said, and she walked around the cars to the back of the garage, where it was darker. He followed warily, shining his flashlight up and down the back of her, exceedingly alert from the volume of caffeine he'd consumed over the past forty hours. Lucky shoes or not, he knew enough to watch her.

'So they found Bobby in the river,' he said. 'Staties, reporters, detectives, the whole nine yards.'

He rocked his head while he watched for her reaction. But she gave him none. Her eyes remained steady. In fact, she was looking at him with a kind of piqued interest, as if there were something about him tonight that fascinated her.

'Jerry, I want you to know that I had nothing to do with that fire.'

He studied her suspiciously for a second. Then his eyes rolled. 'Oh, yeah, well! Pretty big coincidence, then, if you ask me.'

'Shh.'

He whispered forcefully. 'You get me down to Bangor where I almost get my head cut off, then my house burns down. Next thing you know, you put a bullet in my new truck try'na blow me away. Oh yeah, big coincidence, really.'

'I didn't know it was you breaking in. I didn't know who it was.'

Jerry fluttered his lips. 'Just like a woman. I take it up one notch with the plane ticket, and then you take it up twenty-five, burnin down my house and almost gettin me murdered.' He glared, his caffeinated eyes glinting hard. 'I'm right on top of this, Noel. Right on top.'

'Jerry, I'm telling you the truth.'

'Yup, yup, yup.'

'I admit I asked a friend of mine to talk to you about that letter you wrote—'

'Talk, oh yes.'

She inched closer to him. 'But I swear, I don't know anything about that fire.'

'Yup.'

'I was the one who answered the fire phone, how could I have set the fire?' She gave him a look that caught him off guard, her eyes sponge-bathing him.

Jerry leaned back against the Volvo, his own eyes focusing in the vicinity of her hips. 'Well, anyway, they got the dead body now.'

She touched the sleeve of his shirt. 'Is this new?'

Jerry studied her. 'I gotta say, Noel, you don't seem too friggin concerned.'

She laid those eyes on him again. 'Should I be?'

He tipped his head. 'Well, it's not gonna take a brain scientist to figure out that Bobby was buried alive. For starters.'

'Mm-hmm.'

'Alright then,' he said, making his point. It felt good to be in control. The truth was, Jerry was feeling less in control by the minute. Even now, the way Noel gazed at him with that half smile, he felt more like he was being stalked.

'Jerry, I want you to understand something,' she said. 'I didn't kill my husband. Eliot Wicker killed Bobby. And now Eliot Wicker is dead.' She lowered her voice so softly that even if someone else were in the garage with them, he mightn't have heard her. 'And we both know who killed Wicker.'

Jerry's chin doubled, ready to laugh it off. At the same time, his stomach percolated.

'Jerry, it's obvious from your letter that you dug up Bobby's body to blackmail Eliot Wicker—'

'Wrong, wrong—'

'—and then you murdered Wicker.'

'*Wrong!*'

'It's completely obvious. Anyone who read that letter would know exactly what you did.'

Jerry's heel began tapping on the concrete floor. He glanced back at the door, then returned his gaze to her, amazed at how small she was, and how dangerous.

'In the first place,' he said, 'the only reason I dug Bobby up was to save his dumb ass once I figured out that you and Wicker were just gonna leave him down there. Then, alright, *then* I figured since I was too late and he was dead already, and I had the inside information, why not? So I removed his body for safekeeping.'

'And then you murdered Wicker.'

'*No.*' He widened his eyes to make his point. 'I came back here to make a deal with the both of you, but then you went and invited Sal Erickson up – and the next thing I know, here comes Wicker up to see you, and five minutes later there he goes again, spittin and sputterin all the way down to the cemetery, where he digs up the grave and gets even madder when he sees the body's missin. And that's when I went over to make my deal. But Wicker, dumb shit, he pulls a gun on me – which is why I say, self-defense all the way. No question about it.'

'Jerry, you buried him alive.'

'Yeah, well. Not on purpose. He got hit on the head with an oxygen tank, and then he wasn't breathing. Looked dead to me; turns out I only stunned him. Anyway, he got his justice, even if it wasn't from a judge.'

Noel sighed. 'Jerry, you told me that you didn't know anything about Wicker's death, or who took Bobby's body. You lied to me.'

'Oh! Well! Excuse me, Mrs George Washington!'

Noel smiled calmly. 'Jerry, you know we're going to have to be honest with each other now that we're in this together.' She moved closer to him, her eyes *shining*. 'We are in this together, aren't we, Jerry?'

He rocked his head skeptically, but inside his lucky shoes, his toes clenched hard.

Noel's eyes lowered to his chest. 'I really did want to meet you in Bangor, Jerry. I really did. But how could I? You know how I'm being watched.'

Stunned, he folded his arms; looked at her as a dog might look at a grasshopper: playful, distrusting.

'Jerry, I'm serious. You have this *quality* – earthy, physical . . . Do you know what that does to a woman? I feel an animal attraction for you that's – overpowering.'

He felt his trousers tightening.

She gazed at him hungrily, laid her hand on his chest. Then, as if rousted from her fantasy, she spun away from him. 'God, I must be crazy,' she said. 'We can't do this here.'

'No, upstairs,' he said. 'You got a back door up there. Christ, you got three doors. Don't, uh, don't—'

She turned back, silencing him. 'First of all, Jerry, I need to know that you trust me.'

He expelled a column of air, mocking her. But it was easy to see he was transfixed.

'Jerry, you have all the power,' she murmured.

He snorted bitterly. 'That's what I thought.'

'I'm serious. You have the one thing that can save us both. And the thing that can destroy us.'

Jerry was listening; he was also preoccupied with her offer. 'We could go up now,' he said. 'Two in the morning, who's gonna know?'

Her eyes bored into him. 'The oxygen, Jerry.'

'Yeah, no problem. What?'

'When the other two oxygen tanks are found,' she said, 'we'll both be in the clear.'

He tossed his head up and down, eyes bulging. 'Oh, yes, M'am. Like I'm going to give 'em the murder weapon. I just imagine, really!'

She wouldn't stop staring at him. 'Jerry, those oxygen tanks can't be traced to you. Just wipe them off.'

He folded his arms, tapped his heel on the floor. 'You tell me how those tanks are supposed to save us.'

She breathed an exasperated sigh. 'I can see this isn't going to work between us.'

'I'm only askin a question.' He tapped his heel faster.

Now she refused to even meet his eyes.

'Alright, so what about the other thing, the thing that'll destroy us?'

Her words came out cold as polished steel: 'Your letter.'

He folded his arms, folded his face into a scornful mask, once again showing his power.

'Jerry, you are going to have to trust me.'

'Oh, yes, M'am. Trust you?'

'Just like I have to trust you.'

He gawked. 'How the hell do you have to trust me?'

'You say there's only one letter. How do I know there aren't two letters? Or three?'

Jerry flattened his lips. 'I ain't numb, Noel. I don't want that letter found, no more'n you do. There's only the one, and I got it hid in a place where you'll never find it.'

'Jerry, even one letter isn't very smart.'

'Oh, no. That letter's only keeping you from killing me.'

She pinned him with her eyes. 'No, Jerry. It's keeping me from fucking you.'

His knees loosened. He leaned back on the Volvo and peered at her, squinted at her as if he were looking into the sun. Then he slid off the car and moved around her to the outside door.

'That,' he said, 'that right there?' He shuddered as he turned the knob. 'That's what I call head games.'

Halfway to morning, Sal jumped awake.

'*Holy shit!* Bobby, you okay?'

Bouchard left the light off. 'I'm okay,' he answered.

'Oh, man, it's cold. Fuckin whose idea was this?'

Bouchard reached down, felt Sal's arm, taut and trembling; felt the blanket in a humid pile beside him. He tossed the blanket over Sal's back.

'Thanks, man.'

'Yup.'

'Bobby, you sure you're okay?'

'Yup.'

Twenty minutes later, Sal spoke again. 'Anthony, time to go home.'

'Yup.'

'Come on, brother.'

'Yup.'

12

At seven in the morning, when Jerry came into the store, the counter was deserted and Noel was working alone. Jerry had on a short-sleeved madras shirt, a pair of Sal's old khaki pants and his own lucky shoes.

'How about a cup of instant for starters,' he said to Noel. 'Then I guess a stack of pancakes, a half pound of bacon, one of those blueberry muffins toasted, and three eggs, sunny and runny.'

He unscrewed the lid off the big mayonnaise jar beside the register, the one that read: DONATIONS FOR OTIS AND JERRY ROYAL, and emptied the money onto the counter: eighty cents more than the five-dollar bill he had left as bait. 'Thanks, everyone,' he said. He put the five in his pocket, returned the change into the jar and closed the cover. He swung a leg over the stool and started drumming on the counter while he watched Noel break his eggs onto the grill.

'Guess you're the talk of the town today,' he said. His eggs sizzled.

'Word does get around,' Noel replied. Provincialism aside, the extent to which townspeople avoided the Superette this morning surprised even her. Sure, the usuals had all stopped in at the usual time – for gas, or the newspaper, a jug of milk or a loaf of bread – but nobody had sat down for coffee. In fact, even Bonnie had called in sick. A few had mentioned hearing that Herb and Bonnie were going to mind the store while Noel went away on a cruise; a couple of people told Noel, in nice ways, that she should stay longer. That, precisely, was her plan.

She poured Jerry's hot water, set a spoon and the instant coffee in front of him, and then watched as he stirred six teaspoons of granules into the cup. 'I'm on a caffeine diet,' he explained. 'Wicked buzzed, wicked buzzed.' As he poured sugar in, he said without looking up, 'I took care of it, thought you'd oughta know.'

'The letter?' she asked.

He swallowed the coffee, shook his head. 'Oxygen tanks.'

She blinked once, slowly, like an owl.

'Figured with you leavin on your cruise tomorrow,' he said, a shoulder twitching.

'You figured what?'

He swung off his stool, grabbed a ballpoint pen off the cash register. 'Well, I give up certain things, and tonight you go ahead with – your animal attraction, whatever, and I don't get my head bashed in this time.' He underlined the word DONATIONS on the mayonnaise jar, scratching the pen back and forth. 'Better watch my eggs,' he told her. 'Crispy they're no good.'

'Jerry,' she said. 'The letter.'

'I know, the letter for *all-the-way*. But I'm just sayin, okay, up-to-that-point for the oxygen tanks. Preview of coming attractions.'

The scolding, teasing look she gave him made his stomach buzz. 'Where are they?' she said.

'Really, watch my eggs.'

'Jerry, where did you put the tanks?'

Under the word DONATIONS, he wrote PLEASE HELP HIM, but the curve of the jar made his writing a childish scrawl. He looked up at her with a caffeine gleam in his eye.

'You'll find out.'

In Belly Button's backyard, as it turned out. Belly and his wife, both devout Catholics – Jerry had left them a surprise: one tank, propped on an overturned pail, rested against the crotch of their ceramic garden Jesus, like a bright green erection. The Virgin Mary got the other.

The voice on the telephone was British in tone, spiced with West Indian staccato. 'As I explained to your commander, Detective, we have no taxes here in the Caymans; therefore, no tax fraud.' The sentence ended with a lilting brogue that Shepherd found particularly annoying.

'And I'm explaining to you,' he replied, 'that this is not a tax fraud case, but an advanced-stage murder investigation.' He sat on the dispatch desk in the troop barracks, waiting for a reply that turned out to be silence. Seven-thirty in the morning, a half hour before duty, he was the only one on the floor besides Stacy Myotte, the dispatcher, who sat behind the desk buttoning his back pocket for him.

'We have a corpse,' he went on. 'We know that the victim was planning to relocate to your island under an alias, Dale Newman, and that approximately two million dollars of our government's money has been deposited in one of your banks.'

'I see,' the official said. Shepherd slid off the desk and paced toward the wall until Stacy grabbed the phone to keep it from pulling off the desk. He stopped and came back.

'We also know for a fact that the funds are most likely in a joint account, or trust, in the names of Robert Swift, Dale Newman, and a third name – which is the purpose of this inquiry, to verify the identity of the third party, who happens to be our chief suspect.'

'I see,' the Cayman official said again, which Shepherd took as a hopeful sign until the man elaborated. 'If, as you say, your investigation is in an advanced stage, Detective, then surely you must already know the identity of your chief suspect.'

Shepherd turned a circle. Stacy tugged him back.

When he looked up, he saw Sergeant Murdoch walking through the front door. A thick white neck brace holding Murdoch's chin in the air made it necessary for the big man to turn his entire upper body in order to spot Shepherd, and when he did, he came over.

'Look, all we want is a name. I'm asking for a simple professional courtesy.'

'What's he doing?' Murdoch asked the dispatcher, but then another phone line rang before she could reply. She went to a desk on the opposite wall to take the call. Murdoch turned 180 degrees to watch her walk away.

Shepherd covered the phone. 'I'm on my own time here, Sarge.'

'Do you have a confession?' asked the official on the phone. 'Or perhaps the testimony of an accomplice?'

'I told you,' Shepherd said, 'the two accomplices are deceased. They've been murdered. That's why we need the third name.'

The islander cleared his throat. 'I see.'

While Shepherd waited for the bureaucratic kiss-off, he saw Stacy summon Murdoch to the other phone.

'When you have indicted your suspect,' said the Cayman official, 'I have every confidence that we will be able to verify a name for you. Now, was there anything else I might be able to help you with this morning?'

'Yeah,' Shepherd said, 'you could change your goddamned laws.' He slammed the phone down just as Lieutenant Boggs came through the outer door.

Boggs, a tall, white-haired man, was wearing his gray suit, which meant either television cameras would be in today or he was speaking at another Rotary Club meeting. When he spotted Shepherd, he came directly toward him, saying, 'I've got the media coming in this morning, Detective. I want to tell them we're making progress.'

At the other desk, Murdoch hung up the telephone and walked a bisecting route, cutting the lieutenant off. 'I'll be filling you in,' the sergeant said, gesturing in the direction of Boggs's office.

Shepherd cut in. 'Lieutenant, I'd like to speak to you about taking me off the Gravity case.'

Boggs studied Shepherd for a moment. 'Detective, are you saying that you'd like to be taken off the case?'

Confused, Shepherd turned to Murdoch, who abruptly said to the lieutenant, 'I was going to explain that this morning. Last night I made the decision to take charge of this case myself. It's my professional opinion that Detective Shepherd has made some errors of judgment.'

'That's bullshit,' Shepherd said.

Boggs cleared his throat, looked pointedly at Shepherd, then down at the floor. But it was to Murdoch that he finally spoke. 'Sergeant, I don't know what the hell is going on here, but in a few hours I'm going on the noontime news. I plan to announce that our investigation is going forward, that we're examining evidence, conducting interviews, and that an arrest is imminent.' He scowled at Murdoch, then nodded toward the corridor. 'My office,' he said, then started walking.

When he was out of earshot, Murdoch handed Shepherd a note.

'You got your oxygen tanks,' he said. 'Two oxygen tanks turned up in somebody's backyard.'

'Wait a minute. Why two? We're only missing one.'

'That's what I want you to find out,' Murdoch told him. 'Run the tanks down to Augusta and have your friend check 'em out.'

'Wait a minute, you want me down in Augusta? Can't you send somebody else? She's only going to be here one more day.'

Murdoch turned his body toward the corridor to check for Boggs. Then, turning back to Shepherd, he added, 'That's why I want you in Augusta.'

When Sal awoke, it was with a sense of despair that felt bottomless. No longer handcuffed, he found himself sprawled on the floor beside the mattress, feeling like every nerve ending was exposed. His face, in particular, ached from ear to ear. The act of breathing hurt his chest. The sun shone bright on the window shades, and the room was already too warm...

...and Bobby was dead. Sal knew that now, without doubt. Likewise, there was no question that his separation from Iris and Davey was real. Tears burned in his eyes. He felt profoundly, desperately alone.

Images flitted through his mind (the green hand rose out of the river trash, repeatedly) and musical riffs played on and on. Alcohol withdrawal, he knew the symptoms well, the constant tremors. He felt like someone was pumping trash amphetamines into his veins, like he needed to run a twenty-six mile marathon at a flat-out dash. Trouble was, he lacked the desire to even get off the bed. He saw no reason to take another breath.

He looked up at Bouchard, slouched asleep in his wooden chair, backed against the door. The bearded man's eyes were closed, his thick glasses halfway down his nose, a paperback book opened in his hand. On the bureau beside him, the lamp was still lit. A black-haired girl, about eighteen, full-faced and very pretty, smiled out of a framed photo, a sparkle in her dark brown eyes.

'I know what Eliot Wicker did to you,' Sal said. His voice was raspy.

Bouchard stirred, closed his book. He straightened his glasses, pulled himself upright.

'I know what Eliot Wicker did to you,' Sal said again.

Bouchard cleared his throat. 'Didn't do anything to me,' he said quietly. 'Eliot Wicker was just being himself. Wasn't his fault that I lost my family's land. I'd lost everything else, it was just a matter of time.'

Sal stared at him for a number of seconds, then looked back to the picture of the girl on the bureau, realized it was Bouchard's daughter.

'What the hell are you,' he said, 'the A.A. secret police?'

'Fourteen years it's got me through.'

Sal sat up quickly. A rush of dizziness swept over him. 'I've gotta go,' he said.

Bouchard perched his hands on his knees, ready to stand. 'You're not ready, my opinion.'

'Yeah?' Sal studied him, realized that the constable's resolve was as strong as his own. 'Save your breath, I know the program, and it's not for me, okay? Step two: *Came to believe in a power greater than ourselves*. See, that doesn't work for me. I don't believe in myths. I had a drinking problem, so I stopped drinking. That's logic, not magic.'

The men locked eyes.

'I liken it to the geese,' Bouchard said.

Sal scratched at his whiskers. 'Geese—?'

'You take a flock of geese in the air,' Bouchard said. 'When one gets shot or gets sick and falls to the ground, two others'll fly down and stay with him till he dies or gets back to health. They don't know why they do it. They just do. Keeps the flock going, what I say.'

Sal's head throbbed. He leaned forward on the mattress, Bouchard's slow, deliberate speech only intensifying his anxiety.

'Same thing with people, what I've found,' Bouchard continued. 'I've been the same place you are, pretty much. Finally came the day I sawed the barrel off my shotgun and headed up that hill back here. When I got to the top, I heard a truck coming up. See, no one ever came up that hill unless it was the berry crews, in August. This was October. Turned out to be Barlow, the beekeeper

I get my hives from. He asked me what I was hunting. I told him Canada geese. He said he found that peculiar, considering I'd chained my dog down here with enough food and water to keep him alive for a week. He took the gun away from me, brought me down to a meeting, and then he kept going with me every night for three months. He told me some time later he never knew why he came over that day, he just woke up and decided to take a drive.'

Sal took a breath. 'You ever hear the term "captive audience"?'

Leaning forward in his chair, Bouchard fixed Sal in his thick lenses. 'You might be a captured audience, Mister. And you may think this is all a myth. But when you're in need of help, I suggest you keep your eyes wide open, 'cause someone'll be there – every time. You just got to be smart enough to know who it is – and who it isn't.' Bouchard rose off his chair, dropping his book on the floor. Then, as if embarrassed by his outburst, he opened the door to leave the room, saying, 'I'll make us something to eat.'

Murdoch took the boarding house stairs as quietly as his 300 pounds would allow, and the old oak boards cooperated with barely a groan. Less than agile with his weight, his age and his stiff neck, Murdoch wasn't that concerned with agility. He had the element of surprise on his side. He also had his Combat Commander, a particularly convincing .45 automatic that he had yet to use in the Pine Tree State. He didn't knock, didn't even bother to listen at the door, but just turned the knob and walked straight in, his .45 swinging from wall to wall and back again.

That's when his cell phone trilled. He reached back and closed the door behind him, then took the phone off his belt, unfolded it, and answered. 'Yuh.'

'I'm in Augusta with the tanks,' Shepherd told him. 'They finished with the Bobby Swift corpse this morning and they're confirming that he suffocated – probably in his casket, since there's no dirt or water in his lungs. They think he was probably kept frozen till he was dumped in the river.'

'Okay, that's good,' Murdoch said, reaching his hand in the pocket of Sal's sportcoat, feeling along the lining.

While Shepherd talked, his friend Phil Harwood stood at the

end of a long table, examining one of the oxygen tanks under a close, bright light. Two rows of tagged grocery bags and cardboard boxes of various sizes lay scattered around his feet, backlogged evidence from other cases.

'It still doesn't seem right,' Shepherd continued, 'the casket unmarked like it is – that he'd just give up and go to sleep.'

'Well, you keep working on it,' Murdoch said. For the second time, the response seemed too civil for Murdoch. Or too cocky, given the urgency of the investigation, with Noel about to bolt.

'Sarge, has anything come in that I should know about?' Shepherd asked.

'Like what?'

'I don't know. I get the feeling we're working at cross-purposes here.'

'You feel that way, huh?' Murdoch replied, pushing his fingers inside one of Sal's sneakers, feeling around.

'Sarge, we need to get together if we're going to keep her from getting on that plane.'

'No question about it.'

'The other thing,' Shepherd said. 'Those oxygen tanks I just brought down? They've identified marks on one of them that probably correspond with Wicker's hair, where he was struck. The paint's an exact match.'

'Any fingerprints on the tank?' Murdoch asked.

'Only from the man who found the tanks in his yard. They were wiped down before he handled them.'

'Uh-huh.'

'Sarge, I'm going to stop in Belfast on my way back, check out the place where Swift bought the tanks. Only two were signed for, now we've got three. I think this might be the anomaly we've been looking for.'

'That sounds like an anomaly to me. Let me know what you find out.'

Way too cocky.

'Where are you?' Shepherd asked.

'In my car, going down to Pat's for lunch,' Murdoch answered.

Just then the chemist gave a whistle. Shepherd looked up to see him shaking his head. With plain satisfaction, Harwood held a scalpel up for Shepherd to see, a speck of green paint on its tip. 'Hold on, Sarge,' Shepherd said into the phone, then covered the mouthpiece.

'Blue,' the chemist said. 'Under the green paint. The tank's blue. Somebody painted green over it.'

'So, blue – what's the significance?'

'It's not oxygen. Oxygen's green.'

'What's blue?'

His friend smiled. 'Nitrous oxide.'

'Nitrous—?'

'Laughing gas.'

Shepherd stared at Harwood. He uncovered the phone. 'Sarge, I'll call you from Belfast.'

'Yeah, what's up?'

'I'm going to check on that anomaly,' he answered, then hung up.

They sat at the kitchen table over two bowls of corn chowder. Although Sal was anything but hungry, he tried not to let on. In his bowl, a kernel of corn moved through the broth, seemingly under its own strength The Formica pattern swirled dizzily under his arms. Finally he put down his spoon and got to his feet. 'I gotta go,' he said.

Bouchard pushed his chair back an inch or two, enough to prevent Sal from getting to the door. 'You best get some strength first, my opinion.'

'You're entitled to your opinion,' Sal replied, as he pushed for the door.

Bouchard rose to his feet, blocking the path.

Sal grabbed his shirt to pull him out of the way. 'This is not your concern!' he growled. The dog jumped up, barking.

Bouchard, shorter than Sal by an inch but broader all around, took hold of Sal's arms and swung him into the middle of the room, upending a chair.

'You've got to face this!' he said. 'It's already cost you your home, your career—'

Sal lunged to his right, slipping Bouchard's grasp, but the constable caught him again and drove him hard into the counter.

'Your wife,' he said.

Sal closed his eyes.

'Your little girl—'

'Yeah!' Sal drove his elbow into Bouchard's chest. In the next instant, his arm was locked behind his back, his cheek pressed against the cupboard.

'See, I don't understand that logic,' Bouchard said in his ear, 'why anyone would give all that up.'

The dog barked. 'Lay down,' Bouchard told him.

He held onto Sal for a few more moments, then loosened his grip. 'Don't you know,' he said, 'that you're being set up for a murder? A murder you had nothing to do with.'

Sal leaned against the counter. 'You don't know what I did,' he said quietly. 'You don't know anything about me.'

'You got drunk,' Bouchard answered. *'You got drunk.* That's what you did.'

Sal closed his eyes, haunted.

'Noel Swift murdered her husband, as far as I can figure. They were supposed to dig him up, her and Eliot Wicker – but they left him. Killed him for a pile of money stashed in some foreign bank account. And then when things went wrong, she set you up to look guilty.'

Sal shook his head. 'Noel would not do that,' he said. 'Not to Bobby. Not to me.'

'Did you?'

'What?' Sal turned, faced Bouchard.

'Help kill him.'

'Bobby was my best friend.'

'Being his best friend doesn't help.'

Bouchard reached into his back pocket and withdrew a piece of paper, ledger green.

'See, it was someone who cared for him that let him die.' As he unfolded the paper to show Sal, the dog suddenly snapped toward the door and barked – twice, like gunshots.

'Stop!' Bouchard said. He leaned back to look out the low casement window. As the black car crept over the gravel, he folded the paper and stuck it back in his pocket. 'Go in the back and shut the door,' he told Sal, bending to pick up the chair.

'What's that paper?' Sal asked.

A car door closed outside. Bouchard went to the table, grabbed one of the soup bowls and spoons, opened a cupboard and set them inside. A maroon-and-orange checkered blazer strode past the window. Bouchard shot Sal a look, the urgency of which sent Sal backing into the hall as if he'd been shoved.

The dog barked again. Bouchard allowed it to continue.

Sal closed the bedroom door just as he heard Murdoch's voice in the kitchen say, 'Mind if I come in? I didn't think so.' The storm door banged shut.

Shepherd drove north to Belfast, to the company where the two oxygen tanks had been purchased twelve months earlier. But after telling the counterman what he was looking for, he was told that the tank of nitrous couldn't have been bought there.

'Congress says it's a classified hallucinogenic,' said the counterman, an elfish sort of person with a gray beard and light blue, twinkling eyes. 'Christ, you need a special license just to transport the shit.'

'You mean even if I worked for a dentist, I couldn't come down here and pick up a tank of nitrous oxide?'

The small man shook his head. He lifted a thick three-ring notebook from behind the counter and slapped it on the countertop. 'We deliver to dentists' and doctors' offices all over the midcoast area. After we drop it off, who knows? Anybody could've slipped it out. They inhale the shit for recreation, some of 'em. Which is why you need a license.'

Shepherd nodded. The facts told the tale: Bobby Swift had purchased two oxygen tanks to stash in the casket with him. Before the burial, Wicker had replaced one of the tanks with the disguised nitrous – and hidden the oxygen tank under his bed. Therefore, it had to have been either Wicker or Bobby's other accomplice who had signed for the nitrous. Someone with access to a dentist or doctor.

'Could a funeral director sign for nitrous oxide?' Shepherd asked.

'What the hell for?' the counterman said. 'Yeah, right, that'd be one fucked-up funeral.' His laugh sounded like he was choking.

Shepherd opened the book and ran his eye down the signatures on the first page. He knew he wasn't looking for Dale Newman, since Newman was an alias for Bobby Swift, and it was Swift the nitrous had been used against. He was convinced that it wasn't Wicker who had signed for the nitrous. Everything he had learned about the players told him that Wicker would have limited his involvement to the masquerade funeral. No, whoever had procured the nitrous would have been the same person who ended up double-crossing both Bobby and Wicker – someone who had Bobby's trust – the third accomplice.

And Noel still seemed likely, her divorce plans notwithstanding. Of course, the divorce could have been a ruse – Shepherd had suspected that the moment he'd heard it. On the other hand, if she had truly planned to divorce Bobby, then suspicion fell to Bobby's next closest confidant, Sal Erickson. Except something about the man didn't fit; he didn't seem cool enough – or ambitious enough – to have carried out such a deceit. And Noel seemed so perfect.

Ignoring the dog, the sergeant walked stiffly past Bouchard until he was in the center of the kitchen. 'I'm not one to waste time,' he said. With his neck brace, he couldn't move his head without moving his whole body, so he turned a half circle and then stepped to the left in order to look down the hall. 'My colleague Detective Shepherd is down in Belfast right now, at a place called Mid-Maine Supply. Why? Because Mid-Maine Supply sells oxygen – and two oxygen tanks were signed for last spring by a Mr Dale Newman, whose plane ticket ended up in your mailbox, and whose body we fished out of the river yesterday. You ever been in jail yourself, constable?'

Bouchard leaned back against the sink with his arms folded and his dog pressed against his leg.

'Because now we have a third oxygen tank and, frankly, I get the feeling you know why.'

Bouchard blinked.

Murdoch turned his body and peered down the hall again, at the closed door. 'You don't mind if I have a look around your home,' he said.

'I don't believe that'd be proper,' Bouchard answered. 'Not without a search warrant.'

Murdoch bent his knees, getting a lower angle on Bouchard. 'I like to see a man's eyes when I question him. Are you serious about the search warrant?'

'You got a question,' Bouchard told him, 'I suggest you ask it.'

Murdoch snickered. 'Oh, I've got a lot of questions, Mr Magoo. Number one, I've been trying to locate that olive-complected gentleman you absconded with yesterday – the one I was about to arrest – and now nobody seems to know his whereabouts. He didn't sleep in his room last night. His car and motorcycle are both parked in his yard, but his wife and daughter swear they haven't seen him since yesterday.' Murdoch walked to the table and sniffed the air. 'You probably know that the young widow he's taken up with is heading down to Tampa tomorrow for a little cruise.'

Bouchard studied Murdoch to see if he was bluffing.

The sergeant shrugged, as well as he could manage. 'What's the matter, you think he might be going with her? You can see how that would set you up for a little aiding and abetting charge, can't you?'

Bouchard scratched under the dog's ear.

'Your choice, Sparky, you can talk to me here, or we can take a drive.'

Bouchard stood for a second or two, then he stepped to the door and pushed it open. He felt a draft push past his neck, outward.

Murdoch said, 'You trying to tell me something, or just letting more insects in?'

Bouchard replied, 'We're going for a drive, Sergeant Murdoch, as far as I can tell. I don't have any answers for you.'

Murdoch chuckled.

The door remained open.

'Oh, you fuckin country boys,' the sergeant said, stopping beside Bouchard. 'You live in one of these submarines and you think you own a piece of the pie.' He stepped onto the porch, jiggled the railing pointedly. As he sauntered down the steps and to his car, he stopped to look in each of the trailer's windows he passed. Then, stooping to direct his rear end onto his car seat, he looked at Bouchard and said, 'I'll be taking a personal interest in your career, Constable.'

The minute Murdoch's car pulled onto the road, Bouchard went back inside. Locking the kitchen door, he walked down the hall, grabbed the doorknob and pushed. A breeze blew through the open window.

Detective Shepherd sat at a small reception table in the lobby of Mid-Maine Supply and opened another notebook. He had been there for two hours, poring over eighteen months' of medical receipts, occasionally entering a name into his computer, checking for – what? Names that were signed only once in a particular office? Signatures that seemed forced?

'Any luck?' the counterman asked, as he had done every few minutes.

'We're narrowing it down,' Shepherd replied again, as he had replied every time. He was relieved when the telephone rang and the man had to go back behind the counter to answer it.

'He's here, but he's not looking for oxygen,' Shepherd heard the counterman say.

'Is that for me?'

'Nitrous oxide,' the man answered. 'Laughing gas.'

Shepherd pushed away from the table and held his hand out for the telephone, trying to stop the man from saying more.

'Not yet, but he still hasn't gone through the ice-cream accounts.'

'What ice-cream accounts?' Shepherd said. Apparently the caller had asked the same question, because the counterman began answering them both.

'Whipped cream,' he said. 'They use nitrous as a propellant in whipped cream dispensers – it doesn't leave a taste.'

'Let me have the phone,' Shepherd said.

'Hold on, he wants to talk to you himself.' The small man handed over the telephone, saying, 'It's Sergeant Murdoch.'

Shepherd lifted the phone to his ear. 'Yeah, Sarge, I was just gonna call.' Shepherd listened for some nasty witticism; instead, he got the dial tone.

He handed the phone back to the counterman, who said to him,

'I'll tell you right now, ice cream's gonna be harder to track down, being as how the drivers can pick it up right here.'

Shepherd scowled at him. 'Are you telling me a dentist can't transport nitrous oxide, but an ice-cream driver can?'

'Don't ask me,' the counterman said. 'Freakin' Congress.'

At the public telephone inside the school lobby, the phone book lay opened to the Yellow Pages – ICE CREAM MANUFACTURERS. Charlie Walker, the custodian, closed the book and slid it on the shelf. 'Don't worry, I'll put it back,' he muttered, glaring out the glass doors at the Harley rumbling out of the parking lot. 'Friggin wino.'

Sal headed for Ellsworth on the Cooper Road, a winding logging road that crossed the Maine Central Railroad tracks four miles out of Gravity. When he reached the crossing, Sal pulled the Harley onto the tracks and headed west, toward town. Knowing that Murdoch was searching for him, he thought it best to avoid being seen until he could figure out what was going on. He kept the bike between the rails, taking it slow at first, bouncing over the ties and sliding where the gravel was deep. But as he considered the implications of nitrous oxide, he gradually increased his speed, all the while keeping an eye on his rearview, afraid that he wouldn't hear over his own engine if a train were to come up behind him. However, his fear of being rear-ended by a lumber-loaded freighter only approximated the fear he felt knowing that Noel was getting on an airplane in the morning.

Behind the meat counter in the empty store, the door opened, and Noel backed through, carrying two bundled trash bags. She was wearing a faded green SAVE A TREE – KILL A LOGGER T-shirt; a green kerchief, banded around her head, was darkened with her perspiration. When she turned, she saw Detective Shepherd standing by the counter. She ignored him.

Shepherd raised his hands in mock surrender. 'No questions, I promise,' he said.

She set the bags on the floor, then stood and wiped her face with her forearm, giving him a droll glance.

He added, a bit contritely, 'I feel a person should apologize when he's wrong.'

She walked around behind the counter and washed her hands in the sink. 'I find it hard to believe that you're here to apologize.'

He sat down on a counter stool. 'No, you're right. Actually, I've always had a weakness for a good hot fudge sundae. Homemade ice cream, the sign says. Do you make your own?'

'We buy it locally.'

'Oh, where?'

She turned and gave him a look.

'I can't help it, it's in my blood.'

Her expression turned slightly cynical. 'What flavor?' She lifted the scoop out of its cradle.

'Vanilla, chocolate, coffee, whatever's handy,' he replied, 'as long as you load it up with whipped cream.'

She bent low into the freezer. When she straightened, two mounds of pistachio ice cream sat side by side in the bowl.

'Busy packing for your cruise, or just spring cleaning?' he asked. 'The way your dumpster's heaped over, someone might think you were moving out.'

Lifting a lid off a tub, Noel ladled on the hot fudge sauce slowly. 'I buy my ice cream from Windswept Farms. It's on the island. Nuts?'

'No, thanks. Just the whipped cream.'

Noel opened the refrigerator and took out a stainless steel canister, about eight inches high. There was no label on it, no printing. She shook the can, tipped it upside down, slid her thumb down the nozzle, and pushed. A thick cloud mounded up over the ice cream.

'Keep it coming,' he said.

'I thought you'd get a thrill.'

He chuckled. 'It really is amazing how so much whipped cream can come out of such a small can. How do they do that?'

She set his sundae in front of him. 'You'll have to ask Stan the ice-cream man.'

'Stan the ice-cream man.' Shepherd stirred the whipped cream into the ice cream. 'Stan a friend of yours?'

'Oh, absolutely. Stan tells me about the weather and I agree with him. Of course we don't enjoy the sort of rapport that you and I have. But if you take him to dinner sometime and astound him with your investigative prowess, I'm sure he'll tell you how whipped cream comes out of a can.'

Shepherd allowed a penitent smile. 'Noel, if I had known about the divorce, things would have gone differently.' He took a bite of ice cream, tasted it, swallowed. 'While we're on the subject, do you know if Bobby ever told anyone you were leaving him?'

She watched him.

'See, people are different. Man and woman split up – that's tough, emotionally. A lot of guys'd have a friend or somebody close they could confide in.' He stirred the sundae some more. 'The thing is, I haven't been able to find anyone who knew about you and Bobby. Except your lawyer.'

She seemed to smile at Shepherd. 'Who did you confide in, Detective?'

His spoon stopped.

'You hear things in a place like this,' she continued. 'From what I've heard, she got her doctorate degree and left you with the condo. She sounds like a very intelligent, independent woman.'

He acquiesced with a nod. 'That's a fair assessment.'

Noel turned her back to him, casually toweled off the butcher block. 'I only mention it because Mr Jones, my attorney, thinks it may explain your aggression toward me.'

'That's what he thinks, huh?' Shepherd put down his spoon and wiped his mouth with a napkin. 'Listen, before I go, you don't have the phone number of Windswept Farms, do you?'

'Right here,' she answered, nodding to a clipboard that hung beside the wall phone.

'May I?' he said.

'Please.' She folded her arms, sat back against the ice-cream freezer to watch.

He brought his sundae behind the counter and dialed. The man who answered the phone identified himself as Fuzzy O'Coin. As soon as Shepherd introduced himself, the man sighed impatiently. 'We buy our nitrous oxide from Ellsworth Oxy-Acetylene, I just got finished telling your Sergeant Murdoch, thank you very much—'

Shepherd looked over at Noel: 'Has Murdoch been in here?' he asked. She shook her head. 'Has he called?' Again no.

'—I'm sorry, but are you people charging Stanley with a crime?'

'Mr O'Coin, I just want to know if Stanley is the one who signs for shipments of nitrous oxide.' Shepherd kept his eye on Noel.

'What shipments? Stanley picks it up when he's out on deliveries, when we need it, which isn't often.'

'How does he do that?'

'How does he do what? He picks up the full tanks and turns in the empties and signs a book. It's not complicated, Detective.'

'Just like that.'

'Of course, we had to get a license from the FDA, swearing that we were a manufacturer of ice cream and would never use the nitrous for enjoyment. Heaven forbid people should actually *enjoy* themselves.'

While Fuzzy fumed, Shepherd traded another glance with Noel. She seemed to take pleasure in his side of the conversation.

'Mr O'Coin, has Stanley lost that license in the past year? Physically, I mean, has he reported it missing, so that you've had to apply for another one?'

There was a brief pause, and then Fuzzy said, 'You *have* heard of the pursuit of happiness, Detective. It's one of our fundamental rights, you know.'

Shepherd smiled. 'I'll take that as a yes. When did he lose it, do you remember?'

'A year ago, I suppose. My God, crime of the century. Somewhere someone is laughing illegally.'

'Mr O'Coin?'

'*What?*'

'Have a nice day.'

Sal found the oxy-acetylene company in Ellsworth, on a back road that wound through an industrial complex of low, flat-roofed structures that looked like they had been built in a week. Framed by withering potted birches, the orange entrance door led into a small lobby that contained two orange plastic chairs and a collection of *Small Business* magazines fanned neatly on a table. Behind a high orange counter, a young receptionist with piles of blonde hair stopped typing and said, 'Can I help you?'

Sal picked the business card out of his T-shirt pocket and slid it across the counter. 'Sergeant Murdoch,' he said, keeping his eye on her. 'State Police.'

Behind her, a door swung open and a man in a blue suit came through, about forty-five, with round wire-frame glasses, thinning brown hair and a scruffy, reddish beard. 'Now what?' he complained. 'The other guy was in when? Saturday afternoon—?' Redbeard looked at the receptionist, who confirmed eagerly. 'Saturday afternoon.'

'What guy?' Sal asked.

'I don't know. Vice squad, by the looks of him. Scruffy, like you. Black beard, Coke-bottle glasses.'

Bouchard.

Sal's insides clenched. 'What was he looking for?'

'Ask him. He looked through the nitrous book for about ten minutes and then he took off.'

'Yeah, what book is that?'

The man answered by tossing an opened three-ring notebook on the counter in front of Sal. The pages that stared up at him were ledger green.

'Would you like to sit down?' said the woman with the hair, but Sal was already out the door.

Driving to Ellsworth, Shepherd set the blue flasher on his roof. He wanted to reach the company before it closed – and before Murdoch beat him there. He could feel things coming together rapidly. Like maybe last spring Stan the ice-cream man had stepped away from his truck and someone had grabbed his nitrous license. Shepherd figured that Murdoch had already reached the same conclusion. As he crossed the town line into Ellsworth, the sergeant came over the radio.

'Pick up,' Murdoch squawked. 'You pick up.'

Shepherd left the mike in its cradle.

'Listen to me. We just got another call from the lady's lawyer.

They're filing harassment charges. Are you listening? Because you're not only off this case, wise guy, but the next case you're gonna get is a good case of assburn from riding the dispatch desk. You hear that, Mister Dick? Your shift is over.'

Shepherd snatched the microphone, pushed the trigger. 'I'll file with the union, Sarge, I'm telling you now.'

'*Fuck your union!* What are you trying to pull?'

'I'm in Ellsworth,' Shepherd said. 'I'll be there in a minute.'

'Be where?'

'The acetylene place!'

'What acetylene place?'

Shepherd looked at his radio.

'*What acetylene place?*' Murdoch barked.

Shepherd switched him off.

He reached the building in slightly more than a minute, at twenty to five. When he showed his badge over the counter, Redbeard flipped his ballpoint pen into the air. 'Jesus Christ, can't you guys get together?'

'Excuse me?'

'I'm just saying – One comes in Saturday, two today? No wonder we can't pay our goddamn taxes.' He slid the notebook in front of Shepherd. 'Knock yourself out, we close in fifteen minutes.' He opened a side door and disappeared into the warehouse.

Shepherd looked at the receptionist. She smiled.

'He mentioned somebody else—?'

She described Alston Bouchard first, which did not surprise Shepherd.

'Who was in today?' he said, as he opened the book.

'Undercover,' the receptionist said. 'He just left a few minutes ago. On a Harley.'

Shepherd looked up from the book. 'What did he want?'

'To see the book.'

'These detectives,' Shepherd said, 'did they show you their shields?'

She scowled apologetically. 'When somebody says they're a detective, I guess you don't ask.'

He nodded. 'How about when somebody wants to pick up a tank of nitrous oxide, do you check their licenses?'

She hunched her shoulders. 'Always. Until I get to know them.'

He began turning pages again. 'You make them sign the book?'

She nodded. 'Always.'

He fanned the pages back to May of the previous year, when the oxygen tanks had been bought. From there he started flipping forward. 'How about the driver from Windswept Farms?'

'That'd be Stan. He's wicked nice.'

'Do you remember anybody else from that company ever coming in? Maybe last summer—?'

She hunched her shoulders again. 'I only just started in January.'

Shepherd stopped on June 25. Turned back a page, to June 23. The missing page had been ripped at the perforation; specks of paper still clung to the tear.

Shepherd closed the book and walked around the counter, a heady sensation coming over him. It was a feeling he loved, the rush of facts converging. With a quick thank-you to the receptionist, he threw open the door and walked quietly to his Cherokee, where he sat inside and turned on his computer. *Search,* he instructed the machine: *Bouchard.*

Sal muscled the Harley up the rocky farm road, the low sun on his back. After finding Bouchard's house trailer empty and the Subaru parked in front, he decided to try the hill. Muscling the Harley up the rock-packed earth that bisected the blueberry hill, halfway up he saw a blue farm truck pulled off to the right, near a birch windbreak. As he drew nearer, he made out Bouchard on the other side of the truck, wearing gray overalls, a corduroy shirt buttoned to the neck and high rubber boots.

Sal pulled up to the farm truck and shut off the engine. Bouchard kept his back to Sal as he worked over a stack of four white boxes sitting on a wooden pallet. Dark shadows breathed around the boxes like a moving storm cloud. Sal could hear the low, sonorous humming of bees.

'Don't worry,' Bouchard said, 'they wouldn't be worried about you.'

Sal could see a bunch of the honeybees crawling on Bouchard's arm.

'I'd pull that motorcycle behind the truck,' Bouchard said as he lifted the lid off one of the hives and shook the bees off his hand. 'Lay it down in the grass.'

'You took that receipt from the acetylene place,' Sal told him. 'I want to know why.'

Bouchard replaced the lid carefully, then took off his gloves, tossed them in the open window of the farm truck and started walking up the hill. He shook more bees off his arm.

Sal stayed where he was, watching. He noticed Bouchard's dog for the first time, sitting nervously in the road about fifty feet ahead. He hadn't seen the black dog at first, blending as it did with the burned-over land to the left. But now the dog rose, wagging its tail, anticipating his master.

'I want an answer,' Sal said.

Bouchard kept walking.

The computer!

The revelation hit Shepherd a minute too late, as the employees were filing out of the building. Spotting the young receptionist, the detective opened his car door. 'Excuse me,' he said.

She glanced over, smiled.

'The information in the receipt book – you enter it in your computer—?'

She thought about the question and nodded. 'Uh-huh.'

'Including the person who signed for it?'

'I knew it!' a voice said – Redbeard, coming out the door. 'No way. My kid's got a ball game. Come back in the morning.' He locked the door behind him.

'It'll only take a minute,' Shepherd said. 'I need one name off your computer. One minute.'

'I don't mind staying with him,' the receptionist volunteered. 'I can lock up.'

Before Redbeard could respond, their attention turned to the parking lot entrance, where a black, unmarked Mercury had turned in from the street, its blue dash light flashing.

'Here we go,' Redbeard said, and he tossed his keys to the receptionist. 'Just remember,' he said to Shepherd, 'we cooperated.'

Murdoch pulled the sedan to the front of the building and pushed himself out the door like something robotic. Falling in step behind Shepherd and the receptionist, he said, 'I'll take over from here. Whadda we got?'

Shepherd led the way into the lobby and around the counter without responding, walked directly to the receptionist's desk, where he turned on her computer. He leaned over the monitor, reading the on-screen menu. 'June twenty-fourth, last year,' he said to the receptionist as she came around beside him.

'The third oxygen tank,' Murdoch said to him. 'You got a name?'

Shepherd looked up at him curiously.

'Let me take a wild guess,' Murdoch continued. There was a light, superior quality in the sergeant's voice that Shepherd could not resist shooting down.

He reached behind the computer monitor and shut it off. 'It's not oxygen we're looking for,' he said.

Murdoch chuckled. 'Whatever,' he replied. 'Your buddy at the crime lab called a while ago. They got a print match on that other champagne glass from the undertaker's house.'

'Yeah?' Shepherd said, studying the sergeant, who was happily hoarding the information.

Murdoch folded his arms. 'You want to work for me on this case?'

Shepherd glared at him.

Murdoch, no less smug: 'I need to know that we're compatible. Which means no union horseshit, pardon my French,' he added, for the receptionist's sake.

Shepherd continued glaring, fighting the impulse to haul off on Murdoch's pink, jeering face. Instead, he flicked on the monitor again.

The receptionist punched a couple of keys. 'Six-twenty-four,' she said. 'Want the name?'

'I already know the name,' Murdoch answered, turning his body and heading for the door. 'You want to be in on the apprehension,' he said to Shepherd, 'I suggest you follow me.'

From the top of Blueberry Hill, the ocean spread flat and silvery against the eastern sky, its dark strands of islands floating like clouds; while off to the west a lone white steeple rose out of the greenery. Just beyond the top of the hill, where the field road ended, the entire ground was black all the way to a low stone wall that rimmed the field and kept back the woods that led down the northern slope.

When the two men reached the stone wall, Bouchard stepped over and pushed his hand into a pocket of his overalls. Sal tensed on the near side of the wall, wondering if he was about to see a gun. But it was the green receipt that Bouchard pulled out. 'See, they let him go easy,' the constable said.

Sal stepped over the wall, took the paper from Bouchard and unfolded it. The page was divided in fourths – four separate receipts, four signatures. One jumped off the page: *Salvatore W. Erickson.*

'Is that your handwriting?'

Sal stared. His chest expanded.

'A year ago you presented your ice-cream manufacturer's license to a clerk at Ellsworth Oxy-Acetylene and signed out a small tank of nitrous oxide. That's what this means.'

The paper shivered in Sal's hand. 'What license?' he said.

'You were drinking heavy back then, most likely. Last June?'

Salvatore W. Erickson. Sal stared at the signature, but it made no sense.

'I think she had you drive into town and pick up the tank for her. Had you show the license and sign for it. You were drunk.'

Sal shook his head. The rest of his body was shaking on its own. He eyed the wooded hillside, ready to bolt.

'She knew you wouldn't remember.'

On the other side of the wall, the black lab looked up, grinning nervously. Suddenly the dog's ears perked; he turned to face the gravel road, which fell out of sight about fifty feet away. Bouchard looked that way too, then said to Sal with sudden, uncommon urgency, 'Go into the woods.'

'What?'

'Go now.' Bouchard tapped the receipt page. 'There'll be more.'

Sal stared at him.

'She had a contingency plan, in case something went wrong. The way I see it, you.'

The dog took three steps onto the road and stopped. An explosive bark froze Sal, and then the dog barreled up the road in a cloud. Engines sounded, climbing up the other side.

'They're coming for me,' Bouchard said. 'They won't know you're here. Now go into the woods. There's a path to my sister's house. Tell her I sent you.'

'Wait a minute,' Sal said.

Bouchard pulled him toward an old, spreading oak that was part of the wall. *'You've got to get hid!'* Transmissions whined like insects. 'She's smarter than you. And she's been planning this too long.'

Sal held back, resisting.

'Either that or you did it. You and Bobby and Wicker together. Then you double-crossed them both and set her up. That's the way she's made it look.'

Sal stared at him.

'Where were you the night of Bobby's funeral?'

'I don't know!'

Bouchard grabbed him, swung him around the back of the oak tree, and spoke directly into his face. *'It doesn't matter.* The only way you're not guilty is if you were there digging him up. Anyplace else, you murdered him.'

Sal stood frozen, incapable of absorbing what he was being told. The engines grew louder.

'You stay away from her,' Bouchard warned in a low voice. 'She'll kill you. It'll be self-defense, and she'll go free.' He took the receipt page from Sal, stuffed it in Sal's shirt pocket. Then he pressed a set of keys into Sal's hand.

'Remember, she's not perfect.'

'What?'

Unzipping his fly, Bouchard climbed over the stone wall. Sal heard him pissing on the front of the tree. Suddenly the engines got louder, tires grabbing gravel and rock. Sal's heart pumped another shot of adrenaline. Then car doors opened and closed. Sal stared at the keys in his hand. The first voice he heard made him cringe.

'Destroying more evidence, Mister Magoo?'

Behind the tree, Sal clenched every muscle in his body, trying not to breathe.

'I was relieving myself,' Bouchard answered, walking away from the tree.

A different voice, coming closer: 'You have someone who can take care of your dog, Mr Bouchard?'

'My sister lives over on the next hill.'

'Save yourself the trouble,' Murdoch said. 'Tell us where to find Sacco and Vanzetti.'

'Salvatore Erickson,' Shepherd said. 'You know who we're talking about.'

Sal's stomach floated up.

'And turn over the evidence you took. Hindering the apprehension: that's time, you know.'

'I don't believe I have any evidence.'

'Mr Bouchard, you're protecting a felony suspect.'

'You're looking for the wrong person,' Bouchard said. 'Sal Erickson was set up.'

'We've got a dozen witnesses who place your buddy out on a drunken rampage the night Eliot Wicker was murdered. Half a dozen who put him with Bobby Swift the night before Mr Swift *passed on*.'

'The facts are there,' Shepherd said. 'Bobby Swift wanted to disappear. He needed the undertaker to bury him. And he needed someone he could trust to dig him up – his best friend.'

'And then the best friend does 'em both.' Murdoch hawked a laugh.

'Noel Swift planted the evidence against him,' Bouchard said. 'And she's leaving in the morning.'

'We're well aware of her travel plans, Mr Bouchard. As far as the Constitution is concerned, she has a right to take her vacation.'

'She won't be back,' Bouchard told them, 'and you'll have an innocent man in custody.'

'I'm sorry, Constable, the facts don't support your theory. We have videotape of Erickson's cap at Eliot Wicker's house, his prints on a champagne glass and bottle over there. He and Wicker were going to split Bobby Swift's Cayman money – at least that's what Mr Wicker thought.'

Bouchard's voice again: 'I know these people, Detective. Sal Erickson is a good man. He was Bobby Swift's friend.'

Murdoch smirked. 'I've never yet seen a man double-crossed by his enemy.'

Goose bumps tingled over Sal's arms. He pressed against the back of the tree.

'Why do you suppose he'd leave his fingerprints at the victim's house?' Bouchard said. 'Or sign his own name on the receipt?'

Murdoch answered, thick with satisfaction: 'Guy kills his best friend and then diddles the widow. I don't know, maybe he's feeling a little guilty and he wants to be punished. I'll tell you what. Detective Shepherd is our resident psychologist. Why don't you take a ride with him, and you can discuss your theories while he reads you your rights. Or save yourself the trouble and give up the greaseball.'

Bouchard remained silent.

'That's actually good,' Murdoch said. 'I was hoping you wouldn't cooperate. Detective, take Ray Charles for a ride and introduce him to the inside of the county jail. I'm going down to say hello to some of the townspeople.'

As Sal heard the footsteps scratching away on the hardpack, he heard Murdoch say, 'Put the nips on him, detective. This ain't a joyride.' The footsteps stopped, replaced by the metallic jangle of handcuffs – and Shepherd's attempts to lighten the circumstance.

'One thing I can say for you, Mr Bouchard, I respect your loyalty.'

'I'm trying to do my job,' Bouchard answered. 'Seems all you want is a closed case.'

'Not at all. We're entirely directed by the evidence.'

'You know he's not guilty.'

'I think we can prove he did it.'

'You know he didn't do it.'

'We can prove he's guilty, then!' Shepherd snapped. 'Either way.'

The footsteps started up again, and then a car door slammed

shut. Another car door closed, and then another. The engines started up again, revved, and then the vehicles drove over the rocks and gravel and were gone. Sal remained motionless behind the tree, his body quivering, his mind racing with confusion, while overhead a flock of swallows darted about, chittering madly.

13

Sal waited until dusk settled before coming off the hill. Knowing that Murdoch and other police would be patrolling the town for him, he took Bouchard's prescription sunglasses off the constable's dashboard, popped out the lenses with his thumb and fit the frames on his face. He pulled one of Bouchard's caps over his brow and drove the Subaru toward the coast. He had no idea where he was going. The fuel gauge registered a quarter tank. He had less than eighty dollars in his pockets; and even though his Visa and ATM cards were in his wallet, he had no doubt the police would have traces on them by now. He wasn't going far.

All he really wanted was to be in his own warm living room again, sitting on the couch with Iris on one side and Davey on the other. He knew the police would have already been there. He wondered what they had told Iris, wondered what she believed, and what she chose to tell Davey.

He felt the paper in his shirt pocket, took it out and turned on the interior light. *Salvatore W. Erickson.* QUANTITY ONE, NITROUS OXIDE, RECEIVED BY ... Not a forgery, but his actual signature. According to the date, he had signed for the tank almost a year ago, beginning of summer, right after school got out. He was drinking heavily then, he and Bobby both, going to ball games and bars. He could remember only isolated patches of those months, nothing of a plan with Bobby and Wicker.

He did remember the day Bobby died: jogging to the store; the way Wicker went speeding past ... and at the funeral, thinking it strange that Bobby was wearing a wristwatch ... The signs were there, now that he had an idea what they meant. And then the reception at Noel's – when the wall went up, when he'd started drinking again. He remembered the way Noel had come up behind him with the drink in her hand...

wearing her gloves ...

The champagne glass—

He pulled off the road about a mile outside of town, in the Oyster Cove Post Office.

She'd planted the glass at Wicker's. Same time she'd planted his cap. Sal felt a terrible sinking in his chest. Simultaneously, an irrepressible need arose in him to see her, to confront her. But he couldn't go over there, not if Bouchard was right—

and Bouchard was right. Sal could deny it no longer.

He wheeled the Subaru around the parking lot and turned back toward Gravity. He avoided the main road, cut back into town on a dirt road that wound through miles of disused blueberry flats and woods. The road would eventually join the River Road, a hundred feet from Sal's house.

You stay away from her.

Going home. He would see Iris and Davey. Profess his innocence to Iris, kiss Davey goodnight, and then ... play it by ear. Maybe borrow some money from Iris and try to make New Brunswick. Or maybe he'd call the police and give himself up, trust his fate to the courts.

There'll be more evidence against you. She's been planning this too long.

He imagined going over there – if he could get past the police. There were two ways in: through the store or through the garage. He'd wait until just before dawn, when he was sure she was asleep. He'd get inside the garage, then sneak up the stairs, catch her in her bedroom. Force her to confess.

She'll kill you. It'll be self-defense, and she'll go free.

Headlights flashed in his rearview, and his heart jumped. He hit the gas, and the Subaru rattled over the washboard road, its back end sliding out. Behind him, the headlights kept pace. When the blueberry flats ended, the road climbed into the woods and turned to the left. He took the curve and lost the headlights momentarily, but as soon as the road straightened again, the woods in his rearview lit bright green. He went faster, even though he knew he couldn't outrun whoever was following him, with the road so rutted and full of curves. As he watched the mirror, the headlights shot over a rise, nailing him.

The woods in front came up too fast to negotiate. Sal stomped the brakes, and the car swerved to a stop, its right wheels halfway up the bank, its grill two feet from a thick birch. Suddenly the Subaru's interior brightened. Bright lights off his mirror blinded him. He leaned across the passenger seat, took hold of the door handle, ready to bolt.

The approaching vehicle slowed, pulled alongside. With his hand on the door handle, Sal pretended to be searching through his glove compartment. He waved them on, as he imagined Bouchard might, subtly, his arm blocking his face. He heard a sharp roar, and the vehicle shot around him, coming to the road's end just ahead – a Jeep, full of kids. They screeched their tires as they swung out onto the River Road. Sal watched the taillights flicker through the trees and then disappear.

He turned the key, and the Subaru started again. He backed off the banking, then pulled slowly to the stop sign. Looked right and left and saw no other vehicles on the road. He thought of leaving the Subaru where it was and making his way to his house through the woods – sneak in the back door. But Bouchard's car would be spotted in minutes – it would be obvious where Sal had gone. No, he had to ditch the car someplace where he could buy more time. He pulled onto the road and drove past his house slowly – Iris's car and his own, parked side by side; lights on in the living room; he could make out the stairs and the hanging plant through the big front window, as if nothing in the world were wrong. But there was no sign of Iris or Davey, no sign of life. He wondered if they were in on the plan to capture him.

Up ahead, headlights turned toward him from the village. As the vehicle passed slowly under the streetlight, Sal saw the light rack on the roof, saw two heads in the cruiser. State troopers – Sal hoped they wouldn't recognize Bouchard's car. He adjusted his cap, put both hands on the wheel, steadied his foot on the accelerator. As the cruiser approached, he brought his fist to his mouth, pretending to cough, and then he watched his sideview to make sure the car's brake lights didn't flash.

At the Village Road he turned left, drove over the bridge, stayed in second gear up the short hill, and then he was passing the store. He saw two cars in the lot and a pickup truck at the pumps. He didn't want to look in the windows, didn't want the temptation, but he shot a glance just the same. A man at the cash register, but that's all he saw. A hundred feet past the store he checked the mirror to make sure he wasn't being followed, then he doused his headlights and pulled a hard left into the firehouse lot.

Several other vehicles were parked there. The garage doors were opened on the town's two pumpers – the monthly meeting of the volunteers. Sal tucked the Subaru beside a panel truck, slipped out the door and disappeared behind the wooden building.

Keeping to the tree line, he made his way back toward the bridge, running across Herb and Bonnie True's backyard, then veering a ways into the woods to avoid the lights that reached across the road from the Superette. Stopping behind an old pine, he couldn't resist looking for her again; but all he saw were a couple of people through the front windows and one outside pumping gas, none of them Noel. He started moving again to the next tree – and that's when he spotted her. Upstairs, in her living room window. He stepped out from behind the tree and watched as she stood behind the glass – almost like she knew he was out there. Like she was waiting for him. And then her arm went up, and the blinds came down.

All at once headlights shot over his head, and a car engine roared. Sal dropped to the ground. The black sedan tore up Noel's driveway, then cut across the parking lot. With equal urgency, another car suddenly shot up from the River Road, headlights flashing. Sal raised himself on his forearms. It was Shepherd's Cherokee. Both vehicles converged on the firehouse at once, blue lights flashing. At the same time, the store opened up and three men ran diagonally across the road toward the police lights; they didn't appear to be cops themselves. Now the sound of a police radio cut through the air, and Sal knew it wouldn't be long before they'd be coming his way.

He needed to get across the bridge in order to reach the path to the river – which meant he needed to get out to the road – either that or swim, and the river was much too cold, especially when he might be outside for hours in the cold night air.

Staying behind the trees, he made his way to the high riverbank, where he stopped for only a second. Down below, the water was fairly loud – a good sign, if he could judge by the volume – it meant the river was running fast – low tide – and the pool would be traversable. But along with the river sounds, he heard a change in the men's voices at the firehouse. They were starting to move.

He checked to make sure no more cars were coming, and then he ran along the riverbank straight to the bridge, where he ducked behind the low concrete abutment. He looked up the road, where, against the lights of the firehouse, he could see heads moving down, flashlights painting the asphalt. Staying close to the ground, he crawled around the abutment and was about to run across the bridge when headlights swung in off the River Road. Sal pulled behind the concrete again and dropped to his knees.

To his left, he heard the voices getting closer. To his right, the car was approaching dangerously slowly. He lay flat on the gravel, perpendicular to the road. Keep breathing, he told himself, keep moving. He thought of Iris and Davey, steeled his nerves. He shifted to his right until he hit the edge of the bank – a steep fall here, fifteen feet to concrete and rocks. He looked down, thinking if he jumped out far enough, he might make the water, but it was only two or three feet deep. He looked across the span and saw the bright light moving along the opposite bank, dancing across the greenery, then flooding out over the river. Now he heard the tires humming over the steel grating, the engine moving closer to his ear. To his left, the men walking down from the firehouse were almost on top of him. He pressed his cheek to the sand, held his breath. He saw the spotlight touch his left boot. It lingered for a moment and then moved away into the grass as the car passed, its headlights glaring on the men walking down. A rush of urgency overcame Sal. He jumped up into the red glow of taillights while the search party was blinded by headlights, and ran low along the bridge to the other side, where he swung around the abutment and was hidden again. With no thought of safety, he dropped into the darkness, sliding down the steep path on his hands and the soles of his boots. He landed painfully, his right foot twisting against the base of a sapling, and he hobbled to keep from falling.

Despite the pain and the darkness, he immediately resumed his escape, keeping the river noise at his right, climbing over concrete and rocks with diminishing regard for his safety. Behind him, the men mounted the bridge and walked noisily across, shining flashlights down. Sal ducked behind a block, watched the light beams crisscross around him. Then they moved on. He got up and continued making his way downriver.

As his eyes became accustomed to the moonless night, the river began to show itself more clearly on his right, a dim sparkling under the deepening yet still luminous sky. Ahead in the darkness of land, peepers chorused in rapt oblivion. Sal kept to the path as the bank inclined, increasing his pace. But, approaching the pool, a sense of foreboding came over him, far heavier than the danger he was in. He stopped walking. He thought it might be a sixth sense at first, a warning. Then he feared it was something far more ominous.

He stood frozen at the edge of the pool – a tidal bog now, keening with peepers. The entire cove was still, the shallow water taking on the misted sheen of buffed aluminum, broken only by the black shapes of exposed rocks and tussocks – his stepping stones. Sal had crossed the bog dozens of times, knew the way by heart: nine or ten steps to the other side, his fishing rock—

He heard a scratch. He spun around. Heads ducked behind trees, shadows tossed about. *Sins come back*. He closed his eyes, focused his hearing, trying to distinguish any sound other than the flowing water and beckoning tree frogs. And now he could hear whispers … the rustle of leaves … sounds, he told himself, that, like the visions, were merely the by-products of his poisoned imagination. He took a deep breath, let it out.

He opened his eyes again, focused on the bog. Peepers screeched on, unwary of his presence. He looked out and visualized his way across: three staggered rocks and then a wide tussock; then three quick steps – rock, tussock, rock – a short hop to a double tussock; and then the final leap to his fishing rock—

Bobby's hand, reaching up.

Sal refused the image. Iris and Davey, he thought, Iris and Davey – he pictured their faces as he lowered himself down the bank and made the first two rocks in two steps. Arms spread for balance, he did not allow himself to think of anything but the next rock – a flat two-footer about three feet away. He took a deep breath, let it out. *Iris and Davey*. He threw himself at it, landed with his left foot, then brought his right to join it. His sense of balance helped center him. The next step was a couple of feet to his right, a high, wide tussock. Despite his shaking legs, Sal stepped onto it gingerly. The tussock wobbled, but he worked his arms and stayed with it. Balance. In the past, he would offer his sense of balance to Iris as proof that he was not an alcoholic. I never left my feet, he'd tell her, and it was always true – he could sleep standing. Now he shut off his mind again, became automatic. The next three stepping stones were clustered together, right, left, right. And that's how he stepped – right, left, right – until he was standing on a smooth, humpbacked rock, with only two steps to go.

Mentally he prepared to make the jump – first the twin tussocks that stood out of the mist four feet away – then a quick leap to his fishing rock. The fear bubbled to the surface unexpectedly.

Silence.

He realized that the peepers had stopped.

It was as if the bog itself were holding its breath, while the river on the other side of the sandbar continued its malignant whispering. Sal refused to listen. He looked out to his fishing rock, and then beyond, up the rocky bank to the pines. Shadows were everywhere now, shadows crouching behind shadows, shadows walking the tree line ... Sal lowered his eyes, focused only on the distance to the tussocks and not beyond. He knew what was there: his fishing rock, and nothing more.

He would make the leap and then leap again and not stop for anything, not look back. He'd run up the path through the woods and into the field, where he would see his house. He would run across the road and let himself in the back door. He would see Iris and Davey—

He let go, threw himself at the tussocks and landed on his left foot, with which he intended to push himself off again. Instead, the tussocks gave way. Arms outstretched, Sal started to fall, reaching for the rock—

but there were arms below him—

reaching out of the mist—

He slammed down into three inches of water, shattering his own image, then scrambled out of the muck and was racing across the rock, over an upward ledge, breaking through thick dead pine boughs into the field, where he could see his lights across the road, his house—

A beam of light shot toward him—

He threw himself to the ground, flattened himself.

Like a lighthouse beacon, the searchlight brushed the tops of the grass as the patrol car crawled along the road. Panting, Sal stayed down, listened to the car go away. Then he pushed himself to his hands and knees. The *clatch* of a shotgun stopped his heart—

But it was a voice, not a gunshot, that he heard next.

Jerry Royal sauntered out of the pines with the gun under his arm, a cigarette in his mouth.

'Yeah, one day you're the town singin teacher, next thing you know you're a hundred-eighty-pound Caucasian male.' A three-pack of cans hung from Jerry's belt.

'Shh,' Sal said. 'They're looking for me.'

'No shit, they been goin by your house every other minute. I got 'em on the radio. They want you bad, man. What for?'

'They think I killed Bobby.'

Jerry stared at Sal through the darkness.

'Eliot Wicker too.'

'Whoa!' It was a cheer, but the way Sal looked up at him, Jerry turned the sound into a sinus-clearing hawk, which he spat into the grass. 'No, that's bad, really,' he said. There was only one thing that made Jerry happier than seeing someone else in trouble, and that was when someone else was in trouble for something he did. He flipped his cigarette into the air and turned back to the pines. 'Come on, I got a good place,' he said, and he proceeded to lead Sal to a hollow in the trees, where an old flatbed truck was sunk in the ground to its axles, its plank bed overlooking a carpet of flattened cans and half-planted bottles.

'I been up keepin watch,' Jerry explained as he boosted himself onto the truck's bed. 'Break the Guinness record for not sleepin' – three days and nights now. But they think you killed Bobby, no shit.' Jerry acted unnaturally agitated, patting the truck bed beside him, inviting Sal to sit. 'It's a good place, 'cause you're hid up here, but you can still see the road, see all around, in case anyone's got ideas.' He fished a cigarette out of his shirt pocket, snapped fire from his plastic lighter. The flame shivered as he drew. 'Want one? Want one of these?' Holding up a can of cola.

Sal shook his head.

'No, but many's the time I come out here to sort things out,' Jerry continued.

Without a doubt, Jerry had his own sorting out to do. For if Noel had indeed fixed things so that Sal Erickson was about to pay for their crimes, then Jerry was free and clear, just as Noel had promised. Except—

the one thing that could destroy them both—

'This is like a nightmare,' Sal said.

'Hey, tell me about it.'

That fucking letter, again and again. How many times today had Jerry volleyed that thing back and forth, and for how many sleepless nights? Noel was right: It wouldn't take a genius to figure out that the person who wrote the letter was the same person who had killed Wicker. Bottom line: He could leave the letter hidden in the attic where it might remain until he died – of natural causes (as long as he could count on the little girl not to get nosy . . . fat chance). On the other hand, he could destroy the letter and then have sex with Noel – and hope she didn't kill him afterwards. Real fat chance.

'They found my fingerprints in Wicker's house,' Sal said. 'My hat was there.'

Sex. Always sex that confounded things. Even as Sal talked, Jerry couldn't help picturing Noel naked in her bathtub, nipples like twin pink pacifiers. 'So, fingerprints,' Jerry said, cigarette smoke closing his eye. 'Hard to argue with fingerprints.'

'But I didn't know Wicker,' Sal told him. 'I never visited him. I never even talked to him until the day Bobby died.'

Then again he could lie about it. That was always Jerry's first inclination anyway. He could tell Noel that he had destroyed the letter when actually he hadn't. No. That would be double jeopardy. Because not only would the letter still be around for somebody to find, but Noel would think she had nothing to lose by killing him.

'So maybe you'd oughta give yourself up,' Jerry said. 'Sign a confession. They'll prob'ly go easier on you.'

'I'm not confessing to something I didn't do.'

Or he could go ahead and destroy the letter – but not tell Noel about it . . . No, that was even worse. Then he'd not only be out the sex, but if she did kill him, he wouldn't be able to get her back.

'No way I would've done that to Bobby,' Sal said. 'He was my best friend.'

Jerry dragged ponderously – the cigarette glowed. *I feel an animal attraction for you that's overpowering.* Over and over he heard those words: *animal attraction*. Now she was crawling up the aisle of his gospel bus in a leopard-skin corset and a Cat Woman mask . . . Disgusted, Jerry flipped his cigarette into the cans.

'Battle of the sexes,' he said. 'I'll tell you, just once in my life I'd like to find a woman I could trust.'

The words died in the pines, but a reverberation came at Sal with the impact of a slap—

Trust with your life.

Bobby had said the same thing by the river – the night before he had faked his death. It's what Bobby had come to tell him – not that Noel was divorcing him – but that she was about to bury him alive. And he was having second thoughts.

'You alright?' Jerry said. 'Hey—' He poked Sal's arm. 'Christ, don't have a conniption fit on me.'

Sal continued staring at him. Like the perfect break shot, balls began dropping into every hole.

He remembered what Bouchard had told him:

She's not perfect.

'Jerry,' said Sal.

'I'm right here.'

Still staring at him, Sal asked, 'How is it you think that fire started?'

Sal watched as Jerry pulled a cigarette out of his pack, tamped it rapidly on the truck bed. 'What fire we talkin about?'

'I mean, how do you figure your house caught fire that night you were up in Bangor?'

Jerry stuck the cigarette in his mouth, dug his lighter out of his pocket. 'You heard the lady – somethin got in after my chicks.'

'Is that what you think?'

Jerry lit the cigarette, kept the flame going so he could see Sal's face and Sal could see his.

'What I think? I wouldn't get any ideas, that's what I think.'

Sal slid off the truck, took a couple of steps toward the field, stared through the trees at the lights of his house. When he turned around again, Jerry had his shotgun propped under his arm, aimed at Sal's stomach.

Sal stood there, suddenly too sure of himself to feel threatened. 'What are you going to do, Jerry?' he said, in a way that could only be taken as admonishment, a warning.

Jerry's cigarette head brightened. The shotgun didn't move.

'You gonna shoot me?'

Jerry blew the smoke out his nose, and it billowed around his head. 'I guess I'm waitin to see which way this conversation goes.'

'I need your truck,' Sal told him.

'Whoa.'

'Just for an hour.'

Breathing loudly through his nose, Jerry kept his gun trained on Sal. 'That truck, you know – only thing I got anymore with any sentimental value. That and this gun.'

'One hour.'

'Sure, that's what you say now. How do I know you're not gonna—' Jerry stopped, stared off into the darkness, then dragged on his cigarette, transfixed. He set the shotgun noisily onto the bed and stepped down, kicking noisily through the cans. Then he turned back to Sal. 'What the hell,' he said, reaching into his pocket. He came out with a rabbit's foot, a single key hanging from it.

The suddenness of his change might have alerted Sal under different circumstances. But not now, with everything falling.

Dangling the key between them, Jerry said, 'Your car's across the way. You best gimme your own keys in case, you know, an emergency pops up.'

As Sal reached into his pocket, Jerry peeked through the trees at the window lights across the road. 'Be gentle with her,' he said, making the exchange. 'She's barely broke in.'

It was a couple of state troopers, Lemieux and Rolley, out patrolling the roads in search of Sal, who were dispatched to the gospel bus, but Murdoch and Shepherd, having heard the call on their separate radios, got there first.

Jerry had phoned the police from Mrs Abraham's house and reported that his truck had just been stolen with two loaded .38s in the glove compartment, thinking it the perfect brilliant strategy to seal Sal's fate and win favor with Noel. The detectives questioned Jerry for only as long as it took to get the year, make and model, and then they dispersed.

A general broadcast went out across the state, but, with few exceptions, nobody's routine was radically altered. In Bangor, a trooper pulled into a truck stop at the entrance of Route 95 and watched the passing traffic. Guards at the border crossings into Canada were faxed a description of Sal and of Jerry's truck. Troopers patrolling the southbound highways were similarly alerted. The on-duty deputy from the county sheriff's department made a couple of extra passes through Gravity when he did his rounds. In the long run, a stolen truck in Gravity didn't count for more than a stolen vehicle anywhere else, even if the suspect was armed and wanted for questioning in a murder investigation.

For their part, neither Murdoch nor Shepherd believed that Sal Erickson was looking to get far. After briefing Lemieux and Rolley, the four officers divided the town in thirds and went off in three vehicles, scouring fire roads, farm roads and woods roads, aiming their searchlights behind every garage and barn and lobster shack for Jerry Royal's truck.

Sergeant Murdoch, a year from his second retirement, was fiercely determined to make the collar. Equal in his motivation was his animosity for Sal and his particular hunger to exact payback for the damage to his neck. He wanted this one bad.

However, not bad enough to drive into the cemetery, which he had passed once heading out of town and once again heading back in. If he had driven through those iron gates and followed the drive up the terraces to the northeast corner, he would have found Jerry Royal's new Chevy truck parked up against the woods, beside Bobby Swift's grave.

Had he seen the truck, he might have also noticed a thread of cigarette smoke curling out the top of the window. A careful investigator might have wondered about the length of rope that led out of the same window and extended down into the gas tank. He might have noticed that the end of the rope inside the cab seemed to be coiled on a pile of newspapers and rags underneath the ashtray, or detected the smoldering cigarette balanced on the edge of the ashtray. He certainly would have smelled the gasoline fumes. Calculating that such an unattended cigarette would burn itself past the balance point in five to seven minutes and then fall into the gasoline-soaked trash, the detective also would have calculated that by the time the fire worked its way down the rope and the gas tank exploded, the man who had planted this diversion would be eight to fifteen minutes away.

Minute by minute, another hour passed. Iris lay relentlessly in the dark, physically exhausted and emotionally drained, but not tired enough to sleep. Even though the upstairs was warm and stuffy, thc constant passing of patrol cars had made sleeping impossible with the windows open, so she had closed them. But it did little good.

At midnight, when a car stopped outside the house again, its radio barking, Davey came into Iris's bedroom. 'Did they find Daddy?' she asked. Iris lifted the sheet, and Davey climbed in. 'Go to sleep, love,' her mother told her. 'Daddy will be okay.'

Five minutes later Davey was asleep again, breathing deeply. Outside, the last quarter moon was just rising in the sky, while peepers chirred hypnotically down at the river. Any other night, the moon and the breathing and the peepers would have put Iris to sleep. Tonight they only added to the nerve-wracking inertia she felt.

To soothe herself, she thought of Helen Swan. She pictured

Helen smiling. It was a particular smile Helen had given her the last time they'd talked, in response to Iris's maintaining that she didn't feel especially upset about Sal's leaving – or about her father's house burning. She had told Helen that she simply was not an emotional person. That's when Helen had smiled. Helen always seemed to know more than Iris was telling her.

Iris turned over in bed, covered her ear with her arm and tried to occupy her mind with practical things: whether to go through a realtor or advertise the house herself; whether or not to repaper Davey's bedroom. Or to paint the ceiling over the upstairs landing. Something needed to be done, that's how she felt.

Because it was the house that was keeping her awake after all, and not the heat, or the passing cars, or the peepers, or the moon or Davey's breathing. Ever since the fire, ever since Jerry had been inside the house – her mother's house—

Iris sat up in bed. Something needed to be done.

Boxes were packed. Doors were locked. Her father was in the burn ward at Downeast Memorial. Sal was wanted for murder. The peepers chirred. The moon rose. Davey breathed in and out, in and out...

Iris found her glasses and put them on, took the flashlight from her nightstand, slipped out from under the sheet in her jersey and underpants, and padded out of her room. Crossing the polished landing, intending to go downstairs for a cup of tea, she became suddenly conscious – not of the dark, but—

above her

—the attic.

Iris was suddenly, keenly, aware of that musty, wooden room above her, that somehow – somehow her mother was up there, looming over the house, hollow and heartless, always and forever, watching.

She swept the flashlight beam slowly up the wall, across the white ceiling...

Ridiculous!

She knew what Helen would say, so soothing in her abject rationality: 'Do you really believe that if you went up into your attic you would find your mother?'

Iris stood there enraptured by her own silence, hearing another car passing outside.

Going up?

The fear solidified in her, made her almost afraid to move. She stared up at the hatch, the black handle.

'It's only a room,' Helen would have said, smiling. 'What are you afraid you'll find?'

Without knowing what she was about to do, Iris stepped softly across the landing and pulled her bedroom door closed, silently turning the latch to keep from waking Davey. Then she returned to the landing, aiming her flashlight up again. The hatch wasn't two feet over her head. She'd never been tall enough; now she simply reached up. Resisting the impulse to pull her fingers from the cold black handle – *How many more years?* Helen would have said. *How much longer do you want to feel this way?* Iris wrapped her fingers around the handle and gave a tug, just enough to feel it give. She knew precisely how the ladder would unfold.

By road, the village was a mile from the cemetery, half that distance if one could fly. The way Sal ran down the road, he might as well have flown. After leaving Jerry's cigarette burning in the truck's ashtray, he took off down the terraces at a dead-on sprint and didn't miss a beat as he flew out of the gates and hit the asphalt. Just after midnight, the only cars he was likely to encounter would be the police looking for him, so he watched for lights in front and behind as he ran, ready to ditch for cover. At the end of the Townhouse Road he turned onto the River Road, actually picking up speed in his work boots. He made the village in under five minutes.

As he approached the lone streetlight at the corner of the Village Road, he spotted car lights and abruptly cut into the pines. The headlights were coming slowly up the road from his house. He was sure that the police were also watching the store, which was directly uphill from where he stood – across the river and through two hundred feet of woods. Laboring to catch his breath, he did not stop but plowed purposefully through the trees, his elbows around his ears to protect his face from the branches. He knew the river at low tide wouldn't be much more than three feet deep, even though it was fully thirty feet across and frigid. Not taking the time to reconsider – not even removing his pants and boots – he walked steadily down the bank and plunged in. The water was far colder than he'd imagined, its iciness burning him as he stumbled through a current that grew stronger as it deepened, climbing to his hips.

Emerging on the opposite bank, Sal pushed immediately up the hill, his noisy steps through the thicket barely covered by the running water behind him. As the hill leveled off in a stand of scrub fir and wild blueberry vines, Sal could see Noel's upstairs lights. Ahead and to the left, four windows were lit on the side of her apartment – her living room, bedroom and kitchen. He veered further to the right, putting more distance between himself and the building. When vines gave way to lawn and he was at the back of her property, he crouched in the shadows to wait, deeply winded.

He looked up at her kitchen windows for a few moments but saw no movement there. The second floor – store and stockroom – had no windows in the back or sides. Down at ground level, the garage was dark, and her driveway was vacant. Her backyard was rectangular and deep, ornamented with four ancient apple trees that became defined only at the tops, where their branches twisted against the sky. Resisting the temptation to move ahead, Sal stayed put fifty feet behind her swimming pool, deeply inhaling the chlorinated air while he waited. Only when he felt the chill from his wet pants did he begin to consider his various mistakes in coming.

Jerry snored deeply, his shotgun aimed at the door. Between snores he listened. When he was satisfied that the sound he had heard was only a skunk or raccoon rummaging through his stuff outside, he laid the gun back on the table and concentrated on the TV again. He kept the volume down so he could listen for the distant volley of gunshots, the signal that he and Noel were home free.

It was a thirty-minute commercial, some busty woman spray-painting a man's bald spot black while the audience applauded. 'Oh, I imagine,' Jerry muttered. Worse than wrasslin, how people could believe that shit. He drank the rest of his cola and flung the can over his shoulder into the back of the bus.

Jerry was beyond sleep now, way beyond, in some other state of consciousness. Not that he needed to sleep, anyway. He had convinced himself that he remembered a Bible story about Jesus going forty days and forty nights without sleep, to prove a point. Either that or it had something to do with a woman.

Animal attraction.

Jerry's brain brimmed with visions of Noel, his stomach buzzing as though a little motor were going inside. He didn't know what the hell endorphins were, but his sure as hell were boiling over tonight. He reached into his cooler for another cola, popped it, and drank it down till his eyes watered.

Closed his eyes and listened once again for those gunshots, and then he started thinking of last night for the hundredth time. See, it could have gone like this: He goes over there, down in back where it's dark, and he rings her doorbell, then stands and waits all shaved and washed. She comes down the stairs into the garage. In the darkness he can barely make her out – until she emerges into a square of moonlight, and then he sees that she's wearing this sleeveless white undershirt and nothing else. Little red chipmunk fur between her legs. She comes to the door slowly, giving him that animal attraction look. She reaches for the doorknob . . . but then she hesitates . . . looking up at him, teasing. Testing. They both know what she wants.

And so he gives it to her – he raises the letter to the window. She looks. With his other hand, he snaps a spark from his lighter, but he stops short of letting the flame lick the letter, teasing her right back.

The way her lips part . . .

Then he does it, touches the tip of the flame to the paper. Her green eyes flare as the fire climbs higher, digesting his story. Her nipples swell, dark fetching knobs under her T-shirt. And then that crooked little half-smile appears. The flame climbs around Jerry's wrist, but he doesn't mind the heat, because it's making her hot, because she's right now crossing her arms in front of her and peeling that T-shirt slowly up her chest, it catches on her nipples, and her little tits flip when they're freed. Just like that. Totally naked now, bathed in the orange light of his dying flame, she reaches down for the lock. He hears a *click.*

He tries the door—

Wait – not the lock—

—a gun! She swings back, punches the revolver through the glass, aimed dead at his face—

He jumps – bangs his knee on his table.

Fuckin letter.

Jerry drained his cola, slammed the can on the table, pushed to his feet and headed up the aisle to the front. Only thing about drinkin this much, you sure had to piss every other minute.

The hot cedar smell came over Iris, and with it, the first flood of weakness. She pulled herself to a higher rung, rising into darkness, instinctively reaching her right hand over her head, circling around the string until she hit the metal bead. She fingered the tiny bellshaped thing, wrapped the string once around the knuckle of her index finger and gave a tug, hoping the light wouldn't go on. But it did.

click

Brown. Red-brown, yellow-brown, dry-brown rafters crossing overhead, brown roof descending to the two-foot kneewall on both sides. Brown chimney in the center of the room, a vertical fissure snaking down the old bricks. To Iris's left, a wooden chair lay on the floorboards – glossy brown – her mother's kitchen chair. Under the eaves, Jerry's bass fiddle. Iris felt a shaking in her legs, but she kept her perch with her arms, viewing the left side of the room from floor level. A clothesline on its side, the carousel kind – meant nothing to her. But the cedar chest . . . She remembered a wool coat inside, burgundy, with a gray fur collar – her grandmother's. And the cream-colored hat she used to wear when she was four years old, five and six, playing dress-up with her mother—

(No, she was ten, in her Girl Scout uniform. Her brother was seventeen, goat-scented farm boy with whiskers on his chin and dog pads on his palms . . . and her mother . . .)

Iris's heart pounded.

She took a breath. Turned her head to the right and saw the big footprints heading straight through the dust. She gripped the hatch frame to keep from falling . . .

Undone

The mattress, striped and stained, flat on the floor. A small sound came from Iris's chest, like a child's cry.

But there was something else. Standing over the head of the mattress. The wire dress form. Hollow. Fitted with a white wedding dress. Her mother's.

14

14

Jerry stood on the doorstep of his bus, trying to piss into the small riverbed he had created over the past three days and nights, but he overshot the mark and hit a box of dishes. Never easy aiming with a hard-on.

One thing for sure. Just like the old man liked to say, all that blood rushin down to his manhood away from his brain, the thing was gonna get him killed one day. Old man might've been right too. With Noel keeping him awake with all this animal attraction bullshit, he couldn't force a clear thought if his life depended on it. And for once in his life, it did.

When he had finished urinating, he decided that since the thing was in his hand, he'd might as well take care of business and clear his head. Because even if he and Noel got away with this, and Sal Erickson got himself killed in a shoot-out with the cops so that everyone in the world figured he had it coming—

Jerry still needed to hang onto that letter, no matter how many animal attraction looks she gave him. If he had to jack off every fifteen minutes to stay alive, then by God he'd do it and no one was around to tell him otherwise.

'You got that right,' he said, already in motion.

He leaned his head back against the mirror of his bus, looked up at the darkness and started the fantasies rolling, when off in the distance there came a resounding boom that echoed across the sky for a number of seconds. Not the volley of gunshots he had expected to hear, Jerry thought to himself, but then he thought no more about it, because at that moment he was seeing a light that he shouldn't have seen.

He stared across the road at the old family house, the odd, dim illumination high on the gable end. In fact, Jerry wasn't sure that the light wasn't just another one of Noel's tricks on his imagination, so he stepped down from the bus, still masturbating, and walked down to his driveway until—

the attic vent—

Noel! he thought. *She'd found it!*

He turned and hurried back to the bus, stuffing himself into a fly that was way too tight and seemed to have a million teeth. The blood raced back through his veins, engorging his brain now, until at last he knew exactly what he needed to do to stop this chattering once and for all.

On her knees beside the wedding dress, Iris let herself cry. Softly, like a cleansing summer rain. In one way, it was fascinating what her mind had done with its memories. In that way, she marveled how it had protected her, drawing curtains over the reality of her younger life, masking events with bits of dreamlike imagery. The hollow dress form had become her mother, formless and heartless, the specter who looked on scornfully yet silent, always without objection. Yes, Iris had enough appreciation of psychology to be fascinated—

But in another way, she could only begin to fathom what her brother had cost her. The years of pervasive, unfocused shame; the isolation. The way she had become, herself, like the dress form, silent, scornful, hollow. Her brother had even robbed her of her mother's memory.

How many times? Once? Twice? It seemed it must have become a routine occurrence. After school; while their father was down at the clam flats, or tinkering outside with his truck, or sitting downstairs with his bottle and his gospel music.

Up.

Up was the word Jerry had used. *Ready to go up? Time to go up.* Iris's chest heaved. She let the tears flow.

She thought of Davey, realized that she must have been Davey's age when it started. She thought of Sal, imagined how their lives might have been different. She thought of her father and how his alcoholism (and his own pain) had prevented him from protecting her. She thought of his courage in finally getting sober, and his desperate, naive attempts to win her back, and how he never stopped trying. She cried harder when she realized how successfully she had thwarted him. The tears burned. The tears felt wonderful.

She wiped her eyes, then reached out to touch the silk. In fleeting glimpses she envisioned her mother: laughing, trying to pour milk over her Cheerios on the bus …

This—

is a dress form.

This—

my mother's wedding dress.

This—

She heard the floor creak behind her. Thinking it was Davey, she wiped her eyes before she turned.

'Mommy?'

It was Davey, pulling herself up through the hatch, testing her weight on the floor, walking tentatively ahead in her calico nightie. Iris gazed at her daughter as she came barefoot over the loose and dust-covered pine boards.

'I thought you said it was dangerous up here.'

Seeing that her mother had been crying, Davey came directly to Iris and wrapped her arms around her, fit her warm cheek against Iris's neck. Inexplicably, Iris felt a sudden welling of joy, and she almost burst out laughing. But, afraid she might become hysterical, she restrained herself. She breathed deeply the warm cedar air.

'I'm remembering things, love,' she said.

'Bad things?'

'Mm-hm. And some very good.'

Iris reached out and brushed dust off the silk sleeve. 'This was your grandma's wedding dress,' she explained. Neither of them looked back toward the hatch, or they might have seen that the landing light had come on below.

'Maybe it'll be yours someday.' (As her mother used to say to her.)

Iris lifted the sleeve again, and the corner of an envelope poked out between the breasts. Davey spotted it, reached to tuck it back.

Swear to keep a secret?

'Love, what was that?'

Iris unfastened a button, pulled the envelope out – TO BE OPENED ONLY IF GERALD CHRISTIAN ROYAL TURNS UP MISSING OR DEAD. Curious, Iris turned the envelope over, pushed her thumb under the flap and tore it open—

But the look on Davey's face.

'Love, what?'

Davey stared past her mother, terrified. Iris turned. Her heart lurched.

Jerry was peeking over the hatchway.

Shivering from the cold, Sal crouched at the edge of the woods. Listening to a car crawl up the road in front of the store, he saw Noel's building outlined with light, first left, then right. He watched, he waited, he listened.

When the explosion finally sounded, distant as it was, Sal tensed. A dog started barking nearby, but then the dog stopped, and everything once again became quiet and dark, deceptively so. The swimming pool rolled the low moon gently over its surface, chlorine wafting into the air.

Abandoning caution, Sal rose to his feet and began approaching the pool. All at once a man charged out from around the right corner of the building. Sal stopped, braced to break for the woods, but the man showed no sign of seeing him. Instead, the man ran up the driveway, speaking anxiously into a handheld radio. Sal remained motionless while he heard a car's engine start and the car speed off. Simultaneously, up at the firehouse, the fire siren began to wail.

Beneath the din of the fire alarm, Sal walked deliberately around the pool, pulling his T-shirt over his head and wrapping the cloth tight around his fist. Approaching the garage, he stopped in front of the door and tried to see through the window. But all he saw was his own black reflection in front of the moon-shredded water, while apple branches behind his head grappled for the sky. Nothing was innocent anymore.

He punched his wadded fist through the glass, and the pane shattered on the concrete floor like hundreds of bells ringing. But under the wailing siren, Sal was confident that the breaking glass wouldn't be heard. He reached in with his left hand to turn the lock – and found that the door had been left unlocked. Not stopping to wonder why, he pulled the door open and stood there in absolute blackness. He shook the shirt off his hand and dropped it on the floor, then waded into the dark. He reached out with his hands, felt her car with his left. He moved two steps to his right until he could tell that the stairway wall, the half partition, was getting closer – he could sense the change in air pressure. His right hand confirmed his suspicion. He hoped his senses were keen enough to also register someone hiding behind a corner.

When he reached the end of the partition, he turned around it and looked up into more darkness. Again, he could feel a difference in air movement. He could also hear cool saxophone notes rolling like water down the stairwell. Suddenly he hadn't a shred of hope that Bouchard had been wrong about Noel. She was in the building waiting for him, drawing him in. He realized that by causing the diversion that had drawn the cops away, he had inadvertently served them both. With no witnesses, with the broken window, she could eliminate him and nobody alive could call it an ambush.

He knew that the staircase ahead of him reached a landing and then turned to the right. He took the treads as quietly as his waterlogged boots and jeans would allow, thc pants chafing, the wet leather squeaking traitorously with each step. Holding the right handrail, he waved his left hand in front of him to feel the wall at the head of the turn – or to ward off an attack. However, before his fingers touched the facing wall, the change in pressure told him that the right-hand wall had disappeared. And then his toe kicked an angled tread. He swiped the air in front of him and turned right.

From here he was able to make out dim light above the top step. Here, too, the jazz sounded clearer – Coltrane and Miles – like the last time he'd climbed these stairs. Three steps up, he was able to see the origin of the light, a line of it leaking under the stockroom door. He kept his eye on the line and counted his steps as he climbed, thinking that if the door suddenly swung open, he'd know how many steps down before the turn. At the same time, he knew that the nearer he climbed to the door, the less chance he'd have to make that turn.

He knew that she was expecting him, that's why the door had been unlocked and the music left on. He guessed that the stockroom door was also unlocked. He knew that she had a gun.

Very quietly he stepped onto the landing and stood there in front of the door, listening to the steady trumpet, considering his options. Push the door open and stand there looking down those dusky aisles of boxes. That's where she'd be waiting for him – somewhere among the boxes. To his left, another flight of stairs rose eight or ten steps to a wide landing on the southeast corner of the building, where they turned one hundred and eighty degrees for the final ascent to the back door of her apartment.

Sal reached out and touched the stockroom door. It pushed open without a sound, exposing him. He looked in at the shapes, the long, shadowy aisles. Somewhere to the right of the room's center, over her desk, a soft spot of light shone on the ceiling, as Miles blew a doleful line. 'So What' was the name of the tune.

This was where she wanted him.

What he wanted was upstairs.

He broke left, found the handrail and took the stairs at a run, making no effort to disguise his footsteps. He reached the first landing, swung around the partition and continued up. He ran to the top, found the doorknob, turned it and rammed his bare shoulder into the door. Bouncing off, he threw himself at the door again. Now he heard Noel's footsteps drumming across the apartment from the left. Again he drove his shoulder into the wood. It answered with a *crack* but didn't give. He lined up and rammed it again. This time the crack was sharp, startlingly so, and he fell back, catching the handrail to keep from falling.

He noticed two things simultaneously, without realizing they were connected. His left shoulder burned from the impact; and a tiny dot of light shone through the door, off-center. His hand went to his shoulder, felt the wet flap of flesh, the hot cavity – just as another *crack* sounded, and another lighthole appeared, lower, more centered. She was shooting at him!

Had he kept his head, he would have dropped to the floor and rolled down the stairs. But, enraged, he turned his right shoulder to the door and threw himself again. Another *crack!* another hole, and he was stung in the forehead by a shard of oak. He lined up again, gave a long, painful shout and sprang at the wood, splintering the jamb.

Stumbling into her kitchen, he was blinded by the light, but Noel came into focus fast, sprawled on the floor in front of him against the legs of an overturned chair, her arms stretched between her own legs, a black revolver aimed at his midsection.

'Oh, God,' she said, 'I didn't know it was you.' But she didn't lower the gun. Her jeans were bright red, and she wore a black leotard top.

'They said you were dangerous,' she said.

He stared at her. Shirtless, he could feel his blood running warmly under his arm, down his ribs, but he hardly noticed it, struck by the set of her face, the way her finger locked around the trigger.

'You did just break down my door. What was I supposed to do?'

He stepped toward her. Her aim raised to his chest. He stopped. She said, 'I do have to protect myself, you know.' Leaning on the overturned chair, she pulled herself to her knees, then to her feet, keeping the gun on him.

He shook his head at her, showing his confidence. 'You're not going to shoot me, Noel.' He took another step, and she stepped back, keeping the gun on him. 'It's too intimate this way. It's not your style. Through the door, that's different.' She backed around the stove, into the hallway, while he slowly pursued her. 'Like leaving someone in a box underground. No, face to face, you don't have the stomach for it.'

The look of assurance that came over her easily outmatched his own, and he knew it was a mistake to have challenged her. She stopped backing and smiled. He stopped coming forward, while his blood gathered at the waistband of his jeans.

'For what it's worth,' Noel began, 'I don't think people will judge you harshly. Two lives for two million dollars? I think people will say you knew the value of life.'

Her eyes lowered to his chest. Her aim followed. Her finger tensed.

'You should've known the river,' he said.

Noel balked, just for an instant, looked up at him again.

'The reversing falls,' Sal explained, trying not to sound desperate (though he knew he was only buying seconds). He took another step toward her. Although her expression showed no flagging, she stepped back.

'I'm talking about things someone might throw in the river, thinking they'll wash down to the ocean.'

Noel's mouth became cocky, that goading, off-centered smirk.

'I don't think you want to pull that trigger,' he said. 'You know you made a mistake.'

She brushed up against the bookcase on the left wall.

'See, unless you time it right, things you throw in the river don't have time to make it down to the ocean. They come back.'

He took another step, approaching the bookcase – the reason he had come here.

'What I can't figure out is why you burned down Jerry's house. I know you did it, Noel.'

Her pistol swung up and she fired. He saw the flash, felt the percussion slap his face, but the bullet missed him, banged off the stove in the kitchen. Ears ringing from the shot, Sal came forward again, trying to hide the shaking in his legs. When he was even with the bookcase, he took his eyes off her and looked down at the spines.

'See, I remember that book. You said it was for burning down billboards, though. Not houses.' He reached into the case, flipping the books, one by one, onto the floor, looking for the right one.

Keeping the gun on him, Noel reached behind her and pulled open the door to her zebra stairway. 'Actually, I don't know what book you're talking about,' she said, backing through in such a way that Sal should have been alerted, the way she burrowed into the landing so that her arm was the last thing through the door, her arm and the hand holding the gun.

He looked up, too late.

The cylinder twitched—

He dived across the hall, slamming the door against her arm. The shot fired over his back, and she screamed and fired again. Denying the pain in his shoulder, Sal reached up and grabbed the barrel with his left hand while he forced the door open with his knee. But she jerked away, and his shoulder snapped in fiery pain. She swung the revolver down at his face—

He lunged, caught her by the legs, and they fell, tumbling down step after zebra-striped step, both grappling for the gun. When they slammed against the bottom door, Sal threw himself on top of her, crossed his right arm over her throat and caught the small barrel striving for his head. He forced it down, twisting her wrist until the muzzle pressed against her own chin.

'Go ahead,' he whispered, 'pull the trigger. We were gonna do each other anyway, remember? You do me, I do you. Yeah, let's do that.'

Her green eyes drilled into him. With her free hand she tore at his face, his eyes. He twisted his head away, and her knee swung up, thumped his back. He hardly felt it.

'You tell me!' he whispered. The pistol inched down to her throat. But her eyes on him never flickered.

'Tell me what you've done!'

Upstairs, footsteps suddenly thundered down the hall, then down the stairs. Then a voice:

'Get down!'

Sal turned halfway, saw the large figure at the curve in the stairs, unevenly crouched, taking two-handed aim – Murdoch.

'Your legs! Your legs down!'

'Tell him, Noel!'

'Get your legs down!'

'Confess what you did!'

Glaring at Sal, she smiled. Stopped kicking and lowered her legs to the floor. Smiled. Sal jumped at the door—

a shot exploded.

—turned the knob and ran, breaking through rows of cartons, stumbling, racing through the dark, tripping over corners of pallets, careening off shelves. He heard another gunshot as he banged through the swinging door into a blinding, flashing blue light. Ran at the locked door – bounded off and turned – grabbed a bubble-gum dispenser in the crook of his good arm and swung it into the window, bringing the plate glass down in solid, chiming sheets. He leaped through and charged off in the darkness.

* * *

'Real smart,' Jerry said, pulling himself onto the attic floor.

Iris didn't understand the look on his face, why he had the shotgun, or why he was here. She figured he was drunk, and part of the manhunt for Sal – out to make a name for himself. But he seemed strangely agitated, almost afraid – dangerously so. She held onto the envelope and kept her hand on Davey's shoulder.

'Jerry,' she said (it was the first time she had spoken his name as an adult), 'I've been remembering things.'

With a sudden jerk of his arm, he cocked the shotgun, the metallic clatch loud, brutal. 'You stay put,' he told her. His face was drained, his eyes haunted. He held out a hand and said, 'Have her bring it over.'

Before Iris realized what he was talking about, Davey took the envelope from her hand.

'Davey, no—' Iris grabbed Davey's arm.

'Don't worry, I'm not gonna do anything. Just have her bring it to me.'

Iris's gaze turned fiery. 'Do you?'

'Me, what?'

'Remember.' Her voice rang like steel. '*What you did to me up here.*'

He contemplated. 'So? Growin boy, that's all that was.'

'No. No, Jerry. You were seventeen. I was ten. You were my brother.'

'Hey' – he waved the shotgun at Davey's bare feet.

Iris started toward him. '*You get that—*'

He swung the rifle at Iris, stopping her. His eyes sparkled.

'*Jerry, what are you doing?*'

'It's not anybody's fault,' he said, his voice tight and fast. 'Just have her bring the letter and I'll be on my way. Nobody's gonna get hurt.'

'Jerry, I don't know what's in this envelope, and I don't care.'

'Yeah, another woman speaks.' He glared from one to the other, preoccupied, electrified. Then he jerked the shotgun toward the mattress. 'Okay, get down on the bed.'

Davey looked up at her mother, quivering.

'Both of yuhs!' He swung the shotgun back and forth. 'Now! On the bed!'

Iris went cold. 'Love, go downstairs,' she said to Davey.

Jerry stepped in front of the hatchway and took square aim at Iris. 'I'll kill your mother! I'll kill you both, I'm all fucked up!'

'No, you will not!'

'Lay down!' He stamped his foot on a loose board.

Davey shivered quietly, her eyes wide and wet. Iris hugged her to her side, unable to stop her own trembling. 'Jerry, what's the matter with you?'

'Nothin. I got put in this position by dishonest people. Now lay down on your bellies.' His aim lowered to their feet again.

'Jerry, what are you doing?'

He raised the gun back to Iris's chest, and she saw a look come over him that she recognized with horror – a sudden blankness, a detachment from reality. She knew at that moment he was going to kill them both.

'Jerry,' she said. Kneeling on the mattress, she took the envelope from Davey's hand. 'Please. Let Davey go. Whatever it is—'

'Get down on your bellies. Don't make a big deal of it. Nobody's gonna get hurt.'

Davey squeezed Iris's hand. They both knew he was lying.

'Just get down and stop the noise so I can think a minute. Faces down.'

Iris took Davey around the waist. 'It's okay, love,' she whispered, unable to control her own shaking. Together they lay down on the dusty, must-scented mattress. Iris put her arm around Davey, hugged her tightly.

'And I don't want to see any eyes.'

His footsteps approached softly as he talked. Iris pulled Davey's head underneath her own. 'Curl up in a ball,' she whispered, and Davey did.

'Like I said, it's nobody fault—' His sooty blue reef runners stopped beside Iris's face.

Her voice quivered. 'Jerry, you're scaring us.'

'Just close your eyes, I'm gonna take the letter and then I'm gonna go, let bygones be bygones. Just close your eyes.'

She felt the gun barrel rest against the side of her back as he snatched the envelope from her hand. Then the barrel lifted. She heard him take a single step back. Then the snap of a cigarette lighter ... and silence. She opened an eye and turned her head just enough to see the flame climb the corner of the envelope. His shotgun, held under his arm, was aimed vaguely at her legs. She thought about lunging for it. It was her only hope.

'See, that's your problem,' Jerry said, rotating the paper so the flame climbed to the opposite corner. 'You just can't do what a man tells you. It's your own fault, if you hadna been so friggin nosy—'

A creak of wood alerted them. Jerry dropped the envelope, wheeled toward the hatch – a head and shoulder poking up—

'*Freeze, greaseball!*'

Both men fired in a flourish, and Davey screamed. At the hatch there was a spray of white and red, as Murdoch's big head riveted back and plunged from sight, the body cracking once off the ladder, then knocking heavily on the landing below.

Iris pulled Davey beneath her and held her tighter, thinking wildly that if she squeezed hard enough, it would stop both of them from shaking.

Confounded, Jerry turned back toward them, his knee buckling. He staggered a little, clutching his forearm to his stomach, the muzzle of his shotgun scraping over the floorboards. Then he turned his gaze back to the hatch, where white fragments of neck brace were scattered like bloody chicken feathers.

'Oh great,' he strained. 'I suppose this is my fault.'

He lifted his arm from his stomach, saw a solid spot of darkness, and then a thick drop of blood blossomed on his lucky shoe. 'Yeah, just great,' he said. 'Now I'm friggin gut-shot.'

A metallic *pop* alerted him – from the darkness at the back of the room. He snapped his head toward the sound. Thinking it was Noel, he looked down for his burning letter and moved to drag a reef runner over it, to put the fire out. But he was unsteady and slow, and the last corner of the envelope was already folding over, blackening. To his surprise, the voice that came from high on the gable wall was a man's.

'Jerry, what are you doing down there?'

He squinted up at the darkness.
'Daddy?' Davey cried.
Jerry regained his footing. 'No shit, that *is* you.'
'Daddy?'
'I thought you prob'ly bought the farm,' Jerry said.
High on the gable end of the house, Sal stood on the third highest rung of the ladder, two rungs above the danger zone, bracing himself with one hand holding the small wooden frame that surrounded the attic vent. Because of his wounded shoulder, Sal's left hand could only rest against the shingles beside his leg.
'Iris, Davey, are you okay?'
'Daddy?'
'It's okay, hon,' Sal told her. 'Jerry, let them down so we can talk.'
Through the vent screen, Sal could see Jerry silhouetted to the left of the chimney, bent heavily over his shotgun. A finger of smoke was all that remained of the paper by his feet. To the left of Jerry, Iris and Davey lay huddled on the mattress.
'Iris, are you alright?' he called.
'Yes.'
'Jerry, what are you doing? What's that you burned?'
Down in the attic Jerry looked up for the voice, but the chimney threw a black shadow over the middle of the wall where the vent was located. Making a quick, painful grunt, Jerry rocked back on his heels and hoisted his shotgun up under his arm.
'Put that down, Jerry,' Sal told him. 'I've got a gun up here.'
'What, you up on a ladder or something? I can't even see where you are.' Stealthily, Jerry secured the butt of the rifle under his arm.
'I'll shoot you!' Sal cried.
'I'm already shot up pretty friggin good. Can't hardly feel it . . . bleedin like a bastard, though.' Leaning over the barrel, Jerry cocked his gun.
'You let them go, Jerry!'
'You got my truck out there? I'm gonna need some wheels, man.'
'*Let them go!*'
Jerry squeezed his eyes closed. 'Whoa,' he said, 'blackin out

here.' As he wavered, his gun hitched up another two inches, until it was nearly level with Sal's position. 'Hey, no shit, I think I'm blackin out, really—'

Slower than he intended, Jerry jerked the barrel and fired a tremendous boom, knocking himself to the floor.

Through the screen, Sal saw the muzzle explode. In the same instant the top corner of the vent frame blew apart, and Sal fell back off the ladder. Catching his right foot between the rungs, his body went down backwards, slammed against the ladder. He hung by his instep.

Sal's right hand found the rail by his thigh, then a rung. Pocket change dropped out of his pants onto his chest and chin. He heard Davey call for him. Holding his weight with his right arm, he let go of the ladder with his foot. His hip scraped down the rungs until he caught a toehold again, and then he righted himself. He climbed back to the top. At the blown-out corner of the vent, the screen flopped over, so now Sal was able to push his hand inside and catch the interior wallboards.

Down in the attic Jerry was just pushing himself off the floor, using his gun as a crutch.

Sal's voice came down from the darkness. 'Tell me what you burned, Jerry. That paper you burned.'

Hunched over his rifle, Jerry's reef runner slid through his blood, and he almost went down again. His velour jersey hung heavily.

'You knew about her, didn't you, Jerry? You knew what she did.'

Jerry fit his fingers around the gun stock.

'Answer me, Jerry. That paper you burned. You had something on her.'

With a grunt, Jerry lifted the shotgun off the floor.

'Leave it!' Sal said.

'Don't get excited,' Jerry answered, 'it's for self-protection.' His body swayed noticeably; blood transferred from his thumb into the grain of the stock. He took an uncertain step to the right.

'I think she's got something on you too, Jerry. That's why you didn't turn her in after she burned down your house. That's why you're up here now.'

'Wait a minute,' Jerry said. 'I can't hear you.' He took another step, until Sal realized what he was doing – trying to get behind the chimney.

'Don't screw around, Jerry!'

Looking through the screen, Sal saw a sudden, quiet flash, and then darkness overtook the room. Aware that Jerry had popped the lightbulb, Sal leaned to his left, trying to see around the chimney, afraid that Jerry might be making his way downstairs and would have him trapped on the ladder. But as Sal's eyes adjusted to the dark, he saw light glowing out of the hatch from the landing below, vaguely outlining the lower half of the chimney. And then the chimney sprouted an elbow.

'Daddy, get down!'

The elbow jerked, the shotgun cocked.

'Jerry, we don't have to do this!'

'That's alright,' Jerry answered. 'You say you got a gun up there, let 'er rip.' He shuffled slowly out to the left until he was clearly silhouetted by the hatch light. Wavering there, he spread his legs and lifted his arm off his side. 'Gawhead, man, I'll give you first shot.'

'Jerry, listen. She made a mistake.'

'Okay,' Jerry said. Then, as if he were setting up for target practice, he painstakingly raised the shotgun into position, fit his jawbone against the stock, tried to steady the gun while he sighted down the barrel. 'You best take your shot,' he said. 'It's not like I got all night.'

'She screwed up, Jerry.'

As Jerry's sights shivered over the vent, his target slowly materialized: a little piece of metallic sky outlining Sal's head and shoulder.

'Daddy, get down!'

Jerry snickered weakly. 'More or less like a raccoon up a tree,' he said, as his finger curled around the trigger. 'Lookin at the situation, man down here bleedin half to death, I guess we're gonna have to call this one self-defens—'

Jerry saw it too late, swooping up at him—

a ghost in a white wedding dress, headless, hollow—

—solid.

The impact knocked him off his feet, and he sat inside the rising light of the open hatch. His head knocked off the wood frame, his butt scuttered down the ladder rungs, flipping him over in the air so that when he landed, his shotgun muzzle hit the floor and the gun exploded, the butt recoiling into the full weight of his falling body, snapping his right-side ribs like kindling.

On the landing beside him, Sergeant Murdoch lay mortally wounded in his checkered blazer, gaping dark-eyed like a jacked buck, blood pooling from his open neck.

His own wounds notwithstanding, Jerry rolled to his feet, shotgun in hand, eyes flaring. Whether he was escaping the ghost or just anxious to tree Sal, he swung around the banister and started down. But at the head of the stairs his lucky shoe skated over the polished floor, and his upper body, weighted by the shotgun, started down ahead of his legs. Jerry's disconnected feet drummed down the treads to keep up, faster and faster. But his plummeting torso went faster still. He saw the window curtain at the bottom of the stairs fly up at him like another ghost, and he put out his shotgun to stop it. The barrel broke the window first, his head knocked off the planter pot then shattered more glass, and then the white curtain caught his face and hung his body and shotgun out the smashed window like a June bug snagged in a spiderweb—

Immediately a pair of headlights swung at him, flashing bright. Then a spotlight. Then a second car roared up alongside, blue light strobing, car doors opening, someone shouting, *'Drop the gun! Drop the gun!'*

But Jerry, caught in the curtain, could not comply. To make matters worse, his warm shoe was sliding back, while his shotgun pulled him forward. The curtain rod bowed, the nylon stretched.

'Drop it now!'

His blood-soaked jersey pulled up slowly, his glistening torso poised over the jagged glass in the bottom frame. Worst part was, he lacked the strength to resist.

'Drop it or I'll shoot you!'

He lacked the strength to even voice an objection. He saw a figure with a rifle run around the side of the house. He felt a point of window glass poke into his stomach. But, pressed against the curtain, Jerry could not release ballast.

Then two shots barked off behind him. It felt like a finger tapping him on the back – *tap, tap* – followed by the curious sensation that he was deflating. He managed to turn his head to the side, enough to see Murdoch lying red and shiny at the top of the stairs, death mask gaping, his .45 on its side in his hand, glaring down. As Jerry watched, the muzzle barked, and another round punched through his shoulder. Then, for better or worse, the curtain rod snapped free, and the plant pot smashed down on Jerry's back, driving him down on the glass.

He slumped over the sill like a waterlogged rug. Lying there, gazing at the shrubs swallowing his shotgun, imagining that the dark liquid running down the curtain was cola…

'Don't move,' he heard in the retreating distance. *'Don't you move.'*

Jerry managed a flick of his wrist, a final defiance. Then he let go.

15

While Sergeant Murdoch and Jerry Royal were rushed to Downeast Memorial and issued death certificates, and evidence technicians from the local CID drove to Gravity to take videotape and blood samples from the Ericksons' attic, landing and living room, Iris telephoned Helen Swan.

In four minutes Helen was there in her bathrobe to take Iris and Davey back to her house. When she knocked at the back door, however, Iris and Davey were sitting at the kitchen table with Detective Shepherd. Davey drank a glass of orange juice, while Troopers Lemieux and Rolley stood at the sink looking on. It was one-thirty in the morning. Shepherd asked Helen if she'd please wait in her car for a minute while they finished up.

Iris had told the detective about Jerry burning the envelope, but she said she did not know the contents of the letter inside. Davey told about the day Jerry had secreted the letter in the attic, but neither did she know what was in the letter, only that Jerry had told her it was keeping him alive. They both told about Jerry shooting Murdoch in the hatchway, about Sal appearing at the attic vent, and the things he had said to Jerry. Shepherd tape-recorded the interview, and at various, seemingly random, times he would ask them to repeat Sal's words.

When Iris recalled that Sal had warned Jerry that he had a gun, Rolley and Lemieux exchanged a look that didn't escape any of them, least of all Davey.

'Wait outside for me,' Shepherd told the troopers at that point. When they left, he said to Iris, 'But you're saying he never fired the gun?' and she affirmed. In three different ways he asked where they thought Sal might have gone, but each time neither had an answer. '"She screwed up, she made a mistake," you're sure those were the words he used?' Shepherd asked. Iris nodded. Davey looked down at the table, afraid that she had already unwittingly given the police more than enough information to help them arrest her father.

Shepherd shut off the tape recorder, gave Iris a sympathetic smile, Davey a pat on the knee. 'Why don't you go with your friend now and try to get some sleep,' he told them. 'We should be out of here in a few hours.'

When he walked them out to Helen's car, he saw Trooper Lemieux sitting in the cruiser with the door open, his feet out on the lawn, his service piece in his hand, checking his clip. Rolley was standing beside him.

Shepherd left Iris and walked immediately to the troopers. 'Don't do that here,' he said in a low voice.

Lemieux snapped the clip back in the pistol, lifted himself out of the car and holstered the weapon. 'Think we should call in for the dogs?' he said.

Shepherd looked at him, waited for Helen to drive away. After she did, Shepherd said to both troopers, 'No dogs. No canvassing. No guns.'

'She said he was armed, Detective.'

Shepherd looked at them both. 'Listen to me,' he said. 'We're not chasing a cop-killer here. The man who shot Sergeant Murdoch is on his way to the morgue. The man we're looking for is a suspect in a separate crime. You need to disassociate the two.'

Lemieux shifted nervously against the car, stole a glance at Rolley.

'I want you two to split up. Stick to the roads and stay in your vehicles. Rolley, you take Murdoch's car. Keep an eye on the store, go down her driveway from time to time and check the back. You see anything suspicious, you're on the radio to me.'

Shepherd turned to Lemieux. 'You, I want on the telephone.' He reached inside his suitcoat and dug a wallet out of his pocket. 'I found this under the ladder in back, along with some change and a fair amount of blood.'

He flipped Sal's wallet open and squeezed the sides to get at the cards beneath the driver's license. Shuffling through them, he pulled out a card and handed it to Lemieux. 'Blue Cross. Get this number and his description out to all ERs within a two-hour drive.' Shepherd sifted through some more cards and pulled out a Visa card. 'He's gonna need money. He may call to report his credit card stolen and try to get some money wired. You get to them first.' He pulled out another card, AAA. 'He might try to get cash out of these people, or else a loaner car. Call them.' He shuffled through the cards to the bottom of the stack, and then he stopped, separating one from the others. He looked closer.

'What's that?' Lemieux said. 'Another driver's license?'

Shepherd angled the card toward the light. 'From Rhode Island,' he said. Sal's photo was on it. But the name beside the picture—

Shepherd looked up.

Dale Newman.

'Alright, let's go,' he said, sticking the license back in with the other cards. 'Stay in your cars, is that clear?' He addressed the question to Lemieux as he jammed the cards back in the wallet.

'Yes, sir.'

'I don't think he'll come back here, knowing that we're looking for him. The main thing is, I don't want him going anywhere near Noel Swift. She's leaving tomorrow, and he may go over there again to try and stop her.'

'If he tries?' Lemieux said.

The detective nodded. 'Then I guess we're going to have to stop him.'

Shepherd waited until the troopers drove away. Then he went to his Cherokee, checked the clip of his own service piece and holstered it. With the night growing colder, he put on his jacket and zipped it, then walked out behind the house, where he had seen fresh blood on the rungs of the ladder and a sizable puddle in the grass.

He shone his flashlight around and saw another drop not five feet away, and then another in line with it, heading toward the road. The arrival route, Shepherd reasoned. Sal would have escaped the other way, probably around the garden and into the woods in back.

Shepherd returned to the ladder, then walked toward the garden. Ten feet out, as he suspected, he spotted a red drop on a blade of grass to his right. He looked back at the ladder and lined up the drops: heading toward the garage. The next blood drop wasn't for thirty feet, but it led behind the garage. Shepherd walked around the other side and discovered, at the front corner, blotted droppings in the sand the size of a tea rose. He figured that Sal had waited there while the police were engaged with Jerry. Given the activity that had centered around the front of the house thereafter, he guessed that Sal must have headed to the left, keeping the garage between himself and the house. He shone the light off into a thicket of young red pines and spotted the crimson glistening on the fine needles about five feet off the ground; he deduced by the height that Sal was bleeding from his left shoulder, chest.

He pushed through the trees, staying to his right to avoid getting blood on himself. It was like tracking a wounded deer in November, he thought, half expecting to find Sal lying dazed and panting inside the thicket. But than he saw a red smear on a branch to his right, and he stopped. Backed up a step. Sal had turned ninety degrees here, toward the road. Shepherd pushed through another fifteen feet of pines and then was in thick new grass that bordered the drainage ditch alongside the road. Another drop of blood had caught the far side of the ditch.

Shepherd stepped across to the asphalt and toed a line in the sand that pointed to the last blood drop. He imagined Sal would have run across the road here, and he looked out into the dark field, thinking it strange that Sal would have come out in the open so close to his house, unless he'd had a particular destination.

He walked into the road, moving his light slowly over the weeds and blueberry vines on the other side, from right to left and back again, and there he detected a slight depression in the ground cover, recently trodden upon. He joined the path and followed it for about fifty feet, where it cut abruptly to the right. When Shepherd turned that way, he knew where Sal had headed: to a light source that he realized was the open door of Jerry Royal's bus.

Trusting his suspicions, Shepherd doused his flashlight and

stepped quietly over the vines until he reached the Royals' cluttered yard. Coming up quietly behind the burned remains of the house, Shepherd unsnapped his holster and fit his hand over the cold butt. He stopped and listened. Except for the peepers singing down at the river, the night had grown remarkably quiet.

He drew his pistol and then resumed his movement. Approaching the bus, he could see that the windows had been painted black. Quietly approaching the rear corner, he stooped down, turned on his flashlight again and looked for a pair of feet behind the bus. Seeing none, he turned off the light and rose again, aimed his pistol at the open door and proceeded ahead. Fifteen feet away, he stopped.

'Sal Erickson?' he said. He set his flashlight on the ground. 'Sal, why don't you come out now? I'm armed, and I'd rather not come in after you.'

He tried to listen, but the peepers were singing much too loud. He noticed a drop of blood on the bottom step, still liquid. As he wrapped his fingers around the stainless steel rail, he imagined getting shot in the face, and he thought bitterly (as he often did lately) how little cops were paid.

'Sal, I know you're hurt. Let me know if you're in there, please. I want to help you.'

He climbed onto the first step, leaning back so that his head and body remained outside the door. He raised his weapon beside his ear.

'Mr Erickson?'

His suspicion grew that he was talking to himself, and that made him feel at once relieved yet frustrated. Nevertheless, he had to know for sure. He took a breath, counted to three, then poked his head and gun through the door, scanned the inside of the bus in a glance, then pulled out again. Registering what he had seen: table and seats on the left, halfway down; Styrofoam cooler on the right; cola cans strewn all over the aisle. The only place to hide was behind the table.

He swung in again, propped his pistol arm against the railing, aimed just over the seat. 'If you're behind there, Sal, put your hands up. I'm not going to shoot.'

Gratefully, then, Shepherd noticed the mirror at the back

corner of the bus, a round wide angle that confirmed he was alone in the bus. He turned quickly, in case Sal was behind him – and that's when he noticed the overturned cardboard box on the ground, the spilled clothing. He stepped down, picked up his flashlight and illuminated the box. Blood was smeared on the cardboard flap, and there was blood on the ground. With Sal wearing a fresh shirt, there'd be no more blood to track, for a while.

'Shit,' said the detective.

Consumed by cold and weakness, Sal sat high on the bluff above the bog. He had come through the underbrush directly behind the Royals' property and then, to avoid both paths, through a savagely dense growth of pines. Without a light to help him see, and with the thatched ceiling too thick to allow moonlight in, he had scraped his wall through the stiff branches, his wounded arm hanging inside his flannel shirt, taking punishment again and again. Now, in the open moonlight above the river, still wearing his wet jeans and boots, the shirt did little to warm him. The intensity of his shivering, of his pain, made it hard to focus his thoughts.

She would come down, he knew that. She would have to come down – if she wasn't there already, waiting for him. But trying to hear footsteps was futile over the incessant screeching of peepers below. Likewise, the ground fog down on the river made it impossible to see the bank – or even to know how high up he was perched. He pushed himself forward until he felt gravity tugging at his backside. He stared down into the softness, knowing that he had no real choice, this was how he was getting down, wondering if he would survive the fall, wondering why he had come here in the first place, why he didn't just roll back in the grass, close his eyes and let unconsciousness take him. He lost that option when his boot heel lost its purchase on the side of the bluff. Starting to slide, he reached out listlessly, caught a clump of grass, knowing that he lacked the strength to hold on. And then he plummeted, fell ten feet before his legs hit the vertical bank, where he slid another twenty feet down hardpack, trying to slow himself with the sides of his boots and his single hand, but managing instead to turn himself onto his injured side before he was dropped into the air again. He hit bottom twice, once on his heels and again on the flat of his back, with a deafening thud.

Lying there inside the cover of fog, Sal knew he should get to his feet and find cover, but he lay there anyway, dazed, the impact reverberating through his bones. After a minute had passed, he rolled onto his right side and stared off where he thought the path should have been, but the thick, gray gauze in front of his face was all he could see. The only sound in the night was the chorus of peepers. He was surprised they hadn't been silenced by his fall. Shivering weakly, he pushed himself to his knees and rose out of the fog. Suddenly exposed, his heart skipped. The flat surface of smoke was three feet high and moonlit nearly white; trees seemed to grow out of it. Sal looked off down the path, watching for movement. But even with the moonlight, the trail diminished into obscurity thirty or forty feet away.

He struggled to his feet and turned to the fishing pool, looked out over the table of fog. Unable to see even the ground beneath him, he stepped gingerly until his boot found a solid surface – his fishing rock. He crouched inside the fog and, finding the edge of the rock with his hand, sat down with his legs over the edge. Pushing off, his boots met soft resistance, than sank in the mud. Immediately the peepers stopped – a sudden, conspicuous silence. He remained as still as he could, even tried to stop shivering, but he could not, with the freezing water oozing into his boots. Out beyond the sandbar, the river lay quiet, no longer running to the sea, but lolling, fattening, breathing against its banks – the incoming tide.

Because the pool was lower than the bank, Sal now found himself standing up to his neck in fog, and that made him feel safer. He ducked his head and was once again hidden – but now he could not see, either. He stooped to feel the water with his hand and found it about six inches deep.

To reach the river debris, he turned to his right. But when he tried to pull his left foot out of the mud, the bog was reluctant to let him go. Unable to use his left arm, even for balance, he found it easier to lower himself to his knees to break the suction at his heels. Holding the fishing rock with his right hand, he pulled his left leg forward and set it down, then went down to his right knee.

In this way he worked around the rock until finally his knee struck a floating object. He reached out and felt plastic, a hollow handle. He knew he was lifting an empty milk jug out of the pool. He reached out and set it on the grassy bank to his right, then felt around him again, found a plastic sandwich bag – put that on the bank too. In the same way he removed and identified each bit of trash: a deflated kickball; a rectangular plastic bottle that might have once contained motor oil; a hollow doll with a missing leg; a plastic ice cube tray; a rubber glove, its fingers stuck together. He folded the glove and stuffed it in his pocket, then felt for more: a small plastic bottle with a cone top – maybe a mustard dispenser; a fishing bobber attached to a few feet of line; a short string of Christmas tree lights; a flat slab of Styrofoam that might have been insulation or the broken lid to a cooler; Sal skimmed his hand over the water and couldn't find anything more – until he reached under the bank. That's where he found the empty tube, and then something close to warmth went through him. Stuffing the tube in his other pocket, he crawled onto the bank and then quietly lowered the rest of the debris back into the pool.

It was the tube of hair cream that Davey had joked about when they were fishing, the hair goop. It was his one chance – if he could convince anybody that this wasn't some last-ditch fantasy of his. He was about to stand again when he heard the noise out ahead of him – a slight crack. He stopped moving. Cocked his ear to the left and heard it again. He looked out over the fog toward the river, where the trees stopped. There he knew the firm bank gave way to a grassy sandbar that curved around to form the outer boundary of the pool, holding out the river on its other side. He heard a squirrel start to chatter ahead on the path, a nervous warning.

He stepped over the rock and very slowly, very quietly, made his way along the edge of the bank, past the last scrub alder, until he felt the ground soften under his feet. As the bar curved around to the left, heading downriver, the sand became even softer and wetter, spreading into a grassy swail, the inlet for the reversing tidal waters. When Sal felt water filling his boots again, he turned and climbed back onto the bar where the grass grew thicker and the sand was firmer. There he sank to his knees beneath the fogbank, to wait.

It seemed a fair place strategically, across the pool so he could see both approaches – that is, if someone came with a flashlight. He knew that Noel would come in from the left (where he had heard the noises); the police, if they came at all, would follow the path down from the right.

Sal had no idea what time it was – two? three? four o'clock? – nor if his position was indeed as advantageous as he'd first thought. Now it occurred to him that he had trapped himself on the sandbar along with the only piece of evidence that might incriminate Noel. The river behind him was twenty feet across, and the woods beyond thick and unfriendly – assuming he had enough strength to mount an escape, which he doubted. His body was dominated by uncontrollable shivering and pain. Yet he felt nothing as much as his fatigue.

He pulled the tube of hair cream out of his pocket, intending to bury it in the sand beneath him. But needing to preserve the silence, and wanting to warm himself, he closed the tube tightly in his hand and pulled his knees into his chest, making as compact a shape as possible in the marsh grass. With the toes of his boots, he dug small holes in the sand, thinking even that might help warm him. He laid his cheek in the grass and stared into the cold, blind fog that surrounded his face, shivering, keeping his ears attuned for the slightest rustle.

But the night had fallen so brutally still. The night, the pool, the river. The only sound he heard was the little plop of a tree frog going into the pool in front of him. It wasn't long before a frog on the opposite bank called out with a single, daring peep. Moments later, there came an answering peep from off to his right. An unsolicited response from the left. Then two and three and four more, and all at once the entire bog was once again awash in the mating concerto. The music surrounded Sal, became synonymous with his shivering, a pleasant, buoyant life raft on which he willfully floated away from his weariness and pain. The loss of feeling, the loss of heat, the loss of blood – the accumulation of losses finally took his consciousness.

A whisper gave it back. He was aware of nothing at first, and then a sudden, furious cold – but it was the whisper that had roused him. The whisper of water. He realized that he was hearing the falls reversing, the tidal waters fighting their way over the rocks down-river – and then he remembered where he was. And why. He opened his eyes and could see nothing but an impenetrable grayness, black wires of marsh grass in front of his face. He had fallen asleep, he didn't know for how long. Now he was awake; cold, stiff and shivering to his core. The falls whispered on, the unnatural act continuing, tidal water flowing uphill, washing the darkened woods with ocean life. The sound was so soothing he started to doze again. But something else—

He realized that something else had awakened him: The peepers had stopped.

She was there.

He caught his breath. Silently he lifted his cheek off the sand, his eyes out of the grass, afraid of even a rustle of cloth, the snap of cartilage. And he saw her. On the far side of the pool, a bare dot of light appeared to float in the air, and then it lowered to the pool, making a smudge reflection. She was bending, looking through the debris—

The hair cream. He realized that the empty tube was still in his hand.

He knew she wouldn't have come down without her gun. He knew also that he had given her no choice but to use it – unless he could hide the tube.

He looked up through the fog, saw that the sky was half a shade lighter than the bog, just enough to give objects a shadowy definition. But where he lay, forty feet away, he realized that he must have looked no more distinctive than any other part of the bank, if she could see the sandbar at all.

As slowly as he could manage, he raised his body enough to free his right arm. Then he lowered his hand until he felt the flat bottom of the tube meet the sand. He pushed it about a half inch deep and very slowly plowed a short furrow.

Suddenly in front of his face, he heard a snick of sound – a tiny shadow leaping out of the grass – a tree frog – and then its small splash in the pool.

The light whipped around in the fog, no bigger than a dim, searching eye. It hovered above the water, not moving.

The moment remained motionless, poised. Sal stared, wondering if his own eyes reflected the light back to her, bracing for the muzzle flash, the clap of gunpowder. When he couldn't wait any longer, he rose to his knees.

'I got what you're looking for,' he said, his voice slicing the fog.

For a moment, her light remained still. Then it rose into the air, and he heard her leg suck out of the mud. He knew that she was aiming her revolver at him.

'I buried it,' he said.

She pulled her other foot up, made a soft, water sound as she took another step. 'I really don't know what you're talking about. Buried what?'

Gradually he could make out the outline of her head and shoulders in the fog, then her torso and hips. He moved his hand, furtively plowing sand over the tube as he talked. 'It's all in your book,' he said. 'Hair cream and swimming pool cleaner. It's how Jerry Royal's house burned down.'

'Jerry's house?'

She took another step, and her outline suddenly became clearer, her light beam brighter. 'I'm not sure I understand how that relates to me.'

'Jerry knew what you did, Noel. He put it in a letter, to protect himself. And then he tried to blackmail you. That's why you burned down his house, to destroy the letter.'

'You really are delusional,' she said. 'That's what people say about you, you know, that you've had a breakdown.' Her foot made a sucking sound.

'It didn't make sense at first, I mean why he didn't turn you in. But then I realized – he couldn't. Because it was Jerry who killed Eliot Wicker.'

Noel sighed. 'Sal, you know you murdered Wicker, just like you deceived Bobby. Like you deceived me into coming down here so you could attack me.'

Now he could make out her features enough to see that she was barelegged under a dark, hooded sweatshirt. And that she did indeed have her pistol with her. Aimed squarely at him.

'Psychologically, it's not hard to understand. You had sex with me. You betrayed your best friend and your wife, and now you need someone to blame. Poor, innocent Salvatore, victimized by the evil seductress.'

She took another step, and then she stopped. The light flared in his eyes.

'So, I guess whatever it is you buried,' she said—

and that's when Sal realized his fatal mistake—

—'well, that's exactly what I was planning to do.'

She hesitated, as if giving him a chance to respond. But he just stared into her light without recourse, exhausted, targeted. A wave of weak emotion passed over him, knowing he was about to die. He lowered his eyes. He pictured Iris . . . Davey . . .

With no trace of regret, she said simply, 'Nobody's innocent, Sal. And you're nobody's victim.'

A thick shaft of light flashed across the bog.

'Noel, don't you move!'

To Sal's left, at the source of the light, all he could see was the shape of a man standing amongst the vaporous trees.

'Drop that gun in the water, Noel.'

It was Shepherd, perched at the foot of the sandbar, not thirty feet away. His light, diffused through the fog, gave Noel's face a reddish, eerie glow. She shielded her eyes with the hand that held her own penlight, but her revolved remained point-blank at Sal.

'I'm sorry, *Detective*, I need to protect myself. In case you haven't heard, he broke into my apartment and tried to kill me earlier. He murdered Bobby. I came down here because I knew this was where he'd be.'

'You came down to get something out of the water,' Shepherd replied. 'I've been right here watching you.'

Standing up to her knees in the pool, Noel sneered. 'You're just so clever. But if you'll take your flashlight out of my eyes and shine it on him, you'll see that he also has a gun in his hand.'

Shepherd didn't budge. He kept his flashlight – and his eyes – on her. 'Noel,' he said, softening his voice, 'I know you can't see me here, but I have a nine millimeter semiautomatic aimed at you. I have fourteen rounds, and you're making me very nervous. Drop your weapon now.'

She smirked. 'Do they teach you to talk like that at detective school, or did you pick it up at the movies?'

'Drop it.'

'He murdered my husband,' she said, 'and he murdered Eliot Wicker. He's got nothing to lose by killing both of us.'

'Mr Erickson, did you kill those men?'

'Oh, right, ask him, asshole.'

'Noel—'

'I've done a lot of things I can't undo,' Sal said. 'I'm a drunk. I destroyed my family. But I've never killed anybody.'

'Sal, I found your wallet,' Shepherd said.

For a moment, the only response was the sound of the pool quietly rising up its banks. 'Okay,' Sal answered.

'I have it with me.'

'I don't mean to sound ungrateful, Detective, but I don't need my wallet right now.'

'Sal, you need to explain your driver's license,' Shepherd told him.

Noel broke in, keeping her gun on Sal. 'You are questioning him,' she said, 'but you are still shining your light on me. I find that extremely annoying.'

'It's a Rhode Island license with your picture on it, Sal.'

Noel continued. 'Are you going to let him murder me in cold blood while you're standing right there?'

'You keep quiet.'

'Look at him! He has a gun!'

'Noel, I'm not taking my eyes off you. Sal, I want you to explain the name on your license.'

'What name?'

There was a pause. 'Dale Newman.'

'*Bastard!*' Noel said.

'*Noel!*' Two corners of the triangle leaned in, Noel aiming her light and gun at Sal, Shepherd aiming at Noel.

'He murdered my husband!' she snapped. 'I have the right to protect myself!'

'You do anything other than dropping that gun,' he replied, 'and I'll shoot you dead.'

'I'd love to be there when you explain that,' she replied.

Shepherd kept his pistol trained on her chest. 'Sal, we have more than enough evidence for an indictment. I need to know why I shouldn't arrest you.'

Sal dug his fingers in the sand.

'He's got a gun!'

'Sal – Don't you move!'

Sal pulled out the tube and tossed it. It hit Shepherd's leg, made him jump back, ready to swing toward Sal. 'Jesus Christ, I said don't move!'

'Hair cream,' Sal told him. 'She burned down Jerry Royal's house with it. He was blackmailing her.'

'With hair cream—?'

'You mix it with swimming pool cleaner to start a fire. The directions are in a book she had in her apartment. I saw the empty tube here yesterday when I was fishing with my daughter.'

'We have videotape of the area,' Shepherd said. 'If it was in the water, we'll see it.'

Noel glared down the barrel at Sal. 'And you'll send it down to the lab for analysis, and you'll find my fingerprints on it. So what? Of course my fingerprints are on it. I sell that brand of hair cream in my store.'

'I don't think so,' Sal said. 'You're too smart to leave fingerprints.' He leaned forward, his right hand going behind him.

Hearing the movement, Shepherd tensed again. 'Just tell me!'

'Watch him!'

'Noel!'

Sal snapped the glove from his pocket. Shepherd caught his breath, remained riveted on Noel.

'It's a rubber glove,' Sal said. 'I don't have a gun.'

'Okay, that's enough,' Shepherd told him. 'I'd rather you didn't say any more.'

Noel sighed impatiently. Her right leg moved in the water. 'Detective, if I agree to—'

'Noel, don't you even think about turning toward me or I'll shoot you.'

'The fingers are stuck together,' Sal said, 'like they've been melted.'

'Enough!' Shepherd told him. 'Don't you say another word.'

Sal heard the detective's foot enter the pool, saw the light beam shift on Noel's right side. 'Okay, I'm coming out where I can see you both. Noel, for all I know, you could be thinking that the only way out of this is to kill me first, and then shoot him.'

'I'm sorry, but you have it exactly wrong, as usual,' she scoffed. 'He's the one who has to get out of this, and right now he's aiming his gun right at the side of your face.'

Shepherd put his other foot in the water. 'Calm down, Noel. Now I need you to drop your weapon in the water.'

'I don't believe this,' she said. 'A tube of hair cream and a rubber fucking glove. Listen to me – I have a seven-thirty flight!'

Shepherd kept his gun on her, while his voice grew steady and soothing. 'It's important that we all stay calm. There's nothing we have to solve here and now. That's what lawyers are for. Now lower your weapon, Noel. Nice and easy.'

But she kept her revolver trained on Sal.

As Shepherd came closer to her, his beam intensified on the side of her face, her shining eye. 'That's right, everyone stay cool, and we'll all get out of here without anyone getting hurt.'

Sal knew differently. There were three possible ways this would end, none of them calm. Only one way had him walking out alive. He swallowed.

'Detective Shepherd,' he said.

'Not now—'

'Is it possible to take fingerprints from inside a rubber glove?'

Shepherd stopped. Extended his gun toward Noel.

'Don't move, Noel—'

Her green eye, sideswiped by the light, narrowed in the fog.

'Noel, please,' he said quietly. 'Drop it in the water.'

For several beats, the only sound in the pool was breathing.

'Noel, we're about one second from becoming very bloody here.'

Her mouth contorted in a crooked, haughty smile. 'Are you serious?' she said, turning toward him.

The gunshots cracked off the bluff – three, in quick succession, from Shepherd's pistol.

Sal fell back.

Noel dropped into the pool as if she'd been pulled down by the legs. She curled away from Sal, looking like she wanted to return fire at Shepherd, but her feet were stuck and she couldn't seem to raise her arm. Slumping forward, she managed to draw a knee up under her. In the water, her small haze of light drifted away.

Sal pulled himself to his feet, legs shaking.

Shepherd took a step toward her, his gun trained on the top of Noel's head, his flashlight beam searching the murky water for her right hand, her weapon.

'Let go of the gun, Noel. Let me help you.'

As the pool rose to her face, Noel turned her head groggily, her eyes rolling over to Sal, dark and glazed.

He stepped toward her in the mud.

'You stay back,' Shepherd told him, but Sal wasn't hearing. He took another step.

Noel continued staring at him as the pool licked her chin. Her head hitched forward once. Then, sucking in a shallow breath, she slid under.

Sal pushed through the muck, sloshing forward. Shepherd moved forward, trying to stop him. 'Get back—'

Sal dropped to his knees, got his right arm under Noel's arm and started to lift. She felt heavier than possible, at first, then suddenly weightless—

'*Look out!*'

Her face flew out of the water, gasping the air, eyes flaring. Her elbow followed, the revolver splashing up.

Sal froze in front of her, pinned.

The pistol shot blew behind Sal's ear with tremendous volume, the echo absorbed by the dense fog, the surrounding trees, and as Sal watched, horrified, Noel slipped heavily from his arms, seeming to dive away from him, moving the water back.

For most of a minute, the entire bog lay perfectly still. Neither man moved.

Than Sal rose to his feet.

Shepherd let out a low sigh. 'You can't help her now,' he said.

Engulfed by shivering, Sal took a step deeper into the pool. Shepherd slogged toward him, caught hold of his shirt with his flashlight hand. 'Listen—' His right arm went around Sal's back, to keep him from falling. 'She did it herself.' He raised his flashlight to the middle of the pool as the body stopped drifting. 'She did it herself,' Shepherd said again.

'I know. I know.'

Sal stared into the dusky fog. From where he stood, the lifeless form that protruded from the pool, still as one of the rocks or tussocks around it, could have been mistaken for anything – another rock, a discarded milk jug, a child's broken kickball. But it was Noel Swift in the water, Bobby's Noel, the last part of her cooling body to go down, her buttock and thigh.

16

The morning newspaper ran a photo of Jerry Royal's body draped out of the front window of the Ericksons' house, with the headline 'Suspect at Large in Gravity Carnage,' although the accompanying article failed to draw a relationship between the deaths of Jerry Royal and Sergeant Murdoch and the pursuit of Sal Erickson. By the time the papers came off the trucks, Sal was in the emergency ward of Downeast Memorial Hospital with a mild case of hypothermia, serious blood loss and a fractured shoulder.

By seven o'clock, Lieutenant Boggs found himself standing in front of television cameras lamenting Sergeant Murdoch's untimely death and painting him as a hero, telling the viewing audience that even after Murdoch was mortally wounded, he had taken down his assailant while the man engaged police in an armed standoff. Boggs went on to say that a second suspect in the case was now in custody, although he did not make it clear what Sal was suspected of.

Reporters, eager to profile Sal Erickson and his family and photograph the house where Murdoch and Jerry Royal had been gunned down, were kept away from the scene in the early morning, until evidence technicians had finished processing the house. Then, when a crew of carpenters and cleaners took over, there was nothing newsworthy to see, nor anyone knowledgeable to interview.

Despite the calamitous events – or maybe because of them – a stony reticence overspread the town. Even the coffee crowd, who had gathered outside the closed Superette to discuss the news, steadfastly refused to talk to reporters. At seven-fifteen, when they all went off about their day's business, the newspeople gave up and returned to Bangor to await the police report.

It wasn't that townspeople were unmoved about what had befallen the victims; they were just relieved that the ordeal was finally over. They longed for the Gravity they knew, slow and warm in the summertime, with haying and berrying and lawn-mowing and half-witted tourists and lobster bakes; with their Fourth of July parade, their oxen pulls, their Blueberry Queen.

For Iris, the hours that followed were, in various ways, the saddest yet most liberating time of her life, and so she was careful with her emotions. At seven-thirty in the morning, after staying up all night talking to Helen, she telephoned the clinic to say she was taking a month off (despite protests from the two doctors, who owed her twenty-four weeks in accumulated time). At eight, she called the university and canceled her summer semester. It was the first time in her memory that she had no schedule to keep. Then, leaving Davey with Helen Swan, Iris walked out to her car and began the long journey of reclaiming her life.

She started by visiting an Ellsworth funeral director. In the slow hours before dawn, over two pots of tea, Helen had told Iris that one day she would learn to forgive her brother. By the time Iris had finished making arrangements for Jerry's burial, she believed that one day she would.

After leaving the funeral home, she drove to the hospital to visit her father. She brought him a can of vegetable juice and a straw from the cafeteria. She held his hand while she told him about Jerry. She didn't tell everything. When the nurse brought lunch, she fed her father with a spoon; she brushed his hair with a soft baby brush; then she stayed for a while and watched him sleep.

Before she left the hospital, she stopped at the desk to ask for Sal. She hadn't planned to, not exactly. But thinking that she might, she had brought a tulip that Davey had picked from Helen's bulb garden, along with a get-well card that Davey had made. The receptionist told Iris that Sal was recovering from surgery and that, since he was still in police custody, he could not have visitors.

She went up to the recovery room anyway and looked in the window while Sal slept. He looked old – that was Iris's first thought – whether because of the cast on his arm, his pallid complexion, his growth of beard or the weight he had lost. A uniformed policeman sitting in the room with him glanced up from his magazine. Iris held the flower and card to the window. The cop set his magazine on the radiator and came to the door to take them.

It was another twenty-four hours before Sal opened his eyes. When he did, the tulip was the first thing he saw. The card beside the red plastic vase said 'I love you Daddy.' He went to reach for the card but found his arm unmovable, bound in a stiff cast.

'Still pretty tender, I guess,' a voice said.

Sal raised his head, saw Alston Bouchard sitting at the foot of his bed. The constable lifted two pill bottles from his shirt pocket. 'I've got a ten-day supply of painkillers for you,' he said. 'Plus tetracycline, to ward off infection.'

Sal cleared his throat, coming to full, painful consciousness. His shoulder throbbed intensely, his back and ribs hurt when he breathed. Even his jaw still ached where Bouchard had punched him.

'I thought you were in jail,' Sal said, his voice raspy from the long sleep.

'They let me go,' Bouchard told him. 'Detective Shepherd stopped by a while ago. He said they found that book you were looking for. It was in her dumpster with a lot of other things she was throwing out.'

Sal laid his head back on the pillow. Memories began seeping in, carrying far more pain than he felt physically.

'Also' – Bouchard leaned forward in his chair – 'he wanted me to show you this.' He took a Polaroid photo out of his pocket, got to his feet and came to Sal's bedside. 'They went through her suitcases and such. 'Course, they found her round-trip plane ticket to Tampa.'

He put the picture in Sal's hand, a close-up of a green airline ticket. 'This one they found in the lining.'

Sal's eyes sharpened. 'Swissair?'

'Miami to Zurich,' Bouchard said. 'The money'd been transferred to Switzerland.'

Sal's eyes stung. He closed them, the photo hanging from his fingers.

'See the name on the ticket?'

Sal opened his eyes again, saw the way Bouchard was looking at him. He didn't have to look at the ticket.

'They found black hair dye too. She would've been on that plane today.'

Sal remained silent. Bouchard took the photo from him.

'I brought you a change of clothes. They want to check you over once more, then you're free to go.'

Sal laid his head back on the pillow.

Bouchard's car radio didn't work, so it was a quiet ride back to town. Sal wore a pair of corduroy trousers and a dark cotton shirt that Bouchard had brought for him; the left sleeve was cut off at the shoulder to make room for his cast and sling. Sal had shaved before he left, and he'd eaten some mashed potatoes and apple-sauce, his first solid food in days.

They drove on over the frost-heaved road, the late afternoon sun flickering through the windows. Sal put his visor down, opened his window. The warm air, laced with lilacs, fluttered against his face.

'Windy,' Bouchard said, the only thing he had said since they'd left the hospital.

Sal did not respond. They drove on further, eventually crossing into Gravity.

'Your motorcycle's up to my place,' Bouchard told him. 'But with that arm...'

'I'll get my car,' Sal agreed.

'I'll drop you off at...' Bouchard flipped his hand. *Your house* were the words he did not say.

They drove the next three miles without speaking. When they reached the Superette, the building was deserted, ringed with yellow police tape. Sal stared straight ahead out the windshield as they drove by. Crossing over the bridge to the stop sign, Bouchard stepped on his brakes, then started to turn.

'I'll get out here,' Sal told him.

Bouchard pulled over, shifted into neutral. Sal pushed against the door, popped it open. He got out, then reached into the back seat with his good arm and picked up the plastic bag containing his clothes. Somebody at the hospital had laundered them. Halfway out, he stopped. 'Listen—'

'Yup.'

'I've been thinking, next time you go to one of those meetings...'

Bouchard nodded, his hands rubbing the steering wheel. 'I was going to say, you ever go fishing and want some company...' He jerked his wrist.

Sal nodded, shut the door. Looked in the open window.

Bouchard raised his fingers off the steering wheel. 'Anyway, about those meetings, we'll be going every night for the next three months, you and me...' He made a fist, bounced it twice off the wheel.

Sal gave him a long look. Then he smiled a little. 'I'm thinking about it,' he said. 'Maybe one of these days I'll come up with a higher power.'

Bouchard gave another nod. Then he drove off.

Sal looked down the road toward his house, and he started walking. It was a bright afternoon, windy and warm. He could hear a lawn mower going, he could hear songbirds in the trees. Off in the eastern sky a noisy flock of Canada geese rode the wind northward in a V, following the coast. Any other day like this, after supper, he'd be mowing his own lawn, or out in his garden, or playing catch with Davey, or heading down to the fishing pool with his rod and net. Now that he was this close to home, his heart sank inside him, knowing that those days were gone. The wind gusted behind him, pushing him down the road. But he held back, favoring his left ankle. He was in no hurry.

He figured he'd drive into Ellsworth and buy a newspaper, start looking for a job, maybe do some house painting. Or he'd go up to the university and see about giving private lessons. Approaching his house, he saw Mrs Abraham standing in her sunporch, looking out at him. Sal knew she'd be on the telephone in the next minute.

When he could see his own house, the first thing he noticed was the new front window and patch of new shingles around it. His shoulder ached.

Then he saw them both, Iris and Davey, out behind the house in the garden. He was glad their backs were to him. It looked like Iris was pushing the rototiller, fighting to steady the machine while it rocked her along. He could hear the motor sputtering. Davey was crouched in the garden behind her – weeding? He could see the row of pea plants – already up past Davey's ankles. The row of spinach was thick and green. A twinge of pride mixed with his sadness. They were doing without him.

Sal reached the property without their seeing him, cut across the front lawn so they were out of sight behind the house. He went to his car, looked in the window and saw the back seat packed with cardboard boxes of his things. What he wanted to do was to go out to the garden and see them both, tell them that he'd been cleared, but he figured they must already know. He'd wait till he looked better, dressed in clothes that fit him; without the cast. He'd come back when he was settled and he felt stronger, when he could face Davey without feeling ashamed. When he could face them both – although right now he couldn't see that day ever coming. He opened the car door and slid in on the seat. He reached in the ashtray and took out his spare key, and that's when he heard the rototiller die. He put the key in the ignition and sat for a moment to listen, while Iris pulled the starter cord again and again, and the rototiller did nothing but cough. He heard Davey's voice, like a sweet song; Iris's voice, patient and soothing.

Sal took a long breath, got out of the car. He walked up the driveway and then stopped tentatively between the garage and the house, where he could see them: Davey kneeling in the peas, Iris bent over the machine. 'This must be the choke,' Iris was saying, making an adjustment. Sal walked under the clothesline while she gave another pull. This time the motor sputtered, and Iris adjusted the choke until the motor evened out. She increased the throttle, and the rototiller sang. She started the tines revolving and then went churning up the dark soil.

Yes, they would do without him. He started to turn, wanting to get out of there before he was spotted.

But then Davey turned too, as if she had sensed his presence. At first she gazed with disbelief, then she sprang to her feet and came running through the garden, and she was in his arms. Iris stopped tilling, looked back at them both, Davey with her long limbs wrapped around her father, hugging Sal as if she'd never let him go. Sal held her just as tightly with his one good arm, his face reddening.

Iris disengaged the tines, slowed the throttle, took off her glasses to wipe her dirty face with the back of her arm. She stopped the motor with her foot and then walked across the soft dirt, taking long, purposeful strides toward him.

Sal watched her uncertainly, not knowing what he could possibly say. He cleared his throat and started anyway. 'They let me' – his words caught in his throat. Still holding Davey, he closed his eyes and took a breath. He shook his head, unable to speak.

Iris took another step toward him. 'Be careful of Daddy's shoulder, love.'

The wind came up again, whipped Iris's hair around. Sal could see where her face had been colored by the sun. And then he couldn't look at her any more.

'Davey, I gotta put you down,' he whispered.

But Davey held him tighter, her strong legs squeezing his waist.

'Honey, I have to go.'

'Don't—'

Iris's voice seemed to blow off on a gust of wind. Sal looked at her again. Was she speaking to Davey? She was looking at Sal. A dizziness came over him, and he teetered a bit under Davey's weight.

'Hon, you gotta get down now,' he said to Davey, but he was still captivated by Iris, by the look she was giving him – like she was looking right through him.

She took another step closer, until she was within touch, and then she said clearly, 'Sal, I don't want you to go.' Just like that. So clear there could be no mistake, and Sal lost his balance, lost his legs and staggered backwards, landing softly in a row of soft dirt and radishes. Davey laughed. Still holding on, she braced her feet on the ground to keep him from falling onto his back, and she laughed at him.

And then Iris was there with them both, on her knees, working one arm under Sal's, the other around Davey. The three of them holding one another against the wind, Sal's face caressed by their hair, Iris's mouth at his ear. 'You were right,' she said to him. 'I did come looking for you, Sal. And I found just what I was looking for.'

He leaned into both of them, cradled by their skulls. 'No,' he breathed. 'No.' And Iris angled her face until they found each other's eyes through her hair. 'I came looking for you,' he said. 'And I never even knew it.'

They held each other. They swayed, the three of them in the late afternoon sun, wrapped together like some wild, burgeoning bush. In the soft dirt, in the wind, it was a wonder how they stayed upright.

ACKNOWLEDGMENTS

Thanks to all of you who generously offered or agreed to read this novel in all of its varied forms and then gave me your valuable suggestions and encouragement:

Ron Bourassa
Rich Connor
Chris Fahy
Nancy Gish
Joel Gotler
Rick Hautala
Kyle Jones
Glenna Kimball
Jesse Kimball
Stephen King
Tabitha King
Sue Locsin
Bo Marks
Art Mayers
Allison Mullen
Alan Philbrook
Nessa Reifsnyder
Peter Reifsnyder
Justin Smith
Laurie Stone

For help with research and other things, thank you:

Ladd Alcott

Walter Chapin
David Crook
Meredith DeLoca
Roy Gallant
Dan Guerin
Brent Harrell
Bill Harwood
Al Hendsbee
Joe Jackson
Phil Jones
Ronald Kaufman
Sarah Kimball
Peter and Paula Layton
Bob MacMahon
Dorothy Morang
Howie Nielsen
Andy Pratt
Henry Ryan

Very special thanks to:

Jennifer Hershey, my Avon editor
Billy Massey, my Headline editor
Howard Morhaim, my agent

Bless you, Lou Aronica